D0312031

SAINT PETER'S FAIR

•

THE LEPER OF SAINT GILES

•

THE VIRGIN IN THE ICE

# ELLIS PETERS

## BROTHER CADFAEL OMNIBUS 2

SAINT PETER'S FAIR

•

THE LEPER OF SAINT GILES

•

THE VIRGIN IN THE ICE

LITTLE, BROWN AND COMPANY

A Little, Brown Book
This edition first published in Great Britain in 2000 by
Little, Brown and Company



A CIP catalogue record for this book
is available from the British Library.

ISBN 0 316 85518 9

Printed and bound in Spain

Little, Brown and Company (UK)
Brettenham House
Lancaster Place
London WC2E 7EN

# SAINT PETER'S FAIR

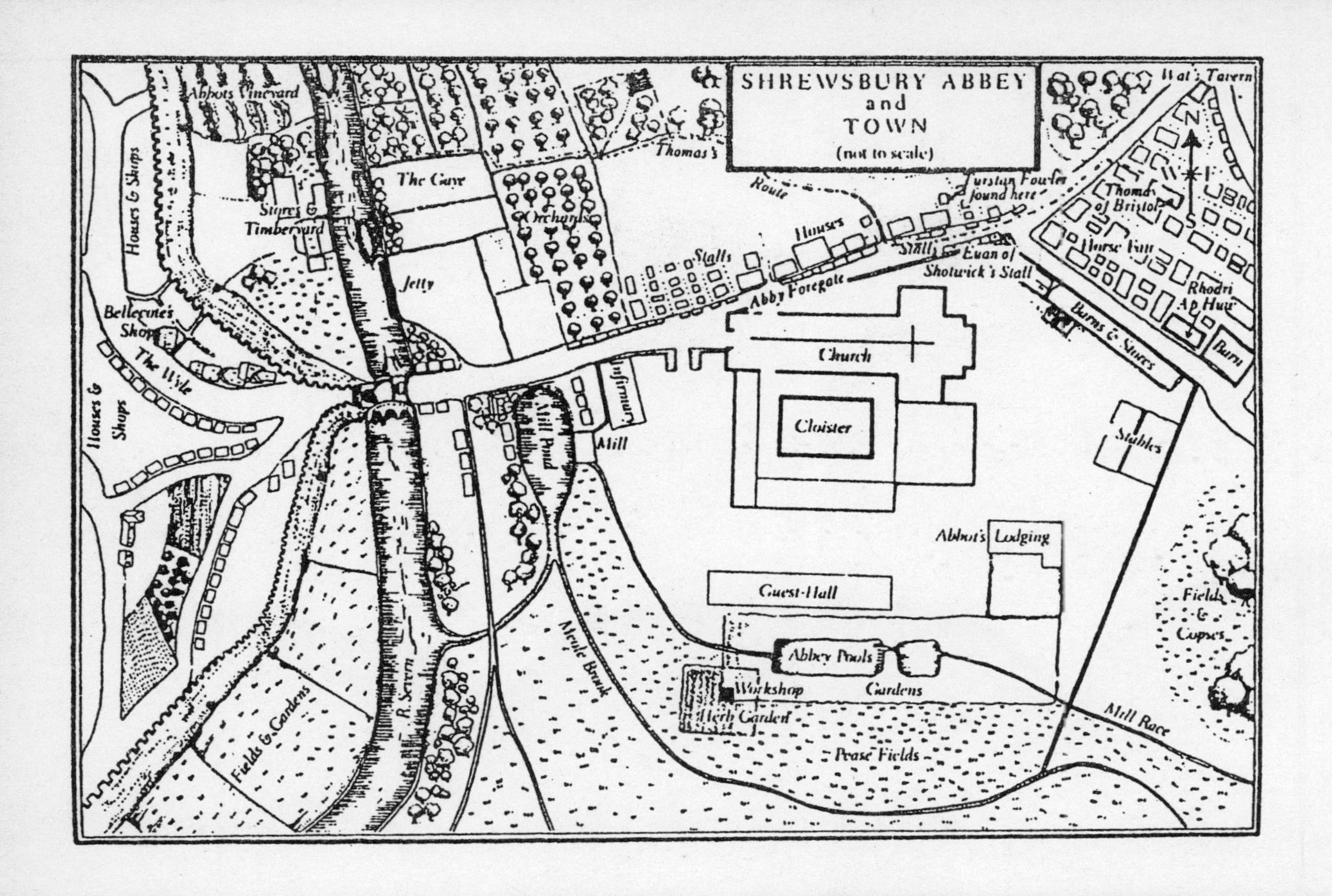
SHREWSBURY ABBEY
and
TOWN
(not to scale)
Abbots Vineyard
Houses & Shops
Stores & Timberyard
The Gaye
Orchards
Thomas's
Route
Turstan Fowler found here
Wat's Tavern
N
Thomas of Bristol
Horse Fair
Rhodri Ap Huw
Barn
Houses
Stalls
Evan of Shotwick's Stall
Abby Foregate
Jetty
Bellecote's Shop
The Wyle
Houses & Shops
Church
Cloister
Infirmary
Mill Pond
Mill
Barns & Stores
Stables
Abbot's Lodging
Guest-Hall
Fields & Copses
Abbey Pools
Workshop
Gardens
Herb Garden
Mill Race
Pease Fields
Meole Brook
R. Severn
Fields & Gardens

# The Eve of the Fair

## Chapter One

It began at the normal daily chapter in the Benedictine monastery of Saint Peter and Saint Paul, of Shrewsbury, on the thirtieth day of July, in the year of Our Lord 1139. That day being the eve of Saint Peter ad Vincula, a festival of solemn and profitable importance to the house that bore his name, the routine business of the morning meeting had been devoted wholly to the measures necessary to its proper celebration, and lesser matters had to wait.

The house, given its full dedication, had two saints, but Saint Paul tended to be neglected, sometimes even omitted from official documents, or so abbreviated that he almost vanished. Time is money, and clerks find it tedious to inscribe the entire title, perhaps as many as twenty times in one charter. They had had to amend their ways, however, since Abbot Radulfus had taken over the rudder of this cloistral vessel, for he was a man who brooked no slipshod dealings, and would have all his crew as meticulous as himself.

Brother Cadfael had been out before Prime in his enclosed herb-garden, observing with approval the blooming of his oriental poppies, and assessing the time when the seed would be due for gathering. The summer season was at its height, and promising rich harvest, for the spring had been mild and moist after plenteous early snows, and June and July hot and sunny, with a few compensatory showers to keep the leafage fresh and the buds fruitful. The hay harvest was in, and lavish, the corn looked ripe for the sickle. As soon as the annual fair was over, the reaping would begin. Cadfael's fragrant domain, dewy from the dawn and already warming into drunken sweetness in the rising sun, filled his senses with the kind of pleasure on which an ascetic church sometimes frowns, finding something uneasily sinful in pure delight. There were times when young Brother Mark, who worked with him this delectable field, felt that he ought to confess his joy among his sins, and meekly accept some appropriate penance. He was still very young, there were excuses to be found for him. Brother Cadfael had more sense, and no such scruples. The manifold gifts of God are there to be delighted in, to fall short of joy would be ingratitude.

Having put in two hours of work before Prime, and having no office in connection with the abbey fair, which was engaging all attention, Cadfael was nodding, as was his habit, behind his protective pillar in the dimmest corner of the chapter-house, perfectly ready to snap into wakefulness if some unexpected query should be aimed in his direction, and perfectly capable of answering coherently what he had only partially heard. He had been sixteen years a monk, by his own considered choice, which he had never regretted, after a very adventurous life which he had never regretted, either, and he was virtually out of reach of surprise. He was fifty-nine years old, with a world of experience stored away within him, and still as tough as a badger – according to Brother Mark almost as bandy-legged, into the bargain, but Brother Mark was a privileged being. Cadfael dozed as silently as a closed flower at night, and hardly ever snored; within the Benedictine rule, and in genial companionship with it, he had perfected a daily discipline of his own, that suited his needs admirably.

It is probable that he was fast asleep when the steward of the grange court, with an appropriate apology, ventured into the chapter-house and stood waiting the abbot's permission to speak. He was certainly awake when the steward reported: 'My lord, here in the great court is the provost of the town, with a delegation from the Guild Merchant, asking leave to speak with you. They say the matter is important.'

Abbot Radulfus allowed his steely, level brows to rise a little, and indicated graciously that the fathers of the borough should be admitted at once. Relations between the town of Shrewsbury on one side of the river and the abbey on the other, if never exactly cordial – that was too much to expect, where their interests so often collided – were always correct, and their skirmishes conducted with wary courtesy. If the abbot scented battle, he gave no sign. But for all that, thought Cadfael, watching the shrewd, lean hatchet-face, he has a pretty accurate idea of what they're here for.

The worthies of the guild entered the chapter-house in a solid phalanx, no less than ten of them, from half the crafts in the town, and led by the provost. Master Geoffrey Corviser, named for his trade, was a big, portly, vigorous man not yet fifty, clean-shaven, brisk and dignified. He made some of the finest shoes and riding-boots in England, and was well aware of their excellence and his own worth. For this occasion he had put on his best, and even without the long gown that would have been purgatory in this summer weather, he made an impressive figure, as clearly he meant to do. Several of those grouped at his back were well known to Cadfael: Edric Flesher, chief of the butchers of Shrewsbury, Martin Bellecote, master-carpenter, Reginald of Aston, the silversmith – men of substance every one. Abbot Radulfus did not know them, not yet.

He had been only half a year in office, sent from London to trim an easy-going provincial house into more zealous shape, and he had much to learn about the men of the borders, as he himself, being no man's fool, was well aware.

'You are welcome, gentlemen,' said the abbot mildly. 'Speak freely, you shall have attentive hearing.'

The ten made their reverences gravely, spread sturdy feet, and stood planted like a battle-square, all eyes alert, all judgments held in reserve. The abbot was concentrating courteous attention upon them with much the same effect. In his interludes of duty as shepherd, Cadfael had once watched two rams level just such looks before they clashed foreheads.

'My lord abbot,' said the provost, 'as you know, Saint Peter's Fair opens on the day after tomorrow, and lasts for three days. It's of the fair we come to speak. You know the conditions. For all that time all shops in the towns must be shut, and nothing sold but ale and wine. And ale and wine are sold freely here at the fairground and the Foregate, too, so that no man can make his living in the town from that merchandise. For three days, the three busiest of the year, when we might do well out of tolls on carts and pack-horses and man-loads passing through the town to reach the fair, we must levy no charges, neither murage nor pavage. All tolls belong only to the abbey. Goods coming up the Severn by boat tie up at your jetty, and pay their dues to you. We get nothing. And for this privilege you pay no more than thirty-eight shillings, and even that we must go to the trouble to distrain from the rents of your tenants in the town.'

'*No more* than thirty-eight shillings!' repeated Abbot Radulfus, and elevated the iron-grey brows a shade higher, but still with an urbane countenace and a gentle voice. 'The sum was appointed as fair. And not by us. The terms of the charter have been known to you many years, I believe.'

'They have, and often before now have been found burdensome enough, but bargains must be kept, and we have never complained. But bad years or good, the sum has never been raised. And it falls very hard on a town so pressed as we are now, to lose three days of trade, and the best tolls of the year. Last summer, as you must know, though you were not then among us, Shrewsbury was under siege above a month, and stormed at last with great damage to the town walls, and great neglect of the streets, and for all our efforts there's still great need of work on them, and it's costly labour, after all last summer's losses. Not the half of the dilapidations are yet put right, and in these troublous times, who knows when we may again be under attack? The very traffic of your fair will be passing through our streets and adding to the wear, while we get nothing to help make good the damage.'

'Come to the point, Master Provost,' said the abbot in the same tranquil tone. 'You are come to make some demand of us. Speak it out plainly.'

'Father Abbot, so I will! We think – and I speak for the whole guild merchant and borough gathering of Shrewsbury – that in such a year we have the best possible case for asking that the abbey should either pay a higher fee for the fair, or, better by far, set aside a proportion of the fair tolls on goods, whether by horse-load or cart or boat, to be handed over to the town, and spent on restoring the walls. You benefit by the protection the town affords you; you ought, we think, to bear a part with us in maintaining its defences. A tenth share of the profits would be welcomed, and we should thank you heartily for it. It is not a demand, with respect, it is an appeal. But we believe the grant of a tenth would be nothing more than justice.'

Abbot Radulfus sat, very erect and lean and lofty,

gravely considering the phalanx of stout burgesses before him. 'That is the view of you all?'

Edric Flesher spoke up bluntly: 'It is. And of all our townsmen, too. There are many who would voice the matter more forcibly than Master Corviser has done. But we trust in your fellow-feeling, and wait your answer.'

The faint stir that went round the chapter-house was like a great, cautious sigh. Most of the brothers looked on wide-eyed and anxious; the younger ones shifted and whispered, but very warily. Prior Robert Pennant, who had looked to be abbot by this time, and been sorely disappointed at having a stranger promoted over his head, maintained a silvery, ascetic calm, appeared to move his lips in prayer, and shot sidelong looks at his superior between narrowed ivory lids, wishing him irredeemable error while appearing to compassionate and bless. Old Brother Heribert, recently abbot of this house and now degraded to its ranks, dozed in a quiet corner, smiling gently, thankful to be at rest.

'We are considering, are we not,' said Radulfus at length, gently and without haste, 'what you pose as a dispute between the rights of the town and the rights of this house. In such a balance, should the judgment rest with you, or with me? Surely not! Some disinterested judge is needed. But, gentlemen, I would remind you, there has been such a decision, now, within the past half-year, since the siege of which you complain. At the beginning of this year his Grace King Stephen confirmed to us our ancient charter, with all its grants in lands, rights and privileges, just as we held them aforetime. He confirmed also our right to this three-day fair on the feast of our patron Saint Peter, at the same fee we have paid before, and on the same conditions. Do you suppose he would have countenanced such a grant, if he had not held it to be just?'

'To say outright what I suppose,' said the provost warmly, 'I never supposed for a moment that the thought of justice entered into it. I make no murmur against what his Grace chose to do, but it's plain he held Shrewsbury to be a hostile town, and most like still does hold it so, because FitzAlan, who is fled to France now, garrisoned the castle and kept it over a month against him. But small say we of the town ever had in the matter, and little we could have done about it! The castle declared for the Empress Maud, and we must put up with the consequences, while FitzAlan's away, safe out of reach. My lord abbot, is that justice?'

'Are you making the claim that his Grace, by confirming the abbey in its rights, is taking revenge on the town?' asked the abbot with soft and perilous gentleness.

'I am saying that he never so much as gave the town a thought, or its injuries a look, or he might have made some concession.'

'Ah! Then should not this appeal of yours be addressed rather to the Lord Gilbert Prestcote, who is the king's sheriff, and no doubt has his ear, rather than to us?'

'It has been so addressed, though not with regard to the fair. It is not for the sheriff to give away any part of what has been bestowed on the abbey. Only you, Father, can do that,' said Geoffrey Corviser briskly. It began to be apparent that the provost knew his way about among the pitfalls of words every bit as well as did the abbot.

'And what answer did you get from the sheriff?'

'He will do nothing for us until his own walls at the castle are made good. He promises us the loan of labour when work there is finished, but labour we could supply, it's money and materials we need, and it will be a year or more before he's ready to turn over even a handful of his men to our needs. In such a case,

Father, do you wonder that we find the fair a burden?'

'Yet we have our needs, too, as urgent to us as yours to you,' said the abbot after a thoughtful moment of silence. 'And I would remind you, our lands and possessions here lie outside the town walls, even outside the loop of the river, two protections you enjoy that we do not share. Should we, then, be asked to pay tolls for what cannot apply to us?'

'Not all your possessions,' said the provost promptly. 'There are within the town some thirty or more messuages in your hold, and your tenants within them, and their children have to wade in the kennels of broken streets as ours do, and their horses break legs where the paving is shattered, as ours do.'

'Our tenants enjoy fair treatment from us, and considerate rents, and for such matters we are responsible. But we cannot be held responsible for the town's dilapidations, as we can for those here on our own lands. No,' said the abbot, raising his voice peremptorily when the provost would have resumed his arguments, 'say no more! We have heard and understood your case, and we are not without sympathy. But Saint Peter's Fair is a sacred right granted to this house, on terms we did not draw up; it is a right that inheres not to me as a man, but to this house, and I in my passing tenure have no authority to change or mitigate those terms in the smallest degree. It would be an offence against the king's Grace, who has confirmed the charter, and an offence against those my successors, for it could be taken and cited as a precedent for future years. No, I will not set aside any part of the profits of the fair to your use, I will not increase the fee we pay you for it, I will not share in any proportion the tolls on goods and stalls. All belong here, and all must be gathered here, according to the charter.' He saw half a dozen mouths open to protest against so summary a dismissal, and rose in his place, very tall and straight, and chill of voice and eye. 'This chapter is concluded,' he said.

There were one or two among the delegation who would still have tried to insist, but Geoffrey Corviser had a better notion of his own and the town's dignity, and a shrewder idea of what might or might not impress that self-assured and austere man. He made the abbot a deep, abrupt reverence, turned on his heel, and strode out of the chapter-house, and his defeated company recovered their wits and marched as haughtily after him.

There were booths already going up in the great triangle of the horse-fair, and all along the Foregate from the bridge to the corner of the enclosure, where the road veered right towards Saint Giles, and the king's highway to London. There was a newly-erected wooden jetty downstream from the bridge, where the long riverside stretch of the main abbey gardens and orchards began, the rich lowland known as the Gaye. By river, by road, afoot through the forests and over the border from Wales, traders of all kinds began to make their way to Shrewsbury. And into the great court of the abbey flocked all the gentry of the shire, and of neighbouring shires, too, lordlings, knights, yeomen, with their wives and daughters, to take up residence in the overflowing guest-halls for the three days of the annual fair. Subsistence goods they grew, or bred, or brewed, or wove, or span for themselves, the year round, but once a year they came to buy the luxury cloths, the fine wines, the rare preserved fruits, the gold and silver work, all the treasures that appeared on the feast of Saint Peter ad Vincula, and vanished three days later. To these great fairs came merchants even from Flanders and Germany, shippers with French wines, shearers with the wool-clip from Wales, and clothiers with the finished goods, gowns, jerkins, hose, town fashions come to the country. Not many of the vendors had yet arrived, most would appear next day, on the eve of the feast, and set up their booths during the long summer evening, ready to begin selling early on the morrow. But the buyers were arriving in purposeful numbers already, bent on securing good beds for their stay.

When Brother Cadfael came up from the Meole brook and his vegetable-fields for Vespers, after a hard and happy afternoon's work, the great court was seething with visitors, servants and grooms, and the traffic in and out of the stables flowed without cease. He stood for a few minutes to watch the pageant, and Brother Mark at his elbow glowed as he gazed, dazzled by the play of colours and shimmer of movement in the sunlight.

'Yes,' said Cadfael, viewing with philosophical detachment what Brother Mark contemplated with excitement and wonder, 'the world and his wife will be here, either to buy or sell.' And he eyed his young friend attentively, for the boy had seen little enough of the world before entering the order, being thrust through the gates willy-nilly at sixteen by a stingy uncle who grudged him his keep even in exchange for hard work, and he had only recently taken his final vows. 'Do you see anything there to tempt you back into the secular world?'

'No,' said Brother Mark, promptly and serenely. 'But I may look and enjoy, just as I do in the garden when the poppies are in flower. It's no blame to men if they try to put into their own artifacts all the colours and shapes God put into his.'

There were certainly a few of God's more charming artifacts among the throng of visitors moving about the great court and the stable-yard, young women as bright and blooming as the poppies, and all the prettier for being in a high state of expectation, looking forward eagerly to their one great outing of the year. Some came riding their own ponies, some pillion behind husbands or grooms, there was even one horse-litter bringing an important dowager from the south of the shire.

'I never saw it so lively before,' said Mark, gazing with pleasure.

'You've not lived through a fair as yet. Last year the town was under siege all through July and into August, small hope of getting either buyers or sellers into Shrewsbury for any such business. I had my doubts even about this year, but it seems trade's well on the move again, and our gentlefolk are hungrier than ever for what they missed a year ago. It will be a profitable fair, I fancy!'

'Then could we not have spared a tithe to help put the town in order?' demanded Mark.

'You have a way, child, of asking the most awkward questions. I can read very well what was in the provost's mind, since he spoke it out in full. But I'm by no means so sure I know what was in the abbot's, nor that he uttered the half of it. A hard man to read!'

Mark had stopped listening. His eyes were on a rider who had just entered at the gatehouse, and was walking his horse delicately through the moving throng towards the stables. Three retainers on rough-coated ponies followed at his heels, one of them with a cross-bow slung at his saddle. In these perilous times, even here in regions summarily pacified so short a time ago, no gentleman would undertake a longer journey without provision for his own defence, and an arbalest reaches further than a sword. This young man both wore a sword and looked as if he could use it, but he had also brought an archer with him for security.

It was the master who held Mark's eyes. He was perhaps a year or two short of thirty, past the uncertainties of first youth – if, indeed, he had ever suffered them – and at his resplendent best. Handsomely appointed, elegantly mounted on a glistening dark bay, he rode with the negligent ease of one accustomed to horses almost from birth. In the summer heat he had shed his short riding-cotte, and had it slung over his lap, and rode with his shirt open over a spare, muscular chest, hung with a cross on a golden chain. The body thus displayed to view in simple linen shirt and dark hose was long and lissome and proud of its comeliness, and the head that crowned it was bared to the light, a smiling, animated face nicely fashioned about large, commanding dark eyes, and haloed in a cropped cap of dark gold hair, that would have curled had it been allowed to grow a little longer. He came and passed, and Mark's eyes followed him, at once tranquil and wistful, quite without any shade of envy.

'It must be a pleasant thing,' he said thoughtfully, 'to be so made as to give pleasure to those who behold you. Do you suppose he realises his blessings?'

Mark was rather small himself, from undernourishment from childhood, and plain of face, with spiky, straw-coloured hair round his tonsure. Not that he ever viewed himself much in the glass, or realised that he had a pair of great grey eyes of such immaculate clarity that common beauty faltered before them. Nor was Cadfael going to remind him of any such assets.

'As the world usually goes,' he said cheerfully, 'he probably has a mind that looks no further ahead or behind than the length of his own fine eyelashes. But I grant you he's a pleasure to look at. Yet the mind lasts longer. Be glad you have one that will wear well. Come on, now, all this will keep till after supper.'

The word diverted Brother Mark's thoughts very agreeably. He had been hungry all his life until he entered this house, and still he preserved the habit of hunger, so that food, no less than beauty, was unflawed pleasure. He went willingly at Cadfael's side towards Vespers, and the supper that would follow. It was Cadfael who suddenly halted, hailed by name in a high, delighted voice that plucked his head about towards the summons gladly.

A lady, a slender, young, graceful lady with a heavy sheaf of gold hair and a bright oval face, and eyes like irises in twilight, purple and clear. Her body, as Brother Mark saw in his first startled glance, though scarcely swollen as yet, and proudly carried, was girdled high, and rounded below the girdle. There was a life there within. He was not so innocent that he did not know the signs. He should have lowered his eyes, and willed to do so, and could not; she shone so that it was like all the pictures of the Visiting Virgin that he had ever seen. And this vision held out both hands to Brother Cadfael, and called him by his name. Brother Mark, though unwillingly, bent his head and went on his way alone.

'Girl,' said Brother Cadfael heartily, clasping the proffered hands with delight, 'you bloom like a rose! And he never told me!'

'He has not seen you since the winter,' she said, dimpling and flushing, 'and we did not know then. It was no more than a dream, then. And *I* have not seen you since we were wed.'

'And you are happy? And he?'

'Oh, Cadfael, can you ask it!' There had been no need, the radiance Brother Mark had recognised was dazzling Cadfael no less. 'Hugh is here, but he must go to the sheriff first. He'll certainly be asking for you before Compline. I have come to buy a cradle, a beautiful carved cradle for our son. And a Welsh coverlet, in beautiful warm wool, or perhaps a sheepskin. And fine spun wools, to weave his gowns.'

'And you keep well? The child gives you no distress?'

'Distress?' she said, wide-eyed and smiling. 'I have

not had a moment's sickness, only joy. Oh, Brother Cadfael,' she said, breaking into laughter, 'how does it come that a brother of this house can ask such wise questions? Have you not somewhere a son of your own? I could believe it! You know far too much about us women!'

'As I suppose,' said Cadfael cautiously, 'I was born of one, like the rest of us. Even abbots and archbishops come into the world the same away.'

'But I'm keeping you,' she said, remorseful. 'It's time for Vespers, and I'm coming, too. I have so many thanks to pour out, there's never enough time. Say a prayer for our child!' She pressed him by both hands, and floated away through the press towards the guest-hall. Born Aline Siward, now Aline Beringar, wife to the deputy sheriff of Shropshire, Hugh Beringar of Maesbury, near Oswestry. A year married, and Cadfael had been close friend to that marriage, and felt himself enlarged and fulfilled by its happiness. He went on towards the church in high content with the evening, his own mood, and the prospects for the coming days.

When he emerged from the refectory after supper, into an evening still all rose and amber light, the court was as animated as at noon, and new arrivals still entering at the gatehouse. In the cloister Hugh Beringar sat sprawled at ease, waiting for him; a lightweight, limber, dark young man, lean of feature and quizzical of eyebrow. A formidable face, impossible to read unless a man knew the language. Happily, Cadfael did, and read with confidence.

'If you have not lost your cunning,' said the young man, lazily rising, 'or met your overmatch in this new abbot of yours, you can surely find a sound excuse for missing Collations – and a drop of good wine to share with a friend.'

'Better than an excuse,' said Cadfael readily, 'I have

an acknowledged reason. They're having trouble in the grange court with scour among the calves, and want a brewing of my cure in a hurry. And I daresay I can find you a draught of something better than small ale. We can sit outside the workshop, such a warm evening. But are you not a neglectful husband,' he reproved, as they fell companionably into step on their way into the gardens, 'to abandon your lady for an old drinking crony?'

'My lady,' said Hugh ruefully, 'has altogether abandoned me! A breeding girl has only to show her nose in the guest-hall, and she's instantly swept away by a swarm of older dames, all cooing like doves, and loading her with advice on everything from diet to midwives' magic. Aline is holding conference with all of them, hearing details of all their confinements, and taking note of all their recommendations. And since I can neither spin, nor weave, nor sew, I'm banished.' He sounded remarkably complacent about it, and being well aware of it himself, laughed aloud. 'But she told me she had seen you, and you needed no telling. How do you think she is looking?'

'Radiant!' said Cadfael. 'In full bloom, and prettier than ever.'

In the herb-garden, shaded along one side by its high hedge from the declining sun, the heavy fragrances of the day hung like a spell. They settled on a bench under the eaves of Cadfael's workshop, with a jug of wine between them.

'But I must start my draught brewing,' said Cadfael. 'You may talk to me while I do it. I shall hear you within, and I'll be with you as soon as I have it stirring. What's the news from the great world? Is King Stephen secure on his throne now, do you think?'

Beringar considered that in silence for a few moments, listening contentedly to the soft sounds of Cadfael's movements within the hut. 'With all the west still holding out for the empress, however warily, I doubt it. Nothing is moving now, but it's an ominous stillness. You know that Earl Robert of Gloucester is in Normandy with the empress?'

'So we'd heard. It's not to be wondered at, he is her half-brother, and fond of her, so they say, and not an envious man.'

'A good man,' agreed Hugh, doing an opponent generous justice, 'one of the few on either side not grasping for what he himself can get. The west, however quiet now, will do what Robert says. I can't believe he'll hold off for ever. And even out of the west, he has kinsmen and influence. The word runs that he and Maud, from their refuge in France, are working away quietly to enlist powerful allies, wherever they see a hope. If that's true, this civil war is by no means over. Promised enough support, there'll be a bid for the lady's cause, soon or late.'

'Robert has daughters married about the land,' said Cadfael thoughtfully, 'and all of them to men of might. One of them to the earl of Chester, I recall. If a few of that measure declared for the empress, you might well have a war on your hands to some purpose.'

Beringar drew a long face, and then shrugged off the thought. Earl Ranulf of Chester was certainly one of the most powerful men in the kingdom, virtually king himself of an immense palatine where his writ ran, and no other. But for that very reason he was less likely to feel the need to declare for either side in the contention for the throne. Himself supreme, and unlikely ever to be threatened in his own possessions by either Maud or Stephen, he could afford to sit back and watch his own borders, not merely with a view to preserving them intact, rather to extending them. A land at odds with itself offers opportunities, as well as threats.

'Ranulf will need a lot of persuading, kinsman or no.

He's very well as he is, and if he does move it will be because he sees profit and power in it for himself, and the empress will come a poor second. He's not the man to risk anything for any cause but his own.'

Cadfael came out from the hut to sit beside him, drawing grateful breath in the evening coolness, for he had his small brazier burning within, beneath his simmering brew. 'That's better! Now fill me a cup, Hugh, I'm more than ready for it.' And after a long and satisfying draught he said thoughtfully: 'There were some fears this disturbed state of things could ruin the fair even this year, but it seems trade keeps on the move while barons skulk in their castles. The prospects are excellent, after all.'

'For the abbey, perhaps,' agreed Hugh. 'The town is less happy about the outlook, from all we heard as we passed through. This new abbot of yours has set the burgesses properly by the ears.'

'Ah, you've heard about that?' Cadfael recounted the course of the argument, in case his friend had caught but one side of it. 'They have a case for seeking relief, no question. But so has he for refusing it, and he's standing firm on his rights. No way round it in law, he's taking no more than is granted to him. And no less!' he added, and sighed.

'Feelings are running high in the town,' warned Beringar seriously. 'I would not be sure you may not have trouble yet. I doubt if the provost made any too much of their needs. The word in the town is that this may be law, but it is not justice. But what's the word with you? How are you faring in the new dispensation?'

'You'll hear murmurs even within our walls,' admitted Cadfael, 'if you keep your ears open. But for my part, I have no complaint. He's a hard man, but fair, and at least as hard on himself as on others. We've been spoiled and easy with Heribert, and the new curb pulled us up pretty sharply, but that's the sum of it. I have much confidence in the man. He'll chasten where he sees fault, but he'll stand by his own against any power where they are threatened blameless. He's a man I'd be glad to have beside me in any battle.'

'But his loyalty's limited to his own?' said Beringar slyly, and cocked a slender black brow.

'We live in a contentious world,' said Brother Cadfael, who had lived more than half his life in the thick of the battles. 'Who says peace would be good for us? I don't know the man well enough yet to know what's in his mind. I have not found him limited, but his vows are to his vocation and this house. Give him room and time, Hugh, and we shall see what follows. Time was when I was in two minds, or more, about *you*!' His voice marvelled and smiled at the thought. 'Not very long, however! I shall soon get the measure of Radulfus, too. Hand me the jug, lad, and then I must go and stir this brew for the calves. How long have we yet to Compline?'

## Chapter Two

On the thirty-first of July the vendors came flooding in, by road and by river. From noon onward the horse-fair was marked out in lots for stalls and booths, and the abbey stewards were standing by to guide pedlars and merchants to their places, and levy the tolls due on the amount of merchandise they brought. A halfpenny for a modest man-load, a penny for a horse-load, from twopence to fourpence for a cart-load, depending on the size and capacity, and higher fees in proportion for the goods unloaded from the river barges that tied up at the temporary landing-stage along the Gaye. The entire length of the Foregate hummed and sparkled with movement and colour and chatter, the abbey barn and stable outside the wall was full, children and dogs ran among the booths and between the wheels of the carts, excited and shrill.

The discipline of the day's devotions within the walls was not relaxed, but between offices a certain air of holiday gaiety had entered with the guests, and novices and pupils were allowed to wander and gaze without penalty. Abbot Radulfus held himself aloof, as was due to his dignity, and left the superintendence of the occasion and the collection of tolls to his lay stewards, but for all that he knew everything that was going on, and had measures in mind to deal with any emergency. As soon as the arrival of the first Flemish merchant was reported to him, together with the news that the man had little French, he dispatched Brother Matthew, who had lived for some years in Flanders in his earlier days, and could speak fluent Flemish, to deal with any problems that might arise. If the fine-cloth merchants were coming, there was good reason to afford them every facility, for they were profitable visitors. It was a mark of the significance of the Shrewsbury fair that they should undertake so long a journey from the East Anglian ports where they put in, and find it worth their while to hire carts or horses for the overland pilgrimage.

The Welsh, of course, would certainly be present in some numbers, but for the most part they would be the local people who had a foot on either side the border, and knew enough English to need no interpreters. It came as a surprise to Brother Cadfael to be intercepted once again as he left the refectory after supper, this time by the steward of the grange court, preoccupied and breathless with business, and told that he was needed at the jetty, to take care of one who spoke nothing but Welsh, and a man of consequence, indeed of self-importance, who would not be fobbed off with the suspect aid of a local Welshman who might well be in competition with him on the morrow.

'Prior Robert gives you leave, for as long as you're needed. It's a fellow by the name of Rhodri ap Huw, from Mold. He's brought a great load up the Dee, and ported it over to Vrnwy and Severn, which must have cost him plenty.'

'What manner of goods?' asked Cadfael, as they made for the gatehouse together. His interest was immediate and hearty. Nothing could have suited him better than a sound excuse to be out among the noise and bustle along the Foregate.

'What looks like a very fine wool-clip, mainly. And also honey and mead. And I thought I saw some bundles of hides – maybe from Ireland, if he trades out of the Dee. And there's the man himself.'

Rhodri ap Huw stood solid as a rock on the wooden planking of the jetty beside his moored barge, and let the tides of human activity flow round him. The river ran green and still, at a good level for high summer; even boats of deeper draught than usual had made the passage without mishap, and were unloading and unbaling on all sides. The Welshman watched, measuring other men's bales with shrewd, narrowed dark eyes, and pricing what he saw. He looked about fifty years old, and so assured and experienced that it seemed strange he had never picked up English. Not a tall man, but square-built and powerful, fierce Welsh bones islanded in a thick growth of thorny black hair and beard. His dress, though plain and workmanlike, was of excellent material and well-fitted. He saw the steward hurrying towards him, evidently having carried out his wishes to the letter, and large, white teeth gleamed contentedly from the thicket of the black beard.

'Here am I, Master Rhodri,' said Cadfael cheerfully, 'to keep you company in your own tongue. And my name is Cadfael, at your service for all your present needs.'

'And very welcome, Brother Cadfael,' said Rhodri ap Huw heartily. 'I hope you'll pardon my fetching you away from your devotions ...'

'I'll do better. I'll thank you! A pity to have to miss all this bustle, I can do with a glimpse of the world now and again.'

Sharp, twinkling eyes surveyed him from head to toe in one swift glance. 'You'll be from the north yourself, I fancy. Mold is where I come from.'

'Close by Trefriw I was born.'

'A Gwynedd man. But one who's been a sight further through the world than Trefriw, by the look of you, brother. As I have. Well, here are my two fellows, ready to unload and porter for me before I send on part of my cargo downriver to Bridgnorth, where I have a sale for mead. Shall we have the goods ashore first?'

The steward bade them choose a stand at whatever point Master Rhodri thought fit when he had viewed the ground, and left them to supervise the unloading. Rhodri's two nimble little Welsh boatmen went to work briskly, hefting the heavy bales of hides and the wool-sacks with expert ease, and piling them on the jetty, and Rhodri and Cadfael addressed themselves pleasurably to watching the lively scene around them; as many of the townsfolk and the abbey guests were also doing. On a fine summer evening it was the best of entertainments to lean over the parapet of the bridge, or stroll along the green path to the Gaye, and stare at an annual commotion which was one of the year's highlights. If some of the townspeople looked on with dour faces, and muttered to one another in sullen undertones, that was no great wonder, either. Yesterday's confrontation had been reported throughout the town, they knew they had been turned away empty-handed.

'A thing worth noting,' said Rhodri, spreading his thick legs on the springy boards, 'how both halves of England can meet in commerce, while they fall out in every other field. Show a man where there's money to be made, and he'll be there. If barons and kings had the same good sense, a country could be at peace, and handsomely the gainer by it.'

'Yet I fancy,' said Cadfael dryly, 'that there'll be some hot contention here even between traders, before the three days are up. More ways than one of cutting throats.'

'Well, every wise man keeps a weapon about him, whatever suits his skill, that's only good sense, too. But we live together, we live together, better than princes manage it. Though I grant you,' he said weightily, 'princes make good use of these occasions, for that matter. No place like one of your greater fairs for exchanging news and views without being noticed, or laying plots and stratagems, or meeting someone you'd liefer not be seen meeting. Nowhere so solitary as in the middle of a market-place!'

'In a divided land,' said Cadfael thoughtfully, 'you may very well be right.'

'For instance – look to your left a ways, but don't turn. You see the meagre fellow in the fine clothes, the smooth-shaven one with the mincing walk? Come to watch who's arriving by water! You may be sure if *he*'s here at all, he's come early, and has his stall already up and stocked, to be free to view the rest of us. That's Euan of Shotwick, the glover, and an important man about Earl Ranulf's court at Chester, I can tell you.'

'For his skill at his trade?' asked Cadfael dryly, observing the lean, fastidious, high-nosed figure with interest.

'That and other fields, brother. Euan of Shotwick is one of the sharpest of all of Earl Ranulf's intelligencers, and much relied on, and if he's setting up a booth here as far as Shrewsbury, it may well be for more purposes than trade. And then on the other side, look, that great barge standing off ready to come alongside – downstream of us. See the cut of her? Bristol-built, for a thousand marks! Straight out of the west country, and the city the king failed to take last year, and has let well alone ever since.'

Above the softly-flowing surface of Severn, its green silvered now with slanting evening sunlight, the barge sidled along the grassy shore towards the end of the jetty. She loomed impressively opulent and graceful, cunningly built to draw hardly more water than boats half her capacity, and yet steer well and ride steadily.

She had a single mast, and what seemed to be a neat, closed cabin aft, and three crewmen were poling her inshore with easy, light touches, and waiting to moor her alongside as soon as there was room. Twenty pence, as like as not, thought Cadfael, before *she* gets her load ashore and cleared!

'Made to carry wine, and carry it steady,' said Rhodri ap Huw, narrowing his sharply-calculating eyes on the boat. 'Some of the best wines of France come into Bristol, they should have a ready sale as far north as this. I should know that rig!'

A considerable number of onlookers, whether they recognised her port and rig or not, were curious enough to come down from the bridge and the highroad to see the Bristol boat come in. She was remarkable enough among her fellow-craft to draw all eyes. Cadfael caught sight of a number of known faces craning among the crowd: Edric Flesher's wife Petronilla, Aline Beringar's maid Constance leaning over the bridge, one of the abbey stewards forgetting his duties to stare; and suddenly sunlight on a head of dark gold hair, cropped short, and a young man came running lightly down from the highway, to halt on the grass slope above the jetty, and watched admiringly as the Bristol boat slid alongside, ready to be made fast. The lordling whose assured beauty had aroused Mark's wistful admiration was evidently just as inquisitive as the raggedest barefoot urchin from the Foregate.

The two Welshmen had completed their unloading by this time, and were waiting for orders, and Rhodri ap Huw was not the man to let his interest in other men's business interfere with his own.

'They'll be a fair while unloading,' he said briskly. 'Shall we go and choose a good place for my stall, while the field's open?'

Cadfael led the way along the Foregate, where

several booths had already been set up. 'You'll prefer a site on the horse-fair itself, I fancy, where all the roads meet.'

'Ah, my customers will find me, wherever I am,' said Rhodri smugly; but for all that, he kept a shrewd eye on all the possibilities, and took his time about selecting his place, even when they had walked the length of the Foregate and come to the great open triangle of the horse-fair. The abbey servants had set up a number of more elaborate booths, that could be closed and locked, and supply living shelter for their holders, and these were let out for rents. Other traders brought their own serviceable trestles and light roofs, while the small country vendors would come in early each morning and display their wares on the dry ground, or on a woven brychan, filling all the spaces between. For Rhodri nothing was good enough but the best. He fixed upon a stout booth near the abbey barn and stable, where all customers coming in for the day could stable their beasts, and in the act could not fail to notice the goods on the neighbouring stalls.

'This will serve very well. One of my lads will sleep the nights here.' The elder of the two had followed them, balancing the first load easily in a sling over his shoulders, while the other remained to guard the merchandise stacked on the jetty. Now he began to stow what he had brought, while Rhodri and Cadfael set off back to the river to dispatch his fellow after him. On the way they intercepted one of the stewards, notified him of the site chosen, and came to terms for the rental. Brother Cadfael's immediate duty was done, but he was as interested in the growing bustle along the road and by the Severn as any other man who saw the like but once a year, and there was time to spare yet before Compline. It was good, too, to be speaking Welsh, there was seldom need within the walls.

They reached the point where the track turned aside from the highway to go down to the waterside, and looked down upon a lively scene. The Bristol boat was moored, and her three crewmen beginning to hoist casks of wine on to the jetty, while a big, portly, red-faced elderly gentleman in a long gown of fashionable cut, his capuchon twisted up into an elaborate hat, swung wide sleeves as he pointed and beckoned, giving orders at large. A fleshy but powerful face, round and choleric, with bristly brows like furze, and bluish jowls. He moved with surprising agility and speed, and plainly he considered himself a man of importance, and expected others to recognise him as such on sight.

'I thought it might well be!' said Rhodri ap Huw, pleased with his own acuteness and knowledge of widespread affairs. 'Thomas of Bristol, they call him, one of the biggest importers of wine into the port there, and deals in a small way in fancy wares from the east, sweetmeats and spices and candies. The Venetians bring them in from Cyprus and Syria. Costly and profitable! The ladies will pay high for something their neighbours have not! What did I say? Money will bring men together. Whether they hold for Stephen or the empress, they'll come and rub shoulders at your fair, brother.'

'By the look of him,' said Cadfael, 'a man of consequence in the city of Bristol.'

'So he is, and I'd have said in very good odour with Robert of Gloucester, but business is business, and it would take more than the simple fear of venturing into enemy territory to keep him at home, when there's good money to be made.'

They had turned to begin the descent to the riverside when they were aware of a growing murmur of excitement among the people watching from the bridge, and of heads turning to look towards the town gates on the other side of the river. The evening light, slanting from the west, cast deep shadows under one parapet and half across the bridge, but above floated a faint, moving cloud of fine dust, glittering in the sunset rays, and advancing towards the abbey shore. A tight knot of young men came into sight, shearing through the strolling onlookers at a smart pace, like a determined little army on the march. All the rest were idling the time pleasurably away on a fine evening, these were bound somewhere, in resolution and haste, the haste, perhaps, all the more aggressive lest the resolution be lost. There might have been as many as five and twenty of them, all male and all young. Some of them Cadfael knew. Martin Bellecote's boy Edwy was there, and Edric Flesher's journeyman, and scions of half a dozen respected trades within the town; and at their head strode the provost's own son, young Philip Corviser, jutting a belligerent chin and swinging clenched hands to the rhythm of his long-striding walk. They looked very grave and very dour, and people gazed at them in wonder and speculation, and drew in at a more cautious pace after their passing, to watch what would happen.

'If this is not the face of battle,' said Rhodri ap Huw alertly, viewing the grim young faces while they were still safely distant, 'I have never seen it. I did hear that your house has a difference of opinion with the town. I'll away and see all those goods of mine safely stacked away under lock and key, before the trumpets blow.' And he tucked up his sleeves and was off down the path to the jetty as nimbly as a squirrel, and hoisting his precious jars of honey out of harm's way, leaving Cadfael still thoughtfully gazing by the roadside. The merchant's instincts, he thought, were sound enough. The elders of the town had made their plea and been sent away empty-handed. To judge by their faces, the younger and hotter-headed worthies of the town of

Shrewsbury had resolved upon stronger measures. A rapid survey reassured him that they were unarmed, as far as he could see not even a staff among them. But the face, no question, was the face of battle, and the trumpets were about to blow.

# Chapter Three

The advancing phalanx reached the end of the bridge, and checked for no more than a moment, while their leader cast calculating glances forward along the Foregate, now populous with smaller stalls, and down at the jetty, and gave some brisk order. Then he, with perhaps ten of his stalwarts on his heels, turned and plunged down the path to the river, while the rest marched vehemently ahead. The interested townspeople, equally mutely and promptly, split into partisan groups, and pursued both contingents. Not one of them would willingly miss what was to come. Cadfael, more soberly, eyed the passing ranks, and was confirmed in believing that they came with the most austere intentions; there was not a bludgeon among them, and he doubted if any of them ever carried knives. Nothing about them was warlike, except their faces. Besides, he knew most of them, there was no wilful harm in any. All the same, he turned down the path after them, not quite easy in his mind. The Corviser sprig was known for a wild one, clever, bursting with hot and suspect ideas, locked in combat with his elders half his time, and occasionally liable to drink rather more than at this stage he could carry. Though this evening he had certainly not been drinking; he had far more urgent matters on his mind.

Brother Cadfael sighed, descending the path to the waterside half-reluctantly. The earnest young are so dangerously given to venturing beyond the point where experience turns back. And the sharper they are, the more likely to come by wounds.

He was not at all surprised to find that Rhodri ap Huw, that most experienced of travellers, had vanished from the jetty, together with his second porter and all his goods. Rhodri himself would not be far, once he had seen all his merchandise well on its way to being locked in the booth on the horse-fair. He would want to watch all that passed, and make his own dispositions accordingly, but he would be out of sight, and somewhere where he could make his departure freely whenever he deemed it wise. But there were half a dozen boats of various sizes busy unloading, dominated by Thomas of Bristol's noble barge. Its owner heard the sudden surge of urgent feet on the downhill track, and turned to level an imperious glance that way, before returning to his business of supervising the landing of his goods. The array of casks and bales on the boards was impressive. The young men surging down to the river could not fail to make an accurate estimate of the powers they faced.

'Gentlemen ...!' Philip Corviser hailed them all loudly, coming to a halt with feet spread, confronting Thomas of Bristol. He had a good, ringing voice; it carried, and lesser dealers dropped what they were doing to listen. 'Gentlemen, I beg a hearing, as you are citizens all, of whatever town, as I am of Shrewsbury, and as you care for your own town as I do for mine! You are here paying rents and tolls to the abbey, while the abbey denies any aid to the town. And we have greater need than ever the abbey has, of some part of what you bring.'

He drew breath hard, having spent his first wind. He was a gangling lad, not yet quite in command of his long limbs, being barely twenty and only just at the end of his growing. Spruce in his dress, but down at the heel, Cadfael noticed – proof of the old saying that the shoemaker's son is always the one who goes barefoot! He had a thick thatch of reddish dark hair, and a decent, homely face now pale, with passion under his summer tan. A good, deft workman, they said, when he could be stopped from flying off after some angry cause or other. Certainly he had a cause now, bless the lad, he was pouring out to these hard-headed business men all the arguments his father had used to the abbot at chapter, in dead earnest, and – heaven teach him better sense! – even with hopes of convincing them!

'If the abbey turns a cold eye on the town's troubles, should you side with them? We are here to tell you our side of the story, and appeal to you as men who also have to bear the burdens of your own boroughs, and may well have seen at home what war and siege can do to your own walls and pavings. Is it unreasonable that we should ask for a share in the profits of the fair? The abbey came by no damage last year, as the town did. If they will not bear their part for the common good, we address ourselves to you, who have no such protection from the hardships of the world, and will have fellow-feeling with those who share the like burdens.'

They were beginning to lose interest in him, to shrug, and turn back to their unloading. He raised his voice sharply in appeal.

'All we ask is that you will hold back a tithe of the dues you pay to the abbey, and pay them instead to the town for murage and pavage. If all hold together, what can the abbey stewards do against you? There need be no cost to you above what you would be paying in any event, and we should have something nearer to justice. What do you say? Will you help us?'

They would not! The growl of indifference and derision hardly needed words. What, set up a challenge to what was laid down by charter, when they had nothing to gain by it? Why should they take the risk? They turned to their work, shrugging him off. The young men grouped at his back set up among themselves a counter murmur, still controlled but growing angry. And Thomas of Bristol, massive and contemptuous, waved a fist in their spokesman's face, and said impatiently: 'Stand out of the way, boy, you are hindering your betters! Pay a tithe to the town indeed! Are not the abbey rights set down according to law? And can you, dare you tell me they do not pay the fee demanded of them by charter? If you have a complaint that they are failing to keep the law, take it to the sheriff, where it belongs, but don't come here with your nonsense. Now be off, and let honest men get on with their work.'

The young man took fire. 'The men of Shrewsbury are as honest as you, sir, though something less boastful about it. We take honesty for granted here! And it is not nonsense that our town goes with broken walls and broken streets, while abbey and Foregate have escaped all such damage. No, but listen ...'

The merchant turned a broad, hunched back, with disdainful effect, and stalked away to pick up the staff he had laid against his piled barrels, and motion his men to continue their labours. Philips started indignantly after him, for the act was stingingly deliberate, as though a gnat, a mere persistent nuisance, had been brushed aside.

'Master merchant,' he called hotly, 'one word more!' And he laid an arresting hand to Thomas's fine, draped sleeve.

They were two choleric people, and it might have come to it even at the best, sooner or later, but Cadfael's impression was that Thomas had been genuinely startled by the grasp at his arm, and believed he was about to be attacked. Whatever the cause, he swung round and struck out blindly with the staff he held. The boy flung up his arm, but too late thoroughly to protect his head. The blow fell heavily on his forearms and temple, and laid him flat on the planking of the jetty, with blood oozing from a cut above his ear.

That was the end of all peaceful and dignified protest, and the declaration of war. Many things happened on the instant. Philip had fallen without a cry, and lay half-stunned, but someone had certainly cried out, a small, protesting shriek, instantly swallowed up in the roar of anger from the young men of the town. Two of them rushed to their fallen leader, but the rest, bellowing for vengeance, lunged to confront the equally roused traders, and closed with them merrily. In a moment the goods newly disembarked were being hoisted and flung into the river, and one of the raiders soon followed them, with a bigger splash. Fortunately those who lived all their lives by Severn usually learned to swim even before they learned to walk, and the youngster was in no danger of drowning. By the time he had hauled himself out and returned to the fray, there was a fully-fledged riot in progress all along the riverside.

Several of the cooler-headed citizens had moved in, though cautiously, to try to separate the combatants, and talk a little sense into the furious young; and one or two, not cautious enough, had come in for blows meant for the foe, the common fate of those who try to make peace where no one is inclined for it.

Cadfael among the rest had rushed down to the jetty, intent on preventing what might well be a second and fatal blow, to judge by the merchant's congested countenance and brandished staff. But someone else was before him. A girl had clambered frantically up out of the tiny cabin of the barge, kilted her skirts and leaped ashore, in time to cling with all her weight to the quivering arm, and plead in agitated tones:

'Uncle, don't, please don't! He did no violence!

You've hurt him badly!'

Philip Corviser's brown eyes, all this time open but unseeing, blinked furiously at the sound of so unexpected a voice. He heaved himself shakily to his knees, remembered his injury and his grievance, and gathered sprawled limbs and faculties to surge to his feet and do battle. Not that his efforts would have been very effective; his legs gave under him as he tried to rise, and he gripped his head between steadying hands as though it might fall off if he shook it. But it was the sight of the girl that stopped him short. There she stood, clinging to the merchant's arm and pleading angelically into his ear, in tones that could have cooled a dragon, her eyes all the time dilated and anxious and pitying on Philip. And calling the old demon 'uncle'! Philip's revenge was put clean out of his reach in an instant, but he scarcely felt a pang at the deprivation, to judge by the transformation that came over his bruised and furious face. Swaying on one knee, still dazed, he stared at the girl as pilgrims might stare at miraculous visions, or lost wanderers at the Pole star.

She was well worth looking at, a young thing of about eighteen or nineteen years, bare-armed and bare-headed, with two great braids of blue-black hair swinging to her waist, and framed between them a round, childish face all roses and snow, lit by two long-lashed dark blue eyes, at this moment huge with alarm and concern. No wonder the mere sound of her voice could tame her formidable uncle, as surely as the sight of her had checked and held at gaze the two young men who had rushed to salvage and avenge their leader, and who now stood abashed, gaping and harmless.

It was at that moment that the fight on the jetty, which had become a melee hopelessly tangled, reeled their way, thudding along the planks, knocked over the stack of small barrels, and sent them rolling thunderously in all directions. Cadfael grasped young Corviser under the arms, hoisted him to his feet and hauled him out of harm's way, thrusting him bodily into the arms of his friends for safe-keeping, since he was still in a daze. A rolling cask swept Thomas's feet from under him, and the girl, flung aside in his fall, swayed perilously on the edge of the jetty.

An agile figure darted past Cadfael with a flash of gold hair, leaped another rolling cask as nimbly as a deer, and plucked her back to safety in a long arm. The almost insolent grace and assurance was as familiar as the yellow hair. Cadfael contented himself with helping Thomas to his feet, and drawing him aside out of danger, and was not particularly surprised, when that was done, to see that the long arm was still gallantly clasped round the girl's waist. Nor was she in any hurry to extricate herself. Indeed, she was gazing at the smiling, comely, reassuring face of her rescuer wide-eyed, much as Philip Corviser had gazed at her.

'There, you're quite safe! But let me help you back aboard, you'd do best to stay there a while, your uncle, too. I advise it, sir,' he said earnestly. 'No one will offer you further offence. With this lady beside you, no one could be so ungallant,' he said, his eyes wide in candid admiration. The cream of the girl's fair skin turned all to rose.

Thomas of Bristol dusted himself down with slightly shaky hands, for he was a big man, and had fallen heavily. 'I thank you, sir, warmly, for your help. You, too, brother. But my wines – my goods –'

'Leave them to us, sir. What can be salvaged, shall be. You stay safe aboard, and wait. This cannot continue, the law will be out after these turbulent young fools any moment. Half of them are off along the Foregate, overturning stalls and hounding the abbey stewards. Before long they'll be in the town gaol with sore heads, wishing they'd had better sense than pick a fight with the abbot of a Benedictine house.'

His eye was on Cadfael, who was busy righting and retrieving the fugitive casks, and still within earshot. He felt himself being drawn companionably into this masterful young man's planning, perhaps as reassurance and guarantee of respectability. The eyes were slightly mischievous, though the face retained its decent gravity. The nearest Benedictine was being gently teased as representative of his order.

'My name,' said the rescuer blithely, 'is Ivo Corbière, of the manor of Stanton Cobbold in this shire, though the main part of my honour lies in Cheshire. If you'll allow me, I'm happy to offer my help ...' He had taken his arm from about the girl's waist by then, decorously if reluctantly, but his gaze continued to embrace and flatter her; she was well aware of it, and it did not displease her. 'There!' cried Corbière triumphantly, as a shrill whistle resounded from a youth hanging over the parapet of the bridge above them. 'Now watch them dive to cover! Their look-out sees the sheriff's men turning out to quell the riot.'

His judgment was accurate enough. Half a dozen heads snapped up sharply at the sound, noted the urgently waving arm, and half a dozen dishevelled youths extricated themselves hastily from the fight, dropped whatever they were holding, and made off at speed in several directions, some along the Gaye, towards the coverts by the riverside, some up the slope into the tangle of narrow lanes behind the Foregate, one under the arch of the bridge, to emerge on the upstream side with no worse harm than wet feet. In a few moments the sharp clatter of hooves drummed over the bridge, and half a dozen of the sheriff's men came trotting down to the jetty, while the rest of the company swept on towards the horse-fair.

'As good as over!' said Ivo Corbière gaily. 'Brother,

will you lend an oar? I fancy you know this river better than I, and there's many a man's hard-won living afloat out there, and much of it may yet be saved.'

He asked no leave; he had selected already the smallest and most manageable boat that swung beside the jetty, and he was across the boards and down into it almost before the sheriff's men had driven their mounts in among the still-locked combatants, and begun to pluck the known natives out by the hair. Brother Cadfael followed. With Compline but ten minutes away, by his mental clock, he should have made his escape and left the salvage to this confident and commanding young man, but he had been sent out here to aid a client of the abbey fair, and could he not argue that he was still about the very same business? He was in the borrowed boat, an oar in his hand and his eye upon the nearest cask bobbing on the bright sunset waters, before he had found an answer; which was answer enough.

The noise receded soon. Everyone left here was busily hooking bales and bundles out of the river, pursuing some downstream to coves where they had lodged, abandoning one or two small items too sodden and too vulnerable to be saved, writing off minor losses, thankfully calculating profits still to be made after fees and rentals and tolls were paid. The damage was not so great, after all, it could be carried. Along the Foregate stalls were being righted, goods laid out afresh. Doubtful if the pandemonium had ever reached the horse-fair, where the great merchants unrolled their bales. In the stony confines of the castle and the town gaol, no doubt, some dozen or so youngsters of the town were nursing their bruises and grudges, and wondering how their noble and dignified protest had disintegrated into such a shambles. As for Philip Corviser, nobody knew where he had fetched up, once he shook off the devotees who had helped him away from the jetty in a daze. The brief venture was over, the cost not too great. Not even the sheriff, Gilbert Prestcote, was going to bear down too hard on those well-meaning but ill-advised young men of Shrewsbury.

'Gentlemen,' said Thomas of Bristol, eased and expansive, 'I cannot thank you enough for such generous help. No, the casks will have taken no hurt. Those who buy my wines should and do store them properly a good while before tapping, their condition will not be impaired. The sugar confections, thanks be, were not yet unloaded. No, I have suffered no real hurt. And my child here is much in your debt. Come, my dear, don't hide there within, make your respects to such good friends! Let me present my niece Emma, my sister's daughter, Emma Vernold, heiress to her father, who was a master-mason in our city, and also to me, for I have no other kin. Emma, my dear, you may pour the wine!'

The girl had made good use of the interval. She came forth now with her braids of hair coiled in a gilded net on her neck, and a fine tunic of embroidered linen over her plain gown. Not, thought Cadfael, for my benefit! It was high time for him to take his leave and return to his proper duties. He had missed Compline in favour of retrieving goods from the waters, and he would have to put in an hour or so in his workshop yet before he could seek his bed. No one would be early to bed on this night, however. Thomas of Bristol was not the man to leave the supervision of his booth and the disposition of his goods to others, however trustworthy his three servants might be; he would soon be off to the horse-fair to see everything safely stowed to his own satisfaction, ready for the morrow. And if he thought fit to leave those two handsome young people together here until his return, that was his affair. Mention of the manor of Stanton Cobbold, and as the least part of Corbière's honour, at that, had made its impression. There had been no real need for that careful mention of Mistress Emma's prospective wealth; but dutiful uncles and guardians must be ever on the alert for good matches for their girls, and this young man was already taken with her face before ever he heard of her fortune. Small wonder, she was a beautiful child by any standards.

Brother Cadfael excused himself from lingering, wished the company goodnight, and walked back at leisure to the gatehouse. The Foregate stretched busy and populous, but at peace. Order had been restored, and Saint Peter's Fair could open on the morrow without further disruption.

## Chapter Four

Hugh Beringar came back from a final patrol along the Foregate well past ten o'clock, an hour when all dutiful brothers should have been fast asleep in the dortoir. He was by no means surprised to find that Cadfael was not. They met in the great court, as Cadfael came back from closing his workshop in the herb-garden. It was still a clear twilight, and the west had a brilliant afterglow.

'I hear you've been in the thick of it,' said Hugh, stretching and yawning. 'Did ever I know you when you were not? Mad young fools, what did they hope to do, that their elders could not! And then to run wild as they did, and ruin their case even with those who had sympathy for them! Now their sires will have fines to pay, and the town lose more for the night's work than ever it stood to gain. Cadfael, I take no joy in heaving decent, silly lads into prison, I have a foul taste in my mouth from it. Come into the gatehouse for a while, and share a cup with me. You may as well stay awake until Matins now.'

'Aline will be waiting for you,' objected Cadfael.

'Aline, bless her good sense, will be fast asleep, for I'm bound to the castle yet to report on this disturbance. I doubt I shall be there over the night. Come and tell me how all this went wrong, for they tell me it began down at the jetty, where you were.'

Cadfael went with him willingly. They sat together in

the anteroom of the gatehouse, and the porter, used to such nocturnal activities when the deputy sheriff of the shire was lodged within, brought them wine, made tolerant enquiry of progress, and left them to their colloquy.

'How many have you taken up?' asked Cadfael, when he had given an account of what had happened by the river.

'Seventeen. And it should have been eighteen,' owned Hugh grimly, 'if I had not hauled Bellecote's boy Edwy aside without witnesses, put the fear of God into him, and sent him home with a flea in his ear. Not sixteen yet! But sharp enough to know very well what he was about, the imp! I should not have done it.'

'His father was one of yesterday's delegates,' said Cadfael, 'and he's a loyal child, as well as a bold one. I'm glad you let him away home. And young Corviser?'

'No, we've not laid hand on him, though a dozen witnesses say he was the ringleader, and captained the whole enterprise. But he has to go home some time, and he'll not get in at the gate a free man. Not a hope of it!'

'He came lecturing like a doctor,' said Cadfael seriously, 'and never a threatening move. It was when he was struck down that the wild lads took the bit between their teeth and laid about them. I saw it! The man who struck him lashed out in alarm, I grant you, but without cause.'

'I take your word for that, and I'll stand by it. But he led the attack, and he'll end with the rest, as he should, seeing he loosed this on us all. They'll be bailed by their fathers, the lot of them,' said Hugh wearily, and passed long fingers over tired eyelids. 'Do I seem to you, Cadfael, to be turning horribly into a crown official? That I should not like!'

'No,' said Cadfael judicially, 'you're not too far gone. Still a glint in the eye and a quirk in the mind. You'll do yet!'

'Gracious in you! And you say this Bristol merchant struck the silly wretch down without provocation?'

'He imagined provocation. The boy laid a detaining hand on his arm from behind, meaning no ill, but the man took fright. He had a staff in his hand, he turned on him and hit out. Felled him like an ox! I doubt if he had the strength to knock the trestle from under a stall, after that. For all I know, he may be fallen out of his senses, somewhere, unless his friends have kept their hands on him.'

Hugh looked at him across the trestle on which their own elbows were spread, and smiled. 'If ever I want for an advocate, I'll come running to you. Well, I do know the lad, he has a well-hung tongue, and lets it wag far too freely, and he has a hot temper and a warm heart, and lets the pair of them run away with his own sense – if you claim he has any!'

The lay porter put his bald brown crown and round red face into the room. 'My lord, there's a lady here at the gate has a trouble on her mind, and asks a word. One Mistress Emma Vernold, niece to the merchant Thomas of Bristol. Will you have her come in?'

They looked at each other across the board with raised brows and startled eyes. 'The same man?' said Beringer, marvelling.

'The same man, surely! And the same girl! But the uproar was all over. What can she be wanting here at this hour, and what's her uncle about, letting her venture loose into the night?'

'We'd best be finding out,' said Hugh, resigned. 'Let the lady come in, if I'm the man she wants.'

'She asked first for a guest here, Ivo Corbière, but I know he's still out viewing the preparations along the Foregate. And when I mentioned that you were here, she begged a word with you. Glad to find the law here and awake, seemingly.'

'Ask her to step in, then. And Cadfael, stay, if you'll be so good, she's had speech with you already, she may be glad of a known face.'

Emma Vernold came in hurriedly yet hesitantly, unsure of herself in this unfamiliar place, and made a hasty reverence. 'My lord, I pray your pardon for troubling you so late ...' She saw Brother Cadfael, and half-smiled, relieved but distracted. 'I am Emma Vernold, I came with my uncle, Thomas of Bristol, we have our own living-space on his barge by the bridge. And this is my uncle's man Gregory.' It was the youngest of the three who attended her, a gawky, lean but powerful fellow of about twenty.

Beringar took her by the hand and put her into a seat by the table. 'I'm here to serve you, as best I can. What's your trouble?'

'Sir, my uncle went to see to the stocking of his booth at the horse-fair, it was not long after the good brother here left us. You'll have heard all that happened, below there? My uncle went to join his other two men, who were busy there before him, and left only Gregory with me. But that's nearly two hours ago, and he has not come back.'

'He will have brought a great deal of merchandise with him,' suggested Hugh reasonably. 'It takes time to arrange things to the best vantage, and I imagine your uncle will have things done well.'

'Oh, yes, indeed he will. But it isn't just that he is so long. The two men with him were his journeyman, Roger Dod, and the porter Warin, and Warin sleeps in the booth to mind the goods. Roger came back to the barge an hour ago, and was surprised not to find my uncle back, for he said he left the booth well before him. We thought perhaps he had met some acquaintance on the way, and stopped to exchange the news with him, so we waited some while, but still he did not come. And now I have been back to the booth with

Gregory, to see if by some chance he had turned back there for something, something forgotten, perhaps. But he has not, and Warin says, as Roger does, that my uncle left first, intending to come straight home to me, it being so late. He never liked – he does not like,' she amended, paling, 'for me to be alone with the men, without his company.' Her eyes were steady and clear, but her lip quivered, and there was the faint suggestion of disquiet even in the unflinching firmness of her regard.

She knows she is fair, Cadfael thought, and she's right to take account of it. It may even be that one of them – Roger Dod, the most privileged of the three, perhaps? – has a fancy for her, and she knows that, too, and has no fancy for him, and whether justly or not, is uneasy about being close to him without her guardian by.

'And you are sure he has not made his way home by some other way,' asked Hugh, 'while you've been seeking him at his booth?'

'We went back. Roger waited there, for that very case, but no, he has not come. I asked those still working in the Foregate if they had seen such a man, but I could get no news. And then I thought that perhaps –' She turned in appeal to Cadfael. 'The young gentleman who was so kind, this evening – he is staying here in the guest-hall, so he told us. I wondered if perhaps my uncle had met him again on his way home, and lingered ... And he, at least, knows his looks, and could tell me if he has seen him. But he is not yet back, they tell me.'

'He left the jetty earlier than your uncle, then?' asked Cadfael. The young man had looked very well settled to spend a pleasant hour or two in the lady's company, but perhaps her formidable uncle had ways of conveying, even to lords of respectable honours, that his niece was to be approached only when he was present to watch over her.

Emma flushed, but without averting her eyes; eyes which were seen to be thoughtful, resolute and intelligent, for all her milk-and-roses baby-face. 'Very soon after you, brother. He was at all points correct and kind. I thought to come and ask for him, as someone on whom I could rely.'

'I'll ask the porter to keep a watch for him,' offered Cadfael, 'and have him step in here when he returns. Even the horse-fair should be on its way to bed by now, and he'll be needing his own sleep if he's to hunt the best bargains tomorrow, which is what I take it he's here for. What do you say, Hugh?'

'A good thought,' said Hugh. 'Do it, and we'll make provision to look for Master Thomas, though I trust all's well with him, for all this delay. The eve of a fair,' he said, smiling reassurance at the girl, 'and there are contacts to be made, customers already looking over the ground ... A man can forget about his sleep with his mind on business.'

Brother Cadfael heard her sigh: 'Oh, yes!' with genuine hope and gratitude, as he went to bid the porter intercept Ivo Corbière when he came in. His errand could hardly have been better timed, for the man himself appeared in the gateway. The main gate was already closed, only the wicket stood open, and the dip of the gold head stepping through caught the light from the torch overhead, and burned like a minor sun. Bare-headed, with his cotte slung on one shoulder in the warm last night of July, Ivo Corbière strolled towards his bed almost rebelliously, with a reserve of energy still unspent. The snowy linen shirt glowed in the lambent dark with a ghostly whiteness. He was whistling a street tune, more likely Parisian than out of London, by the cadence of it. He had certainly drunk reasonably deep, but not beyond his measure, nor even up to it. He was alert at a word.

'What, you, brother? Out of bed before Matins?' Amiable though his soft laughter was, he checked it quickly, sensing something demanding gravity of him. 'You were looking for me? Something worse fell out? Good God, the old man never killed the fool boy, did he?'

'Nothing so dire,' said Cadfael. 'But there's one within here at the gatehouse came looking for you, with a question. You've been about the Foregate and the fairground all this time?'

'The whole round,' said Ivo, his attention sharpening. 'I have a new and draughty manor to furnish in Cheshire. I'm looking for woollens and Flemish tapestries. Why?'

'Have you seen, in your wanderings, Master Thomas of Bristol? At any time since you left his barge earlier this evening?'

'I have not,' said Ivo, wondering, and peered closely in the strange, soft light of midsummer, an hour short of midnight.

'What is this? The man made it clear – he has practice, which is no marvel! – that his girl is to be seen only in his presence and with his sanction, and small blame to him, for she's gold, with or without his gold. I respected him for it, and I left. Why? What follows?'

'Come and see,' said Cadfael simply, and led the way within.

The young man blinked in the sudden light, and opened his eyes wide upon Emma. It was a question which of them showed the more distracted. The girl rose, reaching eager hands and then half-withdrawing them. The man sprang forward solicitously to welcome the clasp.

'Mistress Vernold! At this hour? Should you ...' He had a grasp of the company and the urgency by then. 'What has happened?' he asked, and looked at Beringar.

Briskly, Beringar told him. Cadfael was not greatly surprised to see that Corbière was relieved rather than dismayed. Here was a young, inexperienced girl, growing nervous all too easily when she was left alone an hour or so too long, while no doubt her uncle, very travelled and experienced indeed, and well able to take care of himself, was in no sort of trouble at all, but merely engaged in a little social indulgence with a colleague, or busy assessing the goods and worldly state of some of his rivals.

'Nothing ill will have happened to him,' said Corbière cheerfully, smiling reassurance at Emma, who remained, for all that, grave and anxious of eye. And she was no fool, Cadfael reflected, watching, and knew her uncle better than anyone else here could claim to know him. 'You'll see, he'll come home in his own good time, and be astonished to find you so troubled for him.'

She wanted to believe it, but her eyes said she could not be sure. 'I hoped he might have met you again,' she said, 'or that at least you might have seen him.'

'I wish it were so,' he said. 'It would have been my pleasure to set your mind at rest. But I have not seen him.'

'I think,' said Beringar, 'this lies now with me. I have still half a dozen men here within the walls, we'll make a search for Master Thomas. In the meantime, the hour is late, and you should not be wandering in the night. It will be best if your man here returns to the barge, while you, madam, if you consent, can very well join my wife, here in the guest-hall. Her maid Constance will make room for you, and find you whatever you need over the night.' There was no knowing whether he had noted her uneasiness about returning to the barge, just as acutely as Cadfael had, or was simply placing her in the nearest safe charge, and the best; but she brightened so eagerly, and thanked him so fervently, that there was no mistaking the relief she felt.

'Come, then,' he said gently, 'I'll see you safely into Constance's care, and then you may leave the searching to us.'

'And I,' said Corbière, shrugging enthusiastically into the sleeves of his cotte, 'will bear a hand with you in the hunt, if you'll have me.'

They combed the whole length of the Foregate, Beringar, with his six men-at-arms, Ivo Corbière, as energetic and wide-awake as at noon, and Brother Cadfael, who had no legitimate reason to go with them at all, beyond the pricking of his thumbs, and the manifest absurdity of going to his bed at such an hour, when he would in any case have to rise again at midnight for Matins. If that was excuse enough for sharing a drink with Beringar, it was excuse enough for taking part in the hunt for Thomas of Bristol. For truly, thought Cadfael, shaking his head over the drastic events of the evening, I shall not be easy until I see that meaty blue-jowled face again, and hear that loud, self-confident voice. Corbière might shrug off the merchant's non-return as a mere trivial departure from custom, such as every man makes now and again, and on any other day Cadfael would have agreed with him; but too much had happened since noon today, too many people had been trapped into outrageous and uncharacteristic actions, too many passions had been let loose, for this to be an ordinary day. It was even possible that someone had stepped so far aside from his usual self as to commit deliberate violence by stealth in the night, to avenge what had been done openly and impulsively in the day. Though God forbid!

They had begun by making certain that there was still no word or sign at the jetty. No, Thomas had neither appeared nor sent word, and Roger Dod's forays among the other traders along the riverside, as far as he dared go from the property he guarded, had elicited no news of his master.

He was a burly, well-set-up young man of about thirty, this Roger Dod, and very personable, if he had not been so curt and withdrawn in manner. No doubt he was anxious, too. He answered Hugh's questions in the fewest possible words, and gnawed an uncertain lip at hearing that his master's niece was now lodged in the abbey guest-hall. He would have come with them to help in their search, but he was responsible for his master's belongings, and would have to be answerable for their safety when his master returned. He stayed with the barge, and sent the mute and sleepily resentful Gregory to lead them straight to the booth Master Thomas had rented. Beringar's sergeant, with three men, was left behind to work his way gradually along the Foregate after them, questioning every waking stallholder as he went, while the rest followed the porter to the fairground. The great open space was by this time half-asleep, but still winking with occasional torches and braziers, and murmuring with subdued voices. For these three days in the year it was transformed into a tight little town, busy and populous, to vanish again on the fourth day.

Thomas had chosen a large booth almost in the centre of the triangular ground. His goods were neatly stacked within, and his watchman was awake and prowling the ground uneasily, to welcome the arrival of authority with relief. Warin was a leathery, middle-aged man, who had clearly been in his present service many years, and was probably completely trusted within his limits, but had not the ability ever to rise to the position Roger Dod now held.

'No, my lord,' he said anxiously, 'never a word since, and I've been on watch every moment. He set off for his barge a good quarter of an hour before Roger left. We had everything stowed to his liking, he was well content. And he'd had a fall not so long before – you'd know of that? – and was glad enough, I'd say, to be off home to his bed. For after all, he's none so young, no more than I am, and he carried more weight.'

'And he set off from here, which way?'

'Why, straight to the highroad, close by here. I suppose he'd keep along the Foregate.'

Behind Cadfael's shoulder a familiar voice, rich and full and merrily knowing, said in Welsh: 'Well, well, brother, out so late? And keeping the law company! What would the deputy sheriff of the shire want with Thomas of Bristol's watchman at this hour? Are they on the scent of all Gloucester's familiars, after all? And I claimed commerce was above the anarchy!' Narrowed eyes twinkled at Cadfael in the light of the dispersed torches and the far-distant stars in a perfect midsummer sky. Rhodri ap Huw was chuckling softly and fatly at his own teasing wit and menacing sharpness of apprehension.

'You keep a friendly eye out for your neighbours?' said Cadfael, innocently approving. 'I see you brought off all your own goods without scathe.'

'I have a nose for trouble, and the good sense to step out of its way,' said Rhodri ap Huw smugly. 'What's come to Thomas of Bristol? He was not so quick on the scent, it seems. He could have loosed his mooring and poled out into the river till the flurry was over, and been as safe as in the west country.'

'Did you see him struck down?' asked Cadfael deceitfully; but Rhodri was not to be caught.

'I saw him strike down the other young fool,' he said, and grinned. 'Why, did he come to grief after I left? And which of them is it you're looking for, Thomas or the lad?' And he stared with marked interest to see the sheriff's men probing at the backs of stalls, and under the trestles, and followed inquisitively on their heels as they worked their way back along the highroad. Evidently nothing of moment was to be allowed to happen at this fair without Rhodri ap Huw being present at it, or very quickly and minutely informed of it. And why not make use of his perspicacity?

'Thomas's niece is in a taking because he has not come back to his barge. That might mean anything or nothing, but now it's gone on so long, his men are getting uneasy, too. Did you see him leave his booth?'

'I did. It might be as much as two hours ago. And his journeyman some little while after him. A fair size of a man, to be lost between here and the river. And no word of him anywhere since then?'

'Not that we've found, or likely to find, without questioning every trader and every idler in all this array. And the wiser half of them getting their sleep in ready for the morning.'

They had reached the Foregate and turned towards the town, and still Rhodri strode companionably beside Cadfael, and had taken to peering into the dark spaces between stalls just as the sheriff's men were doing. Lights and braziers were fewer here, and the stalls more modest, and the quiet of the night closed in drowsily. On their left, under the abbey wall, a few compact but secure booths were arrayed. The first of them, though completly closed in and barred for the night, showed through a chink the light of a candle within. Rhodri dug a weighty elbow into Cadfael's ribs.

'Euan of Shotwick! No one is ever going to get at *him* from the rear, he likes a corner backed into two walls if he can get it. Travels alone with a pack-pony, and wears a weapon, and can use it, too. A solitary soul because he trusts nobody. His own porter – luckily his wares weigh light for their value – and his own watchman.'

Ivo Corbière had loitered to go aside between the

stalls, some of which in this stretch were still unoccupied, waiting for the local traders who would come with the dawn. The consequent darkness slowed their search, and the young man, not at all averse to spending the night without sleep, and probably encouraged by the memory of Emma's bright eyes, was tireless and thorough. Even Cadfael and Rhodri ap Huw were some yards ahead of him when they heard him cry after them, high and urgently:

'Good God, what's here? Beringar, come back here!'

The tone was enough to bring them running. Corbière had left the highway, probing between stacked trestles and leaning canvas awnings into darkness, but when they peered close there was lambent light enough from the stars for accustomed eyes to see what he had seen. From beneath a light wooden frame and stretched canvas jutted two booted feet, motionless, toes pointed skywards. For a moment they all stared in silence, dumbstruck, for truth to tell, not one of them had believed that the merchant could have come to any harm, as they all agreed afterwards. Then Beringar took hold of the frame and hoisted it away from the trestles against which it leaned, and dim and large in the darkness they saw a man's long shape, from the knees up rolled in a cloak that hid the face. There was no movement, and no noticeable sound.

The sergeant leaned in with the one torch they had brought with them, and Beringar reached a hand to the folds of the cloak, and began to draw them back from the shrouded head and shoulders. The movement of the cloth released a powerful wave of an odour that made him halt and draw suspicious breath. It also disturbed the body, which emitted an enormous snore, and a further gust of spirituous breath.

'Dead drunk and helpless,' said Beringar, relieved. 'And not, I fancy, the man we're looking for. The state he's in, this fellow must have been here some hours already, and if he comes round in time to crawl away before dawn it will be a miracle. Let's have a look at him.' He was less gingerly now in dragging the cloak away, but the drunken man let himself be hauled about and dragged forth by the feet with only a few disturbed grunts, and subsided into stertorous sleep again as soon as he was released. The torch shone its yellow, resinous light upon a shock-head of coarse auburn hair, a pair of wide shoulders in a leather jerkin, and a face that might have been sharp, lively and even comely when he was awake and sober, but now looked bloated and idiotic, with open, slobbering mouth and reddened eyes.

Corbière took one close look at him, and let out a gasp and an oath. '*Fowler!* Devil take the sot! Is this how he obeys me? By God, I'll make him sweat for it!' And he filled a fist with the thick brown hair and shook the fellow furiously, but got no more out of him than a louder snort, the partial opening of one glazed eye, and a wordless mumble that subsided again as soon as he was dropped, disgustedly and ungently, back into the turf.

'This drunken rogue is mine ... my falconer and archer, Turstan Fowler,' said Ivo bitterly, and kicked the sleeper in the ribs but not savagely. What was the use? The man would not be conscious for hours yet, and what he suffered afterwards would pay him all his dues. 'I've a mind to put him to cool in the river! I never gave him leave to quit the abbey precinct, and by the look of him he's been out and drinking – Good God, the reek of it, what raw spirit can it be? – since ever I turned my back.'

'One thing's certain,' said Hugh, amused, 'he's in no case to walk back to his bed. Since he's yours, what will you have done with him? I would not advise leaving him here. If he has anything of value on him, even his hose, he might be without it by morning. There'll be scavengers abroad in the dark hours – no fair escapes them.'

Ivo stood back and stared down disgustedly at the oblivious culprit. 'If you'll lend me two of your men, and let us borrow a board here, we'll haul him back and toss him into one of the abbey's punishment cells, to sleep off his swinishness on the stones, and serve him right. If we leave him there unfed all the morrow, it may frighten him into better sense. Next time, I'll have his hide!'

They hoisted the sleeper on to a board, where he sprawled aggravatingly into ease again, and snored his way along the Foregate so blissfully that his bearers were tempted to tip him off at intervals, by way of recompensing themselves for their own labour. Cadfael, Beringar and the remainder of the party were left looking after them somewhat ruefully, their own errand still unfulfilled.

'Well, well!' said Rhodri ap Huw softly into Cadfael's ear, 'Euan of Shotwick is taking a modest interest in the evening's happenings, after all!'

Cadfael turned to look, and in the shuttered booth tucked under the wall a hatch had certainly opened, and against the pale light of a candle a head leaned out in sharp outline, staring towards where they stood. He recognised the high-bridged, haughty nose, the deceptively meagre slant of the lean shoulders, before the hatch was drawn silently to again, and the glover vanished.

They worked their way doggedly, yard by yard, all the way back to the riverside, where Roger Dod was waiting in a fume of anxiety, but they found no trace of Thomas of Bristol.

A late boat coming up the Severn from Buildwas next day, and tying up at the bridge about nine in the morning, delayed its unloading of a cargo of pottery to ask first that a message be sent to the sheriff, for they had other cargo aboard, taken up out of a cove near Atcham, which would be very much the sheriff's business. Gilbert Prestcote, busy with other matters, sent from the castle his own sergeant, with orders to report first to Hugh Beringar at the abbey.

The particular cargo the potter had to deliver lay rolled in a length of coarse sail-cloth in the bottom of the boat, and oozed water in a dark stain over the boards. The boatman unfolded the covering, and displayed to Beringar's view the body of a heavily-built man of some fifty to fifty-five years, fleshy, with thinning, grizzled hair and bristly, bluish jowls, his pouchy features sagging doughily in death. Master Thomas of Bristol, stripped of his elaborate capuchon, his handsome gown, his rings and his dignity, as naked as the day he was born.

'We saw his whiteness bobbing under the bank,' said the potter, looking down upon his salvaged man, 'and poled in to pick him up, the poor soul. I can show you the place, this side of the shallows and the island at Atcham. We thought best to bring him here, as we would a drowned man. But this one,' he said very soberly, 'did not drown.'

No, Thomas of Bristol had now drowned. That was already evident from the very fact that he had been stripped of everything he had on, and hardly by his own hands or will. But also, even more certainly, from the incredibly narrow wound under his left shoulder-blade, washed white and closed by the river, where a very fine, slender dagger had transfixed him and penetrated to his heart.

# The First Day of the Fair

## Chapter One

The first day of Saint Peter's Fair was in full swing, and the merry, purposeful hum of voices bargaining, gossiping and crying wares came over the wall into the great court, and in at the gatehouse, like the summer music of a huge hive of bees on a sunny day. The sound pursued Hugh Beringar back to the apartment in the guest-hall, where his wife and Emma Vernold were very pleasurably comparing the virtues of various wools, and the maid Constance, who was an expert spinstress, was fingering the samples critically and giving her advice.

On this domestic scene, which had brought back the fresh colour to Emma's cheeks and the animation to her voice, Hugh's sombre face cast an instant cloud. There was no time for breaking news circuitously, nor did he think that this girl would thank him for going roundabout.

'Mistress Vernold, my news is ill, and I grieve for it. God knows I had not expected this. Your uncle is found. A boat coming up early this morning from Buildwas picked up his body from the river.'

The colour ebbed from her face. She stood with frightened, helpless eyes gazing blindly before her. The prop of her life had suddenly been plucked away, and for a moment it seemed that all balance was lost to her, and she might indeed fall for want of him. But by the time she had drawn breath deep, and shaped soundlessly: 'Dead!' It was clear that she was firm on her own feet again, and in no danger of falling. Her eyes, once the momentary panic and dizziness passed, looked straight at Hugh and made no appeal.

'Drowned?' she said. 'But he swam well, he was raised by the river. And if he drank at all, it was sparingly. I do not believe he could fall into Severn and drown. Not of himself!' she said, and her large eyes dilated.

'Sit down,' said Hugh gently, 'for we must talk a little, and then I shall leave you with Aline, for of course you must remain here in our care for this while. No, he did not drown. Nor did he come by his death of himself. Master Thomas was stabbed from behind, stripped, and put into the river after death.'

'You mean,' she said, in a voice low and laboured, but quite steady, 'he was waylaid and killed by mere sneak-thieves, for what he had on him? For his rings and his gown and his shoes?'

'It is what leaps to the mind. There are no roads in England now that can be called safe, and no great fair that has not its probable underworld of hangers-on, who will kill for a few pence.'

'My uncle was not a timid man. He has fought off more than one attack in his time, and he never avoided a journey for fear in his life. After all these years,' she said, her voice aching with protest, 'why should he fall victim now to such scum? And yet what else can it be?'

'There are some people recalling,' said Hugh, 'that there was an ugly incident on the jetty last evening, and violence was done to a number of the merchants who were unloading goods and setting up stalls for the fair. It's common knowledge there was bad blood between town and traders, of whom Master Thomas was perhaps the most influential. He was involved bitterly with the young man who led the raid. An attack made in revenge, by night, perhaps in a drunken rage, might end mortally, whether it was meant or no.'

'Then he would have been left where he lay,' said Emma sharply. 'His attacker would think only of getting clean away unseen. Those angry people were not thieves, only townsmen with a grievance. A grievance might turn them into murderers, but I do not think it would turn them into thieves.'

Hugh was beginning to feel considerable respect for this girl, as Aline, by her detached silence and her attentive face, had already learned to do. 'I won't say but I agree with you there,' he admitted. 'But it might well occur to a young man turned murderer almost by mishap, to dress his crime as the common sneak killing for robbery. It opens so wide a field. Twenty young men bitterly aggrieved and hot against your uncle for his scorn of them could be lost among a thousand unknown, and the most unlikely suspects among them, at that, if this passes as chance murder for gain.'

Even in the bleak newness of her bereavement, this thought troubled her. She bit a hesitant lip. 'You think it may have been one of those young men? Or more of them together? That they burned with their grudge until they followed him in the dark, and took this way?'

'It's being both thought and said,' owned Hugh, 'by many people who witnessed what happened by the river.'

'But the sheriff's men,' she pointed out, frowning, 'surely took up many of those young men long before my uncle went to the fairground. If they were already in prison, they could not have harmed him.'

'True of most of them. But the one who led them was not taken until the small hours of the morning, when he came reeling back to the town gate, where he was awaited. He is in a cell in the castle now, like his fellows, but he was still at liberty long after Master Thomas failed to come back to you, and he is under strong suspicion of this death. The whole pack of them will come before the sheriff this afternoon. The rest, I fancy, will be let out on their fathers' bail, to answer the charges later. But for Philip Corviser, I greatly doubt it. He will need to have better answers than he was able to give when they took him.'

'This afternoon!' echoed Emma. 'Then I should also attend. I was a witness when this turmoil began. The sheriff should hear my testimony, too, especially if my uncle's death is in question. There were others – Master Corbière, and the brother of the abbey, the one you know well ...'

'They will be attending, and others besides. Certainly your witness would be valuable, but to ask it of you at such a time ...'

'I would rather!' she said firmly. 'I want my uncle's murderer caught, if indeed he was murdered, but I pray no innocent man may be too hurriedly blamed. I don't know – I would not have thought he looked like a murderer ... I should like to tell what I do know, it is my duty.'

Beringar cast a brief glance at his wife for enlightenment, and Aline gave him a smile and the faintest of nods.

'If you are resolved on that,' he said, reassured, 'I will ask Brother Cadfael to escort you. And for the rest. you need have no anxieties about your own situation. It will be necessary for you to stay here until this matter is looked into, but naturally you will remain here in Aline's company, and you shall have every possible help in whatever dispositions you need to make.'

'I should like,' said Emma, 'to take my uncle's body back by the barge to Bristol for burial.' She had not considered, until then, that there would be no protector for her on the boat this time, only Roger Dod, whose mute but watchful and jealous devotion was more than she could bear, Warin who would take care to notice nothing that might cause him trouble, and poor Gregory, who was strong and able of body but very dull of wit. She drew in breath sharply, and bit an uncertain lip, and the shadow came back to her eyes. 'At least, to send him back ... His man of law there will take care of his affairs and mine.'

'I have spoken to the prior. Abbot Radulfus sanctions the use of an abbey chapel, your uncle's body can lie there when he is brought from the castle, and all due preparations will be made for his decent coffining. Ask for anything you want, it shall be at your disposal. I must summon your journeyman to attend at the castle this afternoon, too. How would you wish him to deal, concerning the fair? I will give him whatever instructions you care to send.'

She nodded understanding, visibly bracing herself again towards a world of shrewd daily business which had not ceased with the ending of a life. 'Be so kind as to tell him,' she said, 'to continue trading for the three days of the fair, as though his master still presided. My uncle would scorn to go aside from his regular ways for any danger or loss, and so will I in his name.' And suddenly, as freely and as simply as a small child, she burst into tears at last.

When Hugh was gone about his business, and Constance had withdrawn at Aline's nod, the two women sat quietly until Emma had ceased to weep, which she did as suddenly as she had begun. She wept, as some women have the gift of doing, without in the least defacing her own prettiness and without caring whether she did or no. Most lose the faculty, after the end of childhood. She dried her eyes, and looked up straightly at Aline, who was looking back at her just as steadily, with a serenity which offered comfort without pressing it.

'You must think,' said Emma, 'that I had no deep affection for my uncle. And indeed I don't know myself that you would be wrong. And yet I did love him, it has not been only loyalty and gratitude, though those came easier. He was a hard man, people said, hard to satisfy, and hard in his business dealings. But he was not hard to me. Only hard to come near. It was not his fault, or mine.'

'I think,' said Aline mildly, since she was being invited closer, 'you loved him as much as he would let you. As he *could* let you. Some men have not the gift.'

'Yes. But I would have liked to love him more. I would have done anything to please him. Even now I want to do everything as he would have wished. We shall keep the booth open as long as the fair lasts, and try to do it as well as he would have done. All that he had in hand, I want to see done thoroughly.' Her voice was resolute, almost eager. Master Thomas would certainly have approved the set of her chin and the spark in her eye. 'Aline, shall I not be a trouble to you by staying here? I – my uncle's men – there's one who likes me too well ...

'So I had thought,' said Aline. 'You're most welcome here, and we'll not part with you until you can be sent back safely to Bristol, and your home. Not that I can find it altogether blameworthy in the young man to like you, for that matter,' she added, smiling.

'No, but I cannot like *him* well enough. Besides, my uncle would never have allowed me to be there on the barge without him. And now I have duties,' said Emma, rearing her head determinedly and staring the uncertain future defiantly in the face. 'I must see to the ordering of a fine coffin for him, for the journey home. There will be a master-carpenter, somewhere in the town?'

'There is. To the right, halfway up the Wyle, Master Martin Bellecote. A good man, and a good craftsman.

His lad was among these terrible rioters, as I hear,' said Aline, and dimpled indulgently at the thought, 'but so were half the promising youth of the town. I'll come in with you to Martin's shop.'

'No,' said Emma firmly. 'It will all be tedious and long at the sheriff's court, and you should not tire yourself. And besides, you have to buy your fine wools, before the best are taken. And Brother Cadfael – was that the name? – will show me where to find the shop. He will surely know.'

'There's very little to be known about this precinct and the town of Shrewsbury,' agreed Aline with conviction, 'that Brother Cadfael does not know.'

Cadfael received the abbot's dispensation to attend the hearing at the castle, and to escort the abbey's bereaved guest, without question. A civic duty could not be evaded, whether by secular or monastic. Radulfus had already shown himself both an austere but just disciplinarian and a shrewd and strong-minded business man. He owed his preferment to the abbacy as much to the king as to the papal legate, and valued and feared for the order of the realm at least as keenly as for the state of his own cure. Consequently, he had a use for those few among the brothers who shared his wide experience of matters outside the cloister.

'This death,' he said, closeted with Cadfael alone after Beringar's departure, 'casts a shadow upon our house and our fair. Such a burden cannot be shifted to other shoulders. I require of you a full account of what passes at this hearing. It was of me that the elders of the town asked a relief I could not grant. On me rests the load of resentment that drove those younger men to foolish measures. They lacked patience and thought, and they were to blame, but that does not absolve me. If the man's death has arisen out of my act, even though I could not act otherwise, I must know it, for I have to answer for it, as surely as the man who struck him down.'

'I shall bring you all that I myself see and hear, Father Abbot,' said Cadfael.

'I require also all that you think, brother. You saw part of what happened yesterday between the dead man and the living youth. Is it possible that it could have brought about such a death as this? Stabbed in the back? It is not commonly the method of anger.'

'Not commonly.' Cadfael had seen many deaths in the open anger of battle, but he knew also of rages that had bred and festered into killings by stealth, with the anger as hot as ever, but turned sour by brooding. 'Yet it is possible. But there are other possibilities. It may indeed be what it first seems, a mere crude slaughter for the clothes on the body and the rings on the fingers, opportune plunder in the night, when no one chanced to be by. Such things happen, where men are gathered together and there is money changing hands.'

'It is true,' said Radulfus, coldly and sadly. 'The ancient evil is always with us.'

'Also, the man is of great importance in his trade and his region, and he may have enemies. Hate, envy, rivalry, are as powerful motives even as gain. And at a great fair such as ours, enemies may be brought together, far from the towns where their quarrels are known, and their acts might be guessed at too accurately. Murder is easier and more tempting, away from home.'

'Again, true,' said the abbot. 'Is there more?'

'There is. There is the matter of the girl, niece and heiress to the dead man. She is of great beauty,' said Cadfael plainly, asserting his right to recognise and celebrate even the beauty of women, though their enjoyment he had now voluntarily forsworn, 'and there are three men in her uncle's service, shut on board a river barge with her. Only one of them old enough, it may be, to value his peace more. One, I think, God's simpleton, but not therefore blind, or delivered from the flesh. And one whole, able, every way a man, and enslaved to her. And this one it was who followed his master from the booth on the fairground, some say a quarter of an hour after him, some say a little more. God forbid I should therefore point a finger at an honest man. But we speak of possibilities. And will speak of them no more until, or unless, they become more than possibilities.'

'That is my mind, also,' said Abbot Radulfus, stirring and almost smiling. He looked at Cadfael steadily and long. 'Go and bear witness, brother, as you are charged, and bring me word again. In your report I shall set my trust.'

Emma had on, perforce, the same gown and bliaut she had worn the evening before, the gown dark blue like her eyes, but the tunic embroidered in many colours upon bleached linen. The only concession she could make to mourning was to bind up her great wealth of hair, and cover it from sight within a borrowed wimple. Nevertheless, she made a noble mourning figure. In the severe white frame her rounded, youthful face gained in concentrated force and meaning what it lost in pure grace. She had a look of single-minded gravity, like a lance in rest. Brother Cadfael could not yet see clearly where the lance was aimed.

When she caught sight of him approaching, she looked at him with pleased recognition, as the man behind the lance might have looked round at the fixed, partisan faces of his friends before the bout, but never shifted the focus of her soul's intent, which reached out where he could not follow.

'Brother Cadfael – have I your name right? It's

Welsh, is it not? You were kind, yesterday. Lady Beringar says you will show me where to find the master-carpenter. I have to order my uncle's coffin, to take him back to Bristol.' She was quite composed, yet still as simple and direct as a child. 'Have we time, before we must go to the castle?'

'It's on the way,' said Cadfael comfortably. 'You need only tell Martin Bellecote, whatever you ask of him he'll see done properly.'

'Everyone is being very kind,' she said punctiliously, like a well brought-up little girl giving due thanks. 'Where is my uncle's body now? I should care for it myself, it is my duty.'

'That you cannot yet,' said Cadfael. 'The sheriff has him at the castle, he must needs see the body for himself, and have the physician also view it. You need be put to no distress on that account, the abbot has given orders. Your uncle will be brought with all reverence to lie in the church here, and the brothers will make him decent for burial. I think he might well wish, could he tell you so now, that you should leave all to us. His care for you would reach so far, and your obedience could not well deny him.'

Cadfael had seen the dead man, and felt strongly that she should not have the same experience. Nor was it for her sake entirely that he willed so. The man she had respected and admired in his monumental dignity, living, had the right to be preserved for her no less decorously in death.

He had found the one argument that could deflect her absolute determination to take charge of all, and escape nothing. She thought about it seriously as they passed out at the gatehouse side by side, and he knew by her face the moment when she accepted it.

'But he did believe that I ought to take my full part, even in his business. He wished me to travel with him, and learn the trade as he knew it. This is the third such journey I have made with him.' That reminded her that it must also be the last. 'At least,' she said hesitantly, 'I may give money to have Masses said for him, here where he died? He was a very devout man, I think he would like that.'

Well, her reserves of money might now be far longer than her reserves of peace of mind were likely to be; she could afford to buy herself a little consolation, and prayers are never wasted.

'That you may surely do.'

'He died unshriven,' she said, with sudden angry grief against the murderer who had deprived him of confession and absolution.

'Through no fault of his own. So do many. So have saints, martyred without warning. God knows the record without needing word or gesture. It's for the soul facing death that the want of shriving is pain. The soul gone beyond knows that pain for needless vanity. Penitence is in the heart, not in the words spoken.'

They were out on the highroad then, turning left towards the reflected sparkle that was the river between its green, lush banks, and the stone bridge over it, that led through the drawbridge turret to the town gate. Emma had raised her head, and was looking at Brother Cadfael along her shoulder, with faint colour tinting her creamy cheeks, and a sparkle like a shimmer of light from the river in her eyes. He had not seen her smile until this moment, and even now it was a very wan smile, but none the less beautiful.

'He was a good man, you know, Brother Cadfael,' she said earnestly. 'He was not easy upon fools, or bad workmen, or people who cheated, but he was a good man. Good to me! And he kept his bargains, and he was loyal to his lord ...' She had taken fire, for all the softness of her voice and the simplicity of her plea for him; it was almost as though she had been about to say 'loyal to his lord to the death!' She had that high, heroic look about her, to be taken very seriously, even on that child's face.

'All which,' said Cadfael cheerfully, 'God knows, and needs not to be told. And never forget you've a life to live, and he'd want you to do him justice by doing yourself justice.'

'Oh, yes!' said Emma, glowing, and for the first time laid her hand confidingly on his sleeve. 'That's what I want! That's what I have most in mind!'

# Chapter Two

At Martin Bellecote's shop, off the curve of the rising street called the Wyle, which led to the centre of the town, she knew exactly what she wanted for her dead, and ordered it clearly; more, she knew how to value a matching clarity and forthrightness in the master-carpenter, and yet had time to be pleasantly distracted by the invasion of his younger children, who liked the look of her and came boldly to chatter and stare. As for the delinquent Edwy, sent home overnight after his tongue-lashing from Hugh Beringar, the youngster worked demurely with a plane in a corner of the shop, and was not too subdued to cast inquisitive glances of bright hazel eyes at the lady, and one impudent wink at Brother Cadfael when Emma was not noticing.

On the way through the town, up the steep street to the High Cross, and down the gentler slope beyond to the ramp which led up to the castle gateway, she fell into a thoughtful silence, putting in order her recollections. The shadow of the gate falling upon her serious face and cutting off the sunlight caused her eyes to dilate in awe; but the casual traffic of the watch here was no longer reminiscent of siege and battle, but easy and brisk, and the townspeople went in and out freely with their requests and complaints. The sheriff was a strong-minded, taciturn, able knight past fifty, and old in experience of both war and office, and while he could be heavy-handed in crushing disorder, he was trusted to be fair in day to day matters. If he had not given the goodmen of the town much help in making good the dilapidations due to the siege, neither had he permitted them to be misused or heavily taxed to restore the damage to the castle. In the great court one tower was still caged in timber scaffolding, one wall shored up with wooden buttresses. Emma gazed, great-eyed.

There were others going the same way with them, anxious fathers here to bail their sons, two of the abbey stewards who had been assaulted in the affray, witnesses from the bridge and the jetty, all being ushered through to the inner ward, and a chill, stony hall hung with smoky tapestries. Cadfael found Emma a seat on a bench against the wall, where she sat looking about her with anxious eyes but lively interest.

'Look, there's Master Corbière!'

He was just entering the hall, and for the moment had no attention to spare for anyone but the hunched figure that slouched before him; blear-eyed but in his full wits today, going softly in awe of his irate lord, Turstan Fowler made his powerful form as small and unobtrusive as possible, and mustered patience until the storm should blow over. And what had he to do here, Cadfael wondered. He had not been on the jetty, and by the state in which he had been found near midnight, his memories of yesterday should in any case be vague indeed. Yet he must have something to say to the purpose, or Corbière would not have brought him here. By his mood last night, he had meant to leave him locked up all day, to teach him better sense.

'Is this the sheriff?' whispered Emma.

Gilbert Prestcote had entered, with a couple of lawmen at his elbows to advise him on the legalities. This was no trial but it rested with him whether the rioters would go home on their own and their sires' bond to appear at the assize, or be held in prison in the meantime. The sheriff was a tall, spare man, erect and vigorous, with a short black beard trimmed to a point, and a sharp and daunting eye. He took his seat without ceremony, and a sergeant handed him the list of names of those in custody. He raised his eyebrows ominously at the number of them.

'All these were taken in riot?' He spread the roll on his table and frowned down at it. 'Very well! There is also the graver matter of the death of Master Thomas of Bristol. At what hour was the last word we have of Master Thomas alive and well?'

'According to his journeyman and his watchman, he left his booth on the horse-fair, intending to return to his barge, more than an hour past the Compline bell. That is the last word we have. His man Roger Dod is here to testify that the hour was rather more than a quarter past nine of the evening and the watchman bears that out.'

'Late enough,' said the sheriff, pondering. 'The fighting was over by then, and Foregate and fairground quiet. Hugh, prick me off here all those who were then already in custody. Whatever their guilt for damages to goods and gear, they cannot have had any hand in this murder.'

Hugh leaned to his shoulder, and ran a rapid hand down the roster. 'It was a sharp encounter, but short. We had it in hand very quickly, they never reached the end of the Foregate. This man was picked up last, it might be as late as ten, but in an ale-house and very drunk, and the ale-wife vouches for his having been there above an hour. A respectable witness, she was glad to get rid of him. But he's clear of the killing. This one crept back to the bridge a little later, and owned to having been one among the rabble, but we let him home, for he's very lame, and there are witnesses to all his moves since before nine. He's here to answer for his part in the muster, as he promised. I think you may safely write him clear of any other blame.'

'It leaves but one,' said Prestcote, and looked up sharply into Beringar's face.

'It does,' said Hugh, and committed himself to nothing further.

'Very well! Have in all the rest, but keep him aside. Let us hold these two matters apart, and deal with the lesser first.'

Into the space roped off along one side the hall, the sheriff's officers herded their prisoners, a long file of sullenly sheepish young men, bruised, dishevelled and sorry for themselves now, but still nursing the embers of a genuine resentment. There were some torn coats among them, and a purple eye or two, and the lingering signs of bloody noses and battered crowns, and a night on the stones of indifferently swept cells had done their best clothes, donned for dignified battle as knights case themselves in ceremonial armour, no good at all. There would be indignant mothers scolding bitterly as they scrubbed and mended, or here and there a young wife doing the nagging on behalf of all women. The offenders stood in line doggedly, set their jaws, and braced themselves to endure whatever might follow.

Prestcote was thorough. Plainly he was preoccupied with the more serious evil, and little disposed to fulminate overmuch about this civic discord, which in the end had done comparatively little harm. So though he called every culprit separately, and had him answer for his own part in the affray, he got through them rapidly and reasonably. Most of them freely owned that they had taken part, maintained that the intention had been entirely lawful and peaceable, and the disintegration later had been unintentional and none of their making. Several bore witness that they had been with Philip Corviser on the jetty, and told how he had been assaulted, thus letting loose the riot that followed. Only one here and there sought to prove that he had never so much as overset one trestle under a stall, nor even been on the abbey side of Severn that evening. And those few were already committed deep on the evidence of law-abiding citizens.

Agitated fathers, vengeful rather than doting, came forward to claim each dejected hero, pledged attendance at the assize, and offered surety for the pledge. The lame lad was lectured perfunctorily, and dismissed without penalty. Two who had been particularly voluble in asserting that they were elsewhere at the time, and unjustly accused, were returned to their prison for a day or two, to reconsider the nature of truth.

'Very well!' said Prestcote, dusting his hands irritably. 'Clear the hall, but for those who have evidence to give concerning Master Thomas of Bristol. And bring in Philip Corviser.'

The line of young men had vanished, hustled out and shepherded away by loyal but exasperated families. At home they would have to sit and nurse sore heads and sore hearts while fathers hectored and dames wept, pouring out on them all the fear and worry they had suffered on their behalf. Emma looked after the last of them with round, sympathetic eyes, as he was haled away by the ear by a diminutive mother half his size, and shrill as a jay. Poor lad, he needed no other punishment, he was drowning in mortification already.

She turned about, and there where his fellows had been, but monstrously alone in the middle of that stony wall, was Philip Corviser.

He gripped the rope with both hands, and stood rigidly erect, neck as stiff as a lance, though for the rest he looked as if his flesh might melt and droop off the bone, he was so haggard. His extreme pallor, which

Cadfael knew for what raw wine can do to the beginner, the day after his indulgence, Emma almost certainly took for the fruit of dire injury and great anguish of mind. She paled in reflection, staring piteously, though he was nothing to her, except that she had seen him struck down, and been afraid he might not rise again.

For all his efforts, he was a sorry figure. His best cotte was torn and soiled, and worse, speckled with drops of blood under his left ear, and vomit about the skirts. He mustered his gangling limbs gallantly but somewhat uncertainly, and his harmless, sunburned face, unshaven now and ashen under its tan, blushed to an unbecoming and unexpected purple when he caught sight of his father, waiting with laboured patience among the onlookers. He did not look that way again, but kept his bruised brown eyes fixed upon the sheriff.

He answered to his name in a voice too loud, from nervous defiance, and agreed to the time and place of his arrest. Yes, he had been very drunk, and hazy about his movements, and even about the circumstances of his arrest, but yes, he would try to answer truthfully to what was charged against him.

There were several witnesses to testify that Philip had been the originator and leader of the whole enterprise which had ended so ignominiously. He had been in the forefront when the angry young men crossed the bridge, he had given the signal that sent some of the party ahead along the Foregate, while he led a handful down to the riverside, and entered into loud argument with the merchants unloading goods there. Thus far all accounts tallied, but from then on they varied widely. Some had the youths beginning at once to toss merchandise into the river, and were certain that Philip had been in the thick of the battle. One or two of the aggrieved merchants alleged with righteous indignation that he had assaulted Master Thomas, and so began the whole turmoil. Since they would all have their say, Hugh Beringar had held back his preferred witnesses until last.

'My lord, as to the scene by the river, we have here the niece of Master Thomas, and two men who intervened, and afterwards helped to rescue much of what had been cast into the river: Ivo Corbière of Stanton Cobbold, and Brother Cadfael of the abbey, who was assisting a Welsh-speaking trader. There were no others so close to the affair. Will you hear Mistress Vernold?'

Philip had not realised until that moment that she was present. The mention of her caused him to look round wildly, and the sight of her stepping shyly forward to stand before the sheriff's table brought out a deep and painful blush, that welled out of the young man's torn collar and mounted in a great wave to his red-brown hair. He averted his eyes from her, wishing, thought Cadfael, for the floor to open and swallow him up. It would not have mattered so much looking a piteous object to others, but before her he was furious and ashamed. Not even the thought of his father's mortification could have sunk his spirits so low. Emma, after one rapid glance, sympathetic enough, had also turned her eyes away. She looked only at the sheriff, who returned her straight gaze with concern and compunction.

'Was it needful to put Mistress Vernold to this distress, at such a time? Madam, you could well have been spared an appearance here, the lord Corbière and the good brother would have been witness enough.'

'I wished to come,' said Emma, her voice small but steady. 'Indeed I was not pressed, it was my own decision.'

'Very well, if that is your wish. You have heard these

varying versions of what happened. There seems little dispute until these disturbers of the peace came down to the jetty. Let me hear from you what followed.'

'It is true that young man was the leader. I think he addressed himself to my uncle because he seemed the most important merchant then present, but he spoke high to be heard by all the rest. I cannot say that he uttered any threats, he only stated that the town had a grievance, and the abbey was not paying enough for the privilege of the fair, and asked that we, who come to do business here, should acknowledge the rights of the town, and pay a tithe of our rents and tolls to the town instead of all to the abbey. Naturally my uncle would not listen, but stood firm on the letter of the charter, and ordered the young men out of his way. And when he – the prisoner here – would still be arguing, my uncle turned his back and shrugged him off. Then the young man laid a hand on his arm, wanting to detain him still, and my uncle, who had his staff in his hand, turned and struck out at him. Thinking, I suppose, that he intended him offence or injury.'

'And did he not?' The sheriff's voice indicated mild surprise.

She cast one brief glance at the prisoner, and one in quest of reassurance at Brother Cadfael, and thought for a moment. 'No, I think not. He was beginning to be angry, but he had not said any ill word, or made any threatening movement. And my uncle, of course in alarm, hit hard. It felled him, and he lay in a daze.' This time she did turn and look earnestly at Philip, and found him staring at her wide-eyed. 'You see he is marked. His left temple.' Dried blood had matted the thick brown hair.

'And did he then attempt retaliation?' asked Prestcote.

'How could he?' she said simply. 'He was more than

half stunned, he could not rise without help. And then all the others began to fight, and to throw things into the river. And Brother Cadfael came and helped him to his feet and delivered him to his friends, and they took him away. I am sure he could not have walked unaided. I think he did not know what he was doing, or how he came to such a state.'

'Not then, perhaps,' said Prescote reasonably. 'But later in the evening, somewhat recovered, and as he has himself admitted, very drunk, he may well have brooded on a revenge.'

'I can say nothing as to that. My uncle would have struck him again, and might have done him desperate hurt if I had not stopped him. That is not his nature,' she said firmly, 'it was most unlike him, but he was in a rage, and confused. Brother Cadfael will confirm what I say.'

'At all points,' said Brother Cadfael. 'It is a perfectly balanced and just account.'

'My lord Corbière?'

'I have nothing to add,' said Ivo, 'to what Mistress Vernold has so admirably told you. I saw the prisoner helped away by his fellows, and what became of him after that I have no knowledge. But here is a man of mine, Turstan Fowler, who says he did see him later in the evening, drinking in an ale-house at the corner of the horse-fair. I must say,' added Ivo with resigned disgust, 'that his own recollection of the night's events ought to be as hazy as the prisoner's, for we took him up dead drunk past eleven, and by the look of him he had been in the same state some time then. I had him put into a cell in the abbey overnight. But he claims his head is clear now, and he knows what he saw and heard. I thought it best he should speak here for himself.'

The archer edged forward sullenly, peering up under thick frowning brows, as though his head still rang.

'Well, what is it you claim to know, fellow?' asked Prestcote, eyeing him narrowly.

'My lord, I had no call to be out of the precinct at all, last night, my lord Corbière had given me orders to stay within. But I knew he would spend the evening looking the ground over, so I ventured. I got my skinful at Wat's tavern, by the north corner of the horse-fair. And this fellow was there, drinking fit to beat me, and I'm an old toper, and can carry it most times. The place was full, there must be others can tell you the same. He was nursing his sore head, and breathing fire against the man that gave it him. He swore he'd be up with him before the night was out. And that's all the meat of it, my lord.'

'At what hour was this?' asked Prestcote.

'Well, my lord, I was still firm on my feet then, and clear in my mind, and that I certainly was not later in the evening. It must have been somewhere halfway between eight and nine. I should have borne my drink well enough if I had not gone from ale to wine, and then to a fierce spirit, and that last was what laid me low, or I'd have been back within the wall before my lord came home, and escaped a night on the stones.'

'It was well earned,' said Prestcote dryly. 'So you took yourself off to sleep off your load – when?'

'Why, about nine, I suppose, my lord, and was fathoms deep soon after. Troth, I can't recall where, though I remember the inn. They can tell you where I was found who found me.'

At this point it dawned abruptly upon Brother Cadfael that by pure chance this whole interrogation, since Philip had been brought in, had been conducted without once mentioning the fact that Master Thomas at this moment lay dead in the castle chapel. Certainly the sheriff had addressed Emma in tones of sympathy and consideration appropriate to her newly-orphaned state, and her uncle's absence might in itself be suggestive, though in view of the importance of his business at the fair, and the fact that Emma had once, at least, referred to him in the present tense, a person completely ignorant of his death would hardly have drawn any conclusion from these hints, unless he had all his wits about him. And Philip had been all night in a prison cell, and haled out only to face this hearing, and moreover, was still sick and dulled with his drinking, his broken head and his sore heart, and in no case to pick up every inference of what he heard. No one had deliberately laid a trap for him, but for all that, the trap was there, and it might be illuminating to spring it.

'So these threats you heard against Master Thomas,' said Prestcote, 'can have been uttered only within an hour, probably less, of the time when the merchant left his booth to return alone to his barge. The last report we have of him.'

That was drawing nearer to the spring, but not near enough. Philip's face was still drawn, resigned and bewildered, as though they had been talking Welsh over his head. Brother Cadfael struck the prop clean away; it was high time.

'The last report we have of him *alive*,' he said clearly.

The word might have been a knife going in, the slender kind that is hardly felt for a moment, and then hales after it the pain and the injury. Philip's head came up with a jerk, his mouth fell open, his bruised eyes rounded in horrified comprehension.

'But it must be remembered,' continued Cadfael quickly, 'that we do not know the hour at which he died. A body taken from the water may have entered it at any time during the night, after *all* the prisoners were in hold, and all honest men in bed.'

It was done. He had hoped it would settle the issue of guilt and innocence, at least to his satisfaction, but now he still could not be quite sure the boy had not known the truth already. How if he had only held his peace and listened to the ambiguous voices, and been in doubt whether Master Thomas's corpse had yet been found? On the face of it, if he had had any hand in that death, he was a better player than any of the travelling entertainers who would be plying their trade among the crowds this evening. His pallor, from underdone dough, had frozen into marble, he tried to speak and swallowed half-formed words, he drew huge breaths into him, and straightened his back, and turned great, shocked eyes upon the sheriff. On the face of it – but every face can dissemble if the need is great enough.

'My lord,' pleaded Philip urgently, when he had his voice again, 'is this truth? Master Thomas of Bristol is dead?'

'Known or unknown to you,' said Prestcote dryly, '– and I hazard no judgment – it is truth. The merchant is dead. Our main purpose here now is to examine how he died.'

'Taken from the water, the monk said. Did he drown?'

'That, if you know, you may tell us.'

Abruptly the prisoner turned his back upon the sheriff, took another deep breath into him, and looked directly at Emma, and from then on barely took his eyes from her, even when Prestcote addressed him. The only judgment he cared about was hers.

'Lady, I swear to you I never did your uncle harm, never saw him again after they hauled me away from the jetty. What befell him I do not know, and God knows I'm sorry for your loss. I would not for the world have touched him, even if we had met and quarrelled afresh, knowing he was your kinsman.'

'Yet you were heard threatening harm to him,' said the sheriff.

'It may be so. I cannot drink, I was a fool ever to try that cure. I recall nothing of what I said, I make no doubt it was folly, and unworthy. I was sore and bitter. What I set out to do was honest enough, and yet it fell apart. All went to waste. But if I talked violence, I did none. I never saw the man again. When I turned sick from the wine I left the tavern and went down to the riverside, away from the boats, and lay down there until I made shift to drag myself back to the town. I admit to the trouble that arose out of my acts, and all that has been said against me, all but this. As God sees me, I never did your uncle any injury. Speak, and say you believe me!'

Emma gazed at him with parted lips and dismayed eyes, unable to say yes or no to him. How could she know what was true and what was lies?

'Let her be,' said the sheriff sharply. 'It is with us you have to deal. This matter must be probed deeper than has been possible yet. Nothing is proven, but you stand in very grave suspicion, and it is for me to determine what is to be done with you.'

'My lord,' ventured the provost, who had kept his mouth tightly shut until now, against great temptation, 'I am prepared to stand surety for my son to whatever price you may set, and I guarantee he shall be at your disposal at the assize, and at whatever time between when you may need to question him. My honour has never been in doubt, and my son, whatever else, has been known as a man of his word, and if he gives his bond here he will keep it, even without my enforcement. I beg your lordship will release him home to my bail.'

'On no terms,' said Prestcote decidedly. 'The matter is too grave. He stays under lock and key.'

'My lord, if you so order, under lock and key he shall be, but let it be in my house. His mother –'

'No! Say no more, you must know it is impossible. He

stays here in custody.'

'There is nothing against him in the matter of this death,' offered Corbière generously, 'as yet, that is, except my rogue's witness of his threats. And thieves do haunt such gatherings as the great fairs, and if they can cut a man out from his fellows, will kill him for the clothes on his back. And surely the fact that the body was stripped accords better with just such a foul chance crime for gain? Vengeance has nothing to feed on in a bundle of clothing. The act is all.'

'True,' agreed Prestcote. 'But supposing a man had killed in anger, perhaps simply gone too far in an assault meant only to injure, he might be wise enough to strip his victim, to make it appear the work of common robbers, and turn attention away from himself. There is much work to be done yet in this case, but meantime Corviser must remain in hold. I should be failing in my duty if I turned him loose, even to your care, master provost.' And the sheriff ordered, with a motion of his hand: 'Take him away!'

Philip was slow to move, until the butt of a lance prodded him none too gently in the side. Even then he kept his chin on his shoulder for some paces, and his eyes desperately fixed upon Emma's distressed and doubting face. 'I did not touch him,' he said, plucked forcibly away towards the door through which his guards had brought him. 'I pray you, believe me!' Then he was gone, and the hearing was over.

Out in the great court they paused to draw grateful breath, released from the shadowy oppression of the hall. Roger Dod hovered, with hungry eyes upon Emma.

'Mistress, shall I attend you back to the barge? Or will you have me go straight back to the booth? I had Gregory go there to help Warin, while I had to be absent, but trade was brisking up nicely, they'll be hard pushed by now. If that's what you want? To work the fair as he'd have worked it?'

'That is what I want,' she said firmly. 'To do all as he would have done. You go straight back to the horse-fair, Roger. I shall be staying with Lady Beringar at the abbey for this while, and Brother Cadfael will escort me.'

The journeyman louted, and left them, without a backward glance. But the very rear view of him, sturdy, stiff and aware, brought back to mind the intensity of his dark face and burning, embittered eyes. Emma watched him go, and heaved a helpless sigh.

'I am sure he is a good man, I know he is a good servant, and has stood loyally by my uncle many years. So he would by me, after his fashion. And I do respect him, I must! I think I could like him, if only he would not want me to love him!'

'It's no new problem,' said Cadfael sympathetically. 'The lightning strikes where it will. One flames, and the other remains cold. Distance is the only cure.'

'So I think,' said Emma fervently. 'Brother Cadfael, I must go to the barge, to bring away some more clothes and things I need. Will you go with me?'

He understood at once that this was an opportune time. Both Warin and Gregory were coping with customers at the booth, and Roger was on his way to join them. The barge would be riding innocently beside the jetty, and no man aboard to trouble her peace. Only a monk of the abbey, who did not trouble it at all. 'Whatever you wish,' he said. 'I have leave to assist you in all your needs.'

He had rather expected that Ivo Corbière would come to join her once they were out of the hall, but he did not. It was in Cadfael's mind that she had expected it, too. But perhaps the young man had decided that it was hardly worthwhile making a threesome with the desired lady and a monastic attendant, who clearly had his mandate, and would not consent to be dislodged. Cadfael could sympathise with that view, and admire his discretion and patience. There were two days of the fair left yet, and the great court of the abbey was not so great but guests could meet a dozen times a day. By chance or by rendezvous!

Emma was very silent on the way back through the town. She had nothing to say until they emerged from the shadow of the gate into full sunlight again, above the glittering bow of the river. Then she said suddenly: 'It was good of Ivo to speak so reasonably for the young man.' And on the instant, as Cadfael flashed a glance to glimpse whatever lay behind the words, she flushed almost as deeply as the unlucky lad Philip had blushed on beholding her a witness to his shame.

'It was very sound sense,' said Cadfael, amiably blind. 'Suspicion there may be, but proof there's none, not yet. And you set him a pace in generosity he could not but admire.'

The flush did not deepen, but it was already bright as a rose. On her ivory, silken face, so young and unused, it was touching and becoming.

'Oh, no,' she said, 'I only told simply truth. I could do no other.' Which again was simple truth, for nothing in her life thus far had corrupted her valiant purity. Cadfael had begun to feel a strong fondness for this orphan girl who shouldered her load without timidity or complaint, and still had an open heart for the burdens of others. 'I was sorry for his father,' she said. 'So decent and respected a man, to be denied so. And he spoke of his wife ... she will be out of her wits with worry.'

They were over the bridge, they turned down the green path, trodden almost bare at this busy, hot time, that led to the riverside and the long gardens and orchards of the Gaye. Master Thomas's deserted barge nestled into the green bank at the far end of the jetty, close-moored. One or two porters laboured along the boards with fresh stocks from the boats, shouldered them, and tramped away up the path to replenish busy stalls. The riverside lay sunlit, radiantly green and blue, and almost silent, but for the summer sounds of bees drunkenly busy among the late summer flowers in the grass. Almost deserted, but for a solitary fisherman in a small boat close under the shadow of the bridge; a comfortable, squarely-built fisherman stripped to shirt and hose, and bristling thornily with black curls and black bush of beard. Rhodri ap Huw clearly trusted his servant to deal profitably with his English customers, or else he had already sold out all the stock he had brought with him. He looked somnolent, happy, almost eternal, trailing his bait along the current under the archway, with an occasional flick of a wrist to correct the drift. Though most likely the sharp eyes under the sleepy eyelids were missing nothing that went on about him. He had the gift, it seemed, of being everywhere, but everywhere disinterested and benevolent.

'I will be quick,' said Emma, with a foot on the side of the barge. 'Last night Constance lent me all that I needed, but I must not continue a beggar. Will you step aboard, brother? You are welcome! I'm sorry to be so poor a hostess.' Her lips quivered. He knew the instant when her mind returned to her uncle, lying naked and dead in the castle, a man she had revered and relied on, and perhaps felt to be eternal in his solidity and self-confidence. 'He would have wished me to offer you wine, the wine you refused last night.'

'For want of time only,' said Cadfael placidly, and hopped nimbly over on to the barge's low deck. 'You go get what you need, child, I'll wait for you.'

The space aboard was well organised, the cabin aft rode low, but the full width of the hull, and though Emma had to stoop her neat head to enter, stepping down to the lower level within, she and her uncle would have had room within for sleeping. Little to spare, yet enough, where no alien or suspect thing might come. But taut, indeed, when she was short of her natural protector, with three other men closely present on deck outside. And one of them deeply, hopelessly, in love. Uncles may not notice such glances as his, where their own underlings are concerned.

She was back, springing suddenly to view in the low doorway. Her eyes had again that look of shock and alarm, but now contained and schooled. Her voice was level and low as she said: 'Someone has been here! Someone strange! Someone has handled everything we left here on board, pawed through my linen and my uncle's, too, turned every board or cover. I do not dream, Brother Cadfael! It is true! Our boat has been ransacked while it was left empty. Come and see!'

It was without guile that he asked her instantly: 'Has anything been taken?'

Still possessed by her discovery, and unguardedly honest, Emma said: 'No!'

# Chapter Three

Everything in the boat, and certainly in the small cabin, seemed to Cadfael to be in immaculate order, but he did not therefore doubt her judgment. A girl making her third journey in this fashion, and growing accustomed to making the best use of the cramped space, would know exactly how she had everything folded and stowed, and the mere disturbance of a fold, the crumpling of a corner in the neat low chest under her bench-bed would be enough to alert her, and betray the intervention of another hand. But the very attempt at perfect restoration was surprising. It argued that the interloper had had ample time at his disposal, while all the crew were absent. Yet she had said confidently that nothing had been stolen.

'You are sure? You've had little time to examine everything here. Best look round thoroughly and make sure, before we report this to Hugh Beringar.'

'Must I do that?' she asked, a little startled, even, he thought, a little dismayed. 'If there's no harm? They are burdened enough with other matters.'

'But do you not see, child, that this comes too aptly on the other? Your uncle killed, and now his barge ransacked ...'

'Why, there can surely be no connection,' she said quickly. 'This is the work of some common thief.'

'A common thief who took nothing?' said Cadfael.

'Where there are any number of things worth the taking!'

'Perhaps he was interrupted ...' But her voice wavered into silence, she could not even convince herself.

'Does it look so to you? I think he must have been through all your belongings at leisure, to leave them so neat for you. And removed himself only when he was satisfied.' But of what? That what he wanted was not there?

Emma gnawed a dubious lip, and looked about her thoughtfully. 'Well, if we must report it ... You're right, I spoke too soon, perhaps I should go through everything. No use telling him but half a tale.'

She settled down methodically to take out every item of clothing and equipment from both chests, laying them out on the beds, even unfolding those which showed, to her eyes at least, the most obvious signs of handling, and refolding them to her own satisfaction. At the end of it she sat back on her heels and looked up at Cadfael, thoughtfully frowning.

'Yes, there have been some things taken, but so cunningly. Small things that would never have been missed until we got home. There's a girdle of mine missing, one with a gold clasp. And a silver chain. And a pair of gloves with gold embroidery. If my thumbs had not pricked when I came in here, I should not have missed them, for I shouldn't have wanted to wear any of them. What could I want with gloves in August? I bought them all in Gloucester, on the way up the river.'

'And of your uncle's belongings?'

'I think there is nothing missing. If some moneys were left here, certainly none are here now, but his strong-box is at the booth. He never carried valuables on such journeys as this, except the rings he always wore. I should not have had such rich trifles here myself, if I had not but newly bought them.'

'So it seems,' said Cadfael, 'whoever took the opportunity of stepping aboard boldly, to see what he could pick up, had the wit to take only trifles he could slip in his sleeve or his pouch. That makes good sense. However, naturally it was done, he'd be likely to cause some curiosity if he stepped ashore with his arms full of your uncle's gowns and shirts.'

'And we must trouble Hugh Beringar and the sheriff over so trivial a loss?' wondered Emma, jutting a doubtful lip. 'It seems a pity, when he has so many graver matters on his mind. And you see this is only an ordinary, vulgar filching, because the boat was left empty a while. Small creatures of prey have an eye to such chances.'

'Yes, we must,' said Cadfael firmly. 'Let the law be the judge whether this has anything to do with your uncle's death or no. That's not for us to say. You find what you need to take with you, and we'll go together and see him, if he's to be found at this hour.'

Emma put together a fresh gown and tunic, stockings and shift and other such mysteries as girls need, with a composure which Cadfael found at once admirable and baffling. The immediate discovery of the invasion of her possessions had startled and disturbed her, but she had come to terms with it very quickly and calmly, and appeared perfectly indifferent to the loss of her finery. He was just considering how odd it was that she should be so anxious to disconnect this incident from her uncle's death, when she herself, in perverse and unthinking innocence, restored the link.

'Well, at any rate,' said Emma, gathering her bundle together neatly in the skirt of the gown, and rising nimbly from her knees, 'no one can dare say that the provost's son was to blame for this. He's safe in a cell in the castle, and the sheriff himself can be his witness this time.'

*

Hugh Beringar had shrugged off his duties to enjoy at least the evening meal with his wife. Mercifully the first day of the fair had passed so far without further incident, no disorders, no quarrels, no accusations of cheating or overcharging, no throat-cutting or price-cutting, as though the uproar of the previous evening, and its deadly result, had chastened and subdued even the regular offenders. Trade was thriving, rents and tolls bringing in a high revenue for the abbey, and sales seemed set to continue peacefully well into the night.

'And I have bought some spun wool,' said Aline, delighted with her day's shopping, 'and some very fine woollen cloth, so soft – feel it! And Constance chose two beautiful fleeces from Cadfael's Welsh merchant, she wants to card and spin them herself for the baby. And I changed my mind about a cradle, for I saw nothing in the fair to match what Martin Bellecote can do. I shall go to him.'

'The girl is not back yet?' said Hugh, mildly surprised. 'She left the castle well before me.'

'She'll have gone to bring some things from the barge. She had nothing with her last night, you know. And she was going to Bellecote's shop, too, to bespeak the coffin for her uncle.'

'That she'd done on the way,' said Hugh, 'for Martin came to the castle about the business before I left. They'll be bringing the body down to the chapel here before dark.' He added appreciatively: 'A fair-minded lass, our Emma, as well as a stout-hearted one. She would not have that fool boy of Corviser's turned into the attacker, even for her uncle's sake. A straight tale as ever was. He opened civilly, was brusquely received, made the mistake of laying hand on the old man, and was felled like a poled ox.'

'And what does he himself say?' Aline looked up intently from the bolt of soft stuff she was lovingly stroking.

'That he never laid eyes on Master Thomas again, and knows no more about his death than you or I. But there's that falconer of Corbière's says he was breathing fire and smoke against the old man in Wat's tavern well into the evening. Who knows! The mildest lamb of the flock – but that's not his reputation! – may be driven to clash foreheads when roused, but the knife in the back, somehow – that I doubt. He had no knife on him when he was taken up at the gate. We shall have to ask all his companions if they saw such a thing about him.'

'Here is Emma,' said Aline, looking beyond him to the doorway.

The girl came in briskly with her bundle, Brother Cadfael at her shoulder. 'I'm sorry to have been so long,' said Emma, 'but we had reason. Something untoward has happened – oh, it is not so grave, no great harm, but Brother Cadfael says we must tell you.'

Cadfael forbore from urging, stood back in silence, and let her tell it in her own way, and a very flat way it was, as though she had no great interest in her reported loss. But for all that, she described the bits of finery word for word as she had described them to him, and went into greater detail of their ornaments. 'I did not wish to bother you with such trumpery thefts. How can I care about a lost girdle and gloves, when I have lost so much more? But Brother Cadfael insisted, so I have told you.'

'Brother Cadfael was right,' said Hugh sharply. 'Would it surprise you, child, to know that we have had not one complaint of mispractice or stealing or any evil all this day, touching any other tradesman at the fair? Yet one threat follows another where your uncle's business is concerned. Can that truly be by chance? Is there not someone here who has no interest in any other, but all too much in him?'

'I knew you would think so,' she said, sighing helplessly. 'But it was only by chance that our barge was left quite unmanned all this afternoon, by reason of Roger being needed with the rest of us at the castle. I doubt if there was another boat there unwatched. And common thieves have a sharp eye out for such details. They take what they can get.'

It was a shrewd point, and clearly she was not the girl to lose sight of any argument that could serve her turn. Cadfael held his peace. There would be a time to discuss the matter with Hugh Beringar, but it was not now. The questions that needed answers would not be asked of Emma; where would be the use? She had been born with all her wits about her, and through force of circumstances she was learning with every moment. But why was she so anxious to have this search of her possessions shrugged aside as trivial, and having no bearing on Master Thomas's murder? And why had she stated boldly, in the first shock of discovery, indeed without time to view the field in any detail, that nothing had been taken? As though, disdaining the invasion, she had good reason to know that it had been ineffective?

And yet, thought Cadfael, studying the rounded resolute face, and the clear eyes she raised to Hugh's searching stare, I would swear this is a good, honest girl, no way cheat or liar.

'You'll not be needing me,' he said, 'Emma can tell you all. It's almost time for Vespers, and I have still to go and speak with the abbot. There'll be time later, Hugh, after supper.' Abbot Radulfus was a good listener. Not once did he interrupt with comment or question, as Brother Cadfael recounted for him all that had passed at the sheriff's hearing and the unexpected discovery at the barge afterwards. At the end of it he sat for a brief while in silence still, pondering what he had heard.

'So we now have one unlawful act of which the man charged cannot possibly be guilty, whatever may be the truth concerning the other. What do you think, does this tend to weaken the suspicion against him, even on the charge of murder?'

'It weakens it,' said Cadfael, 'but it cannot clear him. It may well be true, as Mistress Vernold believes, that the two things are no way linked, the filching from the barge a mere snatch at what was available, for want of a watchman to guard it. Yet two such assaults upon the same man's life and goods looks like methodical purpose, and not mere chance.'

'And the girl is now a guest within our halls,' said Radulfus, 'and her safety our responsibility. Two attacks upon one man's life and goods, you said. How if there should be more? If a subtle enemy is pursuing some private purpose, it may not end with this afternoon's violation, as we have seen it did not end with the merchant's death. The girl is in the care of the deputy sheriff, and could not be in better hands. But like them, she is a guest under our roof. I do not want the brothers of our community distracted from their devotions and duties, or the harmony of our services shaken, I would not have these matters spoken of but between you and me, and of course as is needful to aid the law. But you, Brother Cadfael, have already been drawn in, you know the whole state of the case. Will you have an eye to what follows, and keep watch on our guests? I place the interests of the abbey in your hands. Do not neglect your devotional duties, unless you must, but I give you leave to go in and out freely, and absent yourself from offices if there is need. When the fair ends, our halls will empty, our tenant merchants depart. It will be out of our hands then to protect the just or prevent the harm that threatens from the unjust. But while they are here, let us do what we can.'

'I will undertake what you wish, Father Abbot,' said Cadfael, 'to the best I may.'

He went to Vespers with a burdened heart and a vexed mind, but for all that, he was glad of the Abbot's charge. It was, in any case, impossible to give up worrying at so tangled a knot, once it had presented itself to his notice, even apart from the natural concern he felt for the girl, and there was no denying that the Benedictine round, dutifully observed, did limit a man's mobility for a large part of the day.

Meantime, he drove the affairs of Emma Vernold from his thoughts with a struggle that should have earned him credit in heaven, and surrendered himself as best he could to the proper observance of Vespers. And after supper he repaired to the cloister, and was not surprised to find Hugh Beringar there waiting for him. They sat down together in a corner where the evening breeze coiled about them very softly and gratefully, and the view into the garth was all emerald turf and pale grey stone, and azure sky melting into green, through a fretwork of briars blowsy with late, drunken-sweet roses.

'There's news in your face,' said Cadfael, eyeing his friend warily. 'As though we have not had enough for one day!'

'And what will you make of it?' wondered Hugh. 'Not an hour ago a lad fishing in Severn hooked a weight of sodden cloth out of the water. All but broke his line, so he let it back in, but was curious enough to play it to shore until he could take it up safely. A fine, full woollen gown, made for a big man, and one with money to spend, too.' He met Cadfael's bright, alerted eyes, rather matching certainties than questioning. 'Yes, what else? We did not trouble Emma with it – who would have the heart! She's drawing Aline a pattern for an embroidered hem for an infant's robe, one she got from France. They have their heads together like sisters. No, we fetched Roger Dod to swear to it. It's Master Thomas's gown, no question. We're poling down the banks now after hose and shirt. To any wandering thief that gown was worth a month's hunting.'

'So no such leech would have thrown it away,' said Cadfael.

'Never!'

'There were also rings taken from his fingers. But rings, I suppose, might be too good to discard, even to prove that this was a murder for hate, not for gain. Rings would sink even if hurled into the Severn. So why hurl them?'

'As usual,' said Hugh, elevating thin black brows, 'you're ahead of me rather than abreast. On the face of it, this was a killing for private malice. So while we examine it, Ivo Corbière very sensibly points out that a murderer so minded would not have stayed to strip the body and put it into the river, but left it lying, and made off as fast as he could. Vengeance, he says rightly, has nothing to feed on in a bundle of clothing. The act is all! And that moved my sheriff to remark that the same thought might well have occurred to the murderer, and caused him to strip his victim naked for that very reason, a hoodwink for the law. Now we drag out of the river the dead man's gown. And where does that leave you and me, my friend?'

'In two minds, or more,' said Cadfael ruefully. 'If the gown never had been found, the notion of common robbery would have held its ground and told in young Corviser's favour. Is it possible that what was said in the sheriff's court put that thought into someone's mind for the first time, and drove him to discard the gown where it was likely to be found? There's one person it would suit very well to have the case against your prisoner strengthened, and that's the murderer himself. Supposing yon fool boy is not the murderer, naturally.'

'True, half a case can come to look almost whole by the addition of one more witness. But what a fool your man would be, to toss the gown away for proof the killing was not for robbery, thus turning suspicion back upon Philip Corviser, and then creep aboard the barge and steal, when Philip Corviser is in a cell in the castle, and manifestly out of the reckoning.'

'Ah, but he never supposed the theft would be discovered until the barge was back in Bristol, or well on the way. I tell you, Hugh, *I* could see no trace of an alien hand anywhere among those stores on deck or the chattels in the cabin, and Emma herself said she would not have missed the lost things until reaching home again. They were bought on this journey, she had no intention of wearing them. Nothing obvious was stolen, she had almost reached the bottom of her chest before she found out these few bits of finery were gone. But for her sharp eye for her own neat housekeeping, she would not have known the boat had been visited.'

'Yet robbery points to two separate villains and two separate crimes,' pointed out Hugh with a wry smile, 'as Emma insists on believing. If hate was the force behind the man's death, why stoop to pilfer from him afterwards? But do *you* believe the two things are utterly separate? I think not!'

'Strange chances do jostle one another sometimes in this world. Don't put it clean out of mind, it may still be true. But I cannot choose but believe that it's the same hand behind both happenings, and the same purpose, and it was neither theft nor hatred, or the death would have ended it.'

'But Cadfael, in heaven's name, what purpose that demanded a man's death could get satisfaction afterwards from stealing a pair of gloves, a girdle and a chain?'

Brother Cadfael shook his head helplessly, and had no answer to that, or none that he was yet prepared to give.

'My head spins, Hugh. But I have a black suspicion it may not be over yet. Abbot Radulfus has given me his commission to have an eye to the matter, for the abbey's sake, and permission to go in and out as I see fit for the purpose. It's as the back of his mind that if there's some malignant plot in hand against the Bristol merchant, his niece may not be altogether safe, either. If Aline can keep her at her side, so much the better. But I'll be keeping a watchful eye on her, too.' He rose, yawning. 'Now I must be off to Compline. If I'm to scamp my duties tomorrow, let me at least end today well.'

'Pray for a quiet night,' said Hugh, rising with him, 'for we've not the men to mount patrols through the dark hours. I'll take one more turn along the Foregate with my sergeant, as far as the horse-fair, and then I'm for my bed. I saw little enough of it last night!'

The night of the first of August, the opening day of Saint Peter's Fair, was warm, clear, and quiet enough. Traders along the Foregate kept their stalls open well into the dark hours, the weather being so inviting that plenty of customers were still abroad to chaffer and bargain. The sheriff's officers withdrew into the town, and even the abbey servants, left to keep the peace if it were threatened, had little work to do. It was past midnight when the last lamps and torches were quenched, and the night's silence descended upon the horse-fair.

Master Thomas's barge rocked very softly to the motion of the river. Master Thomas himself lay in a chapel of the abbey, decently shrouded, and in his workshop in the town Martin Bellecote the master-carpenter worked late upon the fine, lead-lined coffin

Emma had ordered from him. And in a narrow and dusty cell in the castle, Philip Corviser tossed and turned and nursed his bruises on a thin mattress of straw, and could not sleep for fretting over the memory of Emma's doubting, pitying face.

# The Second Day of the Fair

## Chapter One

The second day of the fair dawned brilliantly, a golden sun climbing, faint mist hanging like a floating veil over the river. Roger Dod rose with the dawn, shook Gregory awake, rolled up his brychan, washed in the river, and made a quick meal of bread and small ale before setting off along the Foregate to his master's booth. All along the highroad traders were clambering out of their cloaks, yawning and stretching, and setting out their goods ready for the day's business. Roger exchanged greetings with several of them as he passed. Where so many were gathered at close quarters, even a dour and silent man could not help picking up acquaintance with a few of his fellows.

The first glimpse of Master Thomas's booth, between the busy stirrings of its neighbours, brought a scowl to Roger's brown and a muttered oath to his tongue, for the wooden walls were still fast closed. Every hatch still sealed, and the sun already climbing! Warin must be fast asleep, inside there. Roger hammered on the front boards, which should by this hour have been lowered trimly on to their trestles, and set out with goods for sale. He got no response from within.

'Warin!' he bellowed. 'Devil take you, get up and let me in!'

No reply, except that several of the neighbours had

turned curiously to listen and watch, abandoning their own activities to attend to this unexpected clamour.

'Warin!' bawled Roger, and thumped again vigorously. 'You idle swine, what's come to you?'

'I did wonder,' said the cloth-merchant next door, pausing with a bolt of flannel in his arms. 'There's been no sign of him. A sound sleeper, your watchman!'

'Hold hard!' The armourer from the other side leaned excitedly over Roger's shoulder, and fingered the edge of the wooden door. 'Splinters, see?' Beside the latch the boards showed a few pale threads, hardly enough to be seen, and at the thrust of his hand the door gave upon a sliver of darkness. 'No need to hammer, the way in is open. A knife has been used on this!' said the armourer, and there fell a momentary silence.

'Pray God that's all it's been used on!' said Roger in an appalled whisper, and thrust the door wide. He had a dozen of them at his back by then; even the Welshman Rhodri ap Huw had come rolling massively between the stalls to join them, sharp black eyes twinkling out of the thicket of his hair and beard, though what he made of the affair, seeing he spoke no English, no one stopped to consider.

From the darkness within welled the warm scent of timber, wine and sweetmeats, and a faint, strange sound like the breathy grunting of a dumb man. Roger was propelled forward into the dimness by the eager helpers crowding at his back, all agape with curiosity. The stacked bales and small casks of wine took shape gradually, after the brief blindness of entering this dark place from sunlight. Everything stood orderly and handy, just as it had been left overnight, and of Warin there was no sign, until Rhodri ap Huw, ever practical, unbolted the front hatch and let it down, and the brightness of the morning came flooding in.

Stretched along the foot of the same front wall,

where Rhodri must almost have set foot on him, Warin lay rolled in his own cloak and tied at elbows, knees and ankles with cords, so tightly that he could barely wriggle enough to make the folds of cloth rustle. There was a sack drawn over his head, and a length of linen dragged the coarse fibres into his mouth and was secured behind his neck. He was doing his best to answer to his name, and at least his limited jerkings and muted grunts made it plain that he was alive.

Roger uttered a wordless yell of alarm and indignation, and fell on his knees, plucking first at the linen band that held the sack fast. The coarse cloth was wet before with spittle, and the mouth within must be clogged and stung with ropey fibres, but at least the poor wretch could breathe, his strangled grunts were trying to form words long before the linen parted, and let him spit out his gag. Still beneath his sack, his hoarse croak demanded aggrievedly: 'Where were you so long, and me half-killed?'

A couple of pairs of willing hands were at work on the other bonds by that time, all the more zealously now they had heard him speak, and indeed complain, in such reassuringly robust tones. Warin emerged gradually from his swaddlings, unrolled unceremoniously out of the cloak so that he ended face-down on the ground, and still incoherently voluble. He righted himself indignantly, but so spryly that it was plain he had no broken bones, no painful injuries, and had not even suffered overmuch from the cramps of his bonds. He looked up from under his wild grey thatch of hair, half defensive and half accusing, glaring round the circle of his rescuers as though they had been responsible for his hours of discomfort.

'Late's better than never!' he said sourly, and hawked, and spat out fibres of sacking. 'What took you so long? Is everybody deaf? I've been kicking here half the night!'

Half a dozen hands reached pleasurably to hoist him to his feet and sit him down gently on a cask of wine. Roger stood off and let them indulge their curiosity, scowling blackly at his colleague meantime. There was no damage done, not a scratch on the old fool! The first threat, and he had crumpled into a pliable rag.

'For God's sake, what happened to you? You had the booth sealed. How could any man break in here, and you not know? There are other merchants sleep here with their wares, you had only to call.'

'Not all,' said the cloth-merchant fairly. 'I myself lie at a tavern, so do many. If your man was sound asleep, as he well might be with all closed for the night ...'

'It was long past midnight,' said Warin, scrubbing aggrievedly at his chafed ankles. 'I know because I heard the little bell for Matins, over the wall, before I slept. Not a sound after, until I awoke as that hood came over my head. They rammed the stuff into my mouth. I never saw face or form, they rolled me up like a bale of wool, and left me tied.'

'And you never raised a cry!' said Roger bitterly. 'How many were they? One or more?'

Warin was disconcerted, and wavered, swaying either way. 'I think two. I'm not sure ...'

'You were hooded, but you could hear. Did they talk together?'

'Yes, now I recall there was some whispering. Not that I could catch any words. Yes, they were two. There was moving about of casks and bales here, that I know ...'

'For how long? They durst not hurry, and have things fall and rouse the fairground,' said the armourer reasonably. 'How long did they stay?'

Warin was vague, and indeed to a man blindfolded and tied by night, time might stretch out like unravelled thread. 'An hour, it might be.'

'Time enough to find whatever was of most value

here,' said the armourer, and looked at Roger Dod, with a shrug of broad shoulders. 'You'd better look about you, lad, and see what's missing. No need to trouble for anything so weighty as casks of wine, they'd have needed a cart for those, and a cart in the small hours would surely have roused someone. The small and precious is what they came for.'

But Roger had already turned his back on his rescued fellow, and was burrowing frantically among the bales and boxes stacked along the wall. 'My master's strong-box! I built it in behind here, out of sight ... Thank God I took the most of yesterday's gains back to the barge with me last night, and have them safe under lock and key, but for all that, there was a good sum left in it. And all his accounts, and parchments ...'

He was thrusting boxes and bags of spices aside in his haste, scenting the air, pushing out of his way wooden caskets of sugar confections from the east, come by way of Venice and Gascony, and worth high prices in any market. 'Here, against the wall ...'

His hands sank helplessly, he stood staring in dismay. He had bared the boards of the booth; goods stood piled on either side, and between them, nothing. Master Thomas's strong-box was gone.

Brother Cadfael had taken advantage of the early hours to put in an hour or two of work with Brother Mark in the herb-gardens, while he had no reason to anticipate any threat to Emma, for she was surely still asleep in the guest-hall with Constance, and out of reach of harm. The morning was clear and sunny, the mist just lifting from the river, shot through with oblique gold, and Mark sang cheerfully about his weeding, and listened attentively and serenely as Cadfael instructed him in all particulars of the day's work.

'For I may have to leave all things in your hands. And so I can, safely enough, I know, if I should chance to be called away.'

'I'm well taught,' said Brother Mark, with his grave smile, behind which the small spark of mischief was visible only to Cadfael, who had first discovered and nurtured it. 'I know what to stir and what to let well alone in the workshop.'

'I wish I could be as sure of my part outside it,' said Cadfael ruefully. 'There are brews among us that need just as sure a touch, boy, and where to stir and where to let be is puzzling me more than a little. I'm walking a knife-edge, with disastrous falls on either side. I know my herbs. They have fixed properties, and follow sacred rules. Human creatures do not so. And I cannot even wish they did. I would not have one scruple of their complexity done away, it would be lamentable loss.'

It was time to go to Prime. Brother Mark stooped to rinse his hands in the butt of water they kept warming through the day, to be tempered for the herbs at the evening watering. 'It was being with you made me know that I want to be a priest,' he said, speaking his mind as openly as always in Cadfael's company.

'I had never the urge for it,' said Cadfael absently, his mind on other matters.

'I know. That was the one thing wanting. Shall we go?'

They were coming out from Prime, and the lay servants already mustering for their early Mass, when Roger Dod came trudging in at the gatehouse, out of breath, and with trouble plain to be read in his face.

'What, again something new?' sighed Cadfael, and set off to intercept him before he reached the guest-hall. Suddenly aware of this square, sturdy figure bearing down on him with obvious purpose,

Roger checked, and turned an anxious face. His frown cleared a little when he recognised the same monk who had accompanied the deputy sheriff in the vain search for Master Thomas, on the eve of Saint Peter. 'Oh, it's you, brother, that's well! Is Hugh Beringar within? I must speak to him. We're beset! Yesterday the barge, and now the booth, and God knows what's yet to come, and what will become of us before ever we get away from this deadly place. My master's books gone – money and box and all! What will Mistress Emma think? I'd rather have had my own head broke, if need be, than fail her so!'

'What's this talk of broken heads?' asked Cadfael, alarmed. 'Whose? Are you telling me there've been thieves ransacking your booth now?'

'In the night! And the strong-box gone, and Warin tied up hand and foot with a throatful of sacking, and nobody heard sound while they did it. We found him not half an hour ago ...'

'Come!' said Cadfael, grasping him by the sleeve and setting off for the guest-hall at a furious pace. 'We'll find Hugh Beringar. Tell your tale once, and save breath!'

In Aline's apartments the women were only just out of bed, and Hugh was sitting over an early meal in shirt and hose, shoeless, when Cadfael rapped at the door, and cautiously put his head in.

'Your pardon, Hugh, but there's news. May we come in?'

Hugh took one look at him, recognised the end of his ease, and bade them in resignedly.

'Here's one has a tale to tell,' said Cadfael. 'He's new come from the horse-fair.'

At sight of Roger, Emma came to her feet in astonishment and alarm, the soft, bemused bloom of sleep gone from her eyes, and the morning flush from her cheeks. Her black hair, not yet braided, swung in a glossy curtain about her shoulders, and her loose undergown was ungirdled, her feet bare. 'Roger, what is it? What has happened now?'

'More theft and roguery, mistress, and God knows I can see no reason why all the rascals in the shire should pick on us for prey.' Roger heaved in deep breath, and launched headlong into his complaint. 'This morning I go to the stall as usual, and find it all closed, and not a sound or a word from within for all my shouting and knocking, and then come some of the neighbours, wondering, and one sees that the inside bar has been hoisted with a knife – and a marvellous thin knife it must have been. And we go in and find Warin rolled up like baggage in his own cloak, and fast tied, and his mouth stuffed with sacking – a bag over his head, fit to choke him ...'

'Oh, no!' breathed Emma in a horrified whisper, and pressed a fist hard against trembling lips. 'Oh, poor Warin! He's not ... oh, not dead ...?'

Roger gave vent to a snort of contempt. 'Not he! alive and fit as a flea, barring being stiff from the cords. How he could sleep so sound as not to hear the fumbling with the latch, nor even notice when the door was opened, there's no guessing. But if he did hear, he took good care not to give the robbers any trouble. You know Warin's no hero. He says he was only shook awake when the sack went over his head, and never saw face nor form, though he thinks there were two of them, for there was some whispering. But as like as not he heard them come, but chose not to, for fear they'd slip the knife in his ribs.'

Emma's colour had warmed into rose again. She drew a deep breath of thankfulness. 'But he's safe? He's taken no harm at all?' She caught Aline's sympathetic eye, and laughed shakily with relief. 'I *know* he is not brave. I'm *glad* he is not! Nor very clever nor very industrious, either, but I've known him since I was a little girl, he used to make toys for me, and willow whistles. Thank God he is not harmed!'

'Not a graze! I wish,' said Roger, his eyes burning jealously upon her childish morning beauty, not yet adorned and needing no adornment, 'I wish to God I'd stayed there to be watchman myself, they'd not have broken in there unscathed, and found everything handed over on a platter.'

'But then you might have been killed, Roger. I'm glad you were *not* there, you'd surely have put up a fight and come to harm. What, against two, and you unarmed? Oh, no, I want no man hurt to protect my possessions.'

'What followed?' asked Hugh shortly, stamping his feet into his shoes and reaching for his coat. 'You've left him there to mind the stall? Is he fit?'

'As you or me, my lord. I'll send him to you to tell his own tale when I get back.'

'No need, I'm coming with you to view the place and the damage. Finish your tale. They'll scarcely have left empty-handed. What's gone with them?'

Roger turned devoted, humble, apologetic eyes upon Emma. 'Sorrow the day, mistress, my master's strong-box is gone with them!'

Brother Cadfael was watching Emma's face just as intently as was her hopeless admirer, and it seemed to him that in the pleasure of knowing that her old servant had survived unharmed, she was proof against all other blows. The loss of the strong-box she received with unshaken serenity. In these surroundings, safe from any too pressing manifestation of his passion, she was even moved to comfort Roger. A kindhearted girl, who did not like to see any of her own people out of sorts with his competence and his self-respect.

'You must not feel it so sharply,' she said warmly. 'How could you have prevented? There is no fault attaches to you.'

'I took most of the money back to the barge with me last night,' pleaded Roger earnestly. 'It's safe locked away, there's been no more tampering there. But Master Thomas's account books, and some parchments of value, and charters ...'

'Then there will be copies,' said Emma firmly. 'And what is more, if they took the box, supposing it to be full of money, they'll keep what money was left there, and most likely discard the box and the parchments, for what use can they make of those? We may get most of it back, you will see.'

Not merely a kind girl, but a girl of sense and fortitude, who bore up nobly under her losses. Cadfael looked at Hugh, and found Hugh looking at him, just as woodenly, but with one lively eyebrow signalling slightly sceptical admiration.

'Nothing is lost,' said Emma firmly, 'of any value to compare with a life. Since Warin is safe, I cannot be sad.'

'Nevertheless,' said Hugh with deliberation, 'it might be well if one abbey sergeant stood guard on your booth until the fair is over. For it does seem that all the misfortunes that should by rights be shared among all the abbey's clients are falling solely upon you. Shall I ask Prior Robert to see to it?'

She looked down, wary and thoughtful, for a moment, and then lifted deep blue eyes wide and clear as the sky, and a degree more innocent than if they had but newly opened on the world. 'It's kind of you,' she said, 'but surely everything has now been done to us. I don't think it will be necessary to set a guard upon us now.'

Hugh came to Cadfael's workshop after the midday meal, leaving Emma in Aline's charge, helped himself to a horn of wine from Cadfael's private store, and settled down on the bench under the eaves, on the shady side. The fragrance of the herbs lay like a sleepy load on the air within the pleached hedges, and set him yawning against his will and his mood, which was for serious discussion. They were well away from the outer world here, the busy hum of the marketplace drifted to them only distantly and pleasantly, like the working music of Brother Bernard's bees. And Brother Mark, weeding the herb-beds with delicate, loving hands, habit kilted to his knees, was no hindrance at all to their solitude.

'A separate creature,' said Brother Cadfael, eyeing him with detached affection 'My priest, my proxy. I had to find some way of evading the fate that closed on me. There goes my sacrificial lamb, the best of the flock.'

'Some day he will take *your* confession,' said Hugh, watching Mark pluck out weeds as gently as though he pitied them, 'and you'll be a lost man, for he'll know every evasion.' He sipped wine, drew it about his mouth thoughtfully, swallowed it and sat savouring the after-taste for a moment. 'This fellow Warin had little to add,' he said then. 'What do you say now? This *cannot* be chance.'

'No,' agreed Cadfael, propping the door of his workshop wide to let in the air, and coming to sit beside his friend, 'it cannot be chance. The man is killed, stripped, his barge searched, his booth searched. Not a soul besides, at this fair where there are several as wealthy, has suffered any attack or any loss. No, there is nothing done at hazard here.'

'What, then? Expound! The girl claimed there were things stolen from the barge. Now something positive, a strong-box, the single portable thing in the booth that might confidently be supposed to hold valuables, is demonstrably stolen from this last assault. If these are not simple thefts, what are they? Tell me!'

'Stages in a quest,' said Cadfael. 'It seems to me

there's a hunt afoot for something. I do not know what, but some quite single, small thing, and precious, which was, or was thought to be, in the possession of Master Thomas. On the night he came here he was murdered, and his body stripped. The first search. And it was fruitless, for the next day his barge was visited and ransacked. The second search.'

'Not altogether fruitless this time,' said Beringar dryly, 'for we know on the best authority, do we not, that whoever paid that visit left the richer by three things, a silver chain, a girdle with a gold clasp, and a pair of embroidered gloves.'

'Hmmm!' Cadfael twitched his brown nose doubtfully between finger and thumb, and eyed the young man sidewise.

'Oh, come!' said Hugh indulgently, and flashed his sudden smile. 'I may not stumble on these subtleties as quickly as you, but since knowing you I've had to keep my wits about me. The lady has a bold mind and an excellent memory, and I have no hope in the world of getting her to make a mistake in one detail of the embroidery on those lost gloves, but for all that, I doubt if they ever existed.'

'You might,' Cadfael suggested, though without much hope, 'try asking her outright what it is she's hiding.'

'I did!' owned Hugh, ruefully grinning. 'She opened great, hurt eyes at me, and could not understand me! She knows nothing, she's hiding nothing, she has nothing to tell more than she's already told, and every word of that is truth. But for all that, and however angelically, the girl's lying. What was it stuck in your craw, and brought you up against the same shock before ever it dawned upon me?'

'I should be sorry,' said Cadfael slowly, 'if anything I have done or said made you think any evil of the girl, for I think none.'

'Neither do I, you need not fear it. But I do think she may be meddling in something she would do better to let well alone, and I would rather, as you would, as Abbot Radulfus would, that no harm should come to her under our care. Or ever, for that matter. I like her well.'

'When we went together to the barge,' said Cadfael, 'and she took no more than a minute within to cry out that someone had been there, pawing through all their belongings, I never doubted she was telling truth. Women know how they leave things, it needs only a wrong fold to betray an alien hand, and certainly it shocked and startled her, that was no feigning. Nor was it the next moment, when I asked if anything had been taken, and without pause for thought, she said: "No!" An absolute no, I would say even triumphant. I thought little of it, then, but urged her to look thoroughly and make sure. When I said she must report the matter, she thought again, and took pains to discover that indeed a few things had been stolen. I think she regretted that ever she had cried out in the first place, but if the law must know of it, she would ensure that it was accepted as a trivial theft by some common pickpurse. Truth is what she told unguardedly, with that scornful "no" of hers. Afterwards she made to undo the effect by lying, and for one not by nature a liar she did it well. But for all that, I think, like you, those pretty things of hers never existed, or never were aboard the barge.'

'Still remains the question,' said Hugh, considering, 'of why she was so sure in the first place that nothing had been taken.'

'Because,' said Cadfael simply, 'she knew what the thief must have come looking for, and she knew he had not found it, because she knew it was not there to be found. The second search was also vain. Whatever it may be, it was not on Master Thomas's person, which was clearly the most likely place, nor was it on his barge.'

'Hence this third search! So now divine for me, Cadfael, whether this third attempt has succeeded or no. The merchant's strong-box is vanished – again a logical place to keep something so precious. Will this be the end of it?' Cadfael shook his head emphatically. 'This attempt has fared no better than the others,' he said positively. 'You may take that as certain.'

'How can you be so sure of it?' demanded Hugh curiously.

'You saw all that I saw. She does not care a farthing for the loss of the strong-box! As soon as she knew that the man Warin was unhurt, she took everything else calmly enough. Whatever it is the unknown is seeking, she knew it was not in the barge, and she knew it was not in the booth. And I can think of only one reason why she should know so well where it is *not*, and that is that she knows equally well where it *is*.'

'Then the next possibility the enemy will be considering,' said Hugh with conviction, 'is where *she* is – on her person or in some hiding-place only she knows of. Well, we'll keep a vigilant eye on Emma, between us. No,' said Hugh reflectively, 'I cannot imagine any evil of her, but neither can I imagine how she can be tangled in something grim enough to bring about murder, violence and theft, nor why, if she knows herself to be in danger and in need of help, she won't speak out and ask for it. Aline has tried her best to get her to confide, and the girl remains all sweetness and gratitude, but lets no word drop of any burden she may be carrying. And you know Aline, she draws out confidences without ever asking a probing question, and whoever can resist her is beyond the reach of the rest of us ...'

'I'm glad to see you so fond a husband,' said Cadfael approvingly.

'So you should be, it was you tossed the girl into my arms in the first place. You'd best be worrying now about what manner of father I shall make! And you might put in a prayer for me on the issue, some time when you're on your knees. No, truly, Cadfael ... I wonder about this girl. Aline likes her, and that's recommendation enough. And she seems to like Aline – no, more than like! Yet she never lets down her veils. When she seems most to cherish my most cherishable lady, she is also more careful not to let slip one unguarded word about her own situation.'

Brother Cadfael saw no paradox there. 'So she would be, Hugh,' he said gravely. 'If she feels herself to be in danger, the last thing she will do is to draw in beside her someone she values and likes. By every means in her power – and I think she is a clever and resourceful girl – she will stand off her friends from any share in what she is about.'

Beringar considered that long and sombrely, nursing his empty horn. 'Well, all we can do is hedge her about thick enough to stand off, likewise, whatever move may be made against her.'

It had not occurred to him, it was only now insinuating itself into Cadfael's thoughts, that the next decisive move might come from Emma herself, rather than being made against her. A piece of this mystery, apparently the vital piece, she had in her hands; if any use was to be made of it, it might well be at her decree.

Hugh set aside his drinking-horn and rose, brushing the summer dust from his cotte. 'Meantime, the sheriff is left with a murder on his hands, and I tell you, Cadfael, that affair now looks less than ever like a drunken revenge by an aggrieved youth of the town – though to tell truth, it never did look too convincing, even if we could not discard it out of hand.'

'Surely there's good ground now for letting the provost bail his lad out and take him home?' said

Cadfael, encouraged. 'Of all the young men around this town, Philip must be the clearest from any suspicion of this last outrage, or the raid on the barge, either. The gaoler who turns the key on him can witness where *he*'s been all this while, and swear he never left it.'

'I'm off to the castle now,' said Hugh. 'I can't vouch for the sheriff, but I'll certainly speak a word in his ear, and in the provost's, too. It's well worth making the approach.'

He looked down, flashing out of his preoccupation with a sudden mischievous smile, combed the fingers of one hand through the hedge of bushy greying hair that rimmed Cadfael's sunburned tonsure, leaving it bristling like thorn-bushes, snapped a finger painfully against the nut-brown dome between, and took his departure with his usual light stride and insouciant bearing, which the unwary mistook for the mark of a frivolous man. Such small indulgences he was more likely to permit himself, strictly with friends, when he was engaged on something more than usually grave.

Cadfael watched him go, absently smoothing down the warlike crest Hugh had erected. He supposed he had better be stirring, too, and hand over charge here to Brother Mark until evening. It would not do to take his eyes off Emma for any length of time, and Aline, to please a solicitous husband, consented to doze for an hour or two in the afternoon, for the sake of the child. Grandchildren by proxy, Cadfael reflected, might be a rare and pleasurable recompense for a celibate prime. As for old age, he had not yet begun to think about it; no doubt it had its own alleviations.

## Chapter Two

For all I said,' Emma mused aloud, putting fine stitches into a linen band for an infant's cap, in the lofty midday light in the window of Aline's bedchamber, 'I do grieve for those gloves of mine. Such fine leather, supple and black, and a wealth of gold in the embroidery. I never bought such expensive ones before.' She reached the end of her seam, and snipped off the thread neatly. 'They say there's a very good glover has a stall in the fair,' she said, smoothing her work. 'I thought I might take a look at his wares, and see if he has anything as fine as those I've lost. They tell me he's well known in Chester, and the countess buys from him. I think perhaps I'll walk along the Foregate this afternoon, and see what he has. What with all these upsets, I've hardly seen anything of the fair.'

'A good idea,' said Aline. 'Such a fine day, we should not be spending it here within doors. I'll come with you.'

'Oh, no, you should not,' protested Emma solicitously. 'You have not had your sleep this afternoon. No need to keep me company that short way. I should be distressed if you tired yourself on my account.'

'Oh, folly!' said Aline cheerfully. 'I am so healthy I shall burst if I have too little to do. It's Constance and Hugh who want to make an invalid of me, just because I'm in a woman's best and happiest estate. And Hugh is gone to the sheriff, and Constance is visiting with a cousin of hers in the Wyle, so who's to fret? I'll slip on my shoes, and we'll go. I should like to buy a box of those sugared fruits your uncle brought from the east. We'll do that, too.'

It seemed that Emma had, after all, lost her taste for the expedition. She sat stroking the embroidered band she had just finished, and eyed the shape of linen cut for the crown. 'I don't know – I should finish this, perhaps. After tomorrow there may be no choice, and I should be sorry to leave it for someone else to finish. As for the candied fruits, I'll ask Roger to bring you a box, when he comes again this evening to tell me how the day has gone. Tomorrow it will be here.'

'That's kind,' said Aline, slipping on her shoes none the less, 'but he could hardly try on a pair of gloves for you, or choose with your eye. So let's go and see for ourselves. It won't take long.'

Emma sat hesitating, but whether in a genuine endeavour to make up her mind, or in search of a way of extricating herself from an unsatisfactory situation, Aline could not be sure. 'Oh, no, I should not! How can I give my mind to such vanity, at a time like this! I'm ashamed that I ever thought of it. My uncle dead, and here am I yearning after trumpery bits of finery. No, I won't be so shallow. Let me at least go on with my work for the child, instead of thinking only of my own adornment.' And she picked up the cut linen. Aline noted that the hand holding it trembled a little, and wondered whether to persist. Plainly the girl wanted to go forth for some purpose of her own, but would not go unless it could be alone. And alone, said Aline firmly to herself, she certainly shall not go, if I can prevent.

'Well,' she said doubtfully, 'if you're determined to be so penitential, I won't play the devil and tempt you. And I'm the gainer, your sewing is so fine, I could never match it. Who taught you so well?' She slipped off her soft leather shoes, and sat down again. Something, at least, she had learned, better to let well alone now. Emma welcomed the change of subject eagerly. Of her childhood she would talk freely.

'My mother was a famous embroidress. She began to teach me as soon as I could manage a needle, but she died when I was only eight, and Uncle Thomas took me in. We had a housekeeper, a Flemish lady who had married a Bristol seaman, and been widowed when his ship was lost, and she taught me everything she knew, though I could never equal her work. She used to make altar cloths and vestments for the church, such beautiful things ...'

So a plain pair of good black gloves, thought Aline, would have done well enough for you at any time, since you could have adorned them to your own fancy. And those who can do such things exquisitely, seldom prefer the work of others.

It was not difficult to keep Emma talking, but for all that, Aline could not help wondering what was going through the girl's mind, and how soon, and how cunningly, she would make the next bid to slip away solitary about her mysterious business. But as it fell out, she need not have troubled, for late in the afternoon came a lay brother from the gatehouse, to announce that Martin Bellecote had brought down Master Thomas's coffin, and desired permission to proceed with his business. Emma rose instantly, laying down her sewing, her face pale and intent. If there was one thing certain, it was that no other matter, however urgent, would take her away from the church until her uncle was decently coffined and sealed down for his journey home, and prayers said for his repose, as later she would attend the first Mass for him. Whatever he had been to others, he had been uncle and father and friend to his orphaned kinswoman, and no reverence, no tribute, would be omitted from his obsequies.

'I will come myself,' said Emma. 'I must say farewell to him.' She had not yet seen him, dead, but the brothers, long expert in the gentle arts that reconcile life to death, would have made sure that she would be able to remember him without distress.

'Shall I come with you?' offered Aline.

'You are very good, but I would rather go alone.'

Aline followed as far as the great court, and watched the little procession cross to the cloister, Emma walking beside the handcart on which Martin and his son wheeled the coffin. When they had lifted the heavy box and carried it in by the south door of the church, with Emma following, Aline stood for some minutes looking about her. At this hour most of the guests and many of the lay servants were out at the fair, only the brothers went about their business as usual. Through the wide gate of the distant stable-yard she could see Ivo Corbière's young groom rubbing down a pony, and the archer Turstan Fowler sitting on a mounting-block, whistling as he burnished a saddle. Sober and recovered from his debauch, he was a well-set-up and comely fellow, with the open face of one who has not a care in the world. Evidently he was long since forgiven, and back in favour.

Brother Cadfael, coming from the gardens, saw her still gazing pensively towards the church. She smiled at sight of him.

'Martin has brought the coffin. They are within there, she'll think of nothing else now. But, Cadfael, she intends to give us all the slip when she can. She has tried. She would see, she said, if the glover at the fair has something to take the place of the ones she lost. But when I said I would go with her, no, that would not do, she gave up the idea.'

'Gloves!' murmured Brother Cadfael, scrubbing thoughtfully at his chin. 'Strange, when you think of it, that it should be gloves she has on her mind, in the middle of summer.'

Aline was in no position to follow that thought, she took it at its surface meaning. 'Why strange? We know there were some stolen from her, and here we are at one of the few fairs where rare goods are to be bought, it follows naturally enough. But of course the glover is only a handy excuse.'

Cadfael said no more then, but he went away very thoughtfully towards the cloister. The strange thing was not that a girl should want to replace, while chance offered, a lost piece of finery. It was rather that when she was suddenly confronted by the need to pass off as simple robbery a raid she knew to be something very different, one of the articles she claimed to have lost should be a thing so inappropriate to the season that she felt obliged to account for it by saying she had newly bought it in Gloucester on the journey. Why gloves, unless she had gloves running in her mind already for another reason? Gloves? Or glovers?

In the transept chapel Martin Bellecote and his young son set up the heavy coffin on a draped trestle, and reverently laid the body of Master Thomas of Bristol within it. Emma stood looking down at her uncle's dead face for a long time, without tears or words. It would not be painful, she found, to remember him thus, dignified and remote in death, the bones of his cheeks and brow and jaw more strongly outlined than in life, his florid flesh contracted and paled into waxen austerity. Now at the last moment she wanted to give him something to take with him into his grave, and realised that in the buffeting of these two days she had not been able to think clearly enough to be ready for the parting. Not the fact of death, but the absolute need of some ceremonial tenderness, separate from the public rites, suddenly seemed to her overwhelmingly important.

'Shall I cover him?' asked Martin Bellecote gently.

Even so soft a sound startled her. She looked round almost wonderingly. The man, large, comely and calm, waited her orders without impatience. The boy, grave and silent, watched her with huge hazel eyes. From her four years' superiority over him she pondered whether so young a creature should be doing this office, and then she understood that those eyes were preoccupied rather with her living self than with the dead, and the vigorous, flowing sap in him reached up towards light and life as to the sun, and recognised shadow only by virtue of its neighbouring brightness. That was right and good.

'No, wait just a moment,' she said. 'I'll come back!'

She went quickly out into the sunlight, and looked about her for the path that led into the gardens. The green lines of a hedge and the crowns of trees within drew her, she came into a walk where flowers had been planted. The brothers were great gardeners, and valued food crops for good reason, but they had time also for roses. She chose the one bush that bore a bloom like no other, pale yellow petals shading into rose at the tips, and plucked one flower only. Not the buds, not even the one perfect globe, but a wide-open bloom just beyond its prime but still unflawed. She took it back, hurrying, into the church with her. He was not young, not even at his zenith, but settling into his autumn, and this was the rose for him.

Brother Cadfael had watched her go, he watched her come again, and followed her into the chapel, but held aloof in the shadows. She brought her single flower and laid it in the coffin, beside the dead man's heart.

'Cover him now,' she said, and stood well back to let them work in peace. When it was done, she thanked them, and they withdrew and left her there, as clearly was her wish. So, just as silently, did Brother Cadfael

Emma remained kneeling on the stones of the transept, unaware of discomfort, a great while, her eyes wide open all that time upon the closed coffin, on its draped stand before the altar. To lie thus in the church of a great abbey, to have a special Mass sung for him, and then to be taken home in a grand coffin for burial with still further rites, surely that was glory, and he would have liked it. All was to be done as he would have liked. All! He would be pleased with her.

She knew her duty; she said prayers for him, a great many prayers, because the form was blessedly laid down, and her mind could range while her lips formed the proper words. She would do what he had wanted done, what he had half-confided to her, as he had to no other. She would see his task completed, and he would rest, pleased with her. And then ... she had hardly looked beyond, but there was a great, summer-scented breeze blowing through her spirit, telling her she was young and fair, and wealthy into the bargain, and that boys like the coffin-maker's young son looked upon her with interest and pleasure. Other young men, too, of less green years ...

She rose from her knees at last, shook out her crumpled skirts, and walked briskly out of the chapel into the nave of the church, and rounding the clustered stone pillars at the corner of the crossing, came face to face with Ivo Corbière.

He had been waiting, silent and motionless, in his shadowy corner, refraining even from setting foot in the chapel until her vigil was over, and the resolution with which she had suddenly ended it flung her almost into his arms. She uttered a startled gasp, and he put out reassuring hands to steady her, and was in no haste to let go. In this dim place his gold head showed darkened to bronze, and his face, stooped over her solicitously, was so gilded by the summer that it had almost the same fine-metal burnishing.

'Did I alarm you? I'm sorry! I didn't want to disturb you. They told me at the gatehouse that the master-carpenter had come and gone, and you were here. I hoped if I waited patiently I might be able to talk with you. If I have not pressed my attentions on you until now,' he said earnestly, 'it is not because I haven't thought of you. Constantly!'

Her eyes were raised to his face with a fascinated admiration she would never have indulged in full light, and she quite forgot to make any move to withdraw herself from his hold. His hands slid down her forearms, but halted at her hands, and the touch, by mutual consent, became a clasp.

'Almost two days since I've spoken with you!' he said. 'It's an age, and I've grudged it, but you were well-friended, and I had no right ... But now that I have you, let me keep you for an hour! Come out and walk in the gardens. I doubt if you've even seen them yet.'

They went out together into the sunlight, through the cloister garth and out into the bustle and traffic of the great court. It was almost time for Vespers, the quietest hours of the afternoon now spent, the brothers gathering gradually from their dispersed labours, guests returning from the fairground and the riverside. It was a gratifying thing to walk through this populous place on the arm of a nobleman, lord of a modest honour scattered through Cheshire and Shropshire. For the daughter of craftsmen and merchants, a very gratifying thing! They sat down on a stone bench in the flower-garden, on the sunny side of the pleached hedge, with the heady fragrance of Brother Cadfael's herbarium wafted to them in drunken eddies on a soft breeze.

'You will have troublesome dispositions to make,' said Corbière seriously. 'If there is anything I can arrange for you, let me know of it. It will be my pleasure to serve you. You are taking him back to Bristol for burial?'

'It's what he would have wished. There will be a Mass for him in the morning, and then we shall carry him back to his barge for the journey home. The brothers have been kindness itself to me.'

'And you? Will you also return with the barge?'

She hesitated, but why not confide in him? He was considerate and kind, and quick to understand. 'No, it would be – unwise. While my uncle lived it was very well, but without him it would not do. There is one of our men – I must say no evil of him, for he has done none, but ... He is too fond. Better we should not travel together. But neither do I want to offer him insult, by letting him know he is not quite trusted. I've told him that I must remain here a few days, that I may be needed if the sheriff has more questions to ask, or more is found out about my uncle's death.'

'But then,' said Ivo with warm concern, 'what of your own journey home? How will you manage?'

'I shall stay with Lady Beringar until we can find some safe party riding south, with women among them. Hugh Beringar will advise me. I have money, and I can pay my way. I shall manage.'

He looked at her long and earnestly, until his gravity melted into a smile. 'Between all your well-wishers, you will certainly reach your home without mishap. I'll be giving my mind to it, among the rest. But now let's forget, for my sake, that there must be a departure, and make the most of the hours while you are still here.' He rose, and took her by the hand to draw her up with him. 'Forget Vespers, forget we're guests of an abbey, forget the fair and the business of the fair, and all that such things may demand of you in future. Think only that it's summer, and a glorious evening, and you're young, and have friends ... Come down with me past the fish-ponds, as far as the brook. That is all abbey land, I wouldn't take you beyond.'

She went with him gratefully, his hand cool and vital in hers. By the brook below the abbey fields it was cool and fresh and bright, full of scintillating light along the water, and birds dabbling and singing, and in the pleasure of the moment she almost forgot all that lay upon her, so sacred and so burdensome. Ivo was reverent and gentle, and did not press her too close, but when she said regretfully that it was time for her to go back, for fear Aline might be anxious about her, he went with her all the way, her hand still firmly retained in his, and presented himself punctiliously before Aline, so that Emma's present guardian might study, accept and approve him. As indeed she did.

It was charmingly and delicately done. He made himself excellent company for as long as was becoming on a first visit, invited and deferred to all Aline's graceful questions, and withdrew well before he had even drawn near the end of his welcome.

'So that's the young man who was so helpful and gallant when the riot began,' said Aline, when he was gone. 'Do you know, Emma, I do believe you have a serious admirer there.' A wooer gained, she thought, might come as a blessed counter-interest to a guardian lost. 'He comes of good blood and family,' said the Aline Siward who had brought two manors to her husband in her own right, but saw no difference between her guest and herself, and innocently ignored the equally proud and honourable standards of those born to craft and commerce instead of land. 'The Corbières are distant kin of Earl Ranulf of Chester himself. And he does seem a most estimable young man.'

'But not of my kind,' said Emma, as shrewd and wary as she sounded regretful. 'I am a stone-mason's daughter, and niece to a merchant. No landed lord is likely to become a suitor for someone like me.'

'But it's not someone *like* you in question,' said Aline reasonably. 'It is *you*!'

Brother Cadfael looked about him, late in the evening after Compline, saw all things in cautious balance, Emma securely settled in the guest-hall, Beringar already home. He went thankfully to bed with his brothers, for once at the proper time, and slept blissfully until the bell rang to wake him for Matins. Down the night stairs and into the church the brothers filed in the midnight silence, to begin the new day's worship. In the faint light of the altar candles they took their places, and the third day of Saint Peter's Fair had begun. The third and last.

Cadfael always rose for Matins and Lauds not sleepy and unwilling, but a degree more awake than at any other time, as though his senses quickened to the sense of separateness of the community gathered here, to a degree impossible by daylight. The dimness of the light, the solidity of the enclosing shadows, the muted voices, the absence of lay worshippers, all contributed to his sense of being enfolded in a sealed haven, where all those who shared in it were his own flesh and blood and spirit, responsible for him as he for them, even some for whom, in the active and arduous day, he could feel no love, and pretended none. The burden of his vows became also his privilege, and the night's first worship was the fuel of the next day's energy.

So the shadows had sharp edges for him, the shapes of pillar and capital and arch clamoured like vibrant notes of music, both vision and hearing observed with heightened sensitivity, details had a quivering insistence. Brother Mark's profile against the candle-light was piercingly clear. A note sung off-key by a sleepy elder stung like a bee. And the single pale speck lying under the trestle that supported Master Thomas's coffin was like a hole in reality, something that could not be there. Yet it persisted. It was at the beginning of Lauds that it first caught his eye, and after that he could not get free of it. Wherever he looked, however he fastened upon the altar, he could still see it out of the corner of his eye.

When Lauds ended, and the silent procession began to file back towards the night stairs and the dortoir, Cadfael stepped aside, stooped, and picked up the mote that had been troubling him. It was a single petal from a rose, its colour indistinguishable by this light, but pale, deepening round the tip. He knew at once what it was, and with this midnight clarity in him he knew how it had come there.

Fortunate, indeed, that he had seen Emma bring her chosen rose and lay it in the coffin. If he had not, this petal would have told him nothing. Since he had, it told him all. With hieratic care and ceremony, after the manner of the young when moved, she had brought her offering cupped in both hands, and not one leaf, not one grain of yellow pollen from its open heart, had fallen to the floor.

Whoever was hunting so persistently for something believed to be in Master Thomas's possession, after searching his person, his barge and his booth, had not stopped short of the sacrilege of searching his coffin. Between Compline and Matins it had been opened and closed again; and a single petal from the wilting rose within had shaken loose and been wafted unnoticed over the side, to bear witness to the blasphemy.

# The Third Day of the Fair

# Chapter One

Emma arose with the dawn, stole out of the wide bed she shared with Constance, and dressed herself very quietly and cautiously, but even so the sense of movement, rather than any sound, disturbed the maid's sleep, and caused her to open eyes at once alert and intelligent.

Emma laid a finger to her lips, and cast a meaning glance towards the door beyond which Hugh and Aline were still sleeping. 'Hush!' she whispered. 'I'm only going to church for Prime. I don't want to wake anyone else.'

Constance shrugged against her pillow, raised her brows a little, and nodded. Today there would be the Mass for the dead uncle, and then the transference of his coffin to the barge that would take him home. Not surprising if the girl was disposed to turn this day into a penitential exercise, for the repose of her uncle's soul and the merit of her own. 'You won't go out alone, will you?'

'I'm going straight to the church,' promised Emma earnestly.

Constance nodded again, and her eyelids began to close. She was asleep before Emma had drawn the door to very softly, and slipped away towards the great court.

Brother Cadfael rose for Prime like the rest, but left

his cell before his companions, and went to take counsel with the only authority in whom he could repose his latest discovery. Such a violation was the province of the abbot, and only he had the right to hear of it first.

With the door of the abbot's austere cell closed upon them, they were notably at ease together, two men who knew their own minds and spoke clearly what they had to say. The rose petal, a little shrunken and weary, but with its yellow and pink still silken-bright, lay in the abbot's palm like a golden tear.

'You are sure this cannot have fallen when our daughter brought it as an offering? It was a gentle gift,' said Radulfus.

'Not one grain of dust fell. She carried it like a vessel of wine, in both hands. I saw every move. I have not yet seen the coffin by daylight, but I doubt not it has been dealt with competently, and looks as it looked when the master-carpenter firmed it down. Nevertheless, it has been opened and closed again.'

'I take your word,' said the abbot simply. 'This is vile.'

'It is,' said Cadfael and waited.

'And you cannot put name to the man who would do this thing?'

'Not yet.'

'Nor say if he has gained by it? As God forbid!'

'No, Father! But God will forbid.'

'Give your might to it,' said Radulfus, and brooded for a while in silence. Then he said: 'We have a duty to the law. Do what is best there, for I hear you have the deputy sheriff's ear. As for the affont to the church, to our house, to our dead son and his heiress, I am left to read between rubrics. There will be a Mass this morning for the dead man. The holy rite will cleanse all foulness from his passing and his coffin. As for the child, let her be at peace, for so she may, her dead is in the hand of God, there has no violence been done to his soul.'

Brother Cadfael said, with hearty gratitude: 'She will rest the better if she knows nothing. She is a good girl, her grief should have every consolation.'

'See to it, brother, as you may. It is almost time for Prime.'

Cadfael was hurrying from the abbot's lodging towards the cloister when he saw Emma turn in there ahead of him, and slowed his steps to be unnoticed himself while he watched what she would do. On this of all days Emma was entitled to every opportunity of prayer and meditation, but she also had a very private secular preoccupation of her own, and which of these needs she was serving by this early-rising zeal there was no telling.

In at the south door went Emma, and in after her, just as discreetly, went brother Cadfael. The monks were already in their stalls, and concentrating all upon the altar. The girl slipped silently round into the nave, as though she would find herself a retired spot there in privacy; but instead of turning aside, she continued her rapid, silent passage towards the west door, the parish door that opened on to the Foregate, outside the convent walls. Except during times of stress, such as the siege of Shrewsbury the previous year, it was never closed.

In at one door and out at another, and she was free, for a little while, to go where she would, and could return by the same way, an innocent coming back from church.

Brother Cadfael's sandals padded soundlessly over the tiled floor after her, keeping well back in case she should look round, though here within he was reasonably sure she would not. The great parish door was unlatched, she had only to draw it open a little way, her slenderness slipped through easily, and since this was facing due west, no betraying radiance flooded in. Cadfael gave her a moment to turn right or left outside the door, though surely it would be to the right, towards the fairground. What should she have to do in the direction of the river and the town?

She was well in sight when he slid through the doorway and round the corner of the west front, and looked along the Foregate. She did not hurry now, but curbed her pace to that of the early buyers who were sauntering along the highroad, halting at stalls already busy, handling goods, arguing over prices. The last day of the fair was commonly the busiest. There were bargains to be snapped up at the close, and lowered prices. There was bustle everywhere, even at this hour, but the pace of the ambulant shoppers was leisurely. Emma matched hers to it, as though she belonged among them, but for all that, she was making her way somewhere with a purpose. Cadfael followed at a respectful distance.

Only once did she speak to anyone, and then she chose the holder of one of the larger stalls, and it seemed that she was asking him for directions, for he turned and pointed ahead along the street, and towards the abbey wall. She thanked him, and went on in the direction he had indicated, and now she quickened her pace. Small doubt that she had known all along to whom she was bound; apparently she had not known precisely where to find him. Now she knew. By this time all the chief merchants gathered here knew where to find one another.

Emma had come to a halt, almost at the end of the Foregate, where a half-dozen booths were backed into the abbey wall. It seemed that she had arrived at her destination, yet now stood hesitant, gazing a little helplessly, as if what she confronted surprised and baffled her. Cadfael drew nearer. She was frowning doubtfully at the last of the booths, backed into a corner between buttress and wall. Cadfael recognised it; a lean, suspicious face had peered out from that hatch as the sheriff's officers had hoisted Turstan Fowler on to a board and borne him away to an abbey cell on the eve of the fair. The booth of Euan of Shotwick. Here they came again, those imagined gloves, so feelingly described, so soon stolen!

And Emma was at a loss, for the booth was fast-closed, every panel sealed, and business all around in full swing. She turned to the nearest neighbour, clearly questioning, and the man looked, and shrugged, and shook his head. What did he know? There had been no sign of life there since last night, perhaps the glover had sold out and departed.

Cadfael drew nearer. Beneath the austere white wimple, so sharp a change from the frame of blue-black hair, Emma's young profile looked even more tender and vulnerable. She did not know what to do. She advanced a few steps and raised a hand, as though she would knock at the closed shutter, but then she wavered and drew back. From across the street a brawny butcher left his stall, patted her amiably on the shoulder, and did the knocking for her lustily, then stood to listen. But there was no move from within.

A large hand clapped Cadfael weightily on the back, and the cavernous voice of Rhodri ap Huw boomed in his ear in Welsh: 'What's this, then? Master Euan not open for trade? That I should see the day! I never knew him to miss a sale before, or any other thing to his advantage.'

'The stall's deserted,' said Cadfael. 'The man may have left for home.'

'Not he! He was there past midnight, for I took a turn along here to breathe the cool before going to my inn, and there was a light burning inside there then.' No gleam from within now, though the slanting sunlight might well pale it into invisibility. But no, that was not so, either. The chinks between shutter and frame were utterly dark.

It was all too like what Roger Dod had found at another booth, only one day past. But there the booth had been barred from within, and the bar hoisted clear with a dagger. Here there was a lock, to be mastered from within or without, and certainly no visible key.

'This I do not like,' said Rhodri ap Huw, and strode forward to try the door, and finding it, as was expected, locked, to peer squint-eyed through the large keyhole. 'No key within,' he said shortly over his shoulder, and peered still. 'Not a movement in there.' He had Cadfael hard on his heels by then, and three or four others closing in. Give me room!'

Rhodri clenched the fingers of both hands in the edge of the door, set a broad foot against the timber wall, and hauled mightily, square shoulders gathered in one great heave. Wood splintered about the lock, small flinders flying like motes of dust, and the door burst open. Rhodri swayed and recovered in recoil, and was first through the opening, but Cadfael was after him fast enough to ensure that the Welshman touched nothing within. They craned into the gloom together, cheek by jowl.

The glover's stall was in chaos, shelves swept clear, goods scattered like grain over the floor. On a straw palliasse along the rear wall his cloak lay sprawled, and on an iron stand beside, a quenched candle sagged in folds of tallow. It took them a few seconds to accustom their eyes to the dimness and see clearly. Tangled in his spilled stock of belts, baldricks, gloves, purses and saddle-bags, Euan of Shotwick lay on his back, knees drawn up, a coarse sacking bag drawn half-over his lean face and greying head. Beneath the hem of the hood his thin-lipped mouth grinned open in a painful rictus, large white teeth staring, and the angle at which his head lay had the horrible suggestion of a broken wooden puppet.

Cadfael turned and flung up the shutter of the booth, letting in the morning light. He stooped to touch the contorted neck and hollow cheek. 'Cold,' said Rhodri, behind him, not attempting to verify his judgment, which for all that was accurate enough. Euan's flesh was chilling. 'He's dead,' said Rhodri flatly.

'Some hours,' said Cadfael.

In the stress of the moment he had forgotten Emma, but the shriek she gave caused him to swing round in haste and dismay. She had crept in fearfully to peer over the shoulders of the neighbours, and stood staring with eyes wide with horror, both small fists crushed against her mouth. 'Oh, no!' she said in a whisper. 'Not dead! Not he, too ...'

Cadfael took her in his arms, and thrust her bodily before him out of the booth, elbowing the gaping onlookers out of his way. 'Go back! You mustn't stay here. Go back before you're missed, and leave this to me.' He wondered if she even heard his rapid murmur into her ear; she was shaking and white as milk, her blue eyes fixed and huge with shock. He looked about him urgently for someone to whom he could safely confide her, for he doubted if she should be left to return alone, and yet he did not care to leave this scene until Beringar should be here to take charge, or one of the sheriff's sergeants at least. The sudden alarmed shout of recognition that came from the rear of the gathering crowd was a most welcome sound.

'Emma! Emma!' Ivo Corbière came cleaving an unceremonious way through the press, like a sudden vehement wind in a cornfield, bludgeoning the standing stems out of its path. She turned at the call, and a spark of returning life sprang up in her eyes. Thankfully Cadfael thrust her into the young man's arms, which reached eagerly and anxiously to receive her.

'For God's sake, what has happened to her? What ...' His glance flashed from her stunned visage to Cadfael's, and beyond, to the open door with its splintered panel. Over her head his lips framed silently for Cadfael: 'Not again? Another?'

'Take her back,' said Cadfael shortly. 'Take care of her. And tell Hugh Beringar to come. We have sheriff's business here within.'

All the way back along the Foregate, Corbière kept a supporting arm about her, and curbed his long stride to hers, and all the way he poured soothing, caressing words into her ear, while she, until they had almost reached the west door of the church, said nothing at all, simply walked docilely beside him, distantly aware of the lulling sound and the comforting touch. Then suddenly she said: 'He's dead. I saw him, I know.'

'A bare glimpse you had,' said Ivo consolingly. 'It may not be so.'

'No,' said Emma, 'I know the man is dead. How could it happen? Why?'

'There are always such acts, somewhere, robberies, violence and evil. It is sad, but it is not new.' His fingers pressed her hand warmly. 'It is no fault of yours, and alas, there is nothing you or I can do about it. I wish I could make you forget it. In time you will forget.'

'No,' she said. 'I shall never forget this.'

She had meant to return by the church, as she had left, but now it no longer mattered. As far as he or any other was concerned, she had simply set out early to buy some gloves, or at least to view what the glover had to offer. She went in with Ivo by the gatehouse. By the time he had brought her tenderly on his arm to the guest-hall she had regained her composure. There was a little colour in her face again, and her voice was alive, even if its tone indicated that life was painful.

'I'm recovered now, Ivo,' she said. 'You need not trouble for me further. I will tell Hugh Beringar that he is needed.'

'Brother Cadfael entrusted you to me,' said Ivo with gentle and confident authority, 'and you did not reject me. I shall fulfil my errand exactly. As I hope,' he said smiling, 'I may perform any other missions you may care to entrust to me hereafter.'

Hugh Beringar came with four of the sheriff's men, dispersed the crowd that hung expectantly round the booth of Euan of Shotwick, and listened to the accounts rendered by the neighbouring stall-holders, by the butcher from over the road, and by Rhodri ap Huw, for whom Cadfael interpreted sentence by sentence. In no haste to go, for as he said, his best lad was back with the boat from Bridgnorth and competent to take charge of what stock he still had to sell, the Welshman nonetheless showed no unbecoming desire to linger, once his witness was taken. Imperturbable and all-beholding, he ambled away at the first indication that the law had done with him. Others, more persistent, hung about the booth in a silent, watchful circle, but were kept well away from earshot. Beringar drew the door to. The opened hatches gave light enough.

'Can I take the man's account for fair and true?' asked Hugh, casting a glance after Rhodri's retreating back. There was no backward glance from the Welshman, his assurance was absolute.

'To the letter, for all that happened here from the time I came on the scene. He's an excellent observer, there's little he misses of what concerns him, or may concern him, and what does not. He does business, too, his trade here is no pretext. But it may be only half his business that we see.'

There were only the two of them within there now,

two living and the dead man. They stood one either side of him, drawn back to avoid disturbing either his body or the litter of leatherwork scattered about and over him.

'He says there was a light showing through the chinks here past midnight,' said Beringar. 'The light is quenched now, not burned out. And if he locked his door after closing the booth for the night ...'

'As he would,' said Cadfael. 'Rhodri's account of him rings true. A man complete in himself, trusting no one, able to take care of himself, until now. He would have locked his door.'

'Then he also unlocked it, to let in his murderer. The lock never was forced until now, as you saw. Why should a wary man unlock his door to anyone in the small hours?'

'Because he was expecting someone,' said Cadfael, 'though not the someone who came. Because, it may be, he had been expecting someone all these three days, and was relieved when the expected message came at last.'

'So relieved that he ceased to be cautious? Given your Welshman's estimate of him, I should doubt it.'

'So should I,' agreed Cadfael, 'unless there was a private word he was waiting for, and it was known and given. A name, perhaps. For you see, Hugh, I think he was already well aware that the one he had expected to deliver the message was never going to tap at his door by night, or stop in the Foregate to pass the time with him.'

'You mean,' said Hugh, 'Thomas of Bristol, who is dead.'

'Who else? How many strange chances can come together, all against what is likely, or even possible? A merchant is killed, his barge searched, his booth searched, then, dear God, his coffin! I have not yet had time, Hugh, to tell you of that.' He told it now. He had the rose-petal in the breast of his habit, wrapped in a scrap of linen; it still spoke as eloquently as before. 'You may trust my eyes, I know it did not fall earlier, I know it has been in the coffin with him. Now that same man's niece makes occasion to come by stealth to this glover's stall, only to find the glover dead like her uncle. It is a long list of assaults upon all things connected with Thomas of Bristol. Now, since this unknown treasure was not found even in his coffin, for safe-conduct back to Bristol in default of delivery, the next point of search has been here – where Master Thomas should have delivered it.'

'They would need to have foreknowledge of that.'

'Or good reason to guess aright.'

'By your witness,' said Hugh, pondering, 'the coffin was opened and closed between Compline and Matins. Before midnight. When would you say, Cadfael – your experience is longer than mine – when would you say this man died?'

'In the small hours. By the second hour after midnight, I judge, he was dead. After the coffin, it seems, they were forced to the conclusion that somehow, for all they had a watch on Master Thomas from his arrival, and disposed of him before ever the fair started, yet somehow he, or someone else on his behalf, must have slipped through their net, and delivered the precious charge. This poor soul certainly opened his door last night to someone he believed had business with him. The mention of a privileged name ... a password ... He let in his murderer, but what he had expected was the thing promised.'

'Then even now,' said Hugh sharply, 'with two murders on their souls, they have not what they wanted. He thought they were bringing it. They trusted to find it here. And neither of them had it. Both were deceived.' He brooded with a brown fist clamping his jaw, and his black brows down-drawn in unaccustomed solemnity. 'And Emma came here ... by stealth.'

'She did. Not every man,' said Cadfael, 'has your view of women, or mine. Most of your kind, most of mine, would never dream of looking in a woman's direction to find anything of importance in hand. Especially a mere child, barely grown. Not until every other road was closed, and they were forced to notice a woman there in the thick of the matter. Who just might be what they sought.'

'And who has now betrayed herself,' said Hugh grimly. 'Well, at least she reached the guest-hall safely, thanks to Corbière. I have left her with Aline, very shaken, for all her strength of will, and she will not stir a step this day unguarded. That I can promise. Between us I think we can take care of Emma. Now let's see if this poor wretch has anything to tell us that we don't yet know.'

He stooped and drew back the coarse sack that covered half the glover's narrow face, from eyebrow on one side to jaw on the other. A broken bruise in the greying hair above the left temple indicated a right-handed blow as soon as the door was opened to his visitor, meant to stun him, probably, until he could be muffled in the sack and gagged like Warin. Here it was a case of gaining entry and confronting a wide-awake man, not a timid sleeper.

'Much the same manner as the other one,' said Cadfael, 'and I doubt if they ever meant to kill. But he was not so easily put out of the reckoning. He put up a fight. And his neck is broken. By the look of it, one made round behind him to secure this blindfold, and in the struggle he gave them, tried all too hard to haul him backwards by it. He was wiry and agile, but his bones were aging, and too brittle to sustain it. I don't think it was intended. We should have found him neatly bound and still alive, like Warin, if he had not fought them. Once they knew he was dead, they made their search in haste, and left all as it fell.'

Beringar brushed aside the light tangle of girdles and straps and gloves that littered the floor and lay over the body. Euan's right arm was covered from the elbow down by the skirts of his own gown, kicked out of the way of the searchers in their hunt. When the folds were drawn down Hugh let out a sharp whistle of surprise, for in the dead man's hand was a long poniard, the naked blade grooved, and ornamented with gilding near the hilt. At his belt, half-hidden now under his right hip, the scabbard lay empty.

'A man of his hands! And see, he's marked one of them for us!' There was blood on the point of the blade, and drawn up by the grooving for some three fingers' breadth in two thin crimson lines, now drying to black.

'Rhodri ap Huw said of him,' Cadfael remembered, 'that he was a solitary soul who trusted nobody – his own porter and his own watchman. He said he wore a weapon, and knew how to use it.' He went on his knees beside the body, and cleared away the debris that still lay about it, eyeing and handling from head to foot. 'You'll have him away to the castle, I suppose, or the abbey, and look him over more carefully, but I do believe the only blood he's lost is this smear on his brow. This on the dagger is not his.'

'If only we could as easily say whose it is!' said Hugh dryly, sitting on his heels with the nimbleness of the young on the other side of the body. Brother Cadfael eased creaky elderly knees on the hard boards, and briefly envied him. The young man lifted the stiffening arm, and tested the grip of the clenched fingers. 'He holds fast!' It took him some effort to loosen the convulsive grasp enough to slip the hilt of the dagger free. In the slanting light from the open hatch something gleamed briefly, waving at the tip of the blade, and again vanished, as motes of dust come and go in gold in bright sunlight. There was also what seemed at first to be a thin encrustation of blood fringing the steel on one edge. Cadfael exclaimed, leaning to point. 'A yellow hair – There it shows again!' The flashing gleam curled and twisted as Hugh turned the dagger in his hand.

'Not a hair, a fine, yellowish thread. Thread of flax, not bleached. This grooving has ripped out a shred of cloth, and the blood has stuck it fast. See!'

A mere wisp of brown material it was, a fringe along the groove that had held it. Narrow as a blade of grass, but when Cadfael carefully took hold of a thread at the end and drew it out straight, it stretched to the length of his hand. The colour, though fouled by dried blood, showed plain at one edge, a light russet-brown; and at the end of the sliver floated gaily the long, fine flax thread, scalloped like a curly hair.

'A sliced tear a hand long,' said Cadfael, 'and ending at a hem, for surely this thread sewed the edging, and the dagger ripped out a length of the stitching.' He narrowed his eyes, and considered, imagining Euan facing the door as he opened it, the instant blow that failed to tame him, and then his rapid drawing of his poniard and striking with it. Almost brow to brow and breast to breast, a man good with his right hand, and his attacker's heart an open target.

'He struck for the heart,' said Cadfael with conviction. 'So would I, or so would I have done once. The other man, surely, slipped behind him and spoiled the stroke, but that is where he aimed. Someone, somewhere, has a torn cotte. It might be in the left breast, or it might be in the sleeve. The man's arms would be raised, reaching to grapple him. I should say the left sleeve, ripping from the hem halfway to the elbow. The sewing thread was caught first, and pulled out a length of stitches.'

Hugh considered that respectfully, and found no fault with it. 'Much of a scratch, would you guess? He did not drip blood to the doorway. It could not have been enough to need much stanching.'

'The sleeve would hold it. Likely only a graze, but a long graze. It will be there to be seen.'

'If we knew where to look!' Hugh gave a short bark of laughter at the thought of sending sergeants about this teeming marketplace to ask every man to roll up his left sleeve and show his arm. 'A simple matter! Still, no reason why you and I, and all the men I can spare and trust, should not be keeping our eyes open all the rest of this day for a torn sleeve – or a newly cobbled one.'

He rose, and turned to beckon his nearest man from the open hatch. 'Well, we'll have him away from here, and do what we can. A word with your Rhodri ap Huw wouldn't come amiss, and I fancy you might get more out of him in his own tongue than ever I should at second hand. If he knows this man so well, prick him on to talk, and bring me what you learn.'

'That I'll do,' said Cadfael, clambering stiffly from his knees.

'I must go first to the castle, and report what we've found. One thing I'll make certain of this time,' said Hugh. 'The sheriff was in no mood to listen too carefully last night, but after this he'll have to turn young Corviser loose on his father's warranty, like the rest of them. It would take a more pig-headed man than Prestcote to believe the lad had any part in the first death, seeing the trail of offences that have followed while he was in prison. He shall eat his dinner at home today.'

Rhodri was not merely willing to spend an hour pouring the fruits of his wisdom and experience into Brother Cadfael's ear, he was hovering with that very thing in mind as soon as the corpse of Euan of Shotwick had been carried away, and the booth closed, with one of the sheriff's men on guard. Though ever-present, he had the gift of being unobtrusive until he chose to obtrude, and then could appear from an unexpected direction, and as casually as if only chance had brought him there.

'No doubt you'll have sold all you brought with you,' said Cadfael, encountering him thus between the stalls, clearly untroubled by business.

'Goods of quality are recognised everywhere,' said Rhodri, sharp eyes twinkling merrily. 'My lads are clearing the last few jars of honey, and the wool's long gone. But I've a half-full bottle there, if you care to share a cup at this hour? Mead, not wine, but you'll be happy with that, being a Welshman yourself.'

They sat on heaped trestles already freed from their annual use by the removal of small tradesmen who had sold out their stock, and set the bottle between them.

'And what,' asked Cadfael, with a jerk of his head towards the guarded booth, 'do you make of that affair this morning? After all that's gone before? Have we more birds of prey this way than usual, do you think? It may be they've taken fright and left the shires where there's still fighting, and we get the burden of it.'

Rhodri shook his shaggy head, and flashed his large white teeth out of the thicket in a grin. 'I would say you've had a more than commonly peaceful and well-mannered fair, myself – apart from the misfortunes of two merchants only. Oh, tonight's the last night, and there'll be a few drunken squabbles and a brawl or two, I daresay, but what is there in that? But chance has played no part in what has happened to Thomas of Bristol. Chance never goes hounding one man for three days through hundreds of his fellows, yet never grazes one of the others.'

'It has more than grazed Euan of Shotwick,'

remarked Cadfael dryly.

'Not chance! Consider, brother! Earl Ranulf of Chester's eyes and ears comes to a Shropshire fair and is killed. Thomas of Bristol, from a city that holds by Earl Robert of Gloucester, comes to the same fair, and is killed the very night of his coming. And after his death, everything he brought with him is turned hither and yon, but precious little stolen, from all I hear.' And certainly he had a way of hearing most of what was said within a mile of him, but at least he had made no mention of the violation of Master Thomas's coffin. Either that had not reached his ears, and never would, or else he had been the first to know of it, and would be the last ever to admit it. The parish door was always open, no need to set foot in the great court or pass the gatehouse. 'Something Thomas brought to Shrewsbury is of burning interest to somebody, it seems to me, and the somebody failed to get hold of it from man, barge or stall. And the next thing that happens is that Euan of Shotwick is also killed in the night, and all his belongings ransacked. I would not say but things were stolen there. They may have learned enough for that, and his goods are small and portable, and why despise a little gain on the side? But for all that – No, two men from opposite ends of a divided country, meeting midway, on important private business? It could be so! Gloucester's man and Chester's man.'

'And whose,' wondered Cadfael aloud, 'was the third man?'

'The third?'

'Who took such an interest in the other two that they died of it. Whose man would he be?'

'Why, there are other factions, and every one of them needs its intelligencers. There's the king's party – they might well feel a strong interest if they noted Gloucester's man and Chester's man attending the same fair midway between. And not only the king – there are others who count themselves kings on their own ground, besides Chester, and they also need to know what such a one as Chester is up to, and will go far to block it if it threatens their own profit. And then there's the church, brother, if you'll take it no offence is meant to the Benedictines. For you'll have heard by now that the king has dealt very hardly with some of his bishops this last few weeks, put up all manner of clerical backs, and turned his own brother and best ally, Bishop Henry of Winchester, who's papal legate into the bargain, into a bitter enemy. Bishop Henry himself might well have a finger in this pie, though I doubt if he can have had word of things afoot here in time, being never out of the south. But Lincoln, or Worcester – all such lords need to know what's going on, and for men of influence there are always plenty of bully-boys for hire, who'll do the labouring work while their masters sit inviolable at home.'

And so, thought Cadfael, could wealthy men sit inviolable here in their stalls, in full view of hundreds, while their hired bully-boys do the dirty work. And this black Welshman is laying it all out for me plain to be seen, and taking delight in it, too! Cadfael knew when he was being deliberately teased! what he could not be quite sure of was whether this was the caprice of a blameless but mischievous man, or the sport of a guilty one taking pleasure in his own immunity and cleverness. The black eyes sparkled and the white teeth shone. And why grudge him his enjoyment, if something useful could yet be gleaned from it? Besides, his mead was excellent.

'There must,' said Cadfael thoughtfully, 'be others here from Cheshire, even some from close to Ranulf's court. You yourself, for instance, come from not so far away, and are knowledgeable about those parts, and the men and the mood there. If you are right, whoever has committed these acts knew where to look for the thing they wanted, once they gave up believing that it was still among the effects of Thomas of Bristol. Now how would they be able to choose, say, between Euan of Shotwick and you? As an instance, of course! No offence!'

'None in the world!' said Rhodri heartily. 'Why, bless you! The only reason I know myself is because I *am* myself, and know I'm not in Ranulf of Chester's employ. But *you* can't know that, not certainly, and neither can any other. There's a small point, of course – Thomas of Bristol, I doubt, spoke no Welsh.'

'And you no English,' sighed Cadfael. 'I had forgotten!'

'There was a traveller from down towards Gloucester stayed overnight at Ranulf's court not a month ago,' mused Rhodri, twinkling happily at his own omniscience, 'a jongleur who got unusual favour, for he was called in to play a stave or two to Ranulf and his lady in private, after they left the hall at night. If Earl Ranulf has an ear for music, it's the first I've heard of it. It would certainly need more than a French virelai to fetch him in for his father-in-law's cause. He would want to know what were the prospects of success, and what his reward might be.' He slanted a radiant smile along his shoulder at Cadfael, and poured out the last of the mead. 'Your health, brother! You, at least, are delivered from the greed for gain. I have often wondered, is there a passion large enough to take its place? I am still in the world myself, you understand.'

'I think there might be,' said Cadfael mildly. 'For truth, perhaps? Or justice?'

# Chapter Two

The gaoler unlocked the door of Philip's cell somewhat before noon, and stood back to let the provost enter. Father and son eyed each other hard, and though Geoffrey Corviser continued to look grimly severe, and Philip obdurate and defiant, nevertheless the father was mollified and the son reassured. By and large, they understood each other pretty well.

'You are released to my warranty,' said the provost shortly. 'The charge is not withdrawn, not yet, but you're trusted to appear when called, and until then, let's hope I may get some sensible work out of you.'

'I may come home with you?' Philip sounded dazed; he knew nothing of what had been going on outside, and was unprepared for this abrupt release. Hurriedly he brushed himself down, all too aware that he presented no very savoury spectacle to walk through the town at the provost's side. 'What made them change their mind? There's no one been taken for the murder?' That would clear him utterly in Emma's eyes, no doubts left.

'Which murder?' said his father grimly. 'Never mind now, you shall hear, once we have you out of here.'

'Ay, stir yourself, lad,' advised the goodhumoured warder, jingling his keys, 'before they change their minds again. The rate things are happening at this year's fair, you might find the door slammed again before you can get through it.'

Philip followed his father wonderingly out of the castle. The noon light in the outer ward fell warm and dazzling upon him, the sky was a brilliant, deep blue, like Emma's eyes when she widened them in anxiety or alarm. It was impossible not to feel elated, whatever reproaches might still await him at home; and hope and the resilience of youth blossomed in him as his father recounted brusquely all that had happened while his son fretted in prison without news.

'Then there have been two attacks upon Mistress Vernold's boat and booth, her goods taken, her men assaulted?' He had quite forgotten his own bedraggled appearance, he was striding towards home with his head up and his visage roused and belligerent, looking, indeed, very much as he had looked when he led his ill-fated expedition across the bridge on the eve of the fair. 'And no one seized for it? Nothing done? Why, she herself may be in danger!' Indignation quickened his steps. 'For God's sake, what's the sheriff about?'

'He has enough to do breaking up unseemly riots by you and your like,' said his father smartly, but could not raise so much as a blush from his incensed offspring. 'But since you want to know, Mistress Vernold is in the guest-hall of the abbey, safe enough, in the care of Hugh Beringar and his lady. You'd do better to be thinking about your own troubles, my lad, and mind your own step, for you're not out of the wood yet.'

'What did I do that was so wrong? I went only one pace beyond what you did yourself the day before.' He did not even sound aggrieved about being judged hard, he made that brief defence only absently, his mind all on the girl. 'Even in the guest-hall she may not be out of reach, if this is all some determined plot against her uncle and all his family.' In the death of one more tradesman at the fair he showed less interest, shocking though it was, since it seemed to have little or nothing to do with the vindictive catalogue of offences against Master Thomas and all his possessions. 'She spoke so fairly,' he said. 'She would not have me accused of worse than I did.'

'True enough! She was a fine, honest witness, no denying it. But no business of yours now, she's well cared for. It's your mother you need to be thinking of, she's been in a fine taking over you all this while, and now they're looking in other directions for the one who did the killing – with one eye still on you, though, mind! – she'll likely take some sweetening. One way or another, you'll get a warm welcome.'

Philip was far beyond minding that, though as soon as he entered the house behind the shoemaker's shop he did indeed get a warm welcome, not one way or another, but both ways at once. Mistress Corviser, who was large, handsome and voluble, looked round from her fireside hob, uttered a muted shriek, dropped her ladle, and came billowing like a ship in full sail to embrace him, shake him, wrinkle her nose at the prison smell of him, abuse him for the damage to his best cotte and hose, box his ears for laughing at her tirade, exclaim lamentably over the dried scar at his temple, and demand that he sit down at once and let her crop the hair that adhered to the matted blood, and clean up the wound. By far the easiest thing to do was to submit to all, and let her talk herself out.

'The trouble and shame you've put us to, the heartaches you've cost me, wretch, you don't deserve that I should feed you, or wash and mend for you. The provost's son in prison, think of our mortification! Are you not ashamed of yourself?' She was sponging away the encrusted blood, and relieved to find so insignificant a scar remaining; but when he said blithely: 'No, mother!' she pulled his hair smartly.

'Then you should be, you good-for-nothing! There,

that's not so bad. Now I hope you're going to settle down to work, and make up for all the trouble you've made for us, instead of traipsing about the town egging on other people's sons to mischief with your wild ideas ...'

'They were the same ideas father and all the guild merchant had, mother, you should have scolded them. And you ask those who're wearing my shoes whether there's much amiss with my work.' He was a very good workman, in fact, as she would have asserted valiantly if anyone else had cast aspersions on his diligence and ability. He hugged her impulsively, and kissed her cheek, and she put him off impatiently, with what was more a slap than a caress. 'Get along with you, and don't come moguing me until you're cleared of the worse charge, and have paid your fine for the riot. Now come and eat your dinner!'

It was an excellent dinner, such as she produced on festivals and saints' days. After it, instead of shedding the clothes he had worn day and night in his cell, he shaved carefully, made a bundle of his second-best suit, and left the house with it under his arm.

'*Now* where are you going?' she demanded inevitably.

'To the river, to swim and get clean again.' They had a garden upstream, below the town hall, as many of the burgesses had, for growing their own fruit and vegetables, and there was a small hut there, and a sward where he could dry in the sun. He had learned to swim there, shortly after he learned to walk. He did not tell her where he was going afterwards. It was a pity he would have to present himself in his second-best coat, but in this hot summer weather perhaps he need not put it on at all; in shirt and hose most men look the same, provided the shirt is good linen and well laundered.

The water was not even cold in the sandy shallow by

the garden, but after his meal he did not stay in long, or swim out into deep water. But it was good to feel like himself again, cleansed even of the memory of his failure and downfall. There was a still place under the bank where the water hung almost motionless, and showed him a fair image of his face, and the thick bush of red-brown hair which he combed and straightened with his fingers. He dressed as carefully as he had shaved, and set off back to the bridge, and over it to the abbey. The town's grievance, which he had had on his mind the last time he came this way, was quite forgotten; he had other important business now on the abbey side of Severn.

'There's one here,' said Constance, coming in from the great court with a small, private smile on her lips. 'Who asks to speak with Mistress Vernold. And not a bad figure of a young fellow, either, though still a thought coltish about the legs. He asked very civilly.'

Emma had looked up quickly at the mention of a young man; now that she had gone some way towards accepting what had happened, and coming to terms with a disaster which, after all, she had not caused, she had been remembering words Ivo had used, almost disregarded then in her shocked daze, but significant and warming now.

'Messire Corbière?'

'No, not this time. This one I don't know, but he says his name is Philip Corviser.'

'I know him,' said Aline, and smiled over her sewing. 'The provost's son, Emma, the boy you spoke for in the sheriff's court. Hugh said he would see him set free today. If there's one soul can say he has done no evil to you or any these last two days, he's the man. Will you see him? It would be a kindness.'

Emma had almost forgotten him, even his name, but she recalled the plea he had made for her belief in him.

So much had happened between. She remembered him now, unkempt, bruised and soiled, pallid-sick after his drunkenness, but still with a despairing dignity. 'Yes, I remember him. Of course I'll see him.'

Philip followed Constance into the room. Fresh from the river, with damp hair curling thickly about his head, shaven and glowing and in fierce earnest, but without the aggression of the manner she had first seen in him, this was a very different person from the humiliated prisoner of the court. The last look he had given her, chin on shoulder, as he was dragged out ... yes, she saw the resemblance there. He made his reverence to Aline, and then to Emma.

'Madam, I am released on my father's bail. I came to say my thanks to Mistress Emma for speaking so fairly for me, when I had no right to expect goodwill from her.'

'I'm glad to see you free, Philip,' said Aline serenely, 'and looking none the worse. You will like to speak with Emma alone, I daresay, and company other than mine may be good for her, for here we talk nothing but babies.' She rose, folding her sewing carefully to keep the needle in view as she carried it. 'Constantine and I will sit on the bench by the hall door, in the sun. The light is better there, and I am no such expert needlewoman as Emma. You can be undisturbed here.'

Out she went, and they saw a ray of sun from the open outer door sparkle in her piled gold hair, before Constance followed, and closed the door between. The two of them were left, gazing gravely at each other.

'The first thing I wanted to do with freedom,' said Philip, 'was to see you again, and thank you for what you did for me. As I do, with all my heart. There were some who bore witness there who had known me most of my life, and surely had no grudge against me, and yet testified that I had been the first to strike, and done all manner of things I knew I had not done. But you, who had suffered through my act, though God knows I never willed it, you spoke absolute truth for me. It took a generous heart and a fair mind to do so much for an unknown whom you had no cause to love.' He had not chosen that word, it had come naturally in the commonplace phrase, but when he heard it, it raised a blush like fire in his own face, faintly reflected the next moment in hers.

'All I did was to tell the truth of what I had seen,' she said. 'So should we all have done, it's no virtue, but an obligation. It was shame that they did not. People do not think what it is they are saying, or trouble to be clear about what they have seen. But that's all by now. I'm very glad they've let you go. I was glad when Hugh Beringar said they must, taking into account what has been happening, for which you certainly can bear no blame. But perhaps you have not heard ...'

'Yes, I have heard. My father has told me.' Philip sat down beside her in the place Aline had vacated, and leaned towards her earnestly. 'There is some very evil purpose against you and yours, surely, how else to account for so many outrages? Emma, I am afraid for you ... I fear danger threatening even you. I'm grieved for your loss, and all the distress you've suffered. I wish there might be some way in which I could serve you.'

'Oh, but you need not be troubled for me,' she said. 'You see I am in the best and kindest hands possible, and tomorrow the fair will all be over, and Hugh Beringar and Aline will help me to find a safe way to go home.'

'Tomorrow?' he said, dismayed.

'It may not be tomorrow. Roger Dod will take the barge down-river tomorrow, but it may be that I must stay a day or two more. We have to find a party going south by Gloucester, for safe-conduct, and with some other women for company. It may take a day or two.'

Even a day or two would be gold; but after that she would be gone, and he might never see her again. And still, confronted by this cause for unhappiness on his own part, he could only think of her. He could not rid himself of the feeling that she was threatened.

'In only two days, see how many ill things have happened, and always close to you, and what may not still happen in a day or two more? I wish you were safe home this moment,' he said passionately, 'though God knows I'd rather lose my right hand than the sight of you.' He was not even aware that that same right hand had taken possession of her left one, and was clasping it hard. 'At least find me some way of serving you before you go. If nothing more, tell me you know that I never did harm to your uncle ...'

'Oh, yes,' she said warmly, 'that I can, most willingly. I never did truly believe it. You are no such person, to strike a man dead by stealth. I never thought it. But still we don't know who did it! Oh, don't doubt me, I'm sure of *you*. But I wish it could be shown clear to the world, for your sake.'

It was said very prettily and sincerely, and he took it to his heart gratefully, but it was said out of generous fellow-feeling, and nothing deeper, and he was gallingly sure of it while he hugged at least the kindness to him.

'For mine, too,' she said honestly, 'and for the sake of justice. It is not right that a mean murderer should escape his due, and it does aggrieve me that my uncle's death should go unpaid for.'

Find me some way of serving you, he had said; and perhaps she had. There was nothing he would not have undertaken for her; he would have lain over the threshold of any room in which she was, like a dog on guard, if she had needed it, but she did not, she was cared for by the sheriff's own deputy and his lady, and they would watch over her until they saw her safely on her way home. But when she spoke of the unknown who had slipped a dagger in her uncle's back, her great eyes flared with the angry blue of sapphires, and her face grew marble-clear and taut. Her complaint was his commission. He would achieve something for her yet.

'Emma,' he began in a whisper, and drew breath to commit himself deep as the sea.

The door opened, though neither of them had heard the knock; Constance put her head into the room.

'Messire Corbière waits to see you, when you are free,' she said, and withdrew, but left the door ajar. Evidently Messire Corbière ought not to be kept waiting long.

Philip was on his feet. Emma's eyes had kindled at the name like distant stars, forgetting him. 'You may remember him,' she said, still sparing a morsel of her attention for Philip, 'the young gentleman who came to help us on the jetty, along with Brother Cadfael. He has been very kind to me.'

Philip did remember, though his bludgeoned senses at the time had seen everything distorted; a slender, elegant, assured lordling who leaped a rolling cask to catch her in his arm at the water's edge, and further, to be just to him, had appeared in the sheriff's court and borne out Emma's honest story – even if he had also produced his falconer to testify to the silly threats Philip had been indulging in, drunk as he was, later that evening. Testimony Philip did not dispute, since he knew he had been incapable of clear thought or positive recollection. He recalled his disgusting self, and smarted at the thought. And the young lord with the bright gold crest and athlete's prowess had showed so admirable by contrast.

'I'll take my leave,' said Philip, and allowed her hand to slip out of his, though with reluctance and pain. 'For the journey, and always, I wish you well.'

'So do I you,' she said, and with unconscious cruelty added: 'Will you ask Messire Corbière to come in?'

Never in his life until then had Philip been required to draw himself to his full stature, body and mind. His departure was made with a dignity he had not dreamed he could achieve, and meeting Corbière face to face in the hall, he did indeed bid him within, at Mistress Emma's invitation, very civilly and amiably, while he burned with jealousy inwardly. Ivo thanked him pleasantly, and if he looked him over, did so with interest and respect, and with no apparent recollection of ever having seen him in less acceptable circumstances.

No one would have guessed, thought Philip, marching out into the sunshine of the great court, that a working shoemaker and a landed lord rubbed shoulders there. Well, he may have several manors in Cheshire and one in Shropshire, and be distant kin of Earl Ranulf, and welcome at his court; but I have something I can try to do for her, and I have a craft as honourable as his noble blood, and if I succeed, whether she comes my way or no, she'll never forget me.

Brother Cadfael came in at the gatehouse after some hours of fruitless prowling about the fair and the riverside. Among hundreds of men busy about their own concerns, the quest of a gashed sleeve, or one recently and hastily mended, is much the same as hunting one straw in a completed stack. His trouble was that he knew no other way to set about it. Moreover, the hot and settled weather continued unbroken, and most of those about the streets and the stalls were in their shirt-sleeves. There was a point there, he reflected. The glover's dagger had drawn blood, therefore it had reached the skin, but never a thread of white or unbleached linen had it brought away with the sliver of brown cloth. If the intruder had worn a shirt, he had worn it with sleeves rolled up, and it had emerged unscathed, and could now cover his graze, and if the wound had needed one, his bandage. Cadfael returned to tend the few matters needing him in his workshop, and be ready for Vespers in good time, more because he was at a loss how to proceed than for any other reason. An interlude of quiet and thought might set his wits working again.

In the great court his path towards the garden happened to cross Philip's from the guest-hall to the gatehouse. Deep in his own purposes, the young man almost passed by unnoticing, but then he checked sharply, and turned to look back.

'Brother Cadfael!' Cadfael swung to face him, startled out of just as deep a preoccupation. 'It is you!' said Philip. 'It was you who spoke for me, after Emma, in the sheriff's court. And I knew you then for the one who came to help me to my feet and out of trouble, when the sergeants broke up the fight on the jetty. I never had the chance to thank you, brother, but I do thank you now.'

'I fear the getting you out of trouble didn't last the night,' said Cadfael ruefully, looking this lanky youngster over with a sharp eye, and approving what he saw. Whether it was time spent in self-examination in the gaol, or time spent more salutarily still in thinking of Emma, Philip had done a great deal of growing up in a very short time. 'I'm glad to see you about again among us, and none the worse.'

'I'm not clear of the load yet,' said Philip. 'The charge still stands, even the charge of murder has not been withdrawn.'

'Then it stands upon one leg only,' said Cadfael heartily, 'and may fall at any moment. Have you not heard there's been another death?'

'So they told me, and other violence, also. But surely

this last bears no connection with the rest? Until this, all was malice against Master Thomas. This man was a stranger, and from Chester.' He laid a hand eagerly on Cadfael's sleeve. 'Brother, spare me some minutes. I was not very clear in my wits that night, now I need to know – all that I did, all that was done to me. I want to trace every minute of an evening I can barely piece together for myself.'

'And no wonder, after that knock on the head. Come and sit in the garden, it's quiet there.' He took the young man by the arm, and turned him towards the archway through the pleached hedge, and sat him down on the very seat, had Philip known it, where Emma and Ivo had sat together the previous day. 'Now, what is it you have in mind? I don't wonder your memory's hazy. That's a good solid skull you have on you, and a blessedly thick thatch of hair, or you'd have been carried away on a board.'

Philip scowled doubtfully into distance between the roses, hesitated how much to say, how much to keep painfully to himself, caught Brother Cadfael's comfortably patient eye, and blurted: 'I was coming now from Emma. I know she is in better care than I could provide her, but I have found one thing, at least, that might still be done for her. She wants and needs to see the man who killed her uncle brought to justice. And I mean to find him.'

'So does the sheriff, so do all his men,' said Cadfael, 'but they've had little success as yet.' But he did not say it in reproof or discouragement, but very thoughtfully. 'So, for that matter, do I, but I've done no better. One more mind probing the matter could just as well be the mind that uncovers the truth. Why not? But how will you set about it?'

'Why, if I can prove – *prove*! – that I did not do it, I may also rub up against something that will lead me to the man who did. At least I can make a start by trying to follow what happened to me that night. Not only for my own defence,' he said earnestly, 'but because it seems to me that I gave cover to the deed by what I had begun, and whoever did it may have had me and my quarrel in mind, and been glad of the opening I made for him, knowing that when murder came of the night, the first name that would spring to mind would be mine. So whoever he may be, he must have marked my comings and goings, or I could be no use to him. If I had been with ten friends throughout, I should have been out of the reckoning, and the sheriff would have begun at once to look elsewhere. But I was drunk, and sick, and took myself off alone to the river for a long time, so much I do know. Long enough for it to have been true. And the murderer knew it.'

'That is sound thinking,' agreed Cadfael approvingly. 'What, then, do you mean to do?'

'Begin from the riverside, where I got my clout on the head, and follow my own scent until I get clear what's very unclear now. I do remember what happened there, as far as you hauling me out of the way of the sheriff's men, and then being hustled away between two others, but my legs were grass and my wits were muddied, and I can't for my life recall who they were. It's a place to start, if you knew them.'

'One of them was Edric Flesher's journeyman,' said Cadfael. 'The other I've seen, though I don't know his name, a big, sturdy young fellow twice your width, with tow-coloured hair ...'

'John Norreys!' Philip snapped his fingers. 'I seem to recall him later in the night. It's enough, I'll begin with them, and find out where they left me, and how – or where I shook them off, for so I might have done, I was no fit company for Christians.' He rose, draping his coat over one shoulder. 'That whole evening I'll unravel, if I can.'

'Good lad!' said Cadfael heartily. 'I wish you success

with all my heart. And if you're going to be threading your way through a few of the ale-houses of the Foregate, as you seem to have done that night, keep your eyes open on my behalf, will you? If you can find your murderer, you may very well also be finding mine.' Carefully and emphatically he told him what to look for. 'An arm raising a flagon, or spread over a table, may show you what I'm seeking. The left sleeve sliced open for a hand's-length from the cuff of a russet-brown coat, that was sewn with a lighter linen thread. It would be on the underside of the arm. Or where arms are bared, look for the long scratch the knife made when it slit the sleeve, or for the binding that might cover it if it still bleeds. But if you find him, don't challenge him or say word to him, only bring me, if you can, his name and where to find him again.'

'This was the glover's slayer?' asked Philip, marking the details with grave nods of his brown head. 'You think they may be one and the same?'

'If not the same, well known to each other, and both in the same conspiracy. Find one, and we shall be very close to the other.'

'I'll keep a good watch, at any rate,' said Philip, and strode away purposefully towards the gatehouse to begin his quest.

# Chapter Three

Afterwards Brother Cadfael pondered many times over what followed, and wondered if prayer can even have a retrospective effect upon events, as well as influencing the future. What had happened had already happened, yet would he have found the same situation if he had not gone straight into the church, when Philip left him, with the passionate urge to commit to prayer the direction of his own efforts, which seemed to him so barren? It was a most delicate and complex theological problem, never as far as he knew, raised before, or if raised, no theologian had ventured to write on the subject, probably for fear of being accused of heresy.

Howbeit, the urgent need came over him, since he had lost some offices during the day, to recommit his own baffled endeavours to eyes that saw everything, and a power that could open all doors. He chose the transept chapel from which Master Thomas's coffin had been carried that morning, resealed into sanctity by the Mass sung for him. He had time, now, to kneel and wait, having busied himself thus far in anxious efforts like a man struggling up a mountain, when he knew there was a force that could make the mountain bow. He said a prayer for patience and humility, and then laid that by, and prayed for Emma, for the soul of Master Thomas, for the child that should be born to Aline and Hugh, for young Philip and the parents who had recovered him, for all who suffered injustice and wrong, and sometimes forgot they had a resource beyond the sheriff.

Then it was high time for him to rise from his knees, and go and see to his primary duty here, whatever more violent matters clamoured for his attention. He had supervised the herbarium and the manufactory derived from it, for sixteen years, and his remedies were relied upon far beyond the abbey walls; and though Brother Mark was the most devoted and uncomplaining of helpers, it was unkind to leave him too long alone with such a responsibility. Cadfael hastened towards his workshop with a lightened heart, having shifted his worries to broader shoulders, just as Brother Mark would be happy to do on his patron's arrival.

The heavy fragrance of the herb-garden lay over all the surrounding land, after so many hours of sunshine and heat, like a particular benediction meant for the senses, not the soul. Under the eaves of the workshop the dangling bunches of dried leafage rustled and chirped like nests of singing birds in waves of warmed air, where there was hardly any wind. The very timbers of the hut, dressed with oil against cracking, breathed out scented warmth.

'I finished making the balm for ulcers,' said Brother Mark, making dutiful report, and happily aware of work well done. 'And I have harvested all the poppy-heads that were ripe, but I have not yet broken out the seed, I thought they should dry in the sun a day or two yet.'

Cadfael pressed one of the great heads between his fingers, and praised the judgment. 'And the angelica water for the infirmary?'

'Brother Edmund sent for it half an hour ago. I had it ready. And I had a patient,' said Brother Mark, busy stacking away on a shelf the small clay dishes he used for sorting seeds, 'earlier on, soon after dinner. A groom with a gashed arm. He said he did it on a nail in the stables, reaching down harness, though it looked like a knife-slash to me. It was none too clean, I cleansed it for him, and dressed it with some of your goose-grass unguent. They were gambling with dice up there in the loft last night, I daresay it came to a fight, and somebody drew on him. He'd hardly admit to that.' Brother Mark dusted his hands, and turned with a smile to report for the sum of his stewardship. 'And that's all. A quiet afternoon, you need not have worried.' At sight of Cadfael's face his brows went up comically, and he asked in surprise: 'Why are you staring like that? Nothing there, surely, to open your eyes so wide.'

My mouth, too, thought Cadfael, and shut it while he reflected on the strangeness of human effort, and the sudden rewards that fell undeserved. Not undeserved, perhaps, in this case, since this had fallen to Brother Mark, who modestly made no demands at all.

'Which arm was gashed?' he asked, further baffling Brother Mark, who naturally could not imagine why that should matter.

'The left. From here, the outer edge of the wrist, down the underside of the forearm. Almost to the elbow. Why?'

'Had he his coat on?'

'Not when I saw him,' said Mark, smiling at the absurdity of this catechism. 'But he had it over his sound arm. Is that important?'

'More than you know! But you shall know, later, I am not playing with you. Of what colour was it? And did you see the sleeve that should cover that arm?'

'I did. I offered to stitch it for him – I had little to do just then. But he said he'd already cobbled it up, and so he had, very roughly, and with black thread. I could have done better for him, the original was unbleached linen thread. The colour? Reddish dun, much like most of the grooms and men-at-arms wear, but a good cloth.'

'Did you know the man? Not one of our own abbey servants?'

'No, a guest's man,' said Brother Mark, patient in his bewilderment. 'Not a word to his lord he said! It was one of Ivo Corbière's grooms, the older one, the surly fellow with the beard.'

Gilbert Prestcote himself, unescorted and on foot, had taken an afternoon turn about the fairground to view the public peace with his own eyes, and was in the great court on his way back to the town, conferring with Hugh Beringar, when Cadfael came in haste from the garden with his news. When the blunt recital was ended, they looked at him and at each other with blank and wary faces.

'Corbière's within at this moment,' said Hugh, 'and I gather from Aline has been, more than an hour. Emma has him dazed, I doubt if he's had any other thought, these last two days. His men have been running loose much as they pleased, provided the work was done. It could be the man.'

'His lord has the right to be told,' said Prestcote. 'Households grow lax when they see the country torn, and their betters flouting law. There's nothing been said or done to alarm this fellow, I take it? He has no reason to make any move? And surely he values the shelter of a name like Corbière.'

'No word has been said to any but you,' said Cadfael. 'And the man may be telling the truth.'

'The tatter of cloth,' said Hugh, 'I have here on me. It should be possible to match or discard.'

'Ask Corbière to come,' said the sheriff.

Hugh took the errand to himself, since Ivo was a

guest in his rooms. While they waited in braced silence, two of the abbey's men-at-arms came in at the gatehouse with unstrung long-bows, and Turstan Fowler between them with his arbalest, the three of them hot, happy and on excellent terms. On the last day of the fair there were normally matches of many kinds, wrestling, shooting at the butts along the river meadows, long-bow against cross-bow, though the long-bow here was usually the short bow of Wales, drawn to the breast, not the ear. The six-foot weapon was known, but a rarity. There were races, too, and riding at the quintain on the castle tiltyard. Trade and play made good companions, and especially good profits for the ale-houses, where the winners very soon parted with all they had won, and the losers made up their losses.

These three were wreathed together in argumentative amity, passing jokes along the line; each seemed to be vaunting his own weapon. They had strolled no more than halfway across the court when Hugh emerged from the guest-hall with Ivo beside him. Ivo saw his archer crossing towards the stable-yard, and made him an imperious signal to stay.

There was no fault to be found with Turstan's service since his disastrous fall from grace on the first evening; motioned to hold aloof but remain at call, he obeyed without question, and went on amusing himself with his rivals. He must have done well at the butts for they seemed to be discussing his arbalest, and he braced a foot in the metal stirrup and drew the string to the alert for them, demonstrating that he lost little in speed against their instant arms. No doubt the dispute between speed and range would go on as long as both arms survived. Cadfael had handled both in his time, as well as the eastern bow, the sword, and the lance of the mounted man. Even at this grave moment he spared a long glance for the amicable wrangle going on a score of paces away.

Then Ivo was there among them, and shaken out of his easy confidence and grace. His face was tense, his dark eyes large and wondering under the proudly raised auburn brows and golden cap of curls. 'You wanted me, sir? Hugh has not been specific, but I took it this was urgent matter.'

'It is a matter of a man of yours,' said the sheriff.

'My men?' He shook a doubtful head, and gnawed his lip. 'I know of nothing ... Not since Turstan drank himself stiff and stupid, and he's been a penitent and close to home ever since, and he did no harm then to any but himself, the dolt. But they all have leave to go forth, once their work's done. The fair is every man's treat. What's amiss concerning my men?'

It was left to the sheriff to tell him. Ivo paled visibly as he listened, his ruddy sunburn sallowing. 'Then my man is suspect of the killing I brushed arms with – Good God, this very morning! That you may know, his name is Ewald, he comes from a Cheshire manor, and his ancestry is northern, but he never showed ill traits before, though he is a morose man, and makes few friends. I take this hard. I brought him here.'

'You may resolve it,' said Prestcote.

'So I may. His mouth tightened. 'And will! About this hour I appointed to ride, my horse has had little exercise here, and he'll be bearing me hence tomorrow. Ewald is the groom who takes care of him. He should be saddling him up in the stables about this time. Shall I send for him? He'll be expecting my summons. No!' he interrupted his own offer, his brows contracting. 'Not send for him, go for him myself. If I sent Turstan, there, you might suspect that a servant would stand by a servant, and give him due warning. Do you think he has not been watching us, this short while? And do you think this colloquy has the look of simple talk among us?'

Assuredly it had not. Turstan, dangling his braced bow, had lost interest in enlightening his rivals, and they, sensing that there was something afoot that did not concern them, were drawing off and moving away, though with discreet backward glances until they vanished into the grange court.

'I'll go myself,' said Ivo, and strode away towards the stable-yard at a great pace. Turstan, hesitant, let him pass, since he got no word out of him in passing, but then turned and hurried on his heels, anxiously questioning. For a little way he followed, and they saw Ivo turn his head and snap some hasty orders at his man. Chastened, Turstan drew back and returned towards the gatehouse, and stood at a loss.

Some minutes passed before they heard the sharp sound of hooves on the cobbles of the stable-yard, brittle and lively. Then the tall, dusky bay, glowing like the darkest of copper and restive for want of work, danced out of the yard with the stocky, bearded groom holding his bridle, and Ivo stalking a yard or so ahead.

'Here is my man Ewald,' he said shortly, and stood back, as Cadfael noted, between them and the open gateway. Turstan Fowler drew nearer by discreet inches, and silently, sharp eyes flicking from one face to another in quest of understanding. Ewald stood holding the bridle, uneasy eyes narrowed upon Prestcote's unrevealing countenance. When the horse, eager for action, stirred and tossed his head, the groom reached his left hand across to take the bridle, and slid the right one up to the glossy neck, caressing by rote, but without for an instant shifting his gaze.

'My lord says your honour has something to ask me,' he said in a slow and grudging voice.

Under his left forearm the cobbled mend in his sleeve showed plainly, the cloth puckered between large stitches, and the end of linen thread shivered in sun and breeze like a gnat dancing.

'Take off your coat,' ordered the sheriff. And as the man gaped in real or pretended bewilderment: 'No words! Do it!'

Slowly Ewald slipped out of his coat, somewhat awkwardly because he was at pains to retain his hold on the bridle. The horse had been promised air and exercise, and was straining towards the gate, the way to what he desired. He had already shifted the whole group, except Cadfael, who stood mute and apart, a little nearer the gate.

'Turn back your sleeve. The left.'

He gave one wild glance round, then lowered his head like a bull, set his jaw, and did it, his right arm through the bridle as he turned up the coarse homespun to the elbow. Brother Mark had bound up the gash in a strip of clean linen over his dressing. The very cleanness of it glared.

'You have hurt yourself, Ewald?' said Prestcote, quietly grim.

He has his chance now, thought Cadfael, if he has quick enough wit, to change his story and say outright that he took a knife-wound in a common brawl, and told Brother Mark the lie about a nail simply to cover up the folly. But no, the man did not stop to think; he had his story, and trusted it might still cover him. Yet if Mark, on handling the wound, could tell a cut from a tear, so at the merest glance could Gilbert Prescote.

'I did it on a nail in the stables, my lord, reaching down harness.'

'And tore your sleeve through at the same time? It was a jagged nail, Ewald. That's stout cloth you wear.' He turned abruptly to Hugh Beringar. 'You have the slip of cloth?'

Hugh drew out from his pouch a folded piece of vellum, and opened it upon the insignificant strip of fabric, that looked like nothing so much as a blade of dried grass fretted into fibres and rotting at the edge.

Only the wavy tendril of linen thread showed what it really was, but that was enough. Ewald drew away a pace, so sharply that the horse backed off some yards towards the gateway, and the groom turned and took both hands to hold and soothe the beast. Ivo had to spring hurriedly backwards to avoid the dancing hooves.

'Hand here your coat,' ordered Prestcote, when the bay was appeased again, and willing to stand, though reluctantly.

The groom looked from the tiny thing he had recognised to the sheriff's composed but unrelenting face, hesitated only a moment, and then did as he was bid, to violent effect. He swung back his arm and flung the heavy cotte into their faces, and with a leap was over the bay's back and into the saddle. Both heels drove into the glossy sides, and a great shout above the pricked ears sent the horse surging like a flung lance for the gateway.

There was no one between but Ivo. The groom drove the bay straight at him, headlong. The young man leaped aside, but made a tigerish spring to grasp at the bridle as the horse hurtled by, and actually got a hold on it and was dragged for a moment, until the groom kicked out at him viciously, breaking the tenuous hold and hurling Ivo out of the way, to fall heavily and roll under the feet of the sheriff and Hugh as they launched themselves after the fugitive. Out at the gateway and round to the right into the Foregate went Ewald, at a frantic gallop, and there was no one mounted and ready to pursue, and for once the sheriff was without escort or archers.

But Ivo Corbière was not. Turstan Fowler had rushed to help him to his feet, but Ivo waved him past, out into the Foregate, and heaving himself breathlessly from the ground, with grazed and furious face ran limping after. The little group of them stood in the middle of the highroad, helplessly watching the bay and his rider recede into distance, and unable to follow. He had killed, and he would get clear away, and once some miles from Shrewsbury, he could disappear into forest and lie safe as a fox in its lair.

In a voice half-choked with rage, Ivo cried: 'Fetch him down!'

Turstan's arbalest was still braced and ready, and Turstan was used to jumping to his command. The quarrel was out of his belt, fitted and loosed, in an instant, the thrum and vibration of its flight made heads turn and duck and women shriek along the Foregate.

Ewald, stooped low over the horse's neck, suddenly jerked violently and reared up with head flung high. His hands slackened from the reins and his arms swung lax on either side. He seemed to hang for a moment suspended in air, and then swung heavily sidewise, and heeled slowly out of the saddle. The bay, startled and shocked, ran on wildly, scattering the frightened vendors and buyers on both sides, but his flight was uncertain now, and confused by this sudden lightness. He would not go far. Someone would halt and soothe him, and lead him back.

As for the groom Ewald, he was dead before ever the first of the appalled stallholders reached him, dead, probably, before ever he struck the ground.

# Chapter Four

He was my villein,' asserted Ivo strenuously, in the room in the gatehouse where they had brought and laid the body, 'and I enjoy the power of the high justice over my own, and this one had forfeited life. I need make no defence, for myself or my archer, who did nothing more than obey my order. We have all seen, now, that this fellow's wound is no tear from a nail, but the stroke of a dagger, and the fret you took from the glover's blade matches this sleeve past question. Is there doubt in any mind that this was a murderer?'

There was none. Cadfael was there with them in the room, at Hugh's instance, and he had no doubts at all. This was the man Euan of Shotwick had marked, before he himself died. Moreover, some of Euan of Shotwick's goods and money had been found among the sparse belongings Ewald had left behind him; his saddle-roll held a pouch of fine leather full of coins, and two pairs of gloves made for the hands of girls, presents, perhaps, for wife or sister. This was certainly a murderer. Turstan, who had shot him down, obviously did not consider himself anything of the kind, any more than one of Prestcote's archers would have done, had he been given the order to shoot. Turstan had taken the whole affair stolidly, as none of his business apart from his duty to his lord, and gone away to his evening meal with an equable appetite.

'I brought him here,' said Ivo bitterly, wiping smears of blood from his grazed cheek. 'It is my honour he has offended, as well as the law of the land. I had a right to avenge myself.'

'No need to labour it,' said Prestcote shortly. 'The shire has been saved a trial and a hanging, which is to the good, and I don't know but the wretch himself might prefer this way out. It was a doughty shot, and that's a valuable man of yours. I never thought it could be done so accurately at that distance.'

Ivo shrugged. 'I knew Turstan's quality, or I would not have said what I did, to risk either my horse or any of the hundreds about their harmless business in the Foregate. I don't know that I expected a death ...'

'There's only one cause for regret,' said the sheriff. 'If he had accomplices, he can never now be made to name them. And you say, Beringar, that there were probably two?'

'You're satisfied, I hope,' said Ivo, 'that neither Turstan nor my young groom Arald had any part with him in these thefts?'

Both had been questioned, he had insisted on that. Turstan had been a model of virtue since his one lapse, and the youngster was a fresh-faced country youth, and both had made friends among the other servants and were well liked. Ewald had been morose and taciturn, and kept himself apart, and the revelation of his villainy did not greatly surprise his fellows.

'There's still the matter of the other offences. What do you think? Was it this man in all of them?'

'I cannot get it out of my mind,' said Hugh slowly, 'that Master Thomas's death was the work of one man only. And without reason or proof, by mere pricking of thumbs, I do not believe it was this man. For the rest – I don't know! Two, the merchant's watchman said, but I am not sure he may not be increasing the odds to excuse his own want of valour – or his very good sense, however you look at it. Only one, surely, would enter the barge in full daylight, no doubt briskly, as if he had an errand there, something to fetch or something to bestow. Where there were two, this must surely be one of them. Who the other was, we are still in the dark.'

After Compline Cadfael went to report to Abbot Radulfus all that had happened. The sheriff had already paid the necessary courtesy visit to inform the abbot, but for all that Radulfus would expect his own accredited observer to bring another viewpoint, one more concerned with the repute and the standards of a Benedictine house. In an order which held moderation in all things to be the ground of blessing, immoderate things were happening.

Radulfus listened in disciplined silence to all, and there was no telling from his face whether he deplored or approved such summary justice.

'Violence can never be anything but ugly,' he said thoughtfully, 'but we live in a world as ugly and violent as it is beautiful and good. Two things above all concern me, and one of them may seem to you, brother, a trivial matter. This death, the shedding of this blood, took place outside our walls. For that I am grateful. You have lived both within and without, what must be accepted and borne is the same to you, within or without. But many here lack your knowledge, and for them, and for the peace we strive to preserve here as refuge for others beside ourselves, the sanctity of this place is better unspotted. And the second thing will matter as deeply to you as to me: Was this man guilty? Is it certain he himself had killed?'

'It is certain,' said Brother Cadfael, choosing his words with care, 'that he had been concerned in murder, most likely with at least one other man.'

'Then harsh though it may be, this was justice.' He

caught the heaviness of Cadfael's silence, and looked up sharply. 'You are not satisfied?'

'That the man took part in murder, yes, I am satisfied. The proofs are clear. But what is justice? If there were two, and one bears all, and the other goes free, is that justice? I am certain in my soul that there is more, not yet known.'

'And tomorrow all these people will depart about their own affairs, to their own homes and shops, wherever they may be. The guilty and the innocent alike. That cannot be the will of God,' said the abbot, and brooded a while in silence. 'Nevertheless, it may be God's will that it should be taken out of our hands. Continue your vigil, brother, through the morrow. After that others, elsewhere, must take up the burden.

Brother Mark sat on the edge of his cot, in his cell in the dortoire, with his elbows on his knees and his head in his hands, and grieved. From a child he had lived a hard life, privation, brutality and pain were all known to him as close companions until he came into this retreat, at first unwilling. But death was too monstrous and too dark for him, coming thus instant in terror, and without the possibility of grace. To live misused, ill-fed, without respite from labour, was still life, with a sky above it, and trees and flowers and birds around it, colour and season and beauty. Life, even so lived, was a friend. Death was a stranger.

'Child, it is with us always,' said Cadfael, patient beside him. 'Last summer ninety-five men died here in the town, none of whom had donc murder. For choosing the wrong side, they died. It falls upon blameless women in war, even in peace at the hands of evil men. It falls upon children who never did harm to any, upon old men, who in their lives have done good to many, and yet are brutally and senselessly slain.

Never let it shake your faith that there is a balance hereafter. What you see is only a broken piece from a perfect whole.'

'I know,' said Brother Mark between his fingers, loyal but uncomforted. 'But to be cut off without trial ...'

'So were the ninety-four last year,' said Cadfael gently, 'and the ninety-fifth was murdered. Such justice as we see is also but a broken shred. But it is our duty to preserve what we may, and fit together such fragments as we find, and take the rest on trust.'

'And unshriven!' cried Brother Mark.

'So went his victim also. And he had neither robbed nor killed, or if he had, only God knows of it. There has many a man gone through that gate without a safe-conduct, who will reach heaven ahead of some who were escorted through with absolution and ceremony, and had their affairs in order. Kings and princes of the church may find shepherds and serfs preferred before them, and some who claim they have done great good may have to give place to poor wretches who have done wrong and acknowledge it, and have tried to make amends.'

Brother Mark sat listening, and at least began to hear. Humbly he recognised and admitted the real heart of his grievance. 'I had his arm between my hands, I saw him wince when I cleansed his wound, and I felt his pain. It was only a small pain, but I felt it. I was glad to help him, it was pleasure to anoint the cut with balm, and wrap it clean, and know he was eased. And now he's dead, with a cross-bow bolt through him ...' Briefly and angrily, Brother Mark brushed away tears, and uncovered his accusing face. 'What is the use of mending a man, if he's to be broken within a few hours, past mending?'

'We were speaking of souls,' said Cadfael mildly, 'not mere bodies. and who knows but your touch with ointment and linen may have mended to better effect the one that lasts the longer? There's no arrow cleaves the soul. But there may be balm for it.

## Chapter Five

Head-down on his own traces, Philip had run his friend John Norreys to earth at last at the butts by the riverside, where the budding archers of the town practised, and together they hunted out Edric Flesher's young journeyman from the yard behind his master's shop. Philip's odyssey on the eve of the fair had begun with these two, who had had him bundled into their arms by Brother Cadfael when the sheriff's men descended on the Gaye.

By their own account, they had hauled him away through the orchards and the narrow lanes behind the Foregate, avoiding the highroads, and sat him down in the first booth that sold drink, to recover his addled wits. And very ungrateful they had found him, as soon as the shock of his blow on the head began to pass, and his legs were less shaky under him.

Furious with himself, he had turned his ill-temper on them, snarled at them, said John tolerantly, that he was capable of looking after himself, and they had better go and warn some of the other stalwarts who had rushed on along the Foregate overturning stalls and scattering goods, before the officers reached them. Which they had taken good-humouredly enough, knowing his head was aching villainously by that time, and had followed him for a while at a discreet distance as he blundered away through the fair-ground, until he turned on them again and ordered them away. They had stood to watch him, and then shrugged and left him to his own devices, since he would have none of them.

'You had your legs again,' said John reasonably, 'and since you wouldn't let us do anything for you, we thought best to let you go your own way. Let alone, you wouldn't go far, but if we followed, you might do who knows what, out of contrariness.'

'There was another fellow who looked after you a thought anxiously,' said the butcher's man, thinking back, 'when we left that booth with you. Came out after us, and set off the same way you took. He thought you were already helpless drunk, I fancy, and might need helping home.'

'That was kind in him,' said Philip, stiffening indignantly, and meaning that it was damned officious of whoever it was. 'That would be what hour? Not yet eight?'

'Barely. I did hear the bell for Compline shortly after, over the wall. Curious how it carries over all the bustle between.' In the upper air, so it would; people in the Foregate regulated their day by the office bells.

'Who was this who followed me? Did you know him?'

They looked at each other and hoisted indifferent shoulders; among the thousands at a great fair the local people are lost. 'Never seen him before. Not a Shrewsbury man. He may not have been following, to call it that, at all, just heading the same way.'

They told him exactly where he had left them,and the direction he had taken. Philip made his way purposefully to the spot indicated, but in that busy concourse, spreading along the Foregate and filling every open space beyond, he was still without a map. All he knew was that before nine, according to the witness in the sheriff's court, he had been very drunk and still drinking in Wat's tavern, and blurting out hatred and grievance and the intent of vengeance against Master Thomas of Bristol. The interval it was hard to fill. Perhaps he had made his way there at once, and been well advanced in drink before the stranger noted his threats.

Philip gritted his teeth and set off along the Foregate, so intent on his own quest that he had no ears for anything else, and missed the news that was being busily conveyed back and forth through the fair, with imaginative variations and considerable embellishments before it reached the far corner of the horse-fair. It was news more than two hours old by then, but Philip had heard no word of it, his mind was on his own problem. All round him stalls were being stripped down to trestle and board, and rented booths being locked up, and the keys delivered to abbey stewards. Business was almost put away, but the evening was not yet outworn, there would be pleasure after business.

Walter Renold's inn lay at the far corner of the horse-fair, not on the London highroad, but on the quieter road that bore away north-eastwards. It was handy for the country people who brought goods to market, and at this hour it was full. It went against the grain with Philip even to order a pot of ale for himself while he was on this desperate quest, but ale-houses live by sales, and at least he was so formidably sober now that he could afford the indulgence. The pot-boy who brought him his drink was hardly more than a child, and he did not remember the tow hair and pock-marked face. He waited to speak with Wat himself, when there was a brief interlude of calm.

'I heard they'd let you go free,' said Wat, spreading brawny arms along the table opposite him. 'I'm glad of it. I never thought you'd do harm, and so I told them where they asked. When was it they loosed you?'

'A while before noon.' Hugh Beringar had said he should eat his dinner at home, and so he had, though at a later hour than usual.

'So nobody could point a finger at you over the latest ill-doings. Such a fair as we've had! Good weather and good sales, and good attendance all round, even good behaviour,' said Wat weightily, considering the whole range of his experience of fairs. 'And yet two merchants murdered, the second of them a northern man found only this morning broken-necked in his stall. You'll have heard about that? When did we ever have such happenings! It's not the lads of Shrewsbury, I said when they asked me, that get up to such villainies, you look among the incomers from other parts. We're decent folk hereabouts!'

'Yes, I know of that,' said Philip. 'But it's not that death they pointed at me, it's the first, the Bristol merchant ...' North and south had met here, he reflected, fatally for both. Now why should that be? Both the victims strangers from far distances, where some born locally were as well worth plundering.

'This one they could hardly charge to your account,' said Wat, grinning broadly, 'even if you'd been at large so early. It's all past and gone. You hadn't heard? There was a grand to-do along the Foregate, a few hours ago. The murderer's found out red-handed, and made a break for his freedom on his lord's horse, and kicked his lord into the dust on the way. And he's shot down dead as a storm-struck tree, at his lord's orders. A master's shot, they say. The glover's soon avenged. And you'd not heard of it?'

'Not a word! The last I heard they were looking for a man who might have a slit sleeve to show, and a gash in his arm. When was this, then?' It seemed that Brother Cadfael must have found his man, unaided, after all.

'Not an hour before Vespers it must have been. All I heard was the shouting at the abbey end of the Foregate. But they tell me the sheriff himself was there.'

About five in the afternoon, perhaps less than an hour after Philip had left Brother Cadfael and gone back into the town to look for John Norreys. A short hunt that had been, no need any longer for him to cast a narrowed eye at men's sleeves wherever he went. 'And it's certain they got the right man?'

'Certain! The merchant had marked him, and they say there were goods and money from the glover's stall found in his pack. Some groom called Ewald, I heard ...'

A mere sneak-thief, then, who had gone too far. Nothing there to bear on Philip's own quest. He was free to concentrate his mind once again, and even more intently, upon his own pilgrimage. It had begun as a penitential exercise, but was gradually abandoning that aspect. Certainly he had made a fool of himself, but the original impulse on which he had acted, and roused others to act, had not been so foolish, after all, and was nothing to be ashamed of. Only when it collapsed about him in ruins had he thrown good sense to the winds, and indulged his misery like a sulking child.

'Now if only I could find out as certainly who it was did for Master Thomas! It was that night there was grave matter urged against me, and I will own I laid myself open. It's all very well being let out on my father's bail, but no one has yet said I'm clear of the charge. The rest I'll pay my score for, but I want to prove I never did the merchant any violence. I know I was here that night – the eve of the fair, you'll remember? From what hour? I've no recollection of times, myself. According to his men, master Thomas was alive until a third of the hour past nine.'

'Oh, you were here, no question!' Wat could not help grinning at the memory. 'There was noise enough, we were busy, but you made yourself heard! No offence, lad, who hasn't made a fool of himself in his cups from time to time? It can't have been more than a quarter after eight when you came in, and I doubt you'd had much, up to then.'

Only a quarter after the hour of Compline – then he must have come straight here after shaking off his friends. Not straight, perhaps that was an inappropriate word, but weavingly and unsteadily, though at that rate not calling anywhere else on the way. It was a natural thing to do, to hurry clean through the thick of the fair, and put as much ground as possible between himself and his solicitous companions before calling a halt.

'I tell you what, boy,' said the expert kindly, 'if you'd taken it slowly you'd have been sober enough. But you had to rush the matter. I doubt I've ever seen a fellow put so much down in the time, no wonder your belly turned against it.'

It was not cheering listening, but Philip swallowed it doggedly. Evidently he had been as foolish as he had been dreading, and the archer's account of his behaviour had not been at all exaggerated.

'And was I yelling vengeance against the man who struck me? That's what they said of me.'

'Well, now, I wouldn't go so far as that, and yet it's not too far off the mark, either. Let's say you were not greatly loving him, and no wonder, we could all see the dunt he'd given you. Arrogant and greedy you called him, and a few other things I don't recall, and mark your words, you kept telling us, pride like his was due for a disastrous fall, and soon. That must be what they had in mind who witnessed against you. I never heard word of any going to this hearing from my tavern, not until afterwards. Who were they that testified, then?'

'It was one man,' said Philip. 'Not that I can blame him, it seems he told no lies – indeed, I never thought he had, I know I was the world's fool that night.'

'Why, bless you, lad, with a cracked head a man's

liable to act like one cracked, he has the right. But who's this one man? What with all the incomers at the fair, I had more strangers than known customers of these evenings.'

'It was a man attending one of the abbey guests,' said Philip. 'Turstan Fowler, they said his name was. He said he was here drinking, and went from ale to wine, and then to strong liquor – it seems he ended up as drunk as I was myself, they took him up helpless later, and slung him into a cell at the abbey overnight. A well-set-up fellow, but slouching and unkempt when I saw him in the court. About thirty-five years old, at a guess, sunburned, a bush of brown hair ...'

Wat shook his head, pondering the description. 'I don't know him, not by that, though I've got a rare memory for faces. An ale-house keeper has to have. Ah, well, if he's a stranger he'd no call to give false witness, I suppose he was but honest, and put the worst meaning on your bletherings for want of knowing you.'

'What time was it when I left here?' Philip winced ever at the recollection of the departure, sudden and desperate, with churning stomach and swimming head, and both hands clamped hard over his grimly locked jaw. Barely time to weave a frantic way across the road and into the edge of the copse beyond, where he had heaved his heart out, and then blundered some distance further in cover towards the orchards of the Gaye, and collapsed shivering and retching into the grass, to pass into a sodden sleep. He had not dragged himself out of it until the small hours.

'Why, reckoning from Compline, I'd say an hour had passed, it would be about nine of the clock.'

Thomas of Bristol had set out from his booth to return to his barge only a quarter of an hour or so later. And someone, someone unknown, had intercepted him on the way, dagger in hand. No wonder the law had looked so narrowly at Philip Corviser, who had reason to resent and hate, and had blundered out of sight and sound of other men around that time, after venting his grievance aloud for all to hear.

Wat rose to go and cope with the custom that was overwhelming his two potboys, and Philip sat brooding with his chin on his fist. Most of the flares must be out by now along the Foregate, most of the stalls packed up and ready for departure. Another balmy summer night, heaven dropping fat blessings on the abbey receipts and the profits of trade, after a lost summer of warfare and a winter of uncertainty. And the town walls still unrepaired, and the streets still broken!

The door stood propped wide on the warm, luminous twilight, and the traffic in and out was brisk. Youngsters came with jugs and pitchers to fetch for their elders, maids tripped in for a measure of wine for their masters, labourers and abbey servants wandered in to slake their thirst between spells of work. Saint Peter's Fair was drawing to its contented and successful close.

Through the open door came a fresh-faced youngster in a fine leather jerkin, and on his heels a sturdy, brown-faced man at least fifteen years older, in the same good livery. It took Philip a long moment of staring to recognise Turstan Fowler, sober, well-behaved, in good odour with his lord and all the world. Still longer to cause him to reflect afresh how he himself must have looked, drunk, if the difference could stretch so far. He watched the little potboy serve them. Wat was busy with others, and the room was full. The end of the fair was always a busy time. Another day, and these same hours would hang heavy and dark.

Philip never quite knew why he turned his head away, and hoisted a wide shoulder between himself and Ivo Corbière's men. He had nothing against either of them, but he did not want to be recognised and condoled with, or congratulated on his release, or in any way, sympathetic or not, have public attention called to him. He kept his shoulder hunched between, and was glad to have the room so full of people, and most of them strangers.

'Fairs are good business,' remarked Wat, returning to his place and plumping down on the bench with a sigh of pleasure, 'but I wish we could spread them round the rest of the year. My feet are growing no younger, and I've hardly been off them an hour in all, the last three days. What was it we were saying?'

'I was trying to describe for you the fellow who reported me as threatening revenge,' said Philip. 'Cast a look over yonder now, and you'll see the very man. The two in leather who came in together – the elder of the two.'

Wat let his sharp eyes rove, and surveyed Turstand Fowler with apparent disinterest, but very shrewdly. 'Slouching and hangdog, was he? Smart as a new coat now.' His gaze returned to Philip's face. 'That's the man? I remember *him* well enough. I seldom forget a man's face, but his name and condition I've no way of knowing.'

'He can't have looked quite so trim that evening,' said Philip, 'seeing he owned to being well soused. He was lost to the world two hours later, by his own tale.'

'And he said he got it all here?' Wat's eyes had narrowed thoughtfully.

'So he said. "Where I got my skinful" is what he said.'

'Well, let me tell you something interesting, friend ...' Wat leaned confidentially across the table. 'Now I see him, I know how I saw him the last time, for if you'll credit me, he looked much as he looks now. And what's more, now I know of the connection he had with you and your affairs, I can recall small things that happened that night, things I never gave a thought to before, and neither would you have done. He was in here twice that evening, or rather, he was in the doorway once, before he came over the threshold later. In that doorway he stood, and looked round him, a matter of ten minutes or so after you came in. I made nothing of it that he gave you a measuring sort of look, for well he might, you were in full cry then. But look at you he did, and weighed you up, and went away again. And the next we saw of him, it might be half an hour later, he came in and bought a measure of ale, and a big flask of strong geneva liquor, and sat supping his ale quietly, and eyeing you from time to time – as again well he might, it was about then you were greenish and going suspicious quiet. But do you know when he drank up and left, Philip, lad? The minute after you made for the door in a hurry. And his flask under his arm, unopened. Drunk? *Him?* He was stone cold sober when he went out of here.'

'But he took the juniper liquor with him,' pointed out Philip, reasonably. 'He was drunk enough two hours later, there were several of them to swear to that. They had to carry him back to the abbey on a trestle-board.'

'And how much of the juniper spirit did they find remaining? Did they ever mention that? Did they find the flask at all?'

'I never heard mention of it,' owned Philip, startled and doubtful. 'Brother Cadfael was there, I could ask him. But why?'

Wat laid a kindly if patronising hand on his shoulder. 'Lad, it's easy to see you never went beyond wine or ale, and if you'll heed me you'll leave the strong stuff to strong stomachs. I said a large flask, and large I meant. There was a quart of geneva spirits in that bottle! If any man drank that dry in two hours, it wouldn't be dead drunk they'd be carrying him away, it would be plain dead. Or if he did live to tell of it, it wouldn't be the next day, nor for several after. Sober as the sheriff himself was that fellow when he went out of here on your heels, and why he should want to lie about it is more than I can say, but lie about it he did, it seems. Now you tell me why a man should go to some pains to convict himself of a debauch he never even had, and get himself slung into a cell for recompense. Unless,' added Wat, considering the problem with lively interst, 'it was to get himself out of something worse.'

The elder potboy, a freckled lad born and bred in the Foregate, came by with a cluster of empties in either hand, and paused to nudge Wat in the ribs with an elbow, and lean to his ear.

'Do you know who you have there, master?' A jerk of his head indicated the two in leather jerkins. 'The young one's fellow-groom to the one that got a bolt through him along the Foregate a while ago. And the other – Will Wharton just told me, and he was close by and saw it all! – that's the fellow who loosed the bolt! His comrade in the same price, mark! Should he be here and in such spirits the same night? That's a stronger stomach than mine. "Fetch him down!" says the master, and down the fellow fetches him, sharp and cool. You'd have thought his hand would have shook too much to get near the target, but no! – thump between the shoulders and through to the breast, so Will says. And that's the very man that did it, supping ale like any Christian.'

They were both of them staring at him open-mouthed, and turned away only to stare again, briefly and intently, at Turstan Fowler sitting at ease with his tankard, sturdy legs splayed under the table. It had never even occurred to Philip to ask in whose service the dead malefactor was employed, and perhaps Wat would not have known the name if he had asked. He would have mentioned it else

'That's the man? You're sure?' pressed Philip.

'Will Wharton is sure, and he helped to pick up the poor devil who was killed.'

'Turstan Fowler? The falconer to Ivo Corbière? And Corbière ordered him to shoot?'

'The name I don't know, for neither did Will. Some young lord at the abbey guest-hall. Very handsome sprig, yellow-haired, Will says. Though it's no great blame to him for wanting a murderer and thief stopped in his tracks, granted, and any road, the man had just stolen his horse, and kicked him off into the dust when he tried to halt him. And I suppose when a lord orders, his man had better jump to obey. Still, it's a grim thing to work side by side with a man maybe months and years, and then to be told, strike him dead! And to do it!' And the potboy rolled up his eyes and loosed a long, soft whistle, and passed on with his handful of tankards, leaving them so sunk in reconsideration that neither of them had anything to say.

But there could not be anything in it of significance for him, surely? Philip looked back briefly as he left the inn, and Turstan Fowler and the young groom were sitting tranquilly with their ale, talking cheerfully with half a dozen other sober drinkers around them. They had not noticed him, or if they had, had not recognised him, and neither of them seemed to have anything of grave moment on his mind. Strange, though, how this same man seemed to be entangled in every untoward episode, never at the centre of things yet always somewhere in view.

As for the matter of the flask of juniper spirits, what did it really signify? The man had been picked up too drunk to talk, no one had looked round for his bottle, it might well have been left lying, still more than half-full, if the stuff was a potent as Wat said, and some scavenger by night might have picked it up and rejoiced in his luck. There were a dozen ways of accounting for the circumstances. And yet it was strange. Why should he have said he was drunk before he left Wat's inn, if he had really left it cold sober? More to the point, why should he have left so promptly on Philip's heels? Yet Wat was a good observer.

The tiny discrepancies stuck like barbs in Philip's mind. It was far too late to trouble anyone else tonight, Compline was long over, the monks of Shrewsbury, their guests, their servants, would all be in their beds or preparing to go there, except for the few lay stewards who had almost completed their labours, and would be glad enough to make a modestly festive night of it. Moreover, his parents would be vexed that he had abandoned them all the day and he could expect irate demands for explanations at home. He had better make his way back.

All the same, he crossed the road and made for the copse, as on the night he was repeating, and found some faint signs of his wallow still visible, dried into the trampled grass. Then back towards the river, avoiding the streets, keeping to the cover of woodland, and there was the sheltered hollow where he had slept off the worst of his orgy, before gathering himself up stiffly and hobbling back to the town. There was enough lambent starlight to see his way, and show him the scuffled and flattened grasses.

But no, this was not the place! Here there was a faint, trodden path, and he had certainly moved much deeper into the bushes and trees, down-river, hiding even from the night. This glade looked very like the other, but it was not the same. Yet someone or something, large as a man, had lain here, and not peacefully. Surely more than one pair of feet had ploughed the turf. A pair of opportunist lovers, enjoying one of the traditional pleasures of the fair?

Or another kind of struggle? No, hardly a struggle, though something had been dragged downhill towards the river, which was just perceptible as a gleam between the trees. There was a patch of bare soil, dry and pale as clay, between the spreading roots of the birch tree against which he leaned, and ribbons of dropped bark littered it. The largest of them showed curiously dark instead of silvery, like the rest. He stooped and picked it up, and his fingertips recoiled from the black, encrusted stain. In the grass, if he searched by daylight, there might well be other such blots.

In looking for the place of his own humiliation, he had found something very different, the place where Master Thomas had been killed. And below, from that spur of grass standing well above the undermined bank, his body had been thrown into the river.

# After the Fair

## Chapter One

Brother Cadfael came out from Prime, next morning, to find Philip hovering anxiously in the great court, fidgeting from one foot to the other as if the ground under him burned, and so intent and grim of face that there was no doubting the urgency of what he had to impart. At sight of Cadfael he came bounding alongside to lay a hand on his sleeve.

'Will you come with me to Hugh Beringar? You know him, he'll listen if you vouch for me. I didn't know if he'd be stirring this early, so I waited for you. I think I've found the place where Master Thomas was killed.'

It was certainly not what he had been looking for, and came as a total irrelevance for a moment to Brother Cadfael, who checked and blinked at an announcement so unexpected. 'You've done *what*?'

'It's true, I swear it! It was so late last night, I couldn't pester anyone with it then, and I've not been there by daylight – but someone bled there – someone was dragged down to the water –'

'Come!' said Cadfael, recovering. 'We'll go together.' And he set out at a brisk trot for the guest-hall, Philip's long strides keeping easy pace with him. 'If you're right ... He'll want you to show the place. Can you find it again with certainty?'

'I can, you'll see why.'

Hugh came out to them yawning, in shirt and hose, but wide awake and shaven all the same. 'Speak low!' he said, finger on lip, and softly closed the door of his rooms behind him. 'The women are still asleep. Now, what is it? I know better than to turn away anyone who comes with Brother Cadfael's warranty.'

Philip told only what was needful. For his own personal need there would be time later. What mattered now was the glade in the edge of the woods, beyond the orchards of the Gaye.

'I was following my own scent, last night, and I made too short a cast at the way I took down to the river. I came on a place in the trees there – I can find it again – where some heavy thing had lain, and been dragged down to the water. The grass is flattened where he lay, and combed downhill, where he was dragged, and for all the three days between, it still shows the traces. I think there are also spots of blood.'

'The merchant of Bristol?' asked Hugh, after an instant of startled silence.

'I think so. Daylight may show for certain.'

Hugh turned to drain his morning ale in purposeful haste, and demolish the end of oatcake he had been eating. 'You slept at home? In the town?' He was brushing his black crest hastily as he talked, tying the laces of his shirt and reaching for his cotte. 'And came to me rather than to the sheriff! Well, no harm, we're nearer than he, it will save time.' Sword and sword-belt he left lying, and thrust his feet into his shoes. 'Cadfael, you'll be missing breakfast, take these cakes with you, and drink something now, while you may. And you, friend, have you eaten?'

'No escort?' said Cadfael.

'To what end? Your eyes and mine are all we require here, and the fewer great boots stamping about the sward, the better. Come, before Aline wakes, she has a bird's hearing, and I'd rather have her rest. Now,

Philip, lead! You're on your home turf, take us the quickest way.'

Aline and Emma were at breakfast, resigned to Hugh's sudden and silent departures, when Ivo came asking admittance. Punctilious as always, he asked for Hugh.

'But as that husband of mine has already gone forth somewhere on official business,' said Aline, amused, 'and as it's certainly you he really wants to see, shall we let him in? I felt sure he would not go away without paying his respects to you yet again. He has probably been exercising his wits to find a way of ensuring it shan't be the last time, either. He was hardly at his best last night, and no wonder, after so many shocks, and grazed and bruised from his fall.'

Emma said nothing, but her colour rose agreeably. She had risen from her bed with a sense of entering a life entirely new, and more her own to determine than ever it had been before. By this hour Master Thomas's barge must be well down the Severn on its way home. She was relieved of the necessity of avoiding Roger Dod's grievous attentions, and eased of the sense of guilt she felt in doing him what was probably the great wrong of fearing and distrusting his intentions towards her. Her belongings were neatly packed for travelling, in a pair of saddle-bags bought at the fair, for whatever was to become of her now, she would be leaving the abbey today. If no immediate escort offered for the south, she would go home with Aline, to await whatever arrangements Hugh could make for her, and in default of any other trustworthy provision, he himself had promised her his safe-conduct home to Bristol.

The bustle of departure filled the stable-yard and the great court, and half the rooms in the guest-hall had already been vacated. No doubt Turstan Fowler and the young groom were also assembling their lord's purchases and effects, and saddling up the bay horse, returned to the abbey by an enterprising errand-boy who had been lavishly rewarded, and their own shaggy ponies. Two of them! The third would be on a leading rein.

Emma felt cold when she remembered what had befallen the rider of the third pony, and the things he had done. So sudden a death filled her with horror. But the man had done murder, and had not scrupled to ride down his own lord when he was unmasked. It was reasonable to blame Ivo for what had happened, even if his order had not been given in an understandable rage at the misuse of his patronage and the assault upon his own person. Indeed, Emma had been touched, the previous evening, when the very vehemence with which Ivo had defended his action had so clearly betrayed his own doubts and regrets. It had ended in her offering reassurance and comfort. It was a terrible thing in itself, she thought, to have the power of life and death over your fellowmen, whatever crimes they might have committed.

If Ivo had lacked something of his normal balance and confidence last night, he had certainly regained them this morning. His grooming was always immaculate, and his dress, however simple, sat upon his admirable body with a borrowed elegance. It had been hateful to him to be spilled into the dust, and rise limping and defaced before a dozen or more witnesses. This morning he had made sure of his appearance, and wore even the healing grazes on his left cheek like ornaments; but as soon as he entered, Emma saw that he was still limping after his fall.

'I'm sorry to have missed your husband,' he said as he came into the room where they were sitting, 'but they tell me he's already gone forth. I had a scheme to put to him for approval. Dare I put it to you, instead?'

'I'm already curious,' said Aline, smiling.

'Emma has a problem, and I have a solution. I've been thinking about it ever since you told me, Emma, two days ago, that you would not be returning to Bristol with the barge, but must find a safe escort south by road. I have no right at all to advance any claim, but if Beringar will consent to trust you to me ... You need to get home, I'm sure, as quickly as you can.'

'I must,' said Emma, eyeing him with wondering expectation. 'There are so many things I must see to there.'

Ivo addressed himself very earnestly to Aline. 'I have a sister at Stanton Cobbold who is determined to take the veil, and the convent of her choice has consented to take her. And by luck it happens that she wished to join a Benedictine house, and the place is the prior at Minchinbarrow, which is some few miles beyond Bristol. She is waiting for me to take her there, and to tell the truth, I've been delaying to give her time to change her mind, but the girl's set on her own way. I'm satisfied she means it. Now if you'll confide Emma to my care, as I swear you may with every confidence, for it will be my pleasure to serve her, then why should not she and Isabel travel down very comfortably together? I have men enough to provide a safe guard, and naturally I should myself be their escort. That's the plan I wanted to put to your husband, and I hope he would have felt able to fall in with it and give his approval. It's great pity he is not here –'

'It sounds admirable,' said Aline, wide-eyed with pleasure, 'and I'm sure Hugh would feel completely happy in trusting Emma to your care. Had we not better ask Emma herself what she has to say?'

Emma's flushed face and dazzled smile were speaking for her. 'I think it would be the best possible answer, for me,' she said slowly, 'and I'm most grateful for so kind a thought. But I must really go as soon as possible, and your sister – you said, you wanted her to have time to be sure ...'

Ivo laughed, a little ruefully. 'I've already reached the point of giving up the hope of persuading her to stay in the world. Never fear that you may be forcing Isabel's hand, ever since she was accepted she has been trying to force mine. And if it's what she wants, whom am I to prevent? She has everything ready, it will give her only pleasure if I come home to say that we can start tomorrow. If you're willing to trust yourself to me alone for the few miles to Stanton Cobbold, and sleep under our roof tonight, we can be on our way in the morning. We can provide you horse and saddle, if you care to ride, or a litter for the pair of you, as you please.'

'Oh, I can ride,' she said, glowing. 'It would be a delight.'

'We would try and make it so. *If*,' said Ivo, turning his grazed smile almost diffidently upon Aline, 'if I may have your approval, and my lord Beringar's. I would not presume without that. But since this is a journey I must make, sooner or later, and Isabel insists the sooner the better, why not take advantage of it to serve Emma's need, too?'

'It would certainly solve everything very happily,' agreed Aline. And there could be no doubt, thought Emma, bolstering her own dear wish with the persuasion of virtue, that Aline would be relieved and happy if Hugh could be spared a journey, and she several days deprived of his company. 'Emma knows,' said Aline, 'that she may choose as she thinks best, for both you and we, it seems, are equally at her service. As for approval, why, of course I approve, and so, I'm sure, would Hugh.'

'I wish he would put in an appearance,' said Ivo, 'I should be the happier with his blessing. But if we are to go, I think we should set out at once. I know I said all's ready with Isabel, but for all that we may need to make the most of this day.'

Emma wavered between her desire and her regret at leaving without making her due and grateful farewell to Hugh. But it was gain for him, great gain, to be rid of the responsibility he had assumed, and so securely as this promised. 'Aline, you have been the soul of kindness to me, and I leave you with regret, but it is better to spare an extra journey, in such times, and then, Hugh has been kept so busy on my account already, and you've seen so little of him these days ... I should like to go with Ivo, if you'll give me your blessing. Yet I hate to go without thanking him properly ...'

'Don't fret about Hugh, he will surely think you wise to take advantage of so kind and fortunate an offer. I will give him all the pretty messages you're thinking of. Once I lose sight of him, now, I never know when he'll return, and I'm afraid Ivo is right, you may yet need every moment of the day, or certainly Isabel may. It's a great step she's taking.'

'So I've told her,' he said, 'but my sister has the boldness of mind to take great steps. You won't mind, Emma, riding pillion behind me, the few miles we have to go today? At home we'll find you saddle and horse and all.'

'Really,' said Aline, eyeing the pair of them with a small and private smile, 'I begin to be envious!'

He sent the young groom to fetch out her saddle-bags. Their light weight was added to the bales of Corbière's purchases on the spare pony, her cloak, which she certainly would not need on so fine a day, folded and stowed away with the bags. It was like setting out into a new world, sunlit and inviting, but frighteningly wide. True, she had solemn duties waiting for her in Bristol, not least the confession of a failure, but for all that, she felt as if she had almost shed the past, and could be glad of the riddance, and was stepping into this unknown world unburdened and unguarded, truly her own mistress.

Aline kissed her affectionately, and wished them both a happy journey. Emma cast frequent glances towards the gatehouse until the last moment, in case Hugh should appear, but he did not; she had still to leave her messages to Aline for delivery. Ivo mounted first, since the bay, as he said, was in a skittish mood and inclined to play tricks, and then turned to give her a steady, sustaining hand as Turstan Fowler hoisted her easily to the pillion.

'Even with two of us up,' said Ivo over his shoulder, smiling, 'this creature can be mettlesome when he's fresh out. For safety hold me fast about the waist, and close your hands on my belt – so, that's well!' He saluted Aline very gracefully and courteously. 'I'll see she reaches Bristol safely, I promise!'

He rode out at the gatehouse in shirt-sleeves, just as he had ridden in, his men, now two only, at his heels, and the pack-pony trotting contentedly under his light load. Emma's arms easily spanned Ivo's slenderness, and the feel of his spare, strong body was warm and muscular and vital through the fine linen. As they threaded the Foregate, now emptying fast, he laid his own left hand over her clasped ones, pressing them firmly against his flat middle, and though she knew he was simply assuring himself that her hold was secure, she could not help feeling that it was also a caress.

She had laughed and shaken her head over Aline's romantic fantasies, refusing to believe in any union between landed nobility and trade, except for mutual profit. Now she was not so sure that wisdom was all with the sceptics.

The hollow where the big, heavy body had lain still showed at least the approximate bulk of Master

Thomas's person, and round about it the grass was trodden, as though someone, or perhaps more than one, had circled all round him as he lay dead. And so they surely had, for here he must have been stripped and searched, the first of those fruitless searches Brother Cadfael had deduced from the events following. Out of the hollow, down to the raised bank of the river, went the track by which he had been dragged, the grass, growing longer as it emerged from shade, all brushed in one direction.

Nor was there any doubt about the traces of blood, meagre though they were. The sliver of birch bark under the tree showed a thin crust, dried black. Careful search found one or two more spots, and a thin smear drawn downhill, where it seemed the dead man had been turned on his back to be hauled the more easily down to the water.

'It's deep here,' said Hugh, standing on the green hillock above the river, 'and undercuts the bank, it would take him well out into the current. I fancy the clothes went after him at once, we may find the rest yet. One man could have done it. Had they been two, they would have carried him.'

'Would you say,' wondered Cadfael, 'that this is a reasonable way he might take to get back to his barge? He'd know his boat lay somewhat down-river from the bridge, I suppose he might try a chance cut through from the Foregate, and overcast by a little way. You see the end of the jetty, where the barge tied up, is only a small way upstream from us. Would you say he was alone, and unsuspecting, when he was struck down?'

Hugh surveyed the ground narrowly. It was not the scene of a struggle, there was the flattened area of the body's fall, and the trampling of feet all round its stillness. The brushings of the grass this way and that were ordered, not the marks of a fight.

'Yes. There was no resistance. Someone crept

behind, and pierced him without word or scruple. He went down and lay. He was on his way back, preferring the byways, and came out a little downstream of where he aimed. Someone had been watching and following him.'

'The same night,' said Philip flatly, 'someone had been watching and following *me*.'

He had their attention at once, both of them eyeing him with sharp interest. 'The same someone?' suggested Cadfael mildly.

'I haven't told you my own part,' said Philip. 'It went out of my head when I stumbled on this place, and guessed at what it meant. What I set out to do was to find out just what I did that night, and prove I never did murder. For I'd come to think that whoever intended this killing had his eye on me from the start. I came from that riot on the jetty, with my head bleeding and my mood for murder, I was a gift, if I could but be out of sight and mind when murder was done.' He told them everything he had discovered, word for word. By the end of it they were both regarding him with intent and frowning concentration.

'The man Fowler?' said Hugh. 'You're sure of this?'

'Walter Renold is sure, and I think him a good witness. The man was there to be seen, I pointed him out, and Wat told me what he'd seen of him that night. Fowler looked in, saw and heard the condition I was in, and went away again for it might be as much as half an hour, says Wat. Then he came back, took one measure of ale to drink, and brought a big flask of geneva spirit.'

'And left with it unopened,' Brother Cadfael recalled, 'as soon as you took yourself off with your misery into the bushes. No need to blush for it now, we've all done as foolishly once or twice in our lives, many of us have bettered it. And the next that's known of him,' he said, meeting Hugh's eyes across the glade, 'is two hours later, when we discover him lying sodden-drunk under a store of trestles by the Foregate.'

'And Wat of the tavern swears he was sober as a bishop when he quit the inn.'

'And I would swear by Wat's judgment,' said Philip stoutly. 'If any man drank that flagon dry in two hours, he says, it would be the death of him, or go very near. And Fowler was testifying in court next day, and little the worse for wear.'

'Good God!' said Hugh, shaking his head. 'I stooped over him, I pulled back the cloak from his shoulders. The fellow reeked. His breath would have felled an ox. Am I losing my wits?'

'Or was it rather the reek you loosed by moving the cloak? I begin to have curious thoughts,' said Cadfael, 'for I fancy that juniper liquor was bought for his outside, not his inside.'

'A costly freak,' mused Hugh, 'the price such liquors are. Cheap enough, though, if it bought him immunity from all suspicion of a thing that could have cost him a deal higher. What was the first thing I said? – more fool I! By the look of him, I said, he must have been here some hours already. And where did he go from there? Safely into an abbey punishment cell, and lay there overnight. How could he be guilty of anything but being a drunken sot? Children and drunken men are the world's only innocents! If murder was done that night, who was to look at a man who had put himself out of the reckoning from the time Master Thomas was last seen alive to the time when his body was brought back to Shrewsbury?'

Cadfael's mind had probed even beyond that point, though nothing beyond was yet clear. 'I have a fancy, Hugh, to look again at the place where we picked up that sodden carcase, if it can be found. Surely an honest drunk should have had his bottle lying beside him for all to see. But I remember none. If we missed it, and some stray scavenger found it by night, still half-full or more, well and good. But if by any chance it was hidden – so that no questions need ever be asked about how much had been drunk, and what manner of head could have borne it – would that be the act of a simple sot? He could not walk through the fairground stinking as he did, whether from outside or in. His baptism was there, where we found him tucked away. So should his bottle have been.'

'And if he was neither simple nor a sot that night, Cadfael, how do you read his comings and goings? He looked in at the tavern, took note of this lad's state, listened to his complaints, and went away – where?'

'As far as Master Thomas's booth, perhaps, to make sure the merchant was there, busy about his wares, and likely to be busy for a while longer? And so back to the tavern to keep watch on Philip, so handy a scapegoat, and so clearly on the way to ending the evening blind and deaf. And afterwards, when he had followed him far enough into the copse to know he was lost to the world, back to dog Master Thomas's footsteps as he made his way back to the barge. Made his way, that is, as far as this place.'

'It is all conjecture,' said Hugh reasonably.

'It is. But read it so, and it makes sense.'

'Then back with his flask of spirits ready, to slip unseen into a place withdrawn and private, and become the wretched object we found. How long would it take, would you say, to kill his man, search and strip him down to the river?'

'Counting the time spent following him unseen, and returning unnoticed to the fairground after all was done, more than an hour of those two hours lost between drunk and sober. No,' said Cadfael sombrely, 'I do not think he spent any of that time drinking.'

'Was it he, also, who boarded the barge? But no, that

he could not, he was at the sheriff's court. Concerning the merchant of Shotwick, we already know his slayer.'

'We know one of them,' said Cadfael. 'Can any of these matters be separated from the rest? I think not. This pursuit is all one.'

'You do grasp,' said Hugh, after a long moment of furious thought, 'what it is we are saying? Here are these two men, one proven a murderer, the other suspect. And yesterday the one of them fetched down the other to his death. Coldly, expertly ... Before we say more,' said Hugh abruptly, casting a final glance about the glade, 'let's do as you suggested, look again at the place where we found him lying.'

## Chapter Two

Philip, who was learning how to listen and be silent, followed at their heels all the way back through the orchards and gardens of the Gaye. Neither of them found fault with his persistence. He had earned his place, and had no intention of being put off. All the larger boats were already gone from the jetty. Soon the labourers would begin dismantling the boards and piers until the following year, and stowing them away in the abbey storehouses. Along the Foregate stalls were being taken down and stacked for removal, while two of the abbey carts worked their way along from the horse-fair towards the gatehouse.

'More than halfway along, I remember,' said Hugh, 'and well back from the roadway. There were few lights, most of the stalls here were for the country people who come in by the day. Somewhere in this stretch.'

There had been trestles stacked that night, and canvas awnings leaning against them ready for use. This morning there were also piles of trestles and boards, ready now to be put away for the next fair. They surveyed all the likely area, but to lay a finger on the exact place was impossible. One of the collecting carts had reached this stretch, and two lay servants were hoisting the heaped planks aboard, and stacking the trestles one within another in high piles. Cadfael watched as the ground was gradually cleared.

'You've found some unexpected discards,' he commented, for a corner of the cart carried a small pile of odd objects, a large shoe, a short cotte, bedraggled but by no means old or ragged, a child's wooden doll with one arm missing, a green capuchon, a drinking-horn.

'There'll be many more such, brother,' said the carter, grinning, 'before the whole ground's cleared. Some will be claimed. I fancy some child will want to know where she lost her doll. And the cotte is good stuff, some young gentleman took a drop too much, and forgot to collect that when he moved. The shoe's as good as new, too, and a giant's size, somebody may sneak in, shamefaced, to ask after that. I hope he had not far to go home with only one. But it wasn't a rowdy night – not like many a night I've seen.' He slid powerful arms under a stack of trestles, and hoisted them bodily. 'You'd hardly credit where we found that flagon there.'

His nod indicated the front of the car, to which Cadfael had hitherto devoted no attention. Slung by a thin leather thong from the shaft hung a flattened glass bottle large enough to hold a quart. 'Stuck on top of the canvas over one of the country stalls. An old woman who sells cheeses had the stall, I know her, she comes every year, and seeing she's not so nimble nowadays, we put up the stall for her the night before the fair opened. The bottle all but brained Daniel here, when we took it down, this morning! Fancy tossing a bottle like that away as if it had no value! He could have got a free drink at Wat's if he'd taken it back, whoever he was.'

His armful of trestles thumped into the cart, and he turned to heave a stack of boards after it.

'It came from Wat's tavern then, did it?' asked Cadfael, very thoughtfully gazing.

'It has his mark on the thong. We all know where

they belong, these better vessels. But they're not often left for us.'

'And where was the stall where this one was left?' asked Hugh over Cadfael's shoulder.

'Not ten yards back from where you're standing.' They could not resist looking back to measure, and it would do. It would do very well. 'The odd thing is, the old woman swore, when she came to put out her wares, that there was a stink of spirits about the place. Said she could smell it in her skirts at night, as if she'd been wading in it. But after the first day she forgot about it. She's half-Welsh, and has a touch of the strange about her, I daresay she imagined it.'

Cadfael would have said, rather, that she had a keen nose, and some knowledge of the distilling of spirits, and had accurately assessed the cause of her uneasiness. Somewhere in the grass close to her stall, he was now certain, a good part of that quart of liquor had been poured out generously over clothing and ground, no wonder the turf retained it. A taste of it, perhaps, to scent the breath and steady the mind, might have gone down a throat; but no more, for the mind had been steady indeed, when stranger stooped over its fleshly habitation, and sniffed at its flagrant drunkenness. Strangers, all but one! Cadfael began to see what could hardly be called light, for he was looking into a profound darkness.

'It so happens,' he said, 'that we have some business with Walter Renold. Will you let us take your bottle back to him? You shall have the credit for it with him.'

'Take it, brother,' agreed the carter cheerfully, unleashing the bottle from the shaft. 'Tell him Rychart Nyall sent it. Wat knows me.'

'Nothing in it, I suppose, when you found it?' hazarded Cadfael, hefting the fated thing in one hand.

'Never a drop, brother! Fair-goers may abandon the bottle, but they make sure of what's inside before they fall senseless!'

The boards were stowed, the stripped ground lay trampled and naked, the cart moved on. It would take no more than a handful of days and the next summer showers, and all the green, fine hair would grow again, and the bald clay coil into ringlets.

'It's mine, surely,' said Wat, receiving the bottle into a large hand. 'The only one of its kind I'm short. Who buys this measure of spirits, even at a fair? Who has the money to afford it? And who chooses it afore decent ale and wine? Not many! I've known men desperate to sink their souls fast, at whatever cost, but seldom at a fair. They turn genial at fairs, even the sad fellows get the wind of it, and mellow. I marvelled at that one, even when he asked for it and paid the price, but he was plainly some lord's servant, he had his orders. He had money, and I sell liquor. But yes, if it's of worth to you, that same fellow Philip here knows of, that's the measure he bought.'

A retired corner of Wat's large taproom was as good a place as any to sit down and think before action, and try to make sense of what they had gathered.

'Wat has just put words to it,' said Cadfael. 'We should have been quicker to see. He was plainly some lord's servant, he had his orders, he had money. One man from a lord's household suborned to murder by an unknown, one such setting out on his own account to enrich himself by murder and theft, that I could believe in. But two? From the same household? No, I think not! They never strayed from their own manor. They served but one lord.'

'Their own? *Corbière*?' whispered Philip, the breath knocked out of him by the enormity of the implications. 'But he ... The way I heard it, the groom tried to ride him down. Struck him into the dust when he tried to stop him. How can you account for that? There's no sense in it.'

'Wait! Take it from the beginning. Say that on the night Master Thomas died, Fowler was sent out to deal with him, to get possessions of whatever it is someone so much desires. His lord has spied out the land, told him of a handy scapegoat who may yet be useful, given him money for the drink that will put him out of the reckoning when the deed is done. The man would demand immunity, he must be *seen* to be out of the reckoning. His lord keeps in close touch, joins us when we go forth to look for the missing merchant. Recollect, Hugh, it was *Corbière*, not we, who discovered his truant man. *We* had passed him by, and that would not have done. He must be found, must be seen to be so drunk as to have been helpless and harmless some hours, and must then be manifestly under lock and key many hours more. Ten murders could have been committed that night, and no one would ever have looked at Turstan Fowler.'

'All for nothing,' pointed out Hugh. 'Sooner or later he had to tell his master that murder had been done in vain. Master Thomas did not carry his treasure on him.'

'I doubt if he found that out until morning, when he had his man let out of prison. Therefore he brought Fowler to lay evidence that made sure the finger was pointed at Philip here, and while we were all blamelessly busy at the sheriff's hearing, sent his second man to search the barge. And again, vainly. Am I making sense of it thus far?'

'Sound enough,' said Hugh sombrely. 'The worst is yet to come. Which man, do you suppose, did the work that day?'

'I doubt if they ever involved the young one. Two were enough to do the business. The groom Ewald, I think. Those two were the hands that did all. But they were not the mind.'

'That same night, then, they broke into the booth, and made their search there, and still without success. The next night came the attack that killed Euan of Shotwick.' Hugh said no word of the violation of Master Thomas's coffin. 'And, as I remember you argued, once more in vain. So far, possible enough. But come to yesterday's thorny business. For God's sake, how can sense be made of that affair? I was there watching the man, I saw him change colour, I swear it! Shock and anger and affronted honour, he showed them all. He would not send for the groom, for fear a fellow-servant might warn him, he would fetch him himself. He placed himself between his man and the gate, he risked maiming or worse, trying to halt his flight ...'

'All that,' agreed Cadfael heavily, 'and yet there is sense in it all, though a more abominable sense even than you or I dreamed of. Ewald was in the stables, there was no escape for him unless he could break out of our walls. Corbière came at the sheriff's bidding, and was told all. His man was detected past denying, and driven into a corner, he would pour out everything he knew, lay the load on his lord. Consider the order in which everything happened from that moment. Fowler had been at the butts, and had his arbalest with him. Corbière set off to summon Ewald from the stables, Turstan made to follow him, yes, and some words were exchanged that sent him back. But what words? They were too distant to be heard. Nor could we guess what was said in the stable-yard. We waited – you'll agree? – several minutes before they came. Long enough for Corbière to tell the groom how things stood, bid him keep his head, promise him escape. Bring the horse, *I* will ensure that only I stand between you and the gate, pick your moment, mount and away. Lie up in hiding – doubtless at his manor –

and you shan't be the loser. But make it clear that I have no part in this – attack me, make it good for your part, I will make it good for mine. And so he did – the finest player of a part that ever I saw. He set himself between Ewald and the gate, and between them they used the lively horse to edge us all that way. He made a gallant grab at the rein, and took a heavy fall, and the groom was clear.'

They were both gazing at him in mute fascination, wide-eyed.

'Except that his lord had one more trick to play,' said Cadfael. 'He had never intended to let him go. Escape was too great a risk, he might yet be taken, and open his mouth. "Fetch him down!" said Corbière, and Turstan Fowler did it. Without compunction, like master, like man. A dangerous mouth – dangerous to both of them – closed at no cost.'

There was a long moment of appalled silence. Even Beringar, whose breadth of mind could conceive, though with detestation, prodigies of evil and treachery, was shocked out of words. Philip stared aghast, huge of eye, and came slowly to his feet. His experience was narrow, local and decent, it was hard to grasp that men could be monsters.

'You mean it! You believe it! But this man – he visits her, he pays court to her! And you say there was something he wanted from her uncle, and has missed getting – not on his body, not in his barge, not in his booth – Where is there left, but with Emma? And we delay here!'

'Emma is with my wife,' said Hugh reasonably, 'in the abbey guest-hall, what harm can come to her there?'

'What harm?' cried Philip passionately. 'When you tell me we are dealing not with men, but with devils?' And he whirled on the heel of a trodden shoe and ran, out of the tavern and arrow-straight along the road towards the Foregate, long legs flashing.

Cadfael and Hugh were left regarding each other mutely across the table, but for no more than a moment. 'By God,' said Hugh then, 'we learn of the innocents! Come on, we'd best make haste after. The lad's shaken me!'

Philip came to the guest-hall out of breath. With chest heaving from his running he asked for Aline, and she came out, smiling but alone.

'Why, Philip, what's the matter?' Then she thought she knew, and was sorry for a lovesick boy who came too late even to take a dignified farewell, and receive what comfort a few kind words, costing nothing, could provide him. 'Oh, Philip, I am sorry you've missed her, but they could not linger, it was necessary to leave in good time. She would have wished me to say her goodbye to you, and wish you ... The words faded on her lips. 'Philip, what is it? What ails you?'

'Gone?' he said, hard and shrill. 'She's gone? *They*, you said! Who? *Who* is gone with her?'

'Why, she left with Messire Corbière, he has offered to escort her to Bristol with his sister, who goes to a convent there. It seemed a lucky chance ... *Philip!* What have I said? What is wrong?' He had let out a great groan of fury and anguish, and even reached a hand to grip her wrist.

'Where? Where is he taking her? *Now, today!*'

'To his manor of Stanton Cobbold for tonight – his sister is there ...'

But he was gone, the instant she had named the place, running like a purposeful demon, and not towards the gatehouse, but across the court to the stable-yard. There was no time to ask leave of any man, or respect any man's property, Whatever the consequences. Philip took the best-looking horse he saw ready to hand, which by luck – Philip's luck, not the owner's! – stood saddled and waiting for departure, on a tether in the yard. Before Aline, bewildered and frightened, reached the doorway of the hall, Philip was already out of the gate, and a furious groom was haring across the court in voluble and hopeless pursuit.

Since the nearest way to the road leading south towards Stretton and Stanton Cobbold was to turn left at the gate, and left again by the narrow track on the near side of the bridge, Brother Cadfael and Hugh Beringar, hastening along the Foregate, saw nothing of the turmoil that attended Philip's departure. They came to the gatehouse and the great court without any intimation that things could have gone amiss. There were still guests departing, the normal bustle of the day after the fair, but nothing to give them pause. Hugh made straight for the guest-hall, and Cadfael, following hard on his heels, was suddenly arrested by a large hand on his shoulder, and a familiar, hearty voice hailing him in amiable Welsh.

'The very man I was looking for! I come to make my farewells, brother, and thank you for your companionship. A good fair! I'm off to my boat now, and away home with a handsome profit.'

Rhodri ap Huw beamed merrily from within the covert of his black beard and thorn-bush of black hair.

'Far from a good fair to two, at least, who came looking for a profit,' said Cadfael ruefully.

'Ah, but in cash, or some other currency? Though it all comes down to cash in the end, cash or power. What else do men labour for?'

'For a cause, perhaps, now and then one. You said yourself, I remember, no place like one of the great fairs for meeting someone you'd liefer not be seen meeting. Nowhere so solitary as the middle of a market place!' And he added mildly: 'I daresay Owain

Gwynedd himself may have had his intelligencers here. Though they'd need to have good English,' he said guilelessly, 'to gather much profit from it.'

'They would so. No use employing me. I daresay you're right, though. Owain needs to have forward information, as much as any man, if he's to keep his princedom safe, and add a few more miles to it here and there. Now I wonder which of all these traders I've rubbed shoulders with will be making his report in Owain's ear!'

'And what advice he'll be giving him,' said Cadfael.

Rhodri stroked his splendid beard, and his dark eyes twinkled. 'I think he might take him word that the message Earl Ranulf expected from the south – who knows, maybe even from overseas – will never be delivered, and if he wants to get the best out of the hour, he should be aiming to enlarge his rule away from Chester's borders, for the earl will be taking no risks, but looking well to his own. Owain would do better to make his bid in Maelienydd and Elfael, and let Ranulf alone.'

'Now I come to think,' mused Cadfael, 'it would be excellent cover for Owain's intelligencers to ask the help of an interpreter in these parts, and be seen to need him. Tongues wag more freely before the deaf man.'

'A good thought,' approved Rhodri. 'Someone should suggest it to Owain.' Though there was every indication that the prince of Gwynedd needed no other man's wits to fortify his own, but had been lavishly endowed by God in the first place. Cadfael wondered how many other tongues this simple merchant knew. French, almost certainly enough for his purposes. Flemish, possibly a little, he had undoubtedly travelled in Flanders. It would be no surprise if he knew some Latin, too.

'You'll be coming to Saint Peter's Fair next year?'

'I may, brother, I may, who knows! Will you come forth again and speak for me, if I do?'

'Gladly. I'm a Gwynedd man myself. Take my greetings back with you to the mountains. And good speed on the way!'

'God keep you!' said Rhodri, still beaming, and clapped him buoyantly. on the shoulder, and set off towards the riverside.

Hugh had no sooner set foot in the hall when Aline flew into his arms, with a cry of relief and desperation mingled, and began to pour into his ears all her bewilderment and anxiety.

'Oh, Hugh, I think I must have done something terrible! Either that, or Philip Corviser has gone mad. He was here asking after Emma, and when I told him she was gone he rushed away like a madman, and there's a merchant from Worcester in the stables accusing him of stealing his horse and making off with it, and what it all means I daren't guess, but I'm afraid ...'

Hugh held her tenderly, dismayed and solicitous. 'Emma's gone? But she was coming home with us. What happened to change it?'

'You know he's been paying attentions to her ... He came this morning asking for you – he said he has a sister who is entering the nunnery at Minchinbarrow, and since he must escort her there, and it's barely five miles from Bristol, he could as well take Emma home in his sister's company. He said they'd sleep overnight at his manor, and set off tomorrow. Emma said yes, and I thought no wrong, why should I? But the very name has sent Philip off like a man demented ...'

'Corbière?' demanded Hugh, holding her off by the shoulders to peer anxiously into her face.

'Yes! Yes, Ivo, of course – but what's so wrong in that? He takes her to his sister at Stanton Cobbold – I thought it ideal, so did she, and you were not here to say yes or no. Besides, she is her own mistress …'

True, the girl had a will of her own, and liked the man who had made the offer, and was flattered at being singled out for his favours. Even for the sake of her own independence she would have chosen to go, and Hugh, had he been present, would not then have known or suspected enough to prevent. He tightened his arms comfortingly round his trembling wife, his cheek pressed against her hair. 'My love, my heart, you could not have done anything but what you did, and I should have done the same. But I must go after. No questions now, you shall know everything later. We'll bring her back – there'll be no harm done …'

'It's true, then!' whispered Aline, her breath fluttering against his throat. 'There's reason to fear harm? I've let her go into danger?'

'You could not stop her. She chose to go. Think no more of your part, you played none – how could you know? Where's Constance? Love, I hate to leave you like this …'

He was thinking, of course, like all men, she thought, that any grievous upset to his wife in this condition was a potential upset to his son. That roused her. She was not the girl to keep a man dancing anxious attention on her, even if she had a wife's claim on him, when he was needed more urgently elsewhere. She drew herself resolutely out of his arms.

'Of course you must leave me. I've taken no harm, and shall take none. Go, quickly! They have a good three hours start of you, and besides, if you delay, Philip may run his head into trouble alone. Send quickly for what men you can muster, and I'll go see what I can do to placate the merchant whose horse has been borrowed …' He was loath, all the same, to let go of her. She took his head between her hands, kissed him hard, and turned him about just as Cadfael came in at the hall door.

'She's gone with Corbière,' said Hugh, conveying news in the fewest words possible. 'Bound for his one Shropshire manor. The boy's off after them, and so must I. I'll send word to Prestcote to have a guard follow as fast as may be. You'll be here to take care of Aline ...'

Aline doubted that, seeing the spark flare up in Brother Cadfael's bright and militant eye. Hastily she said: 'I need no one to nurse me. Only go – both of you!'

'I have licence,' said Cadfael, clutching at virtue to cover his ardour. 'Abbot Radulfus gave me the charge of seeing that his guest came to no harm under his roof, and I'll stretch that to extend beyond his roof, and make it good, too. You have a horse to spare, Hugh, besides that raw-boned dapple of yours. Come on! It's a year since you and I rode together.'

## Chapter Three

The manor of Stanton Cobbold lay a good seventeen miles from Shrewsbury, in the south of the shire, and cheek by jowl with the large property of the bishops of Hereford in those parts, which covered some nine or ten manors. The road lay through the more open and sunlit stretches of the Long Forest, and at its southernmost fringe plunged in among the hump-backed hills at the western side of a long, bare ridge that ran for some miles. Here and there a wooded valley backed into its bare flank, and into one of these Corbière turned, along a firm cart-track. It was the height of the early afternoon then, the sun at its highest, but even so the crowding trees cast sudden chill and shadow. The bay horse had worked off his high spirits, and went placidly under his double burden. Once in the forest they had halted briefly, and Ivo had produced wine and oat-cakes as refreshment on the journey, and paid Emma every possible delicate attention. The day was fair, the countryside strange to her and beautiful, and she was embarked on an agreeable adventure. She approached Stanton Cobbold with only the happiest anticipation, flattered by Ivo's deference, and eager to meet his sister.

A rivulet ran alongside the track, coming down from the ridge. The path narrowed, and the trees closed in.

'We are all but home,' said Ivo over his shoulder; and

in a few minutes more the rising ground opened before them into a narrow, level plot enclosed before with a wooden stockade. Within, the manor house backed solidly into the hillside, trees at the back, trees shutting it in darkly at either end. A boy came running to open the gate for them, and they rode into the enclosure. Barns and byres lined the stockade within. The manor itself showed a long undercroft of stone, buttressed, and pierced with two doors wide enough for carts, and a living floor above, also of stone for most of its length, where the great hall and the kitchens and pantries lay, but at the right, stone gave place to timber, and stone mullions to wooden window-frames and stout shutters; and this wooden living apartment was taller than the stone portion, and seemed to have an additional floor above the solar. A tall stone stair led up to the hall door.

'Modest enough,' said Ivo, turning his head to smile at her, 'but it has room and a welcome for you.'

He was well served. Grooms came running before the horse had halted, a maid appeared in the hall doorway, and began to flutter down to meet them.

Ivo kicked his feet free of the stirrups, swung a leg nimbly over the horse's bowing head, and leaped down, waving Turstan Fowler aside, to stretch up his arms to Emma and lift her down herself. Her slight weight gave him no trouble, he held her aloft for a long moment to prove it, laughing, before he set her down.

'Come, I'll take you up to the solar.' He put off the maid with a flick of his hand, and she stood aside and followed them demurely up the steps, but let them go on without her when they reached the hall. The thick stone walls struck inward with a palpable chill. The hall was large and lofty, the high ceiling smoke-stained, but now, in the summer, the huge fireplace was empty and cold. The mullioned windows let in air far more genial than that within, and a comforting light, but they were narrow, and could do little to temper the oppression of the room. 'Not my most amiable home,' said Ivo with a grimace, 'but in these Welsh borders we built for defence, not for comfort. Come up to the solar. The timber end was built on later, but even there this is a chill, dark house. Even on summer evenings we need some firing.'

A short staircase at the end of the hall led up to a broad gallery and a pair of doors. 'The chapel,' he said, indicating that on the left. 'There are two small bedchambers above, dark, since they look into the hillside and the trees at close quarters. And in here, if you'll forgive me while I attend to your baggage and mine, and see the horses stabled, I'll rejoin you shortly.'

The solar into which he led her contained a massive table, a carved bench, cushioned chairs, tapestries draping the walls, and rugs on the floor, and was a place of some comfort and elegance, if also somewhat dim and cold, chiefly by reason of the looming hillside and the shrouding trees, and the narrow windows that let in so little of the day, and so filtered through heavy branches. Here there was no fireplace, the only chimney serving the hall and the kitchens; but the centre of the floor was set with large paving stones to make a hearth proof against cinders, and on this square a brazier burned, even on this summer day. Charcoal and wood glowed, discreetly massed, to give a central spark of comfort without smoke. Summer sunlight failed to warm through the arm's-length thickness of the stone walls below, and here the sun, though confronted only with friendly timber, hardly ever reached.

Emma went forward into the room and stood looking about her curiously. She heard Ivo close the door between them, but it was only a very small sound in a large silence.

She had expected his sister to appear immediately on his return, and felt a pang of disappointment, though she knew it was unreasonable. He had sent no word ahead, how could the girl have known? She might, with good reason, be out walking on the open hill in the full summer warmth, or she might have duties elsewhere. When she did come, it would be to the pleasure of having her brother home, and with a visitor of her own sex and approximate age, into the bargain, and to hear that she was to have her will without further delay. Yet her absence was a disappointment, and his failure to remark on it or apologise for it was a check to her eagerness.

She began to explore the room, interested in everything. Her own city home was cushioned and comfortable by comparison, though no less dark and shut in, if not among trees, among the buildings the trees provided. She was aware that she had been born to comparative wealth, but wealth concentrated into one commodious and well-furbished dwelling, whereas this border manor represented only perhaps a tenth of what Ivo possessed, without regard to the land attached to all those manors. He had said himself that this was not the most genial of his homes, yet it held sway over she could not guess how many miles of land, and how many free tenants and unfree villeins. It was another world. She had looked at it from a distance, and been dazzled, but never to blindness.

She felt a conviction suddenly that it was not for her, though whether she was glad or sorry remained a mystery.

All the same, there was knowledge and taste here beyond her experience. The brazier was a beautiful thing, a credit to the smith who made it; on three braced legs like saplings, the fire-basket a trellis of vine-leaves. If it had a fault, it was that it was raised rather too high, she thought, to be completely stable. The cushions of the chairs were of fine embroidery of hunting scenes, though dulled by use and friction and the touch of slightly greasy fingers. On a shelf built under the table there were books, a psalter, a vellum folder of music, and a faded treatise with strange diagrams. The carving of chairs and table and bench-ends was like live plants growing. The tapestries that covered all the walls between windows and door were surely old, rich, wonderfully worked, and once had had glorious colours that showed still, here and there, in the protected folds; but they were smoke-blackened almost beyond recognition, rotted here and there into tinder. She parted a fold, and the hound, plunging with snarling jaws and stretched paws between her fingers, disintegrated into powdery dust, and floated on the air in slow dissolution. She let fall the threads she held, and retreated in dismay. The very dust on her palms felt like ash.

She waited, but nobody came. Probably the time she waited was not as long as she supposed, by no means as long as it felt to her, but it seemed an age, a year of her life.

In the end, she thought she might not be offending by wandering along the gallery into the chapel. She might at least hear if there was any activity below. Ivo had bought Flemish tapestries for his new Cheshire manor, he might well be unbaling them and delighting in their fresh colours. She could forgive a degree of neglect in such circumstances.

She set her hand to the latch of the door, and trustingly lifted it. The door did not give. She tried it again, more strongly, but the barrier remained immovable. No doubt of it, the door was locked.

What she felt first was sheer incredulity, even amusement, as if some foolish accident had dropped a latch and shut her in by mistake. Then came the instinctive wish of every creature locked in, to get out; and only after that the flare of alarm and the startled and furious reappraisal, in search of understanding. No mistake, no! Ivo's own hand had turned the key on her.

She was not the girl to fall into a frenzy and batter on the door. What good would that do? She stood quite still with the latch in her hand, while her wits ran after truth as fiercely as the hound in the tapestry after the hart. She was here in an upstairs room, with no other door, and windows not only narrow for even her slender body to pass through, but high above ground, by reason of the slope. There was no way out until someone unlocked the door.

She had come with him guilelessly, in good faith, and he turned into her gaoler. What did he want of her? She knew she had beauty, but suddenly was certain he would not go to such trouble on that account. Not her person, then, and there was only one thing in her possession for which someone had been willing to go to extremes. Deaths had followed it wherever it passed. One of those deaths a servant of his had helped to bring about, and he had dealt out summary justice. A sordid attack for gain, a theft that accidentally ended in murder, and the stolen property found to prove it! She had accepted that as everyone had accepted it. To doubt it was to see beyond into a pit too black to be credited, but she was peering into that darkness now. It was Ivo, and no other, who had caged her.

If she could not pass through the windows, the letter she carried could, though that would be to risk others finding it. Its weight was light, it would not carry far. All the same, she crossed to the windows and peered out through the slits at the slope of grass and the fringe of trees below; and there, sprawled at ease against the bole of a beech with his arbalest beside him, was

Turstan Fowler, looking up idly at these very windows. When he caught sight of her face between the timbers of the frame, he grinned broadly. No help there.

She withdrew from the window, trembling. Quickly she drew up, from its resting-place between her breasts, the small, tightly-rolled vellum bag she had carried ever since Master Thomas had hung it about her neck, before they reached Shrewsbury. It measured almost the length of her hand, but was thin as two fingers of that same hand, and the thread on which it hung was of silk, cobweb-fine. It did not need a very large hiding-place. She coiled the silk thread about it, and rolled it carefully into the great swathe of blue-black tresses coiled within her coif of silken net, until its shape was utterly shrouded and lost. When she had adjusted the net to hold it secure, and every strand of hair lay to all appearances undisturbed, she stood with hands clasped tightly to steady them, and drew in long breaths until the racing of her heart was calmed. Then she put the brazier between herself and the door, and looking up across the room, felt the heart she had just steeled to composure leap frantically in her breast.

Once again she had failed to hear the key turn in the lock. He kept his defences well oiled and silent. He was there in the doorway, smiling with easy confidence, closing the door behind him without taking his eyes from her. She knew by the motion of his arm and shoulder that he had transferred the key to the inner side, and again turned it. Even in his own manor, with his household about him, he took no risks. Even with no more formidable opponent than Emma Vernold! It was, in its way, a compliment, but one she could have done without.

Since he could not know whether she had or had not tried the door, she chose to behave as if nothing had happened to disturb her. She acknowledged his entrance with an expectant smile, and opened her lips to force out some harmless enquiry, but he was before her.

'Where is it? Give it to me freely, and come to no harm. I would advise it.'

He was in no hurry, and he was still smiling. She saw now that his smile was a deliberate gloss, as cold, smooth and decorative as a coat of gilt. She gazed at him wide-eyed, the blank, bewildered stare of one suddenly addressed in an unknown tongue. 'I don't understand you! What is it I'm to give you?'

'Dear girl, you know only too well. I want the letter your uncle was carrying to Earl Ranulf of Chester, the same he should have delivered at the fair, by prior agreement, to Euan of Shotwick, my noble kinsman's eyes and ears.' He was willing to go softly with her, since time was now no object, he even found the prospect amusing, and was prepared to admire her playing of the game, provided he got his own way in the end. 'Never tell me, sweet, that you have not even heard of any such letter. I doubt if you make as good a liar as I do.'

'Truly,' she said, shaking her head helplessly, 'I understand you not at all. There is nothing else I could say to you, for I know nothing of a letter. If my uncle carried one, as you claim, he never confided in me. Do you suppose a man of business takes his womenfolk into his confidence over important matters? You're mistaken in him if you believe that.'

Corbière came forward an idle pace or two into the room, and she saw that no trace of his limp remained. The brazier had burned into a steady, scarlet glow, the light from it reflected like the burnish of sunset along the waving gold of his hair. 'So I thought,' he agreed, and laughed at the memory. 'It took me a long time, too long, to arrive at you, my lady. *I* would not have trusted a woman, no ... But Master Thomas, it seems, had other ideas. And I grant you, he had an unusual young woman to deal with. For what it's worth, I admire you. But I shall not let that stand in my way, believe me. What you hold is too precious to leave me any scruples, even if I were given to such weaknesses.'

'But I don't hold it! I can't give you what I have not in my possession. How can I convince you?' she demanded, with the first spurt of impatience and indignation, though she knew in advance that she was wasting all pretences. He knew.

He shook his head at her, smiling. 'It is not in your baggage. We've taken apart even the seams of your saddle-bags. Therefore it is here, on your person. There is no other possibility. It was not on your uncle, it was neither in his barge nor in his booth. Who was left but you? You, and Euan of Shotwick, if I had somehow let a messenger slip through my guard. You, I knew, would keep, and come tamed to my hand – but for a sudden qualm I had, that you might have sent it back in Thomas's coffin for safe-keeping, but that was to overrate you, my dear, clever as you are. And Euan never received it. Who was then left, but you? Not his crew – all of them far too simple, even if he had not had orders to keep strict secrecy, as I know he had. I doubt if he told even you what was in the letter.'

It was true, she had no idea of its contents. She had simply been given it to wear and guard, as the obvious innocent who would never come under suspicion of being anyone's courier, but its importance had been impressed upon her most powerfully. Lives, her uncle had said, hung upon its safe delivery, or, failing that, its safe return to the sender. Or, in the last resort, its total destruction.

'I am tired of telling you,' she said forcefully, 'that you are wrong in supposing that I know anything about it, or believe it ever existed but in your imagination. You brought me here, my lord, on the pretext of providing me the companionship of your sister, and conducting us both to Bristol. Do you intend to do as you promised?'

He threw his head back and laughed aloud, the red glow dancing on his fine cheekbones. 'You would not have come with me if there had not been a woman in the story. If you behave sensibly now you may yet meet, some day, the only sister I have. She's married to one of Ranulf's knights, and keeps me informed of what goes on in Ranulf's court. But devil a nun she'd ever have made, even if she were not already a wife. But send you safe home to Bristol – yes, that I'll do, when you've given me what I want from you. And what I will have!' he added with a snap, and his shapely, smiling lips thinned and tightened into a sword-blade.

There was a moment, then, when she almost considered obeying him, and giving up what she had kept so obstinately through so many shocks. Fear was a reality by this time, but so was anger, all the more fierce because she was so resolutely suppressing it. He came a step towards her, his smile as narrow as a cat's bearing down on a bird, and she moved just as steadily to keep the brazier between them; that also amused him, but he had ample patience.

'I don't understand,' she said, frowning as if she had begun to feel genuine curiosity, 'why you should set such store on a letter. If I had it, do you think I should refuse it to you, when I'm in your power? But why does it matter to you so much? What can there be in a mere letter?'

'Fool girl, there can be life and death in a letter,' he said condescending to her simplicity, 'wealth, power, even land to be won or lost. Do you know what that single packet could be worth? To King Stephen, his kingdom entire! To me, maybe an earldom. And to a number of others, their necks! For I think you must know, for all your innocence, that Robert of Gloucester has his plans made to bring the Empress Maud to England, and make a fight of it for her claim to the throne, and has been touting through his agents here to get Earl Ranulf's support for her cause when they do land. My noble kinsman has a hard heart, and has demanded proof of the strength of that cause before he lifts a hand or stirs a foot to commit himself. Names, numbers, every detail, if I know my Ranulf, they've been forced to set down in writing for him. All the tale of the king's enemies, the names of all those who pay him lip service now but are preparing to betray him. There could be as many as fifty names on the list, and it will serve, believe me, for Ranulf's ruin no less, since if his name is not there, he had reached the point of considering adding it. What will not King Stephen give, to have that delivered into his hand? All committed to writing, it may be even the date they plan to sail, and the port where they hope to land. All his enemies cut off before they can forgather, a prison prepared for Maud before ever she gets foot ashore. That, my child, is what I propose to offer to the king, and never doubt but I shall get my price for it.'

She stood staring at him with drawn brows and shocked eyes across the brazier, and felt her blood chill in her veins and all her body grow cold. And he was not even a partisan! He had killed, or procured others to kill for him, three times already, not for a cause, but coldly and methodically for his own gain and advancement. He cared nothing at all for which of them wore the crown, Stephen or Maud. If he could have got his hands rather on information of value to Maud, and felt that she was likely to prevail and reward him well, he would have betrayed Stephen and all his supporters just as blithely.

For the first time she was terrified, the weight of all those imperilled lives lay upon her heart like a great stone. She had no doubt that this estimate of what would be in the letter must be very close to the truth, close enough to destroy a great many men who adhered to the same side her uncle had served with devotion. He had been a passionate partisan, and it had cost him his life. Now, unless she could bring about a miracle, the message he had carried would cost many more lives, bloodshed, bereavement, ruin. And all for the enrichment and advancement of Ivo Corbière! She had followed and supported Master Thomas as a matter of family loyalty. Now that meant nothing any longer, and all she felt was a desperate desire to avoid more killing, not to betray any man on either side of the quarrel to his enemies on the other. To help every fugitive, to hide every hunted man, to keep the wives unwidowed and the children still fathered, was better by far than to fight and kill either for Stephen or for Maud.

And she would not let him have them! Whatever the cost, he should not tread his way unscathed to his earldom over other men's faces.

'I have nothing against you,' Corbière was saying, confident and at ease. 'Give me the letter, and you shall reach Bristol in safety, and not be the loser. But don't think I'll scruple to pay you in full, either, if you thwart me.'

She stood fixed and still, her hands cupping her face, as though pressing hard to contain fear. The tips of her fingers worked unseen under the edge of her tissue net into the coils of her hair, feeling for the little cylinder of vellum, but face to face with her he saw no movement at all.

'Come, you are not so attractive to me that you need fear rape,' he said, disdainfully smiling, 'provided you are sensible, but for all that, it would be no hardship to me to strip you with my own hands, if you are obstinate. It might even give me pleasure, if the act proves stimulating. Give, or have it taken from you by force. You should know by now that I let no man stand in my way, much less a little shopkeeper's girl of no account.'

Of no account! No, she had never been of any account to him, never for a moment, only of use in his ruthless pursuit of his own ambitous interests. Still she stood as if frozen, except that when he advanced upon her at leisure, his smile now wolfish and hungry, she circled inch by inch to keep the brazier between them. Its heart was a red glow. She stood close, as if only that core of warmth gave her some comfort and protection; and suddenly she tore down the coil of her hair and clawed out the letter, tearing off her silken net with it in her haste. She dared not simply cast it into the fire, it might roll clear or be too easily retrieved. She made a desperate lunge, and thrusting it deep into the heart of the glow, held it there for an agonised moment, snatching back burned fingers with a faint cry that sounded half of pain and half of triumph.

He uttered a bellow of rage, and lunged as quickly to snatch it out again, but the net had flared at a touch, tiny worms of fire climbed to lick his hand, and all he touched of the precious letter, before he recoiled, was the wax of the seal, which had melted at once, and clung searingly to his fingers as he wrung them and whined with pain. She heard herself laughing, and could not believe she was the source of the sound. She heard him frantically cursing her, but he was too intent on recovering his prize to turn upon her then. He tore off his cotte, wrapped a corner of the skirt about his hand, and leaned to grasp again at the glowing cylinder thrust upright in the fire-basket. And he would get it, defaced and incomplete, perhaps, but enough for his purpose. The outer covering was not yet burned through everywhere. He should not have it, she would not bear it! She stooped as he snatched at it, clutched with her good hand at the leg of the brazier, and overturned it over his ankles and feet.

He screamed aloud and leaped back. Glowing coals flew, cascading over the floor, starting a brown furrow, a flurry of smoke and a stink of burning wood across the nearest rug, and reached the tinder-dry skirts of the tapestries on the wall between the two windows. There was a strange sound like a great indrawn breath, and an instant serpent of flame climbed the wall, and after it a tree of fire grew, thickened, put out lightning branches on all sides, enveloped all the space between the windows, and coursed both ways like hounds at fault, to reach the dusty hangings on the neighbouring walls. A brittle shell of fire encased the room before Emma could even stir from her horrified stillness. She saw the huntsmen and huntresses in the tapestries blaze for an instant into quivering life, the hounds leap, the forest trees shimmer in fierce light, before they disintegrated into glittering dust. Smoke rose from a dozen burning fragments over half the floor, and vision dimmed rapidly.

Somewhere in that abrupt hell beyond the hearth, Ivo Corbière, shirt and hair aflame, a length of blazing tapestry fallen upon him, rolled and shrieked in agony, the sounds he made tearing her senses. Behind her one wall of the room was still clean, but the circling flames were licking round both ways towards it.

There was a rug untouched at her back, she dragged it up and tried to reach the burning man with it, but smoke thickened quickly, stinging and blinding her eyes, and flashing tongues of fire jetted out of the smoke and drove her back. She flung the rug, in case he could still clutch at it and roll himself in its smothering folds, but she knew then that it was too late for anyone to help him. The room was already thick with smoke, she clutched her wide sleeve over mouth and nostrils, and drew back from the awful screaming that shrilled in her ears. And he had the key of the room on him! No hope of reaching him now, no hope of recovering the key. The room was ablaze, timber at window and wall and floor began to cry out in loud cracks and splitting groans, spurting strange jets of flame.

Emma drew back, shielding her face, and hammered at the door, shrieking for help against the furious sounds of the fire. She thought she heard cries somewhere below, but distantly. She knotted her hands in the tapestries on either side the door, where the flames had not yet reached, tore the rotting fabric down, rolled it up tightly to resist sparks, and hurled it into the furnace on the other side of the room. Let the door at least remain passable. All the hangings that were not yet burning she dragged down. Her seared hand she had forgotten, she used it as freely as the other. All those other lives, surely, were safe enough, no one was ever going to read the letter that had failed to reach Ranulf of Chester. Even that fearful life shut in this room with her must be all but over, the sounds were almost lost in the voice of the fire. A busy, preoccupied voice, not unlike the obsessed hum of the fairground. She had a life to lose, too. She was young, angry, resolute, she would not lose it tamely. She hammered at the door, and called again. No one came. She heard no voices, no hasty footsteps on the stairs to the gallery, nothing but the singing of the fire, mounting steadily from a hum to a roar, like a rioting crowd, but better harmonised, the triumphant utterance of a single will.

Emma stooped to the keyhole, and called through it as long as breath and strength lasted. She could neither see nor think by then, all about her was gathering blackness, and a throttling hand upon her throat. From stooping she sank to her knees, and from her knees sagged forward along the base of the door, and lay there with mouth and nose pressed against the gap that let in a thread of clean air. After a while she was not aware of anything, even of breathing.

# Chapter Four

Philip lost himself briefly in the tangle of small valley tracks that threaded the hills, after leaving the Long Forest, and was forced to hunt out a local man from the first assart he came to, to put him on the road for Stanton Cobbold. The region he knew vaguely, but not the manor. The cottar gave him precise instructions, and turning to follow his own pointing, saw the first thin column of smoke going up into a still sky, and rapidly thickening and darkening as he stared at it.

'That could be the very place, or near it. The woods are dry enough for trouble. God send they can keep it from the house, if some fool's set a spark going …'

'How far is it?' demanded Philip, wildly staring.

'A mile and over. You'd best …' But Philip was gone, heels driving into his stolen horse's sides, off at a headlong gallop. He kept his eyes upon that growing, billowing column of smoke more often than upon the road, and took risks on those little-used and eccentric paths, that might have fetched him down a dozen times if luck had not favoured him. With every minute, the spectacle grew morc alarming, the red of flames belching upward spasmodically against the black of smoke. Long before he reached the manor, and came bursting out of the trees towards the stockade, he could hear the bursting of beams, splitting apart in the heart with louder reports than any axe-blow. It was the house, not the forest.

The gate stood open, and within, frantic servants ran confusedly, dragging out from hall and kitchen whatever belongings they could, salvaging from the stables and byres, dangerously near to the wooden part of the house, terrified and shrieking horses, and bellowing cattle. Philp stared aghast at the tower of smoke and flames that engulfed one end of the house. The long stone building of hall and undercroft would stand, though as a gutted shell, but the timbered part was already a furnace. Confused men and screaming maids ran about distractedly and paid him no heed. The disaster had overtaken them so suddenly that they were half out of their wits.

Philip kicked his feet out of the stirrups which were short for him, but which he had never paused to lengthen, and vaulted from the horse, leaving it to wander at will. One of the cowmen blundered across his path, and Philip seized him by the arm and wrenched him round to face him.

'Where's your lord? Where's the girl he brought here today?' The man was dazed and slow to answer; he shook him furiously. 'The girl – what has he done with her?'

Gaping helplessly, the man pointed into the pillar of smoke. 'They're in the solar – my lord as well ... It's there the fire began.'

Philip dropped him without a word, and began to run towards the stair to the hall door. The man howled after him: 'Fool, it's the hob of hell in there, nothing could live in it! And the door's locked – he had the key with him ... You'll go to your death!'

Nothing of this made any impression upon Philip, until mention of the locked door checked him sharply. If there was no other way in, by a locked door he would have to enter. He cast about him at all the piles of hangings and furnishings and utensils they had dragged out into the courtyard, for something he could use to break through such a barrier. The kitchen had been emptied, there were meat-choppers and knives, but, better still, there was a pile of arms from the hall. One of Corbière's ancestors, it seemed, had favoured the battle-axe. And these craven creatures of the household had made no attempt to use so handy a weapon! Their lord could roast before they would risk a burned hand for him.

Philip went up the stone steps three at a time, and into the black and stifling cavern of the hall. The heat, after all, was not so intense here, the stone walls were thick, and the floor, too, was laid with stones over the great beams of the undercroft. The worst enemy was the smoke that bit acrid and poisonous into his throat at the first breath. He spared the few moments it took to tear off his shirt and bind it round his face to cover nose and mouth, and then began to grope his way at reckless speed along the wall towards the other end of the hall, whence the heat and the fumes came. He did not think at all, he did what he had to do. Emma was somewhere in that inferno, and nothing mattered but to get her out of it.

He found the foot of the staircase to the gallery by stumbling blindly over the first step, and went up the flight stooped low, because it seemed that the bulk of the smoke was rolling along the roof. The shape of the solar door he found by the framework of smoke pouring in a thin, steady stream all round it. The wood itself was not yet burning. He hammered and strained at the door, and called, but there was no sound from within but the crackling of the fire. No way but to go through.

He swung the axe like a berserker Norseman, aiming at the lock. The door was stout, the wood old and seasoned, but less formidable axes had felled the trees that made it. His eyes smarted, streaming tears that helped by damping the cloth that covered his mouth. The blows started the beams of the door, but the lock held. Philip went on swinging. He had started a deep crack just above the lock, so deep that he had trouble withdrawing the axe. Time after time he struck at the same place, aware of splinters flying, and suddenly the lock burst clear with a harsh, metallic cry, and the edge of the door gave, only to stick again when he had thrust it open no more than a hand's breadth. The upper part, when he groped round it, offered no resistance. He felt along the floor within, and closed his hand upon a coil of silky hair. She was there, lying along the doorway, and though the heat that gushed out at him was terrifying, yet only the smoke, not the flames, had reached her.

The opening of the door had provided a way through for the wind that fed the flames, such a brightness burned up beyond the black that he knew he had only minutes before the blaze swept over them both. Frantically he leaned to get a grasp of her arm and drag her aside, so that he could open the door for the briefest possible moment, just wide enough to lift her through, and again draw it to against the demon within.

There was a great explosion of scarlet and flame, that sent a tongue out through the opening to singe his hair, and then he had her, the soft, limp weight hoisted on his shoulder, the door dragged to again behind them, and he was half-falling, half-running down the staircase with her in his arms, and the devil of fire had done no worse than snap at their heels. He did not even realise, until he took off his shoes much later, that the very treads of the stairs had been burning under his feet.

He reached the hall doorway with head lolling and chest labouring for breath, and had to sit down with his burden on the stone steps, for fear of falling with her. Greedily he dragged the clean outside air into him, and pulled down the smoke-fouled shirt from about his face. Vision and hearing were blurred and distant, he did not even know that Hugh Beringar and his guard had come galloping into the courtyard, until Brother Cadfael scurried up the steps to take Emma gently from him.

'Good lad! I have her. Come away down after us – lean on me as we go, so! Let's find you a safe corner, and we'll see what we can do for you both.'

Philip, suddenly shivering, and so feeble he dared not trust his legs to stand, asked in urgent, aching terror: 'Is she ...?'

'She's breathing,' said Brother Cadfael reassuringly. 'Come and help me care for her, and with God's blessing, she'll do.'

Emma opened her eyes upon a clean, pale sky and two absorbed and anxious faces. Brother Cadfael's she knew at once, for it bore its usual shrewdly amiable aspect, though how he had come to be there, or where, indeed, she was, she could not yet divine. The other face was so close to her own that she saw it out of focus, and it was wild and strange enough, grimed from brow to chin, the blackness seamed with dried rivulets of sweat, the brown hair along one temple curled and brown from burning! but it had two fine, clear brown eyes as honest as the daylight above, and fixed upon her with such devotion that the face, marred as it was, and never remarkable for beauty, seemed to her the most pleasing and comforting she had ever seen. The face on which her eyes had last looked, before it became a frightful lantern of flame, had been the face of ambition, greed and murder, in a plausible shell of beauty. This face was the other side of the human coin.

Only when she stirred slightly, and he moved his position to accommodate her more comfortably, did she realise that she was lying in his arms. Feeling and awareness came back gradually, even pain took its time. Her head was cradled in the hollow of his shoulder, her cheek rested against the breast of his cotte. A craftsman's working clothes, homespun. Of course, he was a shoemaker. A shopkeeper's boy, of no account! There was much to be said for it. The stink of smoke and burning still hung about them both, in spite of Cadfael's attentions with a pannikin of water from the well. The shopkeeper's boy of no account had come into the manor after her, and brought her out alive. She had mattered as much as that to him. A little shopkeeper's girl ...

'Her eyes are open,' said Philip in an eager whisper. 'She's smiling.'

Cadfael stooped to her. 'How is it with you now, daughter?'

'I am alive,' she said, almost inaudibly, but with great joy.

'So you are, God be thanked, and Philip here next after God. But lie still, we'll find you a cloak to wrap you in, for you'll be feeling the cold that comes after danger. There'll be pain, too, my poor child.' She already knew about the pain. 'You've a badly burned hand, and I've no salves here, I can do no more than cover it from the air, until we get back to town. Leave your hand lie quiet, if you can, the stiller the better. How did it come that you escaped clean, but for the one hand so badly burned?'

'I put it into the brazier,' said Emma, remembering. She saw with what startled eyes Philip received this, and realised what she had said; and suddenly the most important thing of all seemed to her that Philip should not know everything, that his candid clarity should not be made to explore the use of lies, deceptions and subterfuges, no matter how right the cause they served. Some day she might tell someone, but it would not be Philip. 'I was afraid of him,' she said, carefully amending, 'and I tipped over the brazier. I never meant to start such a fire ...'

Somewhere curiously distant from the corner of peace where she lay, Hugh Beringar and the sergeant and officers who had followed him from Shrewsbury were mustering the distracted servants in salvage, and damping down all the outhouses that were still in danger from flying sparks and debris, so that the beasts could be housed, and a roof, at least, provided for the men and maids. The fire had burned so fiercely that it was already dying down, but not for some days would the heat have subsided enough for them to sift through the embers for Ivo Corbière's body.

'Lift me,' entreated Emma. 'Let me see!'

Philip raised her to sit beside him in the clean, green grass. They were in a corner of the court, their backs against the stockade. Round the perimeter the barns and byres steamed in the early evening sun from the buckets of water which had been thrown over them. Close to the solar end, men were still at work carrying buckets in a chain from the well. There would be roofs enough left to shelter horses, cattle and people, until better could be done for them. They had the equipment of the kitchen, the stores in the undercroft might be damaged, but would not all be spoiled. In this summer weather they would do well enough, and someone must make shift to have the manor restored before the winter. All that terror, in the end, had taken but one life.

'He is dead,' she said, staring at the ruin from which she, though not he, had emerged alive.

'No other possibility,' said Cadfael simply.

He surmised, but she knew. 'And the other one?'

'Turstan Fowler? He's prisoner. The sergeant has him in charge. It was he, I believe,' said Cadfael gently, 'who killed your uncle.'

She had expected that at the approach of Beringar

and the law he would have helped himself to a horse and taken to his heels, but after all, he had known of no reason why he should. No one had been accusing him when he left Shrewsbury. Everyone at the abbey ought to have taken it for granted that Emma had been duly conducted home to Bristol. Why should they question it? Why *had* they questioned it? She had much to learn, as well as much to tell. There would be time, later. Now there was no time for anything but living, and exulting in living, and being glad and grateful, and perhaps, gradually and with unpractised pleasure, loving.

'What will become of him?' she asked.

'He'll surely tell all he knows, and lay the worst blame where it belongs, on his lord.' Cadfael doubted, all the same, whether Turstan could hope to evade the gallows, and doubted whether he should, but he did not say so to her. She was deeply preoccupied at this moment with life and death, and willed mercy even to the lowest and worst in the largeness of the mercy shown to her. And that was good, God forbid he should say any word to deface it.

'Are you cold?' asked Philip tenderly, feeling her shiver in his arm.

'No,' she said at once, and turned her head a little in the hollow of his shoulder, resting her forehead against his grimy cheek. He felt the soft curving of her lips in the hollow of his throat as she smiled, and was filled with so secure a sense of possession that no one would ever be able to take her away from him.

Hugh Beringar came to them across the trampled grass of the court, even his neatness smoked and odorous.

'What can be done's done,' he said, wiping his face. 'We had better get her back to Shrewsbury, there's no provision here. I'm leaving my sergeant and most of the men here for the time being, but the place for you,' he said, smiling somewhat wearily at Emma, 'is in a comfortable bed, with your hurt properly dressed, and no need for you to think or stir until you're restored. Bristol will have to wait for you. We'll take you to Aline at the abbey, you'll be easy there.'

'No,' said Philip, with large assurance. 'I am taking Emma to my mother in Shrewsbury.'

'Very well, so you shall,' agreed Hugh, 'it's hardly a step further. But give Cadfael time at the abbey to hunt out the salves and potions he wants from his workshop, and let Aline see for herself that we've not let Emma come to any great harm. And don't forget, friend, you owe Aline something for entertaining the fellow you robbed of his horse, and guarding your back for you until you can restore him.'

Beneath his coating of soot Philip could still blush. 'True enough, I'm likely to end in gaol again for theft, but not until I've seen Emma safe lodged in my mother's care.'

Hugh laughed, and clapped him amiably on the shoulder. 'Nor then nor ever, while I'm in office – not unless you choose to kick the law in the teeth on some other occasion. We'll satisfy the merchant, Aline will have sweetened him into complacency, you'll find. And his horse has been rubbed down and watered and rested, while you've been otherwise occupied, and we'll take him back with us unloaded, none the worse for his adventures. There are horses enough here, I'll find you the pick of them, a steady ride fit to bear two.' He had had one eye on Emma while he had been mustering water-carriers and husbanding household effects, he knew better than to try to wrest her out of Philip's arms, or send for a horse-litter to carry her back. There were two here so joined together that only a fool would attempt to part them even for a few hours; and Hugh was no fool.

They wrapped her gently in a brychan borrowed

from the salvaged bedding, rather for comfortable padding than for warmth, for the evening was still serene and mild, though she might yet suffer the cold that comes after effort is all over. She accepted everything with serenity, like one in a dream, though the pain of her hand must, they reasoned, be acute. She seemed to feel nothing but a supreme inner peace that made everything else of no account. They mounted Philip on a great, broad-backed, steady-paced gelding, and then lifted Emma up to him in her swathing blanket, and she settled into the cradle of his lap and arms and braced shoulder as though God had made her to fit there.

'And perhaps so he did,' said Brother Cadfael, riding behind with Hugh Beringar close beside him.

'So he did what?' wondered Hugh, starting out of very different considerations, for two officers brought a bound Turstand Fowler behind them.

'Direct all,' said Cadfael. 'It is, after all, a way he has.'

Halfway back towards Shrewsbury she fell asleep in his arms, nestled on his breast. For the fall of her black, smoke-scented hair he could see only the lower part of her face, but the mouth was soft and moist and smiling, and all her weight melted and moulded into the cradle of his loving body as into a marriage-bed. In her dream she had gone somewhere beyond the pain of her burned hand. It was as if she had thrust her hand into the future, and found it worth the price. The left hand, the unmarked one, lay clasped warmly round him, inside his coat, holding him close to her in her dream.

## Chapter Five

The summer darkness of fine nights, which is never quite dark, showed a horse-fair deserted, no trace of the past three days but the trampled patches and the marks of trestles in the grass. All over for another year. The abbey stewards had gathered in the profits of rent and toll and tax, delivered their accounts, and gone to their beds. So had the monks of the abbey, the lay servants, the novices and the pupils. A sleepy porter opened the gate for them; and mysteriously, at the sounds of their arrival, though circumspect and subdued, the great court awoke to life. Aline came running from the guest-hall with the aggrieved merchant, now remarkably complacent, at her back, Brother Mark from the dortoir, and Abbot Radulfus's own clerk from the abbot's lodging, with a bidding to Brother Cadfael to attend there as soon as he arrived, however late the hour.

'I sent him word what was toward,' said Hugh, 'as we left. It was right he should know. He'll be anxious to hear how it ended.'

While Aline took Emma and Philip, half awake and dazedly docile, to rest and refresh themselves in the guest-hall, and Brother Mark ran to the herbarium to collect the paste of mulberry leaves and the unguent of Our Lady's mantle, known specifics for burns, and the men-at-arms went on to the castle with their prisoner,

Brother Cadfael duly attended Radulfus in his study. Whether at midday or midnight, the abbot was equally wide-awake. By the single candle burning he surveyed Cadfael and asked simply: 'Well?'

'It is well, Father. We are returned with Mistress Vernold safe and little the worse, and the murderer of her uncle is in the sheriff's hands. One murderer – the man Turstan Fowler.'

'There is another?' asked Radulfus.

'There *was* another. He is dead. Not by any man's hand, Father, none of us has killed or done violence. He is dead by fire.'

'Tell me,' said the abbot.

Cadfael told him the whole story, so far as he knew it, and briefly. How much more Emma knew was a matter for conjecture.

'And what,' the abbot wished to show, 'can this communication have been, to cause any man to commit such crimes in pursuit of it?'

'That we do not know, and no man now will know, for it is burned with him. But where there are two warring factions in a land,' said Cadfael, 'men without scruples can turn controversy to gain, sell men for profit, take revenge on their rivals, hope to be awarded the lands of those they betray. Whatever evil was intended, now will never come to fruit.'

'A better ending than I began to fear,' said Radulfus, and drew a thankful sigh. 'Then all danger is now over, and the guests of our house are come to no harm.' He pondered for a moment. 'This young man who did so well for us and for the girl – you say he is son to the provost?'

'He is, Father. I am going with them now, with your permission, to see them safely home and dress their burns. They are not too grave, but they should be cleansed and tended at once.'

'Go with God's blessing!' said the abbot. 'It is

convenient, for I have a message to the provost, which you may deliver for me, if you will. Ask Master Corviser, with my compliments, if he will be kind enough to attend here tomorrow morning, about the end of chapter. I have some business to transact with him.'

Mistress Corviser had undoubtedly been fulminating for hours about her errant son, a good-for-nothing who was no sooner bailed out of prisoner than he was off in mischief somewhere else until midnight and past. Probably she had said at least a dozen times that she washed her hands of him, that he was past praying for, and she no longer cared, let him go to the devil his own way. But for all that, her husband could not get her to go to bed, and at every least sound that might be a footstep at the door or in the street, steady or staggering, she flew to look out, with her mouth full of abuse but her heart full of hope.

And then, when he did come, it was with a great-eyed girl in his arm, a thick handful of his curls singed off at one temple, the smell of smoke in his coat, his shirt in tatters, a monk of Saint Peter's at his heels, and a look of roused authority and maturity about him that quite overcame his draggled and soiled state. And instead of either scolding or embracing him, she took both him and the girl by the hand and drew them inside together, and went about seating, feeding, tending them, with only few words, and those practical and concerned. Tomorrow Philip might be brought to tell the whole story. Tonight it was Cadfael who told the merest skeleton of it, as he cleansed and dressed Emma's hand, and the superficial burns on Philip's brow and arm. Better not make too much of what the boy had done. Emma would take care of that, later; his mother would value it most of all from her.

Emma herself said almost nothing, islanded in her

exhaustion and bliss, but her eyes seldom left Philip, and when they did, it was to take in with deep content the solid, dark furnishings and warm panelling of this burgess house, so familiar to her that being accepted here was like coming home. Her rapt, secret smile was eloquent; mothers are quick to notice such looks. Emma had already conquered, even before she was led gently away to the bed prepared for her, and settled there by Mistress Corviser with all the clucking solicitude of a hen with one chick, with a posset laced with Brother Cadfael's poppy syrup to make sure that she slept, and forgot her pain.

'As pretty a thing as ever I saw,' said Mistress Corviser, coming back softly into the room, and closing the door between. She cast a fond look at her son, and found him asleep in his chair. 'And to think that's what he was about, while I was thinking all manner of bad things about him, who should have known him better!'

'He knows himself a deal better than he did a few days ago,' said Cadfael, repacking his scrip. 'I'll leave you these pastes and ointments, you know how to use them. But I'll come and take a look at her later tomorrow. Now I'll take my leave, I confess I'm more than ready for my own bed. I doubt if I shall hear the bell for Prime tomorrow.'

In the yard Geoffrey Corviser was himself stabling the horse from Stanton Cobbold with his own. Cadfael gave him the abbot's message. The provost raised sceptical eyebrows. 'Now what can the lord abbot want with me? The last time I came cap in hand to chapter, I got a dusty answer.'

'All the same,' advised Cadfael, scrubbing thoughtfully at his blunt brown nose, 'in your shoes I think I'd be curious enough to come and see. Who knows but the dust may have settled elsewhere by this time!'

*

It was no wonder if Brother Cadfael, though he did manage to rise for Prime, took advantage of his carefully chosen place behind a pillar to doze his way through chapter. He was so sound asleep, indeed, that for once he was in danger of snoring, and at the first melodious horn-call Brother Mark took fright, and nudged him awake.

The provost had obeyed the abbot's invitation to the latter, and arrived only at the very end of chapter. The steward of the grange court had just announced that he was in attendance when Cadfael opened his eyes.

'What can the provost be here for?' whispered Mark.

'He was asked to come. Do I know why? Hush!'

Geoffrey Corviser came in in his best, and made his reverence respectfully but coolly. He had no solid cohort at his back this time, and to tell the truth, though he may have felt some curiosity, he was attaching very little importance to this encounter. His mind was on other things. True, the problems of the town remained, and at any other time would have taken foremost place in his concern, but today he was proof against public cares by reason of private elation in a son vindicated and praised, a son to be proud of.

'You sent for me, Father Abbot. I am here.'

'I thank you for your courtesy in attending,' said the abbot mildly. 'Some days ago, master Provost, before the fair, you came with a request to me which I could not meet.'

The provost said not a word; there was none due, and he felt no need to speak at a loss.

'The fair is now over,' said the abbot equably. 'All the rents, tolls and taxes have been collected, and all have been delivered into the abbey treasury, as is due by charter. Do you endorse that?'

'It is the law,' said Corviser, 'to the letter.'

'Good! We are agreed. Right has therefore been done, and the privilege of this house is maintained.

That I could not infringe by any prior concession. Abbots who follow me would have blamed me, and with good reason. Their rights are sacrosanct. But now they have been met in full. And as abbot of this house, it is for me to determine what use shall be made of the monies in our hold. What I could not grant away in imperilment of charter,' said Radulfus with deliberation, 'I can give freely as a gift from this house. Of the fruits of this year's fair, I give a tenth to the town of Shrewsbury, for the repair of the walls and repaving of the streets.'

The provost, enlarged in his family content, flushed into startled and delighted acknowledgement, a generous man accepting generosity. 'My lord, I take your tenth with pleasure and gratitude, and I will see that it is used worthily. And I make public here and now that no part of the abbey's right is thereby changed. Saint Peter's Fair is your fair. Whether and when your neighbour town should also benefit, when it is in dire need, that rests with your judgment.'

'Our steward will convey you the money,' said Radulfus, and rose to conclude a satisfactory encounter. 'This chapter is concluded,' he said.

# Chapter Six

August continued blessedly fine, and all hands turned gladly to making sure of the harvest. Hugh Beringar and Aline set off with their hopes and purchases for Maesbury, as did the merchant of Worcester for his home town, a day late, but well compensated with a fee for the hire of his horse in an emergency, on the sheriff's business, and a fine story which he would retail on suitable occasions for the rest of his life. The provost and council of Shrewsbury drafted a dignified acknowledgement to the abbey for its gift, warm enough to give proper expression to their appreciation of the gesture, canny enough not to compromise any of their own just claims for the future. The sheriff put on record the closure of a criminal affair, as related to him by the young woman who had been lured away on false pretences, with the apparent design of stealing from her a letter left in her possession, but of the contents of which she was ignorant. There was some suspicion of a conspiracy involved, but as Mistress Vernold had never seen nor been told the significance of what she held, and as in any case it was now irrevocably lost by fire, no further action was necessary or possible. The malefactor was dead, his servant, self-confessed a murderer at his master's orders, awaited trial, and would plead that he had been forced to obey, being villein-born and at his lord's mercy. The dead man's overlord had been informed. Someone else, at the discretion of the earl of Chester, would take seisin of the manor of Stanton Cobbold.

Everyone drew breath, dusted his hands, and went back to work.

Brother Cadfael went up into the town on the second day, to tend Emma's hand. The provost and his son were at work together, in strong content with each other and the world. Mistress Corviser returned to her kitchen, and left leech and patient together.

'I have wanted to talk to you,' said Emma, looking up earnestly into his face as he renewed the dressing. 'There must be one person who hears the truth from me, and I would rather it should be you.'

'I don't believe,' said Cadfael equably, 'that you told the sheriff a single thing that was false.'

'No, but I did not tell him all the truth. I said that I had no knowledge of what was in the letter, or even for whom it was intended, or by whom it was sent. That was true, I had no such knowledge of my own, though I did know who brought it to my uncle, and that it was to be handed to the glover for delivery. But when Ivo demanded the letter of me, and I span out the time asking what could be so important about a letter, he told me what he believed to be in it. King Stephen's kingdom stood at stake, he said, and the gain to the man who provided him the means to wipe out his enemies would stretch as wide as an earldom. He said the empress's friends were pressing the earl of Chester to join them, and he would not move unless he had word of all the other powers her cause could muster, and this was the promised despatch, to convince him his interest lay with them. As many as fifty names there might be, he said, of those secretly bound to the empress, perhaps even the date when Robert of Gloucester hopes to bring her to England, even the port where they plan to land. All these sold in advance to the king's vengeance, life and limb and lands, he said, and the earl of Chester with them, who had gone so far as to permit this approach! All these offered up bound and condemned, and *he* would get his own price for them. This is what he told me. This is what I do not know of my own knowledge, and yet in my heart and soul I do know it, for I am sure what he said was true.' She moistened her lips, and said carefully: 'I do not know King Stephen well enough to know what he would do, but I remember what he did here, last summer. I saw all those men, as honest in their allegiance as those who hold with the king, thrown into prison, their lives forfeit, their families stripped of land and living, some forced into exile ... I saw deaths and revenges and still more bitterness if the tide should turn again. So I did what I did.'

'I know what you did,' said Brother Cadfael gently. He was bandaging the healing proof of it.

'But still, you see,' she persisted gravely, 'I am not sure if I did right, and for right reasons. King Stephen at least keeps a kind of peace where his writ runs. My uncle was absolute for the empress, but if she comes, if all these who hold with her rise and join her, there will be no peace anywhere. Whichever way I look I see deaths. But all I could think of, then, was preventing *him* from gaining by his treachery and murders. And there was only one way, by destroying the letter. Since then I have wondered ... But I think now that I must stand by what I did. If there must be fighting, if there must be deaths, let it happen as God wills, not as ambitious and evil men contrive. Those lives we cannot save, at least let us not help to destroy. Do you think I was right? I have wanted someone's word, I should like it to be yours.'

'Since you ask what I think,' said Cadfael, 'I think, my child, that if you carry scars on the fingers of this hand lifelong, you should wear them like jewels.'

'Her lips parted in a startled smile. She shook her head over the persistent tremor of doubt. 'But you must never tell Philip,' she said with sudden urgency, holding him by the sleeve with her good hand. As I never shall. Let him believe me as innocent as he is himself ...' She frowned over the word, which did not seem to her quite what she had wanted, but she could not find one fitter for her purpose. If it was not innocence she meant – for of what was she guilty? – was it simplicity, clarity, purity? None of them would do. Perhaps Brother Cadfael would understand, none the less. 'I felt somehow mired,' she said. '*He* should never set foot in intrigue, it is not for him.'

Brother Cadfael gave her his promise, and walked back through the town in a muse, reflecting on the complexity of women. She was perfectly right. Philip, for all his two years advantage, his intelligence, and his new and masterful maturity, would always be the younger, and the simpler, and – yes, she had the just word, after all! – the more innocent. In Cadfael's experience, it made for very good marriage prospects, where the woman was fully aware of her responsibilities.

On the thirtieth of September, just two months after Saint Peter's Fair, the Empress Maud and her half-brother Robert of Gloucester landed near Arundel and entered into the castle there. But Earl Ranulf of Chester sat cannily in his own palatine, minded his own business, and stirred neither hand nor foot in her cause.

# THE LEPER OF SAINT GILES

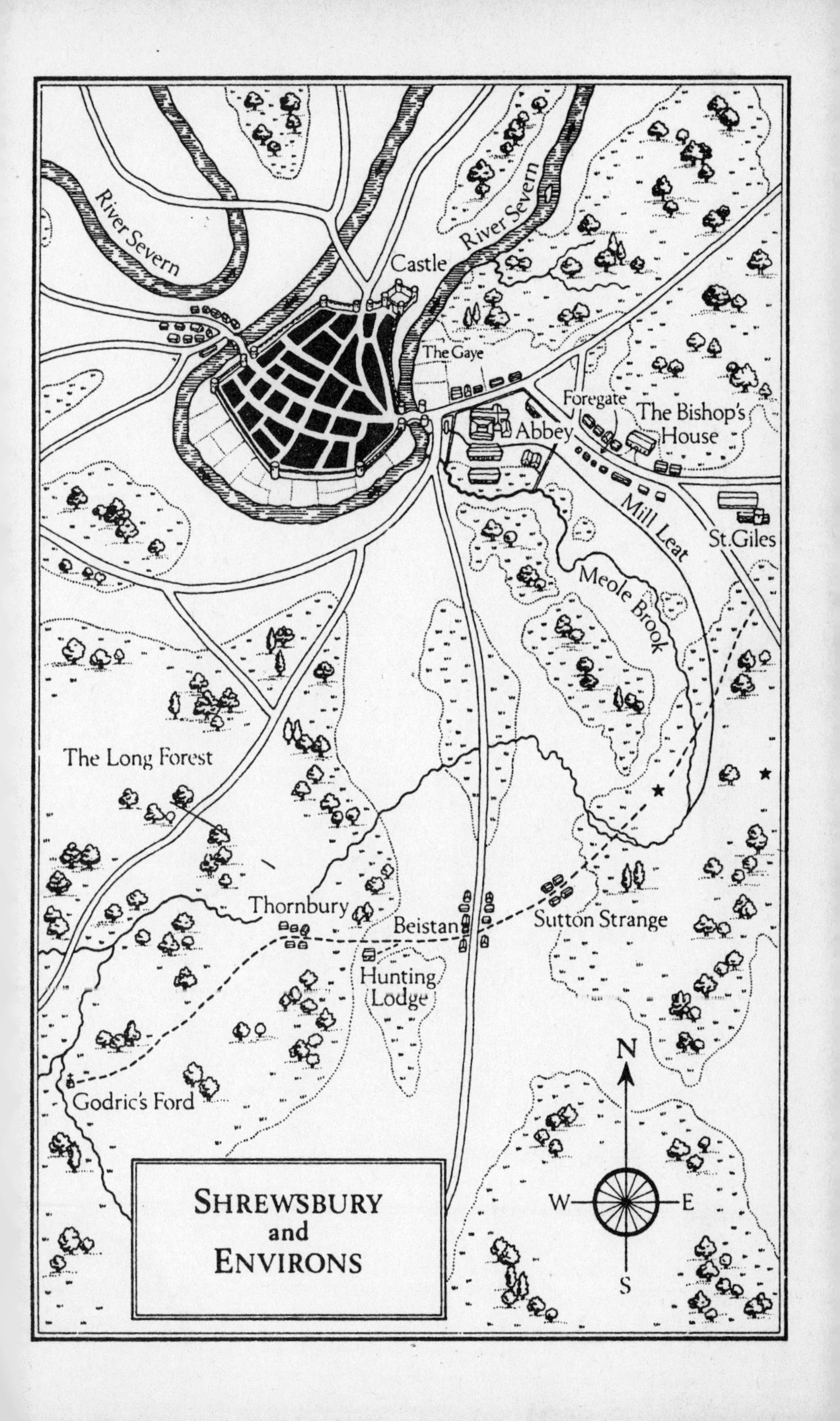
River Severn
River Severn
Castle
The Gaye
Foregate
The Bishop's House
Abbey
Mill Leat
St.Giles
Meole Brook
The Long Forest
Thornbury
Beistan
Sutton Strange
Hunting Lodge
Godric's Ford
SHREWSBURY and ENVIRONS
N
W
E
S

# 1

Brother Cadfael set out from the gatehouse, that Monday afternoon of October, in the year 1139, darkly convinced that something ominous would have happened before he re-entered the great court, though he had no reason to suppose that he would be absent more than an hour or so. He was bound only to the hospital of Saint Giles, at the far end of the Monks' Foregate, barely half a mile from Shrewsbury abbey, and his errand was merely to replenish with oils, lotions and ointments the medicine cupboard of the hospital.

They were heavy on such remedies at Saint Giles. Even when there were few lepers, for whose control and assistance the hospice existed, there were always some indigent and ailing souls in care there, and the application of Cadfael's herbal remedies soothed and placated the mind as well as the skin. He made this pilgrimage on an average every third week, to replace what had been used. These days he made it with all the better will because Brother Mark, his much-prized and dearly-missed assistant in the herbarium, had felt it to be his destiny to go and serve with the unfortunate for a year, and a visit to Saint Giles was now a blessed reminder of peaceful days departed.

For to make all plain, Cadfael's forebodings had nothing whatever to do with the momentous events soon to be visited upon the abbey of Saint Peter and Saint Paul of Shrewsbury, no reference to marrying and giving in marriage, no omens of sudden and violent death. He was expecting, rather, that in his absence some vessel full of precious liquid would be broken, some syrup left to boil over, some pan to burn dry, in his workshop in the herb-gardens, or else that his brazier would be fed too generously, and set light to the parcels of dried herbs rustling overhead and, in the worst case, to the whole workshop.

Mark had been gentle, dutiful and neat-handed. In his place Cadfael had been given, for his sins, the most cheerful, guileless, heedless and handless of cherubs, eternally hopeful, never chastened, a raw novice of nineteen fixed for ever at the age of a happy child of twelve. His fingers were all thumbs, but his zest and confidence were absolute. He knew he could do all, his will being so beneficent, and fumbled at the first baulk, for ever astonished and aghast at the results he produced. To complete the problem he presented, he was the most good-humoured and affectionate soul in the world. Also, less fortunately, the most impervious, since hope was eternal for him. Under reproof, having broken, wrecked, mismanaged and burned, he rode the tide serenely, penitent, assured of grace, confident of avoiding all repetition of failure. Cadfael liked him, as he was infuriated by him, out of all measure, and gloomily made large allowance for the damage the lad was almost certain to do whenever left to follow instructions unsupervised. Still, he had virtues, besides his sweetness of nature. For rough digging, the chief challenge of autumn, he had no peer, he plunged into it with the vigour others devoted to prayer, and turned the loam with a love and fellow-feeling Cadfael could not but welcome. Only keep him from planting what he dug! Brother Oswin had black fingers!

So Brother Cadfael had no thought to spare for the grand wedding which was to take place in the abbey church in two days' time. He had forgotten all about it until he noted, along the Foregate, how people were gathering in voluble groups outside their houses, and casting expectant looks away from town, along the London road. The day was cloudy and chill, a faint mist of rain just perceptible in the air, but the matrons of Shrewsbury were not going to be done out of a spectacle on that account. By this road both wedding parties would enter, and word had evidently gone before them that they were already approaching the town. Since they would not actually enter the walls, a good number of the burgesses had come forth to join the people of the Foregate parish. The stir and hum were almost worthy of a minor fair-day. Even the beggars gathered about the gatehouse had an air of holiday excitement about them. When the baron of an honour scattered over four counties arrived to marry the heiress to lands as great as his own, there must be lavish largesse to be hoped for in celebration.

Cadfael rounded the corner of the precinct wall, by the open green of the horse-fair, and continued along the highroad, where the houses thinned out, and fields and woods began to reach green fingers to touch the rim of the road in between. Here, too, the women stood before their doors, waiting to glimpse bride and groom when they came, and in front of the large house halfway to Saint Giles a knot of interested gazers had gathered to watch the bustle of activity through the open gates of the courtyard. Servants and grooms flickered to and fro between house and stables, flashes of bright liveries crossed the yard. This was where the bridegroom and his retinue were to lodge, while the bride and her party would lie at the abbey guest-hall. Recalled to mild human curiosity, Cadfael loitered for a moment to stare with the rest.

It was a large house, well walled round, with garden and orchard behind, and it belonged to Roger de Clinton, bishop of Coventry, though he rarely used it himself. The loan of it to Huon de Domville, who held manors in Shropshire, Cheshire, Stafford and Leicester, was partly a friendly gesture towards Abbot Radulfus, and partly a politic compliment to a powerful baron whose favour and protection, in these times of civil war, it would be wise to cultivate. King Stephen might be in firm control of much of the country, but in the west the rival faction was strongly established, and there were plenty of lords ready and willing to change sides if fortune blew the opposite way. The Empress Maud had landed at Arundel barely three weeks previously, with her half-brother Robert, earl of Gloucester, and a hundred and forty knights, and through the misplaced generosity of the king, or the dishonest advice of some of his false friends, had been allowed to reach Bristol, where her cause was impregnably installed already. Here in the mellow autumn countryside everything might seem at peace, but for all that men walked warily and held their breath to listen for news, and even bishops might need powerful friends before all was done.

Beyond the bishop's house the road opened between trees, leaving the town well behind; and at the fork, a bow-shot ahead, the long, low roof of the hospice appeared, the wattled fence of its enclosure, and beyond again, the somewhat higher roof of the church, with a small, squat turret above. A modest enough church, nave and chancel and a north aisle, and a graveyard behind, with a carven stone cross set up in the middle of it. The buildings were set discreetly back from both roads that converged towards the town. Lepers, as they may not go among the populous streets of towns, must also keep their distance even to do their begging in the countryside. Saint Giles, their patron, had deliberately chosen the desert and the solitary place for his habitation, but these had no choice but to remain apart.

It was plain, however, that they had their fair share of human curiosity like their fellows, for they, too, were out watching the road. Why should not the unfortunate at least be free to stare at their luckier brethren, to envy them if they could manage no better than that, to wish them well in marriage if their generosity stretched so far? A shifting line of dark-gowned figures lined the wattle fence, as animated if not as agile as their healthy fellow men. Some of them Cadfael knew, they had settled here for life, and made the best of their cramped lives among familiar helpers. Some were new. There were always new ones, the wanderers who made their way the length of the land from lazarhouse to lazarhouse, or settled for a while in some hermitage on the charity of a patron, before moving on to new solitudes. Some went on crutches or leaned hard on staves, having feet maimed by the rot of disease or painful with ulcers. One or two pushed themselves along on little wheeled carts. One hunched shapeless against the fence, bloated with sores and hiding a disfigured face within his cowl. Several, though active, went with veiled faces, only the eyes uncovered.

Their numbers varied as the restless wandered on, shunning the town as they must shun all towns, to some other hospice looking out over another landscape. By and large, the hospital here sheltered and cared for twenty to thirty inmates at a time. The appointment of the superior rested with the abbey. Brothers and lay brothers served here at their own request. It was not unknown that attendant should become attended, but there was never want of another volunteer to replace and nurse him.

Cadfael had done his year or more in this labour, and felt no recoil, and only measured pity, respect being so much greater an encouragement and support. Moreover, he came and went here so regularly that his visits were a part of a patient and permanent routine like the services in the church. He had dressed more and viler sores than he troubled to remember, and discovered live hearts and vigorous minds within the mottled shells he tended. He had seen battles, too, in his time in the world, as far afield as Acre and Ascalon and Jerusalem in the first Crusade, and witnessed deaths crueller than disease, and heathen kinder than Christians, and he knew of leprosies of the heart and ulcers of the soul worse than any of these he poulticed and lanced with his herbal medicines. Nor had he been greatly surprised when Brother Mark elected to follow in his steps. He was well aware that there was one step beyond, which Mark was predestined to take without his example. Brother Cadfael knew himself too well ever to aim at the priesthood, but he recognised a priest when he saw one.

Brother Mark had seen him approaching, and came trotting to meet him, his plain face bright, his spiky, straw-coloured hair erected round his tonsure. He had a scrofulous child by the hand, a skinny little boy with old, drying sores in his thin fair hair. Mark teased aside the hairs that clung to the one remaining raw spot, and beamed down fondly at his handiwork.

'I'm glad you're come, Cadfael. I was running out of the lotion of pellitory, and see how much good it's done for him! The last sore almost healed. And the swellings in his neck are better, too. There, Bran, good boy, show Brother Cadfael! He makes the medicines for us, he's our physician. There, now, run to your mother and keep by her, or you'll miss all the show. They'll be coming soon.'

The child drew his hand free, and trotted away to join the sad little group that yet would not be sad. There was chattering there, a morsel of song, even some laughter. Mark looked after his youngest charge, watched the ungainly, knock-kneed gait that stemmed from under-nourishment, and visibly grieved. He had been here only a month, his skin was still tissue-thin.

'And yet he is not unhappy,' he said, marvelling. 'When no one is by, and he follows me about, his tongue never stops wagging.'

'Welsh?' asked Cadfael, eyeing the child thoughtfully.

He must surely have been named for Bran the Blessed, who first brought the gospel to Wales.

'The father was.' Mark turned to look his friend earnestly and hopefully in the face. 'Do you think he can be cured? Fully cured? At least he's fed, now. The woman will die here. In any case – she has grown indifferent, kind enough, but glad to have him off her hands. But I do believe he may yet go back whole into the world.'

Or out of it, thought Cadfael; for if he follows you so assiduously he cannot but get the savour of church or cloister, and the abbey is close at hand. 'A bright child?' he asked.

'Brighter than many that are brought up to the Latin, and can reckon and read. Brighter than many a one who goes in fine linen, and with a nurse coddling him. I shall try to teach him somewhat, as I can.'

They walked back together to the doorway of the hospital. The hum of expectant voices had risen, and along the highroad other sounds were gradually drawing near, compounded of the jingling of harness, the calls of falconers, conversation, laughter, the muffled beat of hooves using the grassy verge in preference to the naked road. One of the bridal processions was approaching.

'They say the bridegroom will be the first to come,' said Mark, stepping from the open porch into the dimness of the hall, and leading the way through to the corner where the medicine cupboard was kept. Fulke Reynald, a steward of the abbey and superior of the hospital, had one key; Brother Cadfael held the other. He opened his scrip, and began to stow away the preparations he had brought. 'Do you know anything about them?' asked Mark, succumbing to curiosity.

'Them?' murmured Cadfael, preoccupied with his review of the gaps in the shelves.

'These gentlefolk who are coming to marry here. All

I know is their names. I should not have paid so much heed,' said Mark, shame-faced, 'except that our people here, who have nothing but their sores and maimings, have learned more of it than I have, only God knows how, and it is like a spark warming them. As though anything bright that shines on them is more aid than I can give. Yet all it is, is a wedding!'

'A wedding,' said Cadfael seriously, stacking away jars of salves and bottles of lotion made from alkanet, anemone, mint, figwort, and the grains of oats and barley, most of them herbs of Venus and the moon, 'a wedding is the crux of two lives, and therefore no mean matter.' He added the fruits of mustard, which belongs rather to Mars, but provides formidable pastes and poultices to fight malignant ulcers. 'Every man and woman who has faced the ordeal,' he said thoughtfully, 'must feel concern for those about to face it. Even those who have not, may speculate with sympathy.'

Matrimony was one joust he had never attempted, wide as his experience had been before he entered the cloister; but he had brushed fingertips with it once, and circumvented it more than once. He felt some astonishment, once he began remembering.

'This baron has a famous name, but I know no more of him, except that he's in good odour, they say, with the king. I think I may once have known an old kinsman of the lady. But whether she's from the same line is more than I know.'

'I hope she may be beautiful,' said Mark.

'Prior Robert would be interested to hear you say so,' said Cadfael drily, and closed the cupboard door.

'Beauty is a very healing thing,' said Brother Mark, earnest and unabashed. 'If she is young and lovely, if she smiles on them and inclines her head as she rides by, if she does not shrink at seeing them, she will do more for those people of mine out there than I can do with probing and poulticing. Here I begin to know that blessedness is what can be snatched out of the passing day, and put away to think of afterwards.' He added, recoiling into deprecation: 'Of course it need not be someone else's wedding feast. But how can we waste that, when it offers?'

Cadfael flung an arm about Mark's still thin and waiflike shoulders, and hauled him away, out of the dimness within, to the gathering excitement and brightening light without. 'Let's hope and pray,' he said heartily, 'that it may be the source of blessedness even to the pair caught up in it. By the sound of it, one of them is due here this moment. Come and let's see!'

The noble bridegroom and his retinue approached in a shimmer of bright colours, with horn-calls and soft, continuous clamour of harness bells, a cortège stretching fifty paces, and fringed with running servants leading the pack ponies, and two couples of tall deerhounds on leashes. The sorry little straggle of outcasts shuffled forward eagerly the few paces they dared, to see the better those fine fabrics and splendid dyes they could never possess, and set up a muted, awed murmur of admiration as the procession drew level with their wattle fence.

In front, on a tall black horse, his own accoutrements and his mount's very splendid in scarlet and gold, rode a broad-built, gross, fleshy man, inelegant but assured in the saddle, and accorded a station well ahead of all his train, so that his pre-eminence should be seen to be absolute. Behind him came three young squires abreast, keeping a close and wary watch on their lord, as though he might at any moment turn and subject them to some hazardous test. The same tension, just short of fear, passed down the hierarchies that followed, through valet, chamberlain, groom, falconer, down to the boys who were towed along by the hounds. Only the beasts, horse and hound alike, and the hawks on the falconer's frame, went sleek and complacent, in no awe of their lord.

Brother Cadfael stood with Mark at the gate in the wattle fence, and gazed with sharpening attention. For though any one of the three young squires would have done very well for a bridegroom, it was only too plain that none of them was Huon de Domville. It had not entered Cadfael's head until now that this baron might be already well past the prime, no young lover embarking on marriage in the proper years for that undertaking, but with more grey than black in his short, full beard, and only a curled fringe of grey hair and the glisten of a bald crown showing at the temple, where his elaborately twisted capuchon was tilted rakishly aside. A squat, muscular, powerful body still, but well past fifty if he was a day, and more likely nearing sixty. Cadfael hazarded that by now this one must already have used up at least one wife, and probably two. The bride, rumour said, was barely eighteen, fresh from her nurse. Well, these things happen. These things are done.

Then, as the rider drew close, Cadfael could not take his eyes from the face. A wide, flat forehead, rendered tall by the receding hair, cast almost no shadow over the shallow settings of small, black, shrewd eyes, as poorly endowed with lashes as with sockets, but malevolently intelligent. The trimmed beard left uncovered a narrow, implacable mouth. A massive, brutal face, muscled like a wrestler's arm, unsculpted, unfinished. A face that should not have had a subtle mind behind it, to make the man even more formidable, but undoubtedly had. And that was Huon de Domville.

He had drawn close enough now to observe what manner of creatures they were who bobbed and peered and pointed excitedly about the little church, and along the churchyard wall. It did not please him. The black eyes, like small plums embedded in the hard dough of his face, turned dusky red, like smouldering coals.

Deliberately he wheeled his horse to their side of the road, leaving the opposite verge, which was wider, and mounting the grass on the near side, and that solely in order to wave the miserable rabble back to their kennels. And his manner of waving was with the full lash of the riding-whip he carried. Doubtful if he ever used it on his horse, blood-stock of this quality being valuable and appreciated, but for clearing his path of lepers it would serve. The tight mouth opened wide to order imperiously: 'Out of my way, vermin! Take your contagion out of sight!'

They shrank and drew back in humble haste out of reach, if not out of sight. All but one. Half a head taller than his fellows, one lean, cloaked figure stood his ground, whether out of inability to move quickly, or want of understanding, or in mute defiance. He remained erect, intently gazing through the eye-slot in the veil that covered his face. When he did take a pace back, without turning his head, he went heavily upon one foot, and was too slow to avoid the lash of the whip, if indeed he had intended to avoid it. The blow took him on shoulder and breast. His maimed foot turned under him, and he fell heavily in the grass.

Cadfael had started forward, but Mark was before him, darting down with an indignant cry to drop to his knees and spread an arm over the gaunt figure, putting his own braced body between the fallen man and the next blow. But Domville was already past, disdainful of further noticing the dregs of the world. He neither hastened nor slowed his pace, but rode on without a glance aside, and all his train after him, though holding rather to the roadway, and some with averted faces. The three young squires passed, embarrassed and uneasy. The big, tow-headed youngster in the middle actually turned full-face to the two on the ground, flashed them a dismayed stare from eyes as blue as cornflowers, and rode with his chin on his shoulder until both his fellows elbowed him back to caution and his duty.

The whole cortège passed while Mark was helping the gaunt old man to his feet. The servants followed woodenly, armoured against the world by their servitude. Certain more lordly figures, guests or minor relatives, passed blandly, as though nothing whatever had occurred. In their midst a demure cleric fingered his beads, faintly smiling, and ignored all. Rumour said that one Eudo de Domville, a canon of Salisbury, was to perform the marriage ceremony; a man in good odour with the church and the papal legate, and in line for advancement, and probably eager to remain so blessed. He passed with the rest. The grooms, the pages, the deerhounds followed, and all the little bells on bridles and jesses tinkled their way past, and dwindled slowly along the first reach of the Foregate.

Brother Mark came up the incline of grass with his arm about the old leper. Cadfael had drawn back and left them to each other. Mark had no fear of contagion, since he never gave a thought to the peril, all his energy being absorbed into the need. Nor would he ever be surprised, or complain, if at last contagion did seize upon him and draw him even closer to the people he served. He was talking to his companion as they came, mildly and cheerfully, for they were both used to spurning, they did not pay it overmuch notice. Cadfael watched them come, marked the one-sided but steady and forceful gait of the old man, and the breadth of the gesture with which his left hand, emerging momentarily from the shrouding sleeve, put off Mark's embracing arm, and set a space between them. Mark accepted the dismissal with simplicity and respect, and turned to leave him. Cadfael had seen, moreover, that the left hand, once long and shapely, lacked both index and middle fingers, and had but two joints of the third, and the texture of the maimed parts was whitish, wrinkled and dry.

'No very noble proceeding,' said Mark with rueful resignation, shaking the debris of grass from his skirts. 'But fear makes men cruel.'

Brother Cadfael doubted whether fear had played any part. Huon de Domville did not look the man to be afraid of anything short of hellfire, though it was true that the outcasts' disease did not fall far short of hellfire.

'You have a new man there?' he asked, gazing after the tall leper, who had moved along the bank to regain a good view of the road. 'I do not think I have seen him before.'

'No, he came in a week or more ago. He is a wanderer, he goes on perpetual pilgrimage, from shrine to shrine as close as in his condition he may. Seventy years old, he says he is, and I believe him. He will not stay long, I think. He makes a stay here because Saint Winifred's bones rested here in the church before being received into the abbey. There, so close to the town, he may not go. Here he may.'

Cadfael, who had knowledge of that renowned virgin's whereabouts which he could never confide to his innocent friend, scrubbed thoughtfully at his blunt brown nose, and reflected tranquilly that even from her far-distant grave in Gwytherin, Saint Winifred would bestir herself to hear the prayers of a poor, afflicted man.

His eyes followed the tall, erect figure. In the shrouded anonymity of dark cloak and hood, and the cloth veil that hid even the faces of those worst disfigured, men and women, old and young, seemed to go secretly and alone through the remnant of life left to them. No gender, no age, no colouring, no country, no creed: all living ghosts, known only to their maker. But no, it was not so. By gait, by voice, by stature, by a thousand infinitesimal foibles of character and kind that pierced through the disguise, they emerged every one unique. This one in his silence had a dominating presence, and in his stillness even under threat a rare and daunting dignity.

'You have talked with him?'

'Yes, but he says little. From his manner of speaking,' said Mark, 'I think lips or tongue must be corrupted. Words come slowly, a little mangled, and he tires soon. But his voice is quiet and deep.'

'What remedies are you using on him?'

'None, for he says he needs none, he carries his own balm. No one here has seen his face. That is why I think he must be sadly maimed. You'll have noticed one foot is crippled? He has lost all toes on that one, but for the stump of the great toe. He has a special shoe built to give him support, a stable sole to walk on. I think the other foot may also be affected, but not so badly.'

'I saw his left hand,' said Cadfael. Such hands he had seen before, the fingers rotted away until they fell like dead leaves, the corrosion of the flesh gnawing slowly until even the wrist shed its bones. Yet it seemed to him that this devouring demon had died of its own greed. There was no ulcerous crust remaining; the seamed white flesh where the lost fingers had once been was dry and healed, however ugly to the view. Firm muscles had moved in the back of the hand when he gestured.

'Has he given you a name?'

'He says his name is Lazarus.' Brother Mark smiled. 'I think it is a name he gave himself at a late christening – perhaps when he cut himself off from family and home, according to law. It is a second birth, lamentable though it may be. He was godfather at his own second baptism. I don't enquire. But I wish he would use our help, and not rely only on his own tending. He must surely have some sores or ulcers that could benefit by your ointments, before he leaves us as he came.'

Cadfael mused, watching the withdrawn figure, motionless at the head of the slope of grass. 'Yet he is not numbed! He has his powers of body still, in all such members as are left to him? He feels heat and cold? And pain? If he strikes his hand against a nail, or a splinter in the fence, he knows it?'

Mark was at a loss; he knew the disease only as he had encountered it, unsightly, ulcerated, full of sores. 'He felt the sting of the whip, I know, even through the armour of his cloak. Yes, surely he feels, like other men.'

But those who have the true leprosy, thought Cadfael, recalling many he had seen in his crusading days, very long ago, those who whiten like ash, those whose skin powders away in grey patches, in the extreme of their disease do not feel, like other men. They injure themselves, bleed, and are unaware of the injury. They let a foot stray into the fire, sleeping, and only awake to the stench of their own flesh burning. They touch and cannot be sure they touch, hold and cannot lift what they would take up. Without sensation, without purpose, fingers, toes, hands, feet, drop away and rot. As Lazarus had lost fingers and toes. But such victims do not walk, however lamely, as Lazarus walked, do not prise themselves up from the ground with active, effective energy, or grasp a support as Lazarus had grasped the arm Mark offered in his aid, and that with the maimed hand. Not unless, not until, the devil that devoured them has died of his own corruption.

'Are you thinking,' asked Mark hopefully, 'that this may not be leprosy, after all?'

'Oh, yes!' Cadfael shook his head at once. 'Yes, no question of it, this was certainly leprosy.'

He did not add that in his opinion many of the ills they treated here, though they carried the same banishment and were called by the same name, were not true leprosy. Any man who broke out in nodes that turned to ulcers, or pallid, scaly eruptions of the skin, or running sores, was set down as a leper, though Cadfael had his suspicions that many such cases arose from uncleanliness, and many others from too little and too wretched food. He was sorry to see Brother Mark's hopeful face fall. No doubt he dreamed of curing all who came.

Along the road came the first distant murmur of another company approaching the town. The whisperings of the watchers, subdued since Domville's inauspicious passing, took on the cheerful chirping of sparrows again, and they crept a little way down the slope of grass, peering and craning for the first glimpse of the bride. The bridegroom had brought little but dismay with him. The lady might do better.

Brother Mark shook off his small disappointment, and took Cadfael by the sleeve. 'Come, you may as well wait and see the rest of it now. I know you have everything in order there in the herbarium, even without me. Why should you hurry back?'

Remembering the particular gifts of Brother Oswin, Cadfael could think of many reasons why he should not leave his workshop for too long, but also of at least one good reason for remaining. 'I daresay another half-hour will do no harm,' he agreed. 'Let us go and take our stand by this Lazarus of yours, where I may observe him without offending.'

The old man did not stir as he heard them approaching, and they halted somewhat aside, not to disturb his remote contemplation. He had, thought Cadfael, the self-sufficient tranquillity of a desert hermit; as those early fathers had sought out their austere solitudes, so he created his about him, even among men. He towered over both of them by a head, and stood straight as a lance, and almost as meagre, but for the lean, wide shoulders under the shrouding cloak. Only when the sound of the approaching company blew suddenly closer on a stirring wind, and he turned his head to look intently towards the sound, did Cadfael glimpse the face beneath the hood. The hood itself covered the brow, which by the form of the head should be lofty and broad, and the coarse blue cloth of the veil was drawn up to the cheekbones. In the slit between, only the eyes showed, but they were arresting enough, large, unblemished, of a clear, pale but brilliant blue-grey. Whatever deformities he hid, his eyes saw clearly and far, and were accustomed to looking on distances. He paid no heed to the two who stood near to him. His gaze swept beyond them, to where the approaching party showed as a shimmer of colours and a shifting of light.

There was less ceremony here than with Huon de Domville's retinue, and the numbers were smaller. Nor was there a single dominant figure in the lead, but a flurry of mounted grooms as outriders, and within their circle, as though within an armed guard, three came riding abreast. On one side a dark, sinewy, olive-faced man perhaps five and forty years old, very splendidly dressed in sombre, glowing colours, and well mounted on a light, fast grey, surely part Arab, thought Cadfael. The man had plenteous black hair coiling under a plumed cap, and a clipped black beard framing a long-lipped mouth. It was a narrow, closed face, subtle and suspicious. On the other side rode a lady of about the same years, thin and neat and sharply handsome, dark like her lord, and mounted on a roan mare. She had a pursed, calculating mouth and shrewd eyes, beneath brows tending to a frown even when the mouth smiled. Her head-dress was of the most fashionable, her riding habit had the London cut, and she rode with grace and style, but the very look of her struck with a coldness.

And in between these two, dwarfed and overshadowed, there paced a tiny, childlike creature on a palfrey too large for her. Her touch on the rein was light, her seat in the saddle listless but graceful. She was sumptuously arrayed in cloth of gold and dark blue silks, and within the burden of her finery her slight form seemed cramped and straitened, like a body coffined. Her face gazed ahead, beneath a gilded net heavy with dark-gold hair, into emptiness. A softly rounded face, with delicate features and great iris-grey eyes, but so pale and subdued that she might have been a pretty doll rather than a living woman. Cadfael heard Mark draw in startled breath. It was a shame to see youth and freshness so muted and bereft of joy.

This lord, too, had noted the nature of this place, and of those who had come out from it to see his niece go by. He did not, like Domville, spur deliberately at the offence, but swung his mount the other way, to give the infected a wider berth, and turned his head away to avoid even seeing them. The girl might have passed by without so much as noticing them, so deep was she drowned in her submissive sadness, if the child Bran, all shining eyes, had not so far forgotten himself as to run halfway down the hillock for a nearer view. The flash of movement in the corner of her eye caused her to start and look round, and seeing him, she came suddenly to life in the piteous contemplation of an innocent even more wretched than herself. For an instant she stared at him with nothing but horrified compassion, and then, seeing that she mistook him, seeing that he looked up at her smiling, she smiled too. It lasted only the twinkling of an eye, but for that while she shone with a warm, bright, grieving kindness; and before the clear sky clouded again she had leaned across her aunt's saddle-bow, and tossed a handful of small coins into the grass at the child's feet. Bran was so enchanted that he could not even stoop to pick them up, but followed her progress wide-eyed and open-mouthed as she passed by.

No one else in the company offered largesse here. No doubt it was being reserved to make a greater impression at the abbey gatehouse, where there would certainly be a crowd of hopeful beggars waiting.

For no very sound reason, Cadfael turned from the child to look at the old man Lazarus. Bran could afford to take candid delight in the bright colours and pretty clothes of those more fortunate than himself, without envy or greed, but the old in experience might well find a bitter flavour in viewing impossible fruit. The old man had not moved, except that as the riders passed by his head turned to hold those three in sight, with never a glance to spare for the gentlewomen and servants who followed. The eyes staring between hood and veil glittered pale, brilliant and blue as ice, unblinking, as long as the bride remained in sight. When even the last pack-pony had vanished round the curve of the Foregate, he still stood motionless, as though the intentness of his stare could follow them as far as the gatehouse, and pierce the walls to keep unbroken watch on them within.

Brother Mark drew long and rueful breath, and turned to gaze wonderingly at Cadfael. 'And that is she? And they mean to marry her to that man? He could be her grandsire – and no gentle or kindly one, either. How can such things be?' He stared along the road as the old man was staring. 'So small, and so young! And did you see her face – how sad! This is not with her will!'

Cadfael said nothing; there was nothing reassuring or consoling to be said. Such things were the commonplace of marriage where there were lands and wealth and powerful alliances to be gained, and small say the brides – or often enough the young bridegrooms – had in the disposal of their persons. There might even be brides who could see shrewdly enough the advantages of marrying men old enough to be their grandsires, where there was material good to be gained, since death might very soon relieve them of their husbands but leave them their dower and the status of their widowhood, and with some luck and a deal of cleverness they might manage to make a second match more to their liking. But by her face, Iveta de Massard saw the fate that awaited her rather as her own death than her bridegroom's.

'I pray God help her!' said Mark fervently.

'It may be,' said Brother Cadfael, rather to himself than to his friend, 'that he intends to. But it may also be that he has a right to expect a little support from men in setting about it.'

In the courtyard of the bishop's house in the Foregate, Huon de Domville's servants were unloading the pack-horses, and running about with bedding and hangings, and the finery that would grace the marriage service and the bridal bed. Domville's butler already had wine decanted for his master and Canon Eudo, who was a distant cousin, and the chamberlain had seen to it that there was firing and comfort waiting in the best chamber, a loose, warm gown after the rigour of riding clothes, furred slippers after the long, elegant boots had been drawn off. The baron sprawled in his cushioned chair, spread his thick legs, and nursed his mulled wine, well content. It was nothing to him that his bride's procession was drawing near from Saint Giles. He had no need and no desire to waste his time standing to watch his purchase go by; he was already sure of her, and he would be seeing enough of her after the marriage. He was here to conclude a bargain highly satisfactory to himself and to the girl's uncle and guardian, and though it was an agreeable bonus that the child happened to be young, beautiful and appetising, it was of no very great importance.

Joscelin Lucy turned over his horse to a groom, kicked a bale of napery out of his way, and was making off back to the gate and the road when his fellow Simon Aguilon, the oldest of the three squires in Domville's service, caught him by the arm.

'Where are you off to so fast? He'll be bawling for you the minute he's emptied his first cup, you know that. It's your turn to wait on their nobilities!'

Joscelin tugged at his flaxen thatch, and loosed a sharp bay of laughter. 'What nobility? You saw as well as I did. Strike a poor devil who daren't strike back, and as near as death ride him down, for no offence in the world. Devil take such nobility! And devil take him and his thirst, too, until I've seen Iveta go by.'

'Joss, you fool,' cautioned Simon urgently, 'you'll let that tongue of yours wag too loud and once too often. Cross him now, and he'll toss you out naked to go home to your father and explain yourself, and how will that help Iveta? Or you, either?' He shook his head over his friend, though good-humouredly, and kept his hold on him. 'Better go to him. He'll have your hide, else!'

The youngest of the three turned from unsaddling his mount, and grinned at the pair of them. 'Oh, let him have his glimpse, who knows how many more there'll be?' He clouted Joscelin amiably on the shoulder. 'I'll go and run his errands for you this time. I'll tell him you're busy making sure all the butts of wine are handled gently, that'll please him. Go and gaze – though what good it will do either of you . . . .'

'Will you, though, Guy? You're a good fellow! I'll take your turn of duty when you ask it!' And he was off again gatewards, but Simon flung an arm about his shoulders and bounded into step beside him.

'I'll come with you. He won't need me for a while. But hear me, Joss,' he went on seriously, 'you take too many risks with him. You know he can advance you if you please him, it's what your father wants and expects, you're a fool to put your future in peril. And you can please him, if you give your mind to it, he's none so hard on us.'

They passed through the gate and stood in the angle of the wall, leaning shoulder to shoulder against the stone gate-pillar and gazing along the Foregate, two tall, strong young men, Simon the elder by three years, and the shorter by the width of a hand. The sullen, tow-headed lad beside him gnawed a considering lip, and scowled at the ground.

'My future! What can he do to my future, more than toss me back to my father in disgrace, and what the devil need I care about that? There are two good manors will be mine, that he can't take from me, and there are other lords I could serve. I'm a man of my hands, I can hold my own with most . . .'

Simon laughed, shaking him rallyingly in the arm that circled his shoulders. 'You can indeed! I've suffered from it, I know!'

'There are lords enough wanting good men of their hands, now the empress is back in England, and the fight's on in earnest for the crown. I could fend! You could as well be thinking of your own case, lad, you've as much to lose as I have. You may be his sister's son, and his heir now, but how if –' He set his teeth; it was hard to utter it, but he was perversely determined to drive the knife deep into his own flesh, and twist it to double the pain. '– how if things change? A young wife . . . How if he gets a son of this marriage? Your nose will be out of joint.'

Simon leaned his curly brown head back against the stones of the wall, and laughed aloud. 'What, after thirty years of marriage to my Aunt Isabel, and God knows how many passages with how many ladies outside the pale, and never a brat to show for it all? Lad, if he has a seed in him, for all his appetites, I'll eat the fruit myself! My inheritance is safe enough, I'm in no danger. I'm twenty-five, and he's nearing sixty. I can wait!' He straightened alertly. 'Look, they're coming!'

But Joscelin had already caught the first glimmer of

colour and movement along the road, and stiffened to gaze. They came on briskly, Godfrid Picard and his party, in haste to gain the hospitable shelter of the abbey. Simon loosed his clasp, feeling Joscelin draw away.

'For God's sake, boy, what's the use? She's not for you!' But he said it in a despairing sigh, and Joscelin did not even hear it.

They came, and they passed. The ogres on either side of her loomed lean and subtle and greedy, heads arrogantly high, but brows knotted and faces pinched, as though there had already been some happening that had displeased them. And there between them was she, a pale desperation in a golden shell of display, her small face all eyes, but blind eyes, gazing at nothing, seeing nothing. Until she drew close, and something – he wanted to believe his nearness and need – disquieted her, caused her to shiver, and turn her great eyes where she hardly dared turn her whole head, towards the place where he stood. He was not certain that she saw him, but he was certain that she knew he was there, that she had felt, scented, breathed him as she passed between her guards. She did not make the mistake of looking round, or in any way changing the fixed, submissive stillness of her face; but as she passed she lifted her right hand to her cheek, held it so a moment, and again let it fall.

'I do believe,' sighed Simon Aguilon, bringing his friend back in his arm to the courtyard, 'that you haven't given up, even now. For God's sake, what have you to hope for? Two days more, and she's my lady Domville.'

Joscelin held his peace, and thought of the uplifted hand, and knew in his heart that her fingers had touched her lips; and that was more than had been agreed.

The entire guest-hall of the abbey, apart from the common quarters, had been given over to Sir Godfrid Picard and his wedding party. In the privacy of their own chamber, within, Agnes Picard turned to her husband with an anxious face. 'I still do not like this quietness of hers. I do not trust her.'

He shrugged it off disdainfully. 'Ah, you fret too much. She has given over the battle. She is altogether submissive. What can she do? Daniel has his orders not to let her out of the gate, and Walter keeps watch on the parish door of the church. There's no other way out, unless she finds a means to fly over the wall, or leap the Meole brook. No harm in keeping a close eye on her, even within, but not so close as to draw too much attention. But I'm sure you mistake her. That timid mouse has not the courage to stand up at the altar and declare herself unwilling.'

'As well!' said the lady grimly. 'I hear this Abbot Radulfus has a fine conceit of his own rights and powers, and is no respecter of barons if he feels his writ infringed. But I wish I could be as sure of her tameness as you.'

'You fret too much, I tell you, woman. Once bring her to the altar, and she'll speak her words as taught, and no bones about it.'

Agnes gnawed a lip, and still was not quite convinced. 'Well, it may be so . . . But for all that, I wish it was done. I shall breathe the easier when these next two days are over.'

In Brother Cadfael's workshop in the herbarium, Brother Oswin shuffled his feet, folded his large, willing but disastrous hands, and looked sheepish. Cadfael looked apprehensively round the hut, aware of ill news to come, though it was an advance if the lad even realised it when he had done something mad, without having it pointed out to him. Most things appeared to be still in their places. The brazier burned low, there were no noticeable evil smells, the wines in their great flasks bubbled gently to themselves as usual.

Brother Oswin rendered account selfconsciously, gleaning what credit he could before the blow fell. 'Brother Infirmarer has fetched the electuaries and the powders. And I have taken Brother Prior the stomachic you made for him. The troches you left drying I think should be ready now, and the dried herbs for the decoction you spoke of, I have ground to fine powder ready for use tomorrow.'

*But*... Now he was coming to the bad news. That look of astonished reproach, that a thing well-meant and confidently undertaken should so betray him.

'But such a strange thing... I don't understand how it could happen, the pot must surely have been cracked, though I could see no break in it. The linctus you left boiling... I did watch it most carefully, I'm sure I took it from the brazier when it was just the right thickness, and I stirred it as you told me. You know you said it was wanted urgently for old Brother Francis, his chest being so bad... I thought I would cool it quickly, to be able to bottle it for you, so I took the pot from the fire and set it in a bowl of cold water...'

'And the pot burst,' said Cadfael resignedly.

'Fell apart,' owned Oswin, bewildered and grieved, 'in two great pieces, and shed forth all that honey and the herbs into the water. An extraordinary thing! Did you know the pot was cracked?'

'Son, the pot was sound as a bell, and one of my best, but nor it nor any other here is meant to be taken straight from the fire and plumped into cold water. The clay does not like so sharp a change, it shrinks and shatters. And while we are on that, take heed that glass bottles have the same objection,' added Cadfael hastily. 'If warm things are to be put in them, the bottles must be warmed first. Never thrust any matter straight from heat to cold or cold to heat.'

'I have cleared away all,' said Oswin apologetically, 'and thrown out the pot, too. But all the same, I am sure there must have been a crack somewhere in it . . . But I am sorry the linctus is wasted, and I will come back after supper and make a fresh brew in its place.'

God forbid! thought Cadfael, but managed to refrain from saying it aloud. 'No, son!' he said firmly. 'Your duty is to attend Collations and keep the true round of your order. I will see to the linctus myself.' His supply of pots would have to be defended from Brother Oswin's excellent intentions henceforth. 'Now be off and get ready for Vespers.'

Thus Brother Oswin's latest achievement in the herbarium was the reason for Cadfael returning to his workshop that evening after supper, and for his involvement in all that happened afterwards.

## 2

Sir Godfrid Picard and his lady came to Vespers in state, with Iveta de Massard diminutive between them like a lamb led to sacrifice. A hard-faced elderly maid carried Lady Picard's prayer book, and a valet attended Sir Godfrid. The girl had put off her display finery, and came simply dressed in dark colours, with a veil over her great sheaf of gold hair. She stood and knelt throughout with downcast eyes and pale, mute face. Cadfael watched her with curiosity and sympathy from his place among the brethren, and wondered the more, the more he gazed. What kin could she be to the crusader whose name had been a legend among his contemporaries, however this present generation might have forgotten him? Nearly forty years dead, and a man is dead indeed.

At the end of Vespers, as the brothers filed out to supper, Iveta rose, and went swiftly forward, hands clasped, into the Lady Chapel, and there sank to her knees before the altar. It seemed to Cadfael that Agnes Picard would have followed her, but that her husband laid a restraining hand on her arm, for Prior Robert Pennant, ever attentive to Norman nobility of his own kind, was bearing down upon them in all his lofty, silver-haired grandeur, with some civil invitation which could not well be refused. The lady cast one sharp glance at the devout figure of her niece, who seemed to be totally absorbed in fervent prayer, and surrendered gracefully, pacing beside the prior on her husband's arm.

Cadfael made a very hasty supper among his fellows, still disturbed by the events of the day, for which, unhappily, all his herbs had no remedy. As well that he had a specific task to occupy him during the evening, thanks to the inexhaustible optimism of Brother Oswin.

Iveta remained on her knees until all had been silent about her for some minutes, the prior's voice fading away into distance, assiduously attentive. Then she stole up from her place and went to peer cautiously through the south door into the cloister. Robert had drawn the guests into the garth with him to admire the last of the carefully tended roses. Their backs were turned to her, and the western walk of the cloister stood empty before her. Iveta gathered up her skirts and her courage, only she knew with how much heroism and how little hope, and ran like a frightened mouse from cats, out into the great court, and there looked round her desperately.

She knew this enclave not at all, it was the first time she had entered it; but she saw between the buildings of the guest-hall and the abbot's lodging the green of pleached hedges framing a narrow alley, and the heads of trees nodding beyond. There must be the gardens, at this hour surely deserted. Somewhere there he had said he would wait for her, and as she passed him she had given him the signal that she would not fail him. Why had she done so? This could be nothing better than a farewell. Yet she sped towards it with a despairing courage she would have done better to summon up long ago, before it was too late. She was already solemnly affianced, a contract almost as binding as marriage itself. Easier far to slip out of life than out of that bargain.

The thick green walls enclosed her, twilight within twilight. She drew breath and slowed to a walk, uncertain which way to go. The path to the right led between the rear of the guest-hall and the abbey fish-ponds, and beyond the second pool a little foot-bridge crossed the mill leat near the outflow, and brought her to a gateway in a mellow stone wall. With one more wall between herself and detection she felt unaccountably safer, and there was a curious comfort and calm in the wave of spiced sweetness that rose about her as her skirts brushed the greenery within. Rosemary and lavender, mint and thyme, all manner of herbs filled the walled garden with aromatic odours, grown a little rank now with autumn, ready to sink into their winter sleep very soon. The best of their summer was already harvested.

A hand reached out of an arbour in the wall to take her hand, and a voice whispered in haste: 'This way, quickly! There's a hut here in the corner . . . . an apothecary's shop. Come! No one will look for us in there.'

Every time she had ever been able to draw close to him – the times had been very few and very brief – she had been startled and reassured by the very size of him, head and shoulders above her, wide in breast and shoulder, long in the arm, narrow and fleet in the flank, as though his engulfing shadow could wall her in from all threats, like a tower. But she knew it could not, and he was as unblessed and vulnerable as she. The very thought had made her even more timorous than she was for herself. Great lords, if they once take against, can quite destroy young squires, however tall and strong and well versed in arms.

'Someone may come there,' she whispered, clinging to his hand.

'At this time of the evening? No one will come. They're at supper now, they'll be in the chapterhouse afterwards.' He drew her along with him in his arm, under the eaves rustling with dried herbs, into the wood-warm interior where glass gleamed on the shelves, and the brazier, fed to burn slowly until it was needed, provided a small eye of fire in the dimness. The door he left open, just as it stood. Better move nothing, to betray the visit of unauthorised strangers. 'Iveta! You did come! I was afraid . . . .'

'You knew I'd come!'

'. . . afraid you might be watched too closely, and every moment. Listen, for we may not have long. You shall not, you shall not be delivered over to that gross old man. Tomorrow, if you'll trust me, if you will to go with me, come at this hour again, here . . . .'

'Oh, God!' she said in a soft moan. 'Why do we make believe there can be any escape?'

'But there can, there must!' he insisted furiously. 'If you truly want it . . . if you love me . . .'

'*If* I love you . . . .!'

She was in his arms, her own slight arms embracing with all their might as much of his hard young body as they could span, when Brother Cadfael, in all innocence, his sandals silent on his well-kept grass paths, darkened the doorway and startled them apart. He was a good deal more astonished than they, and to judge by their faces, much less terrible than whatever they had momentarily taken him for. Iveta recoiled until her shoulders were brought up against the wooden wall of the hut. Joscelin stood his ground by the brazier, feet solidly spread. Both of them recovered countenance with a gallantry that was more than half desperation.

'I cry your pardon,' said Cadfael placidly. 'I did not know I had patients waiting. Brother Infirmarer will have recommended you to me, I take it. He knew I should be working here until Compline.'

He might have been speaking Welsh to them, of course, but with luck they might pick up the hints he was hastily offering. Desperation does tend to sharpen the wits at need. And he had heard, as they had not, the brushing of garments along the path outside, the rapid, irate tread of a woman's feet bearing down on them. He was standing by the brazier, striking flint and steel to light his little oil-lamp, when Agnes Picard appeared in the doorway, tall and chill, brows drawn together into a level, unbroken line.

Brother Cadfael, having lit and trimmed the wick, turned to gather up into a box the troches Brother Oswin had left drying, little white cakes of carminative powder bound with gum. The act enabled him to keep his back turned serenely upon the woman in the doorway, though he was very well aware of her. Since it was plain that neither of the young people was yet capable of uttering a sensible word, he went on talking for them all.

'It will be the tiring journey,' he said comfortably, closing the box upon his tablets, 'that has brought on your headache. It was wise of you to consult Brother Edmund, a headache should not be neglected, it may deprive you of the sleep you need, otherwise. I'll make you a draught – the young gentleman will not mind waiting a few moments for his lord's needs...'

Joscelin, recovering, and resolutely keeping a shoulder turned on the baleful presence in the doorway, said fervently that he would gladly wait until the Lady Iveta had whatever she required. Cadfael reached for a small cup from a shelf, and selected one from a row of bottles. He was in the act of pouring when a voice cold and piercing as fine steel said behind them, with deliberation: 'Iveta!'

All three of them swung round in a very fair show of being innocently startled. Agnes came forward into the hut, narrowing her eyes suspiciously.

'What are you doing here? I have been looking for you. You are keeping everyone waiting for supper.'

'You lady niece, madam,' said Cadfael, forestalling whatever the girl might have roused herself to say, 'is suffering from a common distress after the exertion of travel, and Brother Infirmarer rightly recommended her to come to me for a remedy.' He held out the cup to Iveta, who took it like one in a dream. She was white and still, the sum of her frustration and fear showed only in her eyes. 'Drink it off now, at once, before you go to supper. You may safely, it will do you nothing but good.'

And so it would, whether her head ached or no. It was one of his best wines, he kept it for his special favourites, since the amount he made of it each year was small. He had the satisfaction of seeing faint astonishment and pleasure sparkle through the desperation of her eyes, even if it faded soon. She put the empty cup back into his hand, and gave him the palest of smiles. At Joscelin she did not venture to look at all.

In a small voice she said: 'Thank you, brother. You are very good.' And to the presence that loomed darkly watching her: 'I am sorry I have delayed you, aunt. I am ready now.'

Agnes Picard said never a word more, but stood aside in cold invitation to the girl to precede her out of the room, eyed her steadily and glitteringly as she passed, and then, before following her, gave the young man a long, intent look that threatened all possible evil. The civilities might have been preserved, but very certainly Agnes had not been deceived, never for a moment.

They were gone, the bride and her keeper, the last rustle of skirts silenced. There was a long moment of stillness while the two left behind gazed helplessly at each other. Then Joscelin let out his breath in a great groan, and threw himself down on the bench that stood against the wall.

'The hag should fall from the bridge and drown in the fish-pond, now, this moment, while she's crossing! But things never work out as they should. Brother, don't think me ungrateful for the goodwill and the wit you've spent for us, but I doubt it was all thrown away. She's had her suspicions of me some while, I fancy. She'll find some way of making me pay for this.'

'At that, she may be right,' said Cadfael honestly. 'And God forgive me for the lies!'

'You told none. Or if she has not a headache, she has what's worse, an ache of the heart.' He ran angry fingers through his shock of flaxen hair, and leaned his head back against the wall. 'What was it you gave her?'

On impulse Cadfael refilled the cup and held it out to him. 'Here! The like potion might not do you any harm. God he knows whether you deserve it, but we'll scamp the judgement until I know more of you.'

Joscelin's eyebrows, winged and expressive, and darker by many shades than his hair, rose in appreciative surprise at the savour of the wine. His forehead and cheeks had the rich golden tan of an outdoor life, rare enough among those of such fair colouring. The eyes, now conning Cadfael rather warily over the rim of the cup, were as radiantly blue as Cadfael remembered them from Saint Giles, like cornflowers in a wheat-field. He did not look like a deceiver or a seducer, rather like an overgrown schoolboy, honest, impatient, clever after his fashion, and probably unwise. Cleverness and wisdom are not inevitable yoke-fellows.

'This is the best medicine I ever tasted. And you have been uncommonly generous to us, as you were uncommonly quick in the uptake,' said the boy, warmed and disarmed. 'And you know nothing about us, and had never seen either of us before!'

'I had seen you both before,' Cadfael corrected him. He began to measure his various pectoral herbs into a mortar, and took a small bellows to rouse the brazier from its quiescent state. 'I have a linctus to make before Compline. You'll not mind if I start work.'

'And I am in the way. I'm sorry! I've put you out enough already.' But he did not want to go, he was too full of matter he needed to unload from his heart, and could not possibly offer to anyone but just such a courteous chance acquaintance, perhaps never to be seen again. 'Or – may I stay?'

'By all means, if you're at leisure to stay. For you serve Huon de Domville, and I fancy his service might be exigent. I saw you pass by Saint Giles. I saw the lady, too.'

'You were there? The old man – he was not hurt?' Bless the lad, he genuinely wanted to know. In the middle of his own troubles, up to the neck, he could still feel indignation at an affront to another's dignity.

'Neither in body nor mind. Such as he live with a humility that transcends all possibility of humiliation. He was above giving a thought to the baron's blow.'

Joscelin emerged from his own preoccupation sufficiently to feel curiosity. 'And you were there among them – those people? You – Forgive me if I offend, it is not meant! – you are not afraid of going among them? Of their contagion? I have often wondered – *someone* tends them. I know they are forced to live apart, yet they cannot be utterly cut out of humanity.'

'The thing about fear,' said Cadfael, seriously considering, 'is that it is pointless. When need arises, fear is forgotten. Would you recoil from taking a leper's hand, if he needed yours, or you his, to be hauled out of danger? I doubt it. Some men would, perhaps – but of you I doubt it. You would grip first and consider afterwards, and by then fear would be clearly a mere waste of time. You are free of your lord's table tonight, are you? Then stay and give account of yourself, if you're so minded. You owe me at worst an excuse – at best, some amends for breaking in uninvited.'

But he was not displeased with his unruly intruder. Almost absent-mindedly Joscelin had taken the bellows from him, and was encouraging the brazier into reviving life.

'He has three of us,' said the boy thoughtfully. 'Simon waits on him at table tonight – Simon Aguilon, his sister's son – and Guy FitzJohn is the third of us, he's in attendance, too. I need not go back yet. And you know nothing about me, and I think you're in doubt whether you did right to try and help us. I should like you to think well of me. I am sure you cannot but think well of Iveta.' The name clouded his face again, he gazed ruefully into the satisfactory glow he was producing. 'She is...' He struggled with adoration, and exploded rebelliously: 'No, she is not perfection, how could she be? Since she was ten years old she has been in wardship to those two! If you were at Saint Giles, you saw them. One on either side, like dragons. Her perfection has been all crushed out of shape, too long. But if she were free, she would grow back into her proper self, she would be brave and noble, like her ancestors. And then I would not care,' he said, turning eyes blindingly blue and bright upon Cadfael, 'if she gave it all to someone else, not to me. No, I lie – I should care infinitely, but I would bear it, and still be glad. Only this – this wicked market-bargaining, this defilement, this I will not endure!'

'Mind the bellows! There, draw it out, you've given me all the fire I want. Lay it by on the stone there. Good lad! A name for a name is fair exchange. My name is Cadfael, a Welsh brother of this house, born at Trefriw.' Cadfael was pounding honey and a morsel of vinegar into his powdered herbs, and warming his pot by the fire. 'Now who may you be?'

'My name is Joscelin Lucy. My father is Sir Alan Lucy, and has two manors in the Hereford borders. He sent me as page to Domville when I was fourteen, as the custom is, to learn my squire-craft in a greater household. And I won't say my lord has been so hard a man to serve. I could not complain for myself. But for his tenants and villeins, and such as fall under his justice...' He hesitated. 'I have my letters, I can read Latin hand. I was at school with monks, it stays with a man. I don't say my lord's worse than his kind, but God knows he's no better. I should have asked my father to take me away to another lord, if...'

If this courtship, to dignify it by that name, had not begun to be mooted between Domville and the Massard heiress. If the boy had not seen, marvelled at, been captivated by, that tiny, fragile, virginal creature between her two dragons. His lord's entry where she was had been entry also, at whatever hopeless distance, for his esquires.

'By staying with him,' said the youth, wrenching at the insoluble complications of his predicament, 'I could at least see her. If I left him, how could I ever get near? So I stayed. And I do try to serve honestly, since I so promised. But oh, Brother Cadfael, is this just? Is it right? For the love of God, she is eighteen years old, and she shrinks from him, and yet, for all I can see, he is better than what she now has. She has no happiness now, and can look for none in her marriage. And I love her! But that's by the way. Of small account, if *she* could be happy.'

'Hmmm!' said Cadfael with mild scepticism, and stirred his gently bubbling pot, which began to fill the hut with a heady aromatic sweetness as it simmered. 'So many a lover has probably vowed, but with one eye on his own advantage, all the same. I suppose you'll tell me you're willing to die for her.'

Joscelin melted suddenly into a boy's grin. 'Well, not with any great eagerness! I'd liefer live for her, if it can be arranged. But if you mean, would I do all in my power to set her free to take another of her own choice, yes, I would. For this match is *not* of her choice, she dreads and loathes it, she is being forced into it utterly against her will.'

There was no need to labour it; the first glimpse of her face and bearing had said it all for him.

'And those who should most guard her and work for

her good are using her for their own ends, and nothing more. Her mother – she was Picard's sister – died when Iveta was born, and her father when she was ten years old, and she was given over into her uncle's ward as her nearest kin, which is natural enough, if her kin had proved natural to her! Oh, I am not so blind as not to know there's nothing new in a guardian making the best profit for himself out of his ward, instead of using his own substance on her behalf, and plundering her lands instead of nourishing them for her future good. I tell you, Brother Cadfael, Iveta is being sold to my lord for his voice and countenance with the king, and advancement under his shadow – but for more than that. She has great lands. She is the only Massard left, all that great honour goes with her hand. And I suspect that the bargain they've struck over her means the carving up of what was once a hero's portion. A great swathe out of those lands of hers will surely stay with Picard, and some of what goes with her to Domville will have been milked hard for years before it passes. A very fine arrangement for both of them, but crying wrong to Iveta.'

And every word could all too well be true. Such things happen where a child is left orphan and heiress to great estates. Even if the child be a boy, and young enough, thought Cadfael, and with no one to protect him, he can be married off to make a profitable alliance for his guardian, to join up lands convenient for exploitation, to spite a rival, just as nimbly and irresistibly as can a girl; but with a girl the thing is more usual, and less to be questioned. No, no one in authority between baron and king will lift a finger to interfere with Iveta's destiny. Only, perhaps, some rash young hothead like this one, at his own risk and hers.

He did not ask what they had been whispering together about, when he stumbled in upon their embrace. However fretted and angry, young Lucy had still something, some faint, hoarded hope in his sleeve, so much was clear. Better not to ask, not to let him utter it, even if he offered. But there was one thing Cadfael needed to know. The only Massard left, he had said.

'What was the name of her father?' he asked, stirring his thickening brew. Before Compline he would be able to set it aside to cool gradually.

'Hamon FitzGuimar de Massard.'

He stressed the patronymic with ceremony and pride. There were still some among the young, it seemed, who had been taught a proper regard for the great names of the dead.

'Her grandsire was that Guimar de Massard who was at the taking of Jerusalem, and was captured afterwards at the battle of Ascalon, and died of his wounds. She has his helm and his sword. She treasures them. The Fatimids sent them back after his death.'

Yes, so they had, in courtesy to a brave enemy. They had been asked also to return his body from its temporary burial, and had received the request graciously, but then the intermittent squabbling among the Crusader leaders had cost them the chance of securing the port of Ascalon, and the negotiations for the return of the paladin's body had been neglected and forgotten. Chivalrous enemies had buried him with honour, and there he rested. It was all very long ago, years before these young people were ever born.

'I remember,' said Cadfael.

'And now it's great shame that the last heiress of such a house should be so misused and defrauded of her happiness.'

'So it is,' said Cadfael, lifting his pot from the fire and standing it aside on the beaten earth of the floor.

'And it must not continue,' said Joscelin emphatically. 'It shall not continue.' He rose, with a vast sigh. 'I must go back, no help for it.' He eyed the array of bottles and jars, and the dangling bunches of herbs that furnished the workshop with infinite possibilities. 'Have you not something among all these wonders that I could slip into his cup? His or Picard's, what does it matter which? Either removed from this world would set Iveta free. And leave the world the sweeter!'

'If that is seriously meant,' said Cadfael firmly, 'you are in peril of your soul, boy. And if it is mere levity, you deserve a great clout on the ear for it. If you were not so big, I might attempt it.'

The flashing smile came and went in an instant, warmly if ruefully. 'I could stoop,' he offered.

'You know as well as I do, child, that you would not touch such foul methods as murder, and you do yourself great wrong to misuse words.'

'Would I not?' said Joscelin softly, the smile clean gone. 'You do not know, brother, how far I would put my soul in peril to make all safe for Iveta.'

Cadfael fretted about it all through Compline, and into the warming-room for the last quiet half-hour before bed. Of course there had been nothing for it but to take the boy sternly to task, tell him firmly and truly that he must abjure all such black thoughts, out of which nothing good could come. None but knightly measures were open to him, since he was destined for knighthood, and he should, he must, forswear all others. The trouble was that the boy had shown very sound sense in retorting that he would be a great fool to challenge his lord to honest combat, after the manner of knighthood, since Domville would not even take such an impertinence seriously, but simply throw him out of his household and be done with him. And how would Iveta be helped then?

But need that mean that he was really capable of contemplating the use of murder? Remembering the open brown face, very poorly provided for dissembling, and the headlong manner, surely not adapted to going roundabout, Cadfael could hardly believe it. And yet there was that fragile golden miniature of a girl with her sad, resigned face and empty eyes, two days from her hated marriage, and her fate was a weighty enough matter to demand, if it could not justify, a death or two.

The urgency touched Cadfael, no less than Joscelin Lucy. For here was Guimar de Massard's granddaughter, stripped of all her kin but these two who hedged her in like guardian dragons. And how could the last of the Massards be left to her fate, without a finger raised from all those who had known her grandfather, and reverenced his memory? As well abandon a comrade wounded and surrounded in battle.

Brother Oswin crept diffidently to Cadfael's side in the warming-room. 'Is the linctus already prepared, brother? The fault was mine, let me do something to make amends. I will rise early and bottle it for you. I have caused you such extra travail, I should make some repayment.'

He had caused more travail than he knew, and more perplexity of mind, but at least he had recalled Cadfael to the remembrance of his first duty here; after, of course, the observance of the rule.

'No, no,' said Cadfael hastily. 'The boiling is very well, and it will cool overnight and thicken, after Prime is time enough before bottling. You are reader tomorrow, you must keep the offices strictly, and think only of your reading.'

And leave my brew alone, he thought, as he went to his cell and his prayers. It came clear to him suddenly how like were Brother Oswin's large hands to those of Joscelin Lucy, and yet how the one pair made havoc of whatever they touched, and the other pair, for all their size, moved with delicate dexterity, whether on the reins of a speckled grey horse, or sword and lance, or circling the tender body of a heart-heavy girl.

And with equal adroitness, thus driven, on the means of murder?

Cadfael arose well before Prime next morning, and went to bottle his overnight brew, and take a measure of it to Brother Edmund at the infirmary. The day had dawned misty and mild, without wind. In the still air sounds were muted and movements softened, and the great court presented an ordinary picture of routine activities from Prime to breakfast, through the first Mass for the lay servants and workmen, the second Mass and the chapter that followed, on this occasion cut short and briskly conducted, there being so much following business to be seen to for the next day's marriage. There was therefore a rather longer interval left for relaxation before High Mass at ten, and Cadfael took the opportunity of returning to the herb-gardens, and earmarking for Brother Oswin's afternoon duty those tasks which seemed best proofed against his knack of well-intentioned devastation. Autumn was a good time, since there was digging to be done, to make the cleared ground ready for the operation of the frosts to come.

Cadfael returned to the great court before ten o'clock, when brothers, pupils, guests and townsmen were beginning to gather for High Mass. The Picards were just issuing forth from the guest-hall, Iveta forlornly small and mute between uncle and aunt, but looking, or so Cadfael thought, resolutely composed, as though a faint, reviving wind had blown through the heavy stillness of her despair, and given her heart at least to hope for a miracle. The elderly maidservant, as forbidding of visage as Agnes herself, walked close behind. The child was hemmed in securely every way.

They were moving at leisure towards the cloister and the south door, with Brother Denis the hospitaller in attendance, when the decorous quiet was rudely broken by a furious clatter of hooves at the gatehouse, and into the court galloped a rider on a speckled grey horse, at such headlong speed that he almost rode down the porter, and scattered the servants like hens before the fox. Reining round abruptly with great slithering of hooves on the moist cobbles, he flung the bridle on his horse's neck, and leaped down with flaxen hair erected and blue eyes blazing, to plant himself squarely in Godfrid Picard's path, feet spread and jaw jutting, a young man in a formidable rage.

'My lord, it's *you* have done this thing to me! I am cast off from my service, thrown out without reason, without fault, with nothing but horse and saddle-bags, and ordered to quit this town before night. This in a moment, and no word of mine will be heard in excuse! And well I know to whom I owe the favour! You, you have complained of me to my lord, and got me turned off like a dog, and I will have satisfaction from you for the favour, man to man, before ever I turn my back on Shrewsbury!'

## 3

Like a flung stone in a placid pool, this violent invasion cast out flurries of ripples in all directions, to beat against gatehouse and guest-hall and cloister. Brother Denis fluttered uncertainly at gaze, unaware even of the identity of this large and very angry youth, and desirous only of restoring peace in the court, but without the least notion of how to set about it. Picard, brought up almost breast to breast with the solid young body and grim face, flamed red to the cheekbones, and then blanched white with answering fury. He could not go forward, he would not go aside, and even if the startled cluster of servants had not been pressing close behind, he would not have given back by an inch. Agnes glared outrage, and quickly reached to grip Iveta by the arm, for the girl had started forward with a faint, desolate cry, the subdued stillness of her face broken, and for one moment sparkling with frantic emotion, as shattered ice takes the light and dazzles. Just for that instant she would have forgotten everything but the boy, sprung to his side without conceal, flung her arms round him, if her aunt's grasp had not plucked her back without gentleness, drawn her close to a rigid, sombrely gowned side, and held her there with steely fingers. Whether from long submission or from newly alerted wit, she shrank and was still, and the light, but not the pain, ebbed out of her face. Cadfael saw it, and was inextricably caught. No young thing hardly out of her nurse's care should so suffer.

He remembered that look later. At this moment he was held by the impact of Joscelin Lucy's wildly unwise youth and Godfrid Picard's subtle, experienced maturity. It was not so unequal a combat as might have been expected. The boy was above himself, and unquestionably a man of his hands, and a son of confident, if minor, privilege.

'I may not ask you to draw, here,' he said high and clearly. Anger raised his voice, as though to reach a marshal in the lists. 'I challenge you to name the place and time where we may draw, to good effect. You have done me an offence, I am cast off by reason of your persuasion, do me right, and stand to what you have urged against me.'

'Insolent rogue!' Picard spat back at him disdainfully. 'I am more likely to set my hounds on you than dignify you by crossing swords with you. If you are dismissed for a profitless, treacherous, meddling, ill-conditioned wretch, you are rightly served, be thankful your lord did not have you whipped from his door. You have got off lightly. Take care you don't provoke worse usage than you already have. Now stand out of my way, and get you gone homewards, as you were ordered.'

'Not I!' vowed Joscelin through his teeth. 'Not until I have said all that I have to say, here before all these witnesses. Nor will I go for being ordered. Does Huon de Domville own the ground I stand on and the air I breathe? His service he can keep, there are other households at least as honourable as his. But to run with mean tales to him, and blacken my name, was that fair dealing?'

Picard gave vent to a wordless bellow of impatient rage, and turned to snap imperious fingers at his menservants, half a dozen of whom, solid men-at-arms of an age to be experienced in rough play, came forth blithely enough, three on either side, closing in a half-circle.

'Take this wastrel out of my sight. The river is handy. Put him to cool in the mud!'

The women drew back in a flurry of skirts, Agnes and

the maid dragging Iveta away by both wrists. The men-at-arms advanced, grinning but wary, and Joscelin was obliged to take some paces back, to avoid being encircled.

'Stand clear!' he warned, glaring. 'Let the coward do his own work, for if you lay hand on me there'll be blood let.'

He had so far forgotten himself as to lay hand to hilt, and draw the blade some inches from the scabbard. Cadfael judged that it was high time to intervene, before the young man put himself hopelessly in the wrong, and both he and Brother Denis were starting forward to thrust between the antagonists, when from the cloister surged the tall presence of Prior Robert, monumentally displeased, and from the direction of the abbot's lodging, swift and silent and thus far unnoticed, the equally tall and far more daunting figure of Abbot Radulfus himself, hawk-faced, shrewd-eyed, and coldly but composedly angry.

'Gentlemen, gentlemen!' Robert spread long, elegant hands between. 'You do yourselves and our house great dishonour. Think shame to touch weapon or threaten violence within these walls!'

The men-at-arms recoiled thankfully into the crowd. Picard stood smouldering but controlled. Joscelin shot his sword very hastily back into the sheath, but stood breathing heavily and cherishing his fury. He was not an easy young man to abash, and harder still to silence. He made a half-turn that brought him eye to eye with the abbot, who had reached the borders of the dispute, and stood lofty, dark and calm, considering all the offenders at leisure. There fell a silence.

'Within the bounds of this abbey,' said Radulfus at last, without raising his voice, 'men do not brawl. I will not say we never hear an angry word. We are also men. Sir Godfrid, keep your men at heel on these premises.

And you, young man, so much as touch your hilt again, and you shall lie in a penitent's cell overnight.'

Joscelin bent head and knee, though the abbot might well have thought the gesture somewhat perfunctory. 'My lord abbot, I ask your pardon! Threatened or no, I was at fault.' But owning his fault, he kept his rage. A close observer might even have wondered if he was not contemplating the possible advantages of offending again, and being cast as promised into a cell within these walls. Locks may be picked, lay brothers suborned or tricked – yes, there were possibilities! He was disadvantaged, however, by a fair-minded disposition not to offend those who had committed no offence against him. 'I stand in your mercy,' he said.

'Good, we understand each other. Now, what is this dispute that troubles the peace here?'

Both Joscelin and Picard began to talk at once, but Joscelin, for once wise, drew back and left the field to his elder. He stood biting a resolute lip and regarding the abbot's face, as Picard brushed him contemptuously aside in the terms he had expected.

'Father, this impertinent squire has been turned off by his lord for a negligent, ill-conditioned fellow, and he credits me with so advising my lord Domville, as indeed I felt it my duty to do. For I have found him presumptuous, pressing his company upon my niece, and in all ways a troubler of the peace. He came here to brawl with me, resenting his well-deserved dismissal. He has no more than his due, but he will not be schooled. And that is all the matter,' he said scornfully.

Brother Cadfael marvelled how Joscelin kept his mouth shut on the flood of his grievance, and his eyes fixed respectfully upon Radulfus, until he was invited to speak. He must surely have acquired in these few moments a healthy respect for the abbot's fairness and shrewd sense, so to contain himself. He had confidence that he would not be judged unheard, and it was worth an effort at self-control to manage his defence aright.

'Well, young sir?' said Radulfus. It could not be asserted that he smiled, his countenance remained judicially remote and calm; but there might have been the suggestion of indulgence in his voice.

'Father Abbot,' said Joscelin, 'all of us of these two houses came here to see a marriage performed. The bride you have seen.' She had been hustled away out of sight, into the guest-hall, long before this. 'She is eighteen years old. My lord – he that *was* my lord! – is nearing sixty. She has been these last eight years orphaned and in her uncle's care, and she has great lands, long in her uncle's administration.' Some indication of his unexpected drift had penetrated by then, Picard was boiling and voluble. But Radulfus dipped a frowning brow, and raised a silencing hand, and they gave way perforce.

'Father Abbot, I pray your help for Iveta de Massard!' Joscelin had gained his moment, and could not hold back. 'Father, the honour of which she is lady spans four counties and fifty manors, it is an earl's portion. They have farmed it between them, uncle and bridegroom, they have parcelled it out, she is bought and sold, without her will – Oh, God, she has no will left, she is tamed! – *against* her will! My offence is that I love her, and I would have taken her away out of this prison . . .'

The latter half of this, though Cadfael had drawn close enough to hear all, was certainly lost to most others under a shrill clamour of refutation, in which Agnes played the loudest part. She had a voice that rode high over opposition, Joscelin could not cry her down. And in the midst of the hubbub, suddenly there were crisp hoofbeats in the gateway, and horsemen pacing into the court with the authority of office, and in numbers calculated to draw ear and eye. The thread alike of Joscelin's appeal and Picard's refutation was broken abruptly; every eye turned to the gate.

First came Huon de Domville, the muscles of his face set like a wrestler's biceps, his small, black, malevolent eyes alertly bright. Close at his elbow rode Gilbert Prestcote, sheriff of Shropshire under King Stephen, a lean, hard, middle-aged knight browed and nosed like a falcon, his black, forked beard veined with grey. He had a sergeant and seven or eight officers at his back, an impressive array. He halted them within the gate, and dismounted as they did.

'And there he stands!' blared Domville, eyes glittering upon Joscelin, who stood startled and gaping. 'The rascal himself! Did I not say he'd be stirring up trouble everywhere possible before he took himself off? Seize him, sheriff! Lay hold on the rogue and make him fast!'

He had been so intent on his quarry that he had not immediately observed that the abbot himself was among those present. His eye lit on the austere and silent figure belatedly, and he dismounted and doffed in brusque respect. 'By your leave, Father Abbot! We have dire business here, and I am all the sorrier that this young rogue should have brought it within your walls.'

'Such disturbance as he has so far caused us,' said Radulfus coolly, 'does not seem of a sort to require the attendance of sheriff and sergeant. I gather that if he has offended, he has also been brought to book for it. To dismiss him your service is your right. To pursue him further seems somewhat excessive. Unless you have further complaint to make against him?' He looked to Prestcote for his answer.

'There is indeed more,' said the sheriff. 'I am instructed by my lord Domville that since this squire was ordered to pack and go, a thing of great value has been missed, and looked for in vain within the household.

There is ground for suspicion that this man may have stolen it in despite of his lord, and in revenge for his dismissal. He stands so charged.'

Joscelin was staring in astonished derision, not yet even angry on this count, and certainly not afraid. 'I, steal?' he gasped in huge contempt. 'I would not touch the meanest thing that belonged to him, I would not willingly take away on my shoes the dust of his courtyard. Go, he bade me, and so I did, out of his house, and have not even stopped to gather together everything that was mine there. All that I brought away is here on my body or in the saddle-bags there.'

The abbot raised a restraining hand. 'My lord, what is this valuable thing which is lost? How does it bulk? When was it missed?'

'It is the wedding gift I intended for my bride,' said the baron, 'a collar of gold and pearls. It could lie in the palm of a man's hand, once out of its case. I meant to bring it to the girl today, after Mass, but when I went to take it, and looked within the case, I found it empty. Nigh on an hour ago, I suppose, for we wasted time hunting for it, though the leaving of the empty case should have told us it was not lost, but stolen. And but for this turbulent boy, who was turned off for good reason and took it very defiantly, no one else has left my household. I charge him with the theft, and I will have the remedy of law, to the last particle.'

'But did this young man know of this collar, and where to lay hand on it?' demanded the abbot.

'I did, Father,' Joscelin acknowledged readily. 'So did all three of us who served him as squires.'

Still more horsemen had appeared in the gateway, several of Domville's outridden retinue, and among them Simon and Guy, by the look of their faces by no means eager to be noticed or take any part in this encounter. They looked on from the background, uncertain and unhappy, as well they might.

'But I have not touched it,' Joscelin went on firmly. 'And here am I, just as I left the house, take me away and strip me if you will, you'll find never a thread that is not mine. And there is my horse and my saddle-bags, turn out whatever you find, and let the lord abbot be witness. But no,' he added vehemently, seeing Domville himself make a move towards the grey horse, 'not you, my lord! I will not have my accuser's hands pawing my belongings. Let an impartial judge do the searching. Father Abbot, I appeal to your justice!'

'That is but fair,' said the abbot. 'Robert, will you do what is needful?'

Prior Robert received the request with a dignified inclination of the head, and made a solemn procession of his advance upon the duty allotted him. Two of Prestcote's men-at-arms unbuckled the saddle-bags from their place, and when the horse, nervous at the press of people, sidled unhappily, Simon impulsively slipped down from his mount and ran to take the bridle and soothe the fidgety grey. The saddle-bags lay open on the cobbles of the court. Prior Robert plunged his hands into the first, and began to hand out the simple items of clothing and accoutrement their raging owner had stuffed unceremoniously within, barely an hour previously. The sergeant received them solemnly, Prestcote standing close by. Linen shirts, crumpled in a furious fist, chausses, tunics, shoes, a few items of spare harness, gloves...

Prior Robert ran his long hand about the interior to show that it was empty. He leaned to the second. Joscelin stood braced on long, shapely legs, barely attentive, his bold brown face arrogantly smiling. Though his mother, Cadfael thought, watching, would have something pithy to say about the way he handled the shirts she made for him, when he got home. *If* he got home...

And how if he did? What followed then for the girl

who had been hustled away and shut up somewhere with the elderly maidservant for gaoler? In all this she was the absent witness. No one asked her what she knew or what she thought. She was not a person, merely a piece of valuable merchandise.

The second bag yielded a handsome gown for best wear, villainously crumpled, sundry belts and baldrics, a blue capuchon, more shirts, a pair of soft shoes, a best pair of chausses, also blue. The mother who had made all these had had an eye fondly to her offspring's fair colouring and blue eyes. And marvel, there was a bound book in thin, carved wooden covers, the young man's prayer book. He had said that he was lettered.

Lastly, Prior Robert plucked out a small roll of fine linen, and began to unwrap it on his palm. He raised a wondering and approving face.

'It is a silver scallop-shell medal. Whoever owned it made the pilgrimage to Compostella, to the shrine of Saint James.'

'It is my father's,' said Joscelin.

'And that is all. This bag is also empty.'

Domville started forward suddenly with a crow of triumph. 'Ah, but what's here? There's something yet in the linen roll – I caught a glint . . .' He plucked at the dangling end of the cloth, almost wrenching it from the prior's hand. The silver medallion fell to the ground, some inches more of its wrapping unrolled, and something flashed and fell after, uncoiling like a little golden snake, to lie in a pool of fine yellow links and creamy pearls between the cobbles at Joscelin's feet.

He was so dumbfounded that he could not find a word to say, but stood staring at the small, precious thing that damned him. When at last he raised his eyes, and caught the intent gaze of all those other eyes, Domville gleefully content, the sheriff grimly satisfied, the abbot aloof and sad, and everywhere mute accusation, he shook violently, stirring out of his shocked stillness. He cried out passionately that he had not taken it, that it was not he who had put it there. But he uttered his denial only once, recognising at once its inevitability and its uselessness. He had some mad thought of putting up a fight for it, but met the abbot's stern, disillusioned eye, and deliberately put away the thought. Not here! He had pledged himself to forswear offence against this place. So here there was nothing he could do but submit. Once outside the gates it would be another matter, and the surer they were of his submission, the fewer crippling precautions they were likely to take. He stood mute and unresisting as the sergeant and his men closed in upon him.

They stripped him of sword and dagger, and kept close hold of him by both arms, but because they were many and he was but one, and seemed utterly subdued, they did not trouble to bind him. Domville stood by, vengefully grinning, and did not deign to stoop to pick up his property, leaving it for Simon to hurry forward, abandoning the grey horse's bridle, to retrieve the collar and hand it to him. He cast a very doubtful and anxious look at Joscelin as he did so, but said never a word. The Picards looked on with evident and malicious satisfaction. A nuisance out of their way, and if Domville pleased, out of everyone's way, for ever. Such a theft, with the additional odour of petty treason about it, even if he had already been dismissed his lord's service, could cost a man his neck.

'I will have the full penalty of law on him,' said Domville, and fixed a commanding stare upon the sheriff.

'That will be matter for the court,' said Prestcote shortly, and turned to his sergeant. 'Have him away to the castle. I must have some talk with Sir Godfrid Picard and the lord abbot, I'll follow you.'

The prisoner went with lamb-like meekness, his fair

head drooping, his arms lax and submissive in the grip of two brawny men-at-arms. Brothers and guests and servants fell away to leave him passage, and a horrified silence closed after his passing.

Brother Cadfael was left gazing as numbly as the rest. It was hard indeed to recognise the belligerent youngster who had galloped into the great court so short a time before, or the audacious lover who had penetrated into the enemy's territory to plot something desperate with a girl too frightened to reach for what her heart desired. Cadfael could not believe in such sudden translations. On impulse he made off towards the gate in haste, to keep the sorry little procession in sight. Behind him as he went he heard Simon Aguilon's voice asking: 'Shall I take his grey back to our stable, sir? We cannot abandon the poor beast, *he*'s done no wrong.' It was not quite clear from the tone whether he believed the poor beast's master had done any, but Cadfael doubted it. He could not be the only one who had reservations about that theft.

Joscelin and his guards were reaching the approaches of the bridge when Cadfael emerged into the Foregate and hastened after them. The hill of Shrewsbury, with its towers and houses cresting the long line of the wall, gleamed fitfully in a moist and feeble sunshine beyond the full flow of the Severn, and far to the right the tall bulk of the castle showed, the prison to which prisoner and escort were now bound. Since the height of the summer there had been heavy rains, and the flood coming down from Wales had swelled the flow here into a rapid high water that swallowed the lower reaches of the islands. The nearest section of the bridge, the drawbridge that could cut off approach to the town at need, was down and bearing plenteous traffic, for the last of the harvest was coming in, fruit and roots for fodder, and the provident were looking to their stores for the winter. Three horsemen rode ahead of the prisoner and his escort, three more brought up the rear, but Joscelin and those who held him went on foot, not briskly, for no prisoner in his right mind is in any haste to have a cell door slammed on him, but not slowly, either, for he was sharply prodded when he hung back. Carts and townspeople afoot drew to the side out of their way, and stood to stare, some so interested that they forgot themselves and closed in again at once, staring after, and barred the way for the following horsemen.

There had frequently been high feeling between the town and the king's sheriff of the shire, and Prestcote's sergeant was wary of using whip or threat on burgesses whose retaliatory sting had sometimes proved sharp. Thus it happened that when the prisoner had passed through the narrowing gate of the drawbridge tower, and the starers turned to gape and blocked the way, the following horsemen contented themselves with calling civilly for passage, and an increasing gap opened between them and their charge. Cadfael, slipping nimbly past the horses to join the curious in the gateway, had a partial view of what followed.

Still dejectedly slouching, Joscelin had reached the crown of the bridge's central span, where the parapet was no more than waist-high. It appeared that he stumbled, allowing the three before, who were archers, to move a yard or so ahead before they realised it. There was a cart drawn aside to the left, the entire group therefore moved to the right to pass by. As they drew near to the wall, Joscelin suddenly braced the deceptively limp sinews of his fine large body, swept both the guards who held him round in a dizzying circle to the right, sweeping them off their feet before they knew what was happening, tore his arms free, and leaped one sprawling adversary to reach the wall. One of those following clawed desperately at his foot as he vaulted to the parapet, but he kicked out vigorously and sent the man staggering. Before any other could get a hand to him, he had leaped strongly out over the flood, and plunged feet-first and cleanly into the centre of the river, and there vanished from sight.

It was beautifully done, and Cadfael, who saw it, could not but rejoice. For no good reason, he was suddenly sure in his own mind that Joscelin Lucy had never laid hand on Domville's gold, that Agnes's report to her husband of the meeting in the herb-garden, and Picard's complaint and warning to the imperilled bridegroom, had occasioned the boy's dismissal, and the dismissal had been expressly designed to make it possible to pursue the young man on a false charge of theft, and cast him safely into prison, out of the way of wide-ranging plans. They could not afford to leave him loose. He must go.

And he was gone, but of his own will, magnificently. Cadfael was leaning breathlessly over the downstream parapet like dozens of other eager watchers. Voices clamoured, some impartial, some partisan. There would always be plenty of law-abiding citizens here to cheer on any prisoner who broke free from the sheriff's hold.

The sergeant, who would certainly be held responsible for the loss, had leaped into action with a bellow of rage, and was roaring orders fore and aft at his men. The two horsemen ahead were sent galloping forward, to ride down to the riverside under the town walls, the three behind were turned back to perform the same service upon the abbey bank, to be ready to pick up the fugitive on whichever shore he tried to land. But both parties had to go roundabout, while the Severn, faster than any of them, went surging serenely forward, bearing away the invisible quarry downstream. The foot soldiers who were left had two archers among them, and at the sergeant's order they strung their bows in haste and thrust their way to the parapet, clearing away the gathering crowds that might hamper their drawing arms.

'Fast as he breaks surface,' yelled the sergeant, 'loose at him! Wing him if you can, kill him if you must!'

Minutes slid by, while the riders reached shore and began to wind a reckless way down to the waterside, and still there was no sign of the flaxen crest breaking the smooth-running surface.

'He's gone!' someone lamented, and some of the women drew pitying sighs.

'Not he!' shrilled an urchin flat on his belly across the parapet. 'See there? Nimble as an otter!'

Joscelin's pale head sprang up for a moment, sleek and streaming, far downstream. An arrow struck and drew shivering ripples only a foot or so aside, but by then he was back under the water, and when he again broke clear to draw breath he was almost out of bowshot. A second shaft fell well short of him, and he stayed in mid-stream, in full view, letting the flow take him with it, apparently as much at home in the water as he was on land. The archers got a derisive cheer for their pains from the imps of the town, or such of them as were safely out of reach, while the glimpse of a long arm impudently waving farewell from downstream raised a great ripple of half-suppressed laughter.

On either bank the horsemen coursed, hopelessly outdistanced, two threading their way along the path under the town wall and the abbot's vineyard, three now far along the rich level on the other side, where the abbey's main vegetable gardens and orchards stretched the length of the fields called the Gaye. They had as much hope of overtaking Joscelin Lucy as of holding their own with the floating leaves that surged past on the central current. The Severn ran silently and without fuss, but deadly fast.

They were craning and straining now after a fair head no larger than a little clot of foam spun by an unexpected eddy. Now barely visible, the next moment not visible at all. He had dived again, to make sure, thought Cadfael, watching intently, that no one should see which shore he approached, or where he drew himself out of the water. He was beyond the vineyard, he had the vast bulk of the castle walls on his left hand, bushes and low trees clothing the waste ground below, and on his right, beyond the orchards, woodlands coming down to the waterside. Small doubt which he would choose, but he refrained from showing himself again until he was ashore and into the trees. Cadfael, selecting carefully what seemed the most favourable cover, thought he caught, not so much a glimpse of the man, as a momentary convulsion of the leaning branches, and a brief sparkle in the water, as Joscelin hauled himself up the bank and vanished into the woods.

There was no more to see or to do here. Cadfael recalled himself to his neglected duty, and made off back to the abbey gatehouse, turning his back upon the gratified urchins and cursing guards. Small profit now in wondering how the boy would fare, weaponless, horseless, without money or dry clothing, and with a certain hue and cry out after him from this moment. Better make himself as scarce as ever he could, on foot or however offered, and put all the space possible between himself and Shrewsbury before night. All the same, Cadfael found himself doubting very much whether he would do anything so sensible.

It came as no great surprise to find that the news had gone before him. Just as he was approaching the gatehouse, Gilbert Prestcote came cantering out with a face of thunder, his remaining men-at-arms hard on his heels. He had nothing against Joscelin Lucy, and by his bearing throughout, no particular reverence for Huon de Domville, but the incompetence of his sergeant would stick in his craw like a nutshell, and unless the prisoner was recovered in short order, there was likely to be a stormy time ahead for all the luckless guards.

The porter emerged cautiously as the dust was settling, to gaze after them, and shook a rueful head as Cadfael came up. 'So the thief got away from them, after all! There'll be the devil to pay now, he'll turn out the whole garrison after the lad. And him on foot to outrun their horses! His own's away back to the bishop's house with the other young squire.'

They were gone, Huon de Domville, Simon Aguilon, Guy FitzJohn, grooms and all, and if the news of the escape had only so far reached the abbey gatehouse, they were gone in the firm belief that the thief was safe in hold.

'Who brought the word?' asked Cadfael. 'He was quick off the mark. He can't have stayed to see the play out.'

'Two lay brothers were just coming up from the Gaye with the last of the late apples. They saw him jump, and came in a hurry to tell. But you're not far behind them.'

So as yet it was cried no further than here. There were plenty of people, brothers, servants and guests, stirring about the great court in excitement and speculation, and some sallying forth to see what was toward along the riverbank. Huon de Domville's displeasure, when the word overtook him, would be vented elsewhere. Here Cadfael observed Godfrid and Agnes Picard in the doorway of the guest-hall, absorbed in some low-voiced and intent colloquy of their own, and their faces were taut and wary, and the way they eyed each other was all calculation and alarm. This development would not suit them at all; they wanted the troublesome boy safe behind locked doors in the castle, with a neck-charge hanging over him if Domville chose to press it to extremes.

There was no sign of Iveta. No doubt she was shut

away within, with Agnes's dragon to guard her. Nor did she appear for some hours, though her uncle and aunt were seen purposefully crossing and recrossing between the abbot's lodging, the guest-hall and the gatehouse on several occasions, and once Picard rode out for the greater part of an hour, surely to the bishop's house to confer with Domville. Cadfael fretted through the early afternoon over his own responsibility, neglectful of his customary watch on Oswin's activities, and somewhat chastened to discover that, for once unregarded, his assistant had spilled nothing, burned nothing, weeded out no precious plants by mistake, and broken nothing. It might, of course, be a special dispensation of providence, a courtesy to Cadfael's obvious preoccupation, but it might just as well be a reproof to him for keeping too unnerving an eye on his pupil.

His problem was simple to state but hard to solve. Ought he to go to Abbot Radulfus, and tell him just what he had witnessed and taken part in, the previous evening? To interfere in the affairs of complete strangers on such brief and suspect evidence may be a dangerous business, however well-meant. For all he knew, the plausible boy might be a fortune-hunter who had attempted to seduce Iveta into decamping with him for his own ends; and certainly he was quite attractive enough to have won her over. Yet however Cadfael tried to view the people concerned from all angles, without prejudice, he could not discover in the Picards any vestige of warmth or tenderness towards the girl.

The matter was solved for him when Abbot Radulfus sent for him, halfway through the afternoon. He obeyed the summons in mild speculation, and even milder apprehension, reflecting philosophically that lies may not always be so easily forgiven, even when well intended. Besides, it would be unwise to under-estimate Agnes Picard, even if he had not so far taken any steps to get in her way, beyond pouring opportunist oil on very stormy waters.

'I have received a complaint about you, Brother Cadfael,' said the abbot, turning with deliberation from his writing-desk. His voice, as always, was cool, incisive and courteous, his face unreadably calm. 'Oh, not by name, but I fancy the brother who was still at work in the herb-garden after supper last night is hardly likely to be any but you.'

'I was there,' said Cadfael readily. There was but one way of dealing with Radulfus, and that was directly and openly.

'In company with the Lady Iveta, and that young man who is now being hunted among the riverside coverts? And conniving with them in so irregular a meeting?'

'Hardly the one or the other,' said Cadfael. 'I walked in upon them in my own workshop, to my discomfort and theirs. So did Lady Picard only a moment later. That I put as soothing a face on it as possible, that I do avow. There was tempest threatening. Let us say I fired an arrow or two to break the clouds.'

'One version,' said the abbot serenely, 'I have heard from Sir Godfrid, who no doubt had it from his lady. Let me hear yours.'

Cadfael told it, as fully as he could recall, though he stopped short of mentioning Joscelin's reckless claim that he would not stop at murder. Hot-headed youngsters say such things, while their faces and their manner belie them. At the end of it Radulfus peered at him long and frowningly, and pondered.

'For your shufflings with truth, Brother Cadfael, I leave that to your confessor. But do you truly believe that this girl is afraid of her kinsman? That she is being enforced to courses hateful to her? I heard for myself what the accused man said. But he stood to gain greatly if he won her away from the marriage planned for her, and his motive may be as rotten as greed always is. A comely person is no warranty of a comely spirit. It may well be that her uncle has planned well for her, and it would be sin to disrupt his plans.'

'There is one particular,' said Cadfael carefully, 'that troubles me most. This girl is never seen alone, but always with uncle and aunt fencing her in on either side. She barely speaks, for someone else always speaks for her. I would be satisfied in my mind if you, Father, could but once speak with her freely alone, without witnesses, and listen to her unprompted.'

The abbot considered, and admitted gravely: 'There is much in what you say. It may be nothing but over-care that hems her so, yet her own voice should also be free to speak. How if I should pay a visit myself to the guest-hall, and see if I cannot make occasion to be alone with her? It would settle my mind, no less than yours. For I tell you frankly, Sir Godfrid assures me this squire has misused the entry he enjoyed as his lord's attendant, to pay furtive court to the girl, who was content enough before, and turn her head with his attentions and compliments. If that is all, this morning's happenings may have opened her eyes, and caused her to reconsider.'

There was no telling from his words or manner whether he accepted unquestioningly the truth of the accusation of theft, or the evidence of his eyes. He was too subtle not to have examined the alternatives.

'I intend,' he said, 'to invite the bridegroom with his nephew, and Sir Godfrid Picard, to sup with me here tonight. It gives me the occasion to carry the invitation myself. Why not now?'

Why not, indeed? Cadfael went out with him into the misty autumn afternoon cautiously pleased with the interview. Radulfus was an aristocrat and the equal of a baron, and entertained austere ideas of the duty of young people to be guided by those set in authority over them; but he was not blind to the frequent failings of elders, thus privileged, to impose benevolent order on the lives of their children. Let him but once gain some moments alone with Iveta, and he could not fail to win her confidence. She would not let slip such a chance. In this household he was master, he could stretch his hand over her and she would be protected even against kings.

They came out through the abbot's garden into the great court, and crossed towards the guest-hall. Cadfael would have taken his leave and returned to the gardens, but instead, they both halted at gaze. For on the stone bench by the wall of the refectory Iveta was sitting, her eyes diligently lowered over the prayer book in her lap, the veiled sunlight a soft sheen over her dark-gold hair. The confutation of everything that had been said of her: she was alone, seated there in the open quietly reading, not another soul of her uncle's household in sight.

Radulfus checked and gazed, and turning, made for the place where she was sitting. She heard, perhaps, the rustle of his habit; his walk was all but silent. She looked up, and her face was almost glacially calm and still. So white was her skin that it was hard to say whether she showed paler than normal, but when she saw the abbot bearing down on her she smiled, at least with her lips, and rose to make him a delicate reverence. Cadfael had drawn close at his back, hardly believing, not at all understanding, what he saw.

'Daughter,' said Radulfus gently, 'I am glad to see you thus at peace. I feared this morning's upsets must have disturbed you sadly, when you are contemplating so solemn a change in your estate, and have need of consideration and calm. You had, I think, a better opinion of that young man than he deserved, and cannot have been prepared for such a discovery. I am sure it distressed you.'

She looked up at him with a clear, still face, and unblinking eyes steady but empty, and said: 'Yes,

Father. I never thought any evil of him. But I have put my doubts by me now. I know my duty.' Her voice was very low, but quite firm and deliberate.

'And your mind is at rest about tomorrow's sacrament? I, too, have a duty, my child, towards all who come within my cure here. I am accessible to all. If there is anything you wish to say to me, do so freely, and there shall no one prevent or persuade but I will hear you faithfully. Your peace, your happiness, is my concern while you are within my walls, and shall have my prayers after you leave them.'

'I do believe it,' said Iveta, 'and I thank you. But my mind is settled and content, Father. I see my way clear, I am not to be swayed any more.'

The abbot looked at her long and earnestly, and she met his eyes without a quiver, and maintained her pale, resolute smile. Radulfus chose to have everything plainly stated, for this might be the only opportunity. 'I understand well that this marriage you will be making tomorrow is very much to the mind of your uncle and aunt, and suitable in rank and fortune. But is it also to your mind, daughter? You undertake it of your own will?'

She opened already wide eyes even wider, purple as irises, and parted innocently wondering lips, and said simply: 'Yes, of course, Father. Certainly of my own will. I am doing what I know it is right and good that I should do, and I do it with all my heart.'

## 4

Simon Aguilon took advantage of the hour while his lord was sleeping off his dinner and his rage together, and slipped away alone and in haste through the bishop's rear garden, down past the barns and orchards, and let himself out through the wicket in the wall, into the belt of scattered woodland that ran parallel with the Foregate. Somewhere well downstream, so the witnesses had said, Joscelin had vanished from view, and somewhere quite close to the spot where he was last seen he must have come ashore. Surely on the right bank, away from the castle. Why heave oneself ashore in the very nest of the enemy, even if there was cover to be had? There was better on the abbey shore, well below the Gaye.

They were hunting him, of course, but methodically, without haste. The first step had been to plant guards on all the roads that radiated from the town, and space roaming patrols between, to make a ring through which he could scarcely hope to break. Once that was done, they could afford to be slow and thorough in sifting all the cover within the ring. He had neither horse nor weapon, nor any means of getting either. Domville, once apprised of his flight, had had the grey horse removed from the common stable where Simon had taken him, and locked away privately, for fear his owner should venture in during the night to get possession of him and make a bid for escape. It was only a matter of time before he was re-taken.

Simon made his way deep into the woods downstream, until he considered he must have penetrated somewhere near the place where Joscelin had come ashore. Here, well inland, the growth was thick, with plenteous underbrush, and he found two separate small streams making their way towards the river. Wet as he would already be, Joscelin could well afford to use the bed of one of these as his path, in case they brought out dogs to hunt him. Simon followed the second stream inland into deep woodland. When he halted to listen, there was no sound anywhere about him but the occasional note of a bird. He stood with pricked ears, and began to whistle a dance tune they had picked up together from Domville's chaplain, who had a gift for music, and relished secular songs as well as the liturgy.

Simon had made his way gradually a further quarter of a mile away from the river, still whistling his estampie at intervals, before he got a response. The thick bushes on his right rustled, a hand was put out to part them, and he caught the gleam of a wary eye peering out.

'Joss?' he said in a whisper. Even if the hunt had not yet come this way, an inquisitive peasant gathering wood could give the alarm and spoil all. But the woodland silence hung undisturbed.

'Simon?' He was slow to trust. 'Are they making you their decoy? I never touched his damned gold.'

'I never thought you did. Hush, keep in cover!' Simon drew nearer, to hear and be heard in whispers. 'I'm here alone, I came to look for you. You can't lie out tonight, soaked from the river. I can't get your horse out to you yet, he's locked away. And all the roads are barred. You'll have to sit it out in hiding a day or so, until they lose interest and grow slack. *He*'ll give over wanting your blood, once tomorrow's over.'

The bushes shook with Joscelin's tremor of protest and detestation, for after tomorrow all would be lost, and all won. 'God witness,' he said through his teeth, 'I'll not give over thirsting for his. If they do marry her, I can still widow her.'

'Hush, you fool, never say such things! Supposing others heard you? You're safe enough with me, I'll help you as best I can, but . . . Be still and let me think!'

'I can shift for myself,' said Joscelin, rising cautiously erect in his covert, soiled and draggled, his fair hair plastered to his head still, but drying in wilful drifts of yellow at his temples. 'You're a good fellow, Simon, but I advise you take no foolish risks for me.'

'What do you want me to do?' Simon sounded exasperated. 'Stand back and let you be taken? See here, the safest place for you now, the one place they'll never think to look, is inside the bishop's grounds. Oh, not in house or stables or court, naturally. But that's the one household and garden this hunt is going to pass by. Everyone else's barns and byres will be ransacked. There's a hut in the corner of the grounds, by the door I came out at, where they store the hay from the back field. You could lie dry enough there, and I could bring you food – and the wicket in the wall we can bar inside, no one can come through from without. Then, if I can get Briar out to you somehow . . . What do you say?'

It was good sense enough, and Joscelin said yes to it with fervour and gratitude. What he did not say was that the want of a horse was nothing to him as yet, for he had no intention of going anywhere until either he had found some way of rescuing Iveta, or lost hope and heart and probably life in the attempt.

'You're a good friend, and I won't forget it. But take care for yourself, one of us in this coil is enough. Listen!' He caught Simon by the wrist, and shook him earnestly. 'If things fall out badly, and I'm ferreted out and taken, you knew nothing of it, I made my own way. Deny me, with all my goodwill. If there's meat or other matter to account for, I'll say I stole, and you'll let it rest at that.

Promise! I should be ashamed if I brought you into question.'

'You'll not be taken,' said Simon firmly.

'No, but promise!'

'Oh, very well, since you're so set, I'll let you stew – or at least go roundabout to hook you out of it. I like my skin whole, like most men, I'll take good care of it, one way or another. Come on, then! While things are quiet and I'm not missed.'

The way back was shorter, since they could make directly for the rear wall of the bishop's garden, and there was cover all the way. Once or twice Simon, going before, set up a soft whistling, and Joscelin dropped into the bushes, but each alarm passed in a moment, the small sounds that had set it off traced to birds taking flight, or wild things creeping among the dry brush. The wicket in the wall stood ajar as Simon had left it. He went first to open it cautiously and look round within, and then beckoned, and Joscelin dived through it thankfully, and heard it closed and barred behind him. And there was the low wooden fodder-store close against the wall. Within, it smelled of dry grass, and the fine dust stirred by their feet tickled the nose, and stung.

'No one will come here,' said Simon, low-voiced. 'The stables in the yard are well stocked. And it's snug enough lying. Keep close and quiet. I go with my uncle to sup with the abbot tonight, but I'll bring you meat and drink before then. You'll dry off nicely here in the hay.'

'It's a palace,' said Joscelin heartily, and squeezed his friend's arm with grateful warmth. 'I'll not forget this to you. Whatever happens now, praise God, I shall know there's one person who refuses to believe me a thief, and one friend I can rely on. But bear in mind, if it comes to it, I'd rather sink alone than drag you down into the muck with me.'

'Leave Simon's well-being,' said that young man with a confident grin, 'to one who loves him well. You take care of your own skin, I'll vouch for mine. And now I'm gone! He'll be yelling for me to help him dress for Vespers. That's the price he pays for supping with the abbot!'

Brother Cadfael marked their presence at Vespers, Huon de Domville sombrely splendid for the abbot's table, in rich crimson and black, Canon Eudo imperturbably demure and ascetic, like a much younger Prior Robert studying for sainthood, but keeping a weather eye on the secular prospects around him, all the same. And in attendance, the young squire Simon Aguilon, curly-haired, athletic and discreet, with a brown, open face stricken into unusual gravity by the events of the day.

The Picards also attended, but the bride, Cadfael noted, did not, nor did the elderly maid. He had caught glimpses of Iveta twice during the later afternoon, but once again with a guardian on either side. She maintained her calm and composed bearing, she wore the same pale but proud and confident face, the slight smile was ready to visit her lips at a glance; but only that once, Cadfael reflected thoughtfully, had she been unquestionably alone, unwatched, at liberty to speak her mind without restraint. And so she had, and confounded all expectation. There was no way of getting round it. She had believed the worst of young Joscelin Lucy, and put him out of her grace with a resolution that seemed far beyond her scope. She was reconciled to her marriage and determined to go through with it, in bitter recoil, perhaps, from a far more pleasing dream which had proved disillusionment on waking.

Then she was all too ingenuous, Cadfael decided, and far too easily convinced. Was there not a cup hidden in the sack of the boy Benjamin, in the Bible story, to make it possible to detain him? And had not the same stratagem been used many times since? But she was very young, and had been, perhaps, so artlessly in love that it took little art to overturn her too rash affection. Yet the trouble with things so obviously suspect, after all, is that they may indeed be true.

He watched the guests cross to the abbot's lodging after Vespers, and observed the return of Agnes Picard to the guest-hall. There was no room for action, nothing to be done about anything. Cadfael went to his own supper in the refectory, and afterwards to the readings in the chapter-house, but had mislaid, for some reason, both his appetite and his concentration.

The abbot's guests, no doubt, supped well, but they did not sit very late afterwards. Cadfael had gone to close his workshop before retiring, well after Compline, and was returning to the dortoir when he saw, by the lantern at the gate, Domville and his squire mounting to return to the bishop's house, and Picard taking his leave of them. Canon Eudo, evidently, was spending the night with the abbot, to see all made ready for the morrow.

They had drunk well enough, by the jovial ring of their voices, but certainly not to excess, since Radulfus was an abstemious man himself, and provided as he thought right and fitting, but not beyond. The sharp yellow light distinguished them scrupulously, showed the baron gross, self-indulgent but powerful still, in purse, possessions, body and mind, in no way a small or inconsiderable man. Picard was slenderer, viewed whichever way, a dark, devious, able man, whose subtlety could well complement Domville's brutal force. Those two together could be formidable to any antagonist. The young man stood patient, assiduous but disinterested, his thoughts probably elsewhere, but his temperament equable. He would not be sorry to heave himself into his bed.

Cadfael watched them ride, saw the youngster hold his lord's stirrup, almost heard his stifled yawn. He mounted after, light and glad, and fell in at Domville's elbow, keeping his station neatly with one hand on the rein. He was certainly sober as stone, aware, probably, of his vulnerable situation, as responsible for getting his lord home and bedded. Picard drew back from them, raising a hand in farewell. The two horses walked at leisure out at the gate, and the measured clop of their hooves on the cobbles of the Foregate faded gradually into silence.

Along the Foregate all was dark, but for the faintly luminous quality of moonless starlight, the sky sparkling after several misted days, the air on the clear, near edge of frost. In one or two windows a candle showed. Outside the bishop's house, where the gate-pillars drew back from the roadway, the wayside trees gave dark green shadow on either flank.

The two horsemen came at an easy walk, and halted briefly in the road, in front of the gates. Their voices, though pitched low, carried clearly in the great stillness.

'Go in, Simon,' said Domville. 'I have a fancy to take the air a while. Send the grooms to bed.'

'And your chamber attendants, sir?'

'Dismiss them. Say I want no service tonight, nor until an hour past Prime tomorrow, unless I call. Make sure it's understood those are my orders.'

The young man bowed his acquiescence without a word. The movement was just perceptible in the utter hush that surrounded it. The man in the shadows, concealing with disciplined stillness an illicit presence thus near the town, heard the slight rustle of a cloak, and the jingle of harness as a horse stirred. Then Simon wheeled obediently and trotted into the courtyard, and Domville shook his bridle and moved onward towards

Saint Giles, first at a walk, then breaking into a brisk and purposeful trot.

A shadow among shadows moved along the grassy border of the road after him, with long, uneven strides that made no sound. For a lame man, going upon one foot mangled by disease, he moved at a surprising speed, but he could not maintain the effort for long. But as long as he could hold the steady hoofbeats within earshot, he followed, along the empty Foregate, past the hospice and church, out along the highway beyond. He recognised the moment when the sound, which had been receding steadily, abruptly fell silent, and judged on which side of the road the rider had turned off on to a grassy track. To that spot he continued, no longer in haste.

To the right of the road the ground fell away towards the valley of the Meole brook, and the mill leat that was drawn off from it. Here open woods and scattered copses clothed the slope, below in the valley the trees grew more thickly. Down through this rolling woodland went a grassy ride, wide enough and smooth enough to be ridden safely in the night, with starlight overhead, and half the leaves already shed. By that path Huon de Domville had descended; here the night was empty of sight or sound of him.

The old man turned, and made his way slowly back to Saint Giles, where all his fellows were within doors and asleep, and only he restless and waking. He did not go in, though the outer door was never locked, in case some unfortunate should come in the chill of the night. Before dawn this night might be chill enough, but it was clean and sweet-smelling, and had the pure stillness proper to solitary thought, and he was not sensitive to cold. Outside the fence, in the angle of the cemetery wall, there was a great pile of dried brushings from the final reaping of the grass slope between the hospital and the road. In a day or two it would be carried within to the barn, to store for fodder and litter for the beasts. The old man wrapped his cloak about him, and sat down there on the grass, drawn well back into the stack to have its softness and warmth about him. The clapper-dish that hung at his belt he laid beside him on the ground. There was no human creature stirring about him now to need warning of the presence of a leper.

He did not sleep. He sat with head erect and straight back, his hands folded together at rest within his lap, the maimed left one within the sound right. Nothing else in the night was quite so still.

Joscelin had slept for a while in his bed of hay. Simon had brought him bread and meat and wine as he had promised, and his clothes had dried on him; he had lain in less comfort many a time. Only his mind was uncomforted. It was all very well for Simon to speak calmly of being able to make the excuse that the grey needed exercise, and get him from behind locked doors in a day or two, and so help his friend to escape when the hunt slackened, as it must. What use was that? In one more day, let alone two, Iveta would have been sacrificed, and escape without her played no part in Joscelin's plans. It was good of Simon to provide him this refuge, and sensible, no doubt, to advise him to stay within here until flight was possible. Very well-meant advice, and Joscelin was grateful, but he had no intention of taking it. A respite was most welcome, but would be wasted if it did not lead to action before ten o'clock on the morrow.

And here was he, alone, due to be pursued, if not shot, at sight, without a weapon, without a clear idea in his head, and only a few hours of grace left to him.

It was a simple conclusion, at any rate, that he could do nothing here, and if he was to remove himself elsewhere it would have to be during darkness. Even if he could have been provided with a dagger, and made his way undetected into the house, to Domville's bedside while he slept, he knew he could not have used his advantage. It was all very fine talking wildly about killing, but Brother Cadfael had been perfectly right, he could not do it, not by stealth. As for an honest challenge in a good quarrel, Domville would laugh in his face before tossing him back to the sheriff. Not out of cowardice, either, Joscelin conceded. There were very few things in this world that Domville was afraid of, and very few antagonists in the lists he need be afraid of. I am no bad swordsman, Joscelin told himself judicially, but for all his years he could carve and eat me for his dinner. No, disdain, not caution, would reject me.

Unless . . . Unless I could beard him before abbot and canon and guests and all, and strike him in the face, something his dignity would not bear, something done publicly that must be wiped out publicly in blood. For that he might even ride roughshod over the sheriff and the law, for that he might forgo destroying me in slower ways, and want nothing but my heart spitted on his blade. For that he would forget Iveta and wedlock and all, until he had wiped out the insult. And what is more, if I could bring him to that point, he would be meticulous to the last hair, give me breathing-time, provide me a sword the length of his own, kill me punctiliously, honourably. Do him that justice, with weapons he fights fair, even if he sees no reason to extend that scruple to such matters as lying charges backed with forged evidence.

And who knows . . . Who knows? With Iveta's prayers on my side, and all the weight of my grudge into the bargain – for he has dealt foully by me! – who knows but I might prevail? Then, even if they wrung my neck for his lying charge, *she* would be delivered.

To be honest, he did not think much of that conclusion, and not all for his own sake. For Iveta needed to be delivered not only from this detestable match, but from the guardian who preyed on her and her inheritance like murderous ivy on an oak, and would sell her to the next compliant bidder as nimbly as to this one. But even delay was salvation. Things could change. Picard could die. Only fend off tomorrow!

If he was to accomplish anything he must get out of here, and somehow make his way in hiding back to the abbey, where all must be enacted. No hope at all by the Foregate, the road would be patrolled, the gatehouse and the parish door guarded, so much was certain. On every side but one the abbey grounds were surrounded by a high boundary wall. The remaining side was bordered by the Meole brook, no mean water hemming the gardens, but fordable or swimmable. Waters were no threat to Joscelin. If he could get across the Foregate, he could make his way down into the valley, and so back beyond the brook to the abbey precincts. There were copses and coverts there for shelter. And it was downstream the sheriff would be hunting him first.

He turned, rustling, in his bed of hay, sneezed at the tickling of dust in his nostrils, and hastily smothered the sneeze. A fine object he must look to confront and blaze defiance at a baron of the realm, but it was the only hope he had. And to retain it even as a hope he must get out of here and across the Foregate into the valley while it was still night. With a rueful obeisance in the direction of Simon, who had wished him well, and wanted him to lie here like a hare in its form until danger passed.

He had no means of knowing the hour, but when he eased open the door of the hut, and looked out into the garden, the darkness was hearteningly deep. The dead silence was less pleasing; a breeze in the bushes would have covered a chance footstep. And once he was out of the shelter of the high walls even the darkness grew faintly luminous. But it was now or never, and everything seemed still and silent. He lifted the bar of the wicket door and slipped through, and began to make his way by touch of the wall round the bishop's garden enclosure. A narrow belt of trees and a footpath separated the house from its neighbour, and brought him to the edge of the Foregate. He paused there to listen, and found all still. But by the degree of faint light he now found over the open roadway, it must be nearer dawn than he would have liked. Better make haste.

He made a dash for it across the open, light on his feet for all his size, and was almost into the grass on the further side when a stone rolled under his foot with a brief, grating sound. Somewhere along the Foregate, towards the town, a voice exclaimed aloud, another answered with a muted shout, and feet began to run in his direction. There were guards still patrolling the roads out of the town. Joscelin darted onward, down the steep slope of grass towards the mill stream, and checked and dived into the cover of the bushes as he caught an echoing shout from below him. That way, too, was stopped. Two of the roving pickets between the roads were down there ahead of him, and climbing towards him now in a hurry.

He had not yet been sighted by any of them, but there was only one hope, and that was to put as much space as possible between himself and pursuit as quickly as possible, and that meant by the road, where he could hope to show fleeter than the hunters. He scrambled back in haste and took to the grassy rim of the road, running like a deer towards Saint Giles. Behind him he heard those below in the valley calling to their companions, heard the answering shout: 'The thief's abroad! Come up!'

The two on the road came pounding after, but he had a good start of them, and was confident he could outrun them and find a place to go to earth, short of the guard-post that would certainly be stationed on every road. But the next moment he heard a sound that chilled his blood, the sudden clatter of hooves emerging from grass on to a hard roadway. The two patrols from the valley were mounted.

'After him! He's for the open, ride him down!' bellowed one of the runners.

And here they came at a canter, and these he could not hope to outrun, nor to evade the four of them for long if he turned from the road here. He reached Saint Giles, running frantically, and looking about him wildly for any hiding-place, and finding none. On his left the slope of grass rose to the wattle fence and the cemetery wall. Behind him the pursuit grew triumphantly vocal, though not yet close. The curve of the road had cut him off from their view.

Out of the darkness along the wall an unexpected voice, low but peremptory, called: 'Come! Quickly!'

Joscelin swung towards the invitation instinctively, panting, and half-fell up the grassy slope and into the grasp of a long arm held out to him. A lean, tall figure in a voluminous dark cloak had risen from the ground and was ripping a hasty tunnel open in the stack of drying herbage in the angle of the wall. 'Here!' said the voice featureless as the face. 'Hide here!'

Joscelin plunged head-first into the heap, and drew it about him frantically. He felt the old man resume his seat on the ground, spread his cloak again, and lean well back against the stack, felt the long spine erect and bony through cloak and gown and grass. Certainly old, certainly a man. The lowered voice might have belonged to either, muffled as it was, but the shoulders pressed well back against him were wide as his own. One hand reached back to grip his knee through the rustling stems, and enjoin stillness, and he froze in instant obedience. The man masking him had a special stillness of his own, a calm that eased Joscelin's heart and mind by its benevolent contagion.

They were coming. He heard the hoofbeats draw close, heard the foremost horse abruptly pulled up on its haunches, feet sliding on the gravel. He thought that the watcher by the wall had been seen; there was pre-dawn light enough for that, and they had a straight stretch of road ahead of them, and certainly empty. He heard one man dismount, and held his breath in the certainty that he was about to climb the slope.

'Unclean!' called the old man warningly, and clashed the clapper of his dish loudly against the wooden rim. There was wary stillness. The climber had taken heed.

Down on the road the second man laughed. 'He'd need to be mad to exchange even a gaol for a lazarhouse.' He raised his voice; the old and diseased must also be hard of hearing. 'Hark, you, fellow! We're on the heels of a wretch who's wanted for thieving. He was headed this way. Have you seen him?'

'No,' said the old man. His voice, besides being muffled behind a veil, was slow in articulation, as if speech gave him trouble; but with labour and patience the words emerged clearly. 'I've seen no thief.'

'How long have you been sitting there? Have you seen any man pass by here?'

'The night long,' said the arduous voice. 'And no one has passed by.'

By the sound of it the two on foot had arrived by this time, out of breath. The four conferred in low tones. 'He must have slipped aside into the trees and turned back,' said one. 'Turn and take the right of the road. We'll ride on to the barrier and make sure he's not wormed his way ahead in cover, and then come back and take the left side.'

The horses stirred and stamped again, and trotted ahead. The two on foot must have turned back to retrace their steps among the trees, beating the bushes for their quarry as they went. There fell a long silence, which Joscelin was afraid to break.

'Stretch out and be easy,' said the old man at last, without turning his head. 'We cannot move yet.'

'I have an errand I must do,' said Joscelin, leaning close to the hooded ear to be heard. 'For this respite God knows I thank you with all my heart, but I must somehow get to the abbey before daylight, or this liberty you've kept for me will not be worth keeping. I have a thing I must do there, for someone else's sake.'

'What is that thing?' asked the old man equably.

'To prevent, if I can, this marriage they're making today.'

'Ah!' said the patient, deliberate voice. 'Wherefore? And by what means? You may not stir yet, they will be back, and they will look this way and must see all as before. An old leper who has preferred a night under the stars to the cover of a roof – nothing more.' The grass rustled; it might have been the very slight stir of a sigh. 'You understood what passed there? Are you afraid of leprosy, boy?'

'No,' said Joscelin, and wavered and reconsidered. 'Yes! I was, or I thought I was. I hardly know. I know I am more afraid of failing in what I must do.'

'We have time,' said the old man. 'If you are willing to tell me, I am listening.'

Only to such a one, chance met and instantly trusted, could Joscelin have poured out the whole load that weighed on his heart. Suddenly it seemed the most natural thing possible that he should confide without restraint, keep nothing back of his indignant love, the wrong done him, and the greater wrongs done to Iveta. In the middle of his narration the controlling hand pressed his knee for silence and stillness, as the two mounted men passed by again towards the town. And when they were gone, the last echo of hooves lost along the road, he resumed as if the thread had never been broken.

'And you have planned to hide yourself somewhere about the cloister,' mused the old man, at the end of it, 'and burst forth to challenge your sometime lord to single combat, and so affront him that he shall not be able to deny you and keep his face?'

'It is the only way I can see,' said Joscelin, though put in such clear terms, he did not think too well of its chances.

'Then be in no haste about it,' said Lazarus, 'until daylight comes, for a clapper-dish and a hood and veil can make you faceless and nameless as well as another. One thing I can tell you. Huon de Domville did not lie in his bed this night. He rode out beyond here, turning right from this road, and I have been here every moment since, and unless he knows of another way back, he has not returned. I think he must ride back by the same way he rode out, and until he passes this place, no bridegroom will present himself at the altar. Between us, you and I can make shift to watch for him. If he comes! But how if he never comes?'

It was the strangest night Joscelin had ever passed, and the strangest dawn. Faint mist came with the light, and the rising sun peered through it overhead, while it lay in great swathes in the valley beyond the road. But no Huon de Domville came trotting back towards the bishop's house.

'Stay in hiding,' said Lazarus at length, 'until I come back.' And he rose and went into the hospice, to return presently with a hooded cloak like his own, and a blue linen cloth for a veil. 'You may creep out and put them on. If you are not afraid to wear the habit of a dead man? He is in the cemetery there. When they come to die here, they leave such clothing behind, there's store enough within. The linen they burn, the habits they clean as best they can. A big man he must have been, you'll find it ample enough.'

Joscelin did all that he was bidden, like a child, or a man in so unpredictable a dream that he must rely on his guide. In such a state it no longer seemed strange that he should open his heart to a leper, accept the protection of the leper cloak, and let himself be led into the hospital where the unfortunates were housed, without conscious fear or revulsion. This was the hand that had been held out to him, and he gripped it warmly and gratefully. He did not even ask how he should pass among the inmates. Surely their number must be known, and he was too large to escape notice. Whether Lazarus had already spoken a word in several ears, or whether the poor know by instinct when one of their fellows is in need, and deploy their movements so subtly as to contain and dissemble him, all those men and women mustered about Joscelin and hid him among them as they assembled in the church for Prime.

Round about him he saw all manner of maimings and disfigurements, and found himself possessed unexpectedly by an overwhelming and unaccustomed humility. Not for a long time had he paid such devout attention to the words of the office, or felt himself so truly drawn into a company at worship.

As for the watch on the road, outside, Lazarus had confided it to the little boy Bran, who knew very well the appearance of the man for whom he was to watch. All was being done for Joscelin by others, and as at this moment there was no resistance he could offer, and no repayment he could make, but to bow his head fervently among the rest and give profound thanks for present mercies. And so he did.

# 5

They had roused Iveta early, for she had an elaborate toilet to make. Agnes and Madlen bathed, dressed and adorned her, swept up the gold mane of her hair in a dozen shining braids, coiled it in a filigree net, and bound it in a gold circlet stuck with stones. From the coronal a veil of gilt thread hung round neck and shoulders, over the stiff gold broidery of her gown. She submitted to all with a mute tongue and and an icy face, so pale that her ivory ornaments looked dun by comparison. She turned obediently under their hands, bent her head as they instructed, did all that was demanded of her. When she was ready they stood her in the midst of the chamber, posed like a gowned statue for a saint's niche, every fold of her dress coaxed out to perfection, and ordered her not to move, for fear of creasing her splendour. She stood as they had placed her and made no complaint, all the time that they were adorning themselves no less splendidly.

Her uncle came, walked round her with narrowed eyes and critical grimace, twitched the folds of her veil into more severe symmetry, and expressed himself satisfied. Canon Eudo came, smooth and sanctimonious, complimented her not so much on her beauty or appropriate grandeur as on her great good fortune in this match, and the gratitude she owed her guardians for achieving it for her. The guests came, admired, envied, and went to take their places in the church.

At the hour of ten, on other days earmarked for High Mass, her attendants formed at her back, and she was led forth into the main porch of the guest-hall on

Picard's arm, ready to go forth to meet her bridegroom when he came.

There was only one thing amiss with the scrupulous arrangements, which up to this moment had worked to perfection. The bridegroom did not come.

No one, not even Picard, ventured to murmur or look askance for the first ten minutes. Huon de Domville was a law to himself, and though this marriage was certainly profitable to him, he regarded it as a condescension on his part. It was ungracious to come late, but no one doubted that he would come. But when ten more minutes had slipped away, and still no formal procession entered at the gatehouse, and no hoofbeats were heard along the Foregate, there began to be a shifting and murmuring, an uneasy shuffling of feet and then a whispering. Iveta stood in the forefront, and awoke out of her frost to the shivering of doubt all round her, and drew breath in wonder. She gave no sign, only the blood began to stir again in her face, and flush into her set lips, softening them into rose-leaves.

Canon Eudo came floating elegantly from the church, but all his graces could not conceal his agitation. He spoke in low tones with Picard, whose brow was growing black and knotted with anxiety. Cadfael, coming late and in haste from the garden to take his place among the brothers, looked only at the bride, and could not take his eyes from the tiny golden doll they had made of her, not a thread of it real but the small, chill face melting among the gilt, and the quickening spark deep in her iris-purple eyes, making its live way up out of drowning fathoms to the light of day.

She was among the first to catch the hurried clatter of hooves along the Foregate. She turned her eyes without daring to turn her head, as Simon Aguilon, in all his wedding finery, rode into the gateway, dropped his bridle into the porter's hand, and swung hastily down to stride across the great court to the door of the guest-hall, in evident agitation.

'My lord, I pray your pardon! Things have somehow gone amiss, we don't know how . . .' He drew in Canon Eudo, the three heads leaned close, and Agnes hovered with pricked ears and drawn brows. The voices spilled abroad, none the less. Both abbot and prior had emerged from the church, and stood at a dignified distance, in contained displeasure. They could not long be ignored.

'Last night, when we left here to return home – I do his bidding, I do not question, how could I? He said to me that he had a fancy to ride a while, and I should go in, and bid the household go to bed, for he wanted no service that night, nor until he should say the word this morning. And so I did! What else? I thought he would be there asleep this morn, when his chamberlain looked in on him. I slept late myself. They shook me awake a good half-hour past Prime, and said he was not in his bed – nor had been, all night long, for the bed was not pressed.' The young man's voice had risen, all those crowding in could hear. They were silent enough, all intent on that knot of consternation in the midst.

'Father Abbot,' Simon turned to him with a hasty reverence, 'we are greatly afraid that something must have happened to my lord. He has not been home all night, since he sent me in and dismissed all attendance. And very surely he would not be absent or late here, had he his freedom and health to keep the tryst. I fear hc may have come by an injury, somehow – a fall, perhaps. . . . Night riding is risky, but he had a fancy for it. It wants only a crippling stone in a hoof, or a fox's earth . . .'

'He left you at the gate of the house?' asked Radulfus. 'And rode on?'

'Yes, towards Saint Giles. But I do not know which way he took, after that, or where he was bound, if indeed he had some purpose in mind. He told me nothing.'

'It would be a first step,' said Radulfus drily, 'to send out along that road for sign or word of him.'

'So we have done, Father, but vainly. The superior at the hospital has seen nothing of him, and we have ridden further along the road without result. Before taking it further I had, of courtesy, to bring word here. But I have spoken to one of the sheriff's sergeants, who was out with a patrol beating the woodlands for the prisoner they lost, and his men will be keeping watch also for any sign of my lord Domville. He has sent a man to tell the sheriff what has happened. Father, you will understand that I dared not be too quick to raise an alarm or question anything my lord does, but I think now it is time there should be a full search for him. He may be lying somewhere hurt and unable to rise.'

'I think as you do,' said the abbot with decision, and turned courteously to Agnes Picard, who stood attentive and alert at her husband's side, one hand closed possessively on Iveta's golden sleeve. 'Madam, I trust this distress may not be long, and that we shall find my lord Domville safe and none the worse, only delayed by some trivial circumstance. But it would be well if you would take your niece within, and have her rest in privacy with you, while these gentlemen – and the brothers of our house, too, if they so choose – go and search for the bridegroom.'

Agnes made brief, anxious acknowledgement, and swept the girl away with her, out of sight. The doors of their apartments closed on them. Iveta had not spoken one word.

They saddled up, mounted and rode, all the men among the wedding guests, all the grooms and pages from the bishop's house, a squad of men-at-arms from the castle, many of the younger brothers and novices on foot, and one of the boy pupils whose long ears had overheard the news, and who had slipped into hiding before he could be herded away into school. He might pay for his truancy later, but he thought it well worth the risk.

Those mounted chose to ride along the Foregate to where Domville had parted from his squire, and been seen continuing towards Saint Giles. Thence they split into two parties, since the roads forked there, and spread out into the verges on either side of either highway. Those afoot took at once to the byways, some threading their way through the woods down-river, some going round by the mill-pond into the valley of the Meole brook, and so upstream through meadows and copses.

Cadfael joined these last. They spread out in a long line, to cover as wide a swathe as possible, and made their way upstream on both sides of the brook from the limit of the abbey grounds. A mounted man would use only good open country or the well-trodden paths and rides in this richly wooded countryside, and to look for him in the first reaches was pointless, if he had begun from his own gateway. They proceeded briskly, therefore, until they had left the abbey precincts well behind, and were strung out across the valley just below the hospital. They could see the little turret of the church just above the bushes at the crest, where the road ran.

From this point they went more slowly and thoroughly, stretching their line to take in more ground. They knew every path here, and threaded each for some distance as they came to it. No doubt others on the opposite side of the Foregate had reached much the same point, and were proceeding in the same way, but as yet there had been no shout anywhere to direct or call off the hunt.

By this time they were probably half a mile beyond Saint Giles, and the sloping fields and light, scattered copses had thickened into woodland. The climb to the road here was steep, and for some distance, until the gradient grew gentler, no paths descended to cross their line. Then they came, as they had known they would, to a broad green ride, a good, smooth plane of turf that came down from the road and narrowed slightly as it entered the denser woods. South-west from the road it ran, twice fording the bends of the brook, which here was narrow and stony, and wandered away, Cadfael recalled, towards the fringe of the Long Forest, a few miles distant.

They had just emerged on to this green track when the truant schoolboy, who had been running in circles ahead of them in his zeal, came rushing back along the path in great excitement, waving an arm towards the groves behind him.

'There's a horse grazing back there in a clearing! Saddle and harness and all, but no rider!'

And he whirled and darted back, with all of them hard on his heels. The path continued clear and well-used, closely hemmed by trees, and then expanded into a small, lush meadow; and there, placidly cropping the grass under the bordering trees, Huon de Domville's tall black horse strolled unalarmed, and raised a mildly wondering stare as so many men suddenly bore down on him. All his harness was in order, nowhere any disarray, but of his rider there was no sign.

'If he'd been near his own home stable,' said the excited boy, proudly possessing himself of the bridle, 'he'd have gone back to it, and they'd have been warned. But he was on strange ground, so when he got over his fright, he wandered.'

It was good sense, and he was all eagerness to press on. But there might well be that ahead that was not good for a child to see. Cadfael looked at Brother Edmund the infirmarer, who was next to him, and saw the same thought reflected back to him. If horse and rider had parted by reason of some shock or alarm, and they met the horse first, then Huon de Domville had probably been on his way back when mischance befell him; and if he had lain out all night, it meant he was in no good case. A tough, determined man, he would not let minor injury hold him helpless.

'A startled horse bolts forward, not back,' pursued the voluble imp, glowing, 'isn't that right? Shall we go on?'

'You,' said Cadfael, 'may have the credit for taking this beast back to the bishop's house, and telling them there where you found him. Then go back to your lessons. If you make a good story of it you may escape punishment for running away.'

The boy looked first dismayed, and then mutinous, and began to argue.

'Hop!' ordered Cadfael briskly, cutting off his objections. 'You may ride him. Here, up with your foot . . . so!' He cupped a hand, and hoisted the boy into the saddle before he had time to decide whether to be aggrieved or flattered. But the feel of the fine beast under him did the trick. His face became one complacent beam, he gathered the reins importantly, ignored the stirrups that were far too long for him, dug his heels into the satin sides, and chirruped at his mount as casually as if he rode such beasts every day.

When they had watched him far enough along the ride to be sure that he was competent, and would do as he had been bidden, they turned and went on. The glade ended, trees closed in again on the track. Here and there, in places where the grass was thin and the ground soft, they saw the mark of a hoof. They had gone perhaps another quarter of a mile before Brother Edmund, who was leading, suddenly halted.

'He is here.'

The thick, powerful body lay sprawled on its back, head against the roots of a great oak, arms spread. The trees grew close here, and the deep shadows swallowed the rich colours of his clothing, so that the upturned face stared out of a green darkness, suffused with blood, open eyes bulging and reddened. The brutal, muscular quality of the face seemed to have melted and run like wax from a candle. As well the child had been sent back before he could run ahead of them and stumble over this in valiant innocence, and sicken in too early knowledge of good and evil.

Cadfael put Edmund aside and went forward, dropping to his knees beside the motionless body, and in a moment Edmund followed him, and crouched on the other side. He was accustomed to easing old men into their deaths, but deaths as gentle as affectionate care and the company of friends could make it, and this abrupt severing of a vigorous life appalled and daunted him. The two novices and the lay brother who had followed them drew near and stood silent.

'Is he dead?' asked Brother Edmund fearfully, and understood at once that it was a foolish question.

'Dead some hours. Around dawn, it might be. He's cooling but not cold.' Cadfael lifted the heavy head on his hand, and felt the sticky foulness of congealed blood on his fingers. High at the back of the head, behind and above the left ear, the bald crown bore a ripped bruise, which had oozed blood from a dozen scratches, now drying. Where his head had lain, and for a hand's-length above, the bole of the oak bore smeared traces of the impact. Cadfael felt delicately over and round the bruise, and the skull seemed to him intact, there was no depression under his touch.

'He was thrown from his horse, and heavily,' ventured Edmund, watching, 'and fell on to this oak-bole. Could such a fall kill him?'

'It could,' said Cadfael distractedly, but did not see fit as yet to make plain that it had not.

'Or if he lay out, not regaining his senses – the chill of the night . . .'

'He has not been here all night long,' said Cadfael.

'The dew of the mist is under him. And if he was thrown, you see he was thrown backwards, not forwards, out of the saddle. The horse did not stumble.' For the body lay diagonally half across the path, head against the tree on the right, his feet towards them as they approached from the brook. 'It was in the early morning, and he was hurled backwards. He was certainly riding back then to his own household. The path is good, at least for a man who knows, but I should guess there was also some light already, for I think he was riding briskly, to come down so heavily.'

'His horse reared,' suggested Edmund. 'Some small night creature started under his feet, and shocked him . . .'

'That could be.' Cadfael laid Domville's head carefully back, and the broken crown rested at the foot of the grazed and bloodied streak on the bole. 'He has not moved since the fall,' he said with certainty. 'Only the heels of his boots, see, have scored deep through the grass, as though in some convulsion.'

He rose to his feet, leaving the body just as it lay, and began to move about the ride, eyeing it from many angles. One of the novices, sensibly enough, had turned back to meet the sheriff's men, who would certainly be despatched from the bishop's house as soon as the boy brought his news. They would need a litter, or a door lifted from its hinges, to carry the dead man back. Cadfael also retraced his steps some dozen yards along the path, and began to work his way back to where the body lay, viewing all the trees on both sides with great care, at a level above his own modest height, as Edmund noted without understanding.

'What is it you're looking for, Cadfael?'

Whatever it was, he had found it. Some four paces from the dead man's feet he had halted, fixing his eyes first on the trunk on his right, well above his own head, and then transferring the same intent stare to the tree opposite.

'Come and see. Come, all, and bear me witness when I tell it.'

On either trunk at the same level there was a thin, scored line, scarring the fine ridges of the bark.

'A rope has been stretched between these trees, throat-height to a man of middle stature and well-mounted, though even at breast-height it would have fetched him down. It was light enough for a canter on so good a pathway, I fancy, for surely he was going briskly. You see how far it toppled him. We shall find the mark of it on his throat.'

They stared, appalled, and had no word to say, as they followed him in awed silence back to where the body lay, and he turned back the collar of the coat, and bared Domville's neck. For the dark-red slash of the cord was not all they found under the beard, on the thick, sinewy flesh. There, plain to be seen, were the wreathing, blackened bruises of two human hands, and the two thumbs, overlapping, had left a great, mangled stain on the Adam's-apple, and possibly crushed the gristle within.

They were still gaping in horrified silence when they heard urgent voices approaching along the ride, the sheriff's loudest among them. The intimation of disaster had gone before, but as yet its magnitude was a secret among these few.

Cadfael drew the collar close over the evidence of strangulation, and turned with his companions to meet Gilbert Prestcote and his officers.

When the sheriff had viewed everything Cadfael had to show him, they brought a litter, and lifted Huon de Domville on to it, drawing the folds of his cloak over his face. At the spot from which they raised him they fixed a cross bound from two sticks, to enable them to find and search the place again at need. Then they carried him back, not to the bishop's house but to the abbey, to be laid in the mortuary chapel there and made decent for burial by the monks of Saint Peter's, who should have witnessed his marriage.

The child Bran, who could pass for any urchin of the Foregate, briefly, at least, and with discretion, simply by shedding his leper cloak, came back from a wary foray along the road, to report to the two tall, veiled men who sat together with their clapper-dishes under the cemetery wall: 'They have found him. I saw them carrying him back. They've taken him past the house. I dared not go further.'

'Alive or dead?' asked the slow, calm voice of Lazarus from behind the faded blue face-cloth. The boy knew death already, no need to shield him.

'His face was covered,' said Bran, and sat down beside them. He felt the silence and tension of the other, the new man, the one who was known to be young and whole, and wondered why he trembled.

'No words,' said Lazarus tranquilly. 'You have your breathing-space. So has she.'

Within the great court of the abbey the men-at-arms laid down the litter they carried, and from all sides, in haste and anxious clamour that died abruptly into silence and stillness, all those bound up in this matter came flooding, to form a mute, wide-eyed audience all about the bier. They halted at an awed distance, all but the sheriff and his men, and Abbot Radulfus, who advanced with authority. From the guest-hall Picard burst forth, obstinately hopeful, to freeze at sight of the shrouded figure and covered face. The women followed fearfully. The little golden image moved as though she could barely sustain the weight of her finery, yet she came, and did not turn her eyes away. No doubt of it now. Shocking though it might be, this death was life to her. Why, why had she so belied herself yesterday?

'My lord abbot,' said Prestcote, 'this is very ill news we bring, for my lord Domville is found indeed, but as you see him. These brothers of your house found him, thrown from his horse on the woodland path that leads out towards Beistan. His horse was grazing unharmed, and is back in his stable. Huon de Domville was thrown against an oak tree, and is dead. It seems that he was on his way home when this thing happened. Father, will you receive him and have body and soul cared for, until due arrangements can be made? His nephew is of his party here, and the canon is also his kinsman...'

Simon hovered, wordless. He inclined his head and swallowed hard, eyeing the body on the litter.

'This is a very ill turn for such a day to take,' said Radulfus heavily, 'and we extend our sorrow and fellow-feeling to all those thus bereaved. And naturally, our hospitality for as long as may be needed, the services of our order, and the privacy of our guest-halls. It is a time for quietness and prayer. Death is present with us every day of our lives, it behoves us to take note of its nearness, not as a threat, but as our common experience on the way to grace. There is no more to be said. It is better to accept the will of God, and be silent.'

'With respect, Father,' Picard spoke up in a voice thin as steel, yet very civil and respectful. Cadfael had been trying to read the man's face, and made little headway; there was dismay there, certainly, and rage, and frustration, but instant calculation, too. 'With respect, I say, should we so tamely accept that this *is* the will of God? Huon de Domville knows this region, he has a hunting-lodge no great way off, near the Long Forest. He has ridden lifelong without mishap, by day or by night, are we to believe he uses less skill and less awareness suddenly on his wedding-eve, when you and I both know he rode from here sober and unwearied? He told his squire he would take the air a little before sleeping. Surely that was all he intended. Now in a moment we have him brought back dead, a man in his prime and in his full powers! No, I do not believe it! There is some evil-dealing here, and I must know more before I can be satisfied.'

It seemed that Prestcote had deliberately delayed the full assault of his news, in order to see if any among his hearers showed signs of gratification at the likelihood that the death would pass as an accident. If so, and if he discovered anything, for all the narrowed glances with which he was sweeping the ring of shocked faces, he was more successful than Cadfael, who was pursuing the same quest. Nowhere could he discover any shadow of guilt or fear in any face, only the expected and obligatory grief and dismay.

'I have not said his death was accidental,' said the sheriff, bluntly now. 'Not even his fall was chance. He was fetched down out of the saddle by a rope stretched across the path between two trees, at a level that took him in the throat. But it was not the fall that killed him. Whoever laid the ambush for him was present to complete his work, while Domville lay senseless. A man's two hands round his throat killed him.'

The whole circle shifted as though a rough wind had shaken them, and drew hard, audible breath. The abbot raised his head to stare.

'You are saying this was murder?'

'As cold and thorough as ever was committed.'

'And we know by whom!' Picard leaned forward, blazing up in malevolent triumph like a thorn fire. 'Did I not say it? This is the work of that thieving youth who was dismissed my lord Domville's service. He has taken his devil's revenge by killing his lord. Who else? Who else had any grudge? Joscelin Lucy did this!'

Light flashed suddenly on darting gold at his back, and there stood Iveta confronting him, yesterday's sacrificial lamb become a spitting yellow wildcat. Dilated iris eyes glittered like amethyst. Her voice rose high and challenging, even triumphant, even derisive, as she cried:

'It's false! You know, you all know, that *cannot* be true! Have you forgotten? He of all men *must* be innocent of this–he's behind locked doors in Shrewsbury castle these two days – and that charge as false as this! – but thank God for it, the sheriff's own gaoler is witness he cannot have done murder.'

Understanding fell upon Brother Cadfael somewhat after the fashion of a great blow on the head, and left him dazed, unable to catch at first the full implications of what she had said. Not so hard now to guess the meaning of her resolute composure when questioned by the abbot. They had cased her up securely within, and kept her from knowing anything of Joscelin's escape, when it would have been comfort and joy to her. Now, when it destroyed all her comfort, they would turn on her and hurl it in her face. They were at it already, both the Picards, Agnes the shriller and more savage of the two.

'Fool girl, he is *not* prisoner. He broke free before ever they got him over the bridge, he's at large with his grudge...'

'Thief he was, and now a hunted wolf in the woods, and has murdered your bridegroom! *And will hang for it!*'

All the brightness, all the valour, was stricken from her face. She hung a moment quite still, and just once her lips formed a protesting 'No!' that made no sound. Then her cheeks blanched whiter than snow. She put up a hand to her heart, and fell down like a shot bird, in a little crumpled heap of gold.

The maid Madlen came rushing officiously, all the women crowded in upon the small, spilled body, Picard gave a cry rather of exasperation than concern, and stooped to gather her up by the wrist and haul her to her feet. She was a reproach and an embarrassment, they wanted her hustled away out of sight and out of mind. Cadfael could not forbear from interfering, before they stifled her among their skirts, or tugged a wrist out of joint. He plunged into the midst of them and spread his arms to press them back from her.

'Peace, let her breathe! She has swooned, don't lift her yet.'

Brother Edmund, versed in such collapses, seconded him valiantly on the other side, and with Abbot Radulfus looking on, the guests could hardly reject the help and authority of those who tended the sick within these walls. Even Agnes stood back, though with a chill and wary face, as Cadfael went on his knees beside the girl, and straightened her tumbled limbs to lie at ease, her head raised on his arm. 'A cloak to fold under her head! And where is Brother Oswin?'

Simon threw off his cloak and rolled it eagerly into a pillow. Oswin came running from among the staring novices.

'Go and fetch me the little flask of mint and sorrel vinegar from the shelf by the door, and a bottle of the draught of bitter herbs. And be quick!'

He laid her head down gently on the pillow Simon had made for it, and took her wrists into his hands and began to chafe them steadily. Her face had the pinched, bluish white of ice. Oswin came back at the same devoted gallop, and moreover, had brought the right medicines. There was hope of him yet. Brother Edmund knelt on the other side, and held the little bottle of vinegar, hot and sharp with mint and sorrel, to her nostrils, and saw them dilate and flutter. A small convulsion like a cough heaved her childish breast, and the steel-sharp lines of cheekbones and chin gradually softened. Over her oblivious head her uncle, having abandoned her to her physicians, returned to his vengeance with renewed venom.

'Can there be any doubt? He broke loose without weapons, and with no means of getting any. Only a man deprived of other means needs to kill with his bare hands. He is a big, strong rogue, capable of such an act. No one else had any grievance against Huon. But *he* had a grudge, and a bitter one, and he has taken to extremes to have his revenge. Now it is mortal! Now he must be hunted down like a mad dog, shot down at sight if need be, for he's perilous to anyone who approaches him. This is a hanging matter.'

'My men are beating the woods and orchards for him at this moment,' said Prestcote shortly, 'and have been ever since a patrol reported flushing a man out of cover into the Foregate early this morning. Though it was not yet light, and they got but the briefest glimpse of him, and for my part I doubt if it was Lucy. More likely some rogue in a small way pilfering from hen-houses and backyards by night. The hunt goes on, and will until we take him. Every man I can spare is out already.'

'Make use of my men also,' offered Picard eagerly, 'and of Huon's. We are all of us bound now to hunt down his murderer. There's surely no doubt in your mind that Joscelin Lucy *is* his murderer?'

'It seems all too clear. This has all the marks of an act of desperate hate. We know of no other present enemy of his.'

Cadfael worked unhurriedly upon Iveta, but listened to all that passed, the abbot's few words and reserved silences, Picard's vindictive urgings, the sheriff's measured dispositions for the continued and extended hunt, all the deployment of the law closing round Joscelin Lucy. In the middle of it he noted that faint colour was returning to Iveta's face, and watched the first delicate flutterings of her eyelids, the shadow of long dark-gold lashes quivering on her cheekbones.

Dazed purple eyes opened at him, and gazed in uncomprehending terror. Her lips parted. As if by chance he laid a fingertip upon them, and briefly closed his own eyes. Joscelin's peril, far more effectively than her own, had made her wits quick. The eyelids, veined like harebells, closed again and remained closed. She lay like one still senseless, but showing signs of returning life.

'She is beginning to stir. We may take her in now.'

He rose from his knees and lifted her in his arms, before Picard or Simon or any other could forestall him.

'She should lie at rest for some hours, after she comes round. It was a bad swoon.' He marvelled how little there was of her, and was convinced her finery weighed more than she did; yet this fragile creature had roused herself to heroic defiance for the sake of Joscelin, she who was so tamed and resigned for herself. Even the charge of theft and a cell in the castle had seemed comfort and joy to her when they served to ward off the infinitely worse charge of murder. Now, when she got her wits back, and remembered, she would be torn in two between terror for his life, since this killing was indeed a hanging matter, and hope for his escape, since thus far he was still at liberty. Hope offered itself and snatched itself away again from Iveta de Massard.

'Madam, if you will show the way . . .'

Agnes gathered her splendid skirts and swept before him into the guest-hall, to her own apartments. It could not be said, Cadfael reflected, that she felt no concern for her niece, since her niece was the greater part of her fortune, and for that she felt a strong defensive care. But her prevailing emotion towards the girl Iveta herself was impatience and displeasure. By this hour she should have been safely married off, a commodity profitably disposed of. However, she was still eminently saleable, she still had all her father's great honour in lands and titles, down to the sword and helmet of the paladin Guimar de Massard, chivalrously restored by the Fatimids of Egypt: the one item of her inheritance, possibly, which Picard did not covet.

'You may lay her here.' By the narrow way she eyed him, Agnes had not forgotten that he was the brother of whose ready prevarications she had complained to the abbot; but that hardly mattered now, since Joscelin Lucy was quarry for a hunt to the death, and no threat to her peace of mind any longer. 'Is there anything needs to be done for her?'

Iveta lay on her covered bed, sighed and was still. All that gold, as though she had been minted.

'If you would be kind enough to find me a small cup, to take a draught of this decoction of herbs when she is with us again. It's a good, bitter restorative, and wards off further fainting. And I think there should be some warmth in the room. A small charcoal brazier would serve.'

These recommendations she took seriously, perforce. He had given her enough to do to remove her from the room, though for perhaps five minutes at best. Her maids had waited in the hall. She swept out to set them to work.

Iveta opened her eyes. The same brother! She had known his voice, and stolen that one glance to make certain. But when she tried to speak, tears rose to hamper her utterance. But he was listening close; he heard.

'They never told me! They said the theft could be pressed to his death . . .'

'I know,' said Cadfael, and waited.

'They said – unless I did all perfectly, spoke the right words, made all above suspicion . . . Huon would have his life . . .'

'Yes . . . Hush now, softly! Yes, I know!'

'But if I did all well, he should go free . . .'

Yes, she had been ready to sell herself, body and will and hopes and all, to see Joscelin delivered. She had her own bravery.

'Help him!' she said, huge eyes like purple flowers overblown, and closed her small hand, fine-boned like a little bird, but with a little bird's strong and compelling grip, on Cadfael's hand. 'He has not stolen or killed . . . I know!'

'If I can!' breathed Cadfael, and stooped to conceal her from Agnes in the doorway. She was very quick, she lay back in mute acceptance, eyes veiled; the hand was empty and limp as before. Not for several more minutes did she raise her lids again and look up, answer faintly and wonderingly when Agnes asked her, with genuine anxiety but little kindness, how she did, and drink the bitter, aromatic draught Cadfael presented to her lips.

'She should be left alone in quietness,' he advised when he took his leave, minded to procure for her, if he could, the solitude she needed, deliverance from the company of people whose very presence was oppression. 'She will sleep. Such seizures are as exhausting as great exertion. If Father Abbot permits, I will look in on her before Vespers, and bring her a syrup that will ensure her a peaceful night.'

That, at least, they might allow her. They had her securely in their power, she could not escape, but at present no more could be done with her or to her. Domville was dead, there would have to be reconsideration now, the field was open to other bidders. It was not deliverance, but it was a respite. Time to give some thought to the circumstances of this violent death, and the fate of the unfortunate young man at whose door it was being laid. There were a great many questions not yet asked, let alone answered.

It was towards noon that one of the men-at-arms combing the copses and gardens behind the houses of the

Foregate on the north side came to his sergeant and said brightly: 'There's but one garden left unexamined in all this array, and now I mind me there could be good sense in looking there, too. Bishop de Clinton's house itself!' And when he was cried down with mention of the folly of hiding in the very lion's mouth, he defended his notion earnestly.

'Not such folly, neither! Suppose this fellow's listening to the pack of you now, making mock of the very idea! He'd have the laugh if he's lying low within there, and you refusing to believe it possible. The one place you put out of the question is the one place he might have wit enough to be. And don't forget his horse is within there, and with all this running hither and thither, who's to care whether the stable's left open?'

The sergeant thought the argument worth considering, and authorised the search of the bishop's garden, byres and stables, his orchard, all the ground within his walls. In due course they arrived at the hay-store by the rear wall. They did not find Joscelin Lucy, but they did find plain evidence that someone had lain there in the hay, and left behind him the heel of a loaf and the core of an apple, besides the impress in the fodder of a long young body, clear to be seen. Joscelin Lucy knew this place, and the wicket in the wall was unbarred. No one had any doubt as to who the vanished guest had been.

So the man-at-arms who had insisted on entry here, though he failed of getting the credit for a capture, did well enough out of his suggestion to be commended by his officer, and was not ill-content with the enterprise.

## 6

Huon de Domville lay naked beneath a linen cerecloth in the mortuary chapel, and round about him stood the abbot and prior, the sheriff of the county, the dead man's nephew and squire, Sir Godfrid Picard, who should by this time have been his uncle by marriage, and Brother Cadfael.

Simon Aguilon was still cloaked and gloved from his strenuous part in the morning's search, and looked haggard and worried, as well he might, at the responsibility that had fallen on him as the dead man's nearest kin here. Picard was gnawing the black, clipped fringe of his beard, and brooding on his losses and the openings now left to him. Radulfus was quietly and scrupulously intent on what Cadfael was expounding.

The abbot was a man of the world and of the church, of wide experience, but not so wide as to include those manifestations of violence which were an open book to Brother Cadfael, who had been soldier and sailor besides. Rare among men of wide experience, Radulfus knew precisely the gaps that were left, and was willing to be instructed. The honour and integrity of his house was his prime concern, and in that criterion pure justice was implied. As for Prior Robert, his Norman loyalties were outraged, since a Norman lord had been removed by murder. In his own way he required a vengeance just as surely as did Picard.

'The head injuries,' said Brother Cadfael, his palm under the newly laved and combed head, 'would have been no danger, had they been all. But the blow stunned him, and laid him open to assault. Now, see . . .' He drew down the linen cloth below the great barrel of a breast and the massive upper arms. 'He fell asprawl on his back, head against the tree, arms and legs spread. My lord Prestcote here saw him so, and so did Brother Edmund and certain novices of our house. I could not then see what I have seen now, by reason of his clothing. Look here at the inner side of his upper arms, those round black bruisings in the muscle. See those arms spread, and consider what fell upon him, senseless as he was. His enemy kneeled here upon these arms, reached here to his throat.'

'And that would not rouse him?' asked the abbot gravely, following Cadfael's blunt brown finger as he traced the prints of murder.

'There was some effort made.' Cadfael recalled the deep pits Domville's boot-heels had scored in the turf. 'But by the body only, as men jerk from wounds when they have no more power to resist them. His senses were out of him, he could not fight his assailant. And these were strong hands, and resolute. See here, where both thumbs, one over the other, were driven in. The apple of his neck is ruptured.'

He had not had the opportunity until now to look more closely at that savage injury. Under the short beard the slash made by the rope drew a dark-red line, from which the beads of blood had been washed away. The black bruises left by the strangler's hands showed up clearly.

'Here is every sign of a madly vindictive attacker,' said Prestcote grimly.

'Or a very frightened one,' Cadfael said mildly. 'Desperate at his own act, an act unlike him, suddenly undertaken and monstrously overdone.'

'You could be speaking of the same man,' said Radulfus reasonably. 'Is there anything more this body can tell us about him?'

It seemed that there was. On the left side of Domville's neck, about where the middle fingers of the right hand must have gripped, and had left their shadowy shape, the bruise was crossed by a short, indented wound, as though a jagged stone had been pressed into the flesh there. Cadfael pondered this small, insignificant thing in silence for a while, and concluded that it might be by no means insignificant.

'A small, sharp cut,' he mused, peering close, 'and this hollow wound beside it. The man who did this wore a ring, on the middle or third finger of his right hand. A ring with a large stone in it, to thrust so into the flesh. And it must hang rather loose on his finger, for it turned partially within as he gripped. On the middle finger, surely . . . if it had hung loose on the third he would have shifted it to the middle one. I can think of no other way such an injury can have been made.' He looked up into the circle of attentive faces. 'Did young Lucy wear such a ring?'

Picard shrugged off all knowledge of such matters. After some thought Simon said: 'I cannot recall ever noticing a ring. But neither can I say certainly that he never wore one. I might ask Guy if he knows.'

'It shall be enquired into,' said the sheriff. 'Is there more to be noticed?'

'I can think of nothing. Unless it is worth wondering where this man had been, and on what errand, to find him on that path at such an hour.'

'We do not know the hour,' said Prestcote.

'No, true. It is not possible to say how long a man has been dead, not within a matter of hours. Yet the turf under him was moist. But there is another point. All the signs show – very well, let us be wary of reading too confidently, they *seem* to show! – that he was riding back towards his house when he was waylaid. And the trap set for him was laid and waiting before he came. Therefore whoever set it, and thereafter killed him, knew where he had gone, and by what road he must return.'

'Or must have followed him in the night, and made his plans accordingly,' said the sheriff. 'We are sure now that Lucy made his way to the hay-store in the bishop's garden and hid there, but after dark he came forth, and may well have lurked to keep watch on his lord's movements, with this fell intent in mind. He knew Domville would be supping here at the abbey, for all the household knew it. It would not be difficult to wait in hiding for his return, and to see him riding on alone and dismissing his squire provided the very chance revenge needed. Small doubt but Lucy is our man.'

There was no more then to be said. The sheriff returned to his hunt, convinced of his rightness; and on the face of it, Cadfael allowed, no blame at all to him, for the case was black. Huon de Domville was left to the care of Brother Edmund and his helpers, and his coffin bespoken from Martin Bellecote, the master carpenter in the town, for whether he was to find his burial here or elsewhere, he must be decently coffined for his journey to the grave, and with suitable grandeur. His body had no more now to tell.

Or so Brother Cadfael thought, until he consented to recount the circumstances of death and enquiry to Brother Oswin in the workshop, over the sorting of beans for the next year's seed. Oswin listened intently to all. At the end he said with apparent inconsequence: 'I wonder that he should ride in a late October night without a capuchon. And he bald, too!'

Cadfael stood at gaze, contemplating him with wonder across a handful of seed. 'What was that you said?'

'Why, for an old man to go bare-headed in the night...'

He had put his finger firmly on the one thing Cadfael had missed. Domville had not ridden away bareheaded from the abbey gatehouse, that was certain. Cadfael himself had seen him depart, the fine crimson capuchon twisted up into an elaborate hat, gold fringe swinging, and yet he had not thought to look for it where the body lay fallen, or question its absence.

'Child,' said Cadfael heartily, 'I am always underestimating you. Remind me of it when next I breathe down your neck over your work, for I shall deserve it. He did indeed have a capuchon, and I had better be about finding it.'

He asked no permission, preferring to consider that the morning's leave to join in the search might reasonably be extended to cover a further stage in the same quest. There was still time before Vespers if he hurried, and the place was marked with their improvised cross.

The turf under the oak still retained the vague shape of Domville's body, but already the grasses were rising again. Cadfael prowled the pathway with his eyes on the ground, penetrated into the trees on both sides, and found nothing. It was a sudden shaft of sunlight through the branches, filtering through thick underbrush, that finally located for him what he sought, by picking out the glitter of the gold fringe that bordered the cape of the capuchon. It had been flung from its wearer's head when he was thrown, and buried itself in a clump of bushes three yards from the path, its fashionable twisted arrangement making it all too easy to dislodge in such a shock. Cadfael hauled it out. The turban-like folds had been well wound, it was still a compact cap, with one draped edge left to swing gracefully to a shoulder. And in the dark crimson folds a cluster of bright blue shone. Somewhere in his nocturnal ride Huon de Domville had added to his adornments a little bunch of frail, straight stems bearing long, fine green leaves and starry flowers of a heavenly blue, even now, when they had lain all day neglected. Cadfael drew the posy out of the folds, and marvelled at it, for though it had commoner cousins, this plant was a rarity.

He knew it well, though it was seldom to be found even in the shady places in Wales where he had occasionally seen it. He knew of no place here in England where it had ever, to his knowledge, been discovered. When he wanted seed to make powders or infusions against colic or stone, he had to be content with the poor relatives of this rarity. Now what, he wondered, viewing its very late and now somewhat jaded flowers, is a bunch of the blue creeping gromwell doing in these parts? Certainly Domville had not had it when he left the abbey.

It was a pity there was no time to go further, since he must be back to attend Iveta and go to Vespers. He was beginning to be very curious indeed about Domville's nightly ramblings. Had not Picard mentioned by the way that the baron had a hunting-lodge near the Long Forest? From the Foregate this path might well be the most direct way to that lodge. True, the place might lie anywhere along some miles of the forest borders, but it would be well worth following the road the dead man had taken. But not today, that was out of the question.

Cadfael tucked the little bunch of blue and the capuchon in the breast of his habit, and made his way back. No doubt it was his duty to hand over both, with due explanations, to the sheriff, but he was not at all sure that he was going to do so. The capuchon, certainly, that added nothing to what was already known. But this small knot of fading beauty was eloquent indeed. Where that grew, Domville had been, and there surely could not be more than one such place in all this shire. He knew of only three in Gwynedd, where it had its home, here he was astonished to find even one. And Prestcote was an honest and just man, but arbitrary in his decisions, and already convinced of Joscelin's guilt. Who else had a grudge against the baron? Cadfael was not convinced. Loose talk about killing did not delude him. There are people who are capable of murder by stealth, and people who are not, and nothing would persuade him to the contrary. Every man may be driven to kill, but not every man can be driven to kill by cunning, the knife in the back, the rope across the path.

He went back dutifully to the abbey, delivered the capuchon to the sergeant Prestcote had left at the gatehouse, and went to fetch the poppy syrup for Iveta from his workshop.

This time they did not leave him alone with her for a moment. The maid Madlen, plainly Agnes's creature to the hilt, stood over them sharp-eyed and prick-eared, all he could give the girl was the reassurance of his continued partisanship by his very presence, and the ministrations he offered. At least they could exchange looks, and interpret what they saw. And he could ensure that she should sleep, and sleep long, while he pondered how best to help her. Also to help Joscelin Lucy? She would not be grateful for a partisanship that did not extend to her lover, for whose life she had been willing to barter all her own future happiness.

Cadfael went to Vespers with the little fading cluster of blue still in his habit.

Brother Mark had been vaguely but persistently troubled, all that day, by the feeling that his grasp on the whole body of his flock at the hospice had somehow been disrupted. It had begun at Prime, when all the household, except the one or two young children, came together in the church. It was not that he ever counted them. If any were sicker or more out of mood than normally, they could remain at rest, no one drove them, so the number need never be the same. Moreover, during even this brief office there were some who for good reason must ease their discomfort by movement, and therefore the whole mass shifted and changed a little.

It was rather that he was haunted by a sense of unexpected bulk, a limitation of the light within the church, which at all times was dim and cramped. There were six or seven big men among his charges, but he knew the manner and gait of them all, the little halts and stoops that identified even the veiled ones among them.

Once or twice during Prime he had thought he detected one lofty, shrouded head and covered face that had an alien look, but always he lost it again. Not until the end did it dawn on him that he was losing it because all his afflicted household was so disposing its people as to swallow up the intruder.

Intruder seemed a hard word where the doors were open to all, yet had the newcomer been truly a leper, here arrived at one more halt in a lifetime's pilgrimage, he would have announced himself, and there would have been no need for this mysterious shifting and dissembling. Yet what whole man in his right mind would choose to hide here? He would have to be desperate.

Mark had almost persuaded himself that he was dreaming. But when he doled out the bread and oatmeal and small ale at breakfast, though again he did not count – for who counts what is given to the unfortunate? – by the end of it he knew that his supplies were depleted beyond what he had expected. Someone among his children had drawn food for another mouth.

He knew, of course, that the sheriff's men were beating the woods and gardens between Saint Giles and the town, and before noon the news of Huon de Domville's death had reached him. The isolation of the outcasts here never kept out the news. Whatever happened in town or abbey was known at once in the hospice, down to the very manner of the baron's death, and the outcry raised against the escaped squire as his murderer. But Brother Mark had work to do, and had not thought much about the rumours. There were all his morning medical duties first, and not until the last dressing was renewed and the last sore anointed did he give much consideration to the discrepancy that was troubling him. Even then there were other matters to be attended to, recording gifts made to the hospital, arranging for a party of the able-bodied to go gleaning for the winter wood-pile in the manor of Sutton, a right granted them by the late lord and continued by his son, helping to prepare the midday meal, checking the superior's accounts, and a dozen other things. Only in the afternoon was he at leisure to pursue some of the duties he had appropriated to himself of his own will, such as reading the office privately to one old man who was too ill to leave his bed, and giving a lesson to the boy Bran. Very easy lessons they usually turned out to be, more than half play, but for all that, the child was thirsty for letters, and drew in learning like mother's milk, as naturally as breathing.

Mark had made a little desk for him, the appropriate size for his spindly eight years, and on this day he trimmed a leaf of old, cleaned vellum for his use, leaving the frayed strips he had removed on his own desk close by. The schoolroom was a cramped corner of the hall, close to a narrow window for light. Sometimes they ended using up the rest of the leaf in children's drawing games, at which Bran could usually win. The leaf could always be cleaned and used again and again, until it wore too thin and frayed away.

Mark went out to find his pupil. The day was clear, but the sunlight moist and mild. Many of the lepers would be out along the fringes of the highroads with their clapper-dishes, keeping their humble distance from all traffic, but crying their appeal to those who passed. But close to his accustomed place beside the cemetery wall Lazarus was sitting, tall, straight-backed, head erect in its shrouding hood and veil. Close beside him, leaning comfortably upon his thighs, was Bran, both hands raised with spread fingers holding a web of coarse thread, with one side of it caught in his teeth. The man's hands shared the spread of the web. They were playing the old game of cat's-cradle, and the boy was bubbling with laughter round the cord he nibbled.

It was pleasant and cheering to see old age and childhood in harmony together, and Brother Mark hesitated to break into their concentration. He was about to withdraw and leave them to their game, but the child had caught sight of him, and let fall his tether to call out hastily: 'I'm coming, Brother Mark! Wait for me!'

He unwound his fingers from the web, said a blithe farewell to his playmate, who unlaced the thread without a word, and ran willingly to slip his hand into Mark's, and skip beside him into the hall.

'We were only filling up the time, till you were ready for me,' said the boy.

'Are you sure you wouldn't rather stay out and play, while the weather's mild like this? You may, of course, if you wish. We can learn in the dark evenings, all the winter long by the fire.'

'Oh, no, I want to show you how well I can do the letters you taught me.'

He had towed Brother Mark indoors, and was at his desk and smoothing the fresh sheet of vellum proudly before him, and still it had not dawned on Mark what he had just witnessed. It was the sight of the thin, careful hand gripping the quill that finally brought enlightenment. He drew in breath so sharply that Bran looked up quickly, in the belief that he must be doing something either very badly, or unexpectedly well, and Mark made haste to reassure and praise him.

But how could he have failed to recognise what he

was seeing? The height matched, the erect carriage was right, the width of the shoulders under the cloak – everything was as it should be. Except that both hands from which Bran had been in the act of lifting their web of thread had all their fingers, and were smooth, supple and shapely, a young man's hands.

Nevertheless, Brother Mark said never a word to the superior of the hospital, or to any other, of what he had discovered, nor did he make any move to confront the interloper. What impressed him most, and caused him to hold his hand, was the unanimity with which his afflicted flock had opened to receive the fugitive, surely with barely a word said, and nothing explained, and had closed about him in the silent solidarity of shared misfortune. Not lightly would he presume to turn back that tide, or dispute the rightness of that judgment.

The hunters came back from their fruitless search with the fall of darkness. Guy, a very reluctant conscript, tramped into the chamber he shared with Simon, kicked off his boots, and lay back on his bed with a great gusty sigh of exasperation.

'Well for you, that you escaped that penance! Hours of draggle-tailing it through the bushes and peering into cottage pig-styes, and scaring out moulting hens. I swear I stink of muck! Canon Eudo came bustling back from the church and hunted us all out, but his zeal didn't run as far as volunteering for the foul work himself. He went back to his prayers – may they do the old man's soul some good!'

'And you've seen nothing of him? Of Joss?' asked Simon anxiously, pausing with one arm in the sleeve of his best cotte.

'If I had, I should have looked the other way, and kept main quiet about it.' Guy smothered a huge yawn, and stretched his long legs at ease. 'But no, never a glimpse.

The sheriff's got a cordon round the town that should keep in even a mouse, and they're planning a slow drive further out on the north side tomorrow, and if that fails, on the brook side the next day. I tell you, Simon, they're set on taking him. Did you hear they even ransacked the grounds of this house? And found he, or some fellow, had been hiding in one of the outhouses down by the wall?'

Simon completed the donning of his coat, glumly thoughtful. 'I heard it. But it seems he was long gone. If it *was* he.'

'Do you think he may be already out and away? Why should we not at least leave the old man's stable unlocked tonight? Or move Briar to the open one in the court? A small chance is better than none.'

'If we even knew where he might be . . .But I've been thinking,' agreed Simon, 'that at least we'd better have the poor beast out into daylight again, and find him some exercise. Who knows, if I was seen riding him, and Joss got word of it, he might get in touch.'

'I see you no more believe in this charge than I do,' observed Guy, lifting his rumpled head to give his friend a sharp glance. 'Nor in that wretched business of the necklace in his saddle-bag, either. I wonder which misbegotten dog among the servants got his orders to hide it there! Or do you suppose the old man saw to it himself? He was never afraid of his own dirty work, as long as I've known him.' Guy had been in the baron's service from twelve years old, beginning as a page fresh from his father's house, and had even acquired a kind of detached affection for his formidable lord, who had never had occasion to turn formidable to him. 'But still, it was a foul way to make away with him,' he said. 'And I do still wonder . . . . If Joss was mad with rage – and he had reason to be – I would not be ready quite to stake my soul he did not kill him. Even that way!'

'But I would,' said Simon with certainty.

'Ah, you!' Guy rose indulgently and clapped his fellow on the shoulder. 'Where others hold opinions, you *know*! Be careful you don't trip yourself some day by trusting too far. And now I look at you,' he added, twitching the collar of Simon's best coat into immaculate neatness, 'you're very fine tonight. Where are you off to?'

'Only to the Picards at the abbey. A common courtesy, now the worst of the day's over and the dust settling. They came close to becoming his kin, they'll have to be allowed a part in the mourning for him. It costs nothing to defer to the man as elder and adviser until my uncle's buried. There'll be messages to send out to my aunt in the nunnery at Wroxall, and one or two distant cousins. Eudo can make himself useful doing the scribing, he has the right flowery style.'

'I warn you,' said Guy, rising lazily to go and demand hot water for his ablutions, 'the sheriff and Eudo between them will drive you out with the rest of us to take part in their sweep tomorrow. They're bent on hanging him.'

'I can always look the other way, like you,' said Simon, and departed to do his duty by one who had almost become a kinsman, and had hoped by this time to have a kinsman's rights.

Iveta lay in her bed, with Brother Cadfael's poppy draught measured and ready to her hand, and his promise that it would bring her sleep like a small, warm core of comfort in her mind. But she did not want to sleep yet. There was a kind of passive pleasure in being here alone in the room, even though she knew that Madlen was within call. They had so seldom left her alone all these weeks, the oppression of their presence had been like a shadow cutting her off from the sun. Only yesterday, and only for those meagre minutes, and even then with an eye on her from the distance, had they sent her out to dispose herself where she must be noticed, and might be questioned, so that she might give the right answers, and display the right assured calmness of consent in her hateful destiny. And all the time they had known that Joscelin was not a prisoner, but somewhere at liberty, even if his liberty was that of a hunted man.

That was over. She could not be cheated like that again. Two things at least she could cling to: he was not taken, and she was not married.

She caught the sound of a hand at the door, and shrank within herself, wary and still. But when the door opened, and Agnes appeared, it was with a face almost benign, and a voice almost solicitous, surely for the benefit of the visitor who came in at her shoulder. Iveta stared in astonishment at the transformation.

'Still awake, child? Then here is a good friend enquiring after you. May he come in for a few moments? You are not too tired?'

He was in already, Simon in his best, and on his best behaviour for her aunt and uncle; and his best behaviour must have made its impression, for he was actually allowed to be alone with her. Agnes was withdrawing, smiling her benevolence in her best public manner. 'Only a few minutes. She should not exert herself longer tonight.'

She was gone, and the door had closed after her. Simon's pleasant, boyish face shed its wariness instantly, and he came striding to Iveta's bedside, pulled up a stool, and sat down beside her. She raised herself gladly on her pillows, the gold mane of her hair loose over the shoulders of her linen gown.

'Softly!' he warned, finger to lip. 'Speak low, your dragon may be set on to listen. I'm let in briefly to pay my respects and enquire how you are. God knows I was sorry to see you so shocked. Did they never tell you he broke free?'

She shook her head, almost too full to speak. 'Oh, Simon, is there news? Not...'

'Not good nor ill,' he said quickly, in the same low and rapid whisper. 'Nothing has changed. He's still at liberty, and pray God he will be. They'll be hunting for him, I know. But so shall I,' he said meaningly, and took the small hand that groped out blindly towards him. 'Take heart! They've searched all day, and no one has laid hand or eye on him yet, who knows but he's away out of the circle long since. He's strong, and bold...'

'Too bold!' she said ruefully.

'And still has friends, for all they've charged against him. Friends who don't believe in his guilt!'

'Oh, Simon, you do me so much good!'

'I would I might do more, for you and for him. But take comfort, all you need do is be patient and wait. One threat is gone from you. Now, if he continues free, there's no urgency, you *can* wait.'

'And truly you don't believe he ever stole? Nor that he has killed?' she pleaded hungrily.

'I *know* he has not,' said Simon firmly, with all the self-assurance with which Guy had goodnaturedly charged him. 'The only wrong he has done is to love where love was not allowed. Oh, I know!' he said quickly, seeing her flinch and turn her face aside. 'Forgive me if I'm presumptuous, but he's my friend and has spoken with me as a friend. I *do* know!' He cast an uneasy glance over his shoulder, and smiled wry reassurance at her. 'Your aunt will be beginning to frown. I should go. But remember, Joss is not friendless.'

'I will,' she said fervently, 'and thank God and you for it. You'll come again, Simon, if you can? You can't imagine how you comfort me.'

'I'll come,' he promised, and stooped hurriedly to kiss her hand. 'Goodnight now! Sleep well, and don't be afraid.'

He was on his way to the door when Agnes opened it, still benevolent, but watchful all the same. This young man was Huon de Domville's nephew, and partook of the deference accorded his uncle in life. But the watch on Iveta would never be wholly relaxed until she was profitably disposed of, and the gains secured.

The door closed. Iveta was ready now for sleep, the load on her heart greatly lightened. She drank Brother Cadfael's potion, honeysweet and heavy, and blew out her candle.

When Madlen came prowling suspiciously, Iveta was already asleep.

After Compline Brother Cadfael asked audience of Abbot Radulfus, in his own study in the abbot's lodging. It was a good hour for grave conversation, a day of many passions over at last, the night's needful composure closing in.

'Father, I have told you all I know of this matter, but for one thing. You know that I have knowledge of herbs. In the capuchon I brought back and delivered to the sheriff this evening, I found a herb which I know to be exceedingly rare, even in Wales, where it does habit in some places. Here I had never before met with it. Yet Huon de Domville, in his last night in this world, was where this herb grows. Father, I think this circumstance of the greatest importance, and it is my wish to find this place, and discover what business the dead man had there, on his marriage eve. I believe it may have a bearing on his death, the manner of it, and the maker of it.'

He had the little faded posy in his palm, a drying bunch of thin stems, thread-like green leaves and wilting, starry flowers, still surprisingly blue.

'Show me,' said the abbot, and gazed with wondering attention. 'And you can say where such a thing grows, and where it does not grow?'

'It grows in a few, a very few places, where the chalk or limestone crops out. I have never before seen it in England.'

'And by this you believe you can divine where our murdered man spent his night?'

'We know the path by which he was returning. By that same path he surely went, when he left his squire at the gate. It is my wish, if you give leave, to follow that path, and find this flower. I believe lives – innocent of anything beyond youth, folly and anger – may hang upon so small a thing.'

'Such things have happened times without number,' said Abbot Radulfus. 'Our purpose is justice, and with God lies the privilege of mercy. You have leave, Brother Cadfael, to pursue this as long as may be needful. You have my trust.'

'God knows I value it,' said Cadfael truly. 'And you have, and shall have, mine. Whatever I may find, I submit to you.'

'Not to the sheriff?' asked Radulfus, and smiled.

'Surely. But through you, Father.'

Brother Cadfael went to his bed in the dortoir, and slept like an innocent babe safely cradled, until the bell rang for Matins.

# 7

When Cadfael emerged from Prime, the following morning, Prestcote was already abroad marshalling his renewed hunt on the northern side of the Foregate. This time they would make a great, slow sweep for some three miles out, so exhaustive that barely a weasel or a hare would elude their net. The sheriff was determined to fetter his quarry this time, and reasonably sure that he had not already slipped through the cordon, which had been strengthened overnight. Picard was out with all the men of his household marshalled at his back, and Canon Eudo was probably exhorting Domville's people at the bishop's house to the same forced service. And though some, no doubt, turned out reluctantly, nevertheless there is something infectious about the zeal of a hunt, that would have most of these beaters in full cry if ever they scented their quarry.

Not for the first time, Brother Cadfael wished heartily that he had Hugh Beringar here, to temper the chill of Prestcote's proceedings. The deputy sheriff had room in his head and conscience for healthy doubts of his own omniscience, and was always perversely suspicious of what seemed a foregone conclusion to others. But Hugh Beringar was in the north of the shire, at his own manor of Maesbury, and certainly would not consent to move from there these coming few weeks, for his wife was near her time with their first child, and that is a peak of experience in any young man's life. No help for it, this matter would have to be settled under Gilbert Prestcote's direction. And at that, thought Cadfael fairly, we're luckier than many a shire. He's an honest, fair-minded man, if he is too urgent for quick resolutions and summary justice, and not inclined to look too far beyond the obvious. Nevetheless, show him a provable truth, and he'll accept it. Provable truths are what we need.

Meantime, he took some care over giving Brother Oswin his tasks for the day. Only a week ago, he would have found him enough rough digging and outdoor work to keep him occupied, and prayed heartily that the great maladroit need not even set foot in the workshop. Today he handed over to him some early winter pruning, but also the tending of a batch of wine just beginning to work, and the making of an ointment for the infirmary. They had made the same ointment together once, the process fully explained as they went. Cadfael nobly refrained from repeating and underlining every stage, and left Oswin with only the most modest and trusting recapitulation.

'I leave the workshop in your hands,' he said firmly. 'I place full confidence in you.'

'And God forgive me the lie,' he muttered to himself when he was out of earshot, 'and turn it to truth. Or at least count it as merit to me rather than sin. If I've been setting your teeth on edge, Oswin, my lad, now's your chance to spread your wings on your own. Make the most of it!'

Now he had the day at his disposal, and his starting-point must be the spot where Domville had died. He took the quickest way to it, a risky and unorthodox route he had sometimes used on more obscure business of his own. The Meole brook, where it bordered the abbey fields and gardens, was fordable except in flood-time, provided a man knew it well, and Cadfael knew it perfectly. He thus cut off a detour by the roads, at the mere cost of kilting his habit above the knees, and sandals let out water as freely as they let it in. By the time chapter ended at the abbey, he was on the path where the baron had been ambushed, and pushing on along it at a good pace.

This part of the path he knew, it lay directly across a great winding bend of the brook, and he was approaching the second ford which would take him out of the loop, and away through woods and fields towards Sutton and Beistan, sparsely peopled country approaching the great stretch of the Long Forest. He did not think that Domville could have had many miles to go, nor that he had spent the night in the open. A man tough enough for that and worse when there was need, but fond of his comforts when things were going easily.

At Sutton Strange the woods fell back before fields. Cadfael exchanged the time of day with a cottar whose children he had once treated for a skin rash, and enquired if the news of Domville's death had reached the village. It had, and was the chief gossip for miles around, and already the inhabitants were expecting that the hunt for the murderer might reach as far as their homes and byres the next day.

'I heard he had a hunting-lodge somewhere in these parts,' said Cadfael. 'On the edge of the forest is what I heard, but that could mean anywhere along ten miles of country. Would you know of the place?'

'Ah, that'll be the house over beyond Beistan,' said the cottar, leaning comfortably on his garden wall. 'He has rights of warren in the forest, but he came there only rarely, and keeps only a local lad there as steward, and the old woman his mother to take care for the house when it's unvisited. As it mostly is. He has better hunts elsewhere. *Had*! Seems someone set a snare for him, this time.'

'And made a thorough job of it,' said Cadfael soberly. 'How do I best go for this place? Through the village at Beistan?'

'That's it, and cross the old road and bear on between the hills. You'll find this path makes a straight run of it. You'll be in the edge of the forest there, sure enough, before ever you see the house.'

Cadfael went on briskly, emerging on to a highroad at the village of Beistan, where the path he was following crossed and moved on, dead straight, past a few scattered holdings beyond, and then into fitful stretches of rising heathland and copses between two gentle slopes. After another mile or so it became a forest path once again, closely hemmed in. Where ground-rock broke through into view, it was white and chalky, and in the more open glades heathers brushed crisp and prickly against his ankles. It was a long time since he had been so far afoot, and if he had not been on so grave a quest his walk would have been pure enjoyment.

He came upon the hunting-lodge quite abruptly, the trees falling away on either side to show him a low boundary wall of stones, and a squat timber building within, raised on an undercroft, with outhouses lining the rear wall of the enclosure. Among the rough white stones of the wall there were all manner of wild herbs growing, toadflax and ivy, stonecrop and selfheal, known by their leaves even now that hardly any flowers remained. There were orchard trees within the wall, but few and old and gnarled, as though someone had once made a garden here, but now it was neglected and forgotten. Some former lord, perhaps, of Domville's line, with a family of children, to turn this quite pleasant fastness into a favourite home, whereas in recent years a childless elderly man had had no use for it but in the hunting season, and even then preferred fatter forests elsewhere in his widespread honour.

Cadfael crossed to the open gate in the wall, and stepped within. Instantly his eye was caught by a broom-bush on the inner side, in a corner near the gate. For it was an unmistakable broom-bush, and yet in this autumn season it was in flower, and its flowers, scattered and starry, were of a bright and limpid blue instead of gold. He went closer, and saw that the three lowest courses of the wall and the ground beside were matted with proliferating stems, thin, straight, branching into long, narrow leaves. The mat on the ground reached the roots of the broom, and sent up long, frail stalks to clamber through its branches, thrusting up to the light these late, radiant clusters of heavenly blue.

He had found his creeping gromwell, and he had found the place where Huon de Domville had spent the last night of his life.

'You are seeking someone, brother?'

The voice behind him was respectful to the point of being obsequious, and yet had a cutting edge like a well-honed knife. He turned alertly to view the speaker, and found the very same ambiguous qualities. He must have come from the outhouses under the rear wall, a fine, well-set-up fellow about thirty-five years old, in country homespun but with a dignity to him that fell just short of a swagger. He had eyes like pebbles under a sunlit brook, as hard and clear, and as fluid and elusive in their glance. He was brown and handsome and altogether pleasant to the view, but he was not quite easy in his authority, and not quite friendly in his civility.

'You are Huon de Domville's steward at this house?' asked Brother Cadfael with wary courtesy.

'I am,' said the young man.

'Then the mission I have is to you,' said Cadfael amiably, 'though I think it may be unnecessary. You may have heard already, for I find it's known in the countryside, that your lord is dead, murdered, and is now lying in the abbey of Saint Peter and Saint Paul of Shrewsbury, from which I come.'

'So we heard yesterday,' said the steward, his manner somewhat easing at this reasonable explanation for the visit, though not as much as might have been expected.

His face remained wary and his voice reserved. 'A cousin of mine brought the word, coming from the town market.'

'But no one has been to you from your lord's household? You've had no orders? I thought Canon Eudo might have sent to let you know. But you'll understand they're all in confusion and consternation yet. No doubt they'll be in touch with you and all his manors when they get round to the proper arrangements.'

'They'll be set first on getting hold of his murderer, no question,' said the man, and moistened his lips, elusive pebble-eyes looking slightly sidelong at Cadfael. 'I shall hear when his kin see fit. Meantime, I'm still in his service until another either confirms me in my stewardship here, or turns me off. I'll keep his property and stock as I should, and turn them over to his heir in good order. Say so for me, brother, and no man need trouble for this place. Let them put their minds at rest.' He veiled his eyes a moment, thinking. 'You did say murdered? Is that certain?'

'Certain,' said Cadfael. 'It seems he rode out after his supper, and was waylaid on his way back. We found him on a path that leads in this direction. It was in my mind he might have been here, seeing this grange is his.'

'He has not been here,' said the steward firmly.

'Not at all, since he came to Shrewsbury three days ago?'

'Not at all.'

'Nor any of his squires or servants?'

'No one.'

'So he did not lodge any guests here for the wedding feast. You keep his lodge alone?'

'I see to grounds and stock and farm, my mother keeps the house. The few times he ever hunted here, he brought his own body servants and cooks and all. But the last time's a good four years gone.'

Now he was lying as roundly and freely as he

breathed. For there were the starry blue flowers that grew here, and could hardly be found anywhere else in the shire. But why so determined to deny that Domville had been here? Any wise man may go to ground when there's a death-hunt up, true, but this young man did not seem the sort to take fright easily. Yet clearly he was determined that no thread should connect this place or anyone in it with the murder of his lord.

'And they've not so far laid hand on his slayer?' No mistake, he would have been glad to have the quarry snared, the hue and cry over, the malefactor safe in prison, and all enquiry at an end.

'Not yet. They're out after him in force. Ah, well,' said Cadfael, 'I'd best be getting back, then, though to tell the truth, I'm in no hurry. It's a fair day, and a good long walk is a pleasure. But would there be a cup of ale and a bench to sit a while, before I set off?'

He had half-expected reluctance, if not some ingenious refusal, to let him into the house; but the young man almost visibly changed his mind, and decided that it would be his best course to invite this monk freely within. Why? To have him see for himself that there was no one here to account for, and nothing to hide? Whatever the motive, Cadfael accepted with alacrity, and followed his host through the open doorway.

The hall was dim and silent, the scent of timber rich and heavy. A little, brisk old woman, very neat and plain, came bustling from the room beyond, and halted in surprise, if not downright alarm, at sight of a stranger, until her son, with slightly suspect speed and emphasis, accounted for the guest.

'Come through, brother, we may as well sit in the best comfort. We very seldom have gentlefolk here to make use of the solar. Mother, will you bring us a stoup? The good brother has a long walk back.'

The solar was light and bright, and furnished with considerable comfort. They sat down together over the ale and oatcakes the old housekeeper brought, and talked of the weather and the season, and the prospects for the winter, and even of the sad state of the country, torn two ways between King Stephen and the empress. Shropshire might be at peace just now, but peace was precarious everywhere in this divided land. The empress had been allowed to join her half-brother Robert of Gloucester in Bristol, and others were throwing in their lot with her, Brian FitzCount, the castellan of Wallingford, Miles, the constable of Gloucester, and others besides. It was rumoured that the city of Worcester was being threatened with attack from Gloucester. Devoutly they agreed to hope that the tide of war would come no nearer, perhaps even spare Worcester.

But for all this innocuous talk, Brother Cadfael's senses were on the alert; and it might, after all, have been a miscalculation on the steward's part to invite him in, so that he could see for himself how all was empty, well-kept and innocent. For it certainly was not the old woman who had brought that faint, indefinable perfume into the room. Nor had the one who distilled it been gone from here very long, for such a fragrance would have faded away within a few days. Cadfael had a nose for floral essences, and recognised jasmine.

There was nothing more to be discovered here within. He rose to take his leave and give thanks for his entertainment, and the steward went out with him dutifully, no doubt to make sure that he set off back to the abbey without deceit. It was pure chance that the old woman should be coming out of the stables in the yard just as they emerged, and had let the door swing wide open behind her before she was aware of them. Her son was deft and quick to spring across and close it, shooting the bar home. But he had not been quite quick enough.

Cadfael gave no sign of having noticed more than he should, but said his farewell cheerfully at the gate, beside the broom-bush that bore blue flowers instead of gold, and set off at a swinging pace back along the path by which he had come.

There was a horse in that stable certainly not built to carry Huon de Domville's lusty weight, or sustain a day's hunting even under one of his retinue. Cadfael had glimpsed the small, delicate white head and curious face peering out, the arched neck and braided mane, and the light, ornate harness hanging on the inner side of the swinging door. A pretty little white jennet, such as a lady would ride, and such elaborate and decorative accoutrements as would be provided for a lady. Yet he would have been prepared to swear that there was no lady there at the hunting-lodge now. There had been no warning of his approach, no time to hide her away. He had been brought in expressly to see for himself that she was not there, that no one was there but the usual custodians.

Why, then, however dismayed she might be at the thought of being hunted out of her privacy, displayed as having some dark connection with Domville's death, perhaps even suspected of collusion in it, why should she choose to depart on foot, and leave her mount idle behind? And where, on foot, in such a remote solitude, could such a lady go?

He did not return directly to the abbey, but continued along the green ride until it emerged on the Foregate, and made his way to the bishop's house. The great courtyard, usually such a bustle, was quiet indeed on this afternoon, for even the grooms and able-bodied servants had been drafted into the hunt as beaters, and were out somewhere in the woods. Only the older men were left here, which suited Cadfael well enough, for the oldest servants were the most likely to know all their lord's private business, whether they ever acknowledged it or not, and the absence of the busy and sharp-eared young made confidences more likely.

He sought out Domville's chamberlain, who had, it seemed, been in his master's service many years, and moreover, had the shrewd good sense to see the force of telling unvarnished truth, now that Domville himself was gone. There was no one else here to be feared, complete frankness would serve his turn best with the sheriff. There would be an inevitable interregnum, and then a new master. The servants were under no suspicion, and had nothing to fear, why conceal anything that might be of significance?

The chamberlain was a man well past sixty, grey-haired and staid, with illusionless eyes and the withdrawn, resigned dignity of most old servants. His name was Arnulf, and he had answered all the sheriff's questions without hesitation, and was willing to answer as candidly any others that Cadfael or any man might put to him. An age had come to an end with his lord's death, he would have to trim his service to quite another rule, now, or go into retirement and take his ease.

Nevertheless, the first question Cadfael asked was one Arnulf had certainly not foreseen.

'Your lord had the name for a womaniser. Tell me this, had he a mistress of such importance – or perhaps a new sweetheart so absorbing – that he could not do without her even for these few days while he married the Massard heiress? Someone he might bring along with him, and install within reach, but apart?'

The old man gaped, as if such forthright words came curiously from one in a Benedictine habit, but after narrow scrutiny appeared to find, after all, nothing so surprising about it. His manner relaxed noticeably. They had a language and an experience of life in common.

'Brother, however you may have hit on it, yes, there is such a woman. They come in all kinds, women. I was never a great one for them myself, I've had troubles enough without courting more. But *he* could not go far or long without them. They came and went, with him. By the score! But there's this one who is different. She stays. Stable as a wife. Like an old gown or a pair of shoes, easy and comfortable, someone he need not make speeches for, or put himself out to flatter and please. I had a feeling always,' said Arnulf reflectively, scrubbing in his beard with thin fingers, 'that wherever he went, she wouldn't be far away. But I know nothing of any plans to bring her here. Not that he ever made use of me in such matters. I helped him into his shirts and hose, and pulled off his boots after hunting, and slept close to fetch him wine in the night if he called. Not for his women. That's another service. What of her? There's been no word of her here. I did wonder.'

'Nor of a palfrey,' asked Cadfael, 'pure white, mane and all? A pretty little lady's jennet out of Spanish stock, I should say by the glimpse I got of her. With a gilded bridle hanging on her stable door.'

'I know the one,' said Arnulf, startled. 'He bought it for her. I was not supposed even to know these things. Where have you seen it?'

Cadfael told him. 'The horse, but not the woman. She left her palfrey and her perfume behind, but she's gone.'

'Well,' allowed Arnulf reasonably, 'I suppose she might well want to avoid being tangled in a matter of murder, and certainly if she was there, and he found on that path, as they tell, it would seem that he rode to her when he sent young Simon in and went on alone. She might well take fright and think it better to vanish.'

'She has also very loyal servants there,' said Cadfael drily, 'who are exerting themselves to convince me and all the world she never was there at all. By this time I daresay that young fellow has moved the jennet away to a safe place.'

It had occurred to him, somewhat belatedly, that the steward might have good reason to do as much for his own sake, as well as the lady's. If she had been in attendance there all this while, waiting for a visit from her lord and keeper, she might well have passed the time pleasantly enough with a younger, handsomer, altogether more personable man who was there to hand. And he, for his part, might have a healthy fear of having the association known, in case it should bring him into suspicion of having made away with his lord for the woman's sake, in jealousy and despite. It was but one step further to wonder if he had not done that very thing. Say that Domville came that night, after the young man had been blessed with the woman's favours to the point where he thought of her as his. Say that he was cast out into the night while they were together, and had nothing to do but brood and grieve, until it came to him that his lord's way home lay clear, and if he removed the act far enough from the lodge, near enough to Shrewsbury, he left the field wide open for any man to be judged the killer. It was possible! It could have happened so. Much depended on the woman. Cadfael wished that he knew more of her.

'The question now is, since she left her mount behind, where could she go from that remote place, on foot?' It was also, why should she choose to go afoot, but that he did not say, that was a more obscure problem.

'The manor where he usually kept her – her home, you might say – is well away in Cheshire.' Arnulf considered, and visibly stirred himself to recall things long neglected or forgotten. 'But it was somewhere in these very parts he found her. Some rustic beauty, a young girl then, twenty years and more ago, that must have been. Yes, more. She used to be known as Avice of Thornbury, they say her father was the village wheelwright there. They were free folk, I recollect, not villeins.' So the village craftsmen usually were, but tied to their tofts just as surely as the villeins to the land. 'Most likely she still has kin there,' said Arnulf. 'Would that be far? I'm strange in these parts.'

'No,' said Cadfael, enlightened, 'it is not far. Thornbury I know. There she could have gone on foot.'

He went away from the bishop's house with much to think about. The vanishing lady became ever more interesting. Since it was more than twenty years that she had been Domville's patient, permanent mistress, so firmly established as to have the respectability and the calm subservience of a wife, she must be fully forty years old, some years senior to that young steward at the hunting-lodge, but no doubt she must still have the charms to dazzle him, if she so wished. Yes, he could have fallen victim to desire and jealousy, and seen fit to rid himself of the old, hard man who was her owner and stood between. But the revelation of her probable years had other implications. So far gone towards middle age, a woman was unlikely to strike up another such comfortable liaison, now Domville was dead. That consideration could well have caused her to reflect that her own people were hardly more than a mile away, and that with them she could vanish, and be hidden for as long as she felt the need to hide.

But why, why should she leave behind a valuable horse, her own property, the gift of her lord? She could just as well have ridden to Thornbury as walked.

Today was more or less spent, he must go back ready for Vespers, and see what prodigies of destruction or genius Brother Oswin had performed in his absence.

But tomorrow he would find her!

At Saint Giles two young men were fretting over their personal problems. Brother Mark had long since made up his mind that the tall leper who matched Lazarus in all particulars but the completeness of his hands was indeed the fugitive squire for whom the sheriff was hunting with such formidable numbers and such ferocious determination. He was therefore caught up in a moral dilemma of some complexity.

He had heard the story of the supposed theft of the bride's necklace, but it was as suspect to him as to Brother Cadfael. Too many men, in all manner of circumstances, had been dragged to ruin and death simply by inserting such valuables into their baggage. It was all too easy a way of wiping out an enemy. He simply did not believe in it. Nor, having observed Huon de Domville, would he willingly have surrendered any man to his vengeance, which was likely to be mortal.

But the murder, that was another matter. He found it all too credible that a young man so wronged, if that accusation had indeed been false, should be driven to brood on revenge even against his nature, and to extremes. Where then was right? And yet the ambush, and the finishing of a stunned man, stuck fast in Mark's humble, unknightly craw. Such a vengeance no man could sanction. He was wrought to the limit, and he could not put off his burden upon any other shoulders. He alone knew what he knew.

He thought of approaching the intruder directly and asking for his confidence, but such a move demanded a privacy hardly to be found in this enclosed community. Not until he was certain of guilt would he make any move that should draw attention to the fugitive. Every man should be adjudged innocent until there was proof against him, and all the more where very suspect and malicious charges had already been thrown at him, and rang leaden as false coin.

If I can find occasion to be alone with him, unobserved of any, Brother Mark decided, I will speak openly and judge as I find. If I cannot, or until I can, I will watch him as best I may, mark all that he does, challenge him if he attempts any ill, stand ready to speak in his defence if he does none. And pray that God may see fit to make use of me for truth, one way or the other.

The object of his concern was sitting with Lazarus at a discreet distance from the highway but within view, some quarter of a mile along the road that led towards the river crossing at Atcham. One of the begging bowls they held, at least, was legitimate, but they made no appeals to any of those who passed by, and used their warning clappers only if some charitably disposed soul showed signs of approaching too closely. They sat cross-legged and shrouded in the bleached autumnal grass under the trees. The attitudes were easily learned.

'Just as you are,' said Lazarus, 'you might walk away through their cordon and go free. They will not believe any man so brave or so mad as to walk in a dead leper's gown, or be themselves so brave or so mad as to risk stripping you to find out.' It was a long speech for him, by the end he stumbled, as if his maimed tongue tired of the effort.

'What, run and save my own skin and leave her still captive? I do not stir from here,' said Joscelin vehemently, 'while she is still in ward to an uncle who plunders her substance, and will sell her for his own profit. To a worse than Huon de Domville, if the price is right! What use is my freedom to me, if I turn my back on Iveta in her need?'

'I think,' said the slow tongue beside him, 'that if truth be told, you want this lady for yourself. Do I belie you?'

'Not by a hair!' said Joscelin with passion. 'I want this lady for myself as I never have wanted and never shall want anything else in this great world. I should want her the same if she lacked not only lands, but shoes on her feet to walk those lands, I should want her if she were what I am feigning to be now, and what you – God be your remedy! – truly are. But for all that, I'd be content – no, grateful! – only to see her safe in the care of a worthy guardian, with all her honours upon her, and free to choose where she would. Surely I'd do my best to win her! But lose her to a better man, yes, that I would, and never complain. Oh, no, you do not belie me! I ache with wanting her!'

'But what can you do for her, hunted as you are? Is there ever a friend among them you can rely on?'

'There's Simon,' said Joscelin, warming. 'He doesn't believe evil of me. He hid me, out of goodwill, it grieves me that I quit the place without a word to him. If I could get a message to him now, he might even be able to speak with her, and have her meet me as she did once before. Now the old man's gone – but how can that ever have come about! – they may not watch her so closely. Simon might even get me my horse . . .'

'And where,' asked the patient, detached voice, 'would you take this friendless lady, if you got her out of ward?'

'I've thought of that. I'd take her to the White Ladies at Brewood, and ask sanctuary for her until enquiry could be made into her affairs, and a proper provision made for her. They would not give her up against her will. It would go as far as the king, if need be. He has a good heart, he'd see her justly used. I would a long sight sooner take her to my mother,' burst out Joscelin honestly, 'but it would be said I coveted her possessions, and that I won't endure. I have two good manors coming to me, I covet no man's lands, I owe no man, and I won't be misprised. If she still chooses me, I'll thank God and her, and be a happy man. But I care most that she should be a happy woman.'

Lazarus reached for his clapper-dish, and set the clapper woodenly clouting, for a plump, solid horseman had halted his pony and turned aside from the road towards them. The rider, nonetheless, smiled from his distance and tossed a coin. Lazarus gathered it and blessed him, and the good man waved a hand and rode on.

'There is still goodness,' said Lazarus, as if to himself.

'Praise God, there is!' said Joscelin with unaccustomed humility. 'I have experienced it. I have never asked you,' he said hesitantly, 'if you have ever had wife and child. It would be great waste if you had always been solitary.'

There was a lengthy silence, though silences at Lazarus's side were neither rare nor troublesome. At last the old man said: 'I had a wife, long dead now. I had a son. He was blessed, in that my shadow never fell upon him.'

Joscelin was startled and indignant. 'I don't find you a shadow. Never speak so! Any son of yours might properly joy in his father.'

The old man's head turned, the eyes above the veil shone steadily and piercingly upon his companion. 'He never knew,' said Lazarus simply. 'Hold him excused, he was only an infant. It was my choice, not his.'

Young and blunt and blundering as he was, Joscelin had learned in haste to understand where he might not pass, and must not and need not wonder. It astonished him, when he looked back, to discover how far his education had progressed in these two days among the outcasts.

'And there is a question you have never asked me,' he said.

'Nor do I ask it now,' said Lazarus. 'It is a question you have not asked me, either, and since a man can hardly say anything but no to it, what sense is there in asking?'

In the mortuary chapel of the abbey, after Vespers, Huon de Domville was coffined, in the presence of Prior Robert, Canon Eudo, Godfrid Picard, and the dead man's two remaining squires. Picard and the two young men had ridden in from the fruitless day's hunting, tired and irritable, still cloaked and gloved, with no captured malefactor to show for their trouble, though whether that was a matter for regret to anyone here but Picard and Eudo seemed to be in some doubt.

The candles on the altar and at the head and foot of the bier guttered gently in a chill draught, and the shadows of those present quivered hugely on the walls. Prior Robert's long white hand took the aspergillum, and shook a few drops of holy water delicately over the dead, and the candle-light caught their flight and turned them to sparks, kindled and dying in the air. Canon Eudo followed, and looking round for the only other kinsman present, handed the aspergillum to Simon, who stripped off his gloves hastily to take it. He stood looking down at his uncle's body with a sombre face as he dipped the brush of sweet herbs, and sprinkled holy water in his turn.

'I had not thought to do this for many a year yet,' he said, and turned to hold out the aspergillum to Picard and withdraw again into the shadows.

The green sprays shook some drops of water on the back of his hand as he relinquished them, and Picard watched them fall, and saw the young man shake them off as if startled at their coldness. There was something fascinating in the way the light of the candles picked out so sharply every detail of those ministering hands, cut off at the wrist by dark sleeves. So many severed hands moving and acting with a life of their own, the only pallors in the enfolding dimness. From Prior Robert's pale, elegant fingers to Guy's smooth brown fist, last of the ministrants, they performed their ritual dance and held all eyes. Only when the act of reverence was done could all those present look up, and find relief in the more human pallor of strained and solemn faces. It seemed that everyone drew a deep breath, like swimmers surfacing.

It was over. The five of them separated, Prior Robert to a brief session of prayers for the dead before supper, Canon Eudo to the abbot's lodging, the two young men to walk their jaded horses back to the bishop's house and see them tended, stabled and fed before seeking their own supper and rest. As for Picard, he bade them all a very short goodnight, and withdrew to the guest-hall, and there drew Agnes with him into their own chamber, and closed the door against all the rest of the household, even those most trusted. He had matter of importance to confide to her, and it was for no other ears.

The little boy Bran had begged and brought away with him from his lesson the strips of worn vellum trimmed from the sheet on which he practised his letters. He got credit with his teacher for wanting them, though his purpose was not quite what Mark supposed. In the dortoir, where he should long ago have been asleep, he crept to Joscelin's side with his prizes, and whispered the secret into his ear.

'For you wanted to send a message. Lazarus told me. Is it true you can write and read?' He was in awe of anyone who had such mysteries at his finger-ends. He nestled close to Joscelin's side, to be heard and to hear in the most private of whispers. 'In the morning you could use Brother Mark's ink-horn, no one will be watching his desk. If you can write it, I could carry it, if you tell me where. They don't notice me. But the best piece of the leaf is not very big, it would have to be a short message.'

Joscelin wrapped the folds of his cloak round the skinny little body against the chill of the night, and drew him into his arm. 'You're a good, gallant ally, and

I'll make you my squire if ever I get to be knight. And you shall learn Latin hand, and reckoning, and matters far beyond me. But yes, I can write a sort of fist that will serve. Where's your vellum?' He felt the meagre width but sufficient length of the strip that was pressed eagerly into his hand. 'It will do very well. Twenty words can say much. Bless you for a clever imp as ever was!'

The head from which Brother Mark's pellitory dressing had erased even the last drying sore of under-feeding and dirt burrowed comfortably into Joscelin's once-privileged shoulder, and he felt nothing but amused and indulgent affection. 'I can get as far as the bridge,' boasted Bran sleepily, 'if I keep to the back ways. If I had a capuchon I could get into the town. I'll go wherever you say . . .'

'Will your mother be missing and wanting you?' Joscelin breathed into the boy's ear. The woman, he knew, had given up all care for the world, and waited only to leave it. Even her son she abandoned thankfully into the hands of Saint Giles, patron of the diseased and shunned.

'No, she's asleep . . .' So, almost, was her busy and contented child, for whom the excitement of study and the small intrigues of friendship opened the world that was closing on her.

'Come, then, shift close, and go to sleep. Creep inside, and get my warmth.' He turned to let the searching face find a nest in the crook of his shoulder, and was startled by the pleasure he got from its delighted confiding. Long after the child was asleep he lay awake wondering that so much of his interest and energy should be directed elsewhere when his own neck was threatened, and so much of his thought devoted to excluding this small, neglected soul from whatever peril he himself had incurred, by his folly or his fate. Yes, he would write, he would try to find a way of getting his message to

Simon, but not by involving the innocent lying easy in his arm.

Joscelin also slept, and with mutual drowsy movements accommodated his guest all night long. Somewhere apart, Lazarus lay wakeful far into the night, long since having discarded his need for sleep.

# 8

Joscelin arose before dawn, with scrupulous care not to awake his bedfellow, who lay now in his abandoned ease and warmth with limbs flung abroad as if discarded. The voluminous leper-cloak Joscelin left draped over the child, for the early air was chilly, and moreover, he dared not draw nearer the town wearing it, though the risk of approaching without its cover was surely as great. He would have to rely on keeping out of sight, and also drew some comfort from the fact that the previous day's drive must have virtually exhausted the possibility of taking the sheriff's quarry on the northern side of the Foregate, and therefore, or so at least he hoped, the watch would be concentrated elsewhere.

He stole out through the hall, and picked up Brother Mark's ink-horn and quill from the desk. He would not wait for light from dawn, and could make none here, but in the church the constant light on the altar, however meagre, would be enough for his young eyes and few words. He had already worked out in his mind what he would write, and managed it legibly, if none too neatly, on his strip of vellum. The quill needed trimming, and tended to spit, but he had no knife to correct it. He was come to the condition of those now his comrades, but that his skin and limbs were whole; otherwise he had nothing but what he stood up in, no possessions of any kind at his disposal.

'Simon, for friendship do me two things, tether Briar in cover across the brook from the abbey, and bid Iveta to the herb-garden after Vespers.'

It would be enough, if he could find some way to get it to the right hands. But if he could not, he must withhold it, since he had written Simon's name. He regretted now the natural impulse to give his missive an address, in case it fell astray, for how could he implicate his friend in his own troubles? But he had no means of cutting off the offending name. It must go as it was, or stay, and destroy the only plan he had. It behoved him to be even more wary and even more audacious, in his attempt to reach the right man.

He went out into just such a pre-dawn dimness and stillness as when he had run from his hiding-place in the bishop's grounds. Warily he made his way behind the hospice and towards the town, keeping well away from the road, where trees and bushes afforded him cover. When he came to the gardens and backyards of houses he was forced further from the highway, but he had time enough to move with caution. No one would stir at the bishop's house until the first light came, no one would quit the courtyard until it was full day, and the gentlefolk had broken their fast. He reached the narrow, tree-shaded path that emerged on the Foregate beside the bishop's boundary wall, and paused to choose his ground. Only by climbing could he see over the wall, and if he must take to the trees it had better be where he could view both the inner and the outer sides of the courtyard, recognise known figures, and watch all the activity about the stables.

He chose his place with care, in the bole of an oak, stretched along a limb still covered well enough to hide him, but affording him views on both sides, and a quick and easy drop to the ground should he have to move in haste. Then there was nothing to be done but wait, for the dawn was still only a grudging pallor in the east. He would miss his breakfast, today nobody need steal for him.

Dawn came at last, in its own good time. The house, the containing wall, the stables and byres and store-houses within, all took shape very gradually out of darkness, and put on colour and life. Sleepy servants, bakers and grooms and dairy-maids, first crept, and then bustled, out about their business. Loaded trays of loaves appeared from the bakehouse, carried indoors by scullions. The morning loitered a further while, and the gentry began to make their appearances, Canon Eudo the first of them, bound for the second Mass of the day, then, some little while later, Simon and Guy together, none too eager, and deep in sombre talk. The grooms were leading out, surely, most of the horses in the stables. It seemed that the morning's hunt was already ordered and preparing to muster.

Muster they did, Guy resigned but sullen among them, and file out from the gate to turn along the Foregate towards the town. But Simon did not mount with them. He was still standing on the steps of the hall, looking after them, and apparently waiting for something. The bishop's own stable was round a corner of the house and out of Joscelin's view, but he pricked his ears to the sound of hooves, urgent and lively, coming round thence into the courtyard. In a moment more he saw his own Briar, silvery grey blotched with darker grey, frisk indignantly out into the open air of the morning, tugging a sweating and voluble groom with him. Simon came down from the steps to meet them, ran a hand over gleaming grey neck and shoulder, and held the silvery head between his palms a moment, in an appreciative caress. Joscelin's heart warmed to him. With all this coil of troubles, he had still spared a thought for the active beast shut up in a stall, and haled him out for exercise. The words he spoke to the groom as he turned back to re-enter the house were not distinguishable at this distance, but his gestures towards horse and gateway had said plainly enough: 'Saddle him up and lead him out for me.'

Joscelin waited long enough to see for himself that the groom was about that very business, and then dropped out of his tree, and moved cautiously forward in cover of the bushes until he could see the outside of the gates. And here they came, Briar mischievously lively, impatient for action. The groom led him out, and hitched him indifferently to one of the rings in the wall beside the mounting-block, and there left him to wait for his rider. It could not have turned out better. As soon as the man had gone back into the yard, and was tramping across the cobbles to the stable, Joscelin was out of cover and darting along the wall to caress and soothe a startled and delighted Briar. There was no time for dalliance, and at first he cursed the chance that a couple of horsemen came jingling along the Foregate at that moment, and he was forced to turn his back on the road and stand stolidly holding the bridle until they passed, as though he had been one of the grooms waiting for his master. But the enforced delay gave time for Briar to feel reassured, and stand in charmed quietness, while Joscelin hurriedly knotted his strip of vellum securely in the silvery forelock.

The riders had passed, for the moment the Foregate here was empty, and there was no one on the path between the trees. Joscelin tore himself away from his favourite perforce, shutting his ears to the protesting whinny that pursued him, and ran like a bolting hare back into cover, and did not stop until he had worked his way some distance back towards Saint Giles.

It was done, he dared not stop to see whether it took immediate effect, for now it was broad day, and growing populous on the roads, and he had better hide himself as quickly as possible in his leper's gown, so much stronger a defence than any weapon, since no one would willingly draw near enough to be contaminated. He could only pray that Simon would find the message – surely before he had been astride Briar long he must notice the knotted mane! – and act on it faithfully. There was at least a safeguard of sorts, Joscelin reflected, for if he made his way to the copses opposite the abbey fields at the time appointed, and failed to find Briar secreted there, he could draw off again, on the assumption that his plea had gone astray, or never been detected. Draw off, and try something else, but never give up, never until Iveta was in better hands, and properly treated.

Meantime, this day of all days, he must remain until evening tamed and exemplary about Saint Giles, taking no risks, drawing no attention to himself.

In the spinney at the edge of the hospital grounds he paused to look ahead before venturing close, suddenly aware of his perilous nakedness without the cloak, now that it was light. And out of the bushes arose a small, hurtling figure with a trailing dark garment bundled under one arm, and embraced him about the thighs with the other arm, reproaching him bitterly in a breathy undertone: 'You never woke me! You went away and left me! *Why* did you?'

Startled and touched, Joscelin sat on his heels and embraced the child heartily in return. 'I was not sleeping, and you were, so soundly it would have been shame to disturb you. And it's done, and I'm back, so hold me excused. I know you'd have done as well or better, never think I didn't trust you . . .'

Bran thrust the gown at him sternly. 'Put it on! And here is the face-cloth . . . How would you have got back into the hospice without it?' He had brought a hunk of bread, too, to make up for the missed breakfast. Joscelin broke it in two, and gave him back the greater half, shaken clean out of his own preoccupations by an irresistible tenderness that filled him with a wild urge to laughter.

'What should I do without you, my squire? You see I'm barely fit to be let out without my keeper. Now I promise you I'll let you bearlead me all this day – except for your lesson-time with Brother Mark, of course!

We'll do whatever you please. You shall call the tune.'

He shrouded himself obediently in the adopted vestments, and they consumed the bread together in silent content before he draped the linen cloth again about his face. Hand in hand they emerged solemnly from the trees, and made their way decorously back into the precincts of Saint Giles.

Simon had trotted an exuberant Briar almost to the abbey gatehouse before he noticed the knotted forelock, and reaching to discover the cause, with some displeasure at such poor grooming, felt the coiled strip of vellum hard under his fingers. He eased to a walk, which did not please his mount, while he disentangled the roll, and uncoiled it curiously.

Joscelin's none too practised fist, further complicated by poor light for the writing, and an unbiddable quill, cut to another man's hand, was nevertheless readable. Simon shut the coil hurriedly in his palm, as though someone might be paying too close attention, and looked back over his shoulder, and all about him, belatedly searching for some sign as to how this sudden message had been placed here for him, and where his elusive correspondent might be. Far too late! He might be anywhere. There was no way of laying hand on him or getting word to him, except by doing what he asked, and setting a scene to which he would certainly come.

Simon put the leaf away carefully in the pouch at his belt, and rode on very thoughtfully. Beyond the gatehouse, towards the bridge that crossed the Severn into the town, the sheriff's forces were beginning to mass. In the great court of the abbey the usual business of the day proceeded. The lay brothers were coming forth briskly to the main gardens at the Gaye, and going about the affairs of the grange court and the stock. Brother Edmund bustled between the herbarium and the wards of his infirmary, and Brother Oswald the almoner was distributing doles to the few beggars at the gate. Simon rode in soberly through the gates, and handed over Briar to a groom. At the guest-hall he asked audience with Godfrid Picard, and was promptly admitted.

Iveta was sitting with Madlen in her own chamber, listlessly sewing at a piece of decorative tapestry for a cushion. It was true that she could go forth now if she wished, but not beyond the gatehouse. She had tried it once, very fearfully, and been turned back by one of her uncle's men, civilly but with a faint, furtive grin that made her cheeks burn. And what was the use of going forth only within this closed ground, however pleasant it might have been in other circumstances, when Joscelin was only God knew where, and she had no means of reaching him? Better to sit here and hold her breath, and listen for a wind of freedom, with word of him. The brother who had warded off the lightnings once, and once conjured her back kindly into a bleak world, he was one friend, even if she had not spoken with him of late. And there was also Simon. He was loyal, he did not believe in the charges made against Joscelin. If the chance ever offered, he would help them.

Iveta stitched away and sat very still, all the more after she had caught the faint sound of voices raised in the next room. Even the inner walls here were solid, and held out sound, she did not think Madlen had noticed anything to arouse her interest. Accordingly Iveta carefully suppressed her own. But it was no mistake. Her uncle was quarrelling with someone. She detected it by the vicious vehemence of his voice rather than by any loudness, indeed it was purposefully quiet, and words quite indistinguishable. The other voice was younger, less cautious, more furiously defensive, surely astonished and aghast, as if this fell on him out of a clear sky.

Still no words, only the thread of significant sound, two voices clashing in bitter conflict. And now she thought she caught an intonation in the second voice which provided a name that could only dismay her. What could have happened between her uncle and Simon? For surely that was Simon's voice. Was her uncle growing suspicious of every young man who came near her? She knew only too well that he had a treasure to guard, herself, the great honour she bore like a millstone round her neck, the use that could be made of her, the profit that could accrue from her. Yet only a day or so ago Simon had been welcome, privileged, smiled upon by Aunt Agnes.

Madlen sat stolidly stitching at a linen coif for herself, and paid no heed. Her ear was older and duller; if she heard the hum of conversation, that was all.

And even that had ceased. A door closed. Iveta thought she caught a renewed murmur next door, urgent and low. Then the door of her own chamber opened, after a round, confident rap, and Simon entered as of right. Iveta was lost, she could only stare; but he had the right note.

'Goodmorrow, Iveta!' he said easily. And to the maid: 'Give me leave a little while, Mistress Madlen!'

Madlen had Agnes's smiles and becks well in mind, he was still privileged to her. She took up her sewing, made her reverence complacently, indulgent as on the last occasion, and left the room.

The door had barely closed on her when Simon was on his knee beside Iveta, and leaning close. And for all his disciplined calm, he was flushed and breathing hard, his nostrils flaring agitatedly.

'Listen, Iveta, for they'll not let me in to you again.... If she tells them I'm here with you now, they'll hunt me out... I've word for you from Joss!' She would have questioned, dismayed and anxious, but he laid silencing fingers on her lips, and rushed on, low and vehemently: 'Tonight, after Vespers, he bids you come to the herb-garden. And I'm to have his horse waiting on the other side of the brook. Don't fail him, as I shall not. Have you understood?'

She nodded, almost speechless with wonder and joy and alarm all mingled. 'Oh, *yes*! Oh, Simon, I would do anything! God bless you for his loyal friend! But you... What can have happened? Why, why turn against *you*?'

'Because I spoke up for Joss. I said he was neither murderer nor thief, and in the end I would see him vindicated, and they'd have to take back all they've said against him. They'll have no more of me, I'm cast off. But here's his message... look!' She knew the scrawl, and read, quivering. She fondled the slip of vellum as if it had been a holy relic, but closed Simon's hand over it again, though reluctantly.

'They might find it... you keep it. I'll do his bidding, and thank you a thousand times for all your goodness. But oh, Simon, I'm sorry that between us we've brought you to grief, too...'

'Grief, what grief?' he whispered fiercely. 'I care nothing for them, if I have *your* goodwill.'

'Always, always... more than goodwill! You have been so good to me, what should I have done without you? If we break free... if we can... we'll find you. You will always be our dearest friend!'

She was clinging to the hand with which he had hushed her, trying to express by touch the gratitude for which words seemed inadequate, but he made a warning grimace and withdrew his hand quickly, rising and standing back from her in one lissome movement, for there was a footstep at the door, a hand at the latch. 'The herb-garden!' he whispered, and noted the answering flash of her eyes, at once resolute and terrified.

'I'm glad to see you so much restored,' he was saying

formally as the door opened. 'I could not take my leave without paying my respects.'

Picard came into the room with deliberate pace, his narrow, subtle face cold, his voice colder still, though carefully civil.

'Still here, Messire Aguilon? Our niece is keeping her room, and should not be disturbed. And I had thought you were in haste to return to your household and make ready. You're pledged to join the sheriff's forces this day, I hope you mean to keep your word.'

'I shall do what is required of me,' said Simon shortly. 'But not on my friend's horse! But rest assured, my lord, I shall join the sheriff's line as I'm ordered, and in good time.'

Agnes had appeared at her lord's shoulder, tight-lipped, with narrowed eyes glittering suspicion. Simon made a deep reverence to Iveta, a stiff and formal one to Agnes, and marched out of the room. Two heads turned to watch him out of the hall in grim silence, and when he was gone, turned with the same chill unanimity to study Iveta. She bent her head meekly over her embroidery, to hide the defiant joy she could not quite banish from her face, and said never a word. The concentrated silence lasted long, but at length they went away, shutting the door upon her. They had asked nothing. She thought they were satisfied. When had she ever shown any spirit on her own account? They did not know, they had no means of understanding, what prodigies she felt she could do now, for Joscelin.

Brother Cadfael had set out, immediately after breaking his fast, on a mule borrowed from the abbey stables, and by the time Iveta received Joscelin's message he had passed Beistan, and was in the open woodland near the hunting-lodge. To reach the hamlet of Thornbury it was not necessary to keep to the path that led to the lodge, he struck off somewhat to the right, westward into the edges of the Long Forest. Between lodge and village the distance was hardly more than a mile, yet still it remained a mystery why a woman should abandon a good horse, and choose to remove herself there on foot..

The trees fell back as he approached the village, and left open to the sun a pleasant bowl of green meadows and striped ploughland, compact and well cared for. Scattered among the surrounding woods there were a few small, new assarts cut out of the forest by enterprising younger sons. And in the midst the low, timbered buildings clustered, fronds of blue smoke and the scent of wood fires hanging over them like a veil. Small, remote and poor, a place for hard-working men, but for all that, with plentiful fuel all around, and excellent poaching, which Cadfael judged might well be a communal enterprise here. Plentiful timber of all kinds, too, for the wheelwright's craft. Elm, essential for the stock, oak, to provide the cleft heartwood for the spokes, with the grain unbroken, and springy, supple ash to make the curved felloes of the rim, they were all here to hand.

Cadfael halted his mule at the first cottage, where a woman was feeding hens in her yard, and asked for the wheelwright.

'You're wanting Ulger?' she said, leaning a plump arm on her fence and viewing him with friendly curiosity. 'His toft's the far end there, past the pond, you'll see it by the timber stacks on your right hand. He has a wagon in for a new wheel, he'll be hard at it.'

Cadfael thanked her and rode on. Beyond the pond, where ducks gossiped and plunged, he saw the stacked wood seasoning, and came at once to the toft, a large undercroft well stocked with tools and materials, a room and a garret above, and in the yard before the house, a wagon standing, propped short of one wheel. The broken halves of it lay on the ground, several spokes shattered, the iron rim salvaged and perhaps to be used again. A new elm stock, already fully provided with spokes, lay star-like on the grass, and the wheelwright, a thickset fellow of about forty-five years, bearded and muscular, was working away with an adze on a length of well-curved ash for the felloes, shaping with the grain of the wood.

'God bless the work!' said Cadfael, halting his mule and lighting down. 'I think you must be Ulger, and it's Ulger I'm seeking. But I looked for an older man.'

The wheelwright rose and abandoned his adze, moving at ease in his own kingdom. He looked at his visitor with amiable curiosity, a round-faced, good-natured soul, but with a dignified reserve about him, too. 'My father in his time was also Ulger, and also wheelwright to this and many another hamlet round here. Belike you had him in mind. God rest him, he died some years back. The toft and the office are mine.' And he added, after a rapid and shrewd scrutiny: 'You'll be from the Benedictines at Shrewsbury. By this way and that way, we do get word.'

'And we have our troubles, and you hear of them,' said Cadfael. He slipped the mule's bridle over a fence-pale, and shook out his habit and stretched his back after the ride. 'I tell you truth as I would be told truth. Huon de Domville was murdered early on his wedding-day, and at his hunting-lodge none so far from here he kept a woman. He was on his way from her when he died. And she is no longer at the hunting-lodge. They called her Avice of Thornbury, daughter to that Ulger who must be also your father. In these parts he found and took up with her. I do not think I tell you anything you did not already know.'

He waited, and there was silence. The wheelwright faced him with countenance suddenly hard and still, for all its native candour, and said no word.

'It is no part of my purpose or my need,' said Cadfael,

'to bring upon your sister any danger or threat. Nevertheless, she may know what justice needs to know, and not only for retribution, but for the deliverance of the innocent. All I want is speech with her. She left behind her at Domville's lodge her horse, and I believe much more that was hers. She left afoot. It is my belief that she came here, to her own people.'

'It is many years,' said Ulger, after a long silence, 'since I had a sister, many years since I and mine were her own people to Avice of Thornbury.'

'That I understand,' said Cadfael. 'Nevertheless, blood is blood. Did she come to you?'

Ulger regarded him sombrely, and made up his mind. 'She came.'

'Two days ago? After the news came from Shrewsbury of Huon de Domville found dead?'

'Two days ago, late in the afternoon she came. No, the news had not reached us then. But it had reached her.'

'If she is here with you,' said Cadfael, 'I must have speech with her.' He looked towards the house, where a sturdy, comely woman moved out and in again as he gazed. In a corner of the yard a boy of about fourteen was fining down cleft oak spokes for some lighter wheel. Ulger's wife and son. He saw no sign of another woman about the toft.

'She is not here,' said Ulger. 'Nor would she be welcome in my house. Only once or twice have we seen her since she chose to go for a Norman baron's whore, a shame to her kin and her race. I told her when she came that I would do for her all that a man should do for his sister, except let her into the house she abandoned long ago for money and ease and rich living. She was not changed nor put down. Make what you can of her, for I'm in many minds about her. She said calmly and civilly that she wanted nothing from me and mine but three things – the loan of my nag, a plain peasant gown in place of her fine clothes, and some hours of my son's time to guide her where she was bound, and bring back the horse safely. She had three miles to go, and her fine shoes were not fit for the way.'

'And these three you granted her?' said Cadfael, marvelling.

'I did. She put off her finery here in the undercroft, and put on an old gown of my wife's. Also she stripped off the rings from her hands and a gold chain from her neck, and gave them to my wife, for she said she had no more need of them, and they might pay a part of her debt here. And she mounted my nag, and the boy there went with her on foot, and before night he rode the horse back to us here. And that is all I know of her, for I asked nothing.'

'Not even where she was bound?'

'Not even that. But my son told me, when he returned.'

'And where is she gone?'

'To a place they call Godric's Ford, west from here and a short way into the forest.'

'I know it,' said Cadfael, enlightened. For at Godric's Ford there was a small grange of Benedictine nuns, a cell of the abbey of Polesworth. So Avice had made for the nearest female sanctuary in her need, for safe hiding under the protection of a powerful and respected abbey until Huon de Domville's murderer was known and taken, his death avenged, his mistress forgotten. From that secure haven she might be quite willing to speak out anything she did know to the purpose, provided she herself remained inviolable in her retreat.

So he was thinking, as he thanked Ulger for his help, and mounted to ride on to Godric's Ford. A very natural course for a discreet woman to take, if she feared she might be drawn into a great scandal and the complex web of a crime.

And yet...! And yet she had left her jennet behind

and gone afoot. And yet she had put off her finery for a homespun gown, and stripped the rings from her fingers, to pay a part of her life's debt to the kin she had deserted long ago . . . .

The grange at Godric's Ford was a decent long, low house in a broad clearing, with a small wooden chapel beside it, and a high stone wall enclosing its well-kept kitchen garden and orchard of fruit trees, now graced with only half their yellowing leaves. In a butt of newly dug ground within the wall a middle-aged novice, comfortably rounded in form and face, was planting out cabbage seedlings for the next spring. Cadfael observed her as he turned in at the gate and dismounted, and with his eye for competence and industry approved the confidence of her manner and the economy of her movements. Benedictine nuns, like Benedictine monks, think well of manual labour, and are expected to expend their energies as generously in cultivation as in prayer. This woman, rosily healthy, went about her work like a good, contented housewife, pressing the soil firm round her transplants with a broad foot, and brushing the loam from her hands with placid satisfaction. She was agreeably plump, and not very tall, and her face, however rounded and well-fleshed, yet had solid, determined bones and a notable firmness of lip and chin.

When she became aware of Cadfael and his mule, she straightened her back with the right cautious gradualness and a true gardener's grunt, and turned upon him shrewd brown eyes under brows quizzically oblique, very knowing eyes that took him in from cowl to sandals in one sweeping glance.

She left her plot, and came unhurriedly towards him.

'God greet you, brother!' she said cheerfully. 'Can any here be of service to you?'

'God bless your house!' said Cadfael ceremoniously. 'I am seeking speech with a lady who has recently sought sanctuary here within. Or so I reason from such knowledge as I have. She is called Avice of Thornbury. Can you bring me to her?'

'Very readily,' said the novice. In her russet apple cheek a sudden, startling dimple dipped and rose like a curtsey. Beauty, in its most mature and tranquil manifestation, flashed and faded with the change, leaving her demure and plain as before. 'If you're seeking Avice of Thornbury, you have found her. That name belongs to me.'

In the dark little parlour of the grange they sat facing each other across the small table, Benedictine monk and Benedictine nun-in-the-making, eyeing each other with mutual close interest. The superior had given them leave, and closed the door upon them, though the postulant's manner was of such assured authority that it seemed surprising she should ask anyone's permission to speak with her visitor, and even more surprising that she did so with such becoming humility. But Cadfael had already come to the conclusion that in dealing with this woman there would be no end to the surprises.

Where now was the expected image of the Norman baron's whore, spoiled, indulged, kept in state for her beauty? Such a creature should have laboured to keep her charms, with paints and creams and secret spells, starved to avoid growing fat, studied the arts of movement and grace. This woman had subsided placidly into middle age, had let the wrinkles form in her face and neck without disguise, and the grey invade her brown hair. Brisk and lively she still was, and would always be, sure of herself, feeling no need to be or seem other than she was. And just as she was she had held Huon de Domville for more than twenty years.

'Yes,' she said immediately, in answer to Cadfael's

question, 'I was at Huon's hunting-lodge. He would always have me close, wherever he went. I have travelled the length and breadth of his honour many times over.' Her voice was low and pleasant, as serene as her person, and she spoke of her past as the most respectable of housewives might, after her man was dead, recalling quiet, domestic affection, customary and unexciting.

'And when you heard of his death,' said Cadfael, 'you thought best to withdraw from the scene? Did they tell you it was murder?'

'By the afternoon of that day it was common knowledge,' she said. 'I had no part in it, I had no means of guessing who had done such a thing. I was not afraid, if that's what you may be thinking, Brother Cadfael. I never yet did anything out of fear.'

She said it quite simply and practically, and he believed her. He would have gone further, and sworn that in her whole life she had never experienced fear. She spoke the very word with a kind of mild curiosity, as if she put her hand into a fleece to judge its weight and fineness.

'No, not fear – reluctance, rather, to play a part in any notorious or public thing. I have been discreet more than twenty years, to become a byword now is something I could not stomach. And when a thing is ended, why delay? I could not bring him back. That was ended. And I am forty-four years old, with some experience of the world. As I think,' she said, eyeing him steadily, and the dimple coming and vanishing in her cheek, 'you also can claim, brother. For I think I do not surprise you as much as I had expected.'

'As at this time,' said Cadfael, 'I cannot conceive of any man whom you would not surprise. But yes, I have been abroad in the world before I took this cowl of mine. Would it be foolish in me to suppose that it was your gift of astonishment that took Huon de Domville's fancy in the first place?'

'If you'll believe me,' said Avice, sitting back with a sigh, and folding plump, homely hands upon a rounding stomach, 'I hardly remember now. I do know that I had wit enough and gall enough to take the best that offered a wench of my birth, and pay for it without grudging. I still have both the wit and the gall, I take the best of what is offered a woman of my years and history.'

She had said far more than was in the words, and knew very well that he had understood all of it. She had recognised instantly the end of one career. Too old now to make a success of another such liaison, too wise to want one, perhaps too loyal even to consider one, after so many years, she had cast about her for something to do now with her powers and energies. Too late, with her past, to contemplate an ordinary marriage. What is left for such a woman?

'You are right,' said Avice, relaxed and easy. 'I made good use of my time while I waited for Huon, as often I have waited, weeks together. I am lettered and numerate, I have many skills. I need to use what I know, and make use of what I can do. My beauty is no longer with me, and never was remarkable, no one is likely to want or pay for it now. I suited Huon, he was accustomed to me. I was his feather-bed when other women had plagued and tired him.'

'You loved him?' asked Cadfael, for her manner with him was such that it was no intrusion to put such a question. And she considered it seriously.

'No, it could not be said that I loved him, that was not what he required. After all these years, certainly there was a fondness, a habit that sat well with us both, and did not abrade. Sometimes we did not even couple,' confided the postulant nun thoughtfully. 'We just sat and drank wine together, played chess, which he taught me, listened to minstrels. Nodded over my embroidery and his wine, one either side the fire. Sometimes we did not even kiss or touch, though we slept snugly in the same bed.'

Like an old, married lord and his plain, pleasant old wife. But that was over, and she was one who acknowledged the realities. She had sincerely regretted her dead companion, even while she was thinking hard, and rubbing her hands in anticipation of getting to work upon a new and different enterprise. So much intelligent life must go somewhere, find some channel it can use. The ways of youth had closed, but there were other ways.

'Yet he came to you,' said Cadfael, 'on his wedding eve.' And the bride, he thought but did not say, is eighteen years old, beautiful, submissive, and has great possessions.

She leaned forward to the table, her face mild and inward-looking, as though she examined honestly the workings of the human spirit, so obdurate and yet so given to conformity.

'Yes, he came. It was the first time since we came to Shrewsbury, and it turned out the last time of all. His wedding eve . . . Yes, marriage is a matter of business, is it not? Like concubinage! Love – ah, well, that's another matter, apart from either of them. Yes, I was expecting him. My position would not have been any way changed, you understand.'

Brother Cadfael understood. The mistress of twenty years standing would not have been dislodged by the equally purchased heiress twenty-six years her junior. They were two separate worlds, and the inhabitant of the alternative world had her own legitimacy.

'He came alone?'

'Yes, alone.'

'And left you at what hour?' Now he was at the heart of the matter. For this honourable whore had certainly never conspired at her lord's end, nor even cuckolded him with his steward, that jealous, faithful, suspicious soul who clove to her out of long-standing loyalty, surely well-deserved. This woman would have both feet firmly on the ground in dealing with those accidentally her servants, and respect them as they would learn to respect her.

She thought carefully about that. 'It was past six in the morning. I cannot be sure how far past, but there was the promise of light. I went out with him to the gate. I remember, there were already colours, it must have been nearing the half-hour. For I went to the patch of gromwell – it went on flowering so late this year – and plucked some flowers and put them in his cap.'

'Past six, and nearer the half than the quarter of the hour,' mused Cadfael. 'Then he could not have reached the spot where he was ambushed and killed before a quarter to the hour of Prime, and probably later.'

'There you must hold me excused, brother, for I do not know the place. For his leaving, as near as I dare state, he rode away about twenty minutes after six.'

A quarter of an hour, even at a speed too brisk for the light, to bring him to the place where the trap was laid. How long to account for the final killing? At the very least, ten minutes. No, the murderer could not have quit the spot before at least a quarter to seven, and most probably considerably later.

There was only one vital question left to ask. Many others, which had been puzzling him before he encountered her, and began to find his way past one misconception after another to the truth, had already become unnecessary. As, for instance, why she had discarded all her possessions, even her rings, left her jennet behind in the stable, denuded herself of all the profits of one career. Haste and fear, he had thought first, a bolt into hiding, putting off without coherent thought everything that could connect her with Huon de Domville.

Then, when he found her already in a novice's habit, he had even considered that she might have been stricken into penitence, and felt it needful to give up all before venturing into the cloister to spend the latter half of her life atoning for the former. Now he could appreciate the irony of that. Avice of Thornbury repented nothing. As she had never been afraid, so he felt certain she had never in her life been ashamed. She had made a bargain and kept it, as long as her lord lived. Now she was her own property again, to dispose of as she saw fit.

She had put off all her finery as an old soldier retiring might put off arms, as no longer of use or interest to him, and turn his considerable remaining energies to farming. Which was just what she proposed to do now. Her farm would be the Benedictine conventual economy, and she would take to it thoroughly and make a success of it. He even felt a rueful sympathy for the handful of sisters into whose dovecote this harmless-looking falcon had flown. Give her three or four years, and she would be the superior here. Give her ten, and she would be abbess of Polesworth, and moreover, would further reinforce that house's stability and good repute, as well as its sound finances. After her death she might well end up as a saint.

Meanwhile, though by this time he was assured of her forthrightness and reliability, she had a right to know that by doing her duty as a citizen she might find her privacy somewhat eroded.

'You must understand,' said Cadfael scrupulously, 'that the sheriff may require you to testify when a man stands trial for his life, and that innocent lives may hang on the acceptance of your word. Will you bear witness to all this in a court of law, as you have here to me?'

'In all my life,' said Avice of Thornbury, 'I have avoided one sin, at least. No, rather I was never tempted to it. I do not lie, and I do not feign. I will tell truth for you whenever you require it.'

'Then there is one matter more, which you may be able to solve. Huon de Domville, as you may not have heard, dismissed all attendance when he rode to you, and no one in his household admits to knowing where he might have gone. Yet whoever waylaid and killed him on that path had either followed him far enough to judge that he must return the same way – or else, and far more likely, knew very well where he was bound. Whoever knew that, knew that you were there at the hunting-lodge. You have said that you always used great discretion, yet someone must have known.'

'Plainly I was not left to travel unescorted,' she pointed out practically. 'I daresay some among his old servants had a shrewd idea I should never be far away, but as for knowing where . . . Who better than the one who brought me there at Huon's orders? Two days before Huon and his party came to Shrewsbury. I was always entrusted to one confidant, and only one. Why let in more? For the last three years it has been this same man.'

'Give him a name,' said Brother Cadfael.

# 9

The sheriff had confined his morning drive to the nearer woods on the southern side of the Meole brook, his line spread like beaters for a hunt, each man just within sight of his neighbours on either hand, and all moving slowly and methodically forward together. And they had netted nothing for all that time and trouble. Nobody broke cover to run from them, nobody they sighted bore any resemblance to Joscelin Lucy. When they drew off to reform and break their fast they had made contact all along their line with the patrols watching the town's borders. The lepers at Saint Giles had come out curiously to watch their activities at the prescribed distance. Gilbert Prestcote was not pleased, and grew markedly short to question or address. Some others were better satisfied.

'The lad's surely away home out of this long ago,' said Guy hopefully to Simon, as they dismounted at the bishop's house to eat a hasty dinner. 'I wish for my life, though, we could be certain of it. I could enjoy the hunt for him if I could be quite sure there's no fear of finding! It would be no hardship to see Picard's face grow blacker and blacker, and a delight if his horse put a foot in a badger's sett and threw him. The sheriff has his work to do, and no avoidance, but Picard has no such duty. Office is one thing, but venom's another.'

'He truly believes Joss killed the old man,' said Simon, shrugging. 'No wonder he's hot after him. All his own plans gone for nothing, and he's a man who'll have his revenge at all costs. Will you believe he's turned against me? I opened my mouth out of turn, and told him flatly I believed Joss never did theft or murder, and he flared at me like wildfire. I'm not welcome to him or his lady any more.'

'Do you tell me?' Guy gaped and sparkled. 'And do you know you're drawn next to him in the line after dinner, when we head further out? Keep a weather eye on Picard, lad, and never turn your back on him, or he might be tempted, if he's at odds with you. I wouldn't trust that temper of his too far, and there's thicker cover where we're bound.'

He was not very serious, merely exuberant in his relief that his comrade and friend was still at liberty. His attention at the time was on his trencher, for the October air was keen, and provided a healthy young man with a voracious appetite.

'The looks he gave me when he turned me out of Iveta's room,' admitted Simon ruefully, 'you could be right! I'll keep an eye on him, and be faster in the draw than he. We're to make our own way back as we please, when the light goes. I'll ensure I'm far enough ahead of him to keep clear of his blade. In any case,' he said, with a swift private smile, 'I have something important to see to before Vespers. I'll make certain he's not there to put a bolt through *that*.' He sat back from the table, satisfied. 'Where are you drawn, this time?'

'Among the sheriff's sergeants, for my sins!' Guy grimaced and grinned. 'Is it possible someone has suspected my heart may not be in it? Well, if I turn a blind eye, and they miss taking me up on it, I'm safe enough, they'll see to that. The sheriff's a decent man, but vexed and frustrated, with a murdered magnate on his hands, and King Stephen beginning to look this way. No wonder he's blowing bitter cold.' He pushed back the bench on which he sat, and stretched, drawing breath deep. 'Are you ready? Shall we go? I'll be main glad when we get home this night, and nothing trapped.'

They went out together, down into the valley below Saint Giles, where the beater line was drawing up afresh, to press onward at the same deliberate speed through thicker copses and woodlands, moving south.

From a hillock on the southern side of the highroad, overlooking the broad valley below, two tall, shrouded figures watched the hunters muster and deploy. Over the meadows the strung line showed clearly, before it moved methodically forward and began to thread the open woodlands ahead, each man keeping his dressing by his neighbour on the right, each man keeping his due distance. The air was very faintly misty, but with sunlight falling through the mist, and as the hunters moved in among the trees their clothing and harness winked and flashed through the leaves like motes of bright dust, scintillating and vanishing, reappearing to vanish again. As they swept slowly south, the watchers above as slowly turned to maintain their watch.

'They will keep up this drive until dark,' said Lazarus, and at length swung about to view the deserted fields from which the hunt had been launched. All was quiet and still there now, the stir, the murmur, the play of colours all past. Two threads of silver made the only sparkles of light in the muted sunbeams, the nearer one the mill leat drawn off to feed the abbey pools and mill, the further one the Meole brook itself, here in a stony and broken bed, and looking curiously small by comparison with its broad flow by the abbey gardens, barely a mile downstream. Geese dabbled in a shallow inlet on the southern side. Upstream from them the child minding them fished in a little rock-fringed pool.

'It's well-timed,' said Joscelin, and drew deep and thoughtful breath. 'The sheriff has emptied the valley of all his armed men for me, yes, surely until twilight. Even then they'll come home out of temper and out of energy. It could not be better.'

'And their mounts ridden out,' said Lazarus drily, and turned his far-sighted, brilliant eyes on his companion.

The absence of a face had ceased to trouble Joscelin at all. The eyes and the voice were enough to identify a friend.

'Yes,' Joscelin said, 'I had thought of that, too.'

'And few remounts to be had, seeing he has called out almost every man he has, and commandeered almost every horse.'

'Yes.'

Bran came darting down the slope of grass towards them, dived confidently between the two, and took possession of a hand of each. It did not trouble him at all that one of the hands lacked two fingers and the half of a third. Bran was putting on a little flesh with every day, the nodes in his neck had shrunk to insignificance, and his fine fair hair was growing in thickly over the scars of old sores on a knowing small head.

'They're away,' he said simply. 'What shall we do now?'

'We?' said Joscelin. 'I thought it was high time for your schooling with Brother Mark? Are you given a day's holiday today?'

'Brother Mark says he has work to do.' By his voice, Bran was not greatly impressed by the argument, since in his experience Brother Mark never ceased working except when he was asleep. The child was even inclined to be a little offended at being put off, if he had not had these two other elect companions to fall back on. 'You said you'd do whatever I wanted today,' he reminded sternly.

'And so I will,' agreed Joscelin, 'until evening. Then I also have work to do. Let's make the most of the time. What's your will?'

'You *said*,' observed Bran, 'you could carve me a little horse out of a piece of wood from the winter pile, if you had a knife.'

'Unbeliever, so I can, and perhaps a little gift for your mother, too, if we can find the right sort of wood. But as for the knife, I doubt if they'd lend us one from the kitchen, and how could I dare take the one Brother Mark uses to trim his quills? More than my life's worth,' said Joscelin lightly enough, and stiffened to recall how little his life might indeed be worth if the hunt turned back too soon. No matter, these few hours belonged to Bran.

'I have a knife,' said the child proudly, 'a sharp one my mother used to use to gut fish, when I was little. Come and let's look for a piece of wood.' The gleaners in the forest had come back well laden, the fuel-store was full, and could spare a small, smooth-grained log to make a toy. Bran tugged at both the hands he held, but the old man slid his maimed member free, very gently, and released himself. His eyes still swept the crowns of the trees below, where even the quiver and rustle of the beaters' progress had ebbed into stillness.

'I have seen Sir Godfrid Picard only once,' he said thoughtfully. 'Which man in the line was he, when they set out?'

Joscelin looked back, surprised. 'The fourth from us. Lean and dark, in black and russet – a bright red cap with a plume . . .'

'Ah, he . . .' Lazarus maintained his steady survey of the woods below, and did not turn his head. 'Yes, I marked the red poll. An easy mark to pick out again.'

He moved forward a few yards more from the highroad, and sat down in the grass of the slope, with his back against a tree. He did not look round when Joscelin yielded to the urging of Bran's hand, and they left him to his preferred solitude.

Brother Mark had indeed work to do that day, though it could as well have waited for another time, if it consisted of the accounts he was casting up for Fulke Reynald. He was meticulous, and the books were never in arrears. The real urgency lay in finding something to do that could enable him to look busily occupied in the open porch of the hall, where the light was best, and where he could keep a sharp eye on the movements of his secret guest without being too obvious about it. He was well aware that the young man who was no leper had been missing from Prime and from breakfast, and had reappeared innocently hand in hand with Bran, somewhat later. Clearly the child had taken a strong fancy to his new acquaintance. The sight of them thus linked, the boy skipping merrily beside the long strides that so carefully but imperfectly mimicked the maimed gait of Lazarus, the man with bent head attentive, and large hand gentle, had moved Mark to believe, illogically but understandably, that one thus kind and generous of his time and interest could not possibly be either thief or murderer. From the first he had found it hard to credit the theft, and the longer he considered this refugee within his cure – for he could pick him out now without difficulty – the more absurd grew the notion that this young man had avenged himself by murder. If he had, he would have plodded away in his present guise, clapping his clapper industriously, and passed through the sheriff's cordon long ago to freedom. No, he had some other urgent business to keep him here, business that might mean greater peril to his own life before he brought it to a good conclusion.

Yet he was on Mark's conscience. No one else had detected him, no one else could answer for him, or answer, if it came to the worst, for sheltering him and keeping silent. So Mark watched, had been watching all this day since the truant's return. And so far the young man had made it easy for him. The whole morning he had kept company with Bran, and been close about the hospital, lending a hand with the work of stacking the gleaned wood, helping to bring in the last mowing from the verges of the road, playing drawing games with the child in a patch of dried-out clay in a hollow where water lay when it rained – good, smooth clay that could be levelled over again and again as a game ended in laughter and crowing. No, a young fellow in trouble who could so blithely accommodate himself to a pauper child's needs and wants could not be any way evil, and Mark's duty of surveillance was rapidly becoming a duty of protection, and all the more urgent for that.

He had seen Joscelin and Lazarus cross the highroad and seek their vantage-point over the valley, to watch the afternoon hunt set forth, and he had seen Joscelin return with Bran dancing and chattering and demanding at his side. Now the two of them were sitting under the churchyard wall, blamelessly absorbed in the whittling of a lump of wood brought from the fuel-store. He had only to take a few steps out from the doorway to see them, Bran's fair head, with its primrose down of new hair, stooped close over the large, deft hands that pared and shaped with such industrious devotion. Now and again he heard gleeful laughter. Something was taking shape there that gave delight. Brother Mark gave thanks to God for whatever caused such pleasure to the poor and outcast, and felt his heart engaged in the cause of whoever brought such blessings about.

He was also human enough to feel curiosity as to what marvels were being produced there under the wall, and after an hour or so he gave in to mortal frailty and went to see. Bran welcomed him with a shout of pleasure, and waved the whittled horse at him, crude, spirited, without details, but an unmistakable horse, one and a half hands high. The carver's hooded and veiled head was bent over a work of supererogation, gouging out from another fistful of wood the features of a recognisable child. Eyes unwarily bright and blue flashed a glance upwards now and then to study Bran, and sank again to the work in hand. In two whole hands, unblemished, smooth, sunburned, young. He had forgotten to be cautious.

Brother Mark returned to his post confirmed in an allegiance for which he had no logical justification. The little head, already live before it had any shaping but in the face, had enlisted him beyond release.

The afternoon passed so, the light faded to a point where artistry was no longer possible. Mark could not see his figures, which in any case were completed, and he was sure that Joscelin Lucy – he had a name, why not acknowledge it? – could not see to continue his carving, and must have abandoned or finished his little portrait of Bran. Just after the lamps were lighted within, the boy burst in, flourishing it for his tutor's approval with small, excited shrieks of joy.

'Look! Look, Brother Mark! This is me! My friend made it.'

And it was he, no question, rough, baulked here and there by the obstinate grain of the wood and an inadequate knife, but lively, pert and pleased. But his friend who had made it had not followed him in.

'Run,' said Brother Mark, 'run and show it to your mother, quickly. Give it to her, and she'll be so cheered – she's down today. She'll like it and praise it. You go and see!' And Bran nodded, and beamed, and went. Even his gait was becoming firmer and more gainly now he had a little more flesh on him and was eating regularly.

Brother Mark rose and left his desk, as soon as the boy was gone. Outside the light was dimming but still day. Almost an hour yet to Vespers. There was no one sitting under the churchyard wall. Down the grassy slope to the verge of the highroad, without haste, as one taking the late air, Joscelin Lucy's tall, straight figure moved, paused at the roadside to see all empty, crossed, and slipped down to where the old man Lazarus still sat alone and aloof.

Brother Mark forsook his desk, and followed at a discreet distance.

Down there beneath Lazarus's tree there was a long pause. In the shadows two men stirred, there were words exchanged, but few; plainly those two understood each other very well. Out of the dimness where a hooded figure had stooped and vanished, another figure emerged, outlined against the pallidly luminous sky, tall, lissome, young, unshrouded and uncowled, in blessedly dark and plain clothing that melted away into shade as he moved. He leaned to the tree again. Mark thought that he stooped to a hand, since there was no cheek offered him. The kiss proper by rights between blood-kin was certainly given.

The leper gown remained among the shades. Evidently he would not take the repute of Saint Giles with him into whatever peril he was going out to encounter. Joscelin Lucy, owner here of nothing in the world but what he was and what he wore, stepped out and dropped away down the slope with long, light strides, into the valley. Half an hour now to Vespers, and still dangerously light in the open.

Brother Mark, determined now on his duty, made a wary circle round the old man's sheltering tree, and followed. Down the steep slope, a light, springy leap over the mill leat for Joscelin, a more awkward and ungainly jump for Mark, and on to the brook. Gleams of light flashed out of the stony bed. Mark got his sandalled feet wet, his vision uncertain in this light, but made the further shore without more damage, and set off along the brookside meadows with the tall young figure still in view.

Halfway along the floor of the valley towards the abbey gardens, Joscelin drew off from the brook into the fringes of woodland and copse that closed in on the meadows. Faithfully Brother Mark followed, slipping from tree to tree, his eyes growing accustomed now to the fading light, so that it did not seem to fade at all, but remained constant and limpid, free as yet of the nightly mist. Looking to his right, Mark could see clearly the outlines of his monastery against the last rosy light of the sunset, roofs and towers and walls, looming above the brook, the serene rise of the pease-fields, and the walls and hedges of the enclosed gardens beyond.

The twilight came; even on the open sward colours put on their final lucent glow before the dusk washed them all into soft shades of grey. Among the trees all was shadow, but Mark, cautiously slipping from bush to bush, could still discern the one shadow that moved. His ear caught also the sounds of movement ahead, deep among the trees, an uneasy stirring and sidling, and then suddenly a soft, anxious whinnying, hastily hushed, he thought, by a caressing hand. A voice whispered, hardly as loudly as the rustle of leaves, and the same hand patted gently at a solid, sleek shoulder. There was joy and hope in the sounds, as clearly as if the words had carried to him.

From his hiding-place among the trees, some yards away, Brother Mark saw dimly the looming pallor that was the head and neck of a horse, silver-grey, an inconvenient colour for such a nocturnal enterprise. Someone had kept faith with the fugitive, and brought his mount to the tryst. What was to happen next?

What happened next was the small sound of the bell for Vespers carried clearly but distantly across the brook.

At about this same hour Brother Cadfael was also brought up short by the apparition of a light grey horse, and halted his mule to avoid startling it away, while he considered the implications.

He had not hurried away from Godric's Ford, feeling it incumbent upon him to give the superior at least a credible account of his errand here, and he had found the ruling sister hospitable and garrulous. They had few visitors, and Cadfael came with the recommendation of his cloth. She was in no hurry to part with him until she had heard all about the frustrated wedding party at the abbey, and the excitement that had followed. Nor was Cadfael disposed to refuse a glass of wine when it was offered. So he took his leave somewhat later than he had expected.

Avice of Thornbury was still at work in the garden when he mounted and rode, tramping the soil firm round her seedlings as vigorously and contentedly as before, and the plot almost filled. With the same purposeful energy she would climb the steps of the hierarchy, as honest and fair-minded as she was ambitious, but ruthless towards weaker sisters who would fall before her for want of her wits, vigour and experience. She gave Cadfael a cheerful wave of her hand, and the dimple in her cheek dipped and vanished again. He mused on the irrepressible imprint of former beauty as he rode away, and wondered if she would not have to find some way of suppressing a quirk that might be so disconcerting to bishops, or whether, on the contrary, it might not yet prove a useful weapon in her armoury. The truth was, he could not choose but respect her. More to the point, such evidence as she gave, with her unmistakable forthrightness, no one would dare try to refute.

He made his way back steadily but without haste, letting the mule choose his own pace. And at about the hour of Vespers he was jogging in deepening twilight along the green ride, not far from the spot where Huon de Domville had died. He recognised the oak as he passed, and it was some minutes later, with the lighter spaces of the meadows already in view between the trees, that he became aware of rustling movements on his right, keeping pace with him at a little distance. Caution prompted him to halt the mule and sit silent, straining his ears, and the sounds continued, with no attempt at stealth. That was reassuring, and he resumed his way quietly, still listening. Here and there, where the bushes thinned, he caught the silvery pallor of the beast that moved with him. A horse, slender and built for speed, pale as a spirit flickering between the branches. In Holy Writ, he thought, it was Death who rode the pale horse. Death, however, appeared to have dismounted somewhere. No one was riding this grey, his elaborate saddle was empty, his rein loose on his neck.

Cadfael dismounted in his turn, and led his mule gently aside towards the apparition, coaxing softly, but the grey, though he had drawn close to them for company, took fright at being approached, and started away into the thicker woods beyond. Patiently Cadfael followed, but as often as he drew near the grey horse cantered away to a distance again, leading him still deeper into the woods. Here the hunters had surely threaded their paths during the afternoon, and through these copses they must have returned only very recently, as the light failed, each man making his own way back. One of them had either been thrown, failed to recapture his startled horse, and ended the journey ignominiously on foot, or else . . .

Suddenly the grey horse appeared ahead, entire and graceful, in the comparative light of a small, grassy clearing, and the faint radiance of starlight, stooped his head for a moment to crop at the turf, and as Cadfael closed in, tossed heels and mane once more, and made off into the trees on the other side. And this time Cadfael did not follow.

In the small arena of grass a man lay on his back, curled black beard pointing at the sky, long black hair flung up from his head, arms spread abroad, crooked and clawing, one at grass, the other at air. A brocaded cap lay in the grass above his head, visible only by reason of its white plume. And aside by some yards from his empty right hand, something long and thin managed to catch out of the dimness enough light to cast a metallic gleam. Brother Cadfael groped cautiously and found a hilt, and a lean blade the length of a man's hand and wrist. He smoothed a finger along it, and finding it unblooded, left it where it lay. Let it speak clearer by a better light. Now in the dusk there was little he could do, beyond feeling after the beat of the blood and the hammer of the heart, and finding neither. On his knees beside the dead man, peering close and avoiding his own shadow, he concentrated upon the face, and even in the dimness knew it congested and gaping, the eyes starting, the tongue protruding and bitten.

Like Huon de Domville, Godfrid Picard had been met in the way, riding home, and had not survived the meeting.

Brother Cadfael left everything here as he had found it, abandoned the half-Arab grey to his own wilful devices, and rode for the abbey at the best pace the surprised mule could be induced to raise.

## 10

Iveta had had all day to compose her mind and learn cunning. Necessity is a great teacher, and it was necessary that by the evening of this day she should be so despised that no one should think it worthwhile to watch her every move, provided she could not pass the gate. In any case, where could she go? Her lover was hunted for his life, her only known friend was banished, even the monk who had been kind to her had not been seen within the precinct since early morning. Where could she go, to whom could she appeal? She was utterly alone.

She had played the part all day, the more thoroughly and convincingly as her rebellious heart rose to the thought of the evening. In the afternoon she complained of a headache, and thought the air would do her good, if she might walk in the garden, and since Madlen was required to work on a gown of Agnes's in which the silver embroidery was fraying, and needed expert repair, she was allowed to go unescorted. Agnes curled a disdainful lip as she gave permission. So tame a creature, what harm could possibly be expected from her?

Iveta went with slow step and languid manner, and even sat for a while on the first stone bench in the flower-garden, in case anyone should be sent spying on her; but as soon as she was sure no one was observing her she skipped nimbly enough through the pleached hedge into the plot beyond, and over the little foot-bridge to the herb-garden. The door of the workshop stood wide open, and someone was moving about within. Iveta began to believe in success. Of course

Brother Cadfael must have an assistant. Medicines might be urgently needed in his absence. Someone must know where to find things, and how to use them, even if he lacked Brother Cadfael's experience and skills.

Brother Oswin was in the act of gathering up the shards of two of the clay saucers they used for sorting seeds, and started guiltily at the sound of footsteps in the doorway. These trifles were the first things he had broken for three days, and as the stock was plentiful, and the dishes themselves easily and quickly replaced, he had hoped to do away with the fragments undetected, and say nothing about the relapse. He turned defensively, and was stricken dumb by the unexpected vision in the doorway. His rosy, guileless face gaped, round-eyed and open-mouthed. It was a question which of them blushed more deeply, Oswin or the girl.

'Pardon if I intrude,' said Iveta hesitantly. 'I wanted to ask . . . Two days ago Brother Cadfael gave me a draught to bring me sleep, when I was not well. He said it was made from poppies. Do you know it?'

Oswin gulped, nodded his head vigorously, and managed speech. 'This is the potion, here in this flask. Brother Cadfael is not here today, but he would wish . . . If I can serve you? He would wish you to have whatever you need.'

'Then may I have such a dose again? For I think tonight I shall need it.' It was no lie, but it was a deliberate deception, and Iveta blushed for it, when this yellow-headed youth, rounded and innocent as a new chick, was offering his services so trustingly. 'May I take double the dose with me? Enough for two nights? I remember how much he bade me take.'

Brother Oswin would have given her all the resources of the workshop, he was so dazzled. His hand shook somewhat as he filled a small vial for her, and stoppered it, and when she put out her hand, just as shyly, to take it from him, he remembered his duty and lowered his eyes before her, rather late in the day for his peace of mind.

It was all over very quickly. She whispered her thanks, looking over her shoulder nervously as though she thought someone might be watching, and hid the vial in her sleeve a good deal more adroitly than Oswin had handled it. His hands and feet seemed to have reverted to their hobbledehoy clumsiness of some years back, in his pimply boyhood, but for all that, the look she gave him in departing made him feel tall, confident and gainly. He was left pensive in the doorway, looking after her as she flitted across the foot-bridge, and wondering if he had not been hasty in deciding that he had a vocation. It was not too late to change his mind, he had not taken his final vows yet.

This time he did not lower his eyes until she vanished along the pleached alley. Even then he stood for some minutes, still pondering. There were drawbacks in any course of life, he supposed sadly. Neither inside nor outside the cloister could a man have everything.

Iveta fled back to her stone bench, sheltered from the breeze, and was sitting there with folded hands and apathetic face when Madlen came out to reclaim her. Iveta rose submissively and went back with her to the guest-hall, and sewed unenthusiastically at the piece of embroidery that had been her cover for weeks, even though her needle was not so industrious that she need unpick at night what she worked during the day, like a certain Dame Penelope, of whom she had once heard tell from a passing jongleur in her father's house, long ago.

She waited until it was almost time for Vespers, and the light fading outside. Agnes had put on the newly mended gown, and Madlen was tiring her hair for the evening. While Sir Godfrid Picard hunted with savage determination for a fugitive murderer, it was his wife's part to maintain the appearance of ritual devotion, attend all the needful services, and retain the good opinion of abbot, prior and brothers.

'It's time you were making ready, girl,' she said, snapping a glance at her niece along a brocaded shoulder.

Iveta let her hands lie in her lap, indifferent, though she kept her wrist pressed firmly upon the vial in her sleeve. 'I think I won't come tonight. My head is so heavy, and I haven't slept well. If you'll be my excuse, madam, I'll eat supper now, with Madlen, and go early to bed.' Naturally if she stayed away, Madlen would inevitably be left to keep guard on her, but she had made her own provision for that.

Agnes shrugged, her fine, steely profile disdainful. 'You are very vapourish these days. Still, stay if you prefer. Madlen will make you a posset.'

It was done. The lady went forth without a qualm. The maid set a small table in Iveta's bedchamber, and brought bread and meat and a brew of honeyed milk and wine, thick and sweet and hot, ideal to drown the heavy sweetness of Brother Cadfael's poppy syrup. She went and came two or three times before she sat down with her charge, ample time to draw a beaker of the innocent brew, and replace it with the whole contents of Oswin's vial. Ample time to stir it and be sure. Iveta made a pretence of eating, and declined more of the drink, and was gratified to see Madlen finish the jug with obvious pleasure. Nor had she eaten much, to temper the effect.

Madlen removed the dishes to the kitchen of the guest-hall, and did not return. Iveta waited almost ten minutes in feverish anxiety, and then went to investigate, and found the maid propped comfortably on a bench in a corner of the kitchen, snoring.

Iveta did not wait for cloak or shoes, but ran in her soft leather slippers, just as she was, out into the dusk, across the great court like a hunted leveret, half-blindly, and along the dark green alley in the garden. The silver streak of the leat gleamed at her, she felt her way along the hand-rail of the bridge. The sky was starry over her, still half-veiled as in the day, but pallidly luminous beyond the veil. The air was chill, fresh, heady, like wine. In the church they were still chanting, leisurely and intently, thank God! Thank God and thank Simon! The only loyal friend . . .

Under the deep eaves of the herbarium workshop Joscelin was waiting, flattened against the wall in the black shade. He reached both arms to her and caught her to him, and she wound her own slight arms about him passionately. They hung silent a long moment, hardly breathing, clinging desperately. Utter silence and stillness, as though the leat, and the brook, and the river itself had stopped moving, the breeze ceased to breathe with them, the very plants to grow.

Then the urgency swept back to swallow everything, even the first stammering utterances of love.

'Oh, Joscelin . . . It *is* you . . . .'

'My dear, my dear . . . Hush, softly! Come, come quickly! This way . . . take my hand!'

She clung obediently and followed blindly. Not by the way she had come. Here they were over the leat, only the brook remained to be crossed. Out from the closed garden into the fringe of the pease-fields, new-ploughed at this season, that ran down to the Meole. Under the hedge he paused a moment to view the empty dusk and listen with stretched ears for any betraying sound, but all was still. Close to his ear she whispered: 'How did you cross? How will you manage with me . . . .?'

'Hush! I have Briar down the field – did Simon not tell you?'

'But the sheriff has every way closed,' she breathed, shivering.

'In the forest . . . in the dark? We'll get through!' He

drew her close in his arm, and began to descend the field, keeping close to the dark shelter of the hedge.

The silence was abruptly torn by a loud, indignant neighing, that halted Joscelin in mid-stride. Below at the water's edge the bushes threshed wildly, hooves stamped, a man's voice bellowed. Confused shouting broke out, and from the covering bulk of the hedge Briar lunged into the open, dragging one man with him. Other moving shadows followed, four at least, dancing to avoid being trampled as they sought to subdue and calm the rearing horse.

Armed men, the sheriff's men, ranged the bank between them and freedom. Escape that way was lost, Briar was lost. Without a word Joscelin turned, sweeping Iveta with him in his arm, and began to retrace his steps in furious haste, keeping close to the bushes.

'The church,' he whispered, when she sought to question in terror, 'the parish door . . .' Even if they were still at Vespers, everyone would be in the choir, and the nave of the great church unlighted. They might yet be able to slip through unseen from the cloister, and out by the west door which alone lay outside the precinct wall, and was never closed but in time of great danger and disorder. But even then he knew it was a very meagre hope. But if it came to the worst, there could be sanctuary within.

Rapid movement betrayed them. Down by the water, where Briar stood now snorting and quivering, a voice bellowed: 'There he goes, back into the garden! We have him in a noose! Come on!' And someone laughed, and three or four men began to surge up the slope, without undue haste. They were quite sure of their prize now.

Joscelin and Iveta fled hand in hand, back through the herb-garden, over the leat, along the alley between the black, clipped hedges, and out into the perilous open spaces of the great court. No help for it now, there was no other way left to them. The gathering darkness might hide identities, but could not hide the haste of their running. They never reached the cloister. An armed man stood blocking the way. They swung towards the gatehouse, where torches were already burning in their sconces on the wall, and two more men-at-arms drew together before the gate. From the garden emerged their pursuers, content and at leisure. The foremost of them swaggered into the flickering light of the torches, and showed the grinning, complacent face of that same astute or well-informed fellow who had suggested to his officer the searching of the bishop's grounds, and been commended for it. He was in luck again. The sheriff and all but a meagre handful of his men out scouring the woods, and the remnant left behind were the ones to run the quarry to ground!

Joscelin drew Iveta into the corner of the guest-hall wall, where the stone steps ascended to the doorway, and put her behind him. Though he was unarmed, they took their time and were cautious of moving in upon him until their circle was drawn tight. Over his shoulder, without taking his eyes from the deployment of his enemies, he said with grim calm: 'Go in, love, and leave me. No one will dare stop you or touch you.'

Instinctively she gasped into his ear: 'No! I'll not leave you!' and as quickly understood that she hampered him at this desperate pass, and turned with a sob to scramble up the steps to the doorway, as he ordered. No further! Not a step! Only far enough to free his arms and stand out of his way, but close enough still to experience in her own flesh whatever befell him, and demand her share in whatever followed, penalty or deliverance. But even the moment's hesitation had undone him, for he had turned his head in furious entreaty to order: 'Go, for God's sake . . . ' And the distraction had given his enemies their best opportunity, and they were on him from three sides like hounds unleashed.

None the less, it was no easy victory over an unarmed

man. Until then all had passed in astonishing silence, suddenly there was chaotic noise, the sergeant hall-ooing on his men, porters, novices, lay brothers, guests, all coming on the run to find out what was happening, voices demanding, others answering, a clamour to rouse the dead. The first man to lunge at Joscelin had misjudged either his own timing, or his quarry's speed of recovery, and ran full tilt into a large fist that sent him reeling, and unbalanced two of his fellows. But from the other side two more got a hold on Joscelin's clothing, and though he jabbed an elbow hard into the midriff of the one who had him by the full of his cotte, and doubled him up retching, the other was able to hold on to his fistful of the dangling capuchon, and twist and tighten it with intent to strangle his opponent into submission. Joscelin wrenched forward, and though he failed to free himself, the cloth tore, and restored him room to breathe, and he kicked backwards at the officer's shins, and raised an aggrieved roar. The man released his hold to hop and rub at his bruises, and Joscelin took his brief chance and lunged after, not at the man but at the hilt of his dagger. It rose into his hand sweetly, smooth as oil, and he made a wide sweep about him, the blade flashing in the torchlight.

'Now come on! Buy me dear, you'll not get me cheaply!'

'His own choice!' yelled the sergeant. 'Draw on him now, it's on his own head!'

Then there were swords out, half a dozen minor lightnings gleaming and vanishing in the dusk. The hubbub sank into a strange, breathless silence. And into the silence, from the cloister, swept the whole brotherhood, startled at the end of Vespers to find so offensive a disturbance in their own peaceful enclave. An outraged voice, loud and authoritative, thundered across the court:

'Stand! Let no man move or strike!'

Everyone froze into stillness, and only dared turn to face the speaker with slow and submissive care. Abbot Radulfus, that austere, dry, stern but composed man, stood at the edge of the battlefield, where the red torchlight caught him, and blazed like an excommunicating angel, fiery-eyed in a face sharp and cold as ice. Prior Robert at his shoulder looked faded and negligible by comparison, with all his noble Norman hauteur and dignity. Behind them the brothers stared and fluttered, and waited for the lightnings to strike.

Iveta's legs gave way under her, and she sat down on the top step and rested her head on her knees in the weakness of relief. The abbot was here, there would not be killing, not yet, not yet, only law, and the killing that law countenances. One step at a time now, and don't look beyond. She prayed passionately without words for a miracle.

When she managed to still the trembling that ran through her whole body, and lifted her head to look again, the entire great court seemed to be full of people, and more were pouring in even as she looked about her. Gilbert Prestcote had just reined in and dismounted within the gates. The members of the hunt, making their ways back at their own speed, were coming in by ones and twos, startled and wondering at what they found here at home, after raising no quarry through all the surrounding countryside. In the flickering light it took the sheriff some moments to recognise in the dishevelled and embattled young man drawn back against the wall of the guest-hall the suspected murderer and thief he had wasted two full days pursuing through the woods.

He came striding forward in haste. 'My lord abbot, what's this? Our wanted man here at bay within your walls? What is happening here?'

'That is what I am bent on discovering,' said Radulfus

grimly. 'Within my walls indeed, and within my jurisdiction. By your leave, Sir Gilbert, it is my right here to enquire into such an unseemly brawl as this.' He cast a glittering look about him at the ring of armed men. 'Put up, every man of you. I will not have drawn steel here on my ground, nor violence done to any.' The same fiery glance lit upon Joscelin, braced and wary in his corner, dagger in hand. 'And you, young man – it seems to me I had occasion to use similar words to you once before, and to warn you that this house also has a punishment cell, and you may find yourself within it if you so much as touch hilt again. What have you to say for yourself?'

Joscelin had regained his breath enough to speak up for himself with spirit. He spread his arms to show there was no scabbard of sword or dagger upon him. 'I brought no weapon within your walls, Father. See how many circle me! I have borrowed what offered, to keep my life, not to take any other man's. My life and my liberty! And for all that these may say against me, I have never stolen or killed, and so I'll maintain within or without your jurisdiction, as long as I have breath.' He was running out of it by then, partly from his exertions, and partly from the choking force of his anger. 'Would you have me offer my neck tamely to be wrung, when I have done no wrong?'

'I would have you abate your tone to me and to these secular authorities,' said the abbot sternly, 'and submit to the law. Give back the dagger, you see it cannot avail you now.'

Joscelin stared back at him for a long moment with grim face and hostile eyes, and then, abruptly, held out the hilt of the dagger to its owner, who took it warily, and was only too glad to slide it into its sheath and back away out of the ring.

'Father,' said Joscelin, and it was a challenge, not an appeal, 'I am in your mercy here. Your justice I might trust more than I trust the law, and I am where your writ runs, and I have obeyed you. Examine me, of all that ever I did, before you give me up to the sheriff, and I swear to you I'll answer all truthfully.' He added quickly and firmly: 'All, that is, as concerning my own acts.' For there were those who had helped and been good to him, and he would do nothing to bring them into question.

The abbot looked at Gilbert Prestcote, who met the glance with a considering smile. There was no great urgency now, the fellow was trapped, and could not escape. There was nothing to be lost by conceding the abbot's prior authority here. 'I bow to your wishes in the matter, Father, but I maintain my claim to this man's person. He is charged with theft and murder, and it is my duty to hold him fast and produce him in time for trial on those charges. And so I shall – unless he can satisfy both you and me, here and now, of his innocence. But let all be done openly and fairly. Question him, if you so please. It would be helpful also to me. I would prefer to turn the key on a manifestly guilty man, and have your own doubts, if you entertain any, set at rest.'

Iveta was on her feet by then, running anxious eyes over every face that showed fitfully in the flickering light. Horsemen were still riding in one by one at the gatehouse, and staring in open-mouthed wonder at the scene within. She caught sight of Simon at the back of the crowd, newly arrived and startled and bewildered like the rest, and Guy behind him, just as dumbfounded. Not everyone here was an enemy. When she met the sharp black eyes of Agnes, there at Prior Robert's shoulder as they had emerged from Vespers, she did not lower her own eyes. This time she had ventured so far out of her old self that there could be no returning. It was not she who showed uneasiness, not she who punctuated a glare of naked dislike with frequent and hurried glances towards the gatehouse, noting each new arrival, and unsatisfied with all. Agnes was waiting and hoping for her husband to come, and resume his authoritative role, which in his absence she felt slipping out of her own fingers. Agnes was afraid of what might yet transpire here while her lord was not there to master it.

Iveta began to descend the steps up which she had groped blindly at Joscelin's entreaty. Very slowly and stealthily she came, stair by stair, not to break the tension below.

'You must be aware,' said Radulfus, surveying Joscelin with face still as grave, but not now so angry, 'that you have been sought by the law ever since your escape into the river, after arrest. You have said you will answer truthfully for your actions. Where have you been hiding all this time?'

Joscelin had promised truth, and must deliver it. 'Under a leper's cloak and veil,' he said bluntly, 'in the hospital at Saint Giles.'

A stir and murmur went round the great court, almost a gasp. Guests and brothers alike stared in awe at a creature so desperate as to choose such an asylum. The abbot neither gasped nor stirred, but accepted the answer gravely, his eyes intent on Joscelin's face.

'Into that sanctuary, I think, you could hardly have penetrated without help. Who was it stretched out a hand to you?'

'I have said I was in hiding there,' said Joscelin steadily. 'I have not said I needed or received any help. I answer for my own actions, not for those of others.'

'Yes,' said the abbot thoughtfully, 'it seems there were others. For instance, I doubt if you thought to hide on your own lord's premises, as it seems for a while you did, without having a friend willing to give you cover. Also, as I remember, that grey horse I observed being led out of the garden just now – there he stands under guard, like you – is the one you rode when we encountered here once before. Did you recover possession of him without help? I doubt it.'

Iveta glanced over Joscelin's shoulder to where Simon stood, and saw him draw back a pace into deeper shadow. He need not have had any qualms. Joscelin closed his mouth very firmly, met the abbot's measuring stare without blinking, and suddenly, though still doubtfully, he smiled. 'Ask me of my own deeds.'

'It seems,' interrupted the sheriff sharply, 'that we have need here of someone in authority at Saint Giles. It's a serious matter to hide a wanted murderer.'

From the rear of the crowd in the direction of the gardens, a deprecating voice piped up none too happily: 'Father Abbot, if it please you, I am willing to speak for Saint Giles, for I serve there.'

Every head turned, all eyes opening wide in astonishment at the sorry little figure advancing meekly to stand before Radulfus. Brother Mark's face was smudged with mud, a trailing wisp of pond-weed adorned his straggling tonsure, his habit trickled water from its skirts at every step, and clung to his thin body in heavy, dripping folds. He was ridiculous enough, and yet the soiled, earnest face and devoted grey eyes had still a bedraggled dignity, and if there were some half-hysterical grins and sniggers among the throng at sight of him, Radulfus was not smiling.

'Brother Mark! What can this mean?'

'It took me a long time to find a fordable place,' said Mark apologetically. 'I am sorry I come so late. I had no horse to carry me over, and I cannot swim. I had to draw back twice, and once I fell, but at the third try I found the shallow place. By daylight it would not have taken so long.'

'We pardon your lateness,' said Radulfus gravely, and for all the composure of his voice and his face, it was no longer quite so certain that he was not smiling. 'It seems you had reason to feel you might be needed here, for you come very aptly, if you come to account for how a wanted man came to find refuge in the hospital. Did you know of this young man's presence there?'

'Yes, Father,' said Brother Mark simply, 'I did know.'

'And was it you who introduced and sheltered him there?'

'No, Father. But I did come to realise, at Prime of that day, that we had one man more among us.'

'And held your peace? And countenanced his presence?'

'Yes, Father, that I did. At first I did not know who he was, nor could I always single him out from others of our flock, for he wore the face-cloth. And when I suspected . . . Father, I do not own any man's life, to give it up to any but God's judgment. So I held my peace. If I was wrong, judge me.'

'And do you know,' asked the abbot impassively, 'who it was who introduced the young man into the hospice?'

'No, Father. I do not even know that anyone did. I may have some thoughts as to that, but I do not *know*. But if I did,' owned Mark with candid-eyed humility, 'I could not give you a name. It is not for me to accuse or betray any man but myself.'

'You are two here of like mind,' said the abbot drily. 'But you have yet to tell us, Brother Mark, how you come to be fording the Meole brook, on the heels, as I understand it – if, indeed, I have yet understood any part of it! – of this young fugitive, who was sensible enough to provide himself with a horse for the venture. Had you been following him?'

'Yes, Father. For I knew I might be answerable for harbouring one less innocent and good than I thought him – for which thought I promise I had good reason. So all this day I have watched him. He has hardly been a moment out of my sight. And when he discarded his cloak in the dusk, and set off this way, I did follow him. I saw him find his horse tethered in the copse across the brook, and I saw him cross. I was in the water when I heard the outcry after him. As for this day I can speak for all he has done, and there was no blame.'

'And the day when he came to you?' the sheriff demanded sharply. 'What of his first appearance among your lepers? At what hour?'

Brother Mark, single-hearted in his allegiance, kept his eyes fixed upon the abbot's face for guidance, and Radulfus nodded gravely that he, too, required an answer.

'It was two days ago, at Prime, as I've told you,' said Mark, 'that I first was aware of him. But at that time he was already provided with the leper cloak, and a face-cloth to hide his face, and behaved altogether conformably with the others. I judge, therefore, he must have been in hiding among us at least some quarter to half an hour, to be so well prepared.'

'And as I have heard,' said the abbot thoughtfully, turning to Prestcote, 'your men on patrol in the Foregate, my lord, started a hare that same morning, and lost him in the neighbourhood of Saint Giles. At what hour did they sight him?'

'They reported to me,' said the sheriff, pondering, 'sighting such a fleeing man the best part of an hour before Prime, and certainly they lost him near Saint Giles.'

Iveta descended one more step. She felt herself suspended in a dream, a double dream that filled her with terror when she looked one way, and wild hope when she looked the other way. For these were not the voices of enemies. And still, blessedly, her uncle did not come, to cast into the balance his black animosity, his narrow malice. She was but two steps behind Joscelin now, she could have stretched out her hand and touched his unkempt flaxen hair, but she was afraid of shattering his braced attention. She did not touch him. She kept an alert eye on the gatehouse, watchful for her chief enemy's return. That was why she was the first to mark Brother Cadfael's arrival. Only she and Agnes were looking that way.

The little mule, which had enjoyed an unhurried day, was resentful at being urged to speed at the end of it, and manifested his displeasure by halting inside the gatehouse and refusing to budge further. And Brother Cadfael, who had been demanding some effort of him until that moment, sat to gaze in mute astonishment as his eyes lit upon the scene in the great court. She saw his rapid glance rove over all those intent faces, she could almost feel him stretch his ears to pick up the words that were passing. He saw Joscelin standing braced and alert at the foot of the steps, saw sheriff and abbot eyeing each other sombrely, and the draggled little figure of the young brother who, for Iveta, spoke with the unwitting tongue of a minor angel, the kind of angel who would descend with disarming apologies, and of whom no sinner would ever be afraid.

Hastily but quietly, Cadfael dismounted, surrendered the mule to the porter, and advanced to the edge of the crowd, himself still unnoticed. Obscurely encouraged, Iveta descended one more step.

'So it would seem,' said Radulfus reasonably, 'that you were at the hospital, young man, by a quarter of an hour at least before Prime of that day, and perhaps as much as half an hour.'

'I had – acquired my cloak,' agreed Joscelin, a little astray now and treading warily, 'some little time before I went to the church.'

'And you were instructed how to behave?'

'I have attended Prime before, I know the office.'

'Perhaps, but it would take some few minutes of

instruction,' persisted Radulfus mildly, 'to pick up the whole order of the day in Saint Giles.'

'I can watch others and do as they do,' said Joscelin flatly, 'as readily as any other man.'

'Granted, Father,' said Gilbert Prestcote impatiently, 'that he was there well before the seventh hour of the morning. That I accept. But we have no way of knowing the hour of my lord Domville's death.'

Brother Cadfael had the whole drift of it by then. Finding his way blocked by spectators so intent that they remained deaf and blind to his civil requests and attempts to make his way through their ranks, he used his elbows sturdily, and butted a path through to the front. And before anyone else could speak up and brush the question of timing aside, he lifted his voice and called loudly as he came: 'True, my lord, but there is a way of knowing when he was last seen alive and well.'

He broke through then, the sudden shout opening a path before him, and emerged face to face with the abbot and the sheriff, both of whom had swung about to face and frown upon the interruption.

'Brother Cadfael! You have something to say in this matter?'

'I have...' began Cadfael, and broke off to gaze in vexed concern at the shivering little figure of Brother Mark. He shook his head in distracted compunction. 'But, Father, should not Brother Mark be changing that wet habit, and getting something hot into him, before he takes his death?'

Radulfus accepted the rebuke with penitent grace. 'You are quite right, I should have despatched him at once. Any further testimony he may have to give can very well wait until his teeth stop chattering. There, brother, get yourself dry garments, go to the kitchen, and have Brother Petrus make you a hot posset. Quick, run.'

'If I may ask but one question first,' said Cadfael hastily, 'before he goes. Did I hear, brother, that you have been following yonder lad as he came here? Have you had him under your eye all this while?'

'All the day from morning,' said Brother Mark, 'he has not been more than a few minutes out of my sight. He left the hospice only an hour or so ago, and I followed him here. Is it of importance?' He meant to Brother Cadfael and whatever cause he had in mind, and Cadfael's satisfied nod comforted and warmed him.

'There, run! You did well.'

Brother Mark made his reverence to the abbot, and dripped and shivered away to the kitchen thankfully enough. If he had done well for Brother Cadfael, he was content.

'And now,' said Radulfus, 'you may explain what you meant by saying you had means of knowing when my lord Domville was last seen alive and in good health.'

'I have found and talked with a witness,' said Cadfael, 'who will testify, whenever the sheriff requires, that Huon de Domville spent the night before his death in his own hunting-lodge, and did not leave it until about a third of the hour after six, next morning. Also that at that time he was in excellent health, and mounted to ride back to his quarters in the Foregate. The path on which we found him is the path he would have to take from that place. And the witness, I dare pledge, is reliable.'

'If what you say is confirmed,' said Prestcote, after a moment's silence, 'this is of the first importance. Who is this witness? Name the man!'

'No man,' said Cadfael simply, 'but a woman. Huon de Domville spent his last night with his mistress of many years, and her name is Avice of Thornbury.'

The shock passed along the ranks of the innocent brethren as a sudden wind-devil whirls through standing wheat in summer, in a great, gusty sigh and a convulsion of rustling garments like shaken stems. On his wedding-eve, to repair to another woman! And after supping with the abbot, at that! To those of lifelong celibacy even the contemplation of a bride, chaste and young, was disturbing. But a kept woman, and visited on the eve of the marriage sacrament, in despite of both the celibate and the marital morality . . .!

The sheriff belonged to a more illusionless world. Not the outrage, only the understandable fact, concerned him. Nor was Abbot Radulfus greatly disconcerted, once the words were spoken. He might have evaded the experiences of the flesh, he had not gone in ignorance of them thus far through a highly intelligent life. The mention of Avice did not shake him.

'You recall, Father,' Cadfael pursued, while he had every man's attention, 'that I showed you the blue flowers of the gromwell he wore in his cap when he was found. The plant grows at this hunting-lodge, I found it there, and it bears out the woman's story. She herself set it in his cap when he left her. It is nearly two miles from the lodge to the spot where he was ambushed and killed. Your own officers, Sir Gilbert, bear witness that they flushed young Lucy here out of cover in the Foregate more than half an hour before Prime. Therefore he could not possibly have been the man who set the springe for Huon de Domville, and killed him. The baron can have been no more than half a mile from his hunting-lodge, when Joscelin Lucy was being hunted along the Foregate to the hospital.'

Iveta took the last step that brought her to Joscelin's side, and slipped her hand into his, and he gripped it convulsively, unaware that he was hurting her, and drew breath into him so deep and hard that she felt he had drawn in the breath of new life for both of them.

Agnes craned and peered towards the gatehouse, but still did not find what she sought. Her face was sharp and icy with malice, but she said never a word. Iveta had expected a blaze of disbelief, casting doubt upon both Brother Cadfael and his witness, even upon the evidence of the sheriff's men. People can be vague and imprecise about time, it is not so hard to argue about the difference a mere half-hour can make. But Agnes kept silence, containing her aching rage and uneasiness.

Abbot Radulfus exchanged a long and thoughtful look with the sheriff, and turned again to Joscelin. 'You promised me truth. I will ask you now what I have not so far asked. Did you play any part in the death of Huon de Domville?'

'I did not,' said Joscelin firmly.

'There remains the charge he himself brought against you. Did you steal from him?'

'No!' He could not keep the scorn out of his voice.

Radulfus turned back to the sheriff with a faint, wry smile. 'For the murder charge, Brother Cadfael will bring you to speak with this woman, and you will judge for yourself what trust to place in her. As for your own officers, there is no need to question their truthfulness. It seems to me that on this count this man must be held guiltless.'

'If this is confirmed,' agreed Prestcote readily, 'he cannot be the murderer. I myself will take this woman's testimony.' He turned to Cadfael with a question: 'She is still at the hunting-lodge?'

'No,' said Cadfael, not without some relish at the stir his answer would make, 'she is now at the cell of the Benedictine sisters at Godric's Ford, where she has entered the order as a novice, and intends to take full vows.'

It was an achievement to have made even Abbot Radulfus blink; shaking the brotherhood was a routine success by comparison. 'And you esteem her an honest witness?' asked the abbot mildly, recovering his control in an instant, while Prior Robert's patrician nose still looked pinched and blue with shock, and the ranks behind his shoulder still quivered.

'As the day, Father. The sheriff will judge for himself. I am convinced that, whatever else she may be, she has no disguises, and does not lie.'

They would get from her, without conceal, the whole story of her life, of which she was not ashamed, and she could not but impress them. He had no fears on that head. Prestcote was a practical man, he would recognise her quality. 'My lord,' said Cadfael, 'and you, Father, may we now understand that you accept – subject to questioning Mistress Avice and finding her testimony true – that Joscelin Lucy is altogether innocent of Huon de Domville's murder?'

Prestcote had no hesitation. 'That seems certain. The charge cannot stand.'

'Then – bear with me! – you cannot but accept, also, that this day he has been under constant watch by Brother Mark, as Mark himself has told us, and has done nothing to occasion suspicion or blame.'

The abbot was regarding him with searching attention. 'That must also be granted. I think, brother, you have some particular reason for calling attention to it in this way. Something has happened!'

'Yes, Father. Something I should have told you at once, if I had not blundered into these equally grave matters as soon as I rode in. Well for any man who can say that today, all day long, he had a good man watching him and seeing no evil. For there has been violence done once again, in the woods beyond Saint Giles. Not an hour ago, as I was coming home, I happened upon a riderless horse, but could not catch him, and following him, I came upon a clearing where another man lies dead, and as I think, strangled like the first. I can lead you to the place.'

In the horrified hush that fell, he turned slowly to

confront Agnes, who stood wild-eyed but still as stone.

'Madam, I grieve to bring you such news, but it is certain, even in the dim light, by the horse he rode . . .

## 11

There was a moment of utter silence, while she stood blanched and stiff like a woman turned to ice. Then, as abruptly, she came to life with a piercing scream of rage and grief, and whirling in a storm of flying skirts, turned her back upon sheriff, abbot, niece and all, and clove like a fury through the startled brothers who gave way hastily before her onslaught. Not one glance at Joscelin Lucy now, she bore down on one man, and one man only, raging.

'You . . . you! Where are you, coward, murderer, come forth and face me! You, you, Simon Aguilon, *you* killed my lord!'

The ranks scattered before her blazing eyes and levelled arm.

'Stand, damned murderer, face me! Hear me!' The whole Foregate, surely, must be hearing her and crossing themselves in superstitious dread, envisaging a demon come after some prodigious sinner. As for Simon, he stood aghast, too taken aback, it seemed, even to retreat before her. He stared open-mouthed, speechless, as she halted challengingly before him, her black eyes huge and flaring redly in the torchlight. Beside him Guy turned a startled stare helplessly from one to the other, and drew back a furtive pace or two from this new and deadly battlefield.

'You killed him! None but you could have done this. You rode off beside him to this hunt, close to him in the line – I know, I heard how it was drawn up. You, FitzJohn, say, let them all hear! Where did this man ride?'

'He was next to Sir Godfrid,' admitted Guy dazedly. 'But . . .'

'Next to him, yes . . . and on the way home, in those thick woods, it was easy to take him by surprise. Late and quiet you come back, Simon Aguilon, and you have made sure he will never come back!'

Sheriff and abbot had drawn close to witness this encounter, startled and appalled like everyone else, and made as yet no attempt to interrupt it. She was past reason. Simon said so, when he could speak at all, swallowing hard, and still breathless.

'For God's sake, what have I done to be so accused? I am altogether innocent of this death, I knew nothing of it . . . I last saw Sir Godfrid Picard three hours ago, well alive, threading the woods like the rest of us. The poor lady is crazed with grief, she strikes at the nearest . . .'

'I strike at *you*,' she cried, 'and would if there were a thousand in between. For *you* are the man! You know it as I know it. Pretence will not save you now!'

Simon appealed wildly to sheriff and abbot, spreading gloved hands. 'Why, why should I so much as think of killing a man who was my friend? With whom I had no quarrel in the world? What possible motive could I have for such a deed? You see she has run mad.'

'Ah, but you did have a quarrel with him,' shrieked Agnes vengefully, 'as well you know. Why? Why? Do you dare ask me why? Because he suspected – he as good as knew – that you had killed your own lord and uncle!'

Wilder and wilder grew the accusations, and yet this time Simon drew in breath sharply, and for an instant was still and pale. He wrenched himself out of shocked silence with a great heave, to defend himself strongly. 'How can that be? Everyone knows that my uncle dismissed me, put off all company and rode out alone. I went to my bed, as I was bidden. I slept late . . . they came to wake me when they found he had not returned...'

She swept that aside with a contemptuous motion of her hand. 'You went to your bed, yes, I make no doubt... and you left it again to steal out in the night and set your trap. Easy enough to leave unseen and return unseen when your wicked work was done. There are more ways in and out of any house than by the hall door, and who was so privileged in going and coming as you? Who else had all the keys he needed? Who stood to gain by the old man's death but you? And not only in being his heir, oh, no! Deny to these here present, if you dare, that in the evening of the day Huon was brought back dead, you came to my lord, before your uncle was cold you came, to make a bargain with us that you would step into his shoes with my niece, inherit bride, and honour, and all. Deny it, and I'll prove it! My maid was there!'

Simon looked round the ring of watching faces wildly, and protested: 'Why should I not fairly offer for Iveta? My estate would match hers, it is no disparagement. I esteem, I honour her. And Sir Godfrid did not reject me. I was willing to wait, to be patient. He agreed to my suit...'

Iveta's hand gripped and clung convulsively in Joscelin's clasp. Her stunned mind went back over those two meetings when Simon had seemed to her the only friend she had in the world, when he had pledged her his help, and Joscelin his loyalty. The first meeting countenanced by a smiling and gracious Agnes, complacently welcoming fortune restored. The second ... yes, that had been different indeed, he had professed himself disapproved and banished, and the event had borne him out in his claim. What could have happened between, to change everything?

'So he did,' shrilled Agnes, glittering with hatred, 'thinking you the honest man you seemed then. But

Huon's throat was bruised and cut – the monk there said it, and my lord heard it, and so did you – bruised and cut by a ring the murderer wore on his right hand. And once you had heard that said, who saw you again without gloves? In season and out! But my husband was at the coffining of Huon de Domville yesterday, and then you were forced – were you not, wretch? – to doff your gloves for once to take the aspergillum. And it was to him you handed it thereafter! He saw – oh, not the ring, no, that you had taken off hastily as soon as the monk here spoke of it, but the pale band where it was wont to be, and the square whiteness under the stone. And he remembered then that you used to wear a ring, just such a ring. And he was fool enough to speak out what he had seen, and what he believed, when you came visiting. He cut off all ado with a man he had cause to think a murderer.'

Yes, so he had. So that was the reason for the change! But not, thought Iveta, grown by force too suddenly into a woman, not because a murderer would not have been acceptable to him, provided no breath of suspicion ever blew his way. No, rather because while suspicion was even possible, he dared not risk contamination. Give him absolute security on that point, and he would have made up his differences quickly enough. And Joscelin had still been the law's quarry, and Joscelin might still have been taken, taken and hanged . . . And she would have been left believing despairingly that she had but one kind friend in the world, and that was Simon Aguilon! He had sworn that the very reason he was banished was because he had declared his faith in Joscelin! And he might – given time enough to dull pain – he might even have prevailed! She pressed close to Joscelin's side, and trembled.

'I urged him, I begged him,' moaned Agnes, writhing, 'to sever all ties with such a man. You knew all too well he might feel it his duty to speak out what he suspected, even without proof. You have made certain he never shall. But you have not reckoned with me!'

'Woman, you are mad!' Simon flung up his hands against her, his voice high almost to breaking. 'How could I have set a snare for my uncle, when I did not know where he had gone, or what he intended, much less by what narrow path he must return? I did not know he had a mistress anywhere within this shire, to tempt him to a night's visit.'

Cadfael had stood silent throughout this duel. He spoke now. 'There is one who will say, Simon Aguilon, that you lie, that you did know, none so well. Avice of Thornbury says, and I fancy there will be two other witnesses to bear her out, once they know she is not at risk and asks no silence, that you, and none other, were the trusted escort who conducted her wherever her lord wanted her. You brought her to the hunting-lodge. The way between was well known to you, for you had ridden it. And Huon de Domville admitted but one man at a time to his private amours. For these last three years you have been that man.'

Agnes uttered a long wail of glee and grief together, that drifted eerily on the blown smoke of the torches. She pointed a triumphant hand. 'Strip him! You will see! The ring is on him now, he never would leave it off his person, for another to see and understand. Search him, and you'll find it. And why should he doff it, if it never left mark on a murdered man?'

The men-at-arms had read the sheriff's signs, and closed in silently, a tight ring of leather and steel about the two antagonists. Simon had been too intent on the threat before him to regard the quiet vigilance behind. He loosed a defiant cry of anger and impatience, and swung on his heel to stride away. 'I need not stay to hear such venom!' he spat, too shrilly.

Only then did he see the solid, silent line of armed men, drawn shoulder to shoulder between him and the gate, and baulked like a headed deer. He looked round wildly, unable to believe the collapse of his fortunes.

The sheriff drew a measured pace nearer, and spoke. 'Take off your gloves!'

It was an unlovely thing to see a human creature break and try to run, see him fight like a wildcat when he was hemmed in, and snarl defiance when he was overcome and pinioned. In deference to the abbot they hauled him out through the gates into the Foregate with as little violence as possible, and dealt with him there. He knotted his hands together to baulk the removal of his gloves, and when his hands were naked, the pale circle on the middle finger of his right hand glared like snow on new-ploughed russet soil, the large blot of the stone clear to be seen. He struggled and cursed when they felt about his body, sank his chin grimly into his chest so that they had to force his head back to withdraw the cord from round his neck, beneath his shirt, and expose the ring to view.

When they had hustled him away, four of them holding him and hard-pressed at that, to a cell in the castle, there fell a dreadful, exhausted silence over the great court. Joscelin, great-eyed, shaken and bewildered, folded his arms about Iveta, and quivered in uncomprehending relief, too shocked to question as yet the devious use that had been made of him throughout. Agnes stood rigid, staring balefully as long as her enemy remained in view, and then, released, clutched her head between her hands and wept, but hardly, in solitary and forbidding grief. Who would have thought she could have loved her unendearing husband?

The virago was gone. She let fall her hands and paced slowly, like one walking in her sleep, through the agitated onlookers who moved aside to give her passage. She looked round once upon them all, from the steps of the guest-hall, having passed by Iveta's extended hand as though the girl did not exist, and then she went in, and vanished.

'Later,' said Abbot Radulfus, heavily but calmly, 'she will speak freely. Her testimony is essential. As for her lord – he is dead already. Need we question, since he cannot be questioned?'

'Not in any tribunal of mine, at any rate,' agreed Gilbert Prestcote drily, and turned to his remaining men. 'You, sergeant, before we set off to bring this dead man home, how comes it that you set so apt a watch about the brook here, while we were beating the forest? We had no intimation that ever reached my ears, that a raid might be attempted on these premises.'

'It was after you were all gone forth, my lord,' said the sergeant, 'that Jehan here came to me with the notion that since the squire was set on the lady, he might take the chance when there were but few of us left here, to try to win her away.' He haled forth the clever fellow who had won commendation for an earlier idea, equally justified in the event. The man was not quite so sure of himself, now that things were turned topsy-turvy, and his patron was become the villain in the web, but he stood his ground. 'It was he who said that the fellow, if he had the wit, might hide in his lord's own gardens, you'll remember, and when we searched, we found he had indeed been there, though he was gone when we came to it. This time it seemed just as good sense, so we kept a vigil in secret.'

'Friend,' said Prestcote, eyeing the man-at-arms somewhat ominously, 'your guesses seem to be blessed by heaven, but I fancy hell had more to do with them. When did Aguilon put it into your head to search the bishop's outhouses for our wanted man? At what hour?'

Jehan had the sense to be open about it, though none too happily. 'My lord, it was after my lord Domville's body was brought back here. When he came back to the bishop's house, then he suggested it. He said I was welcome to the credit if we found our man, and he would as lief keep out of it.'

Joscelin shook his head despairingly between his hands, slow still to understand the whole of it. 'But it was he who helped me – he came to find me, he hid me there himself in goodwill . . .'

'In very evil will!' said Brother Cadfael. 'Son, you had given him not only the opportunity of hastening his inheritance of a great estate, but also of adding to it this lady's person and lands. For you had provided him a perfect scapegoat, one wronged and angry and bearing a grudge. Yours would be the first and only name that came to mind, when Huon de Domville was waylaid and murdered. But with that in view he had to have you still at liberty, hidden away somewhere safe, until well after the death, and where he could point the hunt to take you when that was done. It was your leaving your sanctuary that baulked his plans and saved your neck.'

'Then tonight,' pursued Joscelin, frowning over this chill treachery as if his head ached, 'you mean he set this trap for me, in cold blood? I thought him my one friend, I asked his help . . .'

'How?' asked Cadfael sharply. 'How did you get word to him?'

Joscelin told them the whole of it, though not one word yet of Lazarus or Bran, or any of those who had truly helped him. That he might tell some day, surely to Iveta, perhaps even to Brother Cadfael, but not here, not now.

'So he knew only that you were somewhere close, but not where. He could not send his trusty foil here to lay hands on you, he could only wait for you to come to the law, and you had set the scene yourself. All he had to do was pass on your message to the lady, and see that your horse was waiting for you as you had asked – or you would not have crossed into the garden here to be seized, would you? – and then say the quiet word to Jehan here. He would not wish to appear in the matter himself, certainly,' said Cadfael wryly, 'since his pose of loyalty to you was his best commendation with the lady. You once safely taken and hanged,' he said, making no bones about it, for the good-natured lad was wrenching hard at belief in such devious treason in one he had trusted, 'I doubt if Godfrid Picard would have baulked at matching his niece with a murderer – a *successful* murderer. It was the peril meantime he could not stomach, in case it reached as far as his own credit, if not his own neck.'

'Speak up, Jehan,' ordered the sheriff, grimly smiling. 'Did Aguilon again point you the way to commendation and promotion?'

'This morning,' admitted Jehan unwarily, 'he put the notion into my head . . .'

'This morning! Before ever we set forth! And you said no word to me or to your officer until we were out of the way of your intended feat of arms. Promotion is hardly likely to come your way, fellow, for a while. Think yourself lucky to escape a whipping!'

Jehan was indeed thinking himself well out of a perilous corner, to be dismissed so lightly, and made himself scarce without delay.

'We had best be bringing in this dead man,' said the sheriff, turning brusquely back to the task in hand. 'Will you guide us, brother? We'll go mounted, and with a spare horse for Picard's last ride.'

They were away, half a dozen mounted men, Cadfael in no way displeased to be astride a fine, sturdy rouncey again instead of a modest little mule. The abbot watched them out of the gates, and then turned to dismiss, with even voice and calm face, the disturbed and wondering brotherhood.

'Go, compose your minds, wash your hands, and go in to supper. The rule still orders our day. Traffic with the world is laid upon us for chastening, and for the testing of our vocation. The grace of God is not endangered by the follies or the wickedness of men.'

They went obediently. At a glance from Radulfus, Prior Robert inclined his head and followed the flock. The abbot was left confronting, with a faint, contemplative smile, the two young creatures still clinging hand in hand, eyeing him steadfastly but doubtfully. Too much had happened to them too suddenly, they were like children half-awake, not yet clear what, of their recollections and experiences, was real, and what was dream. But surely the dreams had been terrifying, and the reality must needs be better.

'I think,' said the abbot gently, 'you need not be in any anxiety, my son, about that other charge your lord made against you. In all the circumstances, no just man would consider it safe to believe in such a theft, and Gilbert Prestcote is a just man. I cannot choose but wonder,' he said thoughtfully, 'whether it was Aguilon also who hid the necklace in your saddle-bag with the medal of Saint James.'

'I doubt it, Father.' Joscelin took thought to be fair, even now, to a comrade who had done him such grievous wrong. 'For truly I feel he had not thought of murder until I was cast off and accused, and broke away to freedom as I did. It is as Brother Cadfael said, he was presented with his chance and his scapegoat. My lord Domville most likely did his own meaner work this time. But, Father, it is not my troubles that weigh on me now. It is Iveta.'

He moistened his lips, feeling for the best words, and the abbot stood silent and imperturbable, and gave him no help. Iveta, too, had looked up at him in startled alarm, as though she feared he might too nobly and stupidly let go of her when she thought herself fairly won.

'Father, this lady has been vilely misused by those who were her guardians. Now her uncle is dead, and her aunt, even if she were fit to care for her, would not be allowed to keep the administration of so great an honour. It is my prayer that you, Father, will take her into your own guardianship from this day, for with you I know she will be used with gentleness and honour, and be happy as she deserves. If you put forward such a request to the king, he will not deny you.'

The abbot waited some moments, and his austere lips were very drily smiling. 'And that is all? No plea for yourself?'

'None!' said Joscelin, with the fierce humility that looked and sounded what it was, a nobleman's arrogance.

'But *I* have a prayer of my own,' said Iveta indignantly, keeping fast hold of a hand that would have renounced its claim on her. 'It is that you will look kindly upon Joscelin, and use him as my favoured suitor, for I love him, and he loves me, and though I will be obedient to you in everything else, if you will take me, I will not part with Joscelin, or ever love or marry anyone else.'

Come,' said the abbot, not quite committing himself to a smile, 'I think we three had better sit down to supper together in my lodging, and consider how best to dispose of the future. There's no haste, and much to think about. Thinking is best after prayer, but will be none the worse for a meal and a glass of wine.'

The sheriff and his party brought back Godfrid Picard's body to the abbey before Compline. In the mortuary chapel they laid him straight, and brought candles to examine his injuries. His unblooded dagger, found some yards aside in the grass, where Cadfael had discovered and left it, they slid back into its sheath as they unbuckled his sword-belt, but it cannot be said that much thought had been given to the curious circumstance of its lying thus naked and discarded in the glade.

The man was dead, his murderer, murderer already of one man, and a kinsman at that, was in Shrewsbury castle, safe under lock and key. If there were odd circumstances in this second case, no one but Cadfael noticed them, though for a while they puzzled him as much as they would have puzzled his companions, had they troubled to examine them. A man dies, strangled with a man's hands, yet himself provided with a dagger, and clearly having had time to draw it. To draw, but not to blood it. And those who kill with their hands do so because they are otherwise unarmed.

The night was still. The candles did not flicker, and the light on the dead man's suffused face, bitten tongue and exposed throat was sharp enough to show detail. Cadfael looked closely and long at the marks of the strong fingers that had crushed out life, but he said nothing. Nor was he asked anything. All questions had already been answered to the sheriff's satisfaction.

'We'd best have a mare out tomorrow, to fetch the grey out of the forest,' said Prestcote, drawing up the linen sheet over Picard's face. 'A valuable beast, that. The widow could sell him for a good price in Shrewsbury, if she's so minded.'

Having completed his duty here, Cadfael excused himself, and went to look for Brother Mark. He found him in the warming-room, rosily restored after a kitchen supper and a change of clothes, and about to take his leave, and walk back to Saint Giles and his duty.

'Wait only a brief while for me,' said Cadfael, 'and I'll bear you company. I have an errand there.'

In the meantime, his errand here was to two young

people who had, as he saw when he ran them to earth in the abbot's parlour, of all places, no great need of his solicitude, since they had enlisted a greater patron, and appeared to be on terms of complete confidence with him, partly due, perhaps, to a good wine after extreme stress and rapturous relief. So Cadfael merely paid his respects, accepted their flushed and generous gratitude, exchanged a somewhat ambiguous glance with Radulfus as he made his reverence, and left them to their deliberations, which were certainly proceeding very satisfactorily, but had certain implications for others, not here represented.

Two warm-hearted children, these, radiant with goodwill towards all who had stood by them at need. Very young, very vulnerable, very eager and impulsive now that they were happy. The abbot would keep them on a close rein for a while, her in some sheltered sisterhood or a well-matroned manor of her own, the boy under discreet watch in whatever service he took up, now that he was clean, honourable and his own best guarantor. But Radulfus would not keep them apart, he was too wise to try to separate what God or his angels had joined.

Meantime, there were others to be thought of, and there was need of the coming night, if what Cadfael had divined proved true.

He returned to the warming-room, where Brother Mark, content and expectant, was waiting for him by the fire. He had not sat so long in the warmth since he was a new novice in the order. It had been well worth getting soused in the Meole brook.

'Is everything well?' he asked hopefully, as they set out together along the Foregate in the darkness.

'Very well,' said Cadfael, so heartily that Mark drew pleased and grateful breath, and ceased to question.

'The little lady for whom you prayed God's help, some days ago,' said Cadfael cheerfully, 'will do very well now. The lord abbot will see to that. All I want at the hospital is a pleasant word with your wanderer Lazarus, in case he moves on very soon, before I can come again. You know how they snuff the air and grow uneasy, and up anchor suddenly, and sail.'

'I had wondered,' confided Brother Mark, 'whether he might be persuaded to stay. He has an affection for Bran. And the mother will not live much longer. She has turned her back on the world. Oh, not on her boy – but she feels he has gone beyond her, and has his own saints,' explained one of those saints diffidently, without self-recognition. 'She is certain he is protected by heaven.'

There were those on earth, too, thought Cadfael, who had some interest in the matter. Two grateful, loosened tongues in the abbot's parlour had poured out all their story without reserve, named names confidingly. Joscelin had a mind quick to learn, and a heart tenacious of affections, and Iveta in the fervour of deliverance wanted to take to her heart and hold fast in her life every soul, high or low, whole or afflicted, who had been good to Joscelin.

In the open porch before the hall of the hospice the old man Lazarus sat, mute, motionless, patient, with his erect back braced against the wall, and his legs drawn up beneath him on the bench, crossed after the eastern fashion. Curled up in the circle of the old man's left arm, Bran lay uneasily asleep, with Joscelin's wooden horse clasped to his heart. The small lamp above the door of the hall shed a faint yellow light on his spindly limbs and ruffled fair head, and showed a face smudged with tears. He awoke when Cadfael and Mark entered, starting up dazedly out of his nest, and the long arm withdrew from him silently, and let him scramble down from the bench.

'Why, Bran!' said Brother Mark, concerned and

chiding. 'What are you doing out of your bed at this hour?'

Bran embraced him hard, half-relieved and half-resentful, and accused in muffled tones from within the folds of the new and over-ample habit: 'You *both* went away! You left me alone. I didn't know where you were . . . You might not have come back! *He* hasn't come back!'

'Ah, but he will, you'll see.' Brother Mark gathered the boy to him, and took possession of a groping hand. Its fellow was busy retrieving the wooden horse, momentarily discarded but jealously reclaimed. 'Come, come to bed, and I'll tell you all about it. Your friend is well and happy, and need not hide any more. Everything that was wrong has been put right. Come, and you shall hear it once from me, and he will tell it all over again when next you see him. As you will, I promise.'

'He said I should be his squire, and learn to read Latin hand, and reckon numbers, if ever he came to be knight,' Bran sternly reminded both his present and his absent patron, and allowed himself to be led sleepily towards the inner door. Mark looked back at Cadfael as they went, and at his reassuring nod took the child gently away towards the dortoir.

Lazarus made no movement and said no word when Cadfael sat down beside him. Long ago he had outlived surprise, fear and desire, at least on his own account. He sat gazing out with his far-sighted blue-grey eyes at a night sky now beginning to flow like running water, a lofty, thin stream of cloud carried tranquilly eastwards on a fair breeze, while here on earth the very leaves were still.

'You'll have heard,' said Cadfael, leaning back comfortably against the wall, 'what Mark told the child. It was true, thanks be to God! Everything that was wrong has been put right. The murderer of Huon de

Domville is taken, guilty past doubt. That is over. Pity is out of reach, short of penitence, and of that there's none. The man has not only killed his uncle, but vilely betrayed and misused his friend who trusted him, and shamelessly deceived a harried and forsaken girl. That is over. You need trouble no more.'

The man beside him said no word, asked no question, but he listened. Cadfael continued equably: 'All will be well with her now. The king will surely approve our abbot as her new guardian. Radulfus is an austere and high-minded man, but also a human and humane one. She has nothing more to fear, not even for a lover none too well endowed with worldly goods. Her wishes, her happiness, will no longer be brushed aside as of no account.'

Within the great cloak Lazarus stirred, and turned his head. The deep voice, forming words with deliberate, halting care, spoke from behind the muffling veil: 'You speak only of Domville. What of the second murder?'

'What second murder?' said Cadfael simply.

'I saw the torches among the trees, an hour and more ago, when they came for Godfrid Picard. I know he is dead. Is that, too, laid at this other man's door?'

'Aguilon will be tried for the murder of his uncle,' said Cadfael, 'where there is proof enough. Why look further? If there are some who mistakenly set Picard's death to his discredit, how is his fate changed? He will not be charged with that. It could not be maintained. Godfrid Picard was not murdered.'

'How do you know?' asked Lazarus, untroubled but willing to be enlightened.

'There was no snare laid for him, he had all his senses and powers when he was killed, but all his senses and powers were not enough. He was not murdered, he was stopped in the way and challenged to single combat. He had a dagger, his opponent had only his hands. No doubt he thought he had an easy conquest, an armed man against one weaponless, a man in his prime against one seventy years old. He had time to draw, but that was all. The dagger was wrenched away and hurled aside, not turned against him. The hands were enough. He had not considered the weight of a just quarrel.'

'It must, then, have been a very grave quarrel between these two,' said Lazarus, after a long silence.

'The oldest and gravest. The shameful mistreatment of a lady. She is avenged and delivered. Heaven made no mistake.'

The silence fell between them again, but lightly and softly as a girl's veil might float down and settle, or a moth flutter out of the night and alight without a sound. The old man's eyes returned to the steady, measured flow of wisps of cloud eastward in the zenith. There was diffused light of stars behind the veil, while the earth lay in darkness. Behind the coarse veil of faded blue cloth Cadfael thought there was the faintest and most tranquil of smiles.

'And if you have divined so much from this day's deed,' said Lazarus at length, 'have not others the same knowledge?'

'No other has seen what I have seen,' said Cadfael simply, 'and none will now. The marks will fade. No one wonders. No one questions. And only I know. And only I, and the owner of the hands that did the deed, will ever know that of those hands, the left had but two and a half fingers.'

There was a stir of movement within the mound of dark clothes, and a flash of the ice-clear eyes. Out of the folds of the cloak two hands emerged, and were held to the light of the lamp, the right one whole, long and sinewy, the left lacking index and middle finger and the upper joint of the third, the maimed surfaces showing seamed, whitish and dry.

'Having divined so much from so little, brother,' said the slow, calm voice, 'take me with you one step beyond, and divine me his name, for I think you know it.'

'So I think, also,' said Brother Cadfael. 'His name is Guimar de Massard.'

The night hung motionless over the Foregate and the valley of the Meole, and the woods through which the sheriff and his men had hunted in vain, plotting clearly, for those long-sighted eyes, the passage of Picard's bright red cap through the trees, and mapping the way by which, later, he must return. Overhead, in contrast to this terrestrial stillness, the sky flowed steadily away, like one man's floating, fragile life blown across the constant of life itself, to vanish into the unknown.

'Should I know that name?' asked Lazarus, very still.

'My lord, I, too, was at the storming of Jersusalem. Twenty years old I was when the city fell. I saw you breach the gate. I was at the fight at Ascalon, when the Fatimids of Egypt came up against us – and for my part, after the killing that was done in Jerusalem, of so many who held by the Prophet, I say they deserved better luck against us than they had. But there was never brutality or unknightly act charged against Guimar de Massard. Why, why did you vanish after that fight? Why let us, who revered you, and your wife and son here in England, grieve you for dead? Had any of us deserved that of you?'

'Had my wife, had my son, deserved of me that I should lay upon them the load that had fallen upon me?' asked Lazarus, roused and stumbling for once upon the words that tried his mangled mouth. 'Brother, I think you ask what you already know.'

Yes, Cadfael knew. Guimar de Massard, wounded and captive after Asçalon, had learned from the doctors who attended him in captivity that he was already a leper.

'They have excellent physicians,' said Lazarus, again

calm and still, 'wiser than any here. And who should better know and recognise the first bitter signs? They told me truth. They did what I asked of them, sent word of my death from my wounds. They did more. They helped me to a hermitage where I might live with my enemy, as I had died to my friends, and fight that battle as I had fought the commoner kind. My helm and my sword they sent back to Jerusalem, as I asked.'

'She has them,' said Cadfael. 'She treasures them. You have not been forgotten in your death. I have always known that the best of the Saracens could out-Christian many of us Christians.'

'Chivalrous and courteous I found my captors. At all points they respected and supported me through the years of my penance.'

One nobility is kin to another, thought Cadfael. There are alliances that cross the blood-line of families, the borders of countries, even the impassable divide of religion. And it was well possible that Guimar de Massard should find himself closer in spirit to the Fatimid caliphs than to Bohemond and Baldwin and Tancred, squabbling like malicious children over their conquests.

'How long,' he asked, 'have you been on your way home?' For it was a long, long journey across Europe from the midland sea, on broken feet, with a clapper-dish for baggage, and nothing more.

'Eight years. Ever since they brought word to my hermitage, from the reports of an English prisoner, of my son's death, and told me there was a child, a girl, left orphaned to her dead mother's kin, wanting any remaining of my blood.'

So he had left his cell, the refuge of years, and set off with his begging-bowl and cloak and veil to make that endless pilgrimage to England, to see for himself, at the prescribed distance, that his grandchild enjoyed her lands and had her due of happiness. He had found, instead, her affairs gone far awry, and with his own maimed hands he had straightened them, and set her free.

'She has her due now,' said Cadfael. 'But for all that, I think she might be happy to exchange her title to all that great honour for one living kinsman.'

The silence was long and cold, as if he trod upon forbidden ground. Nevertheless, he persisted doggedly. 'You are a quenched fire. You have been now for years, I judge. Do not deny it, I know the signs. What God imposed, no doubt for his own good reasons, for reasons as good he has lifted away. You know it. You are a peril to no man. And whatever name you have used all these years, you are still Guimar de Massard. If she cherishes your sword, how much more would she revere and delight in you? Why deprive her now of her true shield? Or yourself of the joy of seeing her happy? Of giving her with your own hand to a husband I think you approve?'

'Brother,' said Guimar de Massard, shaking his hooded head, 'you speak of what you do not understand. I am a dead man. Let my grave and my bones and my legend alone.'

'Yet there was one Lazarus,' said Cadfael, venturing far and in great awe, 'who did rise again out of his tomb, to the joy of his kinswomen.'

There was a long hush while the sailing filaments of cloud were the only things that moved in the visible world. Then the old man's unblemished right hand flashed from within the folds of the cloak, and rose to thrust back the hood. 'And was this,' asked Guimar, 'the face that made his sisters glad?'

He plucked away the face-cloth, and uncovered the awful visage left to him, almost lipless, one cheek shrunken away, the nostrils eaten into great, discoloured holes, a face in which only the live and brilliant eyes recalled the paladin of Jerusalem and Ascalon. And Cadfael was silenced.

Lazarus again covered the ruin from sight behind the veil. The quietness and serenity came back, almost stealthily. 'Never seek to roll that stone away,' said the deep, patient voice gently. 'I am content beneath it. Let me lie.'

'I must tell you, then,' said Cadfael after a long silence, 'that the boy has been sounding your praises to her, and she is begging him to bring her to you, since you cannot go to her, that she may thank you in person for your goodness to her lover. And since he can refuse her nothing, I think in the morning they will be here.'

'They will understand,' said Lazarus calmly, 'that there's no relying on us wandering lepers, the pilgrim kind. We have minds incorrigibly *vagus*. The fit comes on us, and the wind blows us away like dust. Relics, we make our way where there are relics to console us. Tell them that all is well with me.'

He put down his feet from the bench, carefully and slowly because of their condition, and courteously shook the skirts of his gown down over them, to hide the deformities. 'For with the dead,' he said, 'all is very well.' He rose, and Cadfael with him.

'Pray for me, brother, if you will.'

He was gone, turning away and withdrawing without another word or look. The heel of the special shoe he wore tapped sharply on the flags of the floor, and changed its note hollowly on the boards within. Brother Cadfael went out from the porch, under the slow-moving clouds that were not drifting, but proceeding with purpose and deliberation on some predestined course of their own, unhurried and unimpeded, like death.

Yes, with the dead, he thought, making his way back to the abbey in the dark, all is surely well. The child will have to find them work for their gratitude, instead.

Their dead has accomplished his own burial, now let them turn rather to the living. Who knows? Who knows but the beggar-woman's scrofulous waif, fed and tended and taught, may indeed end as page and squire to Sir Joscelin Lucy, some day? Stranger things have happened in this strangest, most harrowing and most wonderful of worlds!

The next morning, after Mass, Iveta and Joscelin came to Saint Giles, with the abbot's sanction, and hearts full of goodwill to all those within, but seeking two in particular. The child was easily found. But the old leper called Lazarus had gone forth silently in the night, leaving no word where he was bound, and saying no farewells. They sought for him by all the roads from Shrewsbury, and sent to ask at every place of pilgrimage within three counties, but even on crippled feet he outran pursuit, by what secret ways no one ever discovered. Certain it is he came no more to Shrewsbury.

# THE VIRGIN IN THE ICE

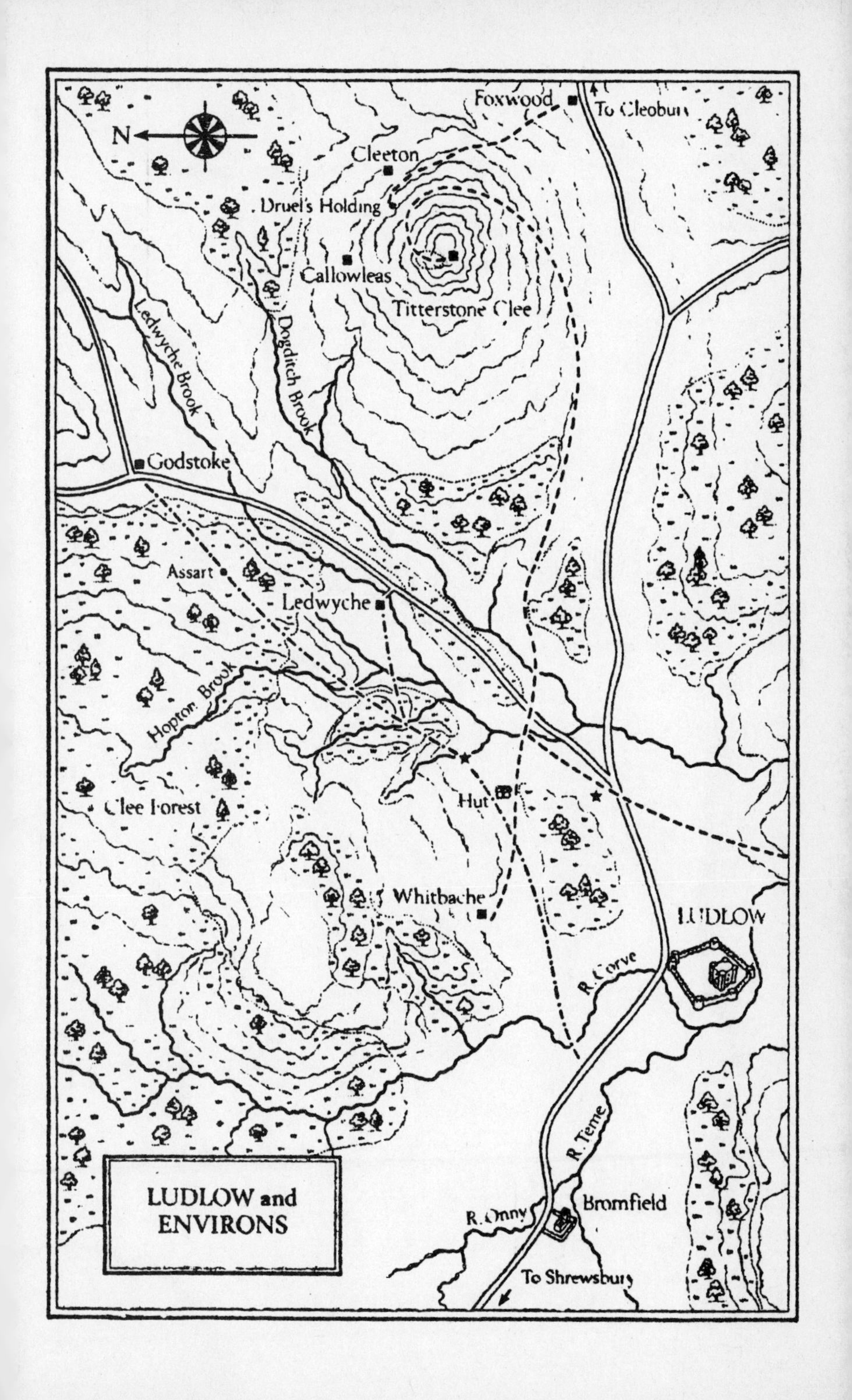
N
Foxwood
To Cleobury
Cleeton
Druel's Holding
Callowleas
Titterstone Clee
Ledwyche Brook
Dogditch Brook
Godstoke
Assart
Ledwyche
Hopton Brook
Hut
Clee Forest
Whitbache
LUDLOW
R. Corve
R. Teme
Bromfield
R. Onny
To Shrewsbury
LUDLOW and
ENVIRONS

# 1

It was early in November of 1139 that the tide of civil war, lately so sluggish and inactive, rose suddenly to sweep over the city of Worcester, wash away half its livestock, property and women, and send all those of its inhabitants who could get away in time scurrying for their lives northwards away from the marauders, to burrow into hiding wherever there was manor or priory, walled town or castle strong enough to afford them shelter. By the middle of the month a straggle of them had reached Shrewsbury, and subsided thankfully into the hospitable embrace of monastery or town, to lick their wounds and pour out their grievances.

They were not in too bad case, apart from the old or sick, for the winter had not yet begun to bite hard. The weather-wise foretold that there was bitter cold in store, heavy snows and hard and prolonged frosts, but as yet the land lay dour, cloudy and mild, with capricious winds, but clear of frost or snow.

'Thanks be to God!' said Brother Edmund, the infirmarer, devoutly. 'Or we should have had more burials on our hands than three, and they all past their three score and ten.'

Even so, he was hard put to it to find beds in his hospice for all those who needed them, and there was thick straw laid down in the stone hall for the overflow. They would live to return to their spoiled city before the Christmas feast, but now, exhausted and apathetic with shock, they needed all his care, and the abbey's resources were stretched to their limits. A few fugitives with distant relatives in the town had been taken into the houses of their kin, and were warmly provided. A pregnant woman near her time had been taken, husband and all, into the town house of Hugh Beringar, the deputy sheriff of the shire, at the insistence of his wife, whom he had brought here to the security of the town, complete with her women, midwife, physician and all, because she, too, looked forward to giving birth before the Nativity, and had a welcome for any who came in the same expectation, and in any kind of need.

'Our Lady,' remarked Brother Cadfael ruefully to his good friend Hugh, 'had no such reception.'

'Ah, there is but one of *my* lady! Aline would take in every homeless dog she saw in the streets, if she could. This poor girl from Worcester will do well enough now, there's nothing amiss with her that rest won't mend. We may yet have two births here for this Christmas, for she can't well be moved until she's safely over her lying-in. But I daresay most of your guests will soon be shrugging off their fears and heading for home.'

'A few have left already,' said Cadfael, 'and more of the hale ones will be off within days. It's natural they should want to get home and repair what they can. They say the king is on his way to Worcester with a strong force. If he leaves the garrison better found, they should be safe over the winter. Though they'll need to draw stores from eastwards, for their own reserves will all have been carried off.'

Cadfael knew from old experience the look, the stench, the desolation of a gutted town, having been both soldier and sailor in his young days, and seen service far afield. 'And besides wanting to reclaim what's left of their store before Christmas,' he said, 'there's the spur of the winter coming. If the roads are cleared of bad customs now, at least they can travel dry-shod and warm enough, but another month, another week it may be, and who knows how deep the snow will be?'

'Whether the roads are cleared of bad customs,' said Beringar in wary reflection, 'is more than I should care to say. We have a pretty firm hold here in Shropshire – thus far! But there's ominous word from east and north, besides this uneasiness along the border. When the king is all too busy in the south, and his mind on where his Flemings' next pay is to come from, and his energy mostly wasted in wavering from one target to another, ambitious men in remoter parts are liable to begin to spread their honours into palatines, and set up kingdoms of their own. And given the example, the lesser fry will follow it.'

'In a land at war with itself,' agreed Cadfael sombrely, 'you may take it as certain that order breaks down, and savagery breaks out.'

'Not here, it shall not,' said Hugh grimly. 'Prestcote has kept a close rein, and in so far as it falls to me as his man, so will I.' For Gilbert Prestcote, King Stephen's sheriff of Shropshire, was planning to keep Christmas in the chief manor of his own honour, in the north of the county, and the castle garrison and the rule of law throughout the southern half of the shire would be left in Beringar's hands. This attack on Worcester might be only a foretaste of further such raids. All the border towns were at risk, as well from the precarious loyalties of constables and garrisons as from the enterprise of the enemy. More than one lord in this troubled land had already changed his allegiance, more than one would do so in the future, some, perhaps, for the second or third time. Churchmen, barons and all, they were beginning to look first to their own interests, and place their loyalty where it seemed likely to bring them the greater profit. And it would not be long before some of them came to the conclusion that their interests could be served just as well by flouting both contendants for the crown, and setting up on their own account.

'There was some talk of your castellan in Ludlow being none too reliable,' observed Cadfael. 'For all King Stephen set him up in the honour of Lacy, and trusted Ludlow castle to him, there have been rumours he was casting his eyes towards the empress. Touch and go with him, as I heard it, if the king had not been close and with a sharp eye on him.'

Anything Cadfael had heard, Hugh had certainly heard. There was not a sheriff in the land who had not all his intelligencers alerted, these days, and his own ear to the ground. If Josce de Dinan, in Ludlow, had indeed been contemplating defection, and thought better of it, Hugh was content to accept his present steadfastness, but with reservations, and was watching him still. Distrust was only one of the lesser horrors of civil war, but saddening enough. It was well that there could still be absolute trust between tried friends. In these days there was no man living who might not suddenly have acute need of a steady and stout back braced against his own.

'Ah, well, with King Stephen on his way to Worcester with an army, no one is going to lift finger or show face until he draws off again. But for all that, I never stop listening and watching.' Hugh rose from the bench against the wall of Cadfael's workshop, brief refuge from the world. 'Now I am going home to my own bed, for once – even if I am banished from my wife's by my own arrogant brat. But what would a devout religious like you know about a father's tribulations!'

What, indeed? 'You must all come to it,' said Brother Cadfael complacently, 'you married men. Third and unwanted where two are lost in admiring each other. I shall go to Compline and say a prayer for you.'

He went first, however, to the infirmary, to check with Brother Edmund on one or two patients who were slow in their recovery from their wanderings, being feeble from age or poverty and hunger, and renew the dressing on a knife-wound which was ill to heal, and only then went to Compline, there to pray for many more, besides his friend, his friend's wife, and his friend's child to come, this winter child.

England was already frozen into a winter years long, and he knew it. King Stephen was crowned, and held, however slackly, most of England. The Empress Maud, his rival for the throne, held the west, and came with a claim the equal of Stephen's. Cousins, most uncousinly, they tore each other and tore England between them, and yet life must go on, faith must go on, the stubborn defiance of fortune must go on in the husbandry of the year, season after season, plough and harrow and seed, tillage and harvest. And here in the cloister and the church, the sowing and tillage and harvest of souls. Brother Cadfael had no fear for mankind, whatever became of mere men. Hugh's child would be a new generation, a new beginning, a new affirmation, spring in midwinter.

It was on the last day of November that Brother Herward, sub-prior of the Benedictine monastery of Worcester, appeared at chapter in the fraternal house of Saint Peter and Saint Paul at Shrewsbury, where he had arrived the previous night, and been entertained in Abbot Radulfus' own lodging as a cherished guest. Most of the brothers had no knowledge of his coming, and wondered who this could be, brought in courteously by their own abbot, and seated at his right hand. For once Brother Cadfael knew no more than his fellows.

The abbot and his guest made a sharp contrast. Radulfus was tall, erect, vigorous, with strong, austere features, magisterially calm. When needed, he could blaze, and those scorched drew back advisedly, but his fire was always in control. The man who entered beside him was meagre, small and slight of body, grey of tonsure, still tired after his journey, but his ageing eyes were direct of gaze, and his mouth set into lines of patience and endurance.

'Our brother, Sub-Prior Herward of Worcester,' said the abbot, 'has come to us with an errand in which I have been unable to help him. Since many of you here have been active in serving those unfortunates who came to us from that city, it is possible that you may have heard from them something which may be to the purpose. I have therefore asked him to repeat his request here to all.'

The visitor rose, to be better seen and heard by all present. 'I am sent to make enquiry after two noble children who were in Benedictine care in our town, and fled from it when the attack fell upon us. They have not returned, and we have traced their steps as far as the borders of this county and there lost them. It was their intention to make for Shrewsbury, and therefore, since our order is responsible for them, I came to find out whether they ever reached here. Father Abbot tells me that to his knowledge they never did, but it may be that some others among the fugitives may have seen them or got word of them in their travels, and spoken of them here among you. I should be grateful for any news that might lead to their safe recovery. And these are their names: the girl Ermina Hugonin, almost eighteen years of age, who was in the care of our sister convent in Worcester, and her brother Yves Hugonin, who was in our charge, and is only thirteen. They are orphaned of both parents, and their uncle and natural guardian has long been overseas in the Holy Land, and is only now returned, to be met by the news of their loss. It will be understood here,' said Brother Herward wryly, 'that we feel ourselves greatly to blame for having failed in our charge, though to say truth, we are not wholly at fault. As this thing befell, it was taken out of our hands.'

'In such confusion and peril,' agreed Radulfus ruefully, 'it would be much to ask of any man that he should order all successfully. But children of such tender age . . .'

Brother Edmund asked hesitantly: 'Are we to understand that they left Worcester alone?' He had not meant to sound either incredulous or censorious, but Brother Herward bowed his head meekly to the implied reproach.

'I would not wish to excuse myself or any of my house. Yet it fell out, perhaps, not quite as you suppose. That attack came in the early morning, but on the south side it was held, and we did not hear how grave it showed, or how great the force coming against us, until later, when they came about, and broke in by the north. It so happened that the boy Yves was visiting his sister, and they were quite cut off from us. The Lady Ermina is, dare I say, a headstrong young woman. In such a case, though the sisters thought best to gather in their church and abide the issue there, trusting that even these marauders – for I must tell you many were already drunk and wild – would respect their cloth, and do them no more harm than to steal, perhaps, their more valuable furnishings – the sisters, I say, held that faith required them to remain, but the Lady Ermina thought otherwise, and would slip away out of the town, as so many did, and make away into some safe and distant refuge. And since she would not be dissuaded, and her brother held with her, the young nun who was her tutor there offered that she would go with them, to see them safe into shelter. When all the raiders were gone, and we had put out the fires, and seen to the dead and wounded, only then did we get word that they had escaped out of the city and intended to reach Shrewsbury. They were well provided, though without horses, since all were seized at sight. The girl had her jewels, and store of money, and wit enough not to let them be seen on the way. And sorry I am to say it, it was well that she would go, for these men of Gloucester did not respect the sisters as they had hoped and trusted, but ravaged and burned, stole away some, the youngest and best-favoured among the novices, and bitterly misused the prioress who tried to prevent. The girl did well to venture, and I pray she and her brother, and Sister Hilaria with them, are safe in shelter somewhere this moment. But alas, I do not know.'

Brother Denis the hospitaller, who knew every soul who came within the gates, said regretfully: 'I grieve to have to tell you, but quite surely they never arrived here. We have had no such party. But come with me and speak with every fugitive we are still sheltering here in the guest-hall, and the few in the infirmary, in case they can tell you anything of use. For of course we knew nothing of these young people until now, and therefore have not asked about them.'

'Or again it may be,' suggested Brother Matthew the cellarer, 'that they knew of some kinsman or tenant or old servant here in the town, and therefore have passed us by, and are now within the walls.'

'It is possible,' agreed Herward, brightening a little. 'But I think Sister Hilaria would prefer to bring them here, to our own order for protection.'

'If there are none here who can help,' said the abbot briskly, 'the next move is certainly to consult the sheriff. He will know who has been received within the town. You did mention, brother, that the uncle of this young pair is newly come home from Palestine. There are channels he may use to approach the authorities here. How is it that he is not pursuing this enquiry in person? For surely he cannot cast the blame all on you.'

Brother Herward heaved a great sigh that first stiffened his little frame, and then let it collapse dispiritedly into limpness. 'Their uncle is a knight of Angevin blood – they are his sister's children – by name Laurence d'Angers. Newly home from the Crusade he is, but to Gloucester, to join the forces of the empress. It is also true that he did not arrive there until after this onslaught, and bears no blame for it, as he took no part in it. But no man from Gloucester dare show his face now in our city. The king is there with a great force, and an angry man, like every ruined burgess of the town. The search for these children is deputed to our house, perforce. Nevertheless, this is a quest for creatures absolutely innocent, and I shall so present it to the sheriff.'

'And you shall have my voice,' Radulfus assured him. 'But first, since none here can provide us news . . . ?' He looked enquiringly round the chapter-house, and found only shaken heads. 'Very well, we must enquire among our guests. The names, the youth of the parties, the presence of the nun, may yield us some useful word.'

Nevertheless Cadfael, filing out from chapter among the rest, could not believe that anything would come of such enquiry. He had spent much of his time, in recent days, helping Brother Edmund house and doctor the exhausted travellers, and never a word had been said of any such trio encountered on the way. Travellers' tales enough there had been, freely spilled for the listening, but none of a Benedictine sister and two noble children loose on the roads with never a man to guard them.

And the uncle, it seemed, was the empress's man, as Gilbert Prestcote was the king's man, to the hilt and bitterness between the factions was flaring up like a torch in tinder over the sack of Worcester. The omens were not good. Abbot Radulfus would lend his own persuasions to the envoy's, and this very day, too, but what countenance the two of them would get for Laurence d'Angers was a dubious speculation.

The sheriff received his petitioners courteously and gravely in his own apartment in the castle, and listened with an impassive face to the story Herward had to tell. A sombre man, black-browed and black-bearded, and his natural cast of countenance rather forbidding than reassuring, but for all that a fair-minded man in his stern fashion, and one who stood by his word and his men, provided they kept the standards he demanded of them.

'I am sorry,' he said when Herward had done, 'to hear of this loss, and sorrier still that I must tell you at once you will be seeking your party in vain here in Shrewsbury. Since this attack took place I have had word brought to me of every soul from Worcester who has entered the town, and these three are not among them. Many have already left again for home, now that his Grace has reinforced the garrison in Worcester. If, as you say, the uncle of these children has now returned to England, and is a man of substance, can he not undertake the search in person?'

It was Herward's weakness that he had withheld, up to that point, all but the name of that nobleman, putting off the evil moment. And as yet the name meant nothing, beyond a knight with the credit of the Crusade shedding lustre upon him, newly arrived from the Holy Land, where a relatively secure peace held at this time. But no help for it, the truth would out.

'My lord,' owned Herward, sighing, 'Laurence d'Angers is willing and anxious to make search for his nephew and niece, but for that he requires your countenance, or the special dispensation of his Grace the king. For he returned home as an Angevin owing allegiance to the Empress Maud, and has attached himself and his men to her forces at Gloucester.' He hurried on, to have all said while speech was allowed him, for the sheriff's level brows had drawn together into a steely bar above eyes now narrowed and bright in understanding. 'He had not arrived in Gloucester until a week after the attack, he took no part in it, knew nothing of it, cannot be held responsible for it. He came only to discover that his kin were lost, and all his desire is to find them and see them into safety. But it is impossible for a man of Gloucester to come near Worcester now, or to enter the king's lands except by special safe-conduct.'

'So you,' said Prestcote after a daunting pause, 'are acting on his behalf – the king's enemy.'

'With respect, my lord,' said Herward with spirit, 'I am acting on behalf of a young girl and a boy of tender years, who have done nothing to make them enemies to king or empress. I am not concerned with faction, only with the fate of two children who were in the charge of our order until this evil befell. Is it not natural that we should feel responsible for them, and do all we can in conscience to find them?'

'Natural enough,' allowed the sheriff drily, 'and moreover, as a man of Worcester yourself you're hardly likely to feel any great warmth towards the king's enemies, or want to give them aid or comfort.'

'We suffered from them, like the rest of Worcester, my lord. King Stephen is our sovereign, and as such we acknowledge him. The only duty I feel here is to the children. Consider what must be the dismay, the anxiety, of their natural guardian! All he asks – all we ask for him – is leave to enter the king's lands, not in arms, and search for his niece and nephew without hindrance. I do not say such a man, however innocent of this murderous raid, and even with his Grace's safe-conduct and countenance, would be utterly safe among the men of our shire or yours, but that risk he is willing to take. If you will give him safe-conduct, he pledges himself to pursue this quest, and no other end. He will go unarmed, and with only one or two attendants to help him. He will take no action but to find his wards. My lord, I entreat it of you, for their sake.'

Abbot Radulfus added his own plea, very restrainedly. 'From a Crusader of unblemished repute, I believe such a pledge may be accepted without question.'

The sheriff considered, darkly and in frowning silence, for some minutes, and then said with chill deliberation: 'No. I will issue no safe-conduct, and if the king himself were here and minded to grant it, I would urge him to the contrary. After what has happened, any man of that faction found in any part of my territory will be treated as a prisoner of war, if not as a spy. If he be taken in any ill circumstances, his life may be forfeit, and even if on no wrong errand, his liberty. It is not a matter of his intent alone. Even a man so pledged, and true enough to his pledge, might take back with him knowledge of castles and garrisons that would stand the enemy in good stead later. Also, and above all, it is my duty to combat the king's enemies and reduce their forces wherever chance offers, and if I can pluck away a good knight from them I will do it. No affront to Sir Laurence d'Angers, whose reputation, as far as I know it, is honourable enough, but he shall not have his safe-conduct, and if he ventures without it, let him look to his head. No doubt he did not come home from Palestine to rot in a prison. If he risks it, it is his own choice.'

'But the girl Ermina,' began Herward in dismayed appeal, 'and her brother, a mere child – are they to be left unsought?'

'Have I said so? Sought they shall be, to the best I can provide, but by my own men. And if found, they shall be delivered safely to their uncle's care. I will send out orders to all my castellans and officers, to look out for such a company of three, and make due enquiries after them. But I will not admit the empress's knight to the lands I administer for the king.'

It was all they would get from him, and they knew it by voice and face, and made the best of it.

'It would help,' suggested Radulfus mildly, 'if Brother Herward gives you some description of the three. Though I do not know if he is well acquainted with the girl, or the nun, her tutor . . .'

'They came several times to visit the boy,' said Herward. 'I can picture them all three. Your officers should enquire after these – Yves Hugonin, thirteen years old, heir to a considerable portion from his father, is not over-tall for his age, but sturdy and well-set-up, with a round, rosy face, and both hair and eyes dark brown. I saw him the morning this coil began, in bright blue cotte, cloak and capuchon, and grey hose. For the women – Sister Hilaria will be known best by her habit, but I should tell you that she is young, not above five and twenty, and well-favoured, a slender woman and graceful. And the girl Ermina . . .' Brother Herward hesitated, gazing beyond the sheriff's shoulder, as if to recall more perfectly someone but seldom seen, yet vividly impressed on his vision.

'She will be eighteen very shortly, I do not know the precise day. Darker than her brother, almost black of hair and eye, tall, vigorous . . . They report her quick of mind and wit, and of strong will.'

It was hardly a detailed description of her physical person, yet it established her with surprising clarity. All the more when Brother Herward ended almost absently, as if to himself: 'She would be reckoned very beautiful.'

Brother Cadfael heard about it from Hugh Beringar, after the couriers had ridden out to the castles and manors, and carried the word to the towns, to be cried publicly. What Prescote had promised, that he performed to the letter before he took himself off to the peace of his own manor to keep Christmas with his family. The very announcement of the sheriff's interest in the missing siblings should cast a protecting shadow over them if anyone in this shire did encounter them. Herward had set off back to

Worcester with a guarded party by then, his errand only partially successful.

'Very beautiful!' repeated Hugh, and smiled. But it was a concerned and rueful smile. Such a creature, wilful, handsome, daring, let loose in a countryside waiting for winter and menaced by discord, might all too easily come to grief.

'Even sub-priors,' said Cadfael mildly, stirring the bubbling cough linctus he was simmering over his brazier in the workshop, 'have eyes. But with her youth, she would be vulnerable even if she were ugly. Well, for all we know they may be snug and safe in shelter this moment. A great pity this uncle of theirs is of the other persuasion, and cannot get countenance to do his own hunting.'

'And newly back from Jerusalem,' mused Hugh, 'no way to blame for what his faction did to Worcester. He'll be too recent in the service to be known to you, I suppose?'

'Another generation, lad. It's twenty-six years since I left the Holy Land.' Cadfael lifted his pot from the brazier, and stood it aside on the earth floor to cool gradually overnight. He straightened his back carefully. He was not so far from sixty, even if he did not look it by a dozen years. 'Everything will be changed there now, I doubt. The lustre soon tarnished. From which port did they say he sailed?'

'Tripoli, according to Herward. In your unregenerate youth I suppose you must have known that city well? It seems to me there's not much of that coast you haven't covered in your time.'

'It was St Symeon I favoured myself. There were good craftsmen in the shipyards there, a fine harbour, and Antioch only a few miles upriver.'

He had good cause to remember Antioch, for it was there he had begun and ended his long career as a crusader, and his love affair with Palestine, that lovely, inhospitable, cruel land of gold and sand and drought. From this quiet, busy harbour in which he had chosen at last to drop anchor, he had had little time to hark back to those remembered haunts of his youth. The town came back to him now vividly, the lush green of the river valley, the narrow, grateful shade of the streets, the babel of the market. And Mariam, selling her fruit and vegetables in the Street of the Sailmakers, her young, fine-boned face honed into gold and silver by the fierce sunlight, her black, oiled hair gleaming beneath her veil. She had graced his arrival in the east, a mere boy of eighteen, and his departure, a seasoned soldier and seafarer of thirty-three. A widow, young, passionate and lonely, a woman of the people, not to everyone's taste, too spare, too strong, too scornful. The void left by her dead man had ached unbearably, and drawn in the young stranger heart and soul into her life, to fill the gap. For a whole year he had known her, before the forces of the Cross had moved on to invest Jerusalem.

There had been other women, before her and after. He remembered them with gratitude, and with no guilt at all. He had given and received pleasure and kindness. None had ever complained of him. If that was a poor defence from the formal viewpoint, nevertheless he felt secure behind it. It would have been an insult to repent of having loved a woman like Mariam.

'They have alliances there that ensure peace now, if only for a time,' he said reflectively, 'I suppose an

Angevin lord might well feel he's more needed here than there, now it's his own liege lady in the lists. And the man bears a good name, from all I hear. A pity he comes when hate's at its height.'

'A pity there should be cause for hate between decent men,' agreed Hugh wryly. 'I am the king's man, I chose him with my eyes open. I like Stephen, and am not likely to leave him for any lure. But I can see just as plainly why a baron of Anjou should rush home to serve his lady every whit as loyally as I serve Stephen. What a bedevilment of all our values, Cadfael, is this civil war!'

'Not all,' said Cadfael sturdily. 'There never was, for all I could ever learn, a time when living was easy and peaceful. Your boy will grow up into a better ordered world. There, I've finished here for tonight, and it must be nearly time for the bell.'

They went out together into the cold and dark of the garden, and felt on their faces the first flakes of the first snow of the winter. The air was full of a drifting unease, but the fall was light and fitful here. Further south it set in heavily, borne on a north-westerly wind, dry, fine snow that turned the night into a white, whirling mist, shrouding outlines, burying paths, blown into smooth, breaking waves only to be lifted and hurled again into new shapes. Valleys filled to a treacherous level, hillsides were scoured clean. Wise men stayed within their houses, clapped to shutter and door, and stopped the chinks between the boards, where thin white fingers reached through. The first snow, and the first hard frost. Thank God, thought Cadfael, hastening his steps as he heard the Compline bell begin to sound,

Herward and his company will be far on their way home now, they'll weather this well enough.

But what of Ermina and Yves Hugonin, astray somewhere between here and Worcester, and what of the young Benedictine sister who had offered, in her gallant innocence, to go with them and see them safe into sanctuary?

## 2

On the fifth day of December, about noon, a traveller from the south, who had slept the night at Bromfield Priory, some twenty-odd miles away, and had the good fortune to find the highroad, at least, in passable condition, brought an urgent message into Shrewsbury abbey. Prior Leonard of Bromfield had been a monk of Shrewsbury until his promotion, and was an old friend of Brother Cadfael's, and familiar with his skills.

'In the night,' the messenger reported, 'some decent fellows of that country brought in a wounded man to the priory, found by the wayside stripped and hacked, and left for dead. And half-dead he is, and his case very bad. If he had lain out all night in the frost he'd have been frozen stiff by morning. And Prior Leonard asked would I bring word here to you, for though they've some knowledge of healing, this case is beyond them, and he said you have experience from the wars, and may be able to save the man. If you could come, and bide until he mends – or until the poor soul's lost! – it would be a great comfort and kindness.'

'If abbot and prior give me leave,' said Cadfael, concerned, 'then most gladly. Footpads preying on the roads so close to Ludlow? What are things come to, there in the south?'

'And the poor man a monk himself, for they knew him by his tonsure.'

'Come with me,' said Cadfael, 'and we'll put it to Prior Robert.'

Prior Robert heard the plea with sympathy, and

raised no objection, since it was not he who must ride out all those miles in haste, in what was now the shrewd grip of winter. He took the request in his turn to the abbot, and came again with his approval granted.

'Father Abbot bids you take a good horse from the stables, for you'll need him. You have leave for as long as may be necessary, and we'll send and have Brother Mark come in from Saint Giles in the meantime, for I think Brother Oswin is not yet practiced enough to be left in charge alone.'

Cadfael agreed, fervently but demurely. A willing and devoted soul, but hardly competent to look after all the winter ailments that might crop up in his tutor's absence. Mark would leave his lepers on the outskirts of the town with regret, but God willing it need not be for very long.

'What of the roads?' he asked the messenger, who was stabling his own beast as Cadfael chose his. 'You made good time here, and so must I back.'

'The worst is the wind, brother, but it's blown the highroad almost clear in all but a few bad places. It's the byways that are clean buried. If you leave now you won't fare too badly. Better going south than north, at least you'll have the wind at your back.'

Cadfael took some thought over filling his scrip, for he had medicines, salves and febrifuges not to be found in every infirmary cupboard, and the commoner sorts Bromfield could provide. The less weight he carried, the better speed he would make. He took stout boots and a thick travelling cloak over his habit, and belted the folds securely about his waist. If the errand had not been so grim, he would have relished the prospect of a justified trip back into the world, and the rare permission to take his pick of the stables. He had campaigned in wintry conditions as well as in burning sun, the snow did not daunt him, though he was shrewd enough to respect it, and treat it with caution.

All these four days since the first snow the weather had followed a fixed pattern, with brief sunshine around noon, gathering cloud thereafter, fresh snow falling late in the evening and well into the night, and always iron frost. Around Shrewsbury the snow-falls had been light and powdery, the pattern of white flakes and black soil constantly changing as the wind blew. But as Cadfael rode south the fields grew whiter, the ditches filled. The branches of trees sagged heavily towards the ground under their load, and by mid-afternoon the leaden sky was sagging no less heavily earthwards, in swags of blue-black cloud. If this went on, the wolves would be moving down from the hills and prowling hungrily among the haunts of men. Better to be an urchin under a hedgerow, sleeping the winter away, or a squirrel holed up snugly with his hoarded stores. It had been a good autumn for nuts and acorns.

Riding was pleasure to him, even riding alone and in the bitter cold. The chance seldom came his way now, it was one of the delights he had given up for the quiet of the cloister and the sense of having discovered his true place. In every decision there must be some regrets. He hunched his back solidly against the malice of the wind, and saw the first driven flakes, fine as dust, whirl by him and outpace his horse, while he felt nothing in his shroud of cowl and cloak. He was thinking of the man who waited for him at the end of this journey.

Himself a monk, the messenger had said. Of Bromfield? Surely not. If he had been one of theirs they would have named him. A monk loose and alone about the roads in the mid of the night? On what errand? Or in flight from what, before he fell into the mercies of robbers and murderers? Others must have ranged through the same countryside, in flight from the rape of Worcester, and where were they now? Perhaps this cowled wanderer had made his way painfully out of the same holocaust?

The snow thickened, two fine curtains of spume driving past him one on either side, cloven by his sturdy body and waving away ahead of him like the ends of a gauze scarf, drawing him forward. Perhaps four times on this ride he had exchanged greetings in passing with other human creatures, and all of them close to home. In such a season only the desperate travel.

It was dark by the time he reached the gatehouse of Bromfield, crossing the foot-bridge over the little River Onny. His horse had had enough by then, and was blowing frostily, and twitching irritable shoulders and flanks. Cadfael lighted down gladly between the torches in the gateway, and let a lay brother take the bridle. Before him the familiar court opened, straighter than at Shrewsbury, and the shapes of the monastic buildings gilded here and there by the flame of a torch. The church of Saint Mary loomed dark in darkness, large and noble for such a modest foundation. And striding out of shadows across the court came Prior Leonard himself, a long, loose-jointed heron of a man, pointed beak anxiously advanced, arms flapping like wings. The court under his feet, surely swept during the day, already bore a smooth, frail coating of snow. By morning it would be crisp and deep underfoot, unless the wind that brought it removed half of it again to hurl it elsewhere.

'Cadfael?' The prior was near-sighted, he had to peer and narrow his eyes even by daylight, but he groped for a hand that came to meet his, and held and knew it. 'Thank God you could come! I fear for him . . . But such a ride . . . Come within, come within, I have provision made for you, and a meal. You must be both hungry and weary!'

'First let me see him,' said Cadfael briskly, and set off purposefully up the slope of the court, leaving his broad boot-prints plain in the new-fallen whiteness. Prior Leonard strode beside him, long legs curbed to his friend's shorter pace, still talking volubly.

'We have him in a room apart, for quietness, and watched constantly. He breathes, but snoringly, like a man with a broken head. He has not spoken word or opened eye since they brought him. Bruises darken on him everywhere, but those would heal. But a knife was used on him, he has bled too much, though the wound is stanched now. Through here – the inner room is less cold . . .'

The infirmary stood a little apart, sheltered from the wind by the mass of the church. They went in, and shut the heavy door against the malice of the night, and Leonard led the way through to the small, bare cell where a little oil-lamp burned beside a bed. A young brother rose from his knees at their entry, and drew back from the sick man's bedside to make room for them.

The patient lay under piled covers, stretched on his back like a man coffined. Certainly he breathed, with a groaning effort, but the intake of breath barely lifted the blanket over his breast, and the face upturned on the pillow was motionless, eyes closed, cheeks hollow and blue beneath thrusting bones. His head was bandaged, covering the tonsure, and the brow beneath the wrappings was swollen and bruised, so misshapen that one eye was sunken in folds of battered flesh. No telling how he would look in health, but Cadfael judged that he was well-made, and certainly not old, probably no older than thirty-five.

'The marvel is,' whispered Leonard, 'that no bones are broken. Unless, indeed, his skull . . . But you'll examine him thoroughly, later . . .'

'No better time than now,' said Cadfael practically, and shed his cloak and went to work, setting down his scrip on the stone floor. There was a small brazier burning in a corner, but for all that, when he slid his hands under the covers and felt at flank and thigh and foot, the unresponsive flesh was everywhere deadly cold. They had wrapped him well, but it was not enough.

'Lay stones over your hob in the kitchen,' said Cadfael, 'get them hot and wrap them in flannel. We'll pack him round with warmth, and change them as they cool. This is not the cold of winter, but the chill of man's mishandling, we must get him out of it, or he never will wake. I've known men shattered by horror or cruelty turn their backs on the world and die, when there was nothing mortal ailed their bodies. Have you made shift to get any food or drink into him at all?'

'We have tried but he cannot swallow. Even a trickle of wine only runs from his mouth again.' A broken mouth, battered by fists or cudgels. Probably he had lost teeth. But no, Cadfael drew back the upper lip delicately, and the strong white teeth showed, even, clenched and large.

The young brother had slipped away silently to see about heating stones or bricks in the kitchen. Cadfael turned back the covers, and viewed the naked body from head to foot. They had left him so, under a linen sheet, to have only a clean, smooth surface touching his many bruises and broken grazes. The knife-wound under his heart was bandaged close. Cadfael did not unbind it; no need to doubt that every wound had been scrupulously cleaned and dressed. But he slid his fingers under the upper folds, and felt along the bones beneath.

'It was meant to finish him. But the knife struck the rib, and they did not wait to make certain. In health this must be a fine man – see the build of him. Three or four at least did this to him.'

He did what he could for the many injuries that showed some angry signs of festering, drawing on his stock of salves tried over years, but let the lesser and clean abrasions alone. They brought the heated stones, two or three eager young brothers hovering anxiously, and packed the battered form round with them, close but not touching, and trotted away devotedly to heat more. A good hot brick at the long, bony feet; for if the feet stay cold, all stays cold, said Cadfael. And then the bludgeoned head. He unwound the bandages, Leonard supporting the man's shoulders. The tonsure emerged unmistakable, thick, bushy brown hair framing a pate scarred by two or three still oozing wounds. So thick and strong the hair, of such vigorous growth, that even the ring of it might well have saved him a broken skull. Cadfael felt delicately all round the cupola of bone, and could not find a hollow that gave to his touch. He drew breath in cautious hope.

'His wits will have been shaken up into confusion, but I do believe his skull is whole. We'll bind it up again for his comfort in lying, and for warmth. I can find no break.'

When all was done, the mute body lay as before; hard to detect any change that did not stem from the handling of others. But the warm stones zealously renewed as they cooled had had their effect. His flesh felt softer and human to the touch, capable of healing.

'We may leave him now,' said Cadfael, staring down at him with a considering frown. 'I'll watch with him through the night, and get my sleep tomorrow by daylight, when we see better how he fares. But I say he'll live. Father Prior, by your leave, I'm ready now for that supper you promised me. And before all, for I'm too stiff to fend for myself, get a stout youngster to haul off these boots.'

Prior Leonard himself waited on his guest at supper, and freely admitted his relief at having a more experienced physician at hand. 'For I never had your knowledge, nor the means of acquiring it, and never, God knows, have I had so wretched and broken a creature left at my door. I thought I had a dead man on my hands, before ever I brought him in and tried to stop the bleeding, and wrap him up against the frost. And how he came by this usage we may never get to know.'

'Who brought him in?' asked Cadfael.

'A tenant of ours near Henley, Reyner Dutton, a good husbandman. That was the first night of snow and frost, and Reyner had lost a strayed heifer, one of the venturesome kind that will wander and break loose, and he was out after her with a couple of his lads. They stumbled on this poor soul by the wayside, and left all to carry him here to shelter as fast as they could. It was a wild night, driving squalls and stone blind when they came. I doubt if he can have lain there long, or he would not be living now, as cold as it was and is.'

'And these who helped him had seen nothing of any footpads? Met with no hindrance themselves?'

'Nothing. But there was no seeing more than a dozen paces, men could pass close and never know it. Likely they were lucky not to meet the same fate, though three of them, perhaps, would be enough to daunt any footpads. They know this countryside like their own palms. A stranger would have had to lie up somewhere and wait till he could see his way. In these drifts, and with such a wind blowing, and the snow so dry and fine, paths appear and vanish twice in a day and more. You could walk a mile, and think you knew every landmark, and see nothing you recognised on the way back.'

'And this sick man of ours – no one knows him here?'

Prior Leonard stared startled and embarrassed surprise. 'Why, yes! Did I never make that plain? Well, my messenger was enlisted in great haste, there was no time to make a long tale of it. Yes, this is a Benedictine brother of Pershore, who came on an errand from his abbot. We have been treating with them for a finger-bone of Saint Eadburga, whose relics, as you know, they possess, and this is the brother who was entrusted with bringing it here to us in its reliquary. He delivered it safely some days ago. The night of the first of the month he arrived here, and stayed to witness the offices when we installed it.'

'Then how,' demanded Cadfael, gaping, 'did he come to be picked out of the snow and brought back to you naked only a day or two later? You're surely grown somewhat careless with your guests, Leonard!'

'But he left us, Cadfael! The day before yesterday he said he must prepare to leave early in the morning, and be on his way. And as soon as he had breakfasted yesterday he left, and I do assure you, well provided for the first part of his journey. We know no more than you how he came to be stricken down still so close to us, and you see he cannot yet speak, to make all plain. Where he has been between yesterday's dawn and the thick of the night no one knows, but certainly not where he was found, or we should be tolling for him, not trying to heal him.'

'Howbeit, at least you know him. How much do you know of him? He gave you a name?'

The prior hoisted bony shoulders. What does a name tell about a man? 'His name is Elyas. I think, though he never said, not long in the cloister. A taciturn man – in particular, I think, he would not speak of himself. He did eye the weather somewhat anxiously. We thought it natural, since he had to brave the way home, but now I fancy there was more in it than that, for he did say something of a party he had left by Foxwood, coming from Cleobury, some people he encountered there in flight from Worcester, and urged to come here with him for safety, but they would push on over the hills for Shrewsbury. The girl, he said, was resolute, and she called the tune.'

'Girl?' Cadfael stiffened erect, ears pricked. 'There was a girl holding the rein?'

'So it seemed.' Leonard blinked in surprise at such interest in the phenomenon.

'Did he say who else was in her company? Was there a boy spoken of? And a nun in charge of them?' He realised ruefully the folly of any such attitude to this relationship. It was the girl who called the tune!

'No, he never told us more. But I did think he was anxious about them, for you see, the snow came after he reached us, and over those bleak hills . . . He might well wonder.'

'You think he may have gone to seek them? To find assurance they had made the crossing safely, and were on a passable way to Shrewsbury? It would not be so far aside from his way.'

'It could be so,' said Leonard, and was mute, searching Cadfael's face with a worried frown, waiting for enlightenment.

'I wonder, I wonder if he found them – if he was bringing them here for refuge!' He was talking to himself, for the prior was left astray, patiently regarding him. And if he was, thought Cadfael silently, what, in God's name, has become of them now? Their only helper and protector battered senseless and left for dead, and those three, where? But as yet there was no proof that these were the hapless Hugonins and their young nun. Many poor souls, girls among them, had fled from the despoiled city of Worcester.

Headstrong girls, who called the tune? Well, he had known them crop up in cottage no less than in castle, in croft and toft, and among the soil-bound villein families, too. Women were as various as men.

'Leonard,' he said earnestly, leaning across the table, 'have you had no proclamation from the sheriff about two young things lost from Worcester in the company of a nun of the convent there?'

The prior shook a vague but troubled head. 'I don't recall such a message, no. Are you telling me that these . . . Brother Elyas certainly felt some anxiety. You think these he spoke of may be the ones being sought?'

Cadfael told him the whole of it, their flight, the search for them, the plight of their uncle, threatened with capture and prison if he ventured across the king's borders in quest of them. Leonard listened in growing dismay. 'It could be so, indeed. If this poor brother could but speak!'

'But he did speak. He told you he left them at Foxwood, and they were bent on crossing the hills still towards Shrewsbury. That would mean their venturing clean over the flank of Clee, to Godstoke, where they would be in the lands of Wenlock priory, and in good enough hands.'

'But a bitter, bleak way over,' mourned the prior, aghast. 'And that heavy snow the next night.'

'There's no certainty,' Cadfael reminded him cautiously. 'Barely a suspicion. A quarter of Worcester fled this way to escape the slaughter. Better I should keep watch on this patient of ours than waste time on speculation. For only he can tell us more, and besides, him we already have, he was laid at our doors, and him we must keep. Go to Compline, Leonard, and pray for him, and I'll do as much by his bed. And if he speaks, never fret, I'll be awake enough to catch his drift, for all our sakes.'

In the night the first sudden but infinitesimal change took place. Brother Cadfael was long accustomed to sleeping with one eye open, and both ears. On his low stool beside the bed he drowsed thus, arms folded, head lowered, one elbow braced on the wooden frame of the bed, to quicken to any move. But it was his hearing that pricked him awake to stoop with held breath. For Elyas had just drawn his first deeper, longer, eased breath, that went down through his misused body from throat to stretched feet, groaning at the disturbed pains that everywhere gored him. The horrid snore in his throat had softened, he drew air, painful though it was, down into his midriff hungrily, like a starving man grasping at food. Gadfael saw a great quiver pass over the mangled face and part the swollen lips. The tip of a dry tongue strove to moisten, and shivered and withdrew from pain, but the lips remained parted. The strong teeth unclenched to let out a long, sighing groan.

Cadfael had honeyed wine standing in a jug beside the brazier, to keep warm. He trickled a few drops between the swollen lips, and had the satisfaction of seeing the unconscious face contort in muscular spasm, and the throat labour to swallow. When he touched a finger to the man's lips, again closed, they parted in thirsty response. Drop by drop, patiently, a good portion of the drink went down. Only when response failed at last did Cadfael abandon the process. Cold, oblivious absence had softened gradually into sleep, now that a little warmth had been supplied him both within and without. A few days of lying still, for his wits to settle again right way up in his head, thought Cadfael, and he'll come round and be on his way back to us. But whether he'll remember much of what befell him is another matter. He had known men, after such head injuries, revive to recall every detail of their childhood and past years, but no recollection whatever of recent injury.

He removed the cooling brick from the foot of the bed, fetched a replacement from the kitchen, and sat down to resume his vigil. This was certainly sleep now, but a very uneasy sleep, broken by whimpers and moans, and sudden shudders that passed all down the long body. Once or twice Elyas laboured in evident distress, throat and lips and tongue trying to frame words, but achieving only anguished, indecipherable sounds, or no sounds at all. Cadfael leaned close, to catch the first utterance that should have meaning. But the night passed, and his vigil had brought him nothing coherent.

Perhaps the sounds that measured out the cloistral day were able to reach some quiet core of habit even within the sufferer's disrupted being, for at the note of the bell for Prime he fell suddenly quiet, and his eyelids fluttered and strove to open, but closed again wincingly against even this subdued light. His throat worked, he parted his lips and began to attempt speech. Cadfael leaned close, his ear to the struggling mouth.

'. . . madness . . .' said Elyas, or so Cadfael thought he said. 'Over Clee,' he grieved, 'in such snows . . .' He turned his head on the pillow, and hissed with the pain. 'So young . . . wilful . . .' He was lapsing again into a better sleep, his disquiet easing. In a voice thread-fine but suddenly clearly audible: 'The boy would have come with me,' said Brother Elyas.

That was all. He lay once again motionless and mute.

'He has the turn for life,' said Cadfael, when Prior Leonard came in to enquire after the patient as soon as Prime ended, 'but there'll be no hurrying him.' An earnest young brother stood dutifully by to relieve him of his watch. 'When he stirs you may feed him the wine and honey, you'll find he'll take it now. Sit close and mark me any word he says. I doubt if you'll have anything more to do for him, while I get my sleep, but there's a ewer for his use if he needs it. And should he begin to sweat, keep him well covered but bathe his face to give him ease. God willing, he'll sleep. No man can do for him what sleep will do.'

'You're content with him?' asked Leonard anxiously, as they went out together. 'He'll do?'

'He'll do very well, given time and quietness.' Cadfael was yawning. He wanted breakfast first, and a bed after, for all the morning hours. After that, and another look at the dressings on head and ribs, and all the minor hurts that had threatened suppuration, he would have a better idea of how to manage both the nursing of Brother Elyas and the pursuit of the lost children.

'And has he spoken? Any sensible word?' pressed Leonard.

'He has spoken of a boy, and of the madness of attempting to cross the hills in such snows. Yes, I believe he did encounter the Hugonin pair and their nun, and try to bring them into shelter here with him. It was the girl who would go her own way,' said Cadfael, brooding on this unknown chit who willed to venture the hills in both winter and anarchy. 'Young and wilful, he said.' But however mad and troublesome they may be, the innocent cannot be abandoned. 'Feed me,' said Cadfael, returning to first needs, 'and then show me a bed. Leave the absent for later. I'll not quit Brother Elyas as long as he needs me. But I tell you what we may well do, Leonard, if you've a guest in your hall here making for Shrewsbury today. You might charge him to let Hugh Beringar know that we have here what I take to be the first news of the three people he's seeking.'

'That I'll certainly do,' said Prior Leonard, 'for there's a cloth merchant of the town on his way home for the Christmas feast, he'll be off as soon as he's eaten, to get the best of the day. I'll go and deliver him the message this minute, and do you go and get your rest.'

Before night Brother Elyas opened his eyes for the second time, and this time, though the return to light caused him to blink a little, he kept them open, and after a few moments opened them wide in blank wonder, astonished by everything on which they rested. Only when the prior stooped close at Cadfael's shoulder did the brightness of recognition quicken in the sick man's eyes. This face, it seemed, he knew. His lips parted, and a husky whisper emerged, questioning but hopeful:

'Father Prior . . . ?'

'Here, brother,' said Leonard soothingly. 'You are here with us, safe in Bromfield. Rest and gather strength, you have been badly hurt, but here you are in shelter, among friends. Trouble for nothing . . . ask for whatever you need.'

'Bromfield . . .' whispered Elyas, frowning. 'I had an errand to that place,' he said, troubled, and tried to raise his head from the pillow. 'The reliquary . . . oh, not lost . . . ?'

'You brought it faithfully,' said Leonard. 'It is here on the altar of our church, you kept vigil with us when we installed it. Do you not remember? Your errand was done well. All that was required of you, you performed.'

'But how . . . My head hurts . . .' The sighing voice faded, the dark brows drew together in mingled anxiety and pain. 'What is this weighs on me? How am I come to this?'

They told him, with cautious gentleness, how he had gone forth again from the priory, to make his way home to his own abbey of Pershore, and how he had been brought back broken and battered and abandoned for dead. At the name of Pershore he grasped gladly, there he knew he belonged, and from there he remembered he had set forth to bring Saint Eadburga's finger-bone to Bromfield, avoiding the perilous route by Worcester. Even Bromfield itself came back to him gradually. But of what had befallen him after his departure he knew nothing. Whoever had so misused him, they were gone utterly from his disturbed mind. Cadfael leaned to him, urging gently:

'You did not meet them again? The girl and boy who would press on over the hills to Godstoke? Foolish, but the girl would go, and her young brother could not persuade her . . .'

'What girl and boy were these?' wondered Elyas blankly, and drew his drawn brows more painfully close.

'And a nun – do you not recall a nun who travelled with them?'

He did not. The effort at recall caused him agitation, he dragged at memory and produced only the panic desperation of failure, and in his wandering state failure was guilt. All manner of undischarged obligations drifted elusive behind his haunted eyes, and could not be captured. Sweat broke on his forehead, and Cadfael wiped it gently away.

'Never fret, but lie still and leave all to God, and under God, to us. Your part was done well, you may take your rest.'

They tended his bodily needs, anointed his wounds and grazes, fed him a broth made from their austere stores of meat for the infirmary, with herbs and oatmeal, read the office with him before bed, and still, by the knotting of his brows, Brother Elyas pursued the memories that fled him and would not be snared. In the night, in the low hours when the spirit either crosses or draws back from the threshold of the world, the sleeper was shaken by recollection and dream together. But his utterances then were broken and mumbled, and so clearly painful to his progress that Cadfael, who had reserved to himself that most perilous watch, bent his energies all to soothing away the torment from his patient's mind, and easing him back into healthful sleep. Cadfael was relieved before dawn, and Elyas slept. The body rallied and healed. The mind wandered and shunned remembrance.

Cadfael slept until noon, and arose to find his patient at rest in wakefulness as he had not been in sleep, very docile, without much pain, and well tended by an elderly brother with long experience of nursing the sick. The day was clear, and the light would last well. Though the frost was unbroken, and without doubt there would be fresh snow in the night, at this hour the sun and the remaining hours of daylight tempted.

'He's well enough cared for,' said Cadfael to the prior. 'I may leave him for a few hours with an easy mind. That horse of mine is rested now, and the ways none so bad until the next fall comes or the wind rises. I'll ride as far as Godstoke, and ask if these truants ever reached there, and whether they've moved on, and by what road. Six days it must be now since he parted from them, at Foxwood you said. If they came safely to the lands of Wenlock priory they may well have made their way either to Wenlock or Shrewsbury by now, and all the coil over them will be done. Then we can all breathe freely.'

# 3

Godstoke, sunk in its deep, wooded valley between the hills, was held by the priory of Wenlock, a third of the manor farmed in demesne, the rest leased out to life tenants, a prosperous settlement, and well-found in stores and firing for the winter. Once over the bleak hills and into this sheltered place, a party of fugitives could rest and be at ease, and make their way onward at their own pace, moving from manor to manor of the prior's wide-ranging properties.

But these fugitives had never reached Godstoke. The prior's steward was quite certain.

'We got word already they were being sought, and though we had no great call to suppose they would be heading this way, any more than by Ludlow or any other road, I've had enquiry made everywhere. You may take it as sure, brother, that they did not reach us.'

'The last known of them,' said Brother Cadfael, 'was at Foxwood. From Cleobury they were in company with a brother of our order, who urged them to come on with him to Bromfield, but they would continue north over the hills. It seemed to me they must make for you.'

'So I would say also,' agreed the steward. 'But they did not come.'

Cadfael considered. He was not perfectly familiar with these parts, yet he knew them well enough to make his way. If they had not passed here, small profit in searching beyond. And though it would be possible to work backwards along the way they should have taken to reach this place, and look for traces of them between here and Foxwood, that would certainly have to wait for another day. This one was already too far spent. Dusk was closing in faintly, and he had better make his way back by the nearest way.

'Well, keep watch in case some word reaches you. I'm for Bromfield again.' He had come by the most used roads, but they were less than direct, and he had a good eye for country. 'If I make straight south-westerly from here, I take it that's the way the crow flies for Bromfield. How are the tracks?'

'You'll be threading part of Clee Forest if you try it, but keep the sunset a little on your right hand and you'll not go wrong. And the brooks are no stay, nor have been since the frost set in.'

The steward started him off in the direction he should go, and saw him out of the wooded hollow and on to the narrow, straight track between gentle hills, turning his back upon the great, hunched bulk of Brown Clee, and his left shoulder on the grimmer, more rugged shape of Titterstone Clee. The sunlight had long withdrawn, though the sun itself had still some way to sink, and hung in a dull red ball behind veils of thin grey cloud. The inevitable nocturnal snow should not begin for an hour or two yet. The air was very still and very cold.

After a mile he was in the forest. The branches still held up roofs of frozen snow, trailing long icicles where the noon sun had had room to penetrate, and the ground underfoot, deep in leaf-mould and needles, was easy riding. The trees even created a measure of warmth. Clee was a royal forest, but neglected now, as much of England was surely being neglected, left to rot or to be appropriated by opportunist local magnates, while king and empress fought out their battle for the crown. Lonely country, this, and wild, even within ten miles of castle and town. Assarts were few and far between. The beasts of the chase and the beasts of the warren had it for their own domain, but in such a winter even the deer would starve without some judicious nursing from men. Fodder too precious to be wasted by the farmer might still be put out by the lord to ensure the survival of his game in a bad season. Cadfael passed one such store, trampled and spread by the hungry beasts, the snow patterned with their slots all around. The hereditary forester was still minding his duties, no matter which of the two rival rulers claimed his estate.

The sun, seen briefly between the trees, hung very low now, evening had begun to gather like an overhanging cloud, while the ground below still had light enough. Before him the trees drew apart, restoring an hour of the failing day. Someone had carved out an assart, a clearing of narrow garden and field about a low cottage. A man was folding his two or three goats, herding them before him into a wattled enclosure. He looked up alertly at the rustle of crisp snow and frozen leaf under hooves. A sturdy, squat husbandman no more than forty years old, in good brown homespun and leggings of home-tanned leather. He had made a good job of his lonely holding, and stood erect to face the traveller as soon as he had penned his goats. Narrowed eyes surveyed the monastic habit, the tall and vigorous horse, the broad, weathered face beneath the cowl.

'God bless the holding and the holder,' said Cadfael, reining in by the wattle fence.

'God be with you, brother!' His voice was even and deep, but his eyes were wary. 'Whither bound?'

'To Bromfield, friend. Am I going right?'

'True enough to your road. Keep on as you are, and in a half-mile you come to the Hopton brook. Cross it, and bear a little to your left over the two lesser brooks that run into it. After the second the track forks. Bear right, level along the slope, and you'll come out to the road beyond Ludlow, a mile from the priory.'

He did not ask how a Benedictine brother came to be riding this obscure way at such an hour. He did not ask anything. He spread his solid bulk across the gateway of his enclosure like a portcullis, but with courteous face and obliging tongue. It was the eyes that said he had somewhat within to cover from view, and also that he was storing every sight and sound to be delivered faithfully elsewhere. Yet whoever hewed this holding out of the forest could be nothing less than a practical, honest man.

'Thanks for your rede,' said Cadfael. 'Now help me with another matter if you can. I am a monk of Shrewsbury, now nursing a brother of our order from Pershore, in the infirmary of Bromfield priory. Our sick brother frets over certain people he met on their way to Shrewsbury from Worcester, in flight from the sacking of the city. They would not turn west with him for Bromfield, they would hold northwards this way. Tell me if you have seen hide or hair of such.' He described them, in doubt of his own intuition until he saw the man cast one swift glance over his shoulder towards his cottage, and again confront him unblinking.

'No such company has come my way in this woodland,' he said steadily. 'And why should they? I'm on the way to nowhere.'

'Travellers in strange country and snow may very well find themselves on the road to nowhere, and lost to anywhere,' said Cadfael. 'You're none so far from Godstoke, where I've already been enquiring. Well, if any or all of these three should come your way, give them the word that they're sought by all the shire and the abbeys of Worcester and Shrewsbury, and when they're found they shall have safe escort wherever they would be. Worcester is re-garrisoned now, and anxious about its strays. Say so, if you meet with them.'

The wary eyes stared him thoughtfully in the face. The man nodded, and said: 'I will say so. If ever I do meet with them.'

He did not move from his place before the gate until Cadfael had shaken his rein and moved on along the track, yet when Cadfael reached the shelter of the trees and turned to look back, the cottager had vanished with some speed into his house, as if he had an errand that would not wait. Cadfael rode on, but at a slow, ambling walk, and once well out of sight, halted and sat listening. The small, cautious sounds of movement behind him were his reward. Someone light-footed and shy was following him, trying at the same time to hurry and to remain unheard. A sly glance over his shoulder afforded him a fleeting glimpse of a blue cloak that whisked aside into cover. He idled, letting the pursuer draw nearer, and then suddenly reined aside and turned to look back openly.

All sounds ceased instantly, but the leaning branches of a beech sapling quivered and shed a few flakes of powdery snow.

'You may come forth,' said Cadfael mildly. 'I am a monk of Shrewsbury, no threat to you or any. The goodman told you true.'

The boy stepped out of hiding and stood in the open ride, legs braced well apart, ready to run if he saw fit, or stand his ground sturdily. A small, stocky boy with a round shock-head of brown hair, large unwavering brown eyes, and a formidably firm mouth and chin belying the childish fullness of his cheeks. The bright blue cotte and cloak were somewhat soiled and crumpled now, as if he had slept wild in the woods in them, as perhaps he had, and there was a tear in one knee of the grey hose, but he still wore them with the large assurance of his own nobility. He had a little dagger at his belt, the sheath ornamented with silver, sign enough of his worth to have tempted many a man. He had fallen into good hands at this recent stay, whatever had happened to him earlier.

'He said . . .' The boy advanced a step or two, reassured. 'His name is Thurstan. He and his wife have been good to me. He said that here was one I could trust, a Benedictine brother. He said you have been looking for us.'

'He said truly. For you, I think, must be Yves Hugonin.'

The boy said: 'Yes. And may I come with you to Bromfield?'

'Yves, very heartily you may, and a warm welcome you'll get from all those who are out hunting for you. Since you fled from Worcester your uncle d'Angers is come back from the Holy Land, and reached Gloucester only to hear you were lost, and he's been sending about to have you sought all through this shire. Main glad he'll be to get you back whole and well.'

'My uncle d'Angers?' The boy's face wavered between eagerness and doubt. 'In Gloucester? But . . . but it was men from Gloucester . . .'

'It was, we know, but none of his doing. Never trouble your head over the divisions that keep him from coming himself to find you, nor you nor I can help those. But we're pledged to return you to him safe and sound, and that you may rely on. But the search is for three, and here we are fobbed off with but one. Where are your sister and her governess?'

'I don't know!' It came almost in a wail. The boy's resolute chin shook for a moment, and recovered gallantly. 'I left Sister Hilaria safe at Cleeton, I hope she is safe there still, but what she would do when she found herself alone . . . And my sister . . . My sister is the cause of all this! She went off with her lover, in the night. He came for her, I am sure she sent him word to fetch her away. I tried to follow them, but then the snow came . . .'

Cadfael drew breath in mingled wonder, dismay and relief. Here was at least one of the three safely netted, another might be snug if distracted at Cleeton still, and the third, even if she had committed a great folly, seemed to be in the hands of someone who held her dear, and presumably meant her nothing but good. There might yet be a happy ending to all. But meantime, it bade fair to be a very long and confused story, and here was dusk falling, the rim of the sun already dipped, and several miles to go, and the best thing to be done was to get this one back to Bromfield, and make sure he did not wander to be lost again.

'Come, let's get you home before night falls on us. Come up before me, your light weight won't worry this fellow. Your foot on mine, so . . .' The boy had to reach high. His hand was firm and eager in Cadfael's, he came up with a spring, and settled himself snugly. His body, at first tensed, relaxed with a great sigh.

'I have thanked Thurstan, and said farewell to him,' he said in a soft, gruff voice, reviewing his own behaviour scrupulously. 'I gave him half what was left in my purse, but it was not very much. He said he did not want nor need it, and I was welcome, but I had nothing else to give him, and I could not go and never leave a token.'

'There may be a time, some day, to visit him again,' said Cadfael comfortably. The boy had been well brought up, and felt his status and its obligations. There was much to be said for the monastic education.

'I should like that,' said the child, wriggling himself warmly into the hollow of Cadfael's shoulder. 'I would have given him my dagger, but he said I should need it, and what would he do with such a thing, when he dared not show it for fear of being thought to have stolen it.'

He seemed to have put away for the present his worries over the two women he had somehow mislaid in the snow, in his gratitude at being relieved of anxiety on his own account. Thirteen years old, they said he was. He had a right to be glad when someone else took charge of him.

'How long have you been there with them?'

'Four days. Thurstan said I'd best wait until someone trusty came by, for there are stories of footpads about the hills and the woods, and in this snow, if I set out alone, I might get lost again. I was lost, two whole days,' said Yves, staring remembered terrors firmly in the eye. 'I slept in a tree, for fear of wolves.' He was not complaining, rather doing his best not to boast. Well, let him talk, easing his heart of loneliness and fright like a man stretching his feet to a good fire after a dangerous journey. The real story he had to tell could wait until proper attention could be paid to it. If all turned out well, he might be able to point the way to both the missing ladies, but what mattered now was to reach Bromfield before complete darkness fell.

They went briskly wherever the forest thinned and the lingering light showed their way clearly. The first floating flakes of new snow drifted languidly on the air as they came down to the Hopton brook, and crossed it on solid ice, Cadfael lighting down to lead the horse over. From that point they bore somewhat to the left, though veering gradually away from the course of the brook, and came to the first of the little tributaries that flowed down into it, from the long, gentle slope on their right hand. Every stream was still, frozen now for many days. The sun was gone, only an angry glow remained in the west, sullen under leaden greyness. The wind was rising, the snow beginning to sting their faces. Here the forest was broken by scattered holdings and fields, and occasionally a sheep shelter, roughly propped with its back to the wind. Shapes began to dissolve into a mere mottle of shadows, but for fugitive gleams of reflected light from surfaces of ice, and the bluish mounds where untrodden snow had drifted deep.

The second brook, still and silent like the rest, was a shallow, reed-fringed, meandering serpent of silver. The horse disliked the feel of the ice under him, and Cadfael dismounted again to lead him over. The wide, glassy surface shone opaque from every angle, except when looking directly down into it, and Cadfael was watching his own foothold as he crossed, for his boots were worn and smooth. Thus his eye caught, for a moment only, the ghostly pallor beneath the ice to his left, before the horse slithered and recovered, hoisting himself into the snowy grass on the further side.

Cadfael was slow to recognise, slower to believe, what he had seen. Half an hour later, and he would not have been able to see it at all. Fifty paces on, with a thicket of bushes between, he halted, and instead of remounting, as Yves expected, put the bridle into the boy's hands, and said with careful calm: 'Wait a moment for me. No, we need not turn off yet, this is not the place where the tracks divide. Something I noticed there. Wait!'

Yves wondered, but waited obediently, as Cadfael turned back to the frozen brook. The pallor had been no illusion from some stray reflected gleam, it was there fixed and still, embedded in the ice. He went down on his knees to look more closely.

The short hairs rose on his neck. Not a yearling lamb, as he had briefly believed it might be. Longer, more shapely, slender and white. Out of the encasing, glassy stillness a pale, pearly oval stared up at him with open eyes. Small, delicate hands had floated briefly before the frost took hold, and hovered open at her sides, a little upraised as if in appeal. The white of her body and the white of her torn shift which was all she wore seemed to Cadfael to be smirched by some soiling colour at the breast, but so faintly that too intent staring caused the mark to shift and fade. The face was fragile, delicate, young.

A lamb, after all. A lost ewe-lamb, a lamb of God, stripped and violated and slaughtered. Eighteen years old? It could well be so.

By this token, Ermina Hugonin was at once found and lost.

# 4

There was nothing to be done here at this hour, alone as he was, and if he lingered, the boy might come to see what kept him so long. He rose from his knees in haste, and went back to where the horse stamped and fidgeted, eager to get back to his stable. The boy was looking round for him curiously, rather than anxiously.

'What was it? Is there something wrong?'

'Nothing to fret you.' Not yet, he thought with a pang, not until you must know. At least let's feed you, and warm you, and reassure you your own life is safe enough, before you need hear word of this. 'I thought I saw a sheep caught in the ice, but I was mistaken.' He mounted, and reached round the boy to take the reins. 'We'd best make haste. We'll have full darkness on us before we reach Bromfield.'

Where the track forked they bore right as they had been instructed, a straight traverse along the slope, easy to follow. The boy's sturdy body grew heavier and softer in Cadfael's arm, the brown head hung sleepy on his shoulder. You at least, thought Cadfael, mute in his anger and grief, we'll put out of harm's way, if we could not save your sister.

'You have not told me your name,' said Yves, yawning. 'I don't know what to call you.'

'My name is Cadfael, a Welshman from Trefriw, but now of Shrewsbury abbey. Where, I think, you were bound.'

'Yes, so we were. But Ermina – my sister's name is Ermina – she must always have her own way. I have far more sense than she has! If she'd listened to me we would never have got separated, and we should all have been safe in Shrewsbury by now. I wanted to come to Bromfield with Brother Elyas – you do know about Brother Elyas? – and so did Sister Hilaria, but not Ermina, she had other plans. This is all her fault!'

And small doubt, by now, that that was true, Brother Cadfael reflected wretchedly, clasping the innocent judge who lay warm and confiding in his arm. But surely our little faults do not deserve so crushing a penalty. Without time to reconsider, to repent, to make reparation. Youth destroyed for a folly, when youth should be allowed its follies on the way to maturity and sense.

They were coming down on to the good, trodden road between Ludlow and Bromfield. 'Praise God!' said Cadfael, sighting the torches at the gatehouse, yellow terrestrial stars glowing through a fragile but thickening curtain of snow. 'We are here!'

They rode in at the gate, to be confronted by a scene of unexpected activity in the great court. The snow within was stamped into intricate patterns of hooves, and about the stables two or three grooms, certainly not of the household, were busy rubbing down horses and leading them to their stalls. Beside the door of the guest-hall Prior Leonard stood in earnest conversation with a lithe young man of middle height, still cloaked and hooded, and his back turned, but it was a back Cadfael knew very well by now. Hugh Beringar had come in person to probe into the first news of the lost Hugonins, and brought, by the look of it, two or three more officers with him.

His ear was as sharp as ever, he turned towards the arrivals and came striding before ever the horse halted. The prior followed, eager and hopeful at sight of two returning where only one went forth.

Cadfael was down by the time they approached, and Yves, dazzled and excited, had recovered from his sleepiness and braced himself to encounter with a nobleman's assurance whoever bore down on him. He set both plump paws to the pommel of the saddle, and vaulted down into the snow. A long way down for his short stature, but he lit like an acrobat, and stretched erect before Beringar's amused and approving eye.

'Make your bow, Yves, to Hugh Beringar, the deputy sheriff of this shire,' said Cadfael. 'And to Prior Leonard of Bromfield, your host here.' And to Hugh, aside, he said fervently, while the boy made his solemn reverences: 'Ask him nothing, yet, get him within!'

Between them they made a reasonable job of it, quick in response to each other from old habit. Yves was soon led away contentedly with Leonard's bony but benevolent hand on his shoulder, to be warmed and fed and made much of before bed. He was young, he would sleep this night. He was cloister-educated, he would stir in response to the bells for office, and find nothing but reassurance, and sleep again heartily.

'For God's sake,' said Cadfael, heaving a great sigh as soon as the boy was safely out of sight, 'come within, somewhere quiet, where we can talk. I never expected you here in person, seeing the ties you have at home . . .' Beringar had taken him companionably by the arm, and was hurrying him into the doorway of the prior's lodging, and eyeing him intently along his shoulder as they shook the snow from boots and cloaks on the threshold. 'We had but a first breath of news of our quarry, I never thought it could tear you away, though thanks be, it did!'

'I've left all in very good order behind me,' said Hugh. He had come to meet his friend expecting a glow of good news, and found himself confronted with a gravity that promised little but trouble. 'If you have burdens on your mind here, Cadfael, at least you may be easy about affairs in Shrewsbury. The very day you left us, our son was born, a fine, lusty lad as yellow-haired as his mother, and the pair of them flourishing. And for good measure, the Worcester girl has given her man a son, too, only one day after. The house is full of exultant women, and no one is going to miss me for these few days.'

'Oh, Hugh, the best of news! I'm happy for you both.' It was right and fitting, Cadfael thought, a life emerging in defiance of a death. 'And all went well for her? She had not too hard a time of it?'

'Oh, Aline has the gift! She's too innocent to understand that there can be pain in a thing so joyful as birth, so she felt none. Faith, even if I hadn't had this errand to occupy me, I was as near being elbowed out of my own house as makes no matter. Your prior's message came very aptly. I have three men here with me, and twenty-two more I have quartered on Josce de Dinan in Ludlow castle, to be at hand if I need them, and to give him a salutary jolt if he really is in two minds about changing sides. He cannot be in any doubt now that I have my eye on him. And now,' said Hugh, drawing up a chair to the fire in the prior's parlour, 'you owe me a story, I fancy, and for my life I can't tell what to expect of it. Here you come riding in with the boy we've been hunting on your saddle-bow, and yet a face on you as bleak as the sky, when you should be beaming. And not a word to be got out of you until he was safe out of earshot. Where did you find him?'

Cadfael sat back with a small groan of weariness and stiffness after his chill ride. There was no longer any urgent need for action. In the night they would never find the place, especially now that the wind was high and the fresh snow altering the landscape on all sides, blowing hillsides naked, filling in hollows, burying what yesterday had uncovered. He could afford to sit still and feel the warmth of the fire on his legs, and tell what he had to tell at his own pace, since there was nothing to be done about it until daylight.

'In an assart in Clee Forest, in shelter with a decent cottar and his wife, who would not let him take his chance alone through the woods until some trustworthy traveller came by to bear him company. Me they considered fit for the task, and he came with me willingly enough.'

'But he was there alone? A pity,' said Hugh with a wry grimace, 'that you did not find his sister, too, while you were about it.'

'I am only too afraid,' said Cadfael, the warmth of the fire heavy on his eyelids, 'that I have indeed found her.'

The silence lasted a shorter time than it seemed. The significance of that last utterance there was no mistaking.

'Dead?' asked Hugh bluntly.

'And cold.' Cold as ice, encased in ice. The first bitter frost had provided her a glassy coffin, preserving her flesh immaculate and unchanged to accuse her destroyer.

'Tell me,' said Hugh, intent and still.

Cadfael told him. The whole story would have to be told again when Prior Leonard came, for he, too, must help to stand between the boy and too early and too sudden knowledge of his loss. But in the meantime it was a relief to heave the burden from his heart, and know that this was now Hugh's responsibility as much as his own.

'Can you find the place again?'

'By daylight, yes, I'll find it. In darkness, no use trying. It will be a fearful thing . . . We shall have to take axes to hew her out of the ice, unless the thaw comes.' It was a forlorn hope, there was no possible sign of a thaw.

'That we'll face when we come to it,' said Hugh sombrely. 'Tonight we'd best get the boy's story out of him, and see if we can gather from it how she ever came where you happened on her. And where, in heaven's name, is the nun who fled with her?'

'According to Yves, he left her in Cleeton, safe enough. And the girl – poor fool! – he says went off with a lover. But I took him no further into matters, it was towards the end of the day, and the most urgent thing was to get one, at least, into safety.'

'True enough, and you did well. We'll wait for the prior, and until the boy's fed and warmed and easy. Then between us we'll hope to get out of him all he knows, and more, perhaps, than he realises he knows, without betraying that he's lost a sister. Though he'll have to learn it soon or late,' said

Hugh unhappily. 'Who else knows the poor girl's face?'

'But not tonight. Let him sleep soundly tonight. Time enough,' said Cadfael heavily, 'when we've brought her in and made her as comely as may be, before he need see her.'

Supper and security had done much for Yves, and his own natural resilience had done even more. He sat in the prior's parlour before Compline, face to face with Hugh Beringar, and with Prior Leonard and Brother Cadfael in watchful attendance, and told his story with bluntness and brevity.

'She is very *brave*,' he said judicially, giving his sister her due, 'but very obstinate and self-willed. All the way from Worcester I did feel she had something up her sleeve, and was taking advantage of having to run away. We had to go roundabout at first, and slowly, because there were bands of soldiers roaming even miles from the town, so it took us a long time to get safely to Cleobury, and there we stayed one night, and that was the night Brother Elyas was there, too, and he came with us as far as Foxwood, and wanted us to come with him into Bromfield for safety, and I wanted that, too, and so did Sister Hilaria. From here we could have got an escort into Shrewsbury, and it would not have been a much longer way. But Ermina would not have it! She must always have her own way, and she *would* go on over the hills to Godstoke. No use my arguing, she never listens, she claims that being the elder makes her the wiser. And if we others had gone with Brother Elyas she would still have gone on over the hills alone, so what could we do but go with her?' He blew out his lips in a disgusted breath.

'Certainly you could not leave her,' agreed Beringar reasonably. 'So you went on, to spend the next night at Cleeton?'

'It's close by Cleeton, a solitary holding. Ermina had a nurse once who married a tenant of that manor, so we knew we could get a bed there. The man's name is John Druel. We got there in the afternoon, and I remembered afterwards that Ermina was talking apart with the son of the house, and then he went away, and we didn't see him again until evening. I never thought of it then, but now I'm sure she sent him with a message. That was what she intended all along. For a man came late in the evening, with horses, and took her away. I heard the stir, and I got up and looked out . . . Two horses there were, and he was just helping her up into the saddle . . .'

'He?' said Hugh. 'You knew him?'

'Not his name, but I do remember him. When my father was alive he used to visit sometimes, if there was hunting, or for Christmas or Easter. Many guests used to come, we always had company. He must be son or nephew to one of my father's friends. I never paid him much attention, nor he never noticed me, I was too young. But I do remember his face, and I think . . . I *think* he has been visiting Ermina now and then in Worcester.'

If he had, they must have been very decorous visits, with a sponsoring sister always in attendance.

'You think she sent him word to come and fetch her?' asked Hugh. 'This was no abduction? She went willingly?'

'She went *gaily*!' Yves asserted indignantly. 'I heard her laughing. Yes, she sent for him, and he came. And that was why she *would go* that way, for he must have a manor close by, and she knew she could whistle him to her. She will have a great dower,' said the baron's heir solemnly, his round, childish cheeks flushing red with outrage. 'And my sister would never endure to have her marriage made for her in the becoming way, if it went against *her* choice. I never knew a rule she would not break, shamelessly . . .'

His chin shook, a weakness instantly and ruthlessly suppressed. All the arrogant pride of all the feudal houses of Anjou and England in this small package, and he loved as much as he hated her, or more, and never, never must he see her mute and violated and stripped to her shift.

Hugh took up the questioning with considerate calm. 'And what did you do?' The jolt back into facts was salutary.

'No one else had heard,' said Yves, rallying, 'unless it was the boy who carried her message, and he had surely been told *not* to hear anything. I was still dressed, there being only one bed, which the women had, so I rushed out to try and stop them. Older she may be, but *I* am my father's heir! I am the head of our family now.'

'But afoot,' said Hugh, pricking him back to the real and sorry situation, 'you could hardly keep their pace. And they were away before you could hale them back to answer to you.'

'No, I couldn't keep up, but I could follow. It had begun to snow, they left tracks, and I knew they could not be going very far. Far enough to lose me!' he owned, and bit a lip that did not quite know whether to curl up or down. 'I followed as long as I could by their tracks, and it was uphill, and the wind rose, and there was so much snow the tracks were soon covered. I couldn't find the way forward or back. I tried to keep what I thought was the direction they'd taken, but I don't know how much I may have wandered, or where I went. I was quite lost. All night I was in the forest, and the second night Thurstan found me and took me home with him. Brother Cadfael knows. Thurstan said there were outlaws abroad, and I should stay with him until some safe traveller came by. And so I did. And now I don't know,' he said, visibly sinking into his proper years, 'where Ermina went with her lover, or what has become of Sister Hilaria. She would wake to find the two of us gone, and I don't know what she would do. But she was with John and his wife, they surely wouldn't let her come to harm.'

'This man who took your sister away,' pressed Beringar. 'You don't know his name, but you do remember he was acceptable in your father's house. If he has a manor in the hills, within easy reach of Cleeton, no doubt we can trace him. I take it he might, had your father lived, have been a possible suitor for your sister, even in a more approved fashion?'

'Oh, yes,' said the boy seriously, 'I think he well might. There were any number of young men used to come, and Ermina, even when she was only fourteen or fifteen, would ride and hunt with the best of them. They were all men of substance, or heirs to good estates. I never noticed which of them she favoured.' He would have been playing with toy warriors and falling off his first pony then, uninterested in sisters and their admirers. 'This one is very handsome,' he said generously. 'Much fairer than me. And taller than you, sir.' That would not make him a rarity, Beringar's modest length of steel and sinew had been under-estimated by many a man to his cost. 'I think he must be about twenty-five or six. But his name I don't know. There were so many came visiting to us.'

'Now there is one more thing,' said Cadfael, 'in which Yves may be able to help us, if I may keep him from his bed a few minutes more. You know, Yves, you spoke of Brother Elyas, who left you at Foxwood?'

Yves nodded, attentive and wondering.

'Brother Elyas is here in the infirmary. After leaving for home, his errand done, he was attacked by footpads in the night and badly hurt, and the countrymen who found him brought him here to be cared for. I am sure he is on the mend now, but he has not been able to tell us anything about what happened to him. He has no memory of these recent days, only in his sleep he seems to struggle with some half-recalled distress. Waking, his mind is blank, but in sleep he has mentioned you, though not by name. The boy would have gone with me, he said. Now if he claps eyes on you, safe and well, it may be the sight will jog his memory. Will you try it with me?'

Yves rose willingly, if somewhat apprehensively, looking to Beringar for confirmation that he had done all that was required of him here. 'I am sorry he has come to harm. He was kind . . . Yes, whatever I can do for him . . .'

On the way to the sickroom, with no other witness by, he slipped his hand thankfully, like an awed child, into Brother Cadfael's comfortable clasp, and clung tightly.

'You mustn't mind that he is bruised and disfigured. All that will pass, I promise you.'

Brother Elyas was lying mute and still, while a young brother read to him from the life of Saint Remigius. His bruises and distortions were already subsiding, he seemed free from pain, he had taken food during the day, and at the office bell his lips would move soundlessly on the words of the liturgy. But his open eyes dwelt unrecognisingly upon the boy who entered, and wandered away again languidly into the shadowy corners of the room. Yves crept to the bedside on tiptoe, great-eyed.

'Brother Elyas, here is Yves come to see you. You remember Yves? The boy you met at Cleobury, and parted from at Foxwood.'

No, nothing, nothing but the faint tremor of desperate anxiety troubling the patient face. Yves ventured close, and timidly laid his hand over the long, lax hand that lay upon the covers, but it remained chill and unresponsive under his touch.

'I am sorry you have been hurt. We walked together those few miles. I wish we had kept your company all the way . . .'

Brother Elyas stared and quivered, shaking his head helplessly.

'No, let him be,' said Cadfael, sighing. 'If we press him he grows agitated. No matter, he has time. Only let his body revive as it is doing, and memory can wait. It was worth the trying, but he is not ready for us yet. Come, you're dropping with sleep, let's get you safely into your bed.'

They arose at dawn, Cadfael and Hugh and his men, and went out into a world which had again changed its shape in the night, hillocks levelled and hollows filled in, and a spume of fine snow waving like a languid plume from every crest, in the subsiding winds. They took axes with them, and a litter of leather thongs strung between two poles, and a linen cloth to cover her, and they went in dour silence, none of them with anything to say until words were to the point for the grim work in hand. The fall had stopped at the coming of daylight, as it had now ever since that first night when Yves had set off doggedly to trail his errant sister. Iron frost had begun the next night, and that same night some nocturnal beast had ravished and murdered the girl they went out now to seek, for the ice had taken her to itself very shortly after she had been put into an already congealing stream. Of that Cadfael was certain.

They found her, after some questing and probing in new snow, swept the fresh fall from the ice, and looked down upon her, a girl in a mirror, a girl spun from glass.

'Good God!' said Hugh in awe. 'She's younger than the boy!' So slight, so childlike, did the shadowy form appear.

But they were there, perforce, to break her rest and take her away for Christian burial, though it seemed almost a violation to shatter the smoothness of the ice that encased her. They did it with care, well aside from the delicate, imprisoned flesh, and it proved hard work enough. For all the bite of the frost, they were sweating when they hoisted out heavily the girl and her cold coffin, laid her like a piece of statuary in the thongs of the litter, covered her with the linen cloth, and carried her slowly back to Bromfield. Not a drop fell from the ice until they had it stowed privately in the chill, bare mortuary of the priory. Then the glittering edges began to soften and slide, and drip into the channel where the water flowed away from the washing of the dead.

The girl lay remote and pale within her lucid shroud, and yet grew steadily more human and closer to life, to pain and pity and violence, and all the mortal lot of mankind. Cadfael dared not leave the place for long, because the boy Yves was now up and active, and inquisitive about everything, and no one could guess where he would appear next. He was well brought up, and his manners were charming, but with his inbred conviction of privilege and his very proper thirteen-year-old energy, he might yet prove a hazard.

It was past ten, and High Mass in progress, when the shell of ice had dwindled so far that the girl began to emerge, the tips of thin, pale fingers and stretched toes, her nose, as yet only a minute pearl, and the first curling strands of hair, a fine lace on either side her forehead. It was those curls that first caught Cadfael's acute attention. For they were short. He wound a few fine threads on his finger, and they made but a turn and a half. And they were no darker than dark gold, and would be even fairer as they dried. Then he bent to the calm stare of her open eyes, still thinly veiled with ice. Their colour seemed to him the soft, dim purple of irises, or the darkest grey of lavender flowers.

The face emerged as Mass ended. After the air touched her, bruises began to darken on cheek and mouth. The tips of her small breasts broke the glaze over them. And now Cadfael could see clearly the smear that darkened her flesh and her linen there, on the right side, a reddish mark like a graze, faintly mottled from shoulder to breast. He knew the traces of blood. The ice had taken her before the stilling water could wash the stain away. Now it might pale as the remaining ice thawed, but he would know how it had lain, and where to look for the source.

Well before noon she was freed of her shell, and softening into his hands, slender and young, her small, shapely head covered all over with an aureole of short bronze curls, like an angel in an Annunciation. Cadfael went to fetch Prior Leonard, and they cared for her together, not yet to wash her body, not until Hugh Beringar had viewed it, but to compose her worthily in her everlasting stillness. To the throat they covered her with a linen sheet, and made her ready to be seen.

Hugh came, and stood by her silently. Eighteen could well be her age, so white and slim and tranquil, gone far beyond them. And beautiful, as reported? Yes, that she was. But was this the dark, headstrong, spoiled daughter of the nobility, who had insisted on her own way in despite of the times, the winter, the war and all?

'Look!' said Cadfael, and turned back the linen to show the crumpled folds of her shift, just as they had emerged from the ice. The dull, reddish smear speckled her right shoulder, the edge of her shift, and the creases over her right breast.

'Stabbed?' said Hugh, looking up into Cadfael's face.

'There is no wound. See now!' He drew down the linen and showed the flesh beneath. Only a smudge or two showed on her pale skin. He wiped them away, and she shone white without blemish. 'Certainly not stabbed. The night frost that took her closed in very quickly, and preserved these marks, faint as they are. But she did not bleed. Or if she did,' he added bleakly, 'it was not from knife-wounds, and not there. More likely she fought him – him or them, such wolves hunt happiest in packs! – and drew blood. A clawed face, it might be, or a hand or wrist as she tried to force him off. Bear it in mind, Hugh, as I will also.' He covered her again reverently. The alabaster face looked up from veiled eyes into the vault, supremely unmoved, and her head of clipped curls was beginning to shine like a halo as it dried.

'She begins to bruise,' said Hugh, and drew a fingertip over her cheekbone and down to the faint discolorations round her lips. 'But her throat is unmarked. She was not strangled.'

'Smothered, surely, in the act of ravishment.'

They were all three so intent upon the dead girl that they had not heard the footsteps that approached the closed door of the room, and even had they been listening, the footsteps were light enough to be missed, though they came briskly and without conceal. The first they knew of the boy's coming was the white burst of reflected light from the snow, as the door was opened wide to the wall, and Yves marched over the threshold with the innocent boldness of his kind. No creeping ingratiatingly through a narrow chink for him, nothing he did was done by half-measures. The abruptness with which they all whirled upon him, and their frowning consternation gave him sharp pause and mild offence. Both Hugh and Prior Leonard stepped quickly between him and the trestle on which the body lay.

'You should not be here, child,' said the prior, flustered.

'Why should I not, Father? No one has told me I should be at fault. I was looking for Brother Cadfael.'

'Brother Cadfael will come out to you in a little while. Go back to the guest-hall and wait for him there . . .'

It was late to ward him off, he had seen, beyond the sheltering shoulders, enough to tell him what lay behind. The linen sheet, quickly drawn up, the unmistakable shape, and one glimpse of short, bright hair where the linen, too hastily drawn, had folded back on itself. His face grew still and wary, his eyes large, and his tongue was silenced.

The prior laid a hand gently on his shoulder and made to turn him back to the doorway. 'Come, you and I will go together. Whatever is to be told, you shall hear later, but leave it now.'

Yves stood his ground, and went on staring.

'No,' said Cadfael unexpectedly, 'let him come.' He came out from behind the trestle, and took a step or two towards the boy. 'Yves, you are a sensible man, no need to pretend to you, after your travels, that violence and danger and cruelty do not exist, and men do not die. We have here a dead body, not known to us. I would have you look at it, if you will, and say if you know this face. You need not fear anything ill to see.'

The boy drew near steadily and with set face, and eyed the shrouded form with nothing worse than awe. Doubtful if it had ever entered his head, thought Cadfael, that this might be his sister, or indeed any woman. He had seen the dilated eyes fix on the short, curling hair; it was a young man Yves expected. Nevertheless, Cadfael would have approached this somewhat differently if he had not been certain already, in his own mind, that this dead girl, whoever she might be, was not Ermina Hugonin. Beyond that he had only a pitiful suspicion. But Yves would know.

He drew down the sheet from her face. The boy's hands, clenched together before him, tightened abruptly. He drew in breath hard, but made no other sound for a long moment. He shook a little, but not much. The wide-eyed stare he raised to Cadfael's questioning face was one of shocked bewilderment, almost of disbelief.

'But how is this possible? I thought . . . I don't understand! She . . .' He gave up, shaking his head violently, and hung over her again in fascinated pity and wonder. 'I do know her, of course I do, but how *can* she be here, and dead? This is Sister Hilaria, who came with us from Worcester.'

# 5

Between them they coaxed and shooed him away across the snowy court. Yves went still in his daze, frowning helplessly over this sudden and inexplicable reappearance in another place of someone he had left safe under a friendly roof some miles away. He was too shaken and puzzled at first to realise fully the meaning of what he had seen, but halfway to the guest-hall it hit him like a blow on the head. He baulked, gulped breath in a great sob, and startled himself, if no one else, by bursting into tears. Prior Leonard would have clucked over him like a dismayed hen, but Cadfael clapped him briskly on the shoulder, and said practically:

'Bear up, my heart, for we're going to need you. We have a malefactor to trace now, and a wrong to avenge, and who but you can lead us straight to the place where you left her? Where else should we start?'

The fit passed as abruptly as it had begun. Yves scrubbed at his smudged cheeks hastily with his sleeve, and looked round alertly enough to see what he could read in Hugh Beringar's face. In Hugh the authority lay. The role of the cloistered was to shelter and counsel and offer prayers, but justice and law were the business of the sheriff. Yves was not a baron's heir for nothing, he knew all about the hierarchies.

'That's true, I can take you straight from Foxwood to John Druel's holding, it lies higher than Cleeton village.' He caught eagerly at Hugh's sleeve, wise enough to ask nicely instead of demanding. '*May* I go with you and show the way?'

'You may, if you'll stay close and do all as you're bidden.' Hugh was already committed, Cadfael had seen to that. But far better for the boy to be out in men's company, and active, than to sit fretting here alone. 'We'll find you a pony your size. Run, then, get your cloak and come after us to the stables.'

Yves ran, restored by the prospect of doing something to the purpose. Beringar looked after him thoughtfully. 'Go with him, Father Prior, if you will, see that he has some food with him, for it may be a long day, and no matter how large a dinner he's eaten half an hour ago, he'll be hungry before night.' And to Cadfael he said, as they turned together towards the stables: 'You, I know, will do whatever you fancy doing, and I'm always glad of your company, if your charges, live and dead, can spare you. But you've had some hard riding these last days . . .'

'For an ageing man,' said Cadfael.

'As well I did not say so! I doubt you could outlast me, for all your great burden of years. What of Brother Elyas, though?'

'He needs no more from me, now, than a visit or two each day, to see that nothing's turned back for him and gone amiss. His body is recovering well. And as for the part of his mind that's astray, my being here won't cure it. It will come back of itself one day, or it will cease to be missed. He's well looked after. As *she* was not!' he said sadly.

'How did you know,' asked Hugh, 'that it could not be the child's sister?'

'The cropped hair, first. A month now since they left Worcester, long enough to provide her that halo we have seen. Why should the other girl clip her locks? And then, the colouring. Ermina, so Herward said, is almost black of hair and eye, darker brown than her brother. So is not this lady. And they did say, as I remember, the nun was also young, no more than five and twenty or so. No, I was sure he was safe from that worst threat. Thus far!' said Cadfael soberly. 'Now we have to find her, and make sure he never shall have to uncover another known face and set a name to it. I have the same obligations as you, and I'm coming with you.'

'Go get yourself booted and ready, then,' said Hugh, without surprise, 'and I'll saddle you one of my own remounts. I came well prepared for any tangles you might get me into. I know you of old.'

To Foxwood was a fairly easy ride, being a used highway, but from Foxwood they climbed by even higher ways, and on tracks more broken and steep. The vast flank of Titterstone Clee rose here to a bleak plateau, with the highest ground towering over them on the left hand, in cloud that dropped lower as the afternoon passed its peak. Yves rode close at Hugh's side, intent and important.

'We can leave the village away on our right, the holding lies above here. Over this ridge there's a bowl of fields John has, and a sheep-pen up the hill.'

Hugh reined in suddenly, and sat with head raised, sniffing the air with stretched nostrils. 'Are you getting the same waft I have in my nose? What should a husbandman be burning at this end of the year?'

The faint but ominous stink hung in the air, stirred by a rising wind. One of the men-at-arms at Beringar's back said with certainty: 'Three or four days old, and snowed over, but I smell timber.'

Hugh spurred forward up the climbing track, between bushes banked with snow, and up to the crest where the ground declined into the hollow. In the sheltered bowl trees grew, providing a wind-break for byre and barn and house, and partly screening the holding from view. They could see the stone walls of the sheep-pen on the rising ground beyond, but not until they had wound their way through the first belt of trees did John Druel's tenant-farm reveal itself to their appalled sight. Yves uttered a muted howl of dismay, and reached to clutch at Brother Cadfael's arm.

The corner-posts of blackened buildings stood stark out of the drifts of snow, the timbers of roof and barn, what remained of them, jutted in charred ruin where they had fallen. A desolation in which nothing moved, nothing lived, even the near-by trees shrivelled and brown. The Druel homestead was emptied of livestock, stores and people, and burned to the ground.

They threaded the forlorn wreckage in grim silence, Hugh's eyes intent on every detail. The iron frost had prevented worse stinks than burning, for in the littered yard they found the hacked bodies of two of the household dogs. Though some two or three fresh falls of snow had covered the traces since the holocaust, it seemed that a party of raiders at least ten or twelve strong had committed this outrage, driving off the sheep and the household cow, emptying the barn, and probably the house, too, of anything portable, stringing the fowls together by the legs, for scattered feathers still blew about the ground and clung to the blackened beams.

Hugh dismounted, and clambered in among the wreckage of the house and barns. His men were quartering all the ground within and without the enclosing wall, probing the drifts.

'They've killed them,' said Yves in a small, hollow voice. 'John and his wife, and Peter, and the shepherd – killed them all, or carried them off, as they carried off Sister Hilaria.'

'Hush!' said Cadfael. 'Never jump to meet the worst until you've looked about you well. You know what they're looking for?' The searchers were turning to exchange looks and shrugs, and drawing together again to the yard. 'Bodies! And they've found none. Only the dogs, poor creatures. They did their proper work, and gave the alarm. Now we'd best hope they gave it in time.'

Hugh came picking his way back from the barn, beating soiled palms together. 'No dead here to find. Either they had warning enough to run for it, or they've been dragged off with the raiders. And I doubt if masterless men living wild would bother with captives. Kill they might, but take prisoners, of this simple kind, that I doubt. But I wonder which way they came? As we did, or by tracks of their own, along the hillside here above? If there were no more than ten of them, they'd keep to their measure, and the village might be too strong to tempt them.'

'There was one sheep slaughtered by the fold,' said his sergeant, back from the hillside. 'There's a traverse comes along the slope there, that might be their path if they wanted to avoid

Cleeton and pick off some meat less well defended.'

'Then Druel may have got his family away towards the village.' Hugh pondered, frowning at the drifts that had covered all traces of coming and going of men and beasts. 'If the dogs gave tongue for the sheep, there may have been time. Let's at least go and ask in the village what they know of it. We may yet find them all alive,' he said, clapping Yves reassuringly on the shoulder, 'even if they've lost their home and goods.'

'But not Sister Hilaria,' said Yves, clinging to a quarrel which had become his own, and bitterly felt. 'If they could run away in time, why could they not save Sister Hilaria?'

'That you shall ask them, if by God's grace we do find them. I do not forget Sister Hilaria. Come, we've found all we are going to find here.'

'One small thing,' said Cadfael. 'When you heard the horses, Yves, in the dark, and ran out to try to follow your sister, which way did they lead you from here?'

Yves turned to view the sorry remains of the house from which he had run. 'To the right, there, behind the house. There's a little stream comes down, it was not frozen then – they started up the slope beside it. Not towards the top of the hills, but climbing round the flank.'

'Good! That direction we may try, another day. I'm done, Hugh, we can go.'

They mounted and turned back by the way they had come, out of the desolation and ruin of the hollow, over the ridge between the trees, and down the track towards the village of Cleeton. A hard place, bleak to farm, meagre to crop, but good for sheep, the rangy upland sheep that brought the leanest meat but the longest fleeces. Across the uphill edge of the settlement there was a crude but solid stockade, and someone was on the watch for strangers arriving, for a whistle went before them into the huddle of houses, shrill and piercing. By the time they rode in there were three or four sturdy fellows on hand to receive them. Hugh smiled. Outlaws living wild, unless they had considerable numbers and sufficient arms, might be wise to fight shy of Cleeton.

He gave them good-day and made himself known. Doubtful if men in isolated places hoped much from the king's protection, or the empress's either, but a county sheriff did offer hope of his being on their side in the fight to survive. They brought their reeve, and answered questions eagerly. Yes, they knew of the destruction of John Druel's holding, and yes, John was safe here, sheltered and fed by the village, at least alive if he had lost everything but life. And his wife and son with him, and the shepherd who laboured for him, all saved. A long-legged boy ran eagerly to bring Druel to answer for himself.

At sight of the lean, wiry husbandman approaching, Yves scrambled down from his saddle and ran to meet him, incoherent in his relief. The man came up with an arm about the boy's shoulders.

'My lord, he says you've been up there . . . where my home was. God knows how grateful I am for the kindness here, that won't let us starve when all our goods and gear are gone, but what's to become of us poor souls that work hard to make a living, if it's to be clawed away in a night, and the roof burned over us? It's hard to live solitary in the hills,' he said roundly, 'at best. But outlawry the like of this we never thought to see.'

'Friend,' said Beringar ruefully, 'you may take it I never looked for it, either. Reparation for your losses I cannot offer, but some of what was yours may still be recovered, if we can trace the raiders who took it from you. The boy, here, lodged with you several nights since, and his sister with him . . .'

'And vanished from us in the night,' said John, and gave Yves a disapproving frown.

'That we know, he has told us, and he, at least, had sound reasons, and took his own grave risks. But what we need from you is some account of this attack that fell upon you . . . when?'

'Two nights after the lady and the lad fled us. The night of the fourth of the month, it was, but very late, towards dawn. We woke to hear the dogs going mad, and rushed out thinking there might be wolves, in such hard weather. For the dogs were chained, d'you see? – and wolves they were, but of the two-legged kind! Once out, we could hear the sheep bellowing up the hill and see torches up there. Then they began to come bounding down the slope, knowing the dogs had given the alarm. I don't know how many men, there might have been a dozen or more. We could not stand, we could only run. From the ridge there we saw the barn take fire. The wind was wild, we knew it must all burn out. And here we are, master, bereft, to make a new start from villeinry, if there's a yardland to be had under any lord. But with our lives, thanks be to God!'

'So they came first to your sheep-fold,' said Hugh. 'From which direction along that slope?'

'From the south,' said John at once, 'but not from the road – higher on the hill. They came down at us.'

'And you have no notion who they may be, or from where? You've had no rumour beforehand of outlaws setting up anywhere near?'

No, there had been no warning until then. It had come out of the blue, between midnight of the fourth, and pre-dawn of the fifth.

'One more question,' said Hugh. 'Since you brought off your family with their lives, what became of the nun of Worcester who lodged with you the night of the second, along with this young man and his sister? That they left you that night we know. What of the nun?'

'Why, she was well out of it,' said Druel thankfully. 'I had not her on my heart that night of the burning. She was gone, the afternoon before. Rather late it was for the daylight, but not too far gone. And a safe escort along the way, I reckoned she would do well enough. In a sad, distracted way she'd been, the poor girl, when she found she'd been left alone, but she did not know where to look for her chicks, and neither did we, and what was she to do?'

'Someone came for her?' asked Hugh.

'A Benedictine brother. She knew him, he had walked a part of the way with them before, and urged them to go with him to Bromfield, she said. So he urged then, and when she told him how she was forsaken, he said all the more she should put herself and her trouble into the hands of others, who would search for her charges for her, and keep her safe until they were found. He'd had to make his way here from Foxwood, asking after her,' said John, making allowance for the waning of the day when he had reached them. 'I never saw woman so thankful to have a friend take her in care. She went with him, and I make no doubt she came safe to Bromfield.'

Yves stood dumb. 'She came,' said Hugh drily, rather to himself than to any other. Safe? Yes, take it as large as words will hold, yes, she came safe. Sinless, conscientious, brave, who at this moment was safer than Sister Hilaria, an innocent gone straight to God?

'A strange thing followed, though,' said Druel, 'for the next day, while we were here telling our tale, and the good folk making room for us in their homes, like Christians as they are, there came a young man afoot, up from the road by the proper way, and asked after just such a party as we had housed. Had any here news, he said, of a young nun of Worcester, in company with two young gentlefolk, brother and sister, making towards Shrewsbury. We were full of our own troubles, but we told him all we knew, and how they were all gone from us before ever this evil befell. And he listened and went away. Up to the wreck of my holding, first, but after that I cannot tell where.'

'A stranger to all here?' asked Hugh, looking round the circle that had gathered, for by then the women had come forth, and hung attentive on the outskirts.

'Never seen before,' said the reeve emphatically.

'What manner of man, then?'

'Why, by his dress husbandman or shepherd like any of us here, a brown homespun man. Not so much as thirty years old, nearer five or six and twenty. Bigger than your lordship, but built like you, light and long. And dark, a black-rimmed eye on him with a yellow glint, like a hawk. And black hair under his hood.'

The women had drawn closer in silence, quiet-eyed and prick-eared. Their interest in the stranger was all the plainer because not one of them voiced it, or volunteered any detail concerning him. Whoever he was, he had made an impression upon the women of Cleeton, and they did not mean to miss anything they could glean about him, or surrender anything they had already gleaned.

'Dark-skinned,' said Druel, 'and beaked like a hawk, too. A very comely man.' Yes, so the attentive eyes of the women said. 'There was something a thought slow about his speech, now I come to recall . . .'

Hugh took him up alertly on that. 'As though he were not at home in the common English?'

John had not thought of that for himself; he considered it stolidly. 'It might be that. Or as if he had a small stumble of the tongue, like.'

Well, if English was not his proper tongue, what was? Welsh? Easily possible here along the borders, but what would a Welshman be doing asking after the fugitives from Worcester? Angevin, then? Ah, that was another matter.

'If ever you should hear or see more of him,' said Hugh, 'send me word into Ludlow or Bromfield, and you shall not be losers. And for you, friend, let's own honestly there's little chance of recovering all or most of your losses, but some of your stock we may yet win back for you if we can trace these outlaws to their lair. We'll do our best to that end, be sure.'

He wheeled his horse, and led the way towards the downward track, the others following, but he did not hurry, for one of the young women had drawn off in that direction, and was eyeing him meaningly over her shoulder. As Hugh came by she closed alongside, and laid a hand to his stirrup-leather. She knew what she was about, she had moved far enough to be out of earshot of the village.

'My lord . . .' She looked up at him with sharp blue eyes, and spoke in a purposeful undertone. 'One more thing I can tell you about the dark man, that no one else saw. I said no word, for fear they would close up against him if they knew. He was a very well-looking man, I trusted him, even if he was not what he seemed . . .'

'In what particular?' asked Hugh, just as quietly.

'He kept his cloak close about him, my lord, and in the cold that was no marvel. But when he went away I followed a little, and I saw how the folds hung at his left side. Country lad or no, he wore a sword.'

'So they went from here together,' said Yves, as they rode down towards the highroad, where they must haste if they were to use the remainder of the daylight. He had been very silent, struggling with revelations that seemed only to make the pattern of events more complex and entangled. 'He came back to look for us all, and found only Sister Hilaria. It was evening already, they would be caught in the darkness and the snow. And these same robbers and murderers who have ruined poor John must have attacked them, and left them both for dead.'

'So it would seem,' said Hugh sombrely. 'We have a plague among us that needs burning out before it spreads. But what are we to make of this simple countryman who wore a sword under his cloak?'

'And asking after us!' Yves recalled, marvelling. 'But I know no one like that.'

'What like was the young lord who took away your sister?'

'Not black, nor like a hawk, rather fair-skinned, and fair in the hair, too. And besides, even if he came seeking the two of us she'd left behind, he would not come up from the highroad, not according to the way we set off when I followed them. And he would not come dressed as a peasant, either. Nor alone.'

All of which was shrewd sense. There were, of course, other possibilities. The men of Gloucester, elated by their gains, might well be sending agents in disguise into these regions, probing for any weak spots, and such envoys, thought Cadfael, might have been told to pursue, at the same time, the search for Laurence d'Angers' nephew and niece, strayed in the Worcester panic.

'Let it lie by a while,' said Beringar, half-grim and half-appreciative, as if he looked forward to interesting encounters. 'We shall certainly hear more of Cleeton's dark stranger, if we just bide quiet and bear his image in mind.'

They were within two miles of Ludlow before the expected snow began with the dusk. They drew close cloak and capuchon, and rode sturdily with heads down, but so close to home that they were in no danger of losing the road. Hugh parted from them under the walls of Ludlow, to ride in to his company there, leaving two of his men to escort Cadfael and the boy the short way on to Bromfield. Even Yves had lost his tongue by then, a little drunk with fresh air and exercise, and already growing hungry, for all he had eaten his hunk of bread and strip of hard bacon long before. He sat braced and stolid in the saddle, hunched under his hood, but emerged from it with a face like a rosy apple as soon as they lighted down in the great court at the priory. Vespers was long over. Prior Leonard was hovering, watchful and uneasy, for the return of his fledgling, and ventured out into the thick haze of snow to reclaim him and bring him in to supper.

It was after Compline when Beringar rode in, let his tired mount be led away to the stables, and came to find Cadfael, who was sitting by the bed where Brother Elyas already slept his secret, remote and troubled sleep. At sight of Hugh's face, full of hard tidings, Cadfael laid a finger to his lip, and rose to steal away from the bedside into the anteroom, where they could talk without disturbing the sleeper.

'Our friend above Cleeton,' said Hugh, sitting back with a great sigh against the panelled wall, 'is not the only one who has fallen victim, Cadfael. We have the devil among us, no question. Ludlow's in a hum tonight. It seems one of Dinan's archers has an old father at a hamlet south of Henley, a free tenant holding from Mortimer, and today the lad went off to visit, to see how the old man was making out in this hard weather. A holding not two miles from Ludlow, though solitary. He found the place as we found Druel's homestead. Not burned, though – smoke or flames would have been seen, and brought Dinan out with all his force like a swarm of bees disturbed. But swept clear of life, goods, gear and all. And there the folk did not escape. Butchered, every one, except for one poor idiot wretch the archer found wandering from house to house, foraging for any crumbs left to live on.'

Brother Cadfael gaped at him in appalled wonder. 'That they should dare, so near a strong town!'

'Trying out their claws, in despite of a well-found garrison. And the one man left alive, who hid in the woods until the raiders left, may be uncertain in his wits, but he saw it all, and has given an account that makes excellent sense, and for my part, I think him a good witness. And he says there were about twenty men, and they had daggers, axes and swords among them. Three, he says, were mounted. They came about midnight, and in a few hours had driven off all the stock and departed into the night. And he has small notion of how many days he has been solitary and starving there, but such things as the changes of weather he understands very well, and he says, and will not be shifted, that this took place on the night of the first hard frost, when all the brooks stopped flowing.'

'I take your meaning,' said Cadfael, and gnawed his knuckles in fierce thought. 'The same two-legged wolves? The same night, surely. The first hard frost! About midnight this slaughter and pillage by Henley . . . As if they set out deliberately to blacken Dinan's face!'

'Or mine,' said Hugh grimly.

'Or King Stephen's! Well, so they moved off with their spoils maybe two hours after midnight. They would not move fast, driving cattle and carrying food and grain. Not long before dawn they ransacked and burned John Druel's holding, high on

Clee. And in between – would you not say, Hugh? – in between they happened on Brother Elyas and Sister Hilaria, and after their fashion let loose in a little exuberant sport, leaving both dead or dying. Could there be two such bands out on their grisly business on the same night? A wild night, a blizzard night, that might well keep even thieves and vagabonds close to home. There are here men who know these parts like their own palms, Hugh, and neither snow nor frost can cage them.'

'Two such bands?' said Hugh, darkly pondering. 'No, that's out of the reckoning. And consider the line they took that night. The night's ventures began here under our noses – that's the furthest range of their foray. They returned eastward, crossing the highway – for somewhere there your Brother Elyas was found – and before dawn they were rounding the high shoulder of Titterstone Clee, where they burned out Druel's holding. It may not even have been in their plan, simply a frolic by men drunk with success. But it was on their way home, for they'd want to be snug and unseen by dawn. Agreed?'

'Agreed. And are you thinking, Hugh, what I am thinking? Yves rushes out to recall his sister from her folly, and strikes off from that holding uphill, perhaps not on the same level, but surely in the same direction your outlaws took on their way home, two nights later. Somewhere in those uplands lies the manor to which his sister fled with her lover. Does it not look as though he may have taken her to a house far too close neighbour to the devil to be a safe place either for him or for her?'

'I have already made my dispositions,' Hugh assured him with grim satisfaction, 'with that in mind.

There's a great swathe of upland there, some of it forested, some of it rock, and bleak as death, too barren even for sheep. The workable manors there go no higher than Druel's homestead, and even there nest in the sheltered places. Tomorrow at first light I'm going out with Dinan to follow that same line the boy took, and see if I can find what he lost himself seeking, the manor where the girl was taken. First, if we can, let's get her safe out of it. Then we may go after this challenger who spits in the face of law, with no hostages at stake.'

'But leave the boy here!' said Cadfael, more peremptorily than he had intended.

Hugh looked down at him with a wry and burdened smile. 'We shall be away before ever he opens his eyes. Do you think I dare risk confronting him with another and dearer corpse, with your fierce eye on me? No, if luck's with us we'll bring him his sister, either intact or a wife irreclaimable, and they shall fight it out between them, he, she and the lover! If luck turns her back on us – well, then you may be needed. But once the girl's well out of it, this burden is mine, and you may take care of your patient and sit quietly at home.'

Cadfael watched the night through with Brother Elyas, and got nothing more for his pains than he had known already. The barrier remained immovable. When a dutiful brother came to relieve him, he went to his bed, and slept as soon as he lay down. He had the gift. There was no profit in lying awake fretting for what would, in any case, have to be faced on awaking, and he had long ago sloughed off the unprofitable. It took too much out of a man, of what would be needed hereafter.

He awoke only when he was roused by Prior Leonard, which was in the early afternoon, a couple of hours at least after he had intended to be up and doing. By which time Hugh was back from his foray into the hills, and tramped in weary and bleak of countenance to share a late dinner, and report the fruits of his labours.

'There is a manor known as Callowleas, a quarter-circle round the flank of Clee from Druel's place, and much on the same level.' Hugh paused to frown over his own choice of words. 'There *was* such a manor! It has been wiped out, drained, filleted like a fish. What we found was Druel's homestead over again, but to another degree. This was a thriving manor, and now it's a snowy waste, a number of bodies buried or frozen there, nothing living left to speak. We've brought back the first of the dead into Ludlow, and left men breaking out others from the drifts. No telling how many they'll find. By the covering of snow, I should judge this raid took place even *before* the frost set in.'

'Do you tell me?' Cadfael sat staring, appalled. 'Then before the raids of which we already know, and before our little nun was killed, and Brother Elyas reduced to this haunted condition he lies in now. Now you have your finger on a fixed place, is there a name and a lord to go with it? Dinan will know all these tenants who hold from him, and it must be his writ, the old Lacy writ, that runs there.'

'It is. The manor of Callowleas is held from him by a young man who came into his father's honour only two years ago. Of suitable fortune, person, and age, yes. His name is Evrard Boterel. Not a great family, but respected. By many tokens, he may well be the man.'

'And this place lies in the right direction? The way the girl fled with her lover?' It was a grim reflection, but Hugh shook his head emphatically at despondency.

'Ah, but wait! Nothing's certain yet, Yves could not name the man. But even if it is so – as I believe it must be – no need yet to bury the girl. For Dinan pointed out that Boterel also holds the manor of Ledwyche, down in the valley of the Dogditch brook, and there's a good downhill track continues on that way from Callowleas, into forest, and thick forest at that. A little over three miles between the two holdings. We followed it a short way, though I own I had little hope of finding any traces, even if some of the household had escaped the slaughter that way. We had better fortune than I expected, or maybe deserved. Look, this is what I found!'

He drew it out from the breast of his cotte, and held it up over his fist, a net of fine gold filigree threads on a band of embroidered ribbon, made to pass round the head when the hair was netted, and tie over the brow. The bow in which it had been tied had been dragged askew, but not undone, for the band had torn apart a little aside from it.

'Caught in thick woodland, well down the path. They were in haste, whoever rode that way, they cut through a dense thicket to come the quickest way down the slope, there were broken twigs hanging to bear witness. I say they, but I fancy one horse only, with two riders. A low branch caught and dragged this from her head. And since that gives us every hope that the wearer got away safely from that terror, we may very well show this to Yves, and say how it was found. If he knows it for hers, then I'm bound for Ledwyche, to see if luck's still on our side.'

There was no hesitation. The moment Yves set eyes on the handful of gold cobweb, his eyes opened wide and grew luminous with hope and eagerness.

'That is my sister's!' he said, shining. 'It was too fine for the journey, but I know she had it with her. For *him* she might wear it! Where did you find it?'

# 6

This time they took Yves with them, partly because, though he might have accepted Hugh's fiat gracefully if refused, he would have been restless and miserable all the time of waiting, and partly because, in addition to being the only one who could positively identify Ermina's suitor when found, he was indeed the man of his blood here, the head of his household, and had every right to partake in the search for his lost sister, now they knew she should be well alive.

'But this is the same way we came down from Thurstan's assart,' he said, after they had turned off the highroad by the bridge over the Corve. 'Must we continue so?'

'We must, for some while. Well past the place where you and I would as soon not be,' said Cadfael simply, divining his unease. 'But we need not turn our eyes away. There is nothing evil there. Neither earth nor water nor air have any part in man's ill-doing.' And with an attentive but cautious eye on the boy's grave face he said: 'You may grieve, but you must not begrudge that she is gone. Her welcome is assured.'

'She was, of all of us, the only best,' said Yves, abruptly eloquent. 'You don't know! Never out of temper, always patient and kind and very brave. She was much more beautiful than Ermina!'

He was thirteen, but taught and gifted, perhaps, somewhat beyond his years, and he had gone afoot in Sister Hilaria's gallant and gentle company many days, close and observant. And if he had glimpsed for the first time a mature kind of love, surely it had been a most innocent and auspicious kind, even now after the apparent mutilation of loss. Yves had come to no harm. In the past two days he seemed to have grown in stature, and taken several long strides away from his infancy.

He did not avert his eyes when they came to the brook, but he was silent, and so remained until after they had crossed the second brook also; but from that point they veered to the right, and came into open woodland, and the new vistas revived his interest in the world about him, and brightened his eyes again. The brief winter sunlight, which had again drawn down slender icicles from eaves and branches, was already past, but the light was clear and the air still, and the patterns of black and white and dusky greens had their own sombre beauty.

They crossed the Hopton brook, still motionless as before, half a mile lower down its course than when they had come to Godstoke together. 'But we must have been very near,' said Yves, marvelling that he might have passed almost within touch of his sister that day, and never known it.

'Still a mile or so to go.'

'I hope she may be there!'

'So do we all,' said Hugh.

They came to the manor of Ledwyche over a slight ridge, and emerged from woodland to look down an equally gentle slope towards the Ledwyche brook, into which all the others drained before it flowed on, mile after mile, southward to join the River Teme. Beyond the watered valley the ground rose again, and there, directly before them in the distance, hung the vast, bleak outline of Titterstone Clee, its top shrouded in low cloud. But in between, the valley lay sheltered on all sides from the worst winds. Trees had been cleared from round the manor, except for windbreaks left for protection to crops and stock in the most open places. From their ridge they looked down at an impressive array of buildings, the manor-house itself built long and steep-roofed over a squat undercroft, the entire visible sweep of the stockade lined within with barn and byre and store. A considerable holding, and surely a temptation to the hungry and covetous, in these lawless times, but perhaps too strongly manned to be easy prey.

It seemed, however, that the holder was not quite easy about his property, for as they drew nearer they could see that on the narrow timber bridge that crossed the brook beyond the manor, men were working busily, erecting a barrier of logs, and above the old, dark wood of the stockade, and especially along that eastward side, glared the white, new wood of recent building. The lord of the manor was heightening his fences.

'They are here, surely,' said Hugh, staring. 'Here lives a man who has taken warning, and does not mean to be caught by surprise a second time.'

They rode down with rising hopes to the open gate in the stockade, which here to the west was still only breast-high. Nevertheless, even on this side an archer rose in the gate to challenge them, and his bow was strung, and if he had not an arrow braced, he had a quiver on his shoulder.

He was a shrewd fellow, so quick to measure the good equipment of the men-at-arms at Hugh's back that he had changed his wary front for a smile before ever Hugh could recite his name and titles.

'My lord, you're very welcome. The lord sheriff's deputy could not come better. If our lord had known you were so near he would have sent to you. For he could not well come himself . . . But ride in, my lord, ride in, and my boy here will run for the steward.'

The boy was already in full flight across the trampled snow within the pale. By the time they had ridden across to the stone stairway that led up to the great door of the hall, the steward was scurrying out to receive them, a stout elderly man, russet of beard and bald of head.

'I am seeking Evrard Boterel,' said Hugh, descending with a flurry of snow at his heel. 'He's within?'

'He is, my lord, but not yet in full health. He has been in a sharp fever, but it mends gradually. I'll bring you to him.'

He went before, stumping up the steep stairs, and Hugh followed him close, with Brother Cadfael and Yves on his heels. Within the great hall, at this hour of this winter day, and with hardly a soul using it and hardly a torch to light it, thick gloom hung heavy, warmed only grudgingly by the damped fire on the stones of the central hearth. All the manor's menfolk were working on the defences. A middle-aged matron jingled her keys along the passage behind the screens, a couple of maids whispered and peered from the kitchen.

The steward brought them with a flourish into a small room at the upper end of the hall, where a man lay back languidly in a great, cushioned chair, with wine and a smoky oil-lamp on a table at his side. One small window was unshuttered, but the light it provided was growing dim, and the yellow flame from the wick of the lamp cast deceptive shadows, and gave them only a dusky view of the face that turned towards them as the door was opened.

'My lord, here are the sheriff's officers come south to Ludlow.' The steward had softened his bluff voice to the coaxing tone he might have used to a child, or a very sick man. 'The lord Hugh Beringar comes to see you. We shall have help if we should need it, you can put your mind at rest.'

A long and muscular but slightly shaky hand was put out to move the lamp, so that it might show host and visitors to each other more clearly. A low-pitched voice said, over somewhat quick and shallow breath: 'My lord, you're heartily welcome. God knows we seem to have need of you in these parts.' And to the steward he said: 'Bring more lights, and some refreshment.' He leaned forward in the chair, gathering himself with an effort. 'You find me in some disarray, I am sorry for it. They tell me I have been in fever some days. I am out of that now, but it has left me weaker than I care to be.'

'So I see, and I am sorry,' said Hugh. 'I brought a force south here, I must tell you, upon other business, but by chance it has taken me to your manor above at Callowleas. I have seen, sir, what has been done to you there. I am glad that you, and some, at least, of your people escaped alive from that massacre, and I intend to make it my business to find and root out whatever nest of vultures brought that upon you. I see you have been busy strengthening your own defences.'

'As best we can.'

A woman brought candles, disposed them silently in sconces on the walls, and withdrew. The sudden brightness brought them all vividly close, eyes startled wide. Yves, who had stood rooted and stiff by Cadfael's side, a lordling ready to confront his enemy, suddenly clutched at Cadfael's sleeve and softened in uncertainty.

The man in the great chair looked no more than twenty-four or twenty-five. He had heaved himself forward, and the cushions had slid down at his back. He presented to the light a face pale and hollow-cheeked, the eyes large and dark, and sunken into bruised hollows, glittering still with the hectic brilliance of fever. His thick fair hair was rumpled and on end from the pillows that had propped him. But no question, this was a very handsome and engaging person, and when in health a tall and athletic one. He was clothed and booted, plainly he had been out during the day among his men, ill-advisedly, for his boots were wet and dark with melted snow. He was bending his brows now and peering attentively at his three visitors, and when his gaze reached the boy, it halted and hung there. He was not sure. He shook his head a little, peered again, and pondered, frowning.

'You know the boy?' asked Hugh mildly. 'He is Yves Hugonin, here seeking a lost sister. If you can help us, we shall be greatly relieved, both he and I. For I think you did not retreat from Callowleas alone. Caught in a tree along the woodland track that bears this way, we found this.' He drew out the thimbleful of gilt thread that expanded to a filigree globe in the palm of his hand. 'Do you know it?'

'Only too well!' said Evrard Boterel harshly, and closed, for an instant, large full eyelids over too-bright eyes. He opened them again to look directly at Yves. 'You are the young brother? Forgive me that I could not be sure of you. I have not seen you but once, I think, since you were a child. Yes, this is hers.'

'You brought her here with you,' said Hugh, not questioning, stating. 'Safe out of that attack.'

'Yes – safe! Yes, I brought her here.' There was a fine dew of sweat on Evrard's broad brow, but his eyes were wide open and clear.

'We have been in search of her and her companions,' said Hugh, 'ever since the sub-prior of Worcester came to Shrewsbury asking after them, since all trace of them had been lost after their flight. If she is here, send for her.'

'She is not here,' said Evrard heavily. 'Nor do I know where she is. All these days between, either I or men of mine have been hunting for her.' He set his long hands to the arms of his chair, and hauled himself shakily to his feet. 'I will tell you!' he said.

He stalked about the room as he told them, a gaunt young man, filled with restless energy, but enfeebled by his days of sickness.

'I was a frequent and welcome guest in her father's house. This boy will know that is truth. She grew up in beauty, and I loved her. I did and do love her! Since she was orphaned I have ridden three times to Worcester to see her, and borne myself as I must to be admitted there, and never did I have any evil design on her, but intended to ask for her hand when I might. For her proper guardian now is her uncle, and he is in the Holy Land. All we could do was wait for his return. When I heard of the sack of Worcester all my prayer was that she should be escaped well out of it. I never thought of any gain to me, nor that she might be fled this way, until she sent her boy up from Cleeton . . .'

'On which day was that?' demanded Hugh, cutting in sharply.

'On the second day of this month. Come by night, she said, and fetch me away, for I am here waiting for you. Never a word of any others along with her. I knew only what she told me, and I went as she asked, with a horse for her, and brought her away to Callowleas. She had taken me by surprise,' he said, jerking up his head in defensive challenge, 'but I wished of all things to wed her, and so did she me. And I brought her there, and used her with all honour, and with her consent I sent out to bring a priest to marry us. But the next night, before ever he reached us, we were all undone.'

'I have seen the ruin they left,' said Hugh. 'From which direction did they come? In what numbers?'

'Too many for us! They were into the bailey and into the house before ever we knew what was happening. I cannot tell whether they came round the flank of the hill, or over the crests at us, for they broke in round half our stockade, ringing us from above and from the east. God knows I may have been too taken up with Ermina to set as strict a watch as I should have done, but there had been no warning, never a word until then of any such banditry in the land. It fell like lightning-stroke. Their numbers I can hardly guess, but surely as many as thirty, and well-armed. We were but half that, and caught easy and half-sleeping after supper. We did what we could – I came by some hurts . . .' Cadfael had already observed how he held one arm and shoulder hunched and still, the left, where a right-handed opponent would lunge for his heart. 'I had Ermina to save, I dared not attempt more. I took her and rode. The downhill way was still possible. They did not follow us. They were busy.' His mouth twisted in a painful grimace. 'We came here safely.'

'And then? How comes it that you have lost her again?'

'You cannot charge me more bitterly than I have accused myself,' said Evrard wearily. 'I am ashamed to face the boy here, and own how I let her slip through my hands. It is little excuse to say, however truly, that I had bled too much, and fell into my bed too weak to move. My leech may say what he can for me, I will not plead. But by the next day this prod here in my shoulder had taken bad ways, and the fever set in. By evening, when I had my wits for a while, and asked for her, they told me she had been frantic with tears for her brother, left behind at the house from which I took her. Now that she knew there were such cutthroats abroad in these parts, she could not rest until she knew him safe, and so she took horse in the middle of the day, and left word she would ride to Cleeton to enquire after him. And she did not return.'

'And you did not follow her!' accused Yves, stiff as a lance and quivering by Cadfael's side. 'You let her go alone, and stayed nursing your grazes!'

'Neither the one nor the other,' said Boterel, but gently and ruefully. 'I did not *let* her go, for I did not know she was gone. And I did, when I learned of it –

as my people here will tell you – I did get up from my bed and go out to hunt for her. It was the cold of that night, I think, and the rubbing of my clothes and the motion of riding, that fetched me down for so long. Sorry I am, I swooned and fell out of the saddle, and those I had with me carried me home the miles I'd ridden. I never reached Cleeton.'

'As well for you,' said Hugh drily, 'for that night the very house she was seeking was gutted and burned, and the family driven out.'

'So I have now been told. You do not think I have left things so, and never stirred to try and find her? But she was not there when the holding was attacked. If you have been there, and spoken with those who sheltered her, you know so much. She never got there. I have had men out hunting for her all this time, even though I myself was a useless wretch laid here shivering and raving. And now that I have my legs under me again I shall go on searching. Until I find her!' he said vehemently, and shut his mouth with a snap of strong teeth.

There was nothing more for them here, nothing to be gained and little to be blamed, it seemed. The girl had set in motion the whole disastrous course, doubly headstrong in decamping with her lover in the first place, and afterwards, because he was stricken down, in setting off alone to try and amend what she had done so sadly amiss.

'If you hear any word of her,' said Hugh, 'send to tell me at Bromfield, where I am lodged, or in Ludlow, where you will find my men.'

'I shall, my lord, without fail.' Evrard fell back again among his untidy pillows, and flinched at a twinge of pain, shifting his shoulder tenderly to ease it.

'Before we go,' said Brother Cadfael, 'can I not dress your wound again for you? For I see that it gives you trouble, and I fancy you have still a raw surface there that sticks to your dressing, and may do further damage. You have a physician here tending you?'

The young man's hollow eyes opened wide at this kindly interest. 'My leech, I called him, I know. He's none, but he has some skill, from experience. I think he has looked after me pretty well. You are wise in such matters, brother?'

'Like your own man, from long practice. I have often dealt with wounds that have taken bad courses. What has he used on you?' He was curious about other men's prescriptions, and there was clean linen bandaging, and a clay ointment jar laid aside on a shelf by the wall. Cadfael lifted the lid and sniffed at the greenish salve within. 'Centaury, I think, and the yellow mild nettle, both good. He knows his herbs. I doubt if you could do better. But since he is not here, and you are in discomfort, may I assay?'

Evrard lay back submissively and let himself be handled. Cadfael unlaced the ties of the young man's cotte, and drew the left shoulder gently out from the wide sleeve, until the shirt could also be drawn down, and his arm freed.

'You have been out and active today, this binding is rubbed into creases, and dried hard, no wonder it hurts you. You should lie still a day or two yet, and let it rest.' It was his physician's voice, practical, confident, even a little severe. His patient listened meekly, and let himself be unwound from his wrappings, which enveloped both shoulder and upper arm. The last folds were stained in a long slash that ran from above the heart down to the underside of the arm, with a thin, dark line of blood that ebbed out on either side into pale, dried fluid. Here Cadfael went delicately, steadying the flesh against every turn of the linen. The folds creaked stiffly free.

A long slash that could have killed him, but instead had been deflected outwards, to slice down into the flesh of his arm. Not deep nor dangerous, though he might well have bled copiously until it was staunched, and since he had ridden hard that same night, no wonder he had lost blood enough to enfeeble him. It was healing now from either end, and healing clean, but certainly, by exertion or some contagion of dirt entering, it had been ugly and festering, and even now, in the centre of the wound, the flesh showed pink, soft and angry. Cadfael cleansed it with a morsel of the linen, and applied a new plaster coated with the herbal salve. The pallid young face stared up at him all the while with unblinking, bruised eyes, wondering and mute.

'You have no other wounds?' asked Cadfael, winding a fresh bandage about his dressing. 'Well, rest this one a day or two longer, and rest your own uneasy mind with it, for we are all on the same quest. Take a little air in the middle of the day, if the sun comes, but keep from cold and give your body time. There, now your sleeve, so . . . But it would be wise to have these boots off, wrap yourself in your gown, and make yourself content.'

The hollow eyes followed his withdrawal, marvelling. He found his voice to follow them with thanks only as they were leaving.

'You have a gifted touch, brother. I feel myself much eased. God be with you!'

They went out to their horses and the gradually fading light. Yves was dumb. He had come to challenge, and remained to feel sympathy, though almost against his will. He was new to wounds and pain and sickness, until the shock of Worcester he had lived indulged, sheltered, a child. And for his sister's sake he was deep in bitter disappointment and anxiety, and wanted no promptings from anyone.

'He has what he claims,' said Brother Cadfael simply, when they were cresting the ridge and heading down into the trees. 'A thrust meant for his heart, rubbed raw again later, and poisoned by some foulness that got into the wound. He has been in fever, sure enough, and fretted gouts from his flesh. Everything speaks him true.'

'And we are no nearer finding the girl,' said Hugh.

The nightly clouds were gathering, the sky drooping over their heads, an ominous wind stirring. They made all the haste they could to get back into Bromfield before the snow began.

# 7

After Vespers that night the wind rose violently, the vague wisps of snow that drifted aimlessly on the air changed to thin, lashing whips, driving horizontally against the walls and piling new layers of white against every windward surface. By the time supper was over, and Brother Cadfael scurried across the great court to the infirmary to look at his patient, the world outside was an opaque, shifting, blinding mass of flakes, growing ever thicker. This was to be a blizzard night. The wolves might well be abroad again. They knew their ground exceedingly well, and weather that might daunt the innocent had no terrors for them.

Brother Elyas had been allowed out of his bed for the first time, and was reclining propped by his pillow, bony and shrunken in his voluminous habit. His head wounds had healed over, his body mended of itself, but the constitution of his mind had not the same strength. With mute submission he did whatever he was bidden, with low and listless voice he gave thanks humbly for all that was done for him, but with sunken eyes and painfully knotted brows he stared beyond the walls of his cell, as if half-seeing and half-deluding himself that he saw that part of him that had been reft away and never returned. Only in sleep, and particularly when falling asleep or awaking out of sleep, was he agitated and shaken, as if between waking life and the gentler semblance of death the veil that hid his lost memory from him thinned but did not quite part.

Yves had followed Cadfael across the court, restless

and anxious. He was hovering outside the door of the sickroom when Cadfael came out.

'Should you not be in your bed, Yves? Such a long, hard day as you've had!'

'I don't want to sleep yet,' pleaded the boy querulously. 'I'm not tired. Let me sit with him for you until after Compline. I'd rather have something to do.' And indeed it might be the best thing for him, to be doing something for someone else, and feeding a draught of herbs to Brother Elyas might spill a drop of comfort to soothe his own troubles and disappointments. 'He still hasn't said anything to help us? He doesn't remember us?'

'Not yet. There is a name he calls sometimes in his sleep, but none of our acquaintance.' He called for her as for a thing hopelessly lost, an irreparable grief but not an anxiety, she being beyond pain or danger. 'Hunydd. In his deepest sleep he calls for Hunydd.'

'A strange name,' said Yves, wondering. 'Is it a man or a woman?'

'A woman's name – a Welshwoman. I think, though I do not know, that she was his wife. And dearly loved, too dearly to leave him in peace if she is only a few months dead. Prior Leonard said of him, not long in the cloister. He may well have tried to escape from what was hard to bear alone, and found it no easier among any number of brethren.'

Yves was looking up at him with a man's eyes, steady and grave. Even sorrows as yet well out of his range he could go far towards understanding. Cadfael shook him amiably by the shoulder. 'There, yes, sit by him if you will. After Compline I'll bring someone to take your place. And should you need me, I'll not be far away.'

Elyas dozed, opened his eyes, and dozed again. Yves sat still and silent beside the bed, attentive to every change in the gaunt but strong and comely face, and pleased and ready when the invalid asked for a drink, or needed an arm to help him turn and settle comfortably. In the wakeful moments the boy tried tentatively to reach a mind surely not quite closed against him, talking shyly of the winter weather, and the common order of the day within these walls. The hollow eyes watched him as though from a great distance, but attentively.

'Strange,' said Elyas suddenly, his voice low and creaky with disuse. 'I feel that I should know you. Yet you are not a brother of the house.'

'You have known me,' said Yves, eager and hopeful. 'For a short time we were together, do you remember? We came from Cleobury together, as far as Foxwood. My name is Yves Hugonin.'

No, the name meant nothing. Only the face, it seemed touched some chord in his disrupted memory. 'There was snow threatening,' he said. 'I had a reliquary to deliver here, they tell me I brought it safely. They tell me! All I know is what they tell me.'

'But you will remember,' said Yves earnestly. 'It will come clear to you again. You may trust what they tell you, no one would deceive you. Shall I tell you more things? True things, that I know?'

The wondering, doubting face watched him, and made no motion of rejection. Yves leaned close, and began to talk solemnly and eagerly about what was past.

'You were coming from Pershore, but roundabout, to avoid the trouble in Worcester. And we had run from Worcester, and wanted to reach Shrewsbury. At Cleobury we were all lodged overnight, and you would have had us come here to Bromfield with you, as the nearest place of safety, and I wanted to go with you, but my sister would not, she would go on over the hills. We parted at Foxwood.' The face on the pillow was not responsive, but seemed to wait with a faint, patient hope. The wind shook the stout shutter covering the window, and filtered infinitely tiny particles of snow into the room, to vanish instantly. The candle flickered. The whine of the gale outside was a piercingly desolate sound.

'But you are here,' said Elyas abruptly, 'far from Shrewsbury still. And alone! How is that, that you should be alone?'

'We were separated.' Yves was not quite easy, but if the sick man was beginning to ask questions thus intelligently, the threads of his torn recollections might knit again and present him a whole picture. Better to know both the bad and the good, since there was no guilt in it for him, he was the blameless victim, and surely knowledge should be healing. 'Some kind country people sheltered me, and Brother Cadfael brought me here. But my sister . . . We are seeking her. She left us of her own will!' He could not resist that cry, but would not accuse her further. 'I am sure we shall find her safe and well,' he said manfully.

'But there was a third,' said Brother Elyas, so softly, so inwardly, that it seemed he spoke to himself. 'There was a nun . . .' And now he was not looking at Yves, but staring great-eyed into the vault above him, and his mouth worked agitatedly.

'Sister Hilaria,' said Yves, quivering in response.

'A nun of our order . . .' Elyas set both hands to the sides of his bed, and sat up strongly. Something had kindled in the deeps of his haunted eyes, a yellow, crazed light too vivid to be merely a reflection from the candle's flame. 'Sister Hilaria . . .' he said, and now at last he had found a name that meant something to him, but something so terrible that Yves reached both hands to take him by the shoulders, and urge him to lie down again.

'You mustn't fret – she is not lost, she is here, most reverently tended and coffined. It is forbidden to wish her back, she is with God.' Surely they must have told him, but maybe he had not understood. Death could not be hidden away. He would grieve, naturally, but that is permitted. But you may not begrudge it that she has left us, Brother Cadfael had said.

Brother Elyas uttered a dreadful, anguished sound, yet so quiet that the howl of the wind at the shutter almost drowned it. He clenched both hands into large, bony fists, and struck them against his breast.

'Dead! Dead? In her youth, in her beauty – trusting me! Dead! Oh, stones of this house, fall and cover me, unhappy! Bury me out of the sight of men . . .'

Barely half of it was clear, the words crowded so thick on his tongue, choking him, and Yves in his alarm and dismay was hardly capable of listening, he cared only to allay this storm he had innocently provoked. He stretched an arm across Elyas' breast, and tried to soothe him back to his pillow, his young, whole strength pitted against this demented vigour.

'Oh, hush, hush, you mustn't vex yourself so. Lie down, you're too weak to rise . . . Oh, don't, you frighten me! Lie down!'

Brother Elyas sat rigidly upright, staring through

the wall, gripping both hands against his heart, whispering what might have been prayers, or self-reproaches, or feverish, garbled recollections of times past. Against that private obsession all the force Yves could exert had no influence. Elyas was no longer even aware of him. If he spoke to any, it was to God, or to some creature invisible.

Yves turned and fled for help, closing the door behind him. Through the infirmary he ran full tilt, and out into the piled, whirling, howling snow of the court, across to the cloister and the warming-room, where surely they would be at this hour. He fell once, and plucked himself shivering out of a drift, halting to clear his eyes. The whole night was a rain of goose-feathers, but cold, cold, and the wind that flung them in his face cut like a knife. He stumbled and slithered to the door of the church, and there halted, hearing the chanting within. It was later than he had thought. Compline had already begun.

He had been too well schooled in the courtesies and proper observancies, he could not for any cause burst in upon the office and bawl for help. He hung still for a few moments to get his breath and shake the snow from his hair and lashes. Compline was not long, surely he could go back and battle with his disordered charge until the office was over. Then there would be help in plenty. He had only to keep Brother Elyas quiet for a quarter of an hour.

He turned, half-blinded as soon as he left cover, and battled his way back through the drifts, labouring hard with his short, sturdy legs, and lowering his head like a little fighting bull against the wind.

The outer door of the infirmary stood open wide, but he was all too afraid that he had left it so in his haste. He blundered along the passage within, fending himself off from the walls with both hands as he shook off the snow that clung to his face. The door of the sickroom was also wide open. That brought him up with a jolt that jarred him to the heels.

The room was empty, the coverings of the bed hung low to the floor. Brother Elyas' sandals, laid neatly side by side under the head of the bed, were gone. And so was Brother Elyas, just as he had risen from his sick-bed, clothed, habited but without cloak or covering, out into the night of the ninth of December, into such a blizzard as had raged the night he came by his all but mortal injuries, and Sister Hilaria by her death. The only name that had reached him in his solitary place.

Yves charged back along the passage to the doorway, and out into the storm. And there were tracks, though he had not seen them when he entered, because he had not expected them to be there, nor would they last long. They were filling fast, but they showed, large feet tramping down the steps and across the court, not towards the church, no – straight for the gatehouse. And Brother Porter had leave to attend Compline.

They were still chanting in the church, and Elyas could not have got far. Yves ran to grab his cloak from the porch of the guest-hall, and bolted like a startled hare, in convulsive leaps, towards the gatehouse. The tracks were filling fast, they lingered only as shallowing pits in the whiteness, picked out by the shadows cast from the few burning torches. But they reached and quitted the gate. The world without was nothing but a boiling whiteness, and the depth of the fall made walking hard labour for his short legs, but he plodded on relentlessly The tracks turned right. So did Yves.

Some way along the road, wading blindly, with no sense of direction left to him in a snowfall that looked the same wherever he turned his face, but where the ground below him was still dimpled faintly with the furrows and pits of passage, he glimpsed in a momentary emptiness cleared by the gale's caprice, a black shadow flitting before him. He fixed his eyes upon it, and plunged determinedly after.

It took him a long time to overtake his quarry. It was incredible how fast Elyas went, striding, thrusting, ploughing his way, so that now a torn furrow showed where he had passed. In sandals, bare-headed, a sick man – only some terrible force of passion and despair could give him such strength. Moreover, which frightened Yves more than ever, he seemed to know where he was going, or else to be drawn to some desperate meeting-place without his own knowledge or will. The line he sheered through the drifts looked arrow-straight.

Nevertheless, Yves did overtake him at last, struggling closer with every step, until he was able to stretch out his hand and catch at the wide sleeve of the black habit. The arm swung steadily, as though Elyas remained totally unaware of the weight dragging at him. Almost he plucked himself clear, but Yves clung with both hands, and heaving himself in front of the striding figure, wound his arms about its middle and held on, blocking the way forward with all his weight, and blinking up through the blinding snow into a face as chill and immovable as a death-mask.

'Brother Elyas, come back with me! You must come back – you'll die out here!'

Brother Elyas moved on inexorably, forcing his incubus before him, hampered but undeterred. Yves maintained his hold, and went with him, but hanging back hard, and pleading insistently: 'You're ill, you should be in your bed. Come back with me! Where is it you want to go? Turn back now, let me take you home . . .'

But perhaps he was not going anywhere, only trying to get away from somewhere, or from someone, from himself, from whatever it was that had come back to him like lightning-stroke, and driven him mad. Yves pleaded breathlessly and insistently, but in vain. He could not turn him or persuade him. There was nothing left but to go with him. He took a firm grip on the black sleeve, and set himself to keep pace with his charge. If they could find any cottage, or meet with any late traveller he could ask for shelter or help. Surely Brother Elyas must weaken and fail at last, and let himself be prevailed upon to accept any aid that offered. But who would be out on such a night? Who but a poor madman and his sorry keeper! Well, he had offered to take care of Brother Elyas, and he would not let go of him, and if he could not protect him from his own frenzy, he could at least share the penalty. And strangely, in a little while they were moving together as one, and Brother Elyas, though his face remained fixed and his purpose secret, laid an arm about Yves' shoulders and drew him close against his side, and small, instinctive motions of mutual kindness arose between them, to ease the labour and the cold and the loneliness.

Yves had no longer any idea of where they were, though he knew that long ago they had left the road. He thought they had crossed a bridge, and that could not have been anything but the River Corve. Somewhere on that upland slope, then. A poor chance of finding a cottage here, even if the snow gave over and let them see their way.

But it seemed that Brother Elyas knew his way, or was guided to the place where he could not choose but go, for some awful, penitential purpose of which only he knew. A thicket of thorny bushes, heaped with snow, snatched at their garments, sheltering a shallow hollow in the slope. Yves stumbled against a hard, dark surface, and grazed his knuckles on rough wood. A low but sturdy hut, built to give shelter to shepherds in the lambing, and store fodder and litter. The door was held by a heavy bar, but Brother Elyas drew it clear and thrust the door open. They burst through into blessed darkness, Elyas stooping his head low beneath the lintel. The door, clapped to against the wind, fitted snugly, and suddenly they were in blindness, stillness and comparative silence. After the blizzard without, this was almost warmth, and the smell of old but dry hay, stirred by their feet, promised bed and blankets together. Yves shook off snow, and his heart lifted hopefully. Here Brother Elyas might survive the night. And before dawn, before he awakes, thought the boy, I can slip out and bar the door on him, while I go to find someone to help me, or carry a message for me. I've held on to him thus far, I won't lose him now.

Brother Elyas had moved away from him. He heard the rustling whisper of the hay as a man's weight was flung down into it. The howl of the wind outside ebbed into a desolate moaning. Yves crept forward with hand extended, and touched a stooped shoulder, caked with snow. The pilgrim had reached his strange shrine, and was on his knees. Yves shook the snow from the folds of the black habit, and felt Elyas shuddering beneath his hand, as though he contained by force what should have been deep and bitter sobbing. Now that they were in utter darkness the thread that bound them seemed to have drawn them closer together. The kneeling man was whispering almost soundlessly, and though all words were lost, the desperation of their import was plain.

Yves felt his way into the pile of hay beside him, and with an arm about the tense shoulders tried to draw Elyas down to lie at rest, but for a long while the pressure was resisted. At last the lean body softened and sank forward with a muted, wordless groan, whether in consent to the boy's urging or in the collapse of exhaustion there was no telling. He lay stretched on his face, his forehead on his arms, and Yves raked up the hay on either side to fold him in with at least a measure of warmth, and lay down beside him.

After a while he knew by the long, deep breathing that Elyas slept.

Yves lay holding him, pressed close to his side, determined not to sleep. He was cold and weary, and in great need of thought, but his mind was numbed and unwilling. He did not want to remember the words Brother Elyas had spoken, much less try to make out their meaning, for whatever it might be, it was terrible. All he could do now for this broken man, for whom he felt so obstinate and strange an affection, having taken the responsibility for him, was to make certain that he could not escape again to wander and be lost, and to go out and seek help for him in the morning. To which end he must stay awake.

For all that, he may have been very close to dozing when he was startled into wakefulness again by a voice beside him, not whispering now, only muffled by the cradling arms.

'Sister . . . my sister . . . Forgive me my weakness, my mortal sin – I, who have been your death!' And after a long pause he said: 'Hunydd – she was like you, even so warm and confiding in my arms . . . After six months starving, suddenly such hunger – I could not bear the burning, body and soul!'

Yves lay still, clasping him, unable to move, unable to stop listening.

'No, do not forgive! How dare I ask? Let the earth close on me and put me out of mind . . . Craven, inconstant – unworthy.'

A longer silence yet. Brother Elyas was still asleep, and out of his sleep he gave voice to his torments, uncovered now, mercilessly remembered. He slept and writhed. Never before had Yves felt himself enlarged to contain either such horror, or such fierce and protective pity.

'She clung to me . . . she had no fear at all, being with me! Merciful God, I am a man, full of blood, with a man's body, a man's desires!' cried Brother Elyas in a muted howl of pain. 'And she is dead, who trusted in me . . .'

# 8

Brother Cadfael came back from Compline to see Elyas settled for the night, and brought a young brother with him to relieve Yves of his watch. They found the door standing open, the bed wildly disturbed, and the room empty.

There might, of course, have been explanations less dire than the obvious one, but Cadfael made straight for the outer door again at a purposeful run, and looked for the signs he had not looked for when entering. The court had been criss-crossed with new tracks at the end of Compline, and even these the continuing snow was rapidly obliterating, but there were still traces of someone who had set a straight course for the gatehouse. Mere dimples in the whiteness, but discernible. And the boy gone, too! What could have erupted there in the sickroom to spur Elyas into such unreasonable and perilous action, after his long apathy and submission? Certainly if he had taken it into his disordered head to do something drastic a half-grown lad would not have been able to stop him, and more than likely pride would not let Yves abandon a creature for whom he had assumed, however briefly, the responsibility. He was getting to know Yves fairly well by now.

'You run to the guest-hall,' he ordered the young brother briskly, 'tell Hugh Beringar what's amiss, and make sure they are not within there. I'll go to Prior Leonard, and we'll have the whole household searched.'

Leonard took the news with concern and distress, and had every brother scouring the enclave at once, even to the grange court and the barns. Hugh Beringar came forth booted and cloaked, in resigned expectation of the worst, and was short with any who got in his way. With both the secular and the cloistral law directing, the search did not take long, and was fruitless.

'My fault entirely,' Cadfael owned bitterly. 'I entrusted the poor wretch to a boy hardly less wretched. I should have had more sense. Though how or why this can have arisen between them is more than I can see. But I should not have taken the least risk with either of them. And now my foolishness has lost them both, the most forlorn pair this house held, who should have been guarded at every step.'

Hugh was already busy disposing the men he had here at hand. 'One to Ludlow, as far as the gate, where either they'll have passed, or you may have them kept safely if they arrive hereafter. And you go with him, but to the castle, have out ten men, and bring them down to the gate, where I'll come. Wake up Dinan, too, let him sweat, the boy's son to a man he must have known, and nephew to one he may well want to have dealings with soon. I won't risk men by sending them out in this beyond a mile or so, or in less than pairs, but our pair can't have got far.' He turned on Cadfael just as vehemently, and clouted him hard between the shoulders. 'And you, my heart, stop talking such arrogant foolery! The man seemed quiet and biddable, and the boy needed using, and could be trusted to the hilt, as you very well know. If they've miscarried, it's none of your blame. Don't arrogate to yourself God's own role of apportioning blame and praise, even when the blame lands on your own shoulders. That's a kind of arrogance, too. Now come on, and we'll see if we can't bring home the two of them out of this cold purgatory. But I tell you what I shall be telling my fellows at Ludlow – move out no more than an hour from home, keep touch, and turn back on the hour, as near as you can judge. I'm not losing more men into the snow this night. At dawn, if we've caught nothing before, we'll take up the search in earnest.'

With those orders they went forth into the blizzard, hunting in pairs, and obscurely comforted, in Cadfael's case at least, by the reflection that it was a pair they were hunting. One man alone can give up and subside into the cold and die, far more easily than two together, who will both brace and provoke each other, wrangle and support, give each other warmth and challenge each other's endurance. In extremes, not to be alone is the greatest aid to survival.

He had taken Hugh's impatient reproof to heart, too, and it gave him reassurance no less. It was all too easy to turn honest anxiety over someone loved into an exaltation of a man's own part and duty as protector, a manner of usurpation of the station of God. To accuse oneself of falling short of infallibility is to arrogate to oneself the godhead thus implied. Well, thought Cadfael, willing to learn, a shade specious, perhaps, but I may need that very argument myself some day. Bear it in mind!

Blundering blindly ahead with a burly young novice beside him, northwards across the Corve, Cadfael groped through a chill white mist, and knew that they were all wasting their time. They might probe the drifts as they would, but the weather had the laugh of them, covering everything in the same blank pall.

They all drew in again resignedly to Bromfield when they judged the time to be spent and the work impossible. The porter had set fresh pine torches in the shelter of the arched gateway to provide a beacon glow homeward, for fear some of the searchers should themselves go astray and be lost, and from time to time he set the bell ringing as an added guide. The hunters came back snow-caked and weary, and empty-handed. Cadfael went to Matins and Lauds before seeking his bed. The order of observances must not be utterly disrupted, even to go out in defence of innocent lives. Nothing could now be done before dawn. Not by men. But God, after all, knew where the lost might be found, and it would do no harm to put in a word in that quarter, and admit the inadequacy of human effort.

He arose at the bell for Prime, and went down with the rest in the winter darkness to the cold church. The snow had ceased at the first approach of morning, as it had done for several days, and the reflected light from all that depth of whiteness brought a pure and ghostly pallor even before dawn. After the office Cadfael ploughed his way alone down towards the gatehouse. The world around him was a waste of white broken by shadowy dark shapes of walls and buildings, but the porter had kept his torches burning hopefully under the archway, and they shed a full, reddish light over the stonework, and into the outer world beyond. To replenish them he had had to open the wicket in the gate and pass through, and as Cadfael approached he was in the act of re-entering, pausing in shelter to stamp off snow before he came within, and closed the wicket again behind him.

Thus it happened that he was facing inwards while Cadfael was facing out, and only Cadfael saw what he saw. The wicket was lofty, to admit mounted men, and Brother Porter was short and slight, and stooping to shake his skirts clear. Behind him, and not many paces behind, two faces suddenly glowed out of the dimness into the flickering light of the torches, and shone clear before Cadfael's eyes. Their suddenness and their beauty took his breath away for a moment, as though a miracle had caused them to appear out of the very air. No heavenly visitors, however, these, but most vividly and vitally of this world.

The girl's hood had fallen back on her neck, the red light flowed over a great disordered coil of dark hair, a wide, clear forehead, arched, imperious black brows, large dark eyes too brilliant to be black, by the reflections in them the darkest and reddest of browns. She had, for all her coarse country clothes, a carriage of the head and a lance-like directness of gaze that queens might have copied. The lines that swooped so graciously over her cheekbones and down to full, strongly folded lips and resolute chin made so suave a moulding that Cadfael's finger-ends, once accomplished in such caresses, stroked down from brow to throat in imagination, and quivered to old memories.

The other face hung beyond and above her left shoulder almost cheek to brow with her. She was tall, but the man behind her was taller, he was stooped protectively and watchfully to bring his face close to hers. A long, spare, wide-browed face with a fine scimitar of a nose and a supple bow of a mouth, and the dilated, fearless golden eyes of a hawk. His head was bared, and capped closely with blue-black hair, coiling vigorously at his temples and sweeping back thick and lustrous over a lofty skull. Cadfael had visions of that face terminating in a short, pointed beard, and with fine-drawn moustaches over the long, fastidious lips. With just such faces had he seen, in his time, proud, mailed Syrians wheeling their line of charge outside Antioch. This face had the same dark colouring and sculptured shape, like cast bronze, but this face was shaven clean in the Norman fashion, the rich hair cropped, the head framed by rough, dun-coloured homespun, a local peasant's wear.

Well, they happen, the lightning-strokes of God, the gifted or misfortunates who are born into a world where they nowhere belong, the saints and scholars who come to manhood unrecognised, guarding the swine in the forest pastures among the beech-mast, the warrior princes villein-born and youngest in a starving clan, set to scare the crows away from the furrow. Just as hollow slave-rearlings are cradled in the palaces of kings, and come to rule, however ineptly, over men a thousand times their worth.

But this one would not be lost. It needed only that flashing glimpse of the black-lashed golden eyes to make it certain they would burn their way before him to wherever he set out to go.

And all in the brief moment while the porter was ridding himself of the snow he had collected on his skirts. For the next moment he had stepped within, and closed the wicket behind him, just in time to cut off, short of the gates, the dual vision of youth that was surely advancing to ask for entry.

Brother Cadfael closed his eyes, opened them hopefully, and closed them again upon dazzled recollection that might almost have been delusion. In the between-light of dawn, in the grip of a hard winter, and complicated by the pleasurable, warming glow of torchlight, what dreams may not come!

He had taken but three more laboured paces through the fall, and the porter had barely reached the door of his lodge, when the bell pealed at the gate.

The porter turned, startled. He had been preoccupied first with reaching up to the sconces in which his torches were set, and then hurrying back into shelter, and he had seen nothing stirring in the lingering darkness without. Only after his back was turned had the two – if they were real indeed! – stepped within range of the light. He hoisted resigned shoulders, and waded back to open the small grid that would show him who stood without. What he saw astonished him still more, it seemed, but it spurred him into instant action. The great latch lifted, and the lofty wicket swung open.

And there she stood, tall, meek and still confronting them, in a too-large gown of faded brown homespun, a coarse short cloak and ragged-edged capuchon flung back from her head, the sheaf of dark hair tumbling to her shoulders. The sting of cold air had brought out a rosy flush on her cheekbones, in a skin otherwise creamy-white and smooth as ivory.

'May I enter and take shelter here a while?' she said in the mildest of voices and humblest of manners, but with that confidence and calm about her that could not be quenched. 'Through weather and mishap and the distresses of war I am here alone. I think you have been looking for me. My name is Ermina Hugonin.'

While the porter was conducting her excitedly into his lodge, and hurrying to inform Prior Leonard and Hugh Beringar of the sudden appearance of the missing lady at their gates, Brother Cadfael lost no time in slipping out into the roadway and casting a shrewd eye on the empty countryside in all directions. Empty it was, to all appearance. There were corners, copses, bushes, any of which could quickly conceal the departure of a young and swift-moving man, and either her companion had chosen to vanish among these, or the falcon had indeed taken wing and flown. As for tracks in the snow, a few early-rising goodmen with sheep to dig out or beasts to feed had already gone to and fro past the gatehouse, and among their traces who was to pick out one man's foot? She had spoken truth, if a somewhat deceptive truth; she entered here alone. But two had approached the gate, though only one rang to ask admittance.

Now why should such a man, bringing a lost girl to safety, avoid showing his face within? And why, pondered Cadfael, should not the one man who was aware of the evasion make it known openly to all? On the other hand, until he knew of a good reason one way or the other, why should he? First hear and consider what the lady had to say.

He went back very thoughtfully to the lodge, where the porter had hurried to prod his fire into life and seat her beside it. She sat self-contained and silent, her wet shoes and skirts beginning to steam gently in the warmth.

'You are also a brother of this house?' she asked, raising dark eyes to study him.

'No, I am a monk of Shrewsbury. I came here to tend a brother who has been lying sick here.' He wondered if any word of Brother Elyas' misfortunes had reached her, but she gave no sign of knowing anything of a wounded monk, and he forbore from mentioning a name. Let her tell her own story once for all, before Hugh and the prior as witnesses, then he might know where he himself stood. 'You know how diligently you have been sought since you fled from Worcester? Hugh Beringar, who is deputy sheriff of the shire, is here in Bromfield, partly on that very quest.'

'I heard it,' she said, 'from the forester who has sheltered me. I know from them, too, that my brother has been here, while I have been hunting for him. And only now that I find my way here myself do I learn that he is again lost, and half the night men have been out searching for him. All this countryside knows of it. I fear you have made a poor exchange,' she said with sudden, flashing bitterness, 'gaining me and losing Yves. For I am the one who has cost you all so much trouble and time.'

'Your brother was safe and in excellent health,' said Cadfael firmly, 'as late as Compline last night. There is no need to suppose that we shall fail of finding him again, for he cannot have gone far. The sheriff's men in Ludlow will have had their orders overnight, and be out by now. And so will Hugh Beringar, as soon as he has seen you safe and well, and heard whatever you can tell him.'

Hugh was at the door by then, and the brothers had hastily cleared a path through the drifts to bring the girl almost dry-shod up to the guest-hall. Prior

Leonard himself led her in to warmth and food and a comfortable seat by the fire. He was distressed that there was no woman guest to provide her a change of clothing.

'That shall be seen to,' said Beringar shortly. 'Josce de Dinan has a household full of women, I'll get from them whatever is needed. But you had better get out of those wet skirts, madam, if it must needs be into habit and sandals. You have nothing with you but what you wear?'

'I gave what I had in exchange for what I wear,' she said with composure, 'and for the hospitality that was given me without thought of reward. But some money I still have about me. I can pay for a gown.'

They left her to strip beside the fire, and provided her the habit and shoes of a novice. When she opened the door to them again, and bade them in, it was with the grace of a countess welcoming guests. She had let down and combed her mass of dark hair, it was drying into curls on her shoulders, and swung like heavy, lustrous curtains either side her face. Wrapped in the black habit, and girdled close about the waist, she returned to her chair and braced herself, facing them squarely, the most beautiful novice Bromfield had ever housed. She had spread out her wet clothes to dry on a bench beside the fire.

'My lord,' she said, 'and Father Prior, to say this briefly, I have been the cause of great trouble and cost to you and many others, and I am sensible of it. It was not intended, but I did it. Now that I am come to make what amends I may, I hear that my brother, who was here in safety, and whom I hoped to join here, has gone forth overnight and vanished again. I cannot but lay this, with the rest, to my own charge, and I am sorry. If there is anything I can do to help in the search for him . . .'

'There is but one thing you can do to help us all,' said Hugh firmly, 'and take one anxiety, at least, off our hands. You can remain here, not setting a foot outside these walls, until we find and bring your brother to join you. Let us at least be sure that *you* are safe, and cannot be lost again.'

'I could wish better, but what you order, I will do. For this while,' she added, and jutted her lip at him.

'Then there are things I need to know from you, now, shortly, and the rest can wait. You are but a part of my business here. The king's peace is also my business, and you, I think, have good reason to know that the king's peace is being flouted in these parts. We know from Yves how you left him and Sister Hilaria at Cleeton, and sent word to Evrard Boterel to come and fetch you away to his manor of Callowleas. We have seen what is left of Callowleas, and we have been to Ledwyche looking for you, and heard from Boterel that you reached there with him safely, but rode out while he lay in fever from his wounds got in the fighting, and went to look for the companions you had left behind. What had befallen Callowleas could well befall others, no wonder you were in desperate anxiety.'

She sat gnawing her underlip and staring at him with unwavering eyes, her brows drawn close. 'Since Evrard has told you all this, I need only confirm it. He is recovered, I trust? Yes, I did fear for them. There was good cause.'

'What happened to you? Boterel has already told us that you did not return, and from the time he recovered his wits and found you were gone, he has been searching for you constantly. It was folly to set out alone.'

Surprisingly, her lips contorted in a wry smile. She had already admitted to folly. 'Yes, I am sure he has been hunting high and low for me. We may set his mind at rest now. No, I did not reach Cleeton. I don't know these ways, and I was benighted, and then the snow came . . . In the dark I lost myself utterly, and had a fall, and the horse bolted. I was lucky to be found and taken in by a forester and his wife, lifelong I shall be grateful to them. I told them about Yves, and how I feared for him, and the forester said he would send up to Cleeton and find out what had happened, and so he did. He brought word how poor John's holding was ravaged, the night after Callowleas, and how Yves was lost even before – the same night I committed my greatest fault and folly.' Her head reared proudly and her back stiffened as she declared her regret, and with fiery stare dared anyone else here present either to echo her self-condemnation, or attempt to deprecate it. 'Thanks be to God, John and his family escaped alive. And as for their losses, I take them as my debts, and they shall be repaid. But one relief they brought me from Cleeton,' she said, quickening into warmth and affection, 'for they told me Sister Hilaria that was gone, well before the raiders came, for the good brother of Pershore came back, in his anxiety over us, and he brought her away safely.'

The dead silence passed unnoticed, she was so glad of that one consolation. One innocent escaped from the landslide her light-hearted escapade had set in motion.

'All this time, while I stayed with them, we have been sending about for news of Yves, for how could

I make any move until I knew how he fared? And only yesterday morning we heard at last that he was here, safe. So I came.'

'Only in time,' owned Hugh, 'to find him lost again just as you are found. Well, I trust he need not be lost for long, and if I leave you without ceremony, it is to look for him.'

Cadfael asked mildly: 'You found your own way here, alone?'

She turned her head sharply, and gave him the wide, challenging gaze of her dark eyes, her face still calm and wary.

'Robert showed me the way – the forester's son.'

'My business,' said Hugh, 'is also with these outlaws who have set up house somewhere in the hills, and hunted you out of Callowleas and Druel out of his holding. I mean to have out enough men to smoke out every yard of those uplands. But first we'll find the two we've lost.' He rose briskly, and with a meaningful gesture of his dark head and lift of an urgent eyebrow drew Cadfael away with him out of the room.

'For all I can see, the girl knows nothing of what happened to Sister Hilaria, and nothing of Brother Elyas. I have my men and as many of Dinan's mustering to take up this hunt, and small time to break unpleasant news gently. Stay here with her, Cadfael, make sure she doesn't elude us again – and tell her! She'll have to know. The more truths we can put together, the nearer we shall be to clearing out this nest of devils once for all, and going home for Christmas to Aline and my new son.'

She was hungry, and had a healthy appetite, Cadfael judged, at any time. It was plenteous activity that kept her slender as a young hind. She ate with pleasure, though her face remained guarded, thoughtful and withdrawn. Cadfael let her alone until she sat back with a sigh of physical content. Her brows were still drawn close, and her eyes looked rather inward than outward. Then, quite suddenly, she was looking at him, and with sharp attention.

'It was you who found Yves and brought him here? So Father Prior said.'

'By chance it was,' said Cadfael.

'Not only chance. You went to look for him.' That commended him; her face warmed. 'Where was it? Was he very cold and wretched?'

'He was in all particulars a young gentleman very much in command of himself. And he had found, as you did, that simple country people can be hospitable and kind without thought of reward.'

'And since then both you and he have been looking for me! While I was looking for him! Oh, God!' she said softly and with dismayed reverence. 'All this I began. And so mistakenly! I did not know even myself. I am not now the same woman.'

'You no longer wish to marry Evrard Boterel?' asked Cadfael placidly.

'No,' she said as simply. 'That is over. I thought I loved him. I did think so! But that was children's play, and this bitter winter is real, and those birds of prey in that eyrie up there are real, and death is real, and very close at every step, and I have brought my brother into danger by mere folly, and now I know that my brother is more to me by far than ever was Evrard. But never say I said so,' she flared, 'when he comes back. He is vain enough already. It was he told you what I had done?'

'It was. And how he tried to follow you, and lost himself, and was sheltered in the forest assart where I found him.'

'And he blamed me?' she said.

'In his shoes, would not you?'

'It seems to me so long ago,' she said, wondering, 'and I have changed so much. How is it that I could do so much harm, and mean none? At least I was thankful when they told me that that good brother from Pershore – how I wish I had listened to him! – had come back to look for us, and taken Sister Hilaria away with him. Were they still here when you came from Shrewsbury? Did she go on, or turn back to Worcester?'

She had arrived at what was for her a simple question before he was ready, and the flat silence fell like a stone. She was very quick. They few seconds it took him to marshal words lasted too long. She had stiffened erect, and was staring at him steadily with apprehensive eyes.

'What is it I do not know?'

There was no way but forward, and plainly. 'What will give you no comfort in the hearing, and me no joy in the telling,' said Brother Cadfael simply. 'On the night when your upland wolves sacked Druel's house, they had already done as much to a lonely hamlet nearer here, barely two miles from Ludlow. Between the two, on their way back to their lair, it seems that they encountered, by cruel ill-luck, the two after whom you ask. It was already evening when they left Druel's holding, and the night was wild, with high winds and blinding snow. It may be they went astray. It may be they tried to take shelter somewhere through the worst. They fell in the way of thieves and murderers.'

Her face was marble. Her hands gripped desperately at the arms of her chair, the knuckles bone-white. In a mere thread of a whisper she asked: 'Dead?'

'Brother Elyas was brought back here barely alive. Your brother was watching with him last night when they both went out into the snow, who can guess why? Sister Hilaria we found dead.'

There was no sound from her for a long moment, no tear, no exclamation, no protest. She sat containing whatever grief and guilt and hopeless anger possessed her, and would show none of it to the world. After a while she asked in a low and level voice: 'Where is she?'

'She is here, in the church, coffined and awaiting burial. In this iron frost we cannot break the ground, and it may be the sisters at Worcester will want to have her taken back to them when that is possible. Until then Father Prior will find her a tomb in the church.'

'Tell me,' said Ermina with bleak but quiet urgency, 'all that befell her. Better to know the whole of it than to guess.'

In simple and plain words he told her the manner of that death. At the end of it she stirred out of her long stillness, and asked: 'Will you take me to her? I should like to see her again.'

Without a word and without hesitation he rose, and led the way. His readiness she accepted thankfully; he knew that he had gained with her. She would not be hemmed in, or sheltered from what was her due. In the chapel where Sister Hilaria lay in her new coffin, made in the brothers' own workshop and lined with lead, it was almost as cold as out in the frost, and the body had not suffered any flawing of its serene beauty. She was not yet covered. Ermina stood motionless by the trestles a long time, and then herself laid the white linen face-cloth back over the delicate face.

'I loved her very much,' she said, 'and I have destroyed her. This is my work.'

'It is nothing of the kind,' said Cadfael firmly. 'You must not take to yourself more than your due. What you yourself did, that you may rue, and confess, and do penance for, to your soul's content, but you may not lift another man's sins from his shoulders, or usurp God's right to be the only judge. A man did this, ravisher and murderer, and he, and only he, must answer for it. Whatever action of any other creature may have thrown our sister in his way, *he* had command of the hands that killed and outraged her, he and no other. It's of him her blood will be required.'

For the first time she shook, and when she would have spoken she had not her voice under control, and was forced to wait and wrestle for clear speech.

'But if I had not set my heart on that foolish marriage, if I had consented to go with Brother Elyas straight here to Bromfield, she would be living now . . .'

'Do we know that? Might not you, too, have fallen into such hands? Child, if men had not done as they did, any time these five centuries, of course things would have gone on differently, but need they have been better? There is no profit in ifs. We go on from where we stand, we answer for our own evil, and leave to God our good.'

Ermina wept, suddenly and irresistibly, but would not be seen to weep. She swept away from him to kneel trembling at the altar, and remained there a long time. He did not follow her, but waited patiently until she chose to rejoin him. When she came back her face was drained but calm. She looked very tired, and very young and vulnerable.

'Come back to the fire,' said Cadfael. 'You'll take cold here.'

She went with him docilely, glad to settle beside the hearth again. The shivering left her, she lay back and half-closed her eyes, but when he made a move as if to leave her she looked up quickly. 'Brother Cadfael, when they sent from Worcester to ask for news of us, was there word said of our uncle d'Angers being in England?'

'There was. Not only in England but in Gloucester, with the empress.' That was what she had meant, though she had been feeling her way towards it cautiously. 'Openly and fairly he asked leave to come into the king's territories himself to look for you, and leave was refused. The sheriff promised a search by his own men, but would not admit any of the empress's party.'

'And should any such be found here and taken – in the search of us – what would happen to him?'

'He would be held prisoner of war. It is the sheriff's duty to deny to the king's enemies the service of any fighting man who falls into his hands, you must not wonder at it. A knight lost to the empress is a knight's gain to the king.' He saw how doubtfully and anxiously she eyed him, and smiled. 'It is the sheriff's duty. It is not mine. Among men of honour and decent Christian life I see no enemies, on either side. Mine is a different discipline. With any man who comes only to rescue and fetch away children to their proper guardian, I have no quarrel.'

She frowned momentarily at the word children, and then laughed, with angry honesty, at the very instinct that showed her still a child. 'Then you would not betray such a man even to your friend?'

Cadfael sat down opposite her and settled himself comfortably, for it seemed she had matters on her mind, and wished to unburden herself. 'I have told you, I take no side here, and Hugh Beringar would not expect me to go always his way in every particular. He does his work and I mine. But I must tell you that he has already some knowledge of a presence in these parts, a stranger, who came to Cleeton enquiring for all you three who left Worcester together. A countryman by his dress, they said, young, tall and dark, eyed and beaked like a hawk, black-haired and dark-skinned.' She was listening intently, her underlip caught between her teeth, and at every detail the colour flamed and faded in her cheeks. 'And one that wore a sword under his cloak,' said Cadfael.

She sat very still, making up her mind. The face at her shoulder in the torchlight of the gatehouse hung vividly in Cadfael's imagination, and surely even more urgently in hers. For a moment he thought she would prevaricate, shrug off the image, declare her guide to be no more than she had said, a forester's son. But then she leaned forward and began to speak with vehement eagerness.

'I will tell you! I will tell you, and not even exact any promise, for I know I need not. You will not give him up. What I said was true, that I was taken in and helped by the forester and his wife. But the second day that I was there with them, there came a youth asking for news of such a company as I had, before I shattered it. Dressed as I was when you first saw me today, still he knew me for what I was, and so did I him, for nothing could show him less than noble. He spoke French freely, but English a little slowly. He told me that my uncle had returned, and was in Gloucester with the empress, and had sent him secretly to find us and bring us safe to him. His errand is that, and nothing more, but here he goes with danger all about him, knowing he may fall into the sheriff's hands.'

'He has eluded them so far,' said Cadfael mildly. 'He may very well go on slipping through our fingers to the end, and hale you away with him to Gloucester.'

'But not without Yves. I will not go without my brother, he knows that. I did not want to come here, but he so wished it. Let me know, he said, that you at least are in safety, and leave the hunt to me. And I have done and I will do what he bids me. But I could not bear it if through his care for us he fell into the king's hands, and was left to rot in a prison.'

'Never go looking for disaster,' said Cadfael cheerfully. 'Expect the best, and walk so discreetly as to invite it, and then leave all to God. You have not given this paladin a name.' No, but he had a face, and a memorable face, too.

She was buoyantly young. Grief was fiercely felt, but so was hope, so was joy, so was the adulation of heroes. The very thought of her champion had lifted her out of the shadows of guilt and death, she glowed as she spoke of him. 'They call him Olivier de Bretagne – it is a name they gave him in his own land, because of his parentage. For he was born in Syria, and his mother was of that country, and his father a Frankish knight of the Crusade, from England. He leaned to his father's faith, and made his way to Jerusalem to join his father's people, and there he took service with my uncle, six years ago now. He is his favourite squire. Now he has come home with him, and who else would be trusted with this search?'

'And with his small experience here and halting English,' said Cadfael appreciatively, 'he was not afraid to venture into these stormy regions, among his lord's enemies?'

'He is not afraid of anything! He is bravery itself! Oh, Brother Cadfael, you do not know how fine he is! If you could only once see him, you must become his friend!'

Cadfael did not say that he had seen him, that requisite first time, briefly, like the blazing recollection of a dream. He was thinking, with nostalgic fondness, that some other lonely soul wearing the Cross had found, somewhere in that burning land of sun and sea and sand, a woman to his liking, who must have liked him no less, if she had borne him such a son. The east was full of glorious bastards. That one of them should come home to his father's land, baptised into his father's faith, was no marvel. No need to look beyond the admirable fruit.

'You have that promise you did not ask,' said Brother Cadfael. 'Olivier is safe with me. I will do nothing to uncover him. In your need or his, I will stand your friend.'

# 9

Yves started awake out of an involuntary doze, instantly aware of movement and sound, though both seemed so distant and faint that they might have been no more than the fading shreds of a dream. Under his arm Brother Elyas lay in exhausted sleep, sunk far too deep for dreaming, and briefly at peace. His breathing was quiet and steady. The boy felt rather than heard by its rhythm how strongly Elyas had survived the night that might well have killed him, tenacious even of a life that tormented him.

Yet something, Yves was sure, he had heard, some human sound. Not the wind, for that had dropped, and as he sat very still, listening with ears stretched, he was sensible of absolute silence. There is nothing more silent than deep snow, until men break the spell. And there it came again, small and distant but no illusion, the faint murmuring of voices, a mere snatch, gone in an instant. And again, some strained moments later, the tiny jingle of metal, a horse's harness clashing. Yves got to his feet stiffly, careful not to disturb the sleeper, and fumbled his way to the door. It was still only the deep twilight that comes before the promise of dawn, but the waste of snow before him cast up an eerie pallor. The night was well advanced, and already there were men abroad. Men with horses! Yves left the door of the hut closed but unbarred, and struggled out into the drifts, in haste lest the promise of help should pass by before he could intercept it.

Somewhere down the slope, out of sight beyond a thicket of snow-heaped bushes and a clump of trees bowed down and turned white like the heads of tired old men, someone laughed, and again a bridle rang. The travellers, as he had hoped, were coming from the direction of Ludlow and Bromfield. Fearful that they might pass by, and never notice the hut at all, Yves plunged downhill, stumbling and wading, found a ridge which the wind had partially stripped, and broke into an eager run. Skirting the bushes, he began to thread the copse, fending his way through the darkness of the close-set trees with hands outstretched. The voices were drawing nearer, loud, unsubdued voices, still wordless, but a most welcome sound. Someone raised a snatch of song, someone broke in with a loud remark, and there was more laughter. Yves was somewhat disconcerted to hear it, even indignant. If these were a party searching for the wanderers, they did not sound too anxious about their errand. But even if he was mistaken in thinking them Hugh Beringar's men, what did that matter? They were men, at any rate, and they could help him.

Nearing the far edge of the copse, and with eyes now growing more accustomed to the eerie twilight, he caught glimpses of movement between the trees. He burst out into the open with their line strung before him, more of them than he had thought, ten or a dozen at least. Three horses, and four pack-ponies, well-loaded, blew forth pale clouds of frosty breath. Even in the dimness he knew the shapes of sword and axe and bow. These men went heavily armed through the ending of the night, but not in the disciplined order of Hugh Beringar's men-at-arms, rather raggedly and merrily, and soiled with smoke. Faintly but unmistakably, the stink of burning wafted from them, and the pack-ponies were loaded high with grain-sacks, wine-skins, pots, bundled clothing, the carcases of two slaughtered sheep.

His heart misgave him. Hastily he made to draw back into cover, but he had been seen, and one of the men afoot loosed a mock hunting-call, and darted into the trees to cut off his retreat. Another took up the cry, and there were the pair of them, with spread arms and broad grins, between him and return. A moment more, and half a dozen were all round him. He tried to slip between them and make off in the opposite direction from the hut, instinctively aware that whatever happened he must not betray the presence close by of Brother Elyas. But a long arm reached for him almost lazily, took him by the liripipe of his capuchon and a fistful of his hair, and hauled him painfully out to the open ride.

'Well, well!' crowed his captor, turning him about by the grip on his hair. 'What's such a small nightbird doing abroad at this hour?'

Yves struggled, but was quick to sense that he achieved nothing. Dignity forbade that he should wriggle or beg. He grew still under the large hand that held him, and said with creditable steadiness: 'Let me go! You're hurting me. I'm doing no harm.'

'Unwary nightbirds get their necks wrung,' said one, and went through the motions of wringing, with lean and dirty hands. 'Especially if they peck.'

The mounted man who led the column had halted and was looking back. A high, peremptory voice demanded: 'What game have you caught there? Bring him, let me see. I want no spies bearing tales back to the town.'

They laid hands willingly on Yves and hauled him forward to where the tallest of the three horses stood.

The horse, being mainly white, was plainly visible, the man on his back loomed only as a great shadow against the sky. When he shifted a little in the saddle to stare down at the captive, some stray gleam of lambent light flowed over the links of chain mail, and flickered out like spent lightning. Afoot, he might not be a very tall man, but the breadth of his shoulders and breast, and the lion's mane of thick hair that covered his head and flowed down on to his chest in a bushy beard made him look immense. He sat his horse as if they made one powerful body between them. He was all the more frightening because his face was but a shadow, and there was nothing to be read in it.

'Hale him close,' he ordered impatiently. 'Here to my knee. Let me see him.'

Yves felt his head yanked back by the hair, to lift his face to view. He stiffened his back and his lips, and stared up in silence.

'Who are you, boy? What's your name?' It was no common country voice, but one accustomed to lordship and to being obeyed.

'They call me Jehan,' lied Yves, and did his best to avoid having his own manner of speech so easily recognised.

'What are you doing here at this hour? Are you here alone?'

'Yes, my lord. My father folds his sheep up yonder.' He pointed firmly in the opposite direction from the hut where Elyas, he hoped, still lay asleep. 'Yesterday some of them strayed, we came out early looking for them. Father went t'other way there, and sent me this. I'm no spy, what should I be spying on? We're only bothered for the sheep.'

'So! A shepherd, eh? And a very pretty little shepherd, too,' said the voice above him drily. 'In good broadcloth that cost enough when it was new. Now take breath and tell me again: who are you?'

'My lord, I've told you true! I'm only Jehan, the shepherd's lad from Whitbache . . .' It was the only manor he could remember to the west and on the near side of Corve. He had no idea why it should raise a bellow of rough laughter from all the listening crew, and his blood chilled at hearing the short, harsh bark of mirth that came from the man above him. His own fright angered him. He set his jaw and glared up into the shadowy face. 'You have no right to question me when I am about lawful business and do no wrong. Tell your man to loose hold of me.'

Instead, the voice, interested but unmoved, said shortly: 'Hand me up that toy he wears at his belt. Let me see what our shepherds are sporting against wolves this year.'

Rough handling had plucked aside the fullness of Yves' cloak, and left his belt exposed to view, the little dagger dangling. Willing hands unbuckled it and handed it up.

'So they favour silver,' said their lord musingly, 'and precious pebbles set in their hilts. Very fine!' He looked up, aware of the first lightening of the sky to eastward. 'Time's too short for starting his tongue wagging here, and my feet grow cold. Bring him! Alive! Amuse yourselves if you must, but stop short of damaging him. He may be valuable.'

He turned at once and spurred forward, his two mounted companions bearing him company. Yves was left to the mercies of the underlings. There was never a moment when he had the remotest chance of breaking away. They valued him, or their lord's orders, so highly that at every turn three of them had a grip on him. They took his own belt, and strapped it round him just above the elbows, to deny him the use of his arms, and though it had a foot to spare about his waist, to close it thus they drew it painfully tight. They found a short cord to tie his wrists before him, palms together, and a long rope to attach him, by a running noose round his neck, to the pack-saddle of the hindmost pony. If he lagged, the noose would tighten. If he hurried he could raise his bound hands high enough to grasp the rope and slacken it enough to breathe, but he could not raise them high enough to get hold of the noose itself and keep it slack. He was shrewd enough to realise that if he fell they would stop to pick him up. They had been told to deliver him wherever their lord was bound, alive and repairable. But short of killing, they were pleased to avail themselves of the permission they had been given to use him for their amusement.

He tried to shrug a fold of his cloak into the noose when they slung it over his head, and someone laughed aloud and clouted him on the ear and dragged the obstruction loose. It was at that moment that Yves remembered that under the collar of that same cloak lay hidden the ring brooch that fastened it. It was very old, a Saxon piece with a formidable pin, the only weapon he had about him now, and they had not discovered it.

'Now, little bird, fly!' said his first captor, wheezing with laughter. 'But bear in mind you're flown on a creance. No making off into the sky for you.' And he strode away to set the column moving again after its master. Between sleep, fright and anger, Yves stood shivering and in a daze so long that the first jerk on his tether half-choked him. He had to gasp and scurry and clutch at his leash to recover, and a wave of raucous laughter washed back over him in recompense.

But after that he soon found that their jest could be made as amusing or as tame as he chose. For they had to move so modestly with their booty that he had no real difficulty in keeping up. Their loads were heavy and unwieldy, his was very light, and once fully awake, very agile. For the first few minutes he took care to give them some occasion for laughter, falling behind and then rushing to preserve his neck. These repeated recoveries brought him well acquainted with the pony to which he was tied, and its load, which was two great sacks of grain, slung in balance, and two equally vast goatskins, surely of wine, behind the grain, with an erection of bundled cloth and slung pots on top. When he scuttled up close he was moving with his cheek almost against the hair of the goatskin on his side. It bulged and undulated with the liquid within. Moreover, when he came thus close he was at the very end of this ponderous procession, and hidden by the lofty load from those who went before. And the way, though clearly they knew it too well to be much aggrieved at its drifts, still put delays enough in their path, they soon forgot to look behind.

Under the lurching load, Yves stretched up his bound hands as far as they would go, and felt under the collar of his cloak for the brooch. No one could see him here, he shrank close to the pony's patient, labouring quarter. Fumbling fingers found the edge of the metal, and felt for the ring of the pin, to draw it forth. His arms, bound cruelly tight, ached with tension, and his finger-ends were growing numb.

Doggedly he kept his hold, and began to coax the brooch loose, terrified that he might drop it, from pure strain, when it came out from the folds of cloth. If he could free it and retain his hold with arms lowered, until the use and the blood returned to his hands, he knew he could manipulate it thereafter.

The point of the pin sprang loose, and the round brooch almost slipped from his hold. He closed both hands upon it in desperation, and the point pierced his finger. He bore the prick gratefully, drew his hands down still impaled, let the blood flow freely down his aching arms and into his hands, and the thin ooze from the wound slide unregarded down his finger until he could feel power there again. He had the precious thing, sharp as a dagger. He took some minutes before he dared try to make use of it, nursing it between his locked palms, flexing his fingertips against it until they felt nimble and supple as ever.

The full goatskin wallowed beside his cheek, the morning twilight hid him. The leather, though rubbed bare of hair in places, and soft and portly with age, was tough, but the pin of the brooch was strong, and protruded the length of his little finger beyond the ring. It took him some moments to work it through the hide at the lowest part of the swaying bag, the yielding folds slithered away from him so vexingly, but he leaned a shoulder hard against it to hold it still, and the pin slid through.

A satisfying spurt of dark red followed as he drew the pin out again, and he looked down in hope, even in elation, to see the sudden red splash like blood in the whiteness of the snow beneath his feet. After the first gush the hole contracted again, but the weight of the wine kept it open, and trickled a thin drip along the way, and he thought it would do. It would not sink into the snow and be lost, for the frost was hard enough to seal it as it fell. And that way, dripping so meagrely, the load would last a long way. He hoped, long enough. But in case it should become too fine to be followed, from time to time he punched the skin, and found he could force out a brief jet, a tiny pool of wine to confirm what had gone before.

The dawn, grey and still and turning now to white mist that cut off all distances, was well upon them. A cold dawn, in which a few starved birds wheeled hopelessly. They had timed their return to the lair to be safe within before full light. If they were now near, Yves thought the depletion in the leaky wineskin might pass for a natural loss. They had been climbing for a long time. Lofty, bleak and inhospitable, the uplands of Titterstone Clee received them. Even in thick mist they knew where they were going, and knew when they drew near; they had begun to prod the pack-beasts and hurry the line along, scenting refuge, food and rest.

Yves took thought for his precious brooch, and managed to thread it inside the hem of his short tunic, out of sight. That freed his bound hands to grasp the rope that had begun to tighten uncomfortably round his neck when he tired, and haul himself along by it. It could not be far now. They had smelled their nest.

From barren, misty desert, without features within the short distance the eye could see, but always climbing, suddenly they were moving between close, low-growing trees, with rising rocks just discernible behind. Then it seemed that they emerged again upon an open summit, and there before them rose a high stockade, with a narrow gate in it, and over it showed a dark, squat, broad tower. There were men on watch, the gate opened as they approached.

Within, there were low, rough lean-to buildings all round the stockade, and men in plenty moving about between them. Below the tower a long hall extended. Yves heard cattle lowing and sheep calling plaintively. All was timber, all was new, raw and crude, but solid and formidably manned. No wonder they moved at ease in the night, insolently aware of their numbers, and of the strength of their secret fortress.

Before they entered the gate Yves had the wit to draw back the length of his leash, well away from the punctured wine-skin, and blunder in droopingly, like one exhausted and cowed. Since sighting the stockade he had let the leaky skin alone, so that it dripped only a meagre droplet by the time they halted in the snowy bailey. A leaky skin was no great marvel, and the pair to it, at least, was sound. And he had luck, for his first captor made haste to undo him and haul him away by the scruff of the neck, before anyone had noticed the thin red drip, and cursed at half a wineskin lost on the journey.

Yves went where he was dragged, scrambling meekly up the steps into the hall, and through the seething warmth and smokiness and stunning noise within. Torches burned along the walls, well primed out from the timber, a great fire blazed on a stone-laid hearth in the midst, and twenty voices at least plaited a lattice of noise though the haze, loud, merry and secure. Of furniture there was little, a few hewn benches, great tables on trestles of rough logs. Men teemed and many turned to stare and grin at the passage of this small prisoner.

At the far end of the hall there was a low dais, and here there were candles in tall sconces, hangings of tapestry, and carved chairs round a table spread with food and drinking horns and pitchers of ale, where three men sat. Yves felt himself hoisted unceremoniously by a fistful of his garments at the neck, heaved bodily to the dais, and flung down on his knees at the feet of the man who sat at the end of the table. Almost he fell flat on his face, but fended himself off with his still bound hands, and hung for a moment knocked clean out of breath.

'My lord, here's your shepherd as you ordered, safe and sound. We're unloading the goods, and all's well. Not a soul stirring on the way.'

Yves gathered himself sturdily and got to his feet. He took time to draw a deep breath and steady the shaking of his knees before he looked up into the face of the chief of these nightbirds.

Mounted and looming in the twilight, the man had seemed immense. Easy now in his great chair, he was seen to be no more than common tall, but very powerfully built, wide-shouldered, deep-chested. After a savage fashion he was very comely. Now with the candlelight to show him clearly he was more like a lion than ever, for the thick mane of curling hair and the glossy, untrimmed beard were tawny, and the large eyes, narrowed but sharp as a cat's beneath heavy lids, were of the same colouring. His lips, left naked among all that profusion of dull gold, were full and curled and proud. He eyed Yves in silence from head to foot, while Yves stared as doughtily back at him, and kept his mouth shut rather out of discretion than fright. There could be worse moments to come. At least now they were back from another successful raid, laden with booty, eating and drinking and in high content with themselves. And the lion seemed in good humour. If his slow smile was mocking, it was at least a smile.

'Loose him,' he said.

The belt was unbuckled from Yves' cramped arms, the cord untied from his wrists. He stood rubbing the blood back into aching arms, kept his eyes warily on the lion's face, and waited. A number of the henchmen in the hall had drawn in at his back, grinning, to watch.

'You've bitten out your tongue on the way?' asked the bearded man amiably.

'No, my lord. I can speak when I have something to say.'

'You might be well advised to think of something to say now, at once. Something nearer truth than you told me under the copse there.'

Yves could not see that boldness was going to do him any harm here, or the discretion of fear very much good. He said bluntly: 'I am hungry, my lord. You would hardly find a truer word than that. And I take it as between gentlemen that you feed your guests.'

The lion threw back his tawny head and loosed a shout of laughter that was echoed down the hall. 'And I take that to be a confession. Gentle, are you? Now tell me more, and you shall eat. No more hunting for lost sheep. Who are you?'

He meant to know. And for all his present easy mood, if he was baulked he would not mind by what means he got what he wanted. Yves spent a few seconds too long considering what he had better say, and got an earnest of what might follow obduracy. A long arm reached out, gripped him by the forearm, and with a casual twist dropped him wincing to his knees. The other hand clenched in his hair and forced his head back, to stare up into a face still calmly smiling.

'When I ask, wise men answer. Who are you?'

'Let me up and I'll tell you,' said Yves through his teeth.

'Tell, brat, and I may let you up. I may even feed you. A strutting little cockerel of the nobility you may be, but many a cock has got his neck wrung for crowing too loud.'

Yves shifted a little to ease his pain, drew deep breath to have his voice steady, and got out his name. This was no time for the stupidity of heroism, not even for obstinate insistence on his dignity.

'My name is Yves Hugonin. My family is noble.'

The hands released him. The bearded man leaned back in his chair at ease. His face had not changed, he had not been at all angry; anger had little part in his proceedings, which were entirely cold. Predatory beasts feel no animosity against their prey, and no compunction, either.

'A Hugonin, eh? And what were you doing, Yves Hugonin, where we found you, alone in the early morning of such a winter day?

'I was trying to find my way to Ludlow,' said Yves. He rose from his knees and shook his disordered hair back from his face. Not a word must be said of anyone but himself; he picked his way delicately between truth and falsehood. 'I was at school with the monks in Worcester. When the town was attacked they sent me away to escape the fighting and slaughter there. I was with some other people, trying to reach any safe town, but in the storms we were separated. Country people have fed and sheltered me, and I was making my way to Ludlow as best I could.'

He hoped it sounded convincing. He did not want to have to invent details. He still recalled with misgivings the shout of laughter it had provoked when he mentioned the manor of Whitbache, and claimed residence there, and wondered uneasily why.

'Where did you spend last night, then? Not in the open!'

'In a hut in the fields. I thought I should get to Ludlow before night, but the snow came on, and I lost my way. When the wind dropped and it stopped snowing,' he said, talking to evade further probing, 'I set out again. And then I heard you, and thought you might set me right.'

The bearded man considered, eyeing him with the disturbing smile that contained merriment without warmth. 'And here you are, with a stout roof over your head, a good fire at your back, and food and drink for you if you behave yourself seemly. There's a price, of course, to pay for your bed and board. Hugonin! And Worcester . . . Are you son to that Geoffrey Hugonin who died a few years back? The most of his lands, I recall, lay in that shire.'

'I'm his son and his heir, if ever I come to it.'

'Ah! There should be no difficulty, then, in paying for your entertainment.' The narrowed eyes gleamed satisfaction. 'Who stands guardian to your lordship now? And why did he let you go stravaging off into the winter so poorly provided, and alone?'

'He was only newly arrived in England from the Holy Land, he knew nothing of it. If you send now, you may hear of him in Gloucester, he is of the empress's party.' The lion shrugged that off indifferently. In the civil war he belonged to neither side, and cared nothing which side others chose. He had set up his own party, and acknowledged no other. But certainly he would extort ransom as cheerfully from one as from the other. 'His name is Laurence d'Angers,' said Yves, 'my mother's brother.' That name was known, and welcomed with satisfaction. 'He will pay handsomely to have me back,' said Yves.

'So sure?' The bearded man laughed. 'Uncles are not always so anxious to ransom nephews who will one day come into great estates. Some have been known to prefer to leave them unredeemed, to be hustled out of the world as unprofitable, and come into the inheritance themselves.'

'He would not come into my inheritance,' said Yves. 'I have a sister, and *she* is not here in this extreme.' It pierced him with sudden renewed dismay that he did not know where she was at this moment, and her situation might be just as dire as his own, but he kept his voice steady and his countenance wooden. 'And my uncle is an honourable man,' he said stiffly. 'He will ransom me and never grudge it. So he gets me back alive and undamaged,' he added emphatically.

'Complete to every hair,' said the lion, laughing, 'if the price is right.' He gestured to the fellow who stood at Yves' shoulder. 'I put him in your charge. Feed him, let him warm himself by the fire, but if you let him slip through your fingers, your own neck pays for it. When he has eaten, lock him away safe in the tower. He'll be worth far more than all the plunder we've brought from Whitbache.'

Brother Elyas awoke from the dreamless peace of sleep to the agonising dream of waking life. It was daylight, lines of pale morning slid between the boards of the hut, cold and white. He was alone. But there had been someone else, that he remembered. There had been a boy, a boy who had kept him company sturdily, and lain by him in the hay, a warmth by his side. Now there was no one. Brother Elyas missed him. In the snow they had clung together in mutual kindness, trying to alleviate more than the cold and the cruelty of the wind. Whatever became of him, he must find the boy, and make sure that no harm should come to him. Children have a right to life, a right so many of their elders have forfeited by follies, by failures, by sins. He was outcast, but the boy was innocent and pure, and must not be surrendered to danger and death.

Elyas rose, and went to open the door. Under the eaves, where the wind had driven the snow away, leaving only a thin layer, the small footmarks showed clearly, only the powdering of a late squall clouding them. They turned right, down the slope, and there in the deeper snow a short, vigorous body had ploughed a jagged furrow, round the bank of bushes, down into the coppice of trees.

Elyas followed where the boy had led. Beyond the belt of trees there was a beaten track that crossed on an almost level course, climbing gently towards the east. Horses had passed this way, and men afoot with them, enough men to carve out a flattened road. They had come from the west. Had they taken the boy away with them towards the east? There would be no tracing one child's passage here, but surely he had run and struggled down the slope to join them.

In his dream, which neither cold nor pain could penetrate, and only the memory of the boy could influence, Brother Elyas turned towards the east, and set out along the track the unknown company had taken. The furrow they had ploughed through barren level, even fall and drift was simple to follow, the weaving route was surely older than all the pathways here, made to render the climb equable and easy. It wound along the hillside in a long curve. Elyas had gone some three hundred paces when he saw beneath him the first splash of dark red in the white.

Someone had shed blood. Only a little blood, but a dotted line of ruby beads continued from it, and in a few moments he found another blossom of blood at his feet. The sun was rising now, pale through the mist, which lifted with the day. The red gleamed, frozen on the surface of the snow. Not even the brief noon sun would thaw it away, though the wind might spread blown snow over it. Brother Elyas followed, drop by drop along the way where someone had bled. Blood can requite blood. If someone had taken and hurt the boy, then a man already fingered by despair and death might still die to some purpose.

Immune from any further onslaughts of cold, pain and fear, on sandalled feet through frozen drifts, Brother Elyas went in search of Yves.

# 10

Brother Cadfael came out from High Mass with Prior Leonard, into the brief and grudging sunshine of the middle hours of the day, and the sudden glitter reflected from the banked piles of snow. A number of the priory tenants had mustered to help in the search for the missing pair, while the light was favourable and no snow falling. Prior Leonard pointed out one of them, a big, bluff fellow in his prime, with red hair just salted with grey, and the weatherbeaten face and far-gazing blue eyes of the hillman.

'That is Reyner Dutton, who brought Brother Elyas in to us in the first place. I feel shame to think what he must be feeling, now the poor man has slipped through our fingers after all.'

'No blame at all to you,' said Cadfael glumly. 'The fault was mine, if there's any question of blame.' He studied Reyner's solid person thoughtfully. 'You know, Leonard, I have been wondering about this flight. Which of us has not! It seems Elyas, once something set him off, went about it with great determination. This was no simple clambering out of bed and wandering at large. Barely a quarter of an hour, and they were well away. And plainly the boy could not turn or dissuade him, but he would go wherever it was he was going. He had an end in view. It need not be a reasonable end, but it meant something to him. How if he had suddenly recalled the attack that all but killed him, and set off to return to that place where it happened? That was the last he knew, before memory and almost life were taken from him. He might feel driven to resume there, in this twilight state of his mind.'

Prior Leonard conceded, though doubtfully: 'It might be so. Or may he not have recalled his own errand from Pershore, and started back to his duty there? It might take a man so, his wits being still so shaken up in him.'

'It comes to me now,' said Cadfael earnestly, 'that I have never been to the spot where Elyas was attacked, though I suppose it must be not far from where our sister was killed. And that again has been fretting me.' But he forbore from spelling out what he found peculiar about it, for Leonard had been a man of the cloister from puberty, serenely content and blissfully innocent, and there was no need to trouble him by reflecting aloud that the night of Hilaria's death had been a blizzard as intense as the night just past, that even lust has its preference for a modicum of shelter, and of shelter he had seen none close to her icy grave. A bed of snow and ice, and a coverlet of howling wind, do not constitute the most conducive of circumstances for rape. 'I was meaning to go out with the rest,' he said, 'as soon as I have taken a bite to eat. How if I should borrow Reyner to bring me to the place where he found Brother Elyas? As well begin there as anywhere.'

'That you could,' agreed the prior, 'if you are sure the girl will bide quietly here, and not try to take some action of her own.'

'She'll bide,' said Cadfael confidently, 'and give you no trouble.' And so she would, but not for his asking. She would wait here obediently because one Olivier, a paragon, had ordered her to do so. 'Come, and we'll ask your man if he'll be my guide.'

The prior drew his tenant out of the group before it moved off from the gatehouse, and made them acquainted. Clearly Reyner had a warm relationship with his lord, and was ready to fall in cheerfully with whatever course Leonard suggested.

'I'll take you there, brother, gladly. The poor man, to be out again in this, when it's almost been the death of him once. And he making such a good recovery. A madness must have come on him, to want out on such a night.'

'Had you not better take two of our mules?' wondered the prior. 'The place may not be far, but how far beyond may it not take you, if you should find a trace to follow? And your horse has been worked hard since coming here, Cadfael. Our beasts are fresh and hardy.'

It was not an offer to be refused. Mounted or afoot, travelling would be slow, but better mounted. Cadfael went to snatch a hasty dinner, and returned to help Reyner saddle the mules. They set forth eastward along a road by this time well trampled. The best of the day would last them perhaps four hours, and after that they must be prepared for a possible return of the snow, as well as fading light. They left Ludlow distant on their right hand, and went on along the beaten road. The sky hung heavy and grey before them, though a feeble sun still shone upon this stretch of their way.

'Surely it was not on the very highroad you found him?' said Cadfael, as Reyner made no move to turn aside.

'Very close, brother, a little to the north of it. We'd come down the slope below the Lacy woods, and all but fell over him lying naked there in the snow. I tell you,' said Reyner forcibly, 'I'll take it very ill if we lose him now, after such an escape, and him as near death when we picked him up as ever man was and lived to tell it. To filch a good man back from the grave, and cheat those devils who did their worst to thrust him under, that did my heart good. Well, please God we'll haul him back from the edge a second time. I hear you had a lad went with him,' said Reyner, turning his far-sighted blue eyes on Cadfael. 'One that was lost beforetime, and now to seek again. I call it handsome, in one so young, to stick like a burr where he could not persuade. We'll be after the pair of them, every hale man who tills or keeps stock around these parts. We are near, brother. Here we leave the road and bear left.'

But not far. A shallow bowl only a few minutes from the road, lined with bushes and two squat hawthorn trees on the upper side, to the north.

'Just here he lay,' said Reyner.

It had been well worth coming, for this posed glaring problems. It fitted the marauding pattern of that night, yes. The outlaws had come from their early raid south of the road, and crossed, it seemed, somewhere here, to climb to some track well known to them, by which they could return unnoticed into the wilderness of Titterstone Clee. Here they could well have happened on Brother Elyas, and killed him more for sport than for his gown and linen, though not despising the small pickings of the supposed corpse. Granted all that, but then, where was Sister Hilaria?

Cadfael turned to look northwards, into the gentle upland across which he had ridden with Yves before him. The brook where he had found Sister Hilaria lay somewhere up there, well away from the road. North and east from here, he judged at least a mile.

'Come up the fields with me, Reyner. There is a place I want to view again.'

The mules climbed easily, the wind having scoured away some of last night's fall. Cadfael set his course by memory, but it did not fall far astray. One thin little brook clashed under the hooves, in the suave hollows the snow lay cushioned over bushes and low trees. They were long out of sight of the road, waves of snowy ground cutting them off, as they continued to climb. They hit the tributary of the Ledwyche brook somewhat downstream, had there been any stream flowing, from the place where Sister Hilaria had been laid, and retraced its gently rising course until they came to the unmistakable spot where the coffin-shaped hole had been hacked in the ice. Even the previous night's snow, though it smoothed off the razor-sharp outlines, kept the remembrance alive. This was the place where her murderers had thrown and abandoned her.

More than a mile from where Brother Elyas had been battered and left for dead!

Not here, thought Cadfael, looking round at a hillside as bare and bleak, almost, as the bald, craggy head of Clee. It did not happen here. She was brought here afterwards. But why? These outlaws otherwise have left all their victims where they fell, and cared nothing to hide them. And if she had been brought here, from where? No one would choose to carry a dead body very far. Somewhere nearby there must be some kind of shelter.

'They'll be running sheep, rather than cattle, up here,' he said, scanning the slopes above them.

'So they do, but they'll have got the most of them folded now. It's ten years since we had a spell such as this.'

'Then there'll be a hut or two, somewhere about, for the shepherds' use. Would you know where the nearest may be?'

'A piece back along the traverse here towards Bromfield, the half of a mile it might be.' That must be along the selfsame track Cadfael had ridden with Yves on his saddle-bow, going home to Bromfield from Thurstan's assart in the forest. He could not recall seeing such a hut that day, but evening had been setting in by then.

'We'll go that way,' he said, and turned his mule back along the path.

A good half-mile it certainly was before Reyner pointed left, to a shallow bowl below the track. The roof of the hut was almost completely screened by the mounds of snow that covered it. Only a straight black shadow under the eaves betrayed its presence from above. They descended the gentle slope to come round to the southern side, where the door was, and found it thrust open, and saw by the sill of the previous night's snow along the threshold that it had not stood thus longer than a matter of hours, for within there was no snow, except for the infinitely fine powder blown between the boards.

Cadfael halted on the brink. In two places, close together, a foot had trampled flat the ridge of snow which had built against the door while it remained closed. A line of icicles fringed the eaves, and successive noons had warmed them enough to drip for a brief while each day, and freeze again before the approach of evening, for the roof was open to the south, and sheltered from the north by the rise of the land. A slow drip fell as Cadfael gazed, and a line of fine black perforations punctured the whiteness of the layer of snow below the eaves, where the wind during the night had already thinned it. At the corner of the hut the drips had bored a small pit, revealing the ripe, rounded brownness of something that was not turf nor soil. Cadfael stirred more snow away with the toe of his boot.

Frost is a great preserver. All the sunshine of all the noons had not produced thaw enough to do more than pierce the crest of this pile of horse-droppings with one tiny shaft. The next snow would cover it again, and the frost seal it. But the hole the drip had bored in it went too deep to be the result of this one day's grudging sun. No knowing exactly how many days had passed since a horse had stood here, but Cadfael judged it might be as many as five or six. Tethered? The wood of the hut was rough-hewn, and there were props under the low, projecting eaves to which a bridle could easily be hitched.

He might never have noticed the hair, pale almost to white as it was, if a sudden rising breeze had not caused it to flutter, somewhat above the level of his eye, from the rough timber of the corner. Had it been motionless it would have passed for one with the snow plastered and frozen there. It was the wind that had shaken the weight from its waving strands, and given it play to catch his eyes. He detached it carefully from the splinters that held it, and smoothed out in his hand a tress of coarse, springy hair the colour of fading primroses. The horse tethered here had rubbed shoulder and mane against the corner of the hut, and left a token behind.

And this must be the nearest roof to the brook where he had found her. And given a horse to carry it, it would be no great labour to transport the body of a murdered girl that distance. But that might be going too fast. Better see what else the place had to tell, before he jumped to such doubtful conclusions.

He stowed away the scrap of horse-hair carefully in the breast of his habit, and went into the hut. The slight tempering of the bitter air without closed round him gratefully, and the dry, faint scent of the piled hay tickled his nostrils. Behind him, Reyner watched in attentive silence.

Someone had done well with his hay harvest in the past season, and had still a plentiful store here. A bed and bedding provided together, a stout roof overhead – yes, anyone benighted would be thankful to hit on such a refuge. Someone had made use of it in the night just past, the great pile of hay was pressed down by the weight of a long body. So it might have been during other nights. So it might have been by two bodies. Yes, this could well be the place he was looking for. Yet even this place was at least half a mile from the spot where Brother Elyas had been left for dead, and his murderers had been making their way home, not scouring half a mile of deserted countryside.

'Are you thinking,' wondered Reyner, watching him, 'that it may be the pair we're seeking who were in here last night? For someone was, and there are two breadths of foot have trampled the snow on the doorsill here.'

'It could be so,' said Cadfael abstractedly. 'Let's hope so, for whoever was here went forth live and able this morning, it seems, and has left tracks we'll follow in a moment. If we've found all there is to be found here.'

'What more can there be, and they gone?' But Reyner watched Cadfael's concentration with respect, and was willing to use his own eyes. He came within, looked all round him sharply, and stirred the great pile of hay with a vigorous foot. 'Not bad lying, if they got this far. They may have taken no real harm, after all.' His disturbance of the pile had loosed a wave of scent and a tickling haze of dust, and uncovered a corner of black cloth, well buried under the load. He stooped and tugged at it, and a long black garment emerged, unrolling in his hands, creased and dusty. He held it up, astonished. 'What's here? Who would throw away a good cloak?'

Cadfael took it from him and spread it out to see. A plain travelling cloak, in the coarse black cloth of the Benedictines. A man's cloak, a monk's cloak. The cloak of Brother Elyas?

He dropped it without a word, and plunged both arms into the pile, scooping a way down to the floor like a terrier after a rat. More black cloth there, rolled up and thrust deep, deep, to be hidden from all eyes. He brought up the roll and shook it out, and a crumpled ball of white fell clear. He snatched it back and smoothed it in his hands, the austere linen wimple of a nun, soiled now and crushed. And the black, held up to view, was a slender habit tied with its own girdle, and a short cloak of the same cloth. And all thrust away into hiding, where no chance shepherd would ever think to delve until all that hay was used.

Cadfael spread out the habit and felt at the right shoulder, sleeve and breast, and the traces, all but invisible in the shrouding black, confided to his touch what his eyes could not distinguish. On the right breast a patch the size of a man's hand was stiff and caked, crusted threads crumbled away as he handled it. The folds of shoulder and sleeve bore streaks and specks of the same corruption.

'Blood?' said Reyner, watching and marvelling.

Cadfael did not answer that. He was grimly rolling up habit and cloaks together, the wimple tucked inside, and hoisting the bundle under his arm. 'Come, let's see where they went, who slept the night here.'

There was no question where the hut's last occupants had gone. From the thin layer of snow before the door, where the prints of large feet and small ones showed clearly, two tracks led downhill and merged, first with the broken slurring of people forging through a moderate fall, then ploughing a furrow to the knee and the hip through fluctuating drifts, down towards the bank of bushes and the coppice of burdened trees below. They followed, leading the mules and keeping to the narrow way carved out by those they pursued. It rounded the bushes, but cleft a passage through the belt of trees, where the branches had held off much of the fall. They emerged upon the level where the tracks of a number of men and horses crossed them, coming from the west and moving east. Cadfael stared eastward, marking the course of the tracks till they faded from sight in distance, bearing downward here towards the drainage valley of the brooks, and surely preserving the same direct line and rising again beyond, pointing straight at the wilderness of Titterstone Clee.

'Did we cross such tracks, coming up from the road? For you see the line they take. We came from below, we end above. We must have crossed.'

'We were not looking for such, then,' said Reyner sensibly. 'And the wind may have blotted them out here and there.'

'True, so it may.' He had been bent on reaching the empty coffin in the ice, he had not been paying attention to the ground. 'Well, let's see what we have here. Whoever they were, they halted, they came circling, here where the tracks from above come forth from the trees.'

'A horse turned and stood, here,' said Reyner, probing ahead. 'Then he wheeled and went on. So did they all. Let's follow a short way.'

The first scarlet flower of blood sprang up under their feet within three hundred paces. A chain of ruby beads wavered on for as far again, and there was a second starry bloom, and beyond, the chain continuing, thin and clear. The frozen snow held its dyes well. They were at the peak of the day, the brief clarity would soon be gone, but while it was at its height it showed them the frowning outline of the Clee straight before them, the goal of this ancient pathway. Distant, savage and lonely, a fit place for wolves.

'Friend,' said Cadfael, halting with his eyes on that ominous skyline, 'I think you and I part company here. By all that I can see, these are last night's tracks, and they mean several horses and many men, and something aboard that dripped blood. Slaughtered sheep, perhaps? Or wounded men? The band we have to root out come from up there, and if they were not out about their grisly business last night, these tracks lie. There's a holding somewhere binding up its wounds and laying out its dead, at the very least grieving for its goods and gear. Turn back, Reyner, follow these traces back to where they burned and stole last night, and go take the word to Hugh Beringar, to save what can be saved. Into Ludlow, if Hugh Beringar is not yet back – Josce de Dinan has as much to lose as any.'

'And you, brother?' demanded Reyner doubtfully.

'I'm going ahead, to follow them the way they took. Whether they've borne our pair away with them or not, this is our best chance to find where they've made their nest. Oh, never fret!' he said, seeing his companion frown and hesitate to leave him, 'I'll mind my going. I'm no beginner at this. But here, take these back with you, and leave them with Prior Leonard until I come.' He drew out the strand of primrose mane, mindful of its importance, and made it secure in the middle of the roll of clothing. 'Tell him I'll be with him before night.'

He had gone no more than a quarter of a mile when he crossed the tracks of Reyner's mule and his own, climbing to the brook. Loose, powdery snow had already been blown over the path there, but if he had been keeping his eyes open he must have seen that a number of travellers had passed that way, though he would not necessarily have read any sinister meaning into that, for the snow-spume had covered the dotted line of red.

From that point on the track dipped gently to cross the Ledwyche brook and the Dogditch brook, its tributary from the north-east, threading its way between holdings on either side without ever sighting them, and at once began to climb again steadily. An old, old road, maintaining its level as easily as possible over undulating country, until it was forced to climb more steeply, as every approach must, to mount to that inhospitable summit, a bleak, blistering mile of rock, starved turf, broken escarpment and treacherous, shivering moss.

The face of Clee thus approached presented surfaces of sheer cliff striated with the brief glare of sunlight. There the path certainly could not go, yet it still aimed like an arrow for the wall of rock. Soon it must veer either to right or left, to circle the hill as it climbed, and remembering the ravaging of John Druel's holding, Cadfael judged that it must bear to the right. That way they had certainly returned home on that night, leaving the village of Cleeton well below, too strongly manned to be a quick or an easy prey so late towards dawn.

Some minutes later his guess was borne out, for the path inclined to the right, and began to follow the course of a small brook, muted now by ice, that flowed down out of the mass, until it dwindled in the higher reaches, and ended in a hollow of frozen moss, which the track carefully skirted. The rocky bulk of the hill loomed on his left hand now, but often hidden from view by the folds of ground near to him, even by rare stands of stunted trees. Circling always, he climbed, until he saw below him in its bowl the desolate remains of Druel's house and byres. The next curve of the spiral took him higher, and the ruin passed from his sight.

In the rocky hillside on his left hand appeared a sudden cleft, so narrow that he might have missed it if the frail string of red drops had not turned into it. The valley within was deep and dark, and cut off at once much of the light and all the force of the wind. Herbage grew here, glad of the shelter, and had built up soil enough to support swart, strong trees. He could not be far from the summit, and he must have made more than half the circuit of the hill by this time. Whatever was at the end of this rough approach must back upon the sheer cliffs of the south-western face, and it might well be that it could be reached by no other way, except by birds.

In that thin and lofty air sounds carried far. Deep into the ravine, Cadfael had already halted to consider his next move when the distant metallic chinking came down to him in a regular rhythm. Somewhere above him a smith was at work. Then, faintly but clearly, he heard cattle lowing.

If this was their gateway, it might be strongly watched, and if he was within earshot the stronghold could not be far. He dismounted, led his mule well into the trees, and there tethered him. There was no longer any question in his mind that he had found his way to the outlaw company who had killed and pillaged across this countryside to the very gates of Ludlow. Who else would have built in this hidden and formidable place?

Where he would not venture in the open he might still penetrate with caution. He threaded a silent way up through the trees, and between their dark tops saw the grey pallor of the sky. Into that pallor a squat dark shape projected, the top of a wooden tower. He was drawing near to the source of the brook which had carved out so deep a cleft, and before him, viewed through the trees, a plateau of rock and snow opened. He saw the long, staked line of a high stockade, the crests of roofs within, the long ridge of the hall, with the tower at its end. Not a high tower, built solid and low to withstand the winds, but tall enough to have the master's view of all that surrounded it. For the outline of wall and tower stood stark on the sky. They had no need to guard their rear, except from falcons. Behind the castle the cliffs fell sheer. From a distance, Cadfael reflected, not even the tower would be visible as separate from the dark rock from which it rose.

He stood for a while memorising what he saw and heard, for Hugh would need every detail he could get. The enclosing wall was high, topped with pointed stakes set close, and by the heads he saw appear and vanish again above the serrated crest, there were watch-platforms at frequent intervals, if not a guard-walk the whole way round. Voices floated clearly from within the pale, wordless but insistent, many voices, shouting, laughing, even singing. The armourer continued his busy hammering, cattle bellowed, sheep bleated, and the hum of much busy coming and going made a confident music. They were quite unafraid, within there, they felt themselves equal to anything the hampered, divided law of the land could do against them. Whoever commanded there must have gathered to him the lawless, restless, masterless men of two or three shires, happy at seeing England torn in two, and its open wounds inviting their teeth.

Cloud was settling low overhead. Cadfael turned and made his way back to his mule, and with heightened care led him, still in the shelter of the trees, down to the opening of the ravine, and waited and listened for a while before mounting and riding. He went back the way he had come, and never encountered a living soul until he was well down towards the lowlands. There he could very well have branched left and descended to the highroad from Cleobury, but he did not do it, preferring to retrace his course all along the road the reivers used. He needed to know it well, for the night's snow, if it came as was now customary, might grievously disguise it.

It was dark by the time he came out on to the road within a mile of Bromfield, and made his way thankfully and wearily home.

Hugh Beringar did not come back until Compline, and rode in tired, hungry, and for all the cold, sweating from his exertions. Cadfael went to join him over his late supper, as soon as he came from the church.

'You found the place, then? Reyner brought you word where last night's devilry fell?' He was answered by the grimness of Hugh's face.

'And told me what you were about at the other end of it. I hardly thought to find you home before me – faith, or at all, undamaged! Need you always be the one to put your hand straight into the hornet's nest?'

'Where was it they burned and slew, last night?'

'At Whitbache. Barely two miles north of Ludlow, and they strode in and out again as freely as in their own bailey.' It fitted well. Their way home from Whitbache would run below the hut to the old road, just as Cadfael had witnessed it. 'I was back in Ludlow when your man came, I fetched Dinan out to come with me. Every house pillaged, every soul hewn down. Two women escaped by running away into the woods, and carried their babes with them, all that ails them is cold and horror, but the rest – one man may live to tell it, and two young lads, but all hurt. And the rest, dead. We've taken them into the town, the quick and the dead. They're Dinan's people, he'll see them cared for. And have blood for their blood, given half a chance.'

'Both you and he may have your chance,' said Cadfael. 'Reyner Dutton found what he was seeking, and so did I.'

Hugh's head, inclined wearily back against the wall, jerked erect again sharply, and his eyes regained their brightness. 'You found the den these wolves are using? Tell!'

Cadfael told the whole story in detail. The clearer the picture they could draw now of the problem confronting them, the better the chance of dealing with it with little loss. For it was not going to be easy.

'As far as I can see, there is but that one road to them. Behind the fortress the ground still rises somewhat, to the rim of the cliff. Whether their stockade continues round the rear of the bailey I could not see. With that drop at their backs they may have felt it unnecessary. I daresay the rocks could be climbed, in a better time of year, but in this ice and snow no one would dare attempt it. And being the men they are, I fancy they have store of stones and boulders ready in case any should venture.'

'And the place is indeed so strong? I marvel how they've contrived so much building in secrecy.'

'A place so remote and harsh, who goes there? A few holdings clinging to the lower slopes, but what is there to draw an honest man above? Not even good grazing. And, Hugh, they have an army within there, the scourings of God knows how wide a swathe of middle England, labour in plenty. And Clee Forest at their feet, and stone all about them, the only crop that summit bears. You know and I know how fast a castle can be reared, given the timber and the need.'

'But runaway villeins turned robber, and petty thieves fleeing from the towns, and such fry, do not build on such a scale, but make themselves hovels in the woods,' said Hugh. 'Someone of more weight has the rule there. I wonder who! I do wonder!'

'Tomorrow, if God please,' said Cadfael, 'we may find out.'

'*We*?' Briefly and distractedly Hugh smiled at him. 'I thought you had done with arms, brother! You think our two are within there?'

'So the tracks would seem to show. It is not certain that those who slept in the hut through the night, and ran down to meet the horsemen, were Yves and Elyas, but man and boy they were, and do you know of any other such couple gone astray in the night? Yes, I do think they have fallen into the hands of these rogues. Armed or unarmed, Hugh, I am coming with you to get them out.'

Hugh regarded him steadily, and said outright what was on his mind. 'Would they bother to burden themselves with Elyas? The boy, yes, his very clothes mark him out as worthy prey. But a penniless monk, wandering in his wits? Once already they've battered him all but to death. You think they would hesitate the second time?'

'If they had discarded him,' said Cadfael firmly, 'I should have found his body lying. I did not find it. There is no way, Hugh, of knowing what is truth, but to go out and exact it from those who know.'

'That we will do,' said Hugh. 'At first light tomorrow I go to the town, to order out on the king's business every man Josce de Dinan can muster, along with my own men. He owes allegiance, and he will pay it. He has no more use for anarchy in his own baileywick than has King Stephen himself.'

'A pity,' said Cadfael, 'that we cannot take them at first dawn, but that would lose us a day. And we need the daylight more than they do, they knowing their ground so much better.' His mind was away planning the assault, which was no business now of his, nor had been for many years, but the old enthusiasm still burned up at the scent of action. He caught Hugh's smiling eye, and was ashamed. 'Pardon, I forget myself, unregenerate as I am.' He turned back to what was his concern, the matter of troubled souls. 'There is more to show you, though it has no immediate link with this devils' castle.'

He had brought the roll of black clothing with him. He unrolled it upon the trestles, drawing aside the creased white wimple and the strand of creamy mane. 'These I found in the hay, in that hut, buried well from sight, if Reyner had not kicked the pile apart. See for yourself what lay in that hiding-place. And this – this from without, snagged in the rough wood at the corner of the hut, and a pile of horse-droppings left at the spot.'

He told that tale with the same exactness, needing another mind at work upon these discoveries. Hugh watched and listened with frowning attention, quickened utterly from his weariness and alert to every implication.

'Hers *and* his?' he said at the end of it. 'Then they were there together.'

'So I read it, also.'

'Yet he was found some distance from this hut. Naked, stripped of his habit – but his cloak left behind where they sheltered. And if you are right, then Elyas sets off wildly back to this very place. By what compulsion? How drawn?'

'This,' said Cadfael, 'I cannot yet read. But I doubt not it can be read, with God's help.'

'And hidden – well hidden, you say. They might have lain unnoticed well into the spring, and been an unreadable riddle when they did reappear. Cadfael, have these wolves hidden any part of their worst deeds? I think not. What they break, they let lie where it falls.'

'Devils do so,' said Cadfael, 'being without shame.'

'But perhaps not without fear? Yet there is no sense in it, take it all in all. I cannot see where this leads. I am none too happy,' owned Hugh ruefully, 'when I try.'

'Nor I,' said Cadfael. 'But I can wait. There will be sense in it, when we know more.' And he added sturdily: 'And it may not be so dismaying as we think for. I do not believe that evil and good can be so dismally plaited together that they cannot be disentangled.'

Neither of them had heard the door of the room open or close, the small anteroom of the guest-hall, where Hugh's supper had been laid. But when Cadfael went out with his bundle of clothing under his arm, she was there outside in the stone passage, the tall, dark girl with her sleepless, proud, anxious eyes huge in her pale face, and her black hair a great, swaying cloud round her shoulders, and he knew by the strained urgency of her face that she had come in innocence, hearing voices, and looked within, and drawn back in awe of what she saw. She had shrunk into the shadows, waiting and hoping for him. She was shivering when he took her firmly by the arm and led her away in haste to where the remnants of the day's fire still burned sullenly in the hall, banked to continue live until morning. But for the surly glow, it was in darkness there. He felt her draw breath and relax a little, being thus hidden. He leaned to stab at the fire, not too roughly, and get an answering red and gratifying warmth out of it.

'Sit down here and warm yourself, child. There, sit back and fear nothing. This same morning, on my life, Yves was live and vigorous, and tomorrow we shall bring him back, if man can do it.'

The hand with which she had gripped his sleeve released him slowly. She let her head rest back against the wall, and spread her feet to the fire. She had on the peasant gown in which she had entered at the gate, and her feet were bare.

'Girl dear, why are you not long ago asleep? Can you not leave anything to us, and beyond us to God?'

'It was God let her die,' said Ermina, and shuddered. 'They are hers – I know, I saw! The wimple and the gown, they are Hilaria's. What was God doing when she was befouled and murdered?'

'God was taking note of all,' said Cadfael, 'and making place beside him for a little saint without spot. Would you wish her back from thence?'

He sat down beside her, not touching, very considerate of her grief and remorse. Who had more to answer for? And who needed more gentle usage and guidance, in respect of her self-destroying rage?

'They *are* hers, are they not? I could not sleep, I came to see if anyone had news, and I heard your voices there. I was not listening, I only opened the door, and saw.'

'You did no harm,' he said mildly. 'And I will tell you all I know, as you deserve. Only I warn you again, you may not take to yourself the guilt of the evil another has done. Your own, yes, that you may. But this death, at whosoever's door it lights, comes not near you. Now, will you hear?'

'Yes,' she said, at once docile and uncompromising in the dark. 'But if I may not arrogate blame, I am noble, and I will demand vengeance.'

'That also belongs to God, so we are taught.'

'It is also a duty of my blood, for so I was taught.'

It was every bit as legitimate a discipline as his own, and she was just as dedicated. He was not even sure, sitting beside her and feeling her passionate commitment, that he did not share her aim. If there was a severance, yet they did not go so far apart. What they had in common, he reasoned, was a thirst for justice, which she, bred into another estate, called vengeance. Cadfael said nothing. A devotion so fierce might burn long enough to carry all before it, or it might soften and concede some degree of its ferocity. Let her find her own way, after eighteen her spirit might abate its fury as it saddened and became reconciled to the human condition.

'Will you show me?' she said almost humbly. 'I would like to handle her habit, I know you have it there.' Yes, almost humbly, she was feeling her way to some end of her own. Humility in her would always be a means to an end. But of her whole-hearted affection for the lost friend there could be no doubt at all.

'It is here,' said Cadfael, and unrolled the bundle on the bench between them, putting aside the cloak that belonged to Brother Elyas. The wisp of creamy mane drifted out of the folds and lay at her foot, stirring like a living thing in the draught along the floor. She picked it up and sat gazing down at it from under drawn brows for some moments, before she looked up questioningly at Cadfael.

'And this?'

'A horse stood tethered under the eaves of that hut for some time, and left his droppings in the snow, and this rubbed off from his mane against the rough boards.'

'That night?' she said.

'Who can be sure? But the droppings were well buried, not new. It could have been that night.'

'The place where you found her,' said Ermina, 'was not close?'

'Not so close that a man would willingly carry a body there, even to hide the circumstances of his guilt – unless he had a horse to bear the burden.'

'Yes,' she said, 'that was my thought, also.' She put the pale strands from her gently, and took the habit into her hands. He watched her drape it over her knees, and run her hands softly over the folds. Her fingers found the stiffened places, halted over the patch on the right breast, traced the folded creases that ran from it, and returned to the source.

'This is blood?' she questioned, wondering. 'But she did not bleed. You told me how she died.'

'That is true. This blood cannot be hers. But blood it is. There were faint traces on her body, where there was no wound.'

'Faint traces!' said Ermina, lifting to his face one flash of her dark eyes. She spread her palm upon the patch that stiffened the breast of the gown, opening her fingers wide to span the clotted stain that was more than a faint trace. A stain from without, then, not from within. 'His blood? The man who killed her? Well done, if she drew blood from him! And yet . . . *I* would have clawed out his eyes, but she? So slight and so gentle . . .'

Suddenly she was still, quite still, brooding with the habit raised in both hands to her breast, as it would hang if she put it on, and the red glow from the fire gilding her face and kindling reflected fires in her eyes. When she stirred again, it was to rise calmly and shake out the creases, and that done, she folded the garment meticulously, smoothing out the edges to make all neat.

'May I keep this in my charge? Until,' she said with considered emphasis, 'it is needed to confront her murderer?'

# 11

In the early morning light Hugh Beringar rode from Bromfield for Ludlow, to muster his forces for the march, and Brother Cadfael pulled on his boots, kilted his habit for riding, took his cloak, and went with him. Besides his function as guide, he had loaded his scrip with dressings and ointments for fresh wounds, of which there might be plenty before this day ended.

He saw nothing of Ermina before they departed, and was glad to believe that she must still be fast asleep, and at peace. There was a tension and withdrawal about her that made him uneasy, for no good reason that he could see. It was not simple fear for her brother that weighed on her heart, nor the grief and guilt she had already confessed and was determined to purge by penitence. That braced, armed stillness with which she had taken her leave the previous night, clasping Sister Hilaria's habit, stayed in his mind as much resembling the virgin knight's bathed and accoutred vigil before his first battle.

Blessed be Olivier de Bretagne, who had somehow found a way to master her, ousting an immature fantasy of love from her heart, and at whose command she would even remain still and inactive, and leave the burden of the day to others, wholly against her nature. But why, then, should he think of her as armed, alert and about to do battle?

Meantime they had their own battle to fight and win.

At Ludlow Josce de Dinan marched out from the

castle the force Hugh demanded of him, and came himself at their head, a big, burly, full-fleshed man of middle age, ruddy of face and well-mounted. Hugh had asked in particular for archers, and got them. In these border shires there were plenty of men skilled with the short bow, and Cadfael estimated that from the rim of the trees at the head of the gully to the stockade should be just within their range. From the shelter of the branches they could provide cover for an advance, by picking off any defenders who mounted the guard-walk within. A pity that the trees spanned barely a quarter of the open plateau, where the ravine still gave them protection from the bleakest winds, and even there they shrank to dwarf size at the crest. That open arena troubled Cadfael. There would be archers within as well as without, and loopholes to allow them a clear field without exposing them to shafts from the attackers. He had no delusions about the quality of the enemy's dispositions. Whoever had erected that fortress in that lofty place knew what he was about, and by the carefree bustle within he had mustered a formidable garrison.

The march was easier than they had expected. The night's snow had begun later and ended earlier than for some days, and without the worst winds, and Cadfael had the path well in mind. The air, still as frosty, was starkly clear here on the lower ground, but thin, bright mist cut off all summits. That might well be to their advantage when they drew close to their goal, affording at least a veil over their movements.

'Such a morning,' judged Cadfael, 'if they have been out at all in the night, they would make sure of being home and invisible early. Given a remission like this, country people will be out betimes. These night-owls have no objection to leaving their traces where they strike, but so far they've avoided being seen, except by their victims. Those who blunder into their way by chance they kill, unless they have a value living. But with one fat plucking only a night ago, maybe they won't have stirred abroad. If that's so, they'll be home and wakeful, and less drunk than after a fat foray, which is a pity.'

He rode ahead, with Hugh on one side, and Josce de Dinan a careless pace to the rear on the other. Dinan was too big a man, in every sense, to strain to keep his horse's nose level with that of Hugh's mount, or resent serving under a younger and less experienced man. He had no need to stress his own worth. Cadfael took to him. He had never before seen this supposedly dubious ally, but he thought him a man to be valued, and lost only with grief.

'They may have outposts at the approaches,' said Hugh.

Cadfael considered, and doubted it. 'Towards the foot or even halfway up, their man would be too distant to give fair warning, and too isolated for his own safety. And the best defence of the gully is that it looks so narrow and blind it must usually pass unnoticed. I was following a plain trail. I shall not miss the place. And in between, all is open. I think they rely on secrecy, and if that's penetrated, on their strength.'

The world before them lay bleak and unpeopled, the great hump of land ahead, turbaned in cloud, was a steely blue shadow. Cadfael viewed the sculptured land, narrowed his eyes, and steered his remembered course. In places the night's fall had smoothed out yesterday's tracks, but here and there they still showed faintly as dimpled hollows in the new surface. When they drew near to the stony bulk before them he slowed his pace, and went with raised head, trying to pierce the haze that hid the crest of the cliffs. He could see no square dark ridge reared above the bulk of the rock, though the outline of the rock itself showed very faintly through the veil. If he could not see the tower, there was hope that no watcher from the tower could see this approaching force, even though they moved openly and in considerable numbers. Better get them past this stage as quickly as possible, and round the first curve of the spiral pathway.

When the long gradual climb brought them out on the bleak waste of the summit, and the fissure in the rocky ground opened on their left, Hugh halted his company and sent scouts ahead. But there was no movement, no sign of life but the wheeling of a few birds in the sky above. The cleft was so narrow that it seemed likely it must close after a few paces, and could hardly be expected to lead anywhere.

'It widens, within,' said Cadfael, 'and goes on opening steadily towards the source of the stream, like most upland brooks. There are trees most of the way, though they're dwarfed above.'

They entered the defile, and deployed their numbers among the trees on either side. The mist was lifting by the time Hugh stood within the highest screen of trees, looking out over the open bowl of sparse grass and rock and snow to the stockade. The first step out of cover by any man, and the alarm would be given at once. From this thin fringe of trees onward there was no cover at all. And the distance, Cadfael saw with concern, was greater than he had thought, great enough to decimate the ranks of any attacking host, if there were competent bowmen and a proper watch within the walls.

Josce de Dinan eyed the length of the stockade and the bulk of the tower within. 'You'll not give them formal call to surrender? I see no need, and good reason against it.'

So did Hugh. Why give away the weapon of surprise, if indeed they had managed to spread their archers and men-at-arms round the meagre crescent of cover without being observed. If they could get even halfway to the walls before the archers sprang into concerted action along the guard-walk, they could save lives.

'No. These men have done pillage, violence and murder without mercy, I need give them nothing. Let's dispose our forces to the best advantage, and then have at them before they're 'ware.'

His bowmen he distributed all round the crescent. His men afoot in three groups were spaced along the rim, and his handful of mounted men in two groups between, to converge on the gate and break their way in, to make a way for the following footmen.

There was a stillness when all was ready, before Hugh, from his place as spear-head of one mounted party, spurred forward and raised his arm for the onset. He from the left and Dinan from the right burst out from cover and charged for the gate, the footmen pouring after them. The bowmen in the edge of the trees loosed one volley together, and then drew and shot at will, watching for any head that appeared above the stockade. Cadfael, left behind with the archers, marvelled that the attack could begin almost in silence but for the thudding of hooves, and even that muffled by the snow. The next moment there was uproar within the walls, a frantic scrambling of men to the loopholes, and then an answering hail of arrows. But that first charge had almost succeeded, for the gate had been unbarred, and by the time the guards had clapped it to, Hugh and Dinan and five or six more were under the wall, hidden from the defenders within, and heaving with all their might to burst into the bailey.

Within, men swarmed to hold the gate closed and bar it securely, and the din of shouted orders and confused movements washed back and forth like storm-water in a foundering ship. The stout gate was ajar, quivering, and the running foot soldiers flung themselves into the human ram to hurl it wide and break into the bailey.

From high above their heads a great voice suddenly bellowed like thunder: 'Hold, you below! King's men or whatever you be, stand, and look up here! Look, I say! Put up and quit my gates, or take this infant carrion with you!'

All heads within and without the gate came up with a jerk to stare at the top of the tower, and on both sides archers froze with bows drawn, and lance and sword were lowered. Between two of the crude timber merlons of the parapet Yves stood balanced, held by a great hand gripping his clothes in the small of the back, and over the merlon beside him leaned a raging, bristling head, tawny gold, long hair and beard streaming in a capricious wind that could hardly be felt below. A mailed hand held a naked dagger at the boy's throat.

'You see him?' roared the lion, glaring down with eyes fire-gold with fury. 'You want him? Living? Then draw off! Haul off out of range, out of sight, or I cut his throat now and throw him down.'

Hugh stood holding the sword he had drawn to probe through the yielding chink of the gate, and stared up with a white, fixed face. Yves was stiff as a beam of wood, looking neither down nor up, but straight before him at empty sky. He never made a sound.

'I do not know you, sir,' said Hugh, carefully and low, 'but I am the king's man here, and I say to you, you have now no refuge, here or anywhere. Harm him, and I will be your death. Be advised. Come down, yield yourself and all these your men and trust to find some mercy that way, for otherwise there is none.'

'And I say to you, king's man, take your rabble out of my sight, now, without argument, or you may have this piglet, bled ready for eating. Now, I say! Turn and go! Shall I show you?' The point of the dagger pricked, in the clear air they saw the little bubble of blood that grew, and burst, and slid down in a fine thread.

Hugh clapped his sword into the scabbard without another word, mounted and wheeled his horse, and waved all his men back from the stockade, back into the trees, back out of sight. Behind him he heard vast laughter that still resembled the hungry roar of a hunting lion.

Archers and all had shrunk far back to be invisible, watching that threat. They drew together in stunned silence, down among the trees. This was deadlock indeed. They knew they dared not advance, and that resplendent wild beast in the tower knew just as surely that they would not depart.

'But I know him, if you do not,' said Josce de Dinan. 'A by-blow of the Lacy clan by a younger son of the house. His brother the right side the sheets, after the father married, is a tenant of mine. This one served in France some years, for Normandy against Anjou. They call him Alain le Gaucher, because he's left-handed.'

Even those who had seen the man now for the first time needed no reminders. It was the left hand that had held the dagger against the boy's throat, and turned the point quite coldly to pierce the skin.

Yves felt himself hoisted by the small of his back, in the fist that gripped the fullness of his clothes and bruised his spine with hard knuckles, and dumped hard upon his feet on the timbers of the roof. The jarring shock ran up from his heels to his head, and shook his eyes wide open. He had been so intent upon uttering no sound that he had bitten his tongue, the blood ran warm within his lower lip. He swallowed it, and braced his quaking feet into the planks under him. The thin thread of blood trickling down his neck from the prick of the dagger hardly troubled him, and was already drying.

He had never yet been so frightened, as he had never been so rough-handled, suddenly plucked erect by the neck, hauled up confusing staircases in the dark, windowless bulk of the tower, finally dragged up a last vertical ladder and through a heavy trap to the dazzle of daylight on the roof. The lion's voice had roared in his ears, the lion's own fist had hoisted him to the parapet, with a furious lunge that might well have hurled him over. By instinct he had held his tongue, and made no sound. Now, suddenly released, he felt his knees give way under him, and stiffened them indignantly. He still had not uttered word or cry. He held that thought to him like an accolade, and stood doggedly waiting for the pounding of his heart to ease. It was an achievement that he stood erect at all.

Alain le Gaucher stood with hands spread along the merlons, grimly watching the besiegers draw off into the gully. The three of his men who had followed him aloft here stood waiting for his orders. So did Yves, bracing himself not to quail when the thick, powerful body swung round on him, and the fiery eyes hung on him with calculating intensity.

'So the brat has his value still, if not in money! Good reason to hold him fast, we may have to make further use of him to the same end. Oh, they'll not go far out of sight, I know – not yet, not until they've tried every roundabout way they can find, and been baulked at every attempt by a small knife at a small piglet's throat. Now we know they'll dance to our tune. Imp, you may yet be worth an army to us.'

Yves found no comfort in that. They would not even seek a ransom for him, his value as a hostage being far higher, now that their fortress was known. They could not hide it again, and enjoy the secrecy of their night exploits by wiping out every witness, as before. But for some while, at least, they could go on repeating the threat to kill their prisoner, perhaps even bargain with his life for freedom to march out unchallenged and resume their activities elsewhere. But no, Hugh Beringar would not so tamely give up, nor would he leave a hostage in such hands a moment longer than he must. He would find some way, short of frontal assault, of breaking into this lair. Yves did his best to believe that, and kept his face expressionless and his mouth shut.

'You, Guarin, stay here with him. You shall be relieved of the watch before dark, and he'll give you no trouble. Short of clambering over the parapet and dashing his brains out below, what can he do? And I fancy he's not yet so mad with fear as to choose that way. Who knows, he may even come to like the life with us – eh, chicken?' He jabbed a hard finger into Yves' ribs and laughed. 'Have your dagger ready. If they come out of hiding, if you see any man of them making roundabout to come at us, challenge on the instant, and repeat the threat. And if they persist,' he said, with a sudden snap of large teeth like a trap closing, 'bleed him! If it comes to worse yet, I'll take the knife myself. Me they'll believe!'

The man called Guarin nodded and grinned, and loosened his dagger in its sheath, suggestively.

'The rest of you, down, and we'll make better dispositions. I want a watch on every foot of our boundaries. They'll be probing busily before they give up from the cold. There's no sheriff born is going to camp in the open up here in such a winter. Not for longer than a night.'

There was a ring set into the trap, by which to lift it. He set his own great hand to it, and heaved it out as easily as lifting a ladle, and dropped it with a hollow thud upon the boards. Below, it could be secured by bolts, the metal rang as it fell.

'We'll shut you up here, for safety's sake. Never fret, you shall have your food brought, and quit your watch by twilight, but with this chick fresh from the egg I take no chances. He's too effective a tool to risk.' He clouted Yves on the shoulder in passing, as forthrightly as he had stroked the knife across his throat, and plunged through the trap, swinging down the tall ladder to the next floor. His men followed him briskly. Guarin hauled the trap into place, and they both heard the bolts slide into their sockets below, and the last man clambering down the ladder.

The two of them were left in their rough timber eyrie, staring at each other. There was frozen snow under their feet, and frost in the air they breathed. Yves licked dried blood from his lip, and looked about him for the most favourable ground. The tower had been built high enough to command as wide a view as possible, without allowing its own outline tc stare too obviously above the line of the rock. The wall surrounding it rose breast-high to him before the merlons began, he could lean between them and look out every way, but to the rear, above the sheer cliffs, he could see only the rim of the escarpment, and beyond, the distant land below. The space up here was too wide and open to be comfortable, wind and weather could make it a bitter ordeal, though this day was better than any that had gone before.

Within his vision nothing now stirred, except for the fierce bustle inside the bailey, where every watch-point was being manned, and every loophole supplied with an archer. The king's men had gone to earth like foxes. Yves selected the snow-free corner of his ground, backing into the wind, and sat down on the boards there with his back hunched against the timbers and his arms hugging his knees. Every contact nursed a shred of warmth. He was going to need all he could get. But so was Guarin.

Not one of the worst of them, this Guarin. Yves had taken the measure of many of those close about their chieftain, by this time, he knew those who took pleasure in hurting, in defiling, in making other human creatures writhe and abase themselves. And there were more than enough of them, but this Guarin was none. The boy had even learned how some of them had come into this service, and could pick out worst from best. Some were footpads, murderers, thieves from choice, born to prey on their own kind. Some were petty tricksters from the towns, who had fled from justice and taken refuge where even their small skills could be used. Some were runaway villeins who had committed some angry revolt against tyranny, and put themselves on the wrong side of the law. Several were of better birth, younger sons and landless knights who considered themselves soldiers of fortune in this company. Some were even men disabled in honest service, and cast off when they were of no further profit; but these were few, and trapped, they did not belong in this garrison, but had blundered into it by ill-fortune, and could not get loose.

Guarin was a big, slow-witted, easy-going soul, without cruelty. He had no objection, as far as Yves could see, to robbing and sacking and burning, provided others did the killing. He would go with the crowd and behave himself conformably, but he would rather not let blood himself if it could be avoided. But for all that, he would carry out his orders. It was the only way he knew of ensuring a share with the rest, all the food he needed, and all the drink, a roof above him, and a fire. If his lord told him point-blank to kill, he would kill and never hesitate.

The day enlarged over the two of them, and brightened. The murderous weather, if it had not yet softened, held a kind of promise. It was past noon when someone thumped merrily at the trap, hauled back the bolts below, and rose out of the dark, wood-scented pit of the tower with a bag of bread and meat and a pitcher of hot, spiced ale for the watchman. There was enough for two, and Guarin spared a portion for his prisoner. They were lavish with their provender. They had the provisions from at least four local holdings to feed them.

The food and drink helped for a while, but as the day wore away the cold came down again and bit hard. Guarin stamped about the boards to keep himself warm, constantly patrolling in order to keep watch in every direction, and paid no attention to his prisoner except for a hard stare now and again to remind him that he was helpless, and had better not attempt anything on his own behalf. Yves fell into an uneasy doze for a while, and awoke so cold and stiff that he found it necessary to get up and stamp his feet and clap his arms vigorously to get his blood flowing again. His guard laughed at that, and let him dance and exercise as he liked. What harm could he do?

The light was beginning to fail. Yves fell to pacing the tower a few steps behind his watchman, peering out at every embrasure upon a world still peopled only by his enemies. On the precipice side, in particular, he craned perilously to see below, but still had only the barren cliff-edge and the distance before him. That entire side of the square tower looked out upon the sky. But at the eastern corner, while Guarin's back was turned, Yves found a rough join in the timbers by which he could gain a foothold and hoist himself up to achieve a better view. Below him the rim of rock levelled out, and by straining perilously round towards the void he could see at last that the stockade did not continue all round the castle, but terminated where it met the cliff-edge. Here at the corner the drop was not quite sheer, he could see the first jagged folds over the edge, every ledge with its smooth burden of untrodden snow. All that motionless, empty whiteness everywhere, as though the friends on whom he relied had deserted him.

But the whiteness was not quite motionless, nor the rocky landscape quite empty. Yves blinked in disbelief, seeing the outline of one hanging drift move, and show for an instant the shape of a raised head, a shadowy visage lifted briefly to judge the next stage of a solitary and perilous climb. The next moment there was nothing to be seen there, at the extreme edge of the stockade and some ten yards down the broken face, but a mound of snow. Yves stared, straining anxious, elated eyes, but there was no more movement.

A shout behind him caused him to slither down frantically from his perch, even before Guarin's hand plucked him down and shook him heartily. 'What are you about? Fool, there's no way down there for you.' He laughed at the thought, but blessedly did not look where the boy had been looking. 'As well get your throat slit as break your bones at the bottom of that fall.'

He kept his grip on the boy's shoulder, and

marched him along before him, as if he really believed his prisoner might yet slip through his fingers and cost him dear. Yves went where he was hustled, and thought it wise to whine a little about his usage, to keep the man amused and distracted.

For now he was sure he had not been deceived. There was a man down there among the rocks, a man who had covered his dark garments with a white linen sheet to move invisibly in the snow, a man who had clambered at his peril, surely not up the whole cliff-face, but laboriously round the rim from the trees, just below vision, to make his way out across the rock face beyond the stockade, and into the bailey where no one watched, where it was thought impenetrable. And in so disciplined a fashion, slow-moving even in this icy coldness, able to freeze into ice himself, and be part of the rocks and the winter. And now he was waiting for the dark, before venturing the last perilous passage.

Yves trotted submissively where the hand gripping his shoulder drove him, and hugged to his heart the blazing conviction that he was not abandoned, that heroes exerted themselves on his behalf, that heroism was also required of him before all was won, and that he must not fall short.

Darkness had closed in, and Guarin was the one complaining, before his relief came clattering up the ladder, shot back the bolts, and heaved up the trap to emerge on the roof.

This one was decidedly not among the least offensive, a bristle-bearded, pock-marked, flat-nosed cutpurse with a malicious fist, and dirty nails that liked pinching. Yves had some few bruises from him already, and gnawed a dubious lip at seeing him burst up out of the depths. He knew no name for him. Possibly he had never had a name, only some epithet by which he might be known, short of proper parentage or Christian baptism.

Guarin was none too fond of him, either, he grunted vexation at such a late relief, when he had been promised it before dark. They snarled at each other before parting, which left Yves time to shrink into his sheltered corner out of sight and mind. There might be a bleak interval. But there was someone out there in the enclosing night, not so far away, coming to his aid.

Guarin grumbled and clumped his way down the long ladder, and Yves heard the bolts shot home. They had their orders. He was left isolated here with this unpredictable cutthroat, who would stop only short of his lord's ban. He dared not kill or maim. Short of either, no doubt he would take it for granted he had free leave to hurt.

Yves sat back against the solid timber wall, shrunken into his corner with back to the wind. It was made clear to him at once that his new guard felt no goodwill towards him, blaming him for the discomfort of being perched up here in the frosty night, instead of below by the fire.

'Pest of a brat,' he snarled, and kicked savagely at the boy's ankles in passing, 'we should have cut your throat there on the road where we first met you. If the king's men had found you dead they'd have had no call to hunt for you living, and we should have been snug and merry here still.' All of which, Yves had to own as he drew in his feet and sat hunched in his corner, was probably true enough. He made himself as small as he could, and held his tongue, but silence did nothing to placate his custodian, rather it seemed to infuriate him.

'If I had my way, you should dangle from one of these merlons for the kites. And never think you'll escape it in the end. Whatever bargain they strike over you, it can be broken once we're clear away. What's to stop you being promised in return for passage, and delivered up carrion? Devil take you, answer me!' He kicked out again viciously, driving his toe deliberately at the boy's groin. The stab was not quite evaded, as Yves rolled hastily away, and cost him a gasp of pain and rage.

'What's to stop it?' he flashed, goaded. 'Only that your lord still keeps some dregs of his breeding, and puts some small value on his word. And you'd best do his bidding to the letter, for this moment he has far more use for me than he has for you. He could swing *you* from a merlon with a light heart and nothing to lose.'

He knew he had been a fool, but he was sick of trying to be wise against his nature. He saw the great fist coming for his hair, and dived below it and sprang clear. On this limited ground he might be cornered in the end, but he was lighter and faster than his tormentor, and at least movement was warmer than keeping still. The man came after him, shrewd enough to do his cursing low-voiced, for any bellowing up here was liable to fetch someone up to enquire the cause. He muttered his obscenities as he charged, both thick arms flailing for a hold. 'What, you naked chick, use such insolence to me, would you? Big talk from a thrapple I could wring one-handed? If your neck's safe, is that warrant for your skin? Or a few teeth down your saucy throat?'

In the act of slipping beneath a grasping arm, Yves saw beyond his enemy's shoulder the heavy trap in the floor beginning to rise. They had been too intent on each other to hear the bolts being withdrawn, even if it had not been done with unusual care and quietness. The head that emerged, though seen only by this late twilight, which below must be already full darkness, was none that Yves knew, and came forth so steadily and silently that his heart leaped with desperate hope. How do you recognise at first sight someone who cannot possibly be a member of an outlaw gang of thieves and murderers? If the guard turned fully about now, he would be looking straight at the newcomer, who was just setting foot to the boards and rising erect. This raving, fumbling wretch must not turn! And if Yves eluded him now he would turn, to follow and punish.

Yves slipped in the frozen snow, or seemed to slip, and the threshing fist had him by the breast of his cotte and slammed him back against the parapet. The fellow to it gripped his hair and forced his head up, as the creature spat copiously in his face, and laughed in triumph. Wrenching aside as best he could from the infamy, and unable to raise a hand to wipe the slime away, Yves saw the invading stranger straighten to his full height, without haste or sound, and lower the trap back into place, eyes fixed all the while on the writhing pair pinned to the wall before him. He did not quit the sensible precaution to rush to the rescue. It was the greatest of praise, and Yves felt his heart swell with gratitude and admiration. For he had just been shown that his act had been understood and appreciated, that he was not a mere victim, but a partner in this secret and splendid war.

He saw the first rapid, silent stride taken towards him, and then his head was buffeted violently aside by a great blow on the cheek, and a second that knocked him back again, and turned him dizzy and faint. To make all sure, he raised his voice in a frantic whine, not too loudly, but enough to cover the movements of one who must be already close: 'Don't! You're hurting me! Let me go! I'm sorry, I'm sorry . . . don't hit me . . .' Something of a crow about the tone, and his hackles erected all the time, but this creature did not know the difference, he was chuckling and quaking with merriment.

He was still laughing when the long arm took him about the face, muzzling his mouth, and jerked him backwards to the boards, and a long-legged, agile, youthful body dropped astride him, drove a knee into his belly, and therewith all the wind out of him, and jolting off his conical steel helmet, calmly hoisted him high enough to drive his skull back against the wood with stunning force, laying him out on the floor limp as a landed fish, and just as silent.

Yves dropped ecstatically upon the pair of them, like a half-trained hawk stooping, and fell to unbuckling the belt that held the guard's sword and dagger. His hands were shaking, but he went about it eagerly, peeled loose the arms, and shoved the belt towards the stranger, who was waiting for it with commending and commendable placidity and patience, and had it drawn tightly round the guard's upper arms, hobbling them behind his back, before he turned to look closely at his helper. He was smiling. The light here was only from a haze of stars, but very pure and clear, and the smile was unmistakable.

He reached a hand into the ample breast of the brown homespun cotte he wore, hauled out a long white roll of linen, and held it out to Yves.

'Wipe your face,' said a calm, low voice, in which both smile and praise were implicit, 'before I use it to make this loud mouth mute.'

# 12

Yves scrubbed the slime from his cheek and brow in awed and fascinated silence, round eyes fixed all the while upon the face that fronted him across the sprawled body of his tormentor. The faint starlight caught the gleam of white teeth, and bright eyes that shone like amber. The capuchon had fallen back from ruffled black hair that did not curl, but curved and clasped in a thick cap about a shapely, vigorous head. Every line and every movement cried out his youth and audacity. Yves gazed and lost his heart. He had had heroes before, his own father among them, but this one was new and young, and above all, present.

'Give!' said his ally briefly, and snapped demanding fingers for the length of linen, which Yves hastily surrendered. An end of the cloth was shoved briskly into the guard's open mouth, the length of it whipped about his head to make him blind as well as dumb, and secured round his shoulders to the belt with which his arms were already pinioned. For want of a cord to bind the prisoner's legs, the lacings of his leather jerkin were stripped out in a moment, made fast around his ankles, and doubled back to tie his feet to his wrists in the small of his back. He lay like a package made compact and neat to be slung one side of a pony for carriage. Yves watched, great-eyed, marvelling at the economy of the movements involved in the process.

They eyed each other, in the breathing space that followed, with mutual content. Yves opened his mouth to speak, and was hushed by a forbidding finger on lips still reassuringly smiling.

'Wait!' said the deep, serene voice, just above a whisper. Whispers have no identity, but carry alarmingly. This muted murmur reached no ears but the boy's. 'Let's see if we may leave the way I came.'

Yves crouched, charmed into stillness, ears pricked, listening and quivering. His companion lay flat over the trap, an ear to the wood, and after a few moments cautiously hoisted one edge to peer down into the timber-scented darkness of the tower below. From outside, about the bailey and the guard-walk along the stockade, came the sounds of movements and voices, from a garrison on the alert, but below among the shadowy beams there was silence and stillness.

'We may essay. Follow close and do as I do.'

He lifted the trap and swung himself down the ladder by his hands, agile as a cat, and Yves scurried after him. In the dimness of the floor below they froze again, backs to the darkest wall, but nothing moved to threaten them. There were fixed stairs, rough but solid, from the corner of this level. They had reached the middle of the flight and could hear the hum and bustle of activity in the hall, and see the flickering of torches and firelight round the rim of a great door below. One more flight, and they would be in the base of the tower, and level with the hall, only that door between them and Alain le Gaucher and his outlaws. A long arm drew Yves close, and again held him still to listen and watch.

The base of the tower was half of rock and half of beaten earth, and the air that came up to them was colder here than between the massive timbers above. Peering down fearfully, Yves could see in a far corner the foot of a deep embrasure, and felt the strong draught that blew from it. There was a narrow outer door upon the night, surely the door by which his rescuer had entered, and if they could but reach it unobserved they might yet make their way back by the same route, out of this enemy stronghold. He would not be afraid, with this superb being as a guide, even to venture the traverse of the rocks in the dark. What one had done alone, surely two could do together.

It was the first tread of that final staircase that undid them. Until then all had been solid and silent, but as soon as a foot was set on this warped board it tilted and settled again with a loud clap, and the echoes took the impact and flung it about the tower in a chain of hollow reverberations. In the hall someone cried out an alarm, there was a rushing of feet, and the great door was flung open, spilling forth firelight and armed men.

'Back!' snapped the stranger instantly, and whipped round without hesitation to hoist the boy before him up the flight they had just descended. 'Up to the roof, quickly!' There was no other way of retreat, and the brief check below to accustom eyes to the darkness after the lighted hall could last only a moment. It was already over, the foremost man loosed a great bellow of alarm and rage, and came for the stairs in a bull's rush, with three or four more on his heels. The blast of the uproar they raised almost blew the fleeing pair up the steps of the tower.

Where the long flight ended, the ladder in sight, Yves felt himself lifted and flung halfway up to the open trap, and that was the height of a tall man. He gripped and climbed, but looking over his shoulder and hesitating, loth to leave his companion behind, until he was ordered sharply: 'Go! Up, quickly!' He completed the climb in a wild scramble, and flung himself down on his belly by the trap, craning anxiously over the rim, just in time to see, in a confusion of shadows further confused by the starlight through the trap, how the foremost pursuer came lurching up the narrow wooden treads of the stairway, drawn sword flailing. A big, bulky man, blocking off from view those who followed him.

Yves had not even noticed, until that moment, that his ally already wore a sword. The one they had taken from the guard still lay here on the roof, though Yves had possessed himself of the dagger and buckled it proudly to his belt as substitute for the one taken from him. The brief flash of a blade, like distant lightning, stabbed the darkness below, a trick of starlight following its slashing course. The outlaw loosed an outraged yell, his short sword struck from his hand and flung below to clatter on the boards. The next moment a braced foot took him in the chest and hurled him backwards while he was off balance. Down he went in a long, echoing fall, and swept his followers down with him. The stairway was narrow and unguarded, two or three went backwards under their leader's massive weight, one at least went over the side, to a heavier fall below.

The young man turned without another glance, and sprang halfway up the ladder to the roof, and in a moment was beside Yves. The naked sword he swung glittering along the ice of the roof, and leaned to grip the uprights of the ladder with both muscular hands, and haul it aloft after him. As soon as Yves had recovered his wits he leaned eagerly to clutch from rung to rung and help to hoist the weight. With all his might, and all the breath he had regained, he heaved and exulted. The ladder had been braced against a wooden bar both below and above, but not fixed. It rose blithely, out of reach of the tallest long before the first of the attackers erupted furiously below and leaped to try and hold it.

The lower end rose clear, tilted aside and clattered on the roof, ringing a glassy cry from the splintered ice. The roars of anger below fumed out of the open trap, and Yves leaned to drag the cover over to shut them out, but his ally waved him aside, and the bewitched boy drew back obediently. Whatever his hero did would be right and wise.

And his hero, palpably smiling, though the smile was hidden in the dark, simply took their prisoner, now uneasily stirring in his bonds, by the cord that bound his feet to his wrists in the small of his back, dragged him to the trap, upended him judiciously so that his head should not take the impact below, and tipped him almost gently through the trap to fall upon his friends, and lay two or three of them flat on the boards. Their startled and aggrieved outcry was cut off when the trap was clapped into place above.

'Quick, now,' said the placid voice almost chidingly, 'here with the ladder, here over the trap. So! Now you lie there upon that end, and I upon this, and who will shift us?'

Yves lay as he had been ordered, flat on his belly on the ladder, his face buried in his arms, panting and shivering, for a long time. The boards under him throbbed to the din below, spent in ugly fury six feet short of reaching the trap. And if they did rear something that would enable them to reach it, how were they to shift it or penetrate it? The trap fitted close, no lance nor sword could be thrust through the cracks. Even if they should climb up and batter a way through with an axe, only one could emerge at a time, and they two above were armed and ready. Yves lay braced, willing his weight to be double, spreading arms and legs, holding his breath. For all the bitter cold, he was in a lavish sweat.

'Look up, my heart,' said the voice at the other end of the ladder, almost gaily, 'and show me that gallant face again, bruises, grime and all. Let me look at my prize!'

Yves lifted his head from his arms and stared dazedly along the ladder into bright, gold-gleaming eyes and an indulgent, glittering smile. A young, oval face under that thick, close cap of black hair, high-cheekboned, thin-black-browed, long-lipped, and with a lean, arrogant beak of a nose, like a scimitar. Smooth-shaven as a Norman, smooth-skinned as a girl, but of an olive, glossy smoothness.

'Take breath, and let them rave, they'll tire of it. If we failed to get past them, neither can they get at us. We have time to think. Only keep well below the parapet. They know their ground, and might think it worth setting their archers to watch for an unwary head.'

'How if they set fire to the tower and burn us out?' wondered Yves, trembling as much with excitement as fear.

'They're no such fools. They could not, without setting the hall ablaze with it. Moreover, why be in haste to do anything, when they know we cannot break out? Here in the cold or in a cell below, they have us cornered. As at this moment, true enough. You and I, Messire Yves Hugonin, have some thinking of our own to do.' He cocked his head, raising a hand for silence, to listen to the babel of voices below, which had sunk into a low, conspiratorial muttering. 'They grow content. We're securely trapped up here, they'll leave us to freeze. They're needed below, all that's wanted here is a couple of men to watch our only way out. They can wait to flay us.'

The prospect did not seem to dismay him at all, he stated it serenely. Below them the hum of consultation receded and stilled. He had judged accurately, Alain le Gaucher knew how to concentrate on what was most urgent, and needed all his company to man his stockade. Let his prisoners, lords though they might be of a tower-top some dozen or so paces square, enjoy their lordship until it chilled them into helplessness, and if need be, killed them. Whatever they did, they could not get away.

A wary, suspicious stillness fell below. And the cold, no question of it, was biting sharply, congealing into the deepest, darkest and deadliest of the night.

The young man eased from his braced listening, and turned to reach a long arm towards the boy. 'Come close, let's share what warmth we have. Come! In a while we may move, but now we'll hold down the lid together over hell a little longer. While we consider what to do next.'

Yves wriggled thankfully along the ladder and was drawn warmly into the embracing arm. They settled together until they found mutual ease, and fitted snugly into one comforting mass. Yves drew breath deep into him, and leaned his cheek almost shyly into this admired and welcoming shoulder.

'You know me, sir,' he said hesitantly. 'I do not know you.'

'You shall, Yves, you shall. I had no leisure until now to present myself respectfully to your lordship. To any but you, my friend, I am Robert, son to one of the foresters of Clee Forest. To you . . .' He turned his head to meet the boy's round-eyed, earnest stare, and smiled. 'To you I can freely be what I really am, if you can keep a blank face and a still tongue when needed. I am one of the newest and least of the esquires of your uncle, Laurence d'Angers, and my name is Olivier de Bretagne. My lord is waiting anxiously in Gloucester for news of you. I am sent to find you, and I have found you. And be sure, I will not now lose you again.'

Yves sat speechless, lost between bewilderment, joy and apprehension. 'Truly? My uncle sent you to find us and take us to him? They did tell me in Bromfield that he was seeking us – my sister and me.' The thought of Ermina made him tremble and falter, for what was the use of being found while she remained lost? 'She – my sister . . . She left us! I don't know where she is!' It ended in a forlorn wisp of sound.

'Ah, but I have the better of you there, for I do know! Make your mind easy about Ermina. She is safe and well in the Bromfield you abandoned. True, believe me! Would I lie to you? I myself took her there to join you, only to find before ever we reached the gate that you were away again on a quest of your own.'

'I couldn't help it, I had to go . . .'

It was almost too much to take in, so suddenly. Yves gulped down wonder and grew coherent. Now that he need no longer worry and grieve over Ermina's fate, whatever the perils hanging over his own, he recoiled for support into resentment against her for ever bringing him and so many others to this pass. 'You don't know her! She won't be bidden,' he warned indignantly. 'When she finds I'm gone she may do *anything*! It was she who caused all this, and if the fit takes her she'll fly off again on some mad folly, You don't know her as I do!'

He thought it an innocent stranger's over-confidence that Olivier laughed, however softly and amiably. 'She'll be bidden! Never fret, she'll be waiting in Bromfield. But I think you have a story to tell me, before I tell mine. Heave it off your heart! You may, we had better not move from here yet. I hear someone stirring below.' Yves had heard nothing. 'You left Worcester a fugitive, that I know, and how your sister left you, and why, that I know, too. She has told me, and made no secret of it. And if it please you to know the best, no, she is not married, nor like to be yet, but thinks herself well out of a foolish mistake. And now what of you, after her going?'

Yves nestled into the rough homespun shoulder, and poured out the whole of it, from his first wanderings in the forest to the remembered comfort and kindness of Father Leonard and Brother Cadfael at Bromfield, the tragedy of Sister Hilaria, and the desperate sally after poor, possessed Elyas.

'And I left him there, never thinking . . .' Yves shrank from remembering the words Brother Elyas had spoken, as they lay side by side in the night. That was something he could not share, even with this admirable being. 'I'm afraid for him. But I did leave the door unbarred. Do you think they would find him? In good time?'

'In God's time,' said Olivier positively, 'which is always good. Your God cares for the sick in mind, and will see to it the lost are found.'

Yves was quick to note the strangeness of the chosen words. '*My* God?' he said, looking up with sharp curiosity into the dark face so close above his own.

'Oh, mine also, though I came to Christendom somewhat roundabout. My mother, Yves, was a Muslim woman of Syria, my father was a crusader of Robert of Normandy's following, from this same England, and sailed for home again before ever I was born. I took his faith and went to join his people in Jerusalem as soon as I came a man. That's where I found service with my lord your uncle, and when he returned here I came back with him. I am a christian soul like you, though I chose it, where you were born to it. And I feel in my bones, Yves, that you will encounter your Brother Elyas again none the worse for the cold night you spent. We'd best be giving our minds rather to how you and I are to get safely out of here.'

'How did you ever get in?' wondered Yves. 'How did you know I was here?'

'I did not *know* it, until this rogue lord of yours hoisted you on the wall there with a knife at your throat. But I saw them pass by with their booty, at some distance, and thought it worth tracking such a company to its den. If they were harrying the countryside by night, and you lost by night . . . It was possible they might take prisoners, if there was profit to be made out of them.'

'Then you saw, you know, that we have an army of our friends close at hand,' said Yves, suddenly glowing with a new and wonderful idea.

'Of your friends, surely. But mine? Friends better avoided, no blame to them. Have you not understood that I am your uncle's man, and your uncle is liegeman to the Empress Maud? I have no wish to fall into the sheriff's hands and sit drumming my heels in a Shropshire prison. Though I owe them a favour, too, for it was under cover of their onslaught that I made my way round and on to the rocks below unnoticed, while these vermin within rushed to slam the gates. I should never have succeeded but for the distraction they provided. And once round the stockade in the dark, what difference between one lumpish ruffian stalking the bailey and all the others? I knew where they had left you. I saw your guard relieved.'

'Then you saw that the only reason Hugh Beringar drew his men off was because they threatened to kill me. And he is not gone far, I know it, he would not give up so easily. And now, don't you see, there is no one holding a knife at my throat, and no reason why they should not attack!'

Olivier had caught his drift, and was eyeing him with respect and amusement. His gaze roved speculatively from the guard's discarded sword, lying in its sheath under the wall, to the battered conical steel helmet which had rolled into a corner beside it. The amber eyes in their deep, black-lashed settings, came back to Yves, dancing.

'A pity we have no trumpets to sound the onset, but the makings of a very serviceable drum we certainly have. Under the wall with it, then, and try what you can do, while I stand guard here. They'll have but a matter of minutes to spend trying to hack their way through at us, after that they'll be busy below, if your friends out there are as quick-witted as you.'

# 13

Brother Cadfael had spent the entire day prowling through the belt of trees, from one end of the crescent to the other, and back again, studying every fold of ground between him and the stockade, in search of even the most tenuous cover by which, once darkness came, a man might hope to approach nearer. Hugh would not allow any man to show himself in the open, and had gone to great pains, while deploying his forces as widely as possible, to keep them well out of sight. Alain le Gaucher could not get out, and the sheriff's powers could not get in, and absolute deadlock had Hugh gnawing his knuckles in frustration. Small doubt but there were lavish supplies of stolen meat and grain within, enough to keep the garrison snugly for some time. Starving them out would be a long business, and starve the unfortunate boy in the process. Le Gaucher might be willing to surrender him in return for free passage out for himself and all his men, but that would only be to place some other unhappy region under the same scourge. Not even a last resort! It was Hugh's business to restore order and do justice in this shire, and he meant to see it done.

He had singled out from his ranks a number of men who claimed skill in climbing, and were born and bred in hill country, and drawn them back out of the ravine, to prospect round the summit in both directions, and see if they could find a level where it might be possible to climb out and penetrate the enclosure from the rear without being seen from above. The slight rise of the lip of land behind the fortress afforded cover, but from below it was seen to be cover for a sheer drop where only birds could hope to find foothold. The only remaining possibility was where they could not reconnoitre without being seen, and provoking a blade at the boy's throat yet again. Close to the stockade there might just be ground enough to let a man inch his way round to the rear, if he had a good head for heights. But to make the assay he would have had to cross a part of that bleak expanse of open rock, making Yves' death likely and his own certain.

But in the darkness, yes, perhaps. If the covering of snow complicated movement, yet there were places where bare rock cropped out to break the betraying pallor. But the night came all too tranquilly, lambent light from snow and stars, a clear sky, crackling with frost. This one night when fresh snow and driving winds might have made vision delusive, and covered dark garments with their own protective veil, no gale blew and no flake descended. And the stillness and silence were such that even the snapping of a buried branch underfoot might carry as far as the stockade.

Cadfael was just reflecting ruefully on this hush when it was abruptly shattered, blasted apart with a violence that made him jump almost out of his skin. Reverberating across from the summit came a loud metallic clanging like a great, ill-made bell, stroke on jarring stroke beating out a merciless peal that went on and on, piercing, demanding, a pain to the ears. Back among the trees men started to their feet, and ventured as near as they dared to the open, to stare across at the castle, and within the stockade, no less, arose shouts and bellowing and clamour that told

Cadfael this music was none of theirs, had not been planned, was neither welcomed nor understood. If something had gone wrong within, then something profitable might yet be made of it without.

The din was coming from the top of the tower. Someone up there was industriously thrashing away at a shield, or a gong of some kind, however improvised. Why should any man of the garrison be sounding so furious a tocsin, when no attack had been threatened? And the noise had provoked other noises within the stockade, muffled and wordless but unmistakably angry, dismayed and vengeful. A great voice that could only belong to le Gaucher was roaring orders. Surely all attention had been diverted from the enemy without to the unexpected onslaught within.

Cadfael acted almost without thought. There was an undulation in the rock surface halfway to the stockade, a narrow black blot breaking the uniform whiteness. He broke from the shelter of the trees and ran for it, and dropped full-length along it, where his black habit could lie motionless and pass unremarked if anyone was still keeping guard. He doubted if they were. The relentless clanging continued tirelessly, though someone's arm must be beginning to ache by this time. Cautiously he raised his head to watch the serrated crest of the tower, clear against the sky. The rhythm of the discordant bell faltered and changed, and as it halted for a moment Cadfael saw a head peep cautiously out between the merlons. There were ominous splintering, crashing sounds now, dulled by the thick timbering of the tower, as though someone was wielding an axe. The head appeared a second time. Cadfael waved an arm, black sleeve plain against the snow, and shouted: 'Yves!'

Doubtful if he was heard, though the clear air carried sounds with meticulous accuracy. Certainly he was seen. The head – it barely topped the parapet – craned into view recklessly for a moment, to shriek in shrillest excitement: 'Come on! Bid them come on! We hold the tower! We are two, and armed!' Then he vanished behind the merlon, and none too soon, for at least one bowman within the stockade had been watching the same serrated outline, and his arrow struck the edge of the embrasure, and stuck there quivering. Defiantly the clangour from the tower resumed its resolute beat.

Cadfael picked himself up from his niche in the rock, regardless of danger, and ran for the trees. At least one arrow followed him, but fell short, somewhat to his surprise when he heard its shuddering flight extinguished in the snow behind him. He must still have a better turn of speed than he had thought, at least when running for his own life and many others. He plunged breathless into cover, and into the arms of Hugh Beringar, and was aware by the stir and quiver all along the fringe of the trees that Hugh also had employed these few minutes to good effect, for his lines were drawn ready for action, waiting only the urgent word.

'Set on!' said Cadfael, puffing for breath. 'That's Yves sounding for us, he says he holds the tower. Someone has reached him, God knows how. No danger now but from our delay.'

There was no more delay. Hugh was away on the instant, and into the saddle before the words were spent. He from the left and Josce de Dinan from the right broke from the trees and drove in upon the gates of Alain le Gaucher's castle, with all their foot-men streaming full tilt behind them, and a file of torches spluttering into life after, to fire the fringe buildings within.

Brother Cadfael, left unceremoniously thus, stood for a while to get his breath back, and then, almost resentfully, resigned himself to the recollected fact that he had long ago forsworn arms. No matter, there was nothing in his vows to prevent him from following unarmed where the armed men led. Cadfael was striding purposefully across the open expanse of snow, torn up now by many hooves and many feet, by the time the assault converged in a spear-head to hurtle against the gates, and drive them in.

For all the industrious din he himself was making, Yves heard the charge of the sheriff's men, and felt the tower shake as they hit the gate like a sledgehammer, and burst the holding timbers in a shower of flying splinters. The clamour of hand-to-hand battle filled the bailey, but about that he could do nothing; but here the very boards under them were heaving and groaning to a fury of axe-blows from below, and Olivier, sword drawn and long legs spread, was holding down ladder and trap against the onslaught. The ladder heaved at every blow, but while it held its place the trap could not be raised, and even if it should be breached, only a hand or a head could be first exposed, and either would be at Olivier's mercy. And at this extreme, Olivier would have no mercy. Braced from crown to heel, he bestrode the enemy's entry, balancing his weight, sword poised to pierce or slash the first flesh that offered.

Yves dropped his aching arm, and let the steel helmet roll away from between his feet, but then, with a better thought, scrambled after it and clapped it on his head. Why refuse any degree of protection that offered? He even remembered to stoop well below the parapet as he flexed his cramped hand, took a fresh grip on the hilt of the sword, and plunged across the roof to embrace Olivier, and plant his own feet on the rungs of the ladder that held them secure, to add his weight to the barrier. There were already splits visible in the wood of the trap, and splinters flew both above and below, but there was nowhere yet that a blade could be thrust through.

'Nor will be,' said Olivier in confident reassurance. 'You hear that?' It was the roaring voice of Alain le Gaucher himself, echoing hollowly up the dark spaces of the tower. 'He's calling off his hounds, they're needed more desperately below.'

The axe struck once more, a mighty blow that clove clean through an already splintered board, and sent a long triangle of shining blade into view beneath the ladder. But that was the last. The striker had trouble freeing his blade again, and cursed over it, but made no further assault. They heard a great scurrying down the stairs, and then all was quiet within the tower. Beneath, in the bailey, the whole enclosure was filled with the babel and struggle and clamour of arms, but up here under the starry calm of the sky the two of them stood and looked at each other in the sudden languor of relief, no longer threatened.

'Not that he would not make the same foul use of you,' said Olivier, sheathing his sword, 'if he could but get his hands on you. But if he spends time on hewing you out of your lair, he will already have lost what your throat might save. He'll seek to fight off this attack before he troubles you again.'

'He will not do it!' said Yves, glowing. 'Listen! They are well within. They'll never give back now, they have him in a noose.' He peered out from behind a merlon over the confused fighting below. All the space of the bailey seethed and swayed with struggling men, a churning, tumultuous darkness like a stormy night sea, but lit by fiery glimpses where the torches still burned. 'They've fired the gatehouse. They're leading out all the horses and cattle – and fetching down all the archers from the walls . . . Should we not go down and help them?'

'No,' said Olivier firmly. 'Not unless we must, not until we must. If you fell into the wrong hands now, all this would be thrown away, all to do again. The best you can do for your friends is to stay out of reach, and deny this rogue baron the one weapon that could save him.'

It was good sense, though none too welcome to an excited boy longing for prodigies to perform. But if Olivier ordered it, Yves accepted it.

'You may be a hero some other day,' said Olivier drily, 'when there's less at stake and you can put only your own neck in peril. Your part now is to wait in patience, even if it cost you more. And since we have time now, and may be mortally short of it before long, listen to me carefully. When we are loosed from here, and all over, I shall leave you. Go back to join your sister at Bromfield, let your friends have the satisfaction of uniting you in safety. I have no doubt they would send you with a good escort to your uncle in Gloucester, as they promised, but I have a fancy to finish my work and deliver you myself, as I was sent out to do. This mission is mine, and I'll complete it.'

'But how will you manage?' Yves wondered anxiously.

'With your help – and certain other help which I know where to find. Give me two days, and I will have horses and supplies ready for us. If all goes well, two nights from this night that's wearing away under us, I will come to Bromfield for you. Tell your sister so. After Compline, when the brothers will be bound for their beds, and you will be thought to be in yours. Ask no more questions, but tell her I shall come. And should I be forced to have speech here with the sheriff's men, or should you be asked about me after I vanish – tell me, Yves, who was it made his way in here to find you?'

Yves understood. He said at once: 'It was Robert, the forester's son who brought Ermina to Bromfield, and happened on this place while he was searching for me.' He added dubiously: 'But they'll wonder at such a deed in a forester, when all the sheriff's men were already searching. Unless,' he went on, curling a disdainful lip, 'they think that every man living will risk his life for Ermina, just because she is handsome. She *is* handsome,' he conceded generously, 'but all too well she knows it and makes use of it. Don't ever let her make a fool of *you*!'

Olivier was peering out over the battlefield below, where a long tongue of fire had sprung from the burning gates and reached the roof of one of the byres. His dark and private smile was hidden from the boy. 'You may let them think me her besotted slave, if it convinces them,' he said. 'Tell them what you please that will serve the purpose. And bear my message, and be ready when I come for you.'

'I will!' vowed Yves fervently. 'I will do all as you tell me.'

They watched the fire spread along the stockade from roof to roof, while the fighting within continued as fiercely and confusedly as ever. The garrison had poured out to the defence greater numbers than anyone had suspected, and all too many of them experienced and powerful fighters. Yves and Olivier looked on from their eyrie intently, as the serpent of fire began to burn uncomfortably near to the corner of the hall itself. If it touched the tower, all that draughty, beam-braced interior would act as a chimney, and they would be isolated at the top of a ferocious blaze. Already the crackling and exploding of burning beams threatened to drown out the din of fighting.

'This grows too hot,' said Olivier, frowning. 'Better brave the devil below than wait for the one that's coming to us here.'

They hauled the ladder aside, and heaved up the mangled trap. Splinters jutted and fell, and a thin curl of smoke, hardly a breath as yet, coiled up out of the recesses of the tower. Olivier did not wait to lower the ladder, but slid through to hang by his hands, and dropped lightly to the floor below, and Yves followed him valiantly, to be caught neatly in mid-air by the waist, and set down silently. Olivier set off down the staircase, a hand extended behind him to hold the boy close. The air here was still cold, but from somewhere smoke was drifting steadily, obscuring the edges of the steps so that they were constrained to feel their way at every tread. The babel of battle grew more distant, a constant buzzing from without the thick walls. Even when they reached the rock floor of the tower, and saw by the dim remains of torches and firelight the outline of the great door to the hall, standing ajar, there was no stir of foot or sound of voices within. Every man must be out in the bailey, battling to fend off the sheriff's forces, or else, by this time just as possibly, to break through the circle somehow and make his escape.

Olivier made for the narrow outer door by which he had entered in the first place, lifted the heavy latch and tugged, but the door did not give. He braced a foot against the wall and heaved again, but the door remained fast shut.

'The devil damn them! They've barred it without, after they treed us. Through the hall, and keep close behind me.'

The very act of thrusting the great door open wide enough for them to slip through, as silently as possible, for fear some cautious or wounded outlaw should still be lurking, brought into play a cross-draught, and a sudden tongue of fire leaped up in the far corner of the hall, licked its way up the beams of the roof, and spat burning splinters below to smoulder in Alain le Gaucher's tapestried chairs, and bring to life three or four new buds of flame that opened marvellously into great crimson flowers. Those red and gold blazons were all they could see clearly through the smoke that thickened as abruptly as the fire had burst in. They groped and stumbled through a deserted wilderness of overturned benches and trampled and spilled dishes, trestle tables fallen aslant, hangings dragged down, torches burned out and adding to the pall of smoke that stung their eyes and was drawn chokingly into their throats. Before them, beyond this obscure and perilous wilderness, the pandemonium of struggle and violence blew in on a freezing draught through the half-open main door of the hall. At the top of the sliver of open air thus uncovered, a single star showed, unbelievably pure and distant. They covered their mouths and nostrils and made for it, with eyes streaming and smarting.

They were almost at the doorway when a ripple of flame flowed suddenly along the surface of a roof-beam, peeling off the unplaned surface in a flurry of sparks, and caught the coarse homespun curtain that served to shut out the cold wind when the doors were closed and the household home at night. The dry, hairy cloth went up in a gush of flame, and fell in their path, a great folded cushion of fire. Olivier kicked it furiously aside, and swung Yves before him round the billowing bonfire towards the doorway.

'Out! Get to the open, and hide!'

If Yves had obeyed him to the letter, he might well have escaped notice, but having reached clear air, with the sweep of the steps and the loud turmoil of the bailey before him, he turned to look back anxiously, for fear the fire, blazing now to a man's height, had trapped Olivier within. The pause cost him and his friends all that they had gained together, for more than half the bailey was then in Beringar's hands, and the remnant of the garrison driven back into a tight knot of fighting round the hall, and while

Yves' back was turned upon his enemies, and he hung hesitating whether to rush back to stretch a hand to his friend, Alain le Gaucher, hard-pressed at the foot of the steps to his own hall, cut a wide swathe before him to clear his ground, and leaped backwards up the wide timber stairway. They all but collided, back to back. Yves turned to run, too late. A great hand shot out and gripped him by the hair, and a roar of triumph and defiance rose even above the clamour of arms and the thunderous crackling of bursting beams. In a moment le Gaucher had his back against the pillar of his doorway, secure from attack from the rear, and the boy clamped to his body before him, with a naked sword, already red, braced across his throat.

'Stand, every man! Down arms and draw off!' bellowed the lion, his tawny mane bristling and glaring in the flickering light of the fires. 'Back! Further, I say! Let me see a clear space before me. If any man so much as draw bow, this imp dies first. I have got my warranty again! Now, king's man, where are you? What will you pay for his life? A fresh horse, free passage out, and no pursuit, on your oath, or I slit his throat, and his blood be on your head!'

Hugh Beringar thrust through to the fore and stood, eyes levelled upon le Gaucher. 'Draw back,' he said without turning his head. 'Do as he says.'

The entire circle, king's men and outlaw's men together, drew back inch by inch and left a great space of trampled and stained snow before the steps of the hall. Hugh moved back with them, though keeping his place in front. What else could he do? The boy's head was strained back against his captor's body, the steel touching his stretched neck. A false move and he would be dead. A few of the garrison began to edge out of the press, backwards towards the stockade and the gate, in the hope of finding a way out while all eyes were on the pair isolated at the top of the steps. The guard on the gate would deal with them, but who would deal with this ruthless and desperate creature? Everyone retreated before him.

Not everyone! Through the press, unnoticed by any until he reached the open space, came lurching a strange and solitary figure, limping and wavering, but marching ahead out of the crowd without pause, straight towards the steps. The red light of the fires trembled over him. A tall, emaciated man in a black habit, the cowl dropped back on his shoulders. Two puckered scars crossed his tonsured head. There was blood on his sandalled feet – he left stains on the snow as he trod – and blood on his brow from a fall in the rocky ground. Great, hollow eyes in a livid face stared upon Alain le Gaucher. A pointing hand accused him. A loud, imperious voice cried out at him:

'Leave go of the boy! I have come for him, he is mine.'

Intent upon Hugh Beringar, le Gaucher had not seen the newcomer until then. His head jerked round, astonished that anyone should break the silence he had imposed, or dare to cross the neutral ground he had exacted.

The shock was brief, but shattering while it lasted, and it lasted long enough. For one moment Alain le Gaucher saw his dead man advancing on him, terrible, invulnerable and fearless, saw the wounds he himself had inflicted still bloody, and the face he had murdered corpse-pale. He forgot the hostage. His hands sank nervelessly, and the sword with them. The next instant he knew past doubt that the dead do not rise, and recovered himself with a scream of rage and scorn, but too late to recover his ascendancy. Yves had slid from between his hands like an eel, dived under his arm and darted away down the steps.

Running blindly, he collided with a welcome solidity and warmth, and clung panting and spent, his eyes closed. Brother Cadfael's voice said in his ear: 'Softly, now, you're safe enough. Come and help me with Brother Elyas, for he'll go nowhere without you, now he's found you. Come, let's get him out of this, you and I together, and do what we can for him.'

Yves opened his eyes, still panting and trembling, and turned to stare back at the doorway of the hall. 'My friend is in there . . . my friend who helped me!'

He broke off there, drawing in breath to heave a huge, hopeful, fearful sigh. For Hugh Beringar, the instant the hostage was free, had darted forward to do battle, but another was before him. Out of the smoke and fire-shot blackness of the doorway surged Olivier, soiled and singed and sword in hand, sprang past le Gaucher to find elbow-room, and in passing struck him on the cheek with the flat of the blade, by way of notice of intent. The tawny mane flew as le Gaucher sprang round to face him. The silence that had exploded in shudderings of wonder at the apparition of Brother Elyas fell again like a stone. Everyone heard clearly the voice that trumpeted disdainfully: 'Now have ado with a man!'

There would be no moving Yves now, not until this last duel was resolved. Cadfael kept hold of him thankfully, though he need not have troubled, for the boy's small fists were clenched in his sleeve for mortal reassurance. Brother Elyas, his bearings lost, looked about him for his boy, and came limping painfully to touch, to comfort and be comforted, and Yves, without for an instant taking his worshipping eyes from Olivier, detached one hand from his hold on Cadfael to accept Elyas' clasp just as fiercely. For him everything now depended on this man to man encounter, from head to foot he was quivering with partisan passion. Both Cadfael and Elyas felt it and were infected by it, and stared as he stared upon this tall, agile, slender person poised with spread feet at the top of the steps. For all his smoke-soiled visage and common country garments, Cadfael knew him again.

And no one meddled, not even Hugh, who might have intervened by virtue of his office. Between his men and these thieves and murderers there would be no more fighting until this fight was over. There was that about the challenge that forbade interference.

It did not appear a very even combat, le Gaucher double his opponent in age and weight and experience, if not in reach and agility. And it did not last long. Le Gaucher, once he had viewed his challenger, came on confidently in a steady, battering onslaught, bent on driving the young man from his stance and backwards down the steps. Yet after long, increasingly furious attacks the boy – a mere half-trained peasant, at that! – had scarcely shifted his balance, not given back a pace, and everywhere the hacking blade crashed in, his sword was there to turn it aside. He stood and seemed at ease, while his adversary flailed at him and wasted energy. Yves gazed with huge, praying eyes, rigid from crown to toe. Elyas clung mutely to the hand he clasped, and quivered to its tension. Brother Cadfael watched the young man Olivier, and recalled disciplines he had almost forgotten, a manner of sword-play bred from the clash of east and west, and borrowing from both.

There was no moving this swordsman, if he gave an inch one moment he regained it the next, added to it the next. It was le Gaucher who was being edged back by degrees to the rim of the steps, while he wasted his strength to no avail.

The lion lunged once more, with all his weight. His heel was too near the edge of the icy stair, his lunge too reckless, the forward pressure slid his rearward foot from under him, and he hung out of balance, struggling for recovery. Olivier sprang forward like a hunting leopard, and drove down with all his weight, clean through the disrupted guard and into the exposed breast. The sword went in halfway to the hilt, and he braced both feet and leaned back on his heel to hoist his blade clear.

The lion's carcase dropped from the withdrawing point, arms spread, flew outwards on its back, landed three steps lower, and rolled ponderously, with an awful dignity, from stair to stair, to come to rest on its face at Hugh Beringar's feet, and bleed what was left of its life away into the defiled snow.

# 14

It was over, once their leader was dead, and seen to be dead. They broke in all directions, some running to try and find a way of escape, some fighting to the death, some bargaining vainly, some having the sense to surrender and hope to make a passable case for themselves thereafter. There were over sixty prisoners to be rounded up, besides the dead, any amount of plunder to drag out from hall and stores before all went up in fire, a passable flock of stolen sheep and herd of cattle to feed and water until they could be driven down to better lodging. Dinan undertook the custody of the prisoners, captured within his lordship. No need to doubt his adherence to law where his own writ was challenged.

The fire spread, and when all that was savable was brought out, they spread the flames of intent. The castle stood solitary, clear of the trees, on solid rock, it could burn to the bone and threaten nothing else. It had been a stain upon the countryside in its short and ignoble life, it might well be a passing blemish in its death.

The strangest thing, though unremarked by most in the general turmoil, was the disappearance of the unknown champion only minutes after he had felled the castellan. Every eye had followed that prodigious fall, and by the time they had stirred out of their daze and looked about, the chaos of flight and capture had broken out all around, and no one had seen the young countryman make off silently into the night.

'Gone like a shadow,' said Hugh, 'when I should have liked to know him better. And never a word as to where he may be found, when the king's Grace owes him a debt any sane man would be eager to collect. You are the only one who has spoken with him, Yves. Who is this paladin?'

Half-drunk with the lassitude of relief after stress, and the exhaustion of safety after terror, Yves said what he had been taught to say, and fronted Hugh with a clear stare and guileless face as he did so. 'That was the forester's son who sheltered Ermina, and brought her to Bromfield. It was he told me she's there. I knew nothing of that until then. She is really there?'

'She is, safe enough. And what is the name of this forester's son? And more to the purpose,' said Hugh thoughtfully, 'where did he learn his sword-craft?'

'His name is Robert. He told me he was searching for me, as he promised Ermina he would, and he saw the raiders coming back here, and followed their tracks. I know no more about him,' said Yves stoutly, and if he blushed as he said it, the night covered the blush.

'Certainly we seem to breed redoubtable foresters in these parts,' said Hugh drily. But he did not press it further.

'And now,' said Cadfael, intent on his own business, 'if you'll lend me four good men, and let us have the use of all these fresh horses, they'll be better on the move to the Bromfield stables, now they've no roof over their heads here, and I can get these two home to their beds. I can leave you my scrip. We'll rig a litter for Brother Elyas, and purloin whatever blankets and brychans are still unburned to wrap him up on the way.'

'Take what you need,' said Hugh. There were seven horses fresh from the stable, besides the common hill-ponies Yves had seen used to bring home plunder. 'Stolen, all or most of them,' said Hugh, looking them over. 'I'll have Dinan give it out wherever they've had losses, they can come to Bromfield and claim their own. The cattle and sheep we'll bring into Ludlow later, after the fellow at Cleeton has picked out his. But best get Brother Elyas away as fast as you can, if he's to live. The marvel is he's survived even this far.'

Cadfael marshalled his helpers to good effect, and took his pick of the furnishings dragged out of the burning hall, to swaddle Brother Elyas in a cocoon of blankets, and fashion a secure cradle for him between two horses. He took thought to load, also, two sacks of fodder from the ransacked stores, in case the sudden arrival of seven horses should tax the resources of Bromfield. The spurt of energy and authority that had animated Elyas when there was most need of him had deserted him as soon as his work was done, and his boy delivered. He yielded himself into their hands docilely, and let them do what they would with him, astray between apathy and exhaustion, and half dead with cold. Cadfael eyed him with much concern. Unless some new fire could be kindled in him, to make life an imperative as it had been when he saw Yves threatened, Elyas would die.

Cadfael took Yves on his own saddle-bow, as once before, for the child was now so weary that he could not walk without stumbling, and if allowed to ride would probably fall asleep in the saddle. A good Welsh brychan wrapped him for warmth, and before they had wound their way down the spiral path and into easier country, as briskly as was safe in the dark, his chin was on his chest, and his breathing had eased and lengthened into deep sleep. Cadfael shifted him gently to rest in the hollow of his shoulder, and Yves stretched a little, turned his face warmly into the breast of Cadfael's habit, and slept all the way back to Bromfield.

Once well away into the fields, Cadfael looked back. The sheer bulk of the hill rose blackly, crested with a coronal of fire. It would take Beringar and Dinan the rest of the night to round up all their prisoners, and shift the beasts down to Cleeton, where John Druel might know his own, and thence on to Ludlow. The terror was over, and more economically that might have been expected. Over for this time, thought Cadfael. Over, perhaps, for this shire, if Prestcote and Hugh can keep their grip as firm in the future. But where royal kinsfolk are tearing each other for a crown, lesser men will ride the time for their own gain, without scruple or mercy.

And where they did so, he reflected, every villainy for miles around would be laid at their door, and some of the crimes might well be laid there unjustly. Even villains should bear only the guilt that belongs to them. And never, now, could Alain le Gaucher speak up in his own defence, and say: 'This, and this, and this I have done – but this, this despoiling and murder of a young nun, this deed is none of mine.'

They came to Bromfield about Prime, and rode in at the gatehouse into a court swept clear. No new snow had fallen in the night. The change was coming, by noon there might even be the brief promise of a thaw. Yves awoke, yawned, stretched and remembered. He was wide awake in a moment, unwinding himself from his wrappings and scrambling down to help carry Brother Elyas back to his forsaken bed. Hugh's men-at-arms took the horses to stable. And Brother Cadfael, glancing up towards the guest-hall, saw the door flung open, and Ermina peering out across the twilit court.

The torch above the door lit up a face utterly vulnerable in its wild mingling of hope and dread. She had heard the horses, and rushed out just as she was, barefoot, her hair loose about her shoulders. Her eyes lit upon Yves, busy unloosing the bindings of Brother Elyas' litter, and suddenly her face softened and glowed into so dazzling a radiance of joy and gratitude that Cadfael stood and stared from pure pleasure. The worst shadow soared from her like a bird rising, and was gone. She still had a brother.

Yves, perhaps fortunately, was so busy with his sick protégé and protector that he never glanced in her direction. And Cadfael was not in any way surprised when she did not rush to welcome and embrace, but withdrew softly and stealthily into the guest-hall, and closed the door.

Accordingly, he did not hurry the boy away too hastily from the small infirmary room where they had brought Brother Elyas, and Yves did not run to be embraced, either. He knew, he had been assured over and over, that she was here waiting for him. Both of them required a little time to prepare for the reunion. Only when he had dressed Brother Elyas' wounded and frost-pinched feet, packed them round with soft wool and warmed tiles, bathed his face and hands and fed him spiced and honeyed wine, and heaped him with the lightest covering he had to hand, did Cadfael take Yves firmly by the shoulder, and steer him towards the guest-hall.

She was sitting by the fire, sewing at a gown brought for her from Ludlow, to alter it to her own measure, and none too willingly to judge by her scowl, when Yves entered with Brother Cadfael's hand on his shoulder. She put her work aside, and rose. Perhaps she saw attack in her brother's jutting lip and levelled eye, for she stepped forward briskly, and kissed him in a chill, admonishing, female manner.

'And a fine dance *you* have led everyone,' she said severely, 'running off into the night like that, without a word to a soul.'

'That *you* should be the one to say so, who have caused all this pother!' Yves retorted loftily. '*I* have brought *my* affair to success, madam. *You* ran off into the night without a word to a soul, and come back profitless and as arrogant as ever, but you had better sing a lower tune if you want to be listened to here. *We* have had more urgent matters to think about.'

'You'll have plenty to say to each other,' said Brother Cadfael, benignly blind and deaf to bickering, 'and plenty of time hereafter to say it. But now Yves should be in his bed, for he's had a couple of nights that could wear out any man. He needs a long day's sleep, and if I have a physician's authority, I order it.'

She rose to it with alacrity, though still scowling. She had his bed ready, probably smoothed with her own hands, she would shoo him into it like a hen-wife harrying her chicks, and when he was in it, and fast asleep, she would probably hang over him possessively, and have food ready for him when he stirred. But never, never would she admit that she had grieved and fretted over him, even wept, or that she had bitterly repented her rash departure. And surely that was well, for the boy would be dismayed and embarrassed if ever she bent her neck to him and begged forgiveness.

'Leave well alone until this evening,' said Cadfael contentedly, and went away and left them to argue their way to a truce. He returned to Brother Elyas, sat beside him a careful while, saw that he slept, corpse-like but deeply, and went to his own bed. Even physicians have need of the simple medicines, now and then.

Ermina came looking for him before Vespers, for which office he had asked Prior Leonard to call him. Hugh Beringar had not yet returned, no doubt he was still busy at Ludlow with the bestowal of the prisoners and the storage of the stock and other plunder brought down from Clee. This day was an interlude of thanksgiving for one peril past, but also a breathing-space in preparation for tasks still to be completed.

'Brother Cadfael,' said Ermina, very neat, grave and quiet in the doorway of the infirmary, 'Yves is asking for you. There is still something on his mind, and I know he will not tell me, of all people. But you he wants. Will you come to him after Vespers? He will have had his supper then, and be ready for you.'

'I will come,' said Cadfael.

'And I have been wondering,' she said, and hesitated. 'Those horses you brought back this morning . . . they came from that thieves' nest there?'

'They did. Stolen from all these local holdings they have preyed on. Hugh Beringar is sending out to all who have had such losses to come and claim their own. The cattle and sheep are penned in Ludlow. John Druel may have picked out already some that are his. The horses I borrowed, they were fresh and ready for work. Why? What's in your mind concerning them?'

'There is one I believe belongs to Evrard.' It was a long time since she had spoken his name, it sounded almost strange on her tongue, as if she remembered him from many years past, and after long forgetfulness. 'They will be sending word to him, too?'

'Surely. Callowleas was stripped bare, there may well be other stock of his to be reclaimed.'

'If he does not already know that I am here,' said Ermina, 'I hope no one will tell him. It is not that I mind him knowing I am safe and well. But I would as soon he did not expect to see me.'

There was nothing strange in that. She had put that whole mistaken episode behind her, she might well wish to avoid the embarrassment and pain of meeting him again face to face, and having to make vain play with words over something already dead.

'I doubt there'll have been any message sent but the same to all,' said Cadfael. 'Come and speak for your stolen property. And come they will. A pity there are losses that can never be made good.'

'Yes,' she said, 'great pity. We can't restore them their dead – only their cattle.'

Yves had risen from his long sleep cleansed of every fear for himself or his sister, and secure in his complete trust in Olivier to accomplish every miracle to which he turned his hand. He had washed and brushed and combed himself fittingly as for a thanksgiving festival, and observed with surprised approval that while he slept, Ermina had mended the rent in the knee of his hose, and laundered his only shirt and dried it by the fire. Her actions often failed to match her words, though he had never really noticed it before.

And then, not forgotten but only put aside while more desperate matters still hounded him, the question of Brother Elyas rose unresolved into his mind, and took possession of it wholly. It grew so monstrous and so insistent that he could not long contain it alone, and though Hugh Beringar was fair and approachable, Hugh Beringar was also the law, and bound by his office. But Brother Cadfael was not the law, and would listen with an open mind and a sympathetic ear.

Yves had finished his supper when Cadfael came, and Ermina wisely took her sewing and went away into the hall to have a better light for her work, leaving them together.

Yves found no way of beginning but directly, a leap into the cold and terror of remembrance. 'Brother Cadfael,' he blurted wretchedly, 'I'm frightened for Brother Elyas. I want to tell you. I don't know what we ought to do. I haven't said a word to anyone yet. He has told me things – no, he was not speaking to me, he did not *tell* me, but I heard. I couldn't choose but hear!'

'There's been no time yet for you to tell what happened when he led you away in the night,' said Cadfael reasonably, 'but you may tell it now. But first, there are things I have not yet told you. If I tell them first, it may be a help to you. I know where he led you, and I know how you left him in the hut, hoping for help, and fell into the hands of outlaws and murderers. Was it there in the hut that he spoke out these things that so trouble you?'

'In his sleep,' said Yves unhappily. 'It is not fair dealing to listen to what a man says in his sleep, but I couldn't help it. I was so anxious about him, I needed to know, if there was any way of helping him . . . Even before, when I was sitting by his bed . . . It was because I spoke of Sister Hilaria, and told him she was dead. Nothing else had touched him, but her name . . . It was terrible! It was as if he had not known till then that she was dead, and yet he blamed himself for her death. He cried out to the stones of the house to fall on him and bury him. And he got up . . . I couldn't stop or hold him. I ran to find you, but everyone was at Compline.'

'And when you ran back to him,' said Cadfael mildly, 'he was gone. And so you went after him.'

'I had to, I was left to care for him. I thought in time he would tire, and I could turn him and lead him back, but I couldn't. So what could I do but go with him?'

'And he led you to the hut – yes, that we understood. And there these words passed, that so torment you. Don't be afraid to speak them. All that you did was done for his sake, believe that this, too, you may be doing for his sake.'

'But he accused himself,' whispered Yves, trembling at the memory. 'He said – he said that it was he who killed Sister Hilaria!'

The very quietness with which this was received shook him into despairing tears. 'He was in such anguish, so torn . . . How can we give him up to be branded a murderer? But how can we hide the truth? Himself he said it. And yet I am sure he is not evil, he is good. Oh, Brother Cadfael, what are we to do?'

Cadfael leaned across the narrow trestle and took firm hold of the boy's tight-clasped hands between his own. 'Look at me, Yves, and I'll tell you what we shall do. What *you* have to do is to put away all fears, and try to remember the very words he used. All of them, if you can. "He said that it was he who killed Sister Hilaria!" Did he indeed say that? Or is that what you understood by what he said? Give me the man's own words and what *I* have to do is listen to those words, and to no others, and see what can be made of them. Now! Go back to that night in the hut. Elyas spoke in his sleep. Begin there. Take your time, there is no haste.'

Yves scrubbed a moist cheek against his shoulder, and raised doubtful but trusting eyes to Cadfael's face. He thought back dutifully, gnawed an unsteady lip, and began hesitantly: 'I was asleep, I think, though I was trying not to sleep. He was lying on his face, but I could hear his voice clearly. He said: My sister – forgive me all my sin, my weakness. I, who have been your death! he said. That I'm sure of, that is word for word. I, who have been your death!' He shook and halted there, afraid that that alone might be enough. But Cadfael held him by the hands and nodded understanding, and waited.

'Yes, and then?'

'Then – do you remember how he called on Hunydd? And you said you thought she was his wife, who died? Well, next he said: Hunydd! She was like you, warm and trusting in my arms. After six months starving, he said, such hunger. *I could not bear the burning*, he said, *body and soul* . . .'

The words were returning in full now, as if they had been carved into his memory. Until now he had wished only to forget them, now, when he consented to remember, they came clearly.

'Go on. There was more.'

'Yes. He changed then, he said no, don't forgive me, bury me and put me out of mind. I am unworthy, he said, weak, inconstant . . .' There was a long pause, as there had been that night, before Brother Elyas cried out his mortal frailty aloud. 'He said: She clung to me, she had no fear, being with me. And then he said: Merciful God, I am a man, full of blood, with a man's body and a man's desires. And she is dead, he said, who trusted me!'

He stared, white-faced, amazed to see Brother Cadfael unshaken, thoughtful and calm, considering him across the table with a grave smile.

'Don't you believe me? I've told you truly. All those things he said.'

'I do believe you. Surely he said them. But think – his travelling cloak was there in the hut, together with her cloak and habit. And hidden! And she taken away from that place, and put into the brook, and he found some distance away, also. If he had not led you back to the hut we should not have known the half of these things. Surely I believe all that you have told me, even so you must believe and consider those things I have been able to tell you. It is not enough to say that a thing is so because of one fragment of knowledge, even so clear as a confession, and put away out of sight those other things known, because they cannot be explained. An answer to a matter of life and death must be an answer that explains all.'

Yves gazed blankly, understanding the words, but seeing no hope or help in them. 'But how can we find such an answer? And if we find it, and it is the wrong answer . . .' he faltered, and shook again.

'Truth is never a wrong answer. We will find it, Yves, by asking the one who knows.' Cadfael rose briskly, and drew the boy up with him. 'Take heart, nothing is ever quite what it seems. You and I will go and speak yet again with Brother Elyas.'

Brother Elyas lay weak and mute as before, yet not as before, for his eyes were open, intelligent and illusionless, windows on a great, contained grief for which there was no cure. He had a memory again, though it brought him nothing but pain. He knew them, when they sat down one on either side his bed, the boy hopelessly astray and afraid of what might come of this, Cadfael solid and practical and ready with an offered drink, and a fresh dressing for the frost-gnawed feet. The fierce strength of a man in his robust prime had stood Brother Elyas, physically at least, in good stead, he would not even lose toes, and his chest was clear. Only his grieved mind rejected healing.

'The boy here tells me,' said Cadfael simply, 'that you have recovered the part of your memory that was lost. That's well. A man should possess all his past, it is waste to mislay any. Now that you know all that happened, the night they left you for dead, now you can come back from the dead a whole man, not the half of a man. Here is this boy of yours to prove the world had need of you last night, and has need of you still.'

The hollow eyes watched him from the pillow, and the face was wrung with a bitter spasm of rejection and pain.

'I have been at your hut,' said Cadfael. 'I know that you and Sister Hilaria took shelter there when the snowstorm was at its worst. A bad night, one of the worst of this bad December. It grows more clement now, we shall have a thaw. But that night was bitter frost. Poor souls caught out in it must lie in each other's arms to live through it. And so did you with her, to keep the woman alive.' The dark eyes had burned into fierce life, even the wandering mind grew intent. 'I, too,' said Cadfael with deliberation, 'have known women, in my time. Never unwilling, never without love. I know what I'm saying.'

A voice harsh with disuse, but intelligent and aware, said faintly: 'She is dead. The boy told me. I am the cause. Let me go after her and fall at her feet. So beautiful she was, and trusted me. Little and soft in my arms, and clung, and confided . . . Oh, God!' pleaded Brother Elyas, 'was it well done to try me so sorely, and I emptied and starving? I could not bear the burning . . .'

'That I comprehend,' said Cadfael. 'Neither could I have borne it. I should have been forced to do as you did. In my fear for her if I stayed, and for my own soul's salvation, which is not such a noble motive as all that, I should have left her there asleep, and gone out into the snow and frost of that night, far away from her, to watch the night out as best I could, and return to her in the dawn, when we could go forth together and finish that journey. As you did.'

Yves leaned forward glittering with enlightenment, holding his breath for the answer. And Brother Elyas, turning his head tormentedly on his pillow, mourned aloud: 'Oh, God, that ever I left her so! That I had not the steadfastness and faith to endure the longing . . . Where was the peace they promised me? I crept away and left her alone. And she is dead!'

'The dead are in God's hand,' said Cadfael, 'Hunydd and Hilaria both. You may not wish them back. You have an advocate there. Do you suppose that she forgets that when you went out into the cold you left her your cloak, wrapped about her for warmth, and fled from her with only your habit, to bear the rigour of the winter all those hours to dawn? It was a killing night.'

The voice from the bed said harshly: 'It was not enough to help or save. I should have been strong enough in faith to bear the temptation laid on me, to stay with her though I burned . . .'

'So you may tell your confessor,' said Cadfael firmly, 'when you are well enough to return to Pershore. But you shall, you must shun the presumption of condemning yourself beyond what he sees as your due. All that you did was done out of care for her. What was amiss may be judged. What was done well will be approved. If you had stayed with her, there is no certainty that you could have changed what befell.'

'At worst I could have died with her,' said Brother Elyas.

'But so you did in essence. Death from violence fell upon you in your loneliness that same night, as death of cold you had accepted already. And if you were delivered from both, and find you must suffer still many years of this life,' said Cadfael, 'it is because God willed to have you so survive and so suffer. Beware of questioning the lot dealt out to you. Say it now, to God and us who hear you, say that you left her living, and meant to return to her with the morning, if you lived out the night, and to bring her safely where she would be. What more was required of you?'

'More courage,' lamented the gaunt mask on the pillow, and wrung out a bitter but human smile. 'All was done and undone as you have said. All was well-meant. God forgive me what was badly done.'

The lines of his face had softened into humility, the stress of his voice eased into submission. There was no more he had to remember or confess, everything was said and understood. Brother Elyas stretched his long body from crown to imperilled toes, shuddered and collapsed into peace. His very feebleness came to his aid, he sank without resistance into sleep. The large eyelids expanded, lines melted from about brow and mouth and deep eye-sockets. He floated down into a prodigious profound of penitence and forgiveness.

'Is it true?' asked Yves in an awed whisper, as soon as they had closed the door softly upon Brother Elyas' sleep.

'It is, surely. A passionate soul, who asks too much of himself, and under-values what he gives. He braved the frosty night and the blinding snow without his cloak, rather than sully Sister Hilaria with even the tormented presence of desire. He will live, he will be reconciled with both his body and his soul. It takes time,' said Brother Cadfael tolerantly.

If a thirteen-year-old boy understood less than all of this, or understood it only in the academic way of one instructed in an art never yet practised, Yves gave no sign of it. The eyes fixed brightly upon

Cadfael's face were sharply intelligent. Grateful, reassured and happy, he put the last burden away from him.

'Then it was the outlaw raiders who found her, after all,' he said, 'alone as she was, after Brother Elyas had left her.'

Cadfael shook his head. 'They found and struck down Brother Elyas, as I think it was their way to kill any who by chance encountered them on their forays, and might bear witness against them. But her – no, I think not. Before dawn followed that same night they had time to strike at Druel's farmstead. I do not believe they went half a mile out of their way to reach the hut. Why should they? They knew of nothing there for them. And besides, they would not have troubled to move her body elsewhere, and the good gowns they would have taken with them. No, someone came by the hut because it *was* on his way, and entered it, I fancy, because the blizzard was at its height, and he thought fit to shelter through the worst of it.'

'Then it could have been *anyone*,' said Yves, indignant and dismayed at the affront to justice, 'and we may never know.'

It was in Cadfael's mind then that there was already one person who knew, and the morrow would see it put to the proof. But he did not say so. 'Well, at least,' he said instead, 'you need have no more anxiety for Brother Elyas. He is as good as shriven, and he will live and thrive, and do honour to our order. And if you are not sleepy again yet, you may sit with him for a while. He claimed you for his boy in a good hour, and you may be his serviceable boy still, while you are here.'

Ermina was sitting by the hall fire, still stitching relentlessly at a sleeve of the gown. Working against time, thought Cadfael, when she looked up only briefly, and at once returned to labour unaccustomed and uncongenial. She gave him a smile, but it was a grave and shadowy one.

'All is well with Yves,' said Cadfael simply. 'He was fretting over words Brother Elyas spoke in his sleep, that seemed to be confession of murder, but were no such thing.' He told her the whole of it. Why not? She was becoming a woman before his eyes, fettered by responsibilities suddenly realised and heroically accepted. 'There is nothing weighing on his heart now, except the fear that the true murderer may go undiscovered.'

'He need not fear,' said Ermina, and looked up and smiled, a different smile, at once secretive and confiding. 'God's justice must be infallible, it would be sin to doubt it.'

'At least,' said Cadfael noncommittally, 'he will be ready and willing to go with you now. Even eager. Your Olivier has a worshipper who would follow him to the world's end.'

The bright, proud stare of her eyes came up to him sharply, the firelight waking sparks of deep red in the depths. 'He has two,' she said.

'When is it to be?'

'How did you know?' she asked, with a little curiosity but no surprise or consternation.

'Would such a man leave his work unfinished, and let another send home, however gallantly, the charges he was sent to find? Of course he means to complete the task himself. What else?'

'You will not stand in his way?' But she waved that aside with the hand that held the needle. 'Pardon! I know you will not. You have seen him now, you know how to recognise a man! He sent me word by Yves. He will come tomorrow, about Compline, when the household makes ready for bed.'

Cadfael thought it over, and said judicially: 'I would leave departure until the brothers rise for Matins and Lauds, there will then be no porter on the gate, he will be in church with the rest. And no further stir until Prime. You and the boy could sleep some hours before riding. I would wake you and see you safe from the gate. And if he comes during Compline, I can bring him within until time to leave. If you will trust me with the charge?'

'And thank you for it,' she said without hesitation. 'We will do as you advise.'

'And you,' said Brother Cadfael, watching her seam lengthen with fierce stitch after stitch, 'will you be as ready as Yves to leave this place by tomorrow's midnight?'

She looked up yet again, without haste or concealment, but without confiding, either, and the sinking firelight caught the red glow again in her eyes, while her face was a pure mask. 'Yes, I shall be ready,' she said, and glanced down at the sewing in her lap before she added: 'My work here will be done.'

# 15

The night was clear, starry and still, barely on the edge of frost. The sun emerged with dawn, and for the second night there had been no fresh snow. The drifts dwindled, even before the slow, quiet thaw set in, the kind of thaw that clears paths by gradual, almost stealthy erosion, and causes no floods.

Hugh Beringar had got back late in the evening, after overseeing the total destruction of what the fire had left, and the removal of a startling collection of plunder. The clutter of lean-to cells along the stockade had yielded up the remains of two murdered prisoners, tortured until they surrendered whatever they had of value, and three more still alive after the same treatment. They were being nursed in Ludlow, where Josce de Dinan had secured the survivors of the garrison in chains. Of the attacking force, there were some eighteen wounded, many more with minor grazes, but none dead. It might have been a deal more costly.

Prior Leonard strode radiantly about his court in the chill but brilliant sunlight, glittering with relief that his region was delivered from a pestilence, the missing pair safe within his walls, and Brother Elyas mute with wonder and grace in his bed, and bent upon life, whether blissful or baleful. He looked up with clear, patient eyes now, and took exhortation and reproof alike with humility and gladness. His mind was whole, his body would not be long in following.

Not long after High Mass the claimants began to come in to look for their horses, as doubtless they were flocking to Ludlow to pick out their own cows and sheep. Some, no doubt, would be claimed by more than one, and give rise to great quarrels and the calling in of neighbours to identify the disputed stock. But here there were only a handful of horses, and little ground for the opportunist greed of the cunning. Horses know their owners as well as the owners know their horses. Even the cows in Ludlow would have plenty to say about where they belonged.

John Druel was among the first to come, having walked all the way from Cleeton, and he had no need to urge his ownership, for the stout brown mountain cob strained and cried after him as soon as he showed his face in the stable-yard, and their meeting was an embrace. The cob blew sweetly in John's ear, and John hugged him about the neck, looked him over from head to hocks, and wept on his cheek. The cob was his only horse, worth a fortune to him. Yves had seen him come, and ran to tell Ermina, and the pair of them came flying to greet him and force on him such favours as they still had about them to give.

A wife from Whitbache came to claim her dead husband's mare. A thin, grave boy from the same manor came in shyly and humbly to call a solid work-horse of hill stock, and it went to him hesitantly, wanting his sire, but acknowledged the child of the same blood with a human sigh.

Not until dinner was over in the refectory, and Brother Cadfael emerged again into the midday sparkle of sun on snow, did Evrard Boterel ride in at the gatehouse, dismount, and look round him for someone to whom he might most properly address himself. He was still somewhat pale and lean from his fever, but much recovered in the vigour of his movements and the clarity of his eye, and he stood with reared head and imperious stare, even frowning a little that no groom ran at once to take his bridle. A fine figure of a young man, fair as his horse's mane, and well aware of his handsome appearance and his dominant nobility. Such comeliness might well take any young woman's fancy. What did a young fellow with these advantages have to do to lose his hold? Reality, Ermina had said, had rudely invaded her idyllic fantasy. Well! But was that enough?

Prior Leonard, all goodwill, came beaming down the court with his gangling stride, to greet the visitor civilly, and conduct him into the stable-yard. One of Hugh's men, seeing the saddled horse untended, and being himself at leisure, came to take the bridle, and Boterel relinquished his mount as to a servant, without a further glance, and went with the prior.

He had come alone. If he had indeed a stolen horse to reclaim, he must take him home on a leading rein.

Brother Cadfael looked round at the guest-hall, very thoughtfully, and saw Ermina in her peasant gown come forth from the doorway and cross to the church, rapid and light, and bearing something rolled up beneath her arm. The dark arch of the porch swallowed her, as the walled enclosure of the stables had swallowed her sometime suitor. Yves would certainly be sitting now with Brother Elyas, his jealously guarded protégé and patient, on whom he waited with proprietorial zeal. Out of sight and out of peril. No arrows loosed here could strike at him.

Without haste, Cadfael stepped out into the cleared court and crossed towards the church, but tempered his going so judiciously that his path converged upon that by which Evrard Boterel and Hugh together emerged from the stables and made for the gatehouse. They, too, were taking their time, and Evrard was sunning into vivacity and smiles; the deputy sheriff was a study worth cultivating. Behind them a lay groom led a fine bay mare, chestnut-maned.

Cadfael reached the spot where their paths would cross, and there halted before the open, dim doorway of the church, so that they, too, came naturally to a halt. Boteral recognised the brother who had dressed his wound once in the manor of Ledwyche, and made gracious acknowledgement.

'I trust I see you fully restored to health,' said Cadfael civilly. His eye was on Hugh, curious to see if he had taken note of the waiting horse, which the man-at-arms was walking to and fro about the court with an admiring eye on his gait and a gentling hand on his neck. There was not much escaped Beringar's eye, but his face gave away nothing of his thoughts. Cadfael's thumbs pricked. He had no part to play here, on the face of it, yet his instinct drew him into a complex affair as yet only partly understood.

'I thank you, brother, I am indeed mending, if not mended,' said Evrard buoyantly.

'Little enough to thank me for,' said Cadfael. 'But have you yet thanked God? It would be a fair return for mercies, from one preserved in life and limb, and in recovery of so fine a property as this mare of yours. After coils and cruelties in which so many have died, honest men and innocent virgins.' He was facing the open door of the church, he caught the dark quiver of movement within, that froze again into stillness. 'For grace, come within now, and say a prayer for those less fortunate – even the one we have coffined here, ready for burial.'

He feared he had said too much, and was relieved to see Boterel confident and unshaken, turning towards the doorway with the light smile of one humouring a well-meaning churchman by consenting to a harmless gesture without significance.

'Very willingly, brother!' Why not? There had been dead left behind to the care of these or others in every rogue raid from Clee, small wonder if one of the last of them lay here newly coffined. He stepped jauntily up the stone stair and into the dim, cold nave, Cadfael close at his shoulder. Hugh Beringar, dark brows drawn down, followed as far as the threshold, and there stood astride, closing the way back.

The radiance of the sunlit snow fell behind them, turning them momentarily half-blind. The great, cold, twilit bulk enclosed them, the lamp on the high altar made an eye of fire ahead, very small and distant, and the only other light within was from the narrow windows, which laid pale bars across the tiles of the floor.

The red eye of the lamp went out suddenly. She must have come quite rapidly the few yards from the mortuary chapel to stand between, but in the brief darkness her movements had been silent and invisible. She came forward in a sweeping, hushed glide, advancing upon Evrard Boterel with hand extended, as in vain entreaty that turned abruptly into a stabbing accusation. He hardly knew what caused the dim air to vibrate until she surged into the first pallid bar of light, veil and cowl drawn close about her face, a slender Benedictine nun in a habit crumpled and soiled from the straw of the hut, the right breast and shoulder clotted and stiffened into a rusty blot of congealed blood. Then pale grey light took her and showed every seamed fold, even the smears that marred her sleeve, as she had fought him and ripped his young wound open again while he lay upon her. She never made a sound, only flew towards him silently along the tiles of the floor.

He gave a great lurch backwards into Brother Cadfael's shoulder, and uttered a muffled moan of terror, whipping up a hand to cross his body against the unbelievable assault. Under the close-drawn hood great eyes blazed at him, and still she came on.

'No – no! Keep from me! You are dead . . .'

It was only a strangled whisper in his throat, as her voice might have been quenched under his hands; but Cadfael heard it. And it was enough, even though Evrard had gathered himself the next moment, and braced himself to stand his ground, stiffening almost breast to breast with her as she stepped into the light and became flesh, tangible and vulnerable.

'What fool's play is this? Do you shelter mad-women here? Who is this creature?'

She flung back the cowl from her head and dragged off the wimple, shaking out her great burden of black hair over the befouled breast of Sister Hilaria's gown, and showed him the fierce, marble face and burning eyes of Ermina Hugonin.

He was as little prepared for that apparition as for the other. Perhaps he had been thinking her safely dead somewhere under the forest drifts, since he had received no news of her. Perhaps he had concluded that he had nothing now to fear from anything she might have to urge against him, at least not in this world, and he had little consideration for any other. He gave back one hasty step before her, but could give no more, because Cadfael and Hugh stood one on either side between him and the open door. But he gathered himself together gallantly, and faced her with a hurt, bewildered countenance, appealing against inexplicable ill-usage.

'Ermina! What can this mean? If you live, why have you not sent me word? What is this you are trying to do to me? Have I deserved it? Surely you know I have been wearing out myself and all my household, searching for you?'

'I know it,' she said, in a voice small and hard, cold as the ice that had prisoned and preserved Sister Hilaria. 'And if you had found me, and no other by, I should have gone the same way my dearest friend went, since you knew by then you would never get me to wed you. Married or buried, there was no third way for me, else I could tell all too much for your comfort and honour. And I have never said one word here to bring you to account, never a word for myself, since I brought it on myself, and was as much to blame as you. But knowing what I know now, and for her – Yes, yes, yes, a thousand times, I accuse you, murderer, ravisher, I name you, Evrard Boterel, as the killer of my sweet Hilaria . . .'

'You are out of your wits!' he cried, riding indignantly over her accusation. 'Who is this woman you speak of? What do I know of any such person? Since the day you left me I've lain in fever and sickness. All my household will say so . . .'

'Oh, no! Oh, no! Not that night! You rode out after me, to recover me for your honour's sake, to silence me, either by marriage or murder. Never deny it! I saw you ride! You think I was fool enough to believe I could outrun you on foot? Or terrified enough to lose my wits and run like a fool hare, zigzag, leaving tracks plain for you? I laid my traces no further than the trees, towards the Ludlow road where you would expect me to run, and made my way back roundabout to hide half the night among the timber you had stacked for your coward defences. I saw you go, Evrard, and I saw you return, with your wound fresh-broken and bloodied on you. I did not run until you were helped within to your bed and the worst of the blizzard over, and I knew I could run at my own pace, with the dawn barely an hour away. And while I was hiding from you, you killed her!' she wrung out, burning up like a bitter fire of thorns. 'On your way back from a fruitless hunt, you found a lone woman, and took your revenge for what I did to you, and all that you could not do to me. We killed her!' cried Ermina. 'You and I between us! I am as guilty as you!'

'What are you saying?' He had called up a little courage, a little confidence. If she had raved, he would have become soothing, solicitous, sure of himself, and even in her cold assurance he could find a foothold for his own. 'Certainly I rode out to look for you, how could I leave you to die in the frost? I had a fall, weak from my wound as I was, and broke it open again and bled – yes, that is truth. But the rest? I hunted you all that night, as long as I could endure, and never did I halt in my search for you. If I came back empty-handed and bleeding, do you accuse me of that? I know nothing of this woman you speak of . . .'

'Nothing?' said Cadfael at his shoulder. 'Nothing of a shepherd's hut close to the track you would be riding, back from the Ludlow road towards Ledwyche? I know, for I've ridden it the opposite way. Nothing of a young nun asleep in the hay there, wrapped in a good man's cloak? Nothing of a freezing brook handy on your way home, afterwards? It was not a fall that ripped your wound open again, it was the doughty fight she made for her honour in the cold night, where you had out your fury and lust upon her for want of another prey, more profitable to your ambitions. Nothing of the cloaks and habit hidden under the straw, to cast the crime on those guilty of everything else that cried to heaven here? Everything but this!'

The cold, pale light cast all shapes into marble, the shadows withdrew and left them stark. It was not long past noon of a sunlit day without. It was moon-chill and white here within. Ermina stood like a carving in stone, staring now in silence upon the three men before her. She had done what she had to do.

'This is folly,' said Evrard Boterel arduously, as against great odds. 'I rode out swathed, after the wounds I got in the storming of Callowleas, I rode back home bleeding through my bindings, what of that? A freezing night of blizzard and snow, and I had taken a fall. But this woman, this nun – the shepherd's hut – these mean nothing to me, I never was there, I do not even know where it is . . .'

'I have been there,' said Brother Cadfael, 'and found in the snow the droppings of a horse. A tall horse, that left a fistful of his mare roven in the rough boards under the eaves. Here it is!' He had the wavy cream-coloured strands in his hand. 'Shall I match them with your gelding, there without? Shall we stretch you over the habit you see before you, and match your wound with the blood that soils it? Sister Hilaria did not bleed. Your wound I have seen, and know.'

Evrard hung for one long moment motionless, drawn up tall like a strung doll between the woman before him and the men behind. Then he shrank and sank, with a long, despairing moan, and collapsed on his knees on the tiles of the nave, fists clutched hard to his heart, and fair hair fallen forward over his face, the palest point in the bar of light where he kneeled.

'Oh, God forgive, God forgive . . . I only meant to hush her, not to kill . . . not to kill . . .'

'And it may even be true,' said Ermina sitting hunched and stiff by the fire in the hall, the storm of her tears past, and nothing left but a great weariness. 'He may not have meant to kill. What he says may be sooth.'

What he had said, bestirring himself out of despair to make the best case he could for his life, was that he had turned for home again from his search by reason of the blizzard, and been driven to take shelter through the worst of it when he came to the hut, never thinking to find anyone there before him. But presented with a sleeping woman at his mercy, he had taken her out of spite and rage against all women for Ermina's sake. And when she awoke and fought him, he owned he had not been gentle. But he never meant to kill! Only to silence her, with the skirts of her habit pressed over her face. And then she lay limp and lifeless, and he could not revive her, and he stripped the gown from her, and hid all the garments under the straw, and took her with him as far as the brook, to make of her merely one more victim of the outlaws who had sacked Callowleas.

'Where he first came by that eloquent wound,' said Brother Cadfael, watching her pale face, and marking the convulsion of a bitter smile, that came and went like a grimace of pain on her mouth.

'I know – so he told you! And I let it stand! In gallant defence of his manor and his men! I tell you, he never drew sword, he left his people to be slaughtered, and ran like a rat. And forced me with him! No man of my blood ever before turned his back and abandoned his own people to die! This he did to me, and I cannot forgive it. And I had thought I loved him! I will tell you,' she said, 'how he got that wound of his that betrayed him in the end. All that first day at Ledwyche he drove his men at cutting fence-pales and building barricades, and he with never a scratch on him. And all that day I brooded and was shamed, and in the evening, when he came, I told him I would not marry him, that I would not match with a coward. He had not touched me until then, he had been all duty and service, but when he saw he would lose both me and my lands, then it was another story.'

Cadfael understood. Marriage by rape, once the thing was done, and privately, would be accepted by most families as preferable to causing an ugly scandal and starting a feud. No uncommon practice to take first and marry after.

'I had a dagger,' she said grimly. 'I have it still. It was I who wounded him, and I struck for his heart, but it went astray and ripped down from shoulder to arm. Well, you have seen . . .' She looked down at the folded habit that lay beside her on the bench. 'And while he was raving and cursing and dripping blood, and they were running to staunch his wound and bandage him, I slipped out into the night and ran. He would follow me, that I knew. He could not afford to let me escape him, after that, marry or bury were the only ways. He would except me to run towards the road and the town. Where else? So I did, but only until the woods covered my traces, and then I circled back and hid. I told you, I saw him ride out, weakened as he was, in a great rage, the way I knew he would go.'

'Alone?'

'Of course alone. He would not want witnesses for either rape or murder. Those within had their orders. And I saw him ride back, freshly bloodied through his bandages, though I thought nothing of it then but that he had exerted himself too rashly.' She shuddered at the thought of that exertion. 'When he was cheated of me, he took out his venom on the first woman who fell in his way, and so avenged himself. For myself I would not have accused him. I had the better of him, and I had brought it on myself. But what had *she* done?'

It was the eternal question, and the one to which there exists no answer. Why do the innocent suffer?

'And yet,' she said doubtfully, 'it may be true what he says. He was not used to being thwarted, it made him mad . . . He had a devil's temper. God forgive me, I used almost to admire him for it once . . .'

Yes, it might be true that he had killed without meaning to, and in panic sought to cover up his deed. Or it might be that he had reasoned coldly that a dead woman could never accuse him, and made sure of her eternal silence. Let those judge who were appointed to do the judging, here in this world.

'Don't tell Yves!' said Ermina. 'I will do that, when the time comes. But not here. Not now!'

No, there was no need to say any word to the boy of the battle that was over. Evrard Boterel was gone to Ludlow under armed escort, and there was no sign in the great court that ever a crime had been uncovered. Peace came back to Bromfield very softly, almost stealthily. In less than half an hour it would be time for Vespers.

'After supper,' said Cadfael, 'you should go to your bed, and get some hours of sleep, and the boy also. I will keep watch and let your squire in.'

He had chosen his words well. It was like the coming of the thaw outside. She lifted her face to him like a flower opening, and all the bitter sadness of guilt and folly regretted melted away and fell from her before such a radiance that Cadfael's eyes dazzled. From death and the past she leaned eagerly to life and the future. He did not think she was making any mistake this time, nor that any power would now turn her from her allegiance.

There was a small congregation in the parish part of the church even at Compline that night, a dozen or so goodmen of the district, come to offer devout thanks for deliverance from terror. Even the weather partook of the general grace, for there was barely a touch of frost in the air, and the sky was clear and starry. Not a bad night for setting out on a journey.

Cadfael knew what to look for by now, but for all that it took him a little time to single out the bowed black head for which he was searching. Marvellous that a creature so remarkable could become at will so unremarked. When Compline ended, it was no surprise to count the villagers leaving, and make them one less than had entered. Olivier could not only look like a local lad when he pleased, he could also vanish into shadow without a sound, and remain as still as the stones about him.

They were all gone, the villagers to their homes, the brothers to the warming-room for half an hour of relaxation before bed. The chill dark bulk of the church was silent.

'Olivier,' said Brother Cadfael, 'come forth and be easy. Your wards are getting their rest until midnight, and have trusted you to me.'

The shadows stirred, and gave forth the shape of a lean, lissome, youthful body, instantly advancing to be seen. He had not thought wise or fit to bring his sword with him into a sacred place. He trod without sound, light as a cat. 'You know me?'

'From her I know you. If the boy promised silence, be content, he has kept his word. She chose to trust me.'

'Then so can I,' said the young man, and drew nearer. 'You have privilege here? For I see you come and go as you please.'

'I am not a brother of the house, but of Shrewsbury. I have a patient here mending, my justification for an irregular life. At the battle up there you saw him – the same distraught soul who marched into peril of his life and gave Yves the chance to break free.'

'I am much in his debt.' The voice was low, earnest and assured. 'And in yours, too, I think, for you must be the brother to whom the boy ran, the same of whom he spoke, the one who first brought him safe to this house. The name he gave you I do not remember.'

'My name is Cadfael. Wait but a moment, till I look out and see if all are within . . .' In the sinking glow of torchlight, the last of the evening, the court showed its pattern of black and white as the paths crossed, empty, quiet and still. 'Come!' said Cadfael. 'We can offer you a warmer place to wait, if not a holier. I advised leaving while the brethren are at Matins and Lauds, for the porter will also attend, and I can let you out at the wicket in peace. But your horses?'

'They are handy, and in shelter,' said Olivier serenely. 'There is a boy goes with me, orphaned at Whitbache, he has them in charge. He will wait until we come. I will go with you, Brother Cadfael.' He tasted the name delicately if inaccurately, finding it strange on his tongue. He laughed, very softly, surrendering his hand to be led half-blind wherever his guide wished. Thus hand in hand they went out by the cloister, and threaded the maze to the infirmary door.

In the inner room Brother Elyas lay monumentally asleep, long, splendid and calm, stretched on his back, with lean hands easy on his breast, and face serene and handsome. A tomb-figure carved to flatter and ennoble the dead man beneath, but this man lived and breathed evenly, and the large, rounded lids over his sleeping eyes were placid as a child's. Brother Elyas gathered within him the grace that healed body and mind, and made no overwheening claim on a guilt beyond his due.

No need to agonise any more over Brother Elyas. Cadfael closed the door on him, and sat down in the dim anteroom with his guest. They had, perhaps, as much as two hours before midnight and Matins.

The small room, bare and stony and lit by only one candle, had a secret intimacy about it at this late hour. They were quiet together, the young man and the elder, eyeing each other with open and amiable curiosity. Long silences did not disturb them, and when they spoke their voices were low, reflective and at peace. They might have known each other life long. Life long? The one of them could surely be no more than five or six and twenty, and a stranger from a strange land.

'You may have a hazardous journey yet,' said Cadfael. 'In your shoes I would leave the highways after Leominster, and avoid Hereford.' He grew enthusiastic, and went into some detail about the route to be preferred, even drawing a plan of the ways as he remembered them, with a charcoal stick on the stones of the floor. The boy leaned and peered, all willing attention, and looked up into Cadfael's face at close quarters with a mettlesome lift of the head and a swift, brilliant smile. Everything about him was stirring and strange, and yet from time to time Cadfael caught his breath as at a fleeting glimpse of something familiar, but so long past that the illusion was gone before he could grasp it, and search back in his memory for the place and the time where it belonged.

'All this you are doing in pure goodwill,' said Olivier, his smile at once challenging and amused, 'and you know nothing of me! How can you be sure I am fit to be trusted with this errand, and take no advantage for my lord and my empress?'

'Ah, but I do know something of you, more than you may think. I know that you are called Olivier de Bretagne, and that you came with Laurence d'Angers from Tripoli. I know that you have been in his service six years, and are his most trusted squire. I know that you were born in Syria, of a Syrian mother and a Frankish knight, and that you made your way to Jerusalem to join your father's people and your father's faith.' And I know more, he thought, recalling the girl's rapt face and devout voice as she praised her paladin. I know that Ermina Hugonin, who is well worth winning, has set her heart on you, and will not easily give up, and by that amber stare of yours, and the blood mounting to your brow, I know that you have set your heart on her, and that you will not undervalue your own worth by comparison with her, or let any other make it a barrier between you, no matter in what obscure way you came into this world. Between the two of you, it would be a bold uncle who would stand in your way.

'She does indeed trust you!' said Olivier, intent and solemn.

'So she may, and so may you. You are here on an honourable quest, and have done well in it. I am for you, and for them, sister and brother both. I have seen their mettle and yours.'

'But for all that,' owned Olivier, relaxing into a rueful smile, 'she has somewhat deceived you and herself. For her every Frankish soldier of the Crusade could be nothing less than a noble knight. And the most of them were none, but runaway younger sons, romantic boys from the byre and the field, rogues one leap ahead of the officers for theft or highway robbery or breaking open some church almsbox. No worse than most other men, but no better. Not even every lord with a horse and a lance was another Godfrey of Bouillon or Guimar de Massard. And my father was no knight, but a simple man-at-arms of Robert of Normandy's force. And my mother was a poor widow who had a booth in the market of Antioch. And I am their bastard, got between faiths between peoples, a mongrel afterthought before they parted. But for all that, she was beautiful and loving, and he was brave and kind, and I think myself well mothered and fathered, and the equal of any man living. And I shall make that good before Ermina's kin, and they will acknowledge it and give her to me!' His deep, soft voice had grown urgent, and his hawk-face passionately earnest, and at the end of it he drew breath deep, and smiled. 'I do not know why I tell you all this, except that I have seen you care for her, and wish her the future she deserves. I should like you to think well of me.'

'I am a common man myself,' said Cadfael comfortably, 'and have found as good in the kennel as in the court. She is dead, your mother?'

'Else I would not have left her. I was fourteen years old when she died.'

'And your father?'

'I never knew him, nor he me. He sailed for England from St Symeon after their last meeting, and never knew he had left her a son. They had been lovers long before, when he came fresh to Syria. She never would tell me his name, though often she praised him. There cannot be much amiss,' said Olivier thoughtfully, 'with a mating that left her such fondness and pride.'

'Half mankind matches without ritual blessing,' said Cadfael, surprised at the stirring of his own thoughts. 'Not necessarily the worse half. At least no money passes then, and no lands are prized before the woman.'

Olivier looked up, suddenly aware of the oddity of these exchanges, and laughed, but softly, not to disturb the sleeper next door. 'Brother, these walls are hearing curious confidences, and I am learning how wide is the Benedictine scope. I might well imagine you speak of your own knowledge.'

'I was in the world forty years,' said Cadfael simply, 'before I chose this discipline for my cure. I have been soldier, sailor and sinner. Even crusader! At least that was pure, however the cause fell short of my hopes. I was very young then. I knew both Tripoli and Antioch, once. I knew Jerusalem. They will all have changed now, that was long ago.'

Long ago, yes–twenty-seven years since he had left those shores!

The young man grew talkative at finding so knowledgeable a companion. For all his knightly ambitions and his dedication to a new faith, a part of him leaned back with longing to his native land. He began to talk of the royal city, and of old campaigns, to question eagerly of events before ever he was born, and to extol the charm of remembered places.

'I wonder, though,' admitted Cadfael wryly, recalling how far his own cause had often fallen short, and how often the paynim against whom he had fought had seemed to him the nobler and the braver, 'I wonder, born into such a faith, that you should find it easy to leave it, even for a father.' He rose as he spoke, recollecting how time must be passing. 'I should be waking them. It cannot be long to the Matins bell.'

'It was not easy at all,' said Olivier, pondering in some surprise that the same doubt had so seldom troubled him. 'I was torn, a long time. It was from my mother I had, as it were, the sign that turned the scale. Given the difference in our tongues, my mother bore the same name as your Lady Mary . . .'

Behind Cadfael's back the door of the little room had opened very softly. He turned his head to see

Ermina, flushed and young from sleep, standing in the doorway.

'. . . she was called Mariam,' said Olivier.

'I have roused Yves,' said Ermina, just above a whisper. 'I am ready.'

Her eyes, huge and clear, all the agonising of the day washed away by sleep, clung to Olivier's face, and at the sound of her voice he flung up his head and answered the look as nakedly as if they had embraced heart to heart. Brother Cadfael stood amazed and enlightened. It was not the name the boy had spoken, it was the wild rise of his head, the softened light over his cheek and brow, the unveiled, unguarded blaze of love, turning the proud male face momentarily into a woman's face, one known and remembered through twenty-seven years of absence.

Cadfael turned like a man in a dream, and left them together, and want to help a sleepy Yves to dress and make ready for his journey.

He let them out by the wicket door while the brothers were at Matins. The girl took a grave and dignified leave, and asked his prayers. The boy, still half asleep, lifted his face for the kiss proper between respected elder and departing child, and the young man, in generous innocence and in acknowledgement of a parting probably lifelong, copied the tribute and offered an olive cheek. He did not wonder at Cadfael's silence, for after all, the night demanded silence and discretion.

Cadfael did not stand to watch them go, but closed the wicket again, and went back to sit beside Brother Elyas, and let the wonder and the triumph wash over him in wave on wave of exultation. *Nunc dimittis!* No need to speak, no need to make any claim, or trouble in any way the course Olivier had set himself. What need had he now of that father of his? But I have seen him, rejoiced Cadfael, I have had him by the hand in the darkness, I have sat with him and talked of time past, I have kissed him, I have had cause to be glad of him, and shall have cause to be glad lifelong. There is a marvellous creature in the world with my blood in his veins, and Mariam's blood, and what does it matter whether these eyes ever see him again? And yet they may, even in this world! Who knows?

The night passed sweetly over him. He fell asleep where he sat, and dreamed of unimaginable and undeserved mercies until the bell rang for Prime.

He thought it politic, on reflection, to be the first to discover the defection and raise the mild alarm. There was a search, but the guests were gone, and it was not the business of the brothers to confine or pursue them, and the only anxiety Prior Leonard expressed was for the fugitives themselves, that they might go in safety, and come safely to their proper guardian. Indeed, Prior Leonard received the whole affair with a degree of complacency that Cadfael found faintly suspicious, though it might have been only a reflection of the distracted elation he himself could not quite dissemble. The discovery that Ermina had stripped the rings from her fingers and left them, with the carefully folded habit, on Sister Hilaria's sealed coffin as an offering, absolved the runaways from the charge of ingratitude.

'But what the deputy sheriff will say is another matter,' signed Prior Leonard, shaking an apprehensive head.

Hugh did not present himself until it was time for High Mass, and heard the news with a very appropriate and official show of displeasure, only to shrug it off as of secondary importance, considering the weightier matters he had dealt with successfully.

'Well, they have saved us an escort, then, and so they get safe to d'Angers, so much the better if it's at his expense. We have rooted out that lair of wolves, and sent a murderer off this morning towards Shrewsbury, and that was the chief of my business here. And I'm off after my men within the hour, and you may as well ride with me, Cadfael, for I fancy your business here is just as well concluded as mine.'

Brother Cadfael thought so, too. Elyas had no more need of him, and to linger where those three had been had no more meaning now. At noon he saddled up and took his leave of Leonard and rode with Hugh Beringar for Shrewsbury.

The sky was veiled but benign, the air cold but still and clear, a good day for going home well content. They had not ridden thus knee to knee in peace and without haste for some time, and the companionship was good, whether in speech or silence.

'So you got your children away without a hitch,' said Hugh innocently. 'I thought it could safely be left to you.'

Cadfael gave him a measuring and mildly resentful look, and could feel no great surprise. 'I should have known! I *thought* you made and kept yourself very scarce overnight. I suppose it wouldn't have done for a deputy sheriff with your reputation for sharpness to sleep the night through while his hostages slipped away quietly for Gloucester.' Not to speak of their escort, he thought, but did not say. Hugh had noted the quality of the supposed forester's son, and even guessed at his purpose, but Hugh did not know his name and lineage. Some day, when wars ended and England became one again, some day Hugh might be told what now Cadfael hugged to his heart in secret. But not yet! It was too new a visitation, he could spare none of the miraculous, the astonishing grace. 'From Ludlow,' he said, 'I grant you could hardly be expected to hear the wicket at Bromfield open and close at midnight. You did not leave Boterel in Dinan's care, then?'

'I was none too sure there would not be another departure in the night,' said Hugh. 'He is Dinan's tenant. We have taken confession from him, but I would rather have him safe under lock and key in Shrewsbury castle.'

'Will he hang, do you think?'

'I doubt it. Let those judge whose work is judging. My work is to hold the ways safe for travellers, as far as man can, and apprehend murderers. And let honest men, women and children go their ways freely, with my goodwill.'

They were more than halfway to Shrewsbury and the light still good, and Hugh's pace began to quicken, and his gaze to prick eagerly ahead, hungry for the first sight of the hill-top towers within the wall. Aline would be waiting for him, proud and fond, and deep in happy preparations for the Christmas feast.

'My son will be grown out of knowledge during these days I've been away. All must be very well with them both, or Constance would have been sending after me. And you have not even seen my son yet, Cadfael!'

But you have seen mine, thought Cadfael, rapt and silent beside him, though you do not know it.

'Long-boned and strong – he'll be taller than his father by a head . . .'

He *is* taller by a head, Cadfael exulted. Taller by a head and something to spare. And what paragons of beauty and gallantry may not spring from his union with that imperial girl!

'Wait until you see him! A son to be proud of!'

Cadfael rode mute and content, still full of the wonder and astonishment, all elation and all humility. Eleven more days to the Christmas feast, and no shadow hanging over it now, only a great light. A time of births, of triumphant begettings, and this year how richly celebrated – the son of the young woman from Worcester, the son of Aline and Hugh, the son of Mariam, the Son of Man . . .

A son to be proud of! Yes, amen!